WILD HEARTS ON THE PENNINE MOORS

ROSIE CLARKE

Boldwood

First published in Great Britain in 2026 by Boldwood Books Ltd.

Cover Design by Colin Thomas

Cover Images: Colin Thomas

A CIP catalogue record for this book is available from the British Library.

Paperback ISBN 978-1-80658-261-7

Large Print ISBN 978-1-80658-263-1

Hardback ISBN 978-1-80658-260-0

Trade Paperback ISBN 978-1-80658-262-4

Ebook ISBN 978-1-80658-264-8

Kindle ISBN 978-1-80658-265-5

Audio CD ISBN 978-1-80658-255-6

MP3 CD ISBN 978-1-80658-256-3

Digital audio download ISBN 978-1-80658-259-4

This book is printed on certified sustainable paper. Boldwood Books is dedicated to putting sustainability at the heart of our business. For more information please visit https://www.boldwoodbooks.com/about-us/sustainability/

Boldwood Books Ltd, 23 Bowerdean Street, London, SW6 3TN

www.boldwoodbooks.com

PROLOGUE

THE YORKSHIRE DALES – PENRITH SCAR, 1890

The man stood on the jutting crag, its surface scarred by long-ago miners in search of iron, his hard eyes surveying the rugged landscape with pride, laced with anger and bitterness. It was all his, the land as far as his eye could see: the rich farms, the stream that made it so fertile, the soft sweeping sea of grass, so green and sweet in summer – and away in the distance, too far for the eye to make out, the dark shadow of the Penrith Mine. Beyond that lay a vast expanse of wild moorland leading to the towering crags that were Malham Cove; the tarn, its water cool and clear, and the beautiful waterfall itself at Janet's Foss, and then on to the small town of Settle. Once, not long ago, these moorlands had been home only to a few, but the coming of the railway, with its great viaduct at the Ribblehead, had opened up the Dales, making them more accessible. Yet still there remained secret ways, known only to those who lived and worked in this harsh environment.

It was his home, his place, and his spirit welcomed the bitterly cold tang of the wind as it blew across the moorlands.

He was back where he belonged and yet nothing held any joy for him now, because *she* was gone.

A shiver went through the man, as for a moment he remembered the smell of long fresh grass as he'd lain in it with *her*, tasting the soft delight of her lips and the joy of her love. Then the memory was gone in a flash, replaced by the bitterness that came after. He returned to his survey of the land. Even the big house that was merely a sprawling grey shadow in the distance, mostly hidden by trees, could be his now, if he chose. He had other choices, other futures, some with a promise beyond his dreams. Yet nothing meant anything. His life was a void, as empty as the cloudless sky above the majestic Pennine Way.

He might have been a part of the rocky range that reared into the heavens above. Not that he believed in Heaven. Death was death and an end – most often to suffering, in his opinion. He'd seen enough of that, experiencing all the emotions, from joyous love to deep despair, culminating in the news of *her* death that had cut him to the heart. Yet there was a spark within that would not let him roll over and die – that would be to let his enemy win.

He cared not for life. It held nothing for him now. Yet there was one more thing he must do – he would taste the bittersweet honey of revenge. If he lost his life for it, then to hell with it!

Throwing back his head, Tor Hardy laughed long and loud. He was as free as the raven that now flew above him, its home somewhere in this rocky outcrop. Nothing they did to him now could matter. It was all gone; all he'd ever wanted and cared for. Money and land brought no joy; he understood that now.

'Oh, God, why?' he cried, his words caught and echoing among these scarred rocks. Rocks as black as his heart was now. 'Why did you let it happen?'

But there was no God. No God and no Heaven. Nothing worth the spit.

In that moment, his face was as hard as the crag on which he stood. A mountain of a man, he might have been a part of the landscape, made of the limestone that formed much of this imposing range. Yet inside he was driven by rage and revenge. *She* – the woman he had loved – was lost to him and *he* – Tor's enemy – must pay!

PART I

THE YORKSHIRE DALES – PENRITH SCAR, 1888

1

'Come 'ere, you bitch, and I'll show you what a real man is!'

Emma Watts shuddered as she heard the jeering words. Ike Hanson was a brute, coarse and foul-mouthed, despite his good looks and broad shoulders. He towered above Emma's five foot four inches, making her feel vulnerable. She was a slender girl, not beautiful but with a sweetness that shone out when she smiled, her skin fair, hair brown with gold lights, and her eyes bright like a robin's.

Ike lived with his mother and sister in a miner's cottage. His father had been a miner before him, and a brute of a man by all accounts, who had beaten his wife and his children. He had been dead some years, having met with an accident one night. Ike had been forced to go down the mines at the age of thirteen to support his family; now, in his mid-twenties, he was both strong and surly. His mother was an invalid and his sister, Marie, looked after her, so Ike was the sole breadwinner. Marie had been asked to wed, but she considered it her duty to care for her mother. Ike was not much liked in the village, but his strength and temper prevented most people from standing up to him and he did much as he wished.

Emma stayed clear of him if she could, but, sometimes, he caught her on her way back from work up at Penrith House.

The house was situated at the top of a gentle rise, protected from the buffeting winds by a stand of trees. Emma was a personal maid to Sylvia, Lady Penrith, a beautiful but selfish woman, hard to please and always complaining.

The money Emma earned was needed, because her father had been injured in an accident at the lead mine three years earlier and was now bedridden. Sir Philip Penrith, owner of the mine and all the rich land for miles around, had allowed the family to stay in Butts Lane and given Jim Watts twenty guineas in compensation. Even such a sum could not keep him, his wife Mary, the two younger children and Emma for long, so, from the age of fourteen, Emma had gone to work at the house. Most maidservants lived in, but Emma's mother needed help in the evenings and so she'd taken the job on the understanding that she could sleep at home, but she was at work by six each morning, come rain or snow, knowing her way by moonlight or dawn. Had she lived in, Emma could have earned an extra two shillings a week, but her mother needed her more.

Every night she walked home alone, often singing in her high clear voice, but sometimes Ike would follow her, jeering at her and saying things that made her shudder. Once, when he'd been drinking, he'd had her pressed against the wall of a barn and she'd had to scratch and fight for her freedom and her virtue. If Tor Hardy hadn't come by on his huge black horse, she knew Ike would have taken her down in the dirt that night. Ike had felt the lash of Tor Hardy's whip on his shoulders, and though he'd flared up in anger, he'd stopped short of attacking him, because Tor was the manager of the mine and Ike needed work like everyone else.

Tor worked for Sir Philip. If you lived in Penrith Scar, in the village, or on the estate and surrounding district, you worked for Sir Philip or you starved. Unless you were fortunate enough to own a farm or have a trade to support yourself, you had to go cap in hand to the house and speak to the bailiff. Otherwise, you might have to walk for miles to the pottery at Black Burton, an area rich in different clays, and one of the biggest employers in the area of the Pennines, but most Penrith Scar men chose to go down the mine.

There had been mines in the Pennine Way for centuries, firstly for iron, but that was mostly gone now, dug out by those long-ago miners. Sir Philip's mine had always been rich in lead and it was the main source of work for those in this vale and miles around. Settle was their nearest town, with a market and good shops and hotels, but there were many small hamlets and farms scattered all the way to the Ribblehead and beyond; an area of heart-wrenching beauty and contrasts, from the crags of limestone to sweeping moorland with hardly a tree in sight. Not far away were rushing streams, the impressive tarn at Malham Cove, where a glacier had carved its way through the earth leaving great scars, and the tumble of water as it cascaded down at Janet's Foss; it was a majestic and beautiful place. Yet here at Penrith Scar were also gentle slopes of green grass dotted with limestone walls where sheep grazed in peace and tranquillity, and, in the spring, there would be wild flowers growing among the lush grasses that grew waist-high in summer. Yorkshire was truly God's own country, Emma thought, for she loved the Dales and the crags, though she had not often time to enjoy them.

Ignoring Ike's insults, Emma walked quickly. The moonlight had guided her homeward, but, as it slipped behind the clouds, shadows were creeping into the small village of Penrith Scar, with only the occasional lantern shedding light through a window. The village consisted of a few rows of shabby cottages that some of the miners inhabited for as long as they could work, two good houses the other side of the stream, which were home to the overseer of Sir Philip's farms, and Tor Hardy's house. Tor's house was the only one at this end of the valley that didn't belong to Sir Philip, and people often wondered that he should own such a house of good buff brick and slate roof. It had belonged to his father, given to him by Sir Philip's own father upon his marriage. Many had wondered why Sir Thomas had given a house to a mere smallholder, until Tor was born just seven months later. After that, they just grinned and whispered of things best left unsaid, but most believed that Millie Hardy had born a second son to Sir Thomas and Tor was therefore Sir Philip's younger brother. There were twenty years between them and a whole world in every other aspect.

Tor could have told them the truth of the story, for his mother had confided her secret to him, before she died of a virulent fever when he was but a young lad, but it amused him that people whispered and named him Sir Thomas's bastard and so the whispers continued.

As well as the two houses and the miners' cottages, there was Butts Lane. The miners often found homes there when their working life was over and the cottages were all in bad repair. One or two had been made more habitable by the men whose families occupied them, because it was useless to ask Sir Philip's bailiff for help. Sir Philip paid his workers the expected rate of a pound and ten shillings plus a cottage to live in, and he was a fair master by repute, but requests for repairs were futile, because they would be told by his overseer that the mine wasn't paying and Sir Philip might have to close it. Work on houses and cottages must wait until things improved. It didn't stop Sir Philip and his wife going off to London for Queen Victoria's Golden Jubilee the previous year. Sir Philip, his son and wife had stayed there for a month. His wife had expensive silk dresses and the finest of everything, and his son went to an elite college in Cambridge, sometimes bringing back his rich friends to stay – but there was no money for repairing the cottages in Butts Lane.

Some of the cottages were occupied by craftsmen who worked by flickering candlelight at their trade from first light to dusk and sometimes beyond. Besides the seamstress at number three, who made clothes for everyone, and the washerwoman next door, there was George Jones the cobbler. A Welshman by birth, he'd found himself here after wandering far and wide, fallen in love with a miner's daughter and settled. He and his wife had two young sons. His boots were famed for their lasting ability and folk came from miles around to buy them. Some of them were bought by a shop in Settle for their customers. George might have moved elsewhere and grown richer, but his wife didn't want to leave her family and so he'd repaired their home at his own expense. Just past George's house lived the farrier, Joe Davies. Joe was tall, dark-haired and handsome, with a smile that made Emma's heart jump. She liked him a lot and wished he would look at her the way he did Sarah Mullens, but he hardly noticed Emma, other than to smile and nod in passing.

Sarah was the miller's daughter and her father's house was further down the valley, just at the edge of the next dale. John Mullens owned his mill, and all the farms for miles around took their grain to him at harvest time. Folk said he was the richest man in the district, apart from Sir Philip. Tall, beautiful, with flaming red hair, Sarah was a catch for any man, but Emma knew she had her eye on Tor Hardy.

Although Sarah Mullens was walking out with Joe Davies, she'd told Emma that she would forsake him if Tor came calling.

'Tor is the mine manager and... well, you know what folk say,' Sarah had confided as they'd walked to church one Sunday that previous summer. 'I wouldn't mind living in his house and having his babies. I reckon he's got more money than anyone knows.'

'What makes you think that?' Emma had asked her.

'I saw him buying a gold watch and chain from a shop in York,' Sarah had replied. 'Father went to York on the train, to talk to some people about selling his flour at a better price. Ma and I accompanied him. We had to change trains at a place named Leeds and 'twas a long journey and a little scary, for the noise there was summat terrible, but then we got to York. Oh, Emma, 'tis such a wonderous place! So grand and beautiful. We walked round the town, just looking in the shop windows, Ma and me. The things they had for sale! Jewels and clothes, the prettiest shoes... and all the books you could wish for! I do so love to read stories of love and adventures.' Sarah had sighed. 'I'd give anything to live there.' She'd giggled; her sapphire eyes filled with longing. 'The railway is a blessing, Emma. It's our gateway to the world, a way to escape, but I know I never shall.' Since the line to Garsdale, and then Carlisle, had opened, the Dales, for so long excluded from the outside world, had begun to hear and know more of what went on outside its secluded community. It was possible to get a London newspaper every day if one went into Settle and collected it when the train brought the mail. So much easier than when everything had to come overland by stage coach and important news would be several days old when it reached them. 'I'll be stuck here for the rest of my life.'

'We none of us know what we'll do,' Emma had teased,

laughing. 'When Sir Philip's son brings his rich friends to stay, one of them might fall madly in love with you, Sarah, and carry you off to York, or even London.'

'I'm not sure I'd want to live in London. I've heard it is a wicked place – but I liked York. It was beautiful; the houses and shops are magical, Emma, especially when the street gas-lamps are lit; it gives them a special glow in that golden light. And the Minster! Well, that is a sight to behold, as glorious as any palace the King ever lived in, thass no doubt.' There were no such street lights in Penrith, just the moon that cast its own enchanted silver glow, and a few lanterns outside the church and the bailiff's house.

'Lucky you.' Emma had envied Sarah the trip, because the only places she ever went were Penrith Manor and church on Sunday, or a very occasional visit to Settle as a young girl.

Settle was a thriving market town, and it was there in the Golden Lion Hotel that Jim Watts, Emma's father, had discovered his love for music. In 1841, he'd been taken to a concert given by an important Italian tenor, Signor Malgarini; he'd stood in the street outside in the rain to listen, because they could not get inside, and his heart had soared with the music. Jim had sung in church and as he walked to work at the mine every day. So when in later life he'd had a daughter, Jim had taken his Emma, the light of his life, to Settle, and they'd attended concerts. However, that was impossible now, because of his disability. Jim no longer sang and his family missed the happy sound, especially Emma. She loved her father dearly and treasured her few memories of sweeter days.

Emma thought it wrong of Sarah Mullens to lead Joe on when she didn't want him, because Joe was an important man and looked after everyone's horses. Next to the Blacksmith, Jack Darrow, and Tor Hardy, he was the most important man in their village. Without the farrier, the horses couldn't work, the blacksmith would have no work, the farms no way of transporting grain, and Tor Hardy couldn't ride his magnificent black stallion about the valley like a lord.

Tor was often to be seen standing on a craggy outcrop, where the old iron mine had been, surveying the land as if he owned it; so often, in fact, that it had become known locally as Hardy's Tor, a pun that made folk chuckle.

So the farrier was a respected man and it was wrong to lead him a dance. Emma wouldn't have done it, but Joe was only interested in Sarah.

'Did you hear what I said, bitch?' Ike's voice was suddenly close behind her, making Emma jump, bringing her wandering thoughts back to the present and danger with a start. She jerked away, sprinting as he lunged and evading him as he made a grab for her, but he shouted after her, 'I'll get you one of these days, girl.'

Emma ran the last few steps to her home and burst in, panting.

Her mother looked up from the fragrant stew she was stirring on the range. 'Did her ladyship keep you late again, love?'

'She always does if she can,' Emma said. 'Sir Philip heard her calling me as I was leaving and told me to go. Mrs Briscoe looks after her in the evenings.'

'The housekeeper?' Emma's mother nodded. 'If her ladyship wasn't so mean with her purse strings, she could get a proper lady's maid to live in – instead of expecting you to look after her and help out in the kitchens.'

'I don't mind helping out,' Emma said and smiled as the children, Pete and Jinny, ran to her. She put her hand in her pocket and brought out a shortbread biscuit, which she divided between them. Their cries of delight were frowned on by her mother, who shook her head.

'You shouldn't bring them treats, Emma. They will have their tea soon, love, and if you got caught stealing, you might lose your job.'

'I don't steal. Cook gives me the treats I bring home. She says I work harder than most and she thinks they don't pay me enough.' Slipping her hand into her pocket, Emma brought out a handful of coins and put them on the kitchen mantle. 'Eighteen shillings this month, Ma. I did some sewing and the mistress was pleased with it. She gave me an extra two shillings.'

Mrs Watts sighed and then kissed her daughter. 'You're a good girl, Emma, but it isn't fair that you should work so hard for so little. If we lived in a town, you might find work at the local foundry or a factory and get paid more.'

'I don't think I'd like it, Ma,' Emma replied. 'Do you remember Mabel Hurst? She lived at Rook Farm but went off to work in Leeds – her sister Rose told me she'd had a letter. Mabel got in trouble and was sacked. She couldn't get another job because she had no references, and she went on the streets to feed herself – now she has a baby. She wrote and asked if she could come home, but her father won't have her. He says she has shamed him.'

'Oh, that poor girl,' Mary Watts cried, lifting the saucepan from the gleaming black range to deposit it on the scrubbed-pine table that occupied much of the kitchen. The cottage might be in need of repair, but it was clean and smelled of baking and lavender polish. 'I know she has disgraced herself, but she had a wretched time of it here – working as a milkmaid on that farm and paid just twelve shillings a month and her board. She thought she'd do better in the town.' Mary shook her head over it as she began to spoon out the delicious stew with its dumplings, potatoes and vegetables, with just enough neck of lamb to flavour the gravy.

'Shall I take Father's through?' Emma asked. Her father's bed was in their parlour, because it saved her mother from running upstairs all the time.

'Yes – that small one is his,' Mrs Watts said. 'He isn't feeling up to much, love, and there's no point in wasting good food. I've made a rice pudding too, and he's more likely to eat a bit of that...'

Emma nodded and picked up the tray, carrying it through to her father's room. He was lying with his eyes closed but opened them as she approached the bed and smiled.

'That smells good,' he said, pushing himself up against the feather pillows. His miner's arms, bulging with muscles, hadn't lost their strength, but he had no feeling below his waist. 'Your mother is a wonderful cook, Emma.'

'Shall I sit with you as you eat?' she asked.

'Nay, lass, get thee back and eat tha's meal – but you can read to me later, if you aren't courting; there's a newspaper just two days old the vicar brought me. I could do without his preaching, but he means well.'

'Courting?' Emma laughed. 'I don't get time for it, Da. Besides, who would have me?'

'Any man with eyes to see,' her father replied with a loving smile. Emma wasn't a beauty, with her little turned-up nose and freckles, but she was lovely, inside and out. Her hair was the shade of brown that went red in the sunshine with golden tips, and her mouth was as sweet and fresh as a new-picked apple. 'I wish I was on my feet, lass. I'd take you about so you could meet a proper lad – one that would look after you. Mebbe to a concert in Settle or even to York. Now there's a fine place, though I saw it but once. I'd like to see you wed to a farmer's son – that's a better life than I gave your ma.'

'Ma wouldn't have it any other way,' Emma assured him. 'She loves you – just the way you love her. I wouldn't mind marrying a miner if he loved me that way...' Her voice was a little wistful. 'A good man... whatever he does...'

Her father looked at her sharply. 'Have you found someone, Emma? If you have, you must marry him, lass.'

'And what would Ma do then?' Emma laughed. 'Don't worry your head, Da. I've not found the one yet.'

'I do worry for you and the little ones,' he said, looking sad. 'Once the railway came, I was going to work hard, save some money and get us away – to a big town where I could find a better job and a decent house. I would have, if that accident hadn't laid me low.'

Emma nodded, though she doubted it would have happened. It took money to up sticks and make a new life, and her father had never had much to spare. Like all those who went down the mines, he'd received a pittance for back-aching, draining work that gradually robbed a man of all hope.

'Well, maybe a prince will come riding by and wed me,' Emma said, eyes sparkling with mischief. 'If he does, the first thing he can do is buy you and Ma a nice house.'

'Oh, aye, tha's fit to be a princess, no doubt,' her father said lovingly. 'Some folks might look at the surface, but others will see you for what you are – a clever, intelligent, loving and passionate woman.'

'Da!' Emma exclaimed, blushing. 'You make me sound—' She was cut off by the sound of her mother's voice calling her. 'Eat your supper, Da. You haven't touched it yet.'

'Not hungry, lass – but I'll try. To please you and your ma...'

Emma smiled and blew him a kiss as she went back to the

kitchen. At times, it broke her heart to see the man he'd become. He'd been such a fine strong man until the rockfall that had damaged his spine. Before the tunnel had collapsed on him, he'd carried three injured colleagues to the surface and was going back for the fourth when the roof caved in, burying him. The other men had dug him out. He was still alive, though barely, but the last man he'd been trying to rescue had died.

Mines were terrible places to work in, Emma thought. Especially when the mine owner kept the maintenance to a minimum; then the accidents started to happen. Sir Philip should have paid hundreds of pounds in compensation, not a measly twenty guineas – and the widow of the dead miner had got only twenty-five. It wasn't right and Emma resented that he and his lady just went on spending money on silks and jewels, on visits to London, Ascot for the racing and Henely for regattas, whatever they were – and her family was reduced to making a stew that lasted a week; each time it was reheated, the meat content got less and less. She couldn't even imagine what it was like to go to balls and prestigious parties, but her mistress had clothes for everything, and sometimes told her what life was like beyond the Dales. Emma did her best to help her family, but her money barely covered what they needed with two growing children in the house: her five-year-old brother Pete and her sister Jinny, just eighteen months older.

If only there was some way she could make their lives better!

2

'Reduce the workforce?' Tor Hardy looked at Sir Philip in shock and barely hidden disgust. 'You can't do that, sir. We've barely enough men to do the maintenance and carry on the new dig. We're bound to find a new seam if we keep trying.'

'It's no good, Tor.' Sir Philip looked both tired and apologetic. At nearly fifty, he was still a young man, but he looked nearer sixty, his face drawn with anxiety. 'Do you imagine I want to shut a mine that has been in my family since my great-grandfather's time? I have no choice. I'm in deep debt to London traders, and I may have to sell some of the farms.'

'If the mine closes what will the families do?' Tor asked, holding his temper by a thread. His face was grim, a pulse beating at his right temple. 'The people will starve come next winter... The mine is all they've known and most would struggle to move their families to find work elsewhere.'

A shudder went through Sir Philip. 'I know that... Look, Tor, I know we are brothers. My father told me what he'd done on his deathbed. I believe he feared hell – and he was certainly bound there...' A look of utter disgust passed across Sir Philip's face, still handsome despite the lines of worry. Tor understood what he spoke of. The rape of a woman, any woman, was bad enough – but what Sir Tomas had done to his wife was unforgivable. He'd raped her and beat her and she'd died of her injuries. Then he'd made Tor's father help him put her body on her horse in the dark of night, pushed her off and left her lying on the moor for others to find, the horse grazing nearby, as if it had thrown her...

And then he'd ordered the horse shot for what it had done to his beloved wife. But Tor's mother had seen it all and she'd threatened him with exposure, so he'd raped and beaten her – but she didn't die. Instead she crawled to Tor's father and told him what she'd seen and who had hurt her. Then, when she knew she was with child and threatened to go to the magistrates, Sir Philip's father had paid Tor's father to take the woman he'd wronged to wife, and keep her quiet.

Unspoken, the old scandal lay between the two men like the spectre at the feast. 'I am aware I owe you,' Sir Philip replied, his expression rueful yet with a hint of resentment. 'I have kept the mine open for the last year for that reason – but now I must regretfully close it.'

'Then sell it to me,' Tor said. It was a request and yet Sir Philip heard the underlying threat. 'I will pay you a thousand pounds for it... land and all rights. Including access across your land. And all minerals I find are mine to sell and benefit from.'

'Do you have such a sum?' Sir Philip stared at him in surprise.

'I would not have offered, else.' Tor's gaze was one of pride and confidence.

For a moment, Sir Philip's eyes simmered with an anger that had always been there but tamped down by the debt owed to Tor's mother. Had she gone to the magistrates with her tale, Sir

Thomas would have been ruined and his family with him. Sir Philip was mindful of what was owed even now. With his fortune dissipated by a spendthrift wife, it was only his reputation as a respectable gentleman that kept the axe from falling and a horde of debtors from his door. To be revealed as the son of a murderer and rapist would shame him, destroy him and his family.

'How will you run the mine? It costs money...'

'I can manage,' Tor replied. 'It may take every penny of my savings if we don't find minerals quickly, but this land is rich in them: iron, lead, and many more I've read of. Perhaps not enough to make it worthwhile for you, but enough for me. I'll make it pay a living, I promise you.'

It was true that there were still small deposits of lead to be found, but only in closed-off tunnels that needed a lot of work to make them safe again. Investment would make it workable, but there was no fortune to be got from a mine Sir Philip considered to be played out. It was not worth spending what little he had from rents to keep the miners in work. Though it went against the grain to part with his heritage, it was simpler to let Tor buy it and work it for a year or two – if he could keep it going that long. He didn't hate his half-brother, though he resented that he knew their father's terrible secret and the hold it gave Tor over him.

'Then good luck to you, brother.' Sir Philip extended his hand. 'I've sold one of my farms and that, with the thousand for the mine, should clear the bills my wife ran up in London. A diamond and ruby tiara...' He shook his head in wonder. 'We were not even invited to the Jubilee ceremony, only a ball to celebrate after...' A look of anger passed across his face. 'I would have returned it or sold it for what I could get, but she put me through hell at the very mention of sending it back.'

'You should divorce her,' Tor said, knowing that it wasn't the first time Sir Philip's wife had run up expensive bills on her visits to London. She was the daughter of an impoverished earl and had brought ten thousand pounds to the marriage, but she must have spent far more since, and Sir Philip was a man of modest means. He had land and property, but the rents were not sufficient for such a lifestyle, without the income from the mine. It had brought in a fair amount each year, until the lead began to run out.

'There are times I wish I might, but my son adores his mother and takes after her, and I suppose I still love her.' Sir Philip sighed. 'It was Ralph's latest debts from college that caused me to decide the mine must close.' A wry smile touched his mouth. 'If you do make a success of it, Tor, I'll be glad. You are a better man than I...'

'I wouldn't say that,' Tor muttered gruffly, for Sir Philip was a decent man in his way, but weak. 'You've done your best, sir – and it isn't your fault that woman has near ruined you.'

'Nay, you are too harsh,' Sir Philip told him. 'She was beautiful, merry, and a little wild once, and she could have married a marquis had she wished; he was wealthy but she chose me. I loved her then. Believed I had caught the prize of the season. I think she loved me – but she craves the London life and hates this place. It makes her ill and unhappy. If I sell everything and rent a modest house in London, I can give her what she needs for a few years.'

'And what then?' Tor asked sceptically.

'I'll either put a pistol to my brain or ask my rich brother to help me out,' Sir Philip said, a glimmer of humour in his eyes. 'You didn't save a thousand pounds from what I pay you, Tor. I don't care how you made your money, but what it says to me is that you'll be rich one day.'

Tor laughed. 'I did nothing very wrong, but I doubt you'd

approve, so I'll keep it to myself,' he said. 'I don't care about riches, but I want land, a wife and two sons. One day I'll own a better farm than my father ever had, maybe more – if my gamble pays off.'

'The iron ran out in my grandfather's day and now the lead is hardly worth the effort,' Sir Philip said reflectively. 'I know some mine owners have found rich sources of other minerals, but I can't hang on any longer – so good luck to you, Tor.'

Tor nodded. 'Will you have your lawyer draw up the bill of sale?'

'Yes, of course – and thank you for your loyalty all these years. We could have been enemies but instead we've been friends. I did resent you when we were younger, but when you became the mine manager, I respected you. The men worked well for you, Tor. That last seam of lead you found kept us going for a couple of years – longer, if my wife did not demand diamond tiaras.' His mouth twisted in a wry smile. 'My advice for what it is worth – be careful who you take for a wife; they can be the very devil to live with.'

'I'll marry a working girl, not a duke's daughter,' Tor said, and they both laughed, for Lady Penrith was but a lord's daughter, though she carried herself with all the regal bearing of a duchess.

'Aye. I'd have done better to do the same – but Sir Thomas wanted good blood in the family and I sought to please him, for I knew not the blackguard he was then.'

They shook hands again and parted.

Tor left the house and mounted his horse; he rode towards the mine. He would go down the old tunnels he'd discovered, again. Sir Philip was correct that the iron had run out years before, but Tor had gone down a small side passage that had not yet been exploited for minerals, and he'd seen a gleam of something halfway up the wall. It might have been just the sheen of water – and yet his instincts told him it was a mineral, though he had no idea what it could be. Silver would be wonderful, yet he hadn't heard of any real finds of that metal in the vicinity, just small deposits here and there. There were, however, many other minerals being found and some of them were worth a fortune.

It had been on the tip of Tor's tongue to tell Sir Philip that he might be on the brink of a great discovery, but he'd been adamant that he wanted to close the mine – and his lack of concern for the miners and their families had made Tor angry. That woman he'd married had run through a small fortune and it looked like their son, Ralph, was about to do the same. Even if Sir Philip sold all his land and perhaps his house, the money would only last a few years in the hands of his family.

Tor frowned, because Sir Philip wasn't a bad man; he was fair, according to his standards, but his family were greedy and grasping. Tor would have to make sure that the bill of sale was waterproof, because if he discovered a rich seam of some mineral, Sir Philip's wife and son might try to snatch back the mine. Sir Philip would stand by his word, but his wife and son were another matter…

* * *

'Going to London for good?' Later that same day, Emma looked at her mistress in dismay. 'You won't be needing me again?'

'Are you deaf, girl?' Lady Penrith gave her a look of disdain. 'My son may visit the house occasionally, but he will not need a personal maid. However, as you have proved your worth in the kitchen, I am prepared to let you stay on until we decide whether or not to sell the house…' Emma's swift thank you died unspoken as she went on. 'Of course, your wage will reduce to eight shillings a month. You are not a qualified cook, just a kitchen maid.'

Emma's breath left her. She'd earned twice that before and that was barely enough to keep her family. Her stomach churned in distress. She wanted to throw the offer back in Lady Penrith's face and walk out, never to return, but she dared not. There was no other work for her, except on a farm and she might have to live in for even less money. It was so unfair. Emma knew that with her skills for sewing and dressing hair, she could earn far more in a town household. Perhaps as much as two pounds a month as a personal maid to a lady. However, it would break her heart if she had to go away to find work, and her father might lose the will to live. Without Emma's help in the evenings, her mother would become tired and ill. She was caught in a trap and could see no way out of it.

'Yes, my lady, thank you for the chance,' Emma replied dutifully and saw the gleam of spite in the older woman's eyes. She was actually enjoying this! It was so mean, so vicious!

Emma was dismissed, her unshed tears burning behind her eyes. She hurried to the kitchen, where she was met by Cook. One look at her face told Emma that she too had been treated unfairly.

'What has she offered you?' Cook asked, her cheeks fiery, eyes gleaming with frustration. 'I'm to be a part-time servant now, if you please – and half the wages I had, which were as low as she dared go. I shall only be needed if they come down for a weekend – or her son wants to bring his friends here. Mrs Briscoe is to stay on to care for the house until it is sold and she may get taken on by the new owner. You'll come in to help her meantime – and Ruby is to clean and scrub twice a week. The horses are to be sold – bar two, which will be stabled with one of the tenant farmers and there will be one outside man to keep the garden tidy.'

'The house will fall into disrepair,' Emma said. 'I am to be a kitchen maid and given eight shillings a month. I don't know how we shall live...' Tears escaped and trickled down her cheek. 'I can't bear the thought of telling my mother...'

'It is downright disgraceful,' Cook said. 'I shan't stay for longer than it takes me to find a new post. I'll go to York – and you should, too, Emma. It is not such a long journey now we have the railway. Happen, you won't find a decent job round here, love, and you don't want the factories of Leeds, nor yet the pottery in Black Burton. Those cotton mills in Lancashire are terrible places to work; besides, some of them are closing these days. York is the place for me – you too, if you can bear to leave your father.'

'I know – but I can sew,' Emma reminded her. 'Mrs Tilley, the seamstress, told me I could do work for her in the evenings. She'll pay me sixpence an hour. I didn't take her up, because I help Ma – but I can scrub the kitchen floor before I come to work.'

'Well, while I'm still here, you can come in an hour later,' Cook told her. 'Why should you work as many hours when you're not paid for them? I can't say what Mrs Briscoe will do. She says she will stay for now. Her wage hasn't changed, but she worries, because she thinks it won't be long before they sell – though, someone better might be mistress here then.'

'If they kept us on...' Emma looked at her hopefully. 'More than likely a new mistress would have her own maid – so I'd still be just a kitchen maid.'

'Not if I teach you to make some fancy dishes,' Cook replied, eyes twinkling with good humour. 'You're a good plain cook already, Emma. Your ma taught you – but she doesn't know the fancy stuff the gentry like. I can help you learn, and I'll let you copy my recipe books. You'd stand a chance of a better life then as a cook...'

'Oh, bless you!' Emma cried and hugged her ample waist. 'You know you are the main reason I've managed to stay here these past three years.'

Cook's cheeks were burning again, but this time with pleasure. 'Well, you're a good girl, Emma Watts, and I'd like to see you have a better life. I'll be off as soon as I can and then you can bargain for your wage – don't take less than four pounds a month. You'd get more in town once you've mastered the dishes I'll show you, more like double – but you'll need to work hard. You'll be helping Ruby clean the house as well as me...'

'I should be very happy with the four pounds,' Emma said wistfully, for it would be riches to her. 'She might not give it to me – but I know the vicar is looking for a cook. Why don't you apply?'

'Because we had a falling out years ago,' Cook replied and started stirring her custard more vigorously. 'He came courting when I was assistant cook here, just a young girl, and there was plenty of money when Sir Thomas was alive – you just had to watch he didn't get you in a corner...'

'What happened?' Emma asked. 'Why would you fall out with the Reverend Henry Joseph?' She'd always thought him pious, if harsh in the pulpit.

'He was the curate then,' Cook replied. 'At the time, I wanted to learn and become a cook. It meant a lot to me – and a curate doesn't earn much of a living. He asked me to wed and I turned him down; he's averted his head each time he sees me from that day to this, and I did truly care for him – but I couldn't ever tell him I'd changed my mind. It was my pride, you see.'

'That is sad,' Emma said. 'You never married?'

'Never wanted anyone else,' Cook replied. 'Henry was wed for a time, but she and the child she carried both died when she was in labour. She was a delicate girl. He went away for years; then, when our old vicar died, he returned to take the living...'

'He didn't marry again,' Emma said, looking thoughtful. 'He has had the same housekeeper for years, but she retires very soon.'

'Aye.' Cook sighed. 'I'd have taken the job gladly – but he wouldn't want me.'

'No, I see how you feel. You must be embarrassed to ask...' Emma said and then smiled. 'What would you like me to do first today?'

'You can peel the spuds and then there's winter cabbage, parsnips and swede. It's saddle of lamb today. Mester bought a sheep from Farmer Mowburry – or, mayhap, it was part of the deal. Mr Blackburn says Mowburry has bought the farm he's been tenant of for the past twenty years.'

'Has Mr Blackburn lost his job too?' Mr Blackburn was their elderly butler and near to retirement age.

'Aye – but he's glad of it,' Cook replied. 'The mester treated him fairly. He is to have a hundred guineas and a cottage the other side of the dale. It's to be his own, so he says. Besides, he has a bit put by him. In the old days, he got a lot of guineas slipped into his hand, and he was always a mean old thing. Never spent a penny if a groat would do...' Cook gave a cackle of laughter. 'I've got a few bob put by, so I'll likely be off once they've gone to London. You'll have to learn sharpish if you want to take my place, Emma.'

'I shall. I promise I shall,' Emma said and smiled as she bent over the large pile of potatoes. Her mind was busy with her future plans and not all of them were for her.

3

'Is it true that bastard is to close the mine?' Ike Hanson demanded when Tor reached the mine entrance the next morning. A group of about twenty men had gathered outside and he could see Ike had been whipping them up and making them angry, their breath, in loud complaint, white smoke on the icy air. It had been a long cold winter and spring was late in coming. 'Don't think to lie to us, Hardy. We know it is the truth.' There was a chorus of 'Aye' from several throats.

'I never lie to you – all here know that,' Tor said, his face like thunder. 'It is true that Sir Philip is giving up – but there is to be a new owner.'

'Who is he?' Ike demanded, his face reddened in the bitter March winds, eyes resentful. 'We've a right to know, Hardy.'

'You will know when I choose to tell you,' Tor said, his voice still calm, toneless. 'And you'll address me as Mr Hardy – or you can take your pick and go home now.'

Fury simmered in Ike Hanson's face, one fist balled at his side, the other hand gripping the handle of his heavy pick. The man was a surly brute with few friends; he'd had a hard upbringing, his father quick with his fist and brutal with the strap. Tor had felt sorry for Ike when he was a boy; he'd come to school barefoot, his clothes often unwashed, and his face pinched with hunger. Only after his father died and Ike had begun work in the mine had the family prospered. The look of fury in his eyes told Tor he burned to strike him, but he was the giver of work and his word was law to these men. They had no choice because there were few enough jobs for men who had no other trade in this valley. Most of the farmers had sons to work the land and only took on extra labour at harvest time; there was seldom a job vacant at the house, and unless you were a carpenter or a thatcher, a farrier or even a boot maker, nothing else was available but the hard slog of the mines, and the only carpenter for miles relied on repairs to the mine for half his living. If Ike lost his job, he would have to look further afield for his living.

Women made their own bread, grew most of their vegetables, scrubbed floors, mended, baked, pickled and, often, made their own clothes. The milkmaids delivered the milk and butter, but the women kept chickens scratching in their back yards and so had their own eggs; a fresh-killed pullet was the meat most families ate; beef and lamb were a treat and bought from one of the larger markets or a farm for special occasions. Sheep were plentiful in the dale and sometimes the families put together to buy a carcass from a farmer. Once a year, a couple of piglets would be purchased at the market in Settle, reared on scraps from every house, then slaughtered and the meat shared by all who had contributed. The women worked from dawn to dusk, as did their men, taking a rest only on the Lord's Day, when they all went to church. Only those bedridden or very sick were excused, for those who didn't received a visit from the vicar, who threatened eternal damnation – and, if the culprit played truant too often, from Sir Philip, who threatened far worse. His workers must be God-fearing or they could seek employment elsewhere. Even Ike paid his respects frequently enough to be sure of his job, if not his eternal soul.

Some men left the valley, taking their families to seek a better life, either in the big towns or perhaps at the coast, but whether or not they succeeded was often never known. None had returned and most could not write more than their own name, despite spending time at the tiny school, which was run by the vicar, but overseen by Mistress Findley. She was entering her sixtieth year, not born in the valley but a woman of learning. She'd come when the old vicar – now long retired – had with great boldness advertised in a national newspaper. Unable to give the school the proper attention, he'd known help could only come from outside the valley. Mistress Findley had arrived over forty years ago and if the vicar knew where she'd come from or why, no one else did. She lived alone in a small cottage near the vicarage and was so strict that even the men of the mine tipped their caps in respect when she was seen in the village.

There were no shops in the valley; food and milk could be bought from the farms, flour from Miller Mullens, but a carrier from Settle visited every few weeks and would take orders for things like cloth and sewing materials, tools that could not be made by the blacksmith. Books, writing paper, inks – something most had no use for – even the London newspapers were also among the goods Jack Jethson delivered on his regular visits. He often brought large parcels for the Manor, smaller ones for the vicar and school, but not many had coin to spare for fripperies like ribbons and lace – apart from the folk at the big house.

So, even though Ike hated him, Tor knew he would not strike

unless pushed to the limit, and he had so far managed to keep from giving him the tongue-lashing he deserved. Sullen and bad-tempered, Ike was strong and a good worker. Most men were too afraid of him to speak against him, but he wasn't liked. Tor was as big as Ike. They stood toe to toe, both solid men with strong backs and even stronger wills. Tor was just luckier. Had his mother not witnessed Sir Thomas murder his wife, Tor would no doubt be one of the mine workers, slogging his guts out day in and day out for a pittance. His mother had married the man she'd wanted all along, but Sir Thomas had never known it, and he'd paid well for their silence over the years – but Sir Philip had behaved like a gentleman. In private he acknowledged Tor as his brother and he'd given him the job when the old mine manager retired, dying soon after of a lung disease. Many of those who worked in the mines would die young of the same disease, or simply because they were worn out.

'Are you working today?' Tor asked, his gaze moving over the assembled men. 'Or shall I tell Sir Philip to just close the mine?'

'We're going,' one of the men answered. 'Thanks for telling us, Mr Hardy. Thass just worried we are for our jobs, sir.'

'I know, Jacob,' Tor answered. Jacob Hymes was a good worker, strong and normally one to keep his mouth shut. 'You can take my word for it – the mine will keep going as long as we have something we can sell. Have any of you noticed new deposits – anything that looks worth investigating?'

Jacob shook his head. 'Just the seam of lead we're working on now.'

'There are older tunnels,' one of the others spoke up. 'You'll need to shore them up, 'cos they're not safe – but my grandfather swore he found silver in one of them. No one believed him, but he kept a small piece until he died...'

'Do you have it still, Jon Reed?' Tor asked, a tingle at the base of his neck.

'Aye, I kept it in memory of him,' the older man replied.

'Then I'll get it analysed in York,' Tor told him. 'Do you know which of the tunnels it came from?'

'I might...' Jon Reed wrinkled his brow. 'Granfer took me down and showed me it once, but it was unsafe even then, because it was one of the ancient workings. He'd gone down there after a dog... Used to take the animal everywhere with him. Risked his life to get it back, he did. Had to crawl over a fall of rock and thass where he saw it.'

'Your granfer was a brave man,' Tor said. 'I'll ask you to show me the tunnel another day, if you can find it.'

'I'll try, sir.'

Tor nodded. He knew the find was unlikely to be silver, but there were so many precious minerals in the ground in this district; it could be one of many things. His instinct was for zinc. He'd taken a sample into York the last time he'd visited and he would get the results when he went in next week on the train. It was an overnight stay, which Tor never minded, for he had friends and business contacts there – business for himself as well as the mine. In York, he'd met someone, a man who could be very helpful and he'd asked him to meet him, but as yet he was not sure the man would come. If he did, it would help Tor make a success of the mine he'd used most of his savings to purchase, though he was determined he would make it pay. Not just for himself. Tor could turn his hand to most things and he didn't mind hard work, but without the mine the village folk would have nothing. Most of them would have to leave, to find work in towns or shipyards, for there was little else, and many would fail, their families cast on the parish. He knew that only the mine would keep the people here – otherwise they would drift away until only the old and sick were left. Some would ask why it mattered, but for Tor it was a burning need. This was his land, his people and they would prosper as he prospered.

While in York, Tor had bought himself a gold watch and chain – well, truth to tell, it was silver with gold plating, but it looked like gold and he wore it proudly when he went to church. He was a single man and could afford a few luxuries for himself, though of late his mind had turned to marriage. The house was empty since his father's death; his mother had gone first, but his father had lingered, suffering a cruel, wracking death that had wasted a once-strong body. Even so, Tor had looked after him. He'd had help from some of the miners' wives, but mostly he'd cared for his father himself, cleaning him up and feeding him, carrying him up and down the stairs so he could sit in his armchair while Tor was at work – or in the garden if the weather was warm. He missed both his parents, though he would never have admitted it. Tor was known as a hard man and that was the way it must remain to keep discipline.

He wasn't sure about romantic love, but he was a man and he'd known women in York. He'd paid a woman of the streets the first time, but after that he'd found a pleasing widow, who had been happy to welcome him and always had clean sheets on her bed when he let her know he would visit her.

Tor wanted a woman who would work hard, as he did; cook, clean and bake, and bear his children – sons preferably. In return, she would have a better life than most in the village. Pretty clothes, a few trinkets – more if he found a rich seam in the mine. He would treat her well. He was not a brute, but neither was he a romantic man. At least he hadn't thought so until... A memory of a girl's scared face and then the relief and her smile had given him some restless nights of late...

Tor thought it was the incident, when he'd saved the girl who worked up at Penrith Manor from certain rape, that had started him thinking about a wife. He'd had no doubt about Ike Hanson's intent as he'd seen her struggling for her life and her virtue – Emma Watts. He'd seen her about, of course, up at the house, in the village. She'd brought refreshments to the study when Sir Philip rang, and he'd noticed her running between the village and the Manor more times than he could recall. Emma was always hurrying from one place to another, but he hadn't taken too much notice until the day he saw Ike Hanson trying to violate her. Rage had built inside him then and for two pins he would have killed the bugger, but Ike had sworn at him, clenched his jaw and walked away. Had he chosen to fight, one of them would be dead.

Tor had never killed anyone, but he could kill, he knew that. He'd had to put down a fox that was caught in a trap. Not in Penrith Valley but in the next. He wouldn't have allowed traps here and nor would Sir Philip. Riding home from the railway station, after one of his business trips, Tor had heard the poor creature's screams. He'd dismounted, followed the sound, but the creature had nearly bitten through its leg in a desperate struggle to get free. Tor knew it couldn't live that way in the wild and would be miserable in captivity, so he'd released it from the trap and then snapped its neck. His hands were very strong. He'd felt pity for the poor beast, but it was his duty to put it out of its misery and so he had. It needed to be done and he'd done it.

The look in the girl's eyes when he'd thrashed Ike had been relief mixed with gratitude and something more. Tor had dismissed her thanks brusquely, but he'd found himself watching for her as she walked home, surveying her from a distance until she was safely inside. He couldn't always be there, because his job involved overseeing the men and checking their work, as well as meetings with Sir Philip and trips into Leeds or York on mine business, but whenever he could, he would make sure that bastard didn't get to her. One day there would be a reckoning between them, but Tor didn't want to swing for murder and so he bided his time – when it happened, it must be Ike who attacked him and it must be witnessed so it was known to be self-defence. But given the chance, he'd break his neck the way he had the fox's.

Soon, Tor would have achieved his first ambition. The mine would be his and then he could think about taking a wife. Emma's family would be cared for; he'd see to that – and she would have a good life. First, he had to make sure he wasn't cheated. Lawyers could insert fancy clauses into a contract, but Tor knew what he was doing. He had to own the mineral rights as well as the land, otherwise the Penrith family could claim a share when a rich seam was found.

Tor was one of the few in the village who could write more than his name; his mother had taught him and she was a clever woman. His father was a crafty one with a nose for the main chance, but Tor's mother was clever; it was she who had seen the way to make their fortunes from the secret she carried to her grave. Now his ambition was within his grasp.

Tor laughed out loud. He was counting his chickens too soon, but he knew he was right – the minerals were there in the mine, enough to make him a rich man. All his instincts told him it was so. He just had to find them. Then he would set about getting all the rest – the farms and the house itself.

Oh yes, he wanted it all. Sir Thomas thought he'd paid for silence and he'd got it, but what about justice? He'd got away with murder and much, much more. Tor had been still a child, too young to take revenge before Sir Thomas died a natural death – and Sir Philip was a decent man, but now Tor's chance had come. He would have all that had belonged to the family for generations and Sir Thomas and his ancestors could turn in their graves!

4

Sarah Mullens looked up into the face of the man who had just taken her down, not with tenderness and love, but with the rough, raw passion she needed. The wild streak in her demanded more than the gentle kisses Joe Davies offered – but this man was rough and strong, and she liked him that way.

'You must marry me, Ike,' she insisted as he turned from her and flopped on his back, satiated by the passionate loving they had both enjoyed so much. 'I'm having a bairn and it's yours.'

'Who says?' Ike demanded carelessly.

'I do,' Sarah said, sitting up to look down at him. Ike was handsome in his own way, despite a scar at his brow, but coarse and harsh. Yet it was that hardness in him that had attracted her. She enjoyed being mastered; she liked the fight and the fierceness of rough love, providing it didn't go too far. 'Who's else would it be?'

'Joe Davies',' he replied, lying there with his eyes closed.

Sarah leaned over him and struck him on his ear with all her strength.

He yelped in pain and jerked up, grabbing her wrist in an iron grip. 'What was that for, vixen?'

'You know the only reason I walk out with Joe,' Sarah replied, angry now. 'My father insists I find a decent man to marry – and that isn't you, Ike. I use my walking out with Joe as a way of being with you.'

'Then marry him,' Ike said, shrugging as he hauled himself to his feet. Sarah was on hers now, sapphire eyes blazing, wild red hair falling about her shoulders in thick waves. 'I'll not marry you, Sarah. I'll not marry any woman.'

'Why?' she demanded. 'I don't understand – you want me and my father has money; it will come to me one day. Why won't you wed me?'

Ike rounded on her furiously, grabbing her by the throat so that she stared up at him with frightened eyes. Breathing heavily, he said, 'That's why. My temper won't stand nagging – and I've enough of it from my mother and sister. Push me too far and I'll do to you what my father did to them – he damned near killed my mother once. Would have if I hadn't hit him with a poker. Thrashed me then, instead of them.' He released her and she rubbed at her throat, looking at him resentfully. 'Besides, why should I bother with a wife when I can get what I want whenever I want it?'

'Then damn you!' Sarah cried and struck out at him again, but he caught her wrist and pulled her in close, pressing his mouth against hers and grinding until she tasted blood. He pulled away from her and she spat in his face. 'I hate you, Ike Hanson.'

'You love me,' he crowed confidently. 'You love what I do to you – crave it, and you'll come back to me after you marry that milksop. Marry him and please your father – when you need me, I'll be around.'

'I'll never lie with you again, you bastard...'

Ike laughed and walked off, leaving Sarah to stare after him in frustration. She'd thought the first time Ike had waylaid her that he truly wanted her, truly cared. He'd told her the other women he'd had meant nothing to him, and she'd believed him. She had given into his pestering to lie with him, because she'd wanted him badly. He filled her with a raging need no other man ever had – including the man she would probably marry, though Joe hadn't asked her yet.

'I hate you...' she whispered to Ike's retreating back. 'I'll get even – see if I don't...'

Sarah thought swiftly. If Ike wouldn't wed her, she didn't have much time. She must get Joe Davies to wed her and soon. He hadn't tried to do more than kiss her yet, but if she encouraged him, he would take what she offered... then she could say it was his child and be wed before she began to show.

Walking home to the mill, Sarah decided that she would put her plan into action the next day. She would be bold and go to Joe's home... Her thoughts gathered pace as she thought of her story. She would tell Joe she loved him but was afraid her father meant her to marry Tor Hardy. Sarah would have taken him like a shot, but when her father hinted at it to Tor, he'd turned him down flat. Told him he had other plans... Sarah wondered who the lucky woman was, but there was no time for regrets. She'd wanted Tor, but her pride had made her angry at his rejection of her father's offer – and then Ike had come after her and she'd gone with him recklessly, perhaps because she needed his lovemaking and perhaps to heal her bruised vanity.

She had to persuade Joe into taking her down, and she had to convince him he was the first with her – but she could whimper with the best of them. A smile touched Sarah's mouth.

Oh yes, Joe wouldn't know whether he was on his head or his heels by the time she'd finished with him.

A sense of searing loss went through her. She doubted that Joe would give her the satisfaction she'd felt with Ike – she doubted any man would be able to satisfy her needs, because she had a hunger inside her that would not be stilled. Even now, when she'd just been with Ike – and hated him! – she craved what he could give her. It would be hard to resist him when he called, and she knew he would. Her blood quickened at the very thought of it, but she could be stubborn. Ike would crawl to her before she lay with him again!

Sarah laughed suddenly and began to run towards her home. She would have Joe as her husband – and if she chose, she would have Ike when she wanted him, too.

Running wildly, her hair flying in the wind, Sarah didn't see the man standing on Hardy's Tor. Her thoughts were too busy with the plans she was weaving to look back, nor did she think to. No one ever came to this place at night – unless it was the smugglers she'd heard whispers of, and Sarah only half believed those tales. Surely that had died out in the last century?

* * *

The man watched her disappear into the darkness, then walked down to where his horse was tethered, quietly grazing. He mounted the fine stallion, which he'd bought at the Appleby horse fair with his first wages as the mine manager. He'd bought him cheaply from the gipsy who owned him, because the fool couldn't handle him, yet he'd responded to Tor like a babe, nuzzling him and eating from his hand.

Tor leaned forward and patted the horse's neck. He'd been waiting for Red Tikka and the men who smuggled illicit goods into the Dales, but the time had passed and he would wait no longer.

'Thass strange what one sees on a dark night,' he murmured. 'The gentlemen won't come now, not tonight. Something must have happened – so we're away, thee to tha' stable, lad, and missen to my bed.'

5

'So her ladyship got off then?' Mary Watts asked her daughter that evening. 'I saw her carriage and all the baggage she took with her as I was in the village.'

'Aye, she has gone and glad to shake the dust from her feet. I heard her say it and that she never wanted to come near again.'

'So you're just a kitchen maid now then?'

'Unless I can persuade the mester to take me on as cook when she leaves.'

'It would be a fine thing for you,' Emma's mother said. 'A cook can always find a job – and there are big houses in the Dales, a way off, but tha's a strong lass and won't mind the walk. We could ask the carter to inquire if there is a job going somewhere else.'

'But if it was too far, I wouldn't get home every night,' Emma objected. 'You would never get any rest then, Ma.'

'You'd get a day off once a month,' her mother told her. 'You could come home then, love. I would miss you and so would your da, but it might be better for you. You'd see more of life, Emma. They might even take you to York or London. Some of the gentry have houses all over the place, and as a fine cook, they might want you wherever they happen to be.'

'Ladies' maids get taken all over, too,' Emma replied. 'I have skill with dressing hair and sewing, too, Ma. I know I could get a better job elsewhere, but I want to stay near my family for as long as I can.'

'We can't manage on what her ladyship intends to pay you – and sooner or later she will let you go, Emma. Then tha'll have to look further afield or it will be up with the lark and the work of a milkmaid. Tha'll not enjoy that, my chick.'

'I know...' Emma sighed. 'Cook says she shall stay for another month and then she is off. She got the *Ladies Monthly* magazine delivered this morning and she has written for three jobs. She will teach me all she can in the meantime, and she has promised me a book of her recipes, but it isn't long to learn everything.'

'You learned to cook at my knee,' her mother said. 'We've never had need of the fancy foods they eat up at the Manor, but there are other houses who would be glad of a good plain cook, my love.'

'Yes, and I'll be able to cook quite a bit of fancy food too,' Emma agreed. She went to give her mother a hug. 'It's just that I don't want to leave you and Da – and the little ones. How will you manage?'

'Jenny Hargreaves is wanting a little job. She is still at school, but she'd help me in the evenings, if I asked. Her mother says two shillings is all she needs, until she leaves school – and your sister will be big enough to help me soon.'

Emma sat on the old oak settle, its hard, carved back made comfortable by cushions she and her mother had sewn. It was true that she could not manage on eight shillings a month, but, when Cook left the Manor and Sir Philip realised there was no one but Emma to cook for him if he visited, he was bound to give her more. She would ask for three pounds a month. Cook had four, but she said she could get more elsewhere. Emma couldn't hope to achieve her standards, but Sir Philip never asked for a lot of fancy puddings when he visited alone. His son was more interested in wine and brandy, but his rich friends might expect more than Emma was capable of producing.

'I'll speak to Sir Philip when he returns,' Emma told her mother after some thought. 'Cook says she shan't tell them she is leaving so they won't have a chance to find anyone else and they'll be glad to have me.'

'That's if he ever returns…'

'Oh, he will. His son is bringing some friends soon. It is the Easter break. Sir Philip is bound to come then, if only to make sure everything is in readiness. They will need to bring in extra staff for a week or two.'

'If anyone will go,' her mother remarked wryly. 'They've not done well by their staff and some folk have looked elsewhere for work. Dick Robinson, the head groom, has gone for a job in the stables at Settle, and his family with him. I heard the mine was to close, but they say now it has been sold, though no one knows who owns it.'

'Cook doesn't know either,' Emma said. 'I'm doing the cooking now, Ma. I'll make some extra and bring a bit home for you and the children. Da might eat a bit of my lemon meringue pie…'

'Aye, lass, he might,' Mrs Watts agreed. 'There was a time when I could make that – when your father was earning good wages. We had it as a treat for his birthday and he loved it.'

'I'll make a big one for the house and a small one for us,' Emma promised. 'Don't look so worried, Ma. No one will know, I swear. Cook often makes treats for us. She orders the kitchen stores herself and a bit extra means we get fed the same as them upstairs.'

'I dare say it happens in most big houses,' her mother said. 'But Lady Penrith is such a miser when it comes to her staff. If she found out, you could all be in trouble. She might accuse you of stealing.'

'If she did, she would have no servants, because no one would work for her,' Emma said and laughed. 'Before I took the job, she couldn't keep a maid more than a month. Besides, she's gone and won't return.'

Emma had stayed because it suited her. She could live at home and run the distance between the village and the big house at the top of the hill, night and morning; it kept her fit and she loved the freedom of being on the open moorland in the fresh air. Cook had always liked her, because she helped her even though she didn't have to, and she'd given Emma bits and pieces to take home for her family – and, occasionally, her ladyship would discard a scarf or a dress that was torn or stained. It was thrown out but Emma took them home and used the good bits of material to make a Sunday blouse for herself and a nightdress for her mother. That was one of the perks, but she had to put up with complaints and grumbling all the time. Some girls might not have been strong enough, but Emma had grown used to the harsh words and didn't let them hurt her.

* * *

'It's nice being here with just you and the others,' Emma told Cook the next day when she was showing her how to make a delicious brandy sauce that accompanied roast pheasant. It was an extravagant meal for the kitchen, but, as Cook said, there was no one around to see, and the game wouldn't keep. 'It's a pity it can't stay this way.'

'Well, most of the others will be off at the end of the week. Mrs Briscoe is having her meals with us now, but she may decide to eat in her room again when it is just you two most of the time...'

Ruby, the kitchen girl, came in with her bucket then and promptly burst into tears. 'I don't want to leave,' she sobbed. 'Ma says I must go scrubbing at the vicarage in the mornings, after I've helped Da milk the cows, and then stay home and help her. She never stops scolding me – and I liked talking to you, Emma, and you, Cook.' Born on a farm, she'd enjoyed coming to the Manor and meeting people instead of working on her father's land, dawn to dusk.

'Stop that wailing, Ruby,' Cook said sternly. 'You're to come twice a week to clean, though you'll find that hard if you've to milk cows first. How often are you needed at the vicarage?' She shook her head as the girl burst into a fresh storm of tears. Her eyes and nose were red, because she hadn't stopped crying since she'd been told she had a week's notice and would then only be needed twice a week in the mornings.

'Ma says I can do the milking, then Dad will let me come to the Manor. I'm to do my work, get my dinner and then walk back to the farm for the second milking. I'm to go two days a week to the vicarage for the scrubbing. I'll never have a day off at all...'

'That's a bit hard,' Emma sympathised. 'Never mind, Ruby. We can chat when you come to the Manor and I'll give you a nice dinner – perhaps your ma will let you have a day off sometimes. I don't go far, but on my day off I occasionally get a lift to the market at Settle. We could go together...'

Ruby's face lit up. 'You're so kind,' she said. 'Perhaps if you spoke to Ma, she might let me – now and then.'

'I expect she was more cross with her ladyship than you,' Emma said. 'She will miss your extra money, Ruby.'

'I used to keep a shilling a week myself,' Ruby said, looking doleful. 'Ma says she'll need all I earn now...'

'I don't keep much either, just a shilling now and then, if I earn extra with my sewing,' Emma told her. 'But it is free to walk to the market, and someone usually offers a lift on a cart, part of the way – and 'tis free to look, Ruby.'

'Yes. I would enjoy just walking there and back with you,' Ruby agreed and stopped crying as Cook placed a mug of tea and a big slice of seed cake on the table in front of her.

'Get that down you, child,' Cook told her. 'There's always a ray of light somewhere. I'll keep an eye out for you – I'll be finding a good place for myself and if I get the chance, I'll ask for you as my kitchen maid. You'd live in and get more than you do here.'

Ruby's face lit up like a candle. 'You and Emma – you're why I like working here. I am going to miss you both.'

'I might tell the mester I can't manage without you,' Emma said. 'He is more generous than her ladyship. I dare say he may realise that if he wishes for some comfort in his house, he needs servants – and not just part-time ones...'

* * *

'Well,' Cook said after Ruby had departed to polish the bannisters on the imposing staircase that ran from the big hall to the first landing. 'I can't blame her for being upset. Her mother is a harridan and she'll make poor Ruby's life a misery.'

She smiled. 'Wouldn't it be good if there was a job for you as an assistant cook as well as Ruby, wherever I go?'

'Oh yes,' Emma replied. 'Ma thinks I should find a place not too far away so that I can come home on my day off – but I liked working here and going home at night.'

'I've no home to go to,' Cook said, and for a moment there was fear in her eyes. 'I'd hoped to end my days here, for I thought Sir Philip might let me live in Butts Lane when my working days are done. I've no relations and I never married...' A shudder ran through her. 'It would have been the workhouse for me a few years ago, but now... many of those places are closing, so I don't know where I'd go. A room in a boarding house for as long as my savings last, I suppose.' A shiver ran through her, for she could end on the streets as a vagrant.

'Don't think about it,' Emma advised. 'You may find a really good mistress who will provide for you... a lot do, so I've been told, but wherever I am, Cook, there will be an armchair for you in my home. I can't promise a bed, except on the kitchen floor, because Da has the parlour and the children occupy the bedrooms.'

'Emma! You sweet angel!' Cook cried and promptly burst into tears. 'I dare say I'll never need it for I have a little nest egg – but the promise is enough to rest my fears.'

Emma smiled and moved towards her. They embraced, friends and allies in a world that was not always fair to women like them. 'I might have a house of my own,' Emma said, eyes dancing with merriment. 'Da has always called me his princess – so perhaps my prince will ride into the valley and claim me.'

'You're a caution, you are,' Cook said. 'Watch that sauce, Emma. The first thing you need to know is never burn an expensive sauce – because if you do, you start all over again and when you've a banquet to provide, you don't have the time...'

* * *

Emma left for home earlier that evening. With the family in London, there was little work to be done after the cleaning was finished, and everyone was fed. It was the end of March now and the weather was still harsh beneath the shadow of the Pennines. A cruel wind blew down the Dales, steep, rolling hills channelling it like a funnel. Emma walked, carrying her treasure carefully. Cook said it was one of the best lemon meringues she'd ever tasted. It was small, but her family would each get a piece to taste and she didn't want it to crumble, because the pastry was so light.

Aware of a horse behind her, Emma stopped walking and moved to the side of the narrow path to allow whoever it was passage, but, to her surprise, the rider brought his horse to a halt beside her. She looked up and saw that it was Tor Hardy.

'Good afternoon, Miss Watts,' he said and bowed his head to her. She knew that when standing he towered over her, a thickset man, attractive but with a hard, stern face and steely eyes, his hair as black as night. 'Thass early you are this evening. 'Tis normally dark when you go home.'

'The family are away and Mrs Briscoe gave me leave,' Emma replied, a little apprehensively. He was after all a man of importance in these parts and respect was due. 'My work is done, sir.'

'Aye, I daresay with the family in London, there's nowt much to do up at the house. My name is Tor Hardy, lass,' he told her, and his mouth softened in a smile. Her heart beat a little faster, because when he smiled, he was an attractive man – and she was alone on the moors with him, some distance from her home. Her mother's warnings sounded in her head, yet she was somehow not afraid of him. 'Tha's no need to call me sir, nor to fear me. I know tha' works hard, Emma. I've seen thissen running in the early mornings and at night.'

'I think I did not thank you properly for what you did that night,' Emma said, suddenly shy. 'I did nothing to encourage him, Mr Hardy. Please believe me.'

'I know Ike Hanson for the brute he is,' Tor replied, his eyes glinting like sunshine on a sword blade. 'I wanted to thrash him harder that night, but he walked away and gave me no chance. Besides, he is one of the best workers in the mine. We needed him.'

'Oh no. You did all that was required – I am grateful.'

'How is your father now?' Tor dismounted and began to walk beside her. 'Are you managing – and what will you do when the family move to London permanently?'

'You think they will?' Emma looked at him uncertainly.

'I believe so – in the next year or two. Sir Philip will try to hold on to the house but he may have to sell in the end...'

'Then I shall have to find work elsewhere,' Emma told him, apprehension in her face. She looked young, innocent, and lovely, her eyes holding the appeal of a young filly, shy but curious. 'Mother says I should, for we shan't manage on what they pay me now. I intended to ask for three pounds as Cook means to leave and I can do her job – not all the fancy sauces yet, but I'm learning.'

'You will make someone a good wife,' Tor observed and smiled in a way that made Emma's heart thud. Why was he looking at her like that?

'I can't think of marriage,' she said, glancing down at the ground. 'I must look after my family.'

'The right man will do that,' Tor said confidently, and Emma felt her heart lurch. She had nothing against him, was grateful for what he'd done when Ike Hanson attacked her – but her heart belonged to Joe Davies. He was so handsome and when he smiled at her, the day always seemed brighter.

'Perhaps...' Emma replied in a voice so low she wasn't sure he could hear her. She couldn't look at him. She was too confused, too anxious, unsure of what she felt – except that she was almost certain he meant to offer for her.

'What are you carrying so carefully?' Tor asked, and she told him. He smiled and nodded, as if it confirmed something in his mind. 'I have a meeting with someone important, so I'll bid you goodnight, Emma – but tell your da he isn't forgotten and I'll be in to see him soon.'

Emma nodded, because she knew he had been to see her father more than once since his accident, and he'd brought gifts that were for the whole family, like a ham he'd said a farmer had given him, and three laying hens that provided them with eggs to this day.

She stood watching as he rode away, trying to make her heart stop thudding. Tor Hardy was a respectable man. If he meant marriage, he would speak to her father first – it was the proper way. What must she do if he asked for her? Emma was tingling with nerves. He was such a formidable man – but fair and respected. She was unlikely to get another offer as good, and yet...

Emma started to run, in a hurry now to get home. She didn't know why, but a shadow seemed to hang over and she had a feeling that something terrible was going to happen.

6

Tor rode on to his meeting. He had found something in the mine a few days earlier and he wanted his opinion confirmed or denied. If he'd found a mineral, it would be worth a lot of money, because there was a good seam of this substance running right through a part of the mine that everyone had thought long played out, but he wasn't certain what it was yet. It wasn't lead; he was certain of that, but his hopes were that it might be zinc. If he told Sir Philip what he suspected and it proved right, he would cancel their contract before it was signed and take the mine over once more. It was the honest thing to do and a part of Tor wanted to take that road; he'd always played fair with Sir Philip, whom he liked – but his half-brother's wife would soon run through whatever the zinc brought in, and then they would be back where they were now. In truth, he owed it to the miners to keep quiet, to prolong their jobs for as many years as possible.

Tor knew that if he didn't speak and the zinc was found, Sir Philip would no longer be his friend. It was a sacrifice, because it was the one link that Tor had with his supposed family – apart from his name. He'd been called Torquil after his great-great-grandfather, but as a child he hadn't been able to say the name and insisted on calling himself Tor. The name had stuck and he liked it; it helped promote the image of a hard man – hard like the very rock of the mountain range he loved so much. To walk in the hills, climb to the platform high above, from where he could survey his kingdom – not his, in truth, but it was his ambition, to own all of it. He believed it was owed for the way his mother had been treated – and to avenge an innocent woman's death.

'Get even for my mistress,' his mother had begged him before she died. 'I hate that family, Tor. I'm not sure how you can bring them down – but I know that you will, for me.' And he'd vowed he would, even as she breathed her last.

Tor had made no move against Sir Philip. How could he harm a man he liked and admired? But Sir Philip had let his wife fritter away the money that should have been spent on securing the mine. A couple of recent small rockfalls had injured two of the older men, though neither had died, but that was luck, and the fact that Tor had initiated a rescue immediately. He'd pulled both the injured men clear after digging them out. It was because of his actions that the men were so loyal to him – apart from Ike. He hated him. It was jealousy, because once they had been as equals, but now Tor was the mine manager, and childhood friends, who had fought and laughed together, were no longer friends. Ike's life had been soured by his brutal father and his nagging mother, making him surly and bad-tempered.

Tor was aware Ike resented him, and it was one of the reasons he watched over Emma. It would be like Ike to strike at him through her. If he'd guessed that Tor was planning to make Emma his wife, he might attack her just to hurt him, but it would destroy Emma, too. If Ike laid a finger on her, Tor would kill him. There were always ways in the mine. It could be arranged that Ike was sent down one of the redundant tunnels and a rockfall might cripple or kill him. It remained an option if Ike continued to upset her, though not one Tor was inclined to take. He would have preferred to offer friendship, as he did to all his men, but Ike's manner made that impossible.

Tor would not marry until he was certain that the mine contained the minerals he believed it did – not only zinc but small deposits of potentially even more lucrative minerals – things he did not yet recognise. The man he was due to meet that evening was an expert. That man had a bad reputation. He had served ten years in prison for murder, but his knowledge was vast, for he had worked in mines in America as well as South Africa. He had killed his wife in a drunken rage for cheating on him, and, because of that, no one would employ him – but Tor was willing to give him a chance. Jonathan Crossly would have to stop drinking, of course, but his expertise would be invaluable.

If Jonathan confirmed Tor's own beliefs, it would make him his fortune and he could overlook a crime that any man might be driven to if he loved a woman enough. It amazed Tor that his father had been willing to accept what had happened to his wife and take the money offered him. Had it been Tor's wife, he knew he would have killed the man who had raped her. Rage filled him whenever he thought of Sir Thomas' crimes. It was lucky for him that he'd died of natural causes before Tor was old enough to take his revenge.

His mother had demanded revenge on the family that had shamed her, but more for the woman she'd loved as a sister despite that she was but her maid. She had accepted dirty money for her own injuries – but her mistress was in her grave and for that the Penrith family should suffer. Tor knew that by keeping his secret concerning the zinc, he would fulfil his mother's wish at the same time as making himself rich. It was the best way – and yet he had a conscience, and he was a God-fearing man. Would he bring divine vengeance upon himself for an act of betrayal against a friend?

Shaking his head, Tor put the doubts from his mind. It was the beginning and, in the end, he would own all that the family at Penrith House had now. A perfect revenge that they'd brought on themselves. If Sir Philip had been more thoughtful for his men, Tor must have told him of his discovery, but he had cared nothing for the miners, and all for his selfish wife.

'You were a fool, Philip,' he muttered to himself as he dismounted and went into the isolated inn. Travellers hardly ever came here, except in high summer, more now that the railway went to Garsdale, but still only modest numbers came this far into the Dales. Most visitors headed for Wensleydale, or Swaledale, and the lakes, ignoring their isolated but beautiful valley, which was fortunate, since the landlord used the inn as cover for smuggling. It had gone on for centuries past, the ships finding anchors and caves at Whitby and using the isolated paths through the hills to known outlets for their wares. Men brought the ponies in from the coast at dead of night, using different routes, sometimes travelling for the best part of a week, but only in the dark hours; the landlord here stored their contraband, until the heat was off, and the French brandy that had seen no taxes could be sold to honest gentlemen for a fair price.

It was an age-old practice, mainly originating in Cornwall, but the net spread far and wide across the country. The trade might not be as frequent as in the last century, because the railways had opened up the previously isolated countryside, making it more likely they would be seen, but it still went on; it probably always would in some form or another, Tor thought. For who would pay tax if they could avoid it? The excisemen who hunted the smugglers up and down the country never thought to look as far afield as this lonely spot – more fool them.

Besides the brandy, there were other things now: rare spices, tobacco from the New World, and silks from the Far East, as fine as any in the grand London drawing rooms. All subject to high taxes and none of it paid – and Tor had dabbled in trading, making more money than his father ever had from his farm. He sold fine silks to a trader in York who asked no questions; there were customers enough for the brandy and tobacco, in the Dales, though he sometimes took a barrel as a gift to a man he counted a good friend. He had money in the form of gold coin stored with Jacob Gregan in York, a man he trusted, and that coin was invested; it brought him a steady income and that suited him, for if he'd flaunted his wealth, Tor would have been suspected of consorting with the gentlemen.

Inside the inn, it was dimly lit, but Tor saw the man he had come to meet sitting in the corner, head down, as though he did not wish to be seen.

The landlord nodded to Tor. He had sold Tor smuggled brandy and wine more times than either of them could remember – some of it bought for Sir Philip, though now and then Tor kept back a barrel for himself.

Tor moved to the table and sat down, acknowledging the other man but neither of them using names. Their business must remain secret. Both knew that and both stood to gain from it – Jonathan Crossly with a job that would give him back his pride and respectability, and Tor with a fortune that would give his mother her revenge, and him the wife he wanted above all else.

* * *

'What's the matter with you, Emma?' her mother asked, looking up from her sewing later that evening. 'Thass something on thy mind, lass. Can thee not tell me and ease thyself, love?'

Emma shook her head. 'I can't, Ma, for I don't know for sure...'

A look of fear passed over her mother's face. 'You've not done anything foolish, lass?'

Emma laughed and shook her head. 'No, Ma – I have not been with a man but...' She hesitated, then, 'Perhaps I should tell you, though I may be wrong, for 'tis only a feeling...'

'A man has spoken to you?' Mary's eyes sharpened.

'No, not outright – but it's the way he looked at me. I do not know if he means marriage or other...' Her cheeks were scarlet as her mother stared at her. 'I think he wants me, but... he did say to tell Father he had not been forgotten and would call on him.'

'Tor Hardy?' Her mother stared in disbelief, her anxiety fading. 'He would make a fine husband – and if he's the one, he means marriage. He would never rape or despoil a woman. I know that for a fact. He isn't like his father. Jon Hardy took the money, but his eyes carried the shame of it for the rest of his life – and Tor is proud, like his mother. It was she who told Jon Hardy to demand payment. No, Tor would never harm a woman.'

'Because it happened to his mother?' Emma asked.

'Aye, but more than that, he is not the sort to harm a woman. Especially you, Emma. He has been good to us, your father, and all of the mining families.' She lifted her eyebrows. 'Where is the problem, my dearest? He is a good man and would make you a fine husband.'

Emma hesitated. 'There is another I have feelings for, Ma. Joe Davies. I know he is courting, but Sarah Mullens doesn't love him – she wants Tor Hardy… She told me so. She wants him for his fine house and his money.'

'Oh, Emma,' her mother sighed. 'Sarah will marry Joe, because Tor wouldn't have her for his wife. It's common knowledge that she has been with Joe in the way she ought not until his ring was on her finger.'

'Ma! You don't know for sure.'

'She is with child, Emma. Mrs Mullens told me in confidence when we met after church, for we were great friends once – so you must keep Sarah's secret. The banns are to be called this Sunday and they will be wed inside a month. She has to or she will be shamed – and folk wouldn't forget. No, Tor wouldn't look at her, Emma.'

Emma's throat caught with regret. Her dreams were ended for she knew that Joe loved Sarah Mullens – and her father had money. Joe had never given Emma more than a smile in passing. It had been a forlorn hope that Tor Hardy would ask Sarah to wed him and Joe turn to her, but now it was ended. There were few other girls in the valley that Tor could choose from, so if he needed a wife, it was probable that her mother was right and he'd settled on Emma. She had wanted to be loved, passionately and deeply, not married because she was suitable and the best there was in his vicinity.

'Why so gloomy?' her mother asked with a smile. 'If you're afeared of marriage itself, don't be, Emma. Men have their needs and it can be pleasant, but lust fades and, when children are born, the man often strays to others and leaves his wife to care for his home.'

'Father is not like that!' Emma cried. 'He would never cheat on you, Ma. You know he wouldn't.'

'Your father is a dear man and he was never a trouble to me, for I enjoyed what we did – but he worked hard all his life and it wasn't often he had the energy for loving. When he did, it was good. Not all men are like that – but Tor Hardy is a decent man. He won't harm you or subject you to unnatural practice, as some do, Emma. Sir Thomas – the old squire – was the other sort. I was glad when he died, for he was a menace to all the young women.'

'Did he harm you, Ma?' Emma looked at her anxiously.

'No, but he would, had he ever caught me. I took care to hide out of his way if he was in the village. Maggie Black, my best friend, was caught and it ruined her life. Her husband wouldn't forgive her and, in the end, she hung herself in the barn.' Emma's mother shook her head sadly. 'She wasn't the only one to suffer death because of him either. Jean Summers was murdered by her husband for he said she encouraged it – and then he killed himself.'

'Sir Thomas must have been a terrible man,' Emma said, shivering. 'Sir Philip is kind – he never tries to touch any of the maids. I think he loves his wife, even though she leads him a merry dance. It's her that caused his downfall. They say he has sold the mine, but no one knows yet who has bought it. Do you think it has played out? Has Da ever said what he thinks?'

'He thought there might be other mineral deposits in the old tunnels,' her mother replied. 'They were played out of iron and now lead, but your father swears he saw metal in at least two of the old tunnels – and he would have told Sir Philip if he'd ever bothered to call and see him, but he sent Tor Hardy instead. I don't know if he told Tor what he'd seen the day of the rock fall or not… but he knows something.'

Emma nodded. 'I suppose the new owner has heard

rumours of new sources, for why else would he buy it? The land it stands on is no use for farming nor yet anything else.'

'We'll find that out when we know who he is,' her mother said and smiled. 'Your father suspects, but he isn't saying...'

Emma stared at her and then the look in her mother's eyes made her gasp. 'You think it is Tor? Surely he would tell Sir Philip if there are mineral deposits – he has always been loyal to him.'

'Loyalty may only go so far,' her mother remarked. 'If it turns out to be Tor, I would bet on there being a rich seam of some mineral, and I think he knows where to find it.'

'That means he'll be wealthy, doesn't it?'

'Thinking he might not make a bad husband now, Emma?' Her mother gave her a sly smile, but Emma angrily denied it.

'Ma, don't think that of me! I'd rather marry a working man who loved me than a rich one that didn't.'

'And where is this working man to come from?' her mother inquired. 'I can't think of another man in the valley who would suit you, Emma. Only if you go away in service might you find a footman or groom to wed you for love – unfortunately, the master or his son might take a fancy to you for another purpose.'

Emma nodded and hung her head. It was true that if Joe married Sarah, there was no one else in the whole valley that she would wish to court her. Tor Hardy had saved her from Ike and perhaps that was a sign. She did not dislike him and perhaps she could learn to love him – if he asked her...

7

Zinc! It was zinc and could be worth a fortune if there was enough of it. The tests in York had proven him right. But Jonathan, a man he'd met by chance and wanted to employ at the mine, hadn't even needed to test it, though he'd taken it with him to ascertain its quality, because higher grade minerals were worth more.

'It is zinc, no doubt,' he'd told Tor in a hushed voice. 'But I'll test it for quality and let you know as soon as I have confirmed it.'

'That's good news,' Tor had said. 'And you'll work for me once I have the mine up and running? With a partnership on offer when I'm on top of things.'

'Aye, I'll do that,' Jonathan promised. 'You will not need to trek into York to discover the worth of your minerals. Don't forget when you sign the contract to make sure the rights are all included – or the family, even the government, could claim a share of your profits. I take it you don't want that?'

'I don't,' Tor said, his resolve hardening. 'They've had their chance – with what result? Five men injured these past three years, two of them badly and one confined to his bed with a broken back. I won't have that happen to my workers, Jonathan. Nay. I'll have it sewn up tight, never fear.'

'Good for you.' Jonathan nodded. 'That's why I'll work for you and keep your secret until it is officially confirmed. I hate people such as the Penriths. It was a man like that who despoiled my wife. I loved her more than life itself, but she betrayed me with that man and my love turned to hatred. I should have killed him instead of her, but she laughed in my face, because he'd promised her diamonds, and I lost my temper. I should not have done it, but she pushed me too far, the hurt beyond bearing. I hit her too hard and regretted it later.'

'You served your time for it,' Tor said gruffly. 'In your shoes, I might have done the same, though I think I would have had him first.'

Jonathan nodded. 'That is my deepest regret. I should have killed him and then her, but I was out of my mind with jealousy, and I'd drunk too much whisky. It's too late now – someone else got to him before me. I'm glad I didn't know before they let me out; it was only the thought of what I'd do to him that kept me sane in there.'

'You won't be drinking if you work for me,' Tor reminded him.

'I've stopped already,' Jonathan promised. 'This is watered ale and not strong enough to start my craving. It is the whisky I can't resist if I start, but I know I am lucky to get another chance and you won't regret it.'

'Good.' They stood and shook hands and Tor went out into the night.

He was thoughtful as he rode home. In a few days, he would sign the contract, providing it was as it should be – and then he could speak to Emma's father. He wouldn't marry her until the mine was producing zinc, but she would know she was spoken for. He smiled as he thought of her lovely face looking up at him so wistful and unsure. Tor would make her smile at him with the eyes of love. He would court her but insist on secrecy, to protect her until she was his wife. After that, he would have Ike Hanson watched – one false move and he would eliminate him. His jaw set hard. No one would lay a finger on his wife – the woman he loved.

Tor had seen more beautiful women in York. Women who dressed in silks and made eyes at him. He was seen as an important man there, known to have money, and would be more so as his fortune built – but Emma was the one he wanted. Without vanity, he knew he could take any one of a dozen women to his bed if he chose, most married, but there was a merchant's daughter who had told him to his face she would wed him and bring him a thousand pounds. For a moment he'd been tempted, but something had held him back – and he'd learned later she'd married an older man to give a name to her unborn child. His instincts had saved him from a trap and he didn't need her money, because he would soon have more than he'd ever dreamed...

A smile touched his mouth as he reached his home. It was in darkness and, as he entered, he felt the loneliness of the big house surround him. One day soon, it would have a mistress and servants who lived in, instead of a woman who came to clean a few times a week. Tor was accustomed to caring for his house. He was used to looking after himself, and bread and cheese was all he needed to fill his stomach in the evening, though on weekends he ate at an inn that did good food. He was capable of cooking bacon and eggs for his breakfast and took cheese and bread for his midday break. Sometimes he bought a ham and ate that with pickles for his evening meal. He could never get through a whole ham, especially in summer when meat turned more quickly, so he normally cut it in half and gave the other half to folk who needed it more, sometimes dividing it into quarters – but sometimes giving half the ham to one family, as he had to Emma's.

He had chickens in a pen in the yard. He fed them in the mornings and either the cleaning woman or the stable boy fed them later in the evening before he got home. Tor kept them for the eggs, but if they didn't lay, he killed them and gave them to one of the villagers – especially the old and those who had been injured in the mine, recently or before his time. It made sense to give what he couldn't use and he wasn't particularly public spirited; he just didn't like waste. Nor did he like the way good workers were treated once they were no longer of use. People he'd helped said he was good and kind, but Tor knew he was just practical and he thought himself a fair man.

It was the reason he had bided his time. He wouldn't deliberately have ruined Sir Philip, but he had ruined himself and Tor was just doing what he thought right. The fact that he had the perfect revenge on the family didn't give him pleasure. Had Sir Philip been a good master to his people, Tor would probably just have gone on working for him – but not for his son. No, Sir Philip's son was rotten to the core, just like his grandfather. The bad blood had skipped a generation, but it was certainly there in the next…

* * *

'Damn you, boy!' Sir Philip looked at his son angrily in the morning room of the house he'd rented in London. 'It is bad enough that your mother spends money as if it were water – but gambling debts! How often have I warned you not to get into that trap?'

Ralph Penrith stared at his father resentfully. He was a mean penny-pincher and always complaining if his son and heir ran up a few thousand guineas in debts, whether it be for clothes, stabling his horses – or gambling on the races, as it was this time.

'I merely laid five hundred pounds on a sure thing, but the stupid beast stumbled ten yards out, fell and broke its leg. It had to be put out of its misery and I lost five thousand pounds in prize money. If I'd won, I could have paid all the bills for everything else and had money to spare. You must see what a wonderful chance it was, Father.'

'No, I don't,' Sir Philip grumbled. 'I could have just about paid your other bills...' He threw a sheaf of tradesmen's notes in his son's face. 'But five hundred pounds on a horse! I can't and I won't pay.'

'You have to – or the family name will be stained,' Ralph muttered, red in the face. 'I'll work – I'll even go down the mine if you insist...'

'The mine no longer belongs to me,' his father told him. 'I sold it to Tor Hardy – signed the papers yesterday.'

'To that bastard!' Ralph cried indignantly. 'How could you, Father? It's all he ever wanted. He'll have the house next and the farms...'

'Don't be ridiculous,' Sir Philip replied coldly. 'The lead was played out – the amount we were taking out these past months was barely enough to cover the costs. I was glad to be rid of it – and I owed him the chance. If he finds enough to cover what he paid and a bit more, good luck to him.'

'And what if he finds other minerals – seams of valuable metals that make him rich? How will you feel then?'

'It won't happen,' his father said. 'I was glad to take what he paid me, otherwise I was going to close down. I had bills to pay – bills I couldn't pay, and still can't if I am to maintain the lifestyle your mother demands. I shall have to sell something else.'

'Not the house,' Ralph said swiftly. 'I want that – it is my heritage.'

'Perhaps,' Sir Philip replied, eyeing him with dislike. 'I have some property in York – a row of terraced houses by the river. They will pay your mother's newest debts and leave a bit over – but not yours. It will have to be another farm then. I wanted to hang on to the land if I could. If it comes to selling piece by piece, I'll let the house go. There is no point in owning a house like that if we don't own the land.'

'We are nothing without it!' his son cried, incensed by his father's casual air. 'Does it mean so little to you?'

'It means more that I can keep your mother happy for a little longer,' Sir Philip said. 'She was very ill two years ago. I thought I should lose her. I was told she might not live more than a few years.' A look of pain came into his eyes. 'If I lose her, the rest means nothing to me. So I give her all I can while she lives.'

'Mother is as tough as old boots,' her incensed son declared. 'She just plays on your love for her – can't you see it? You have no right to waste my inheritance on her whims. Make her behave so that we can all go home.'

'I sometimes wonder where you came from,' Sir Philip replied sadly. 'I do wonder if you are truly mine – and then I remember my father.' He sighed. 'You will just have to work for your living, Ralph. I may be able to pay your debts, given time – but I refuse to continue with it. You can choose from a commission in the army, or a job as a land overseer. I know someone who would take you as a favour to me – or what would you choose?'

Ralph glared at him in frustration. 'If you refuse to support me – the army, I suppose. I couldn't lower myself to work for another, unless he was a marquis or a duke?'

Sir Philip shook his head, 'A plain mister, I am afraid. It is a smallish estate. You would not be overworked and it is not too far away from Penrith. Though that may not be ours before long.'

'No! Never. I should be humiliated.' Ralph cursed beneath his breath. 'It will be the army. I want a commission.' He was furious with his father.

Sir Philip nodded, saddened. 'Of course. I will do my best for you, my son. The army could be the making of you. It will teach you to be strong – and I fear you will need to be. I am sorry I have made such a mess of things, but I was content just to live in peace for years. When I had money to spare, I ought to have invested it, but instead I spent it giving your mother the life she craved. Now there is no going back...'

'You're a fool,' his son hissed and then turned on his heel and walked out. He was furious with his father. How could he just sell the mine to that bastard Tor Hardy? He would bet every penny they still had that the bastard knew something his father did not. Ralph would never have sold to him. He would have found another prospective owner or simply shut it down. His father was too weak, too easily led. Except in his case.

Ralph had never expected him to make a stand, but he had no choice now but to do as his father wanted. Unless his debts were paid, he would be ruined. The tradespeople would dun him and the fellow he'd borrowed the five hundred from would blacken his name in society. At least in the army, he would look good in his uniform and he'd have a chance of picking up some decent prize money if they were sent anywhere there was conflict. He wasn't sure where that would be, but South Africa would be good. The skirmish with the Boers in 1881 had resulted in defeat and loss of face and some territories by the British. It had left things uneasy and a bad taste in the mouth, and it was probable that war would break out again before long – and war meant the chance of rich prizes for soldiers. Besides, Ralph had heard it said that you could pick up gold and precious stones from the earth, if you knew what to look for. Well, he did know, because he'd made a study of minerals and gems at college. It wasn't the course he'd been supposed to take, but he'd seen an opening and he'd taken it, thinking to take charge of the mine. Now his father had given away his birthright!

He was sure there were more minerals in the old mine than his father dreamed – and now Tor Hardy had it! Ralph Penrith's face grew grim. He might have to obey his father for a year or two, but after that he would get home somehow and then – then he would make life hell for the bastard who had ruined his plans...

8

'Have you seen this?' Emma had been using a newspaper the family had discarded to wrap the peelings in, and the headline had caught her attention. 'A woman was attacked in Whitechapel by two or three men and she died the next day. What a terrible thing!' She shook her head. 'Is that in London?' Emma had never heard of it, but it made her shiver to think of a terrible murder happening anywhere.

'Yes, it is a poor part of London. Most unpleasant thing,' Cook said with a little grimace. 'I read she was a prostitute – but she didn't deserve such treatment. I think women of the streets often go in fear of their lives.'

'London must be a wicked place,' Emma said, shaking her head as she finished wrapping the peelings.

'I dare say it may be for some, but a girl like you, of good reputation, could find work in a fine house, Emma. Those pigeons in red wine you cooked last night were as good as I could produce myself.' Cook looked at her with approval, then nodded. After only a month of teaching her, Emma was already proficient in many dishes. Food they and the few servants left had enjoyed, for it was not often they had the chance to dine so well, but Cook had justified it, because it was for a worthwhile end. Emma could now cook dishes Sir Philip would enjoy if he came with his son for a few days. 'You're ready to take over my job, which is just as well.' She beamed happily. 'I've been offered a position in a house in York. The family are well off, and she says they entertain a lot; so she needs someone who can produce a good plain dinner but also a fancy one when the occasion demands it.'

'In York?' Emma asked, feeling a little hollow inside as she congratulated her. Her friend would be going so far away. 'That is wonderful, Cook. What is your new mistress' name?'

'Mrs Maria Madison and they are Americans,' Cook said, beaming. 'Her husband is something in the diplomatic world – and it sounds just the job for me. I'll have my bedroom and a sitting room, six pounds a month, and two weeks' holiday per year – and that means I can come and visit you. Or she says a friend may stay for a short time in my rooms, if I have nieces or respectable lady friends.'

'Oh, Cook,' Emma cried. 'That sounds really nice. I am so pleased for you.'

'So will Ruby be, because they are looking for a reliable kitchen assistant and she could go with me if she chose.' Cook looked at her. 'Unless it would suit you better, Emma? It is two pounds a month.'

'Lucky Ruby!' Emma said, laughing. 'She will think she is in heaven – all that money, and she gets away from her mother, too.'

'You wouldn't consider it? After a while, we could get your wage up, because she might ask you to be her maid, once I tell her how clever you are.'

Emma sighed, because she was going to miss Cook – and

Ruby, too. It would be lonely here without them. Mrs Briscoe wasn't always as friendly as she could be – but Emma's situation had not changed. 'I just can't leave Mum to cope with it all, though she tells me to go – or she did before...'

Cook glanced at her as she broke off. 'Before what, Emma? You're not in any trouble?'

'Not really,' Emma said and then decided to confide in her friend. 'Tor Hardy has spoken to my father. He wants to marry me – not before harvest, because he is too busy at the mine just now.'

'Marriage to Tor Hardy, the new owner of the mine?' Cook looked surprised. 'You'll be a fine lady, Emma, in a big house and with a maidservant, I shouldn't wonder. When is it to be then?'

'Later in the year, when he has the mine up and running properly.'

'Aye, and that was a surprise to most,' Cook replied. 'He's a canny one – buys the mine and then discovers a big seam of zinc...'

'Yes, that's what a lot of folk will think, but it wasn't discovered until after the deal was done – so he told my father. He says he believed it was there, but he'd only seen a small deposit that wouldn't have lasted a month – then they opened up two of the old tunnels and cleared away the fallen rock. It was all over the place and the new man at the mine says there are other minerals that may be worth even more.'

'Well, I wish him good luck with it. The Penrith family have done nothing but waste the fortune they took out of it for years past. Let's hope Tor Hardy will have more sense.'

'Da says he won't waste it and he reckons everyone will prosper because of it. He admires and likes Tor...' Emma faltered and Cook looked at her.

'And you don't?'

'I do like him, and I admire what he is doing a lot,' Emma said. 'He has told Da that once the money comes in, he and the other injured miners will be properly compensated for their injuries.'

'But – and there is a but, because I can see it in your face, Emma.'

'I'm a little afraid of him,' Emma confessed. 'I don't know why, because I know he won't harm me – but something inside me says no...'

'Then don't take him,' Cook said. 'Tell your mother you want to work with me – and let Ruby help her. She could live in and you could pay your ma half your wages. It is more than you earned before – and a lot more than you get now. Ruby would be happy to work for seven shillings and her board; she likes your ma and would be happy to be away from the farm.'

'It would be a solution,' Emma agreed. She sighed deeply. 'Both my parents are delighted with Tor's offer... and he might be angry with them if I turn him down. I've asked Da for a little time and he says I can have a month to decide but must not keep a good man waiting for longer. I know it is what Da wants – he thinks I would be safe then...'

'It might hurt your parents if you tell them you would prefer to go away rather than be the wife of a man who would look after them, but you must think of your happiness, too. You must consider it properly, Emma. I am leaving next week and I'll take either you or Ruby with me. It's your choice.'

'Ma thinks I am being silly. She says I am lucky to get the chance.'

'Well, most girls would think so – and it would be a shame to make the wrong decision,' Cook replied. 'If you stay and then change your mind, I'll look out for another position for you.'

Emma nodded. 'Perhaps it will be better if you take Ruby. I suppose it is only fair to give Tor a chance to walk out with me. It's what I've told Da I will do. He can walk me to church on Sunday and then stay to dinner with us. If I like him, I will consent to a wedding in the autumn.'

'That is a sensible girl,' Cook said and suddenly put her arms about Emma, hugging her. 'If you ever need help, my love, you come to me. I'll find a place for you, wherever I am.'

'And I for you,' Emma replied, hugging her ample waist. Then she laughed. 'I've never called you anything but Cook. I don't know how to address a letter to you.'

Cook nodded. 'It's all I've been called for years – but my name is Eileen; Ellie for short. I am Miss Ellie Blake and I'll give you my address before I leave. I'll be writing to you, because I don't want to lose touch.'

'Oh, Ellie,' Emma said, smiling fondly. 'Our names are so alike and I never knew it.'

'It might have been confusing for others, so I stuck to Cook,' she replied. 'I am going to miss you, Emma, and no mistake – but a good man is hard to find. Don't make the mistake I did; I've regretted it ever since.'

Emma nodded. She had been down to the vicarage and asked to speak to the vicar, but when she'd told him why she was there, he'd refused to listen. Because of her friendship with Ellie, she'd hoped to bring about a reconciliation, but had been politely told that she understood nothing and would do better not to interfere. She had apologised and left, feeling foolish. Emma had merely wanted to help two people she saw as lonely, but at least one of them did not wish for it. Realising that she was dabbling in dark waters, she had put it from her mind. Her friend would be happy now, because she had a new job that seemed to be everything that she'd hoped for. Emma knew she must be happy for her, though she wasn't sure she could bear to go on working at the house for long without her friends. It would either be marriage to Tor Hardy or she must leave and find work elsewhere.

* * *

It was time for Emma to go home when Mrs Briscoe came into the kitchen, looking pleased. 'Sir Philip and Master Ralph are visiting next weekend,' she announced. 'Her ladyship is staying with friends and will not be coming – just the gentlemen.'

'Now is your chance to impress then, Emma,' Cook said, smiling at her.

'What do you mean?' Mrs Briscoe asked, looking at her sharply. 'I am not saying Emma isn't a decent cook – but your dishes are what the master likes.'

'Well, he can eat Emma's version of them; that's why I've been showing her how,' Cook told her. 'I'm off on Saturday morning, Mrs Briscoe. I've a new job in York I start on Monday and I want to look around and settle in first off.'

'You can't just leave like that – you have to give notice,' the housekeeper said, her face red with annoyance. 'You know that is the proper way.'

'Aye, I do and I would have – but her ladyship terminated our contract herself. I told her I should not stay for the wages she offered and would leave as soon as I found work elsewhere – and she said it was a matter of indifference to her as she did not intend to return here ever again.'

The colour faded from Mrs Briscoe's face and she went chalky white. 'I was not informed of that,' she said stiffly. 'I knew the family would be less often in residence but... If that is the case, I too must consider my options. I cannot think Sir Philip will care to visit often without her ladyship.'

'It is my opinion that this house will be sold within the year,' Cook told her. 'Have you somewhere to go, Mrs Briscoe?'

A flicker of fear went through the housekeeper's eyes; she was some ten years older than Cook, and had, no doubt, expected to end her years here, with a little cottage as her reward when her working days were done.

'Nowhere,' she whispered. 'I had hoped for a few more years here.'

'The new owners will be bound to need someone like you,' Emma tried to reassure her, because she did not like to see fear in the older woman's eyes. 'There is no one else for miles around who could take your place.'

'No, you are right.' Mrs Briscoe recovered her composure, at least outwardly. She looked at Emma, doubt in her eyes. 'Are you certain you can cope?'

'If it is just the master and his son, I think so,' Emma replied confidently. 'I'd need some of our old people back if they brought visitors.'

'The letter said just them,' the housekeeper confirmed. 'I feel most uneasy. Why would they come alone? Even if her ladyship did not wish to visit – they normally have guests. Card parties and shooting – just game birds, foxes and rabbits, but gentlemen enjoy sport, do they not? Her ladyship always hated it and I agreed with her – but men will be men.'

'Maybe they've come for one last time, to take away anything they value,' Cook suggested. 'Sir Philip may have a buyer for the house...'

All three women looked at each other solemnly. Penriths had been here for hundreds of years; the village was named for them and was owned by them. Whoever bought the house would buy everything: land, farms, house, the small church and the vicarage. Indeed, almost the whole valley was theirs; no one owned anything much, except Tor Hardy. He owned his house and two fields, and now the mine.

'Why didn't Sir Philip sell the mine with the rest of it?' Mrs Briscoe asked.

'Because Tor Hardy is his half-brother and he wanted it,' Cook said. 'Sir Philip respected him – and... who knows? Happen, he knows something we don't?'

'There were rumours,' Emma said as both older women looked at her. 'Some folk believed them, but Da was never sure – and he made me swear never to tell another living soul. So I can't – and I wouldn't, because I don't know it's true.'

'Keep your secrets.' Mrs Briscoe sniffed. 'I'll borrow your magazine if I may, Cook. I shan't stay here unless Sir Philip tells me what is going on and guarantees me a cottage of my own.'

'Very wise,' Cook told her and grinned at Emma as the housekeeper went off in a miff. 'So, now you can tell me, Emma. I am leaving anyway, so it won't matter...'

'Sorry, Ellie,' Emma said. 'I did promise and I can't break my word – but it was a wicked thing and if Tor Hardy knows it and chose to reveal it, it would ruin the family...'

Cook nodded. 'Say no more. I heard the tale whispered years ago, when I came here as a young woman. I didn't credit it, but now – well, I am glad to be leaving, and that's the truth...'

9

'You can't have sold it all!' Ralph looked at his father in disgust as they stood in what had always been Sir Philip's study and a part of his childhood. He'd wanted to spend a couple of weeks here at the house in the Dales, but now his father was telling him it was no longer theirs – at least it would not be in a few days' time. They had travelled here separately; Sir Philip by train as far as Settle and then in the old-fashioned carriage stabled there, and Ralph in the high perch phaeton his father had purchased for him on his last birthday. He had a team of black horses with gleaming coats that he'd spent a fortune on and cost the earth to feed and maintain. 'What am I supposed to do now – where is my home?'

'You'll be leaving to join the Army in two weeks,' Sir Philip reminded him. He frowned at Ralph. 'You've played your part in this, so don't look at me as if I brought us to ruin. It was your mother that did most of it – and you helped to bring us down. I've discovered your mother has many more undisclosed bills – she owes her dressmaker two thousand pounds, and several other bills of similar amounts. I didn't think it possible...' Sir

Philip shook his head. 'It seems that she is also a gambler and lost the money I gave her for her bills on a horse race and over the table at private gaming parties I knew nothing of.'

'You shouldn't have indulged her!' Ralph raged at him. 'Why did you let the stupid bitch ruin us all?'

His father slapped his face hard, making him recoil, shocked by the strength of the blow from a man he'd always considered weak. 'Never speak of your mother to me like that again or I will horsewhip you! She may have been foolish – but she was brought up in a house where no one ever paid any bills until they were forced. Gamblers all, her father, mother, brothers – the whole damned lot of them, and still are. Fortunately, for them, they have large estates that can be mortgaged piece by piece, and hope of inheritances from various relatives who may leave a fortune to one of them. I have nothing to compare. It is my fault. I should never have wed her and brought her to this place.' He ran fingers through dark hair silvering at the temples. 'This is my last throw of the dice, Ralph. It is down to you now – go and win yourself a fortune in prize money. Or learn to trade overseas. Then you can purchase an estate of your own.'

'Penrith is my birthright,' Ralph muttered. 'You had no right to sell it without my permission.'

'It has never been entailed, because there have always been male heirs and no one ever thought to protect it,' Sir Philip said. 'Besides, there was plenty of money in your grandfather's day.'

'You sold the mine, you fool!' Ralph accused him bitterly. 'To that bastard – Hardy must be laughing at you. Everyone says he will be a rich man…'

'At least he is doing some good with it,' Sir Philip replied, sounding almost as bitter now as his son. 'I had to sell, you selfish wretch. Some of the land was already mortgaged and has been for years. I didn't want to sell – don't you think this is humiliating for me?'

'Why didn't you thrash Mother and make her behave?'

'Because I loved her and I knew she should have married a far richer man than I – I was warned by her father before I took her that she would ruin me, but I didn't listen. She was all I wanted – and she still is... And she's your mother, don't forget!'

Ralph's face twisted in a sneer. 'I'll never let a woman bring me down. I'll marry for money – if you haven't blown my chances.'

'The bank was restless because I couldn't pay the interest last quarter, demanding I pay them the arrears or they would foreclose. I had to do something – and your mother's cousin offered to take the land and the rest of it off my hands for a decent sum. Enough to keep your mother in luxury for a few years.'

'You mean you've sold to that swine Rawlings?' Ralph's face twisted with furious spite. 'He is a devil, Father. In his youth, he killed a man in a duel for daring to suggest he'd cheated at cards – and he's old. What would he need this house and land for?'

'Lord Rolfe of Rawlings has a grandson – about three years older than you,' Sir Philip replied. 'He wants an estate for him and he wants him out of the way, up here where he can conveniently be forgotten, not in London wasting a fortune...'

'Why?' Ralph demanded, his face white with temper. To think a distant relative he hated would own all that should be his! It made his blood boil and he wanted to strike out. There had never been any love lost between them and for two pins he could have killed his father in that moment, but it would complete his ruin if he did. 'Damned fool!'

'I understand it is young women,' Sir Philip replied, his mouth twisting in disgust. 'Stephen has got two young women in trouble and their fathers are both demanding marriage – they are both daughters of prominent citizens.'

Ralph threw back his head and laughed scornfully. 'You've sold Penrith to a rogue like that – after all your preaching! For years you've told me I must respect women and never force myself on even a kitchen maid – and now you sell to that bastard.'

'You think I wanted it that way?' Sir Philip glared at him. 'God knows, I've lived in fear that people would discover your grandfather's secret...'

'What secret?' Ralph's eyes narrowed. 'I know he raped Hardy's mother – but that is no secret.'

Sir Philip turned away, muttering a curse. 'Perhaps it is time you knew the whole truth, boy! Your grandfather raped and murdered his own wife – your grandmother. He smuggled her body out of the house at night, put her on a horse and took her out into the Dales. He let her fall off her horse, but attached the reins to her wrist so it looked as if she'd become entangled and then sent the horse running. She was discovered the next day after he raised a search party to look for her.' Sir Philip took a deep breath. 'Then, when her maid accused him of murder, he raped and beat her. She managed to wind him by use of her knee and escape, or he might have killed her too.'

Ralph stared at him in horror. 'That's a lie... it can't be true.'

'It is the truth and Tor knows it all – so just remember that before you pick a quarrel with him over the mine.'

Ralph stared at him with undisguised disgust. 'My God! That's... that's foul, sickening. That I should be descended from such a man... it demeans me.'

Ralph rushed from the room out into the gardens that surrounded the house, where he vomited violently. Loathing for his grandfather and anger raged through him. Reared to respect women by both his parents, he had taken a few carelessly during his life, both here at Penrith and at college – but never an unwilling one, and never a respectable girl. There were enough disappointed wives and widows to fulfil his purpose of having fun. He'd never met a girl who filled him with the warmer feelings of love. Ralph was not sure whether he was capable of it. Yet to know that his grandfather was both a rapist and a murderer stunned him, hitting at his pride in his name and family. How could he bear such a stain on his honour? And that bastard Tor Hardy knew it all! Had profited because of it. Somehow that was the worst of it.

Striding away from the house, Ralph made up his mind to get drunk. His world had crumbled about his ears for he'd lost everything: the estate, his leisurely life at college, which he'd enjoyed to the full – and now his sense of pride in his family. His mouth tasted of ashes and his fury was building.

His father had had no right to let his debts run on until they were out of control. He had deceived his son into thinking they were a decent family that could hold their heads up, and now he'd been told that was not so – the grandson of a murderer and a coward; for it was the way it had been covered up that made it ten times worse.

Ralph strode into the stables, demanded his horse and swung up into the saddle when it was led out. Kicking his heels into the animal's flanks, he set off, racing away from the house towards the open moorland. He didn't see or hear his father come to the French window and call to him – all he could see was the red mist in front of his eyes...

* * *

Emma backed away from the study door. She had been about to take a tray of drinks in, but she'd stopped as she'd heard them arguing. Every sentence of their quarrel had been clear to her and she'd been too stunned by the bitterness of their words to either go in or walk away.

She retreated down the hall and sat on one of the old oak chairs that had stood there for a hundred years or more, trembling. Yes, she'd heard the old whispers from her father, but neither of them had truly credited it. Sir Thomas had murdered his wife – and covered it up. He'd then raped Tor Hardy's mother, which everyone knew – which meant that he was Tor's father...

For a few moments, she felt a little sick. She was still sitting there when Sir Philip opened the door. He looked out into the hall, frowning as he saw her. She got to her feet instantly. 'I was just bringing this tray, sir,' she said, not meeting his eyes.

'I suppose you heard us arguing,' Sir Philip sighed. 'Please, come into the study, Emma. I wish to speak with you.'

Emma followed, her stomach twisting with nerves. Was she about to be threatened if she spoke of what she'd heard?

'You are not in trouble.' Sir Philip's first words brought her head up. He looked so sad and downcast that she lost her fear of him, moved to pity. 'I just wanted to ask if you were prepared to stay on as our cook until the new owner takes over. I am not certain when he will choose to come, but we need to rehire a few of the staff – if any will oblige temporarily. Just a couple of housemaids to keep the place ticking over. Mrs Briscoe tells me Cook is leaving and the kitchen girl, too. May I rely on you, Emma? I have things to do here before the handover and I enjoyed the meal you did for us today. My son will be leaving next week, but I shall stay for at least a fortnight. I cannot say what Mr Rawlings will require...'

'Yes, I will stay, sir – for a fair wage.'

'Mrs Briscoe suggested three pounds, ten shillings a month – will that be satisfactory?'

It was more than she had expected, but Emma hid her surprise.

'Yes, sir. Thank you.'

'Very well. I have work to do, please do not disturb me until dinner. I want nothing more and I must go through a lifetime of paperwork.'

Emma dipped a curtsey and left. She had never thought to feel pity for her employer; he had not treated his workers at the mine well. Now, she understood at least some of the burdens he carried and it made her feel sad that he'd had such an unhappy life. Strangely enough, it also made her feel inclined to favour Tor Hardy's courtship of her more than she had. To be in such a position of power and never speak of it – that took a special kind of strength. Some might have used it to take what he wanted, but from what she'd heard, Tor had paid a fair price for a worked-out mine; it was his good luck that he'd found new sources of mineral deposits.

* * *

After Emma had gone, Sir Philip sank down into an armchair, covering his face with his hands. For a few moments, he considered taking his own life – it would be easier to put a pistol to his head and press the trigger than to face the shambles he'd made of his life. Yet his wife was not strong. How could he leave her to fend for herself? Her brother would take what little Sir Philip still owned and use it for his own devices. His wife would live in his house, but as what – a poor relation, dependent on others for the clothes on her back?

No, he would go on, though his pride was in tatters and his heart torn to shreds. Yes, perhaps he'd been a fool to let the mine go, but he'd always hated it and would never go down even as a young man. He didn't believe Tor had deliberately cheated him, as Ralph accused. Besides, he'd always liked Tor, admired him – even wished on occasion that he could change places. Tor was everything he would have liked to be. Had he been stronger, his wife might have heeded him, and his son respected him. It was their betrayal of his values that hurt him the most, he decided.

Shaking his head, he stood and went to his desk. He must clear this lot out – and pray that he didn't find yet another sheaf of unpaid bills.

10

Ralph stayed in the isolated inn until late that night. His head was whirling with all the brandy he'd drunk – good French cognac, and none of it had paid tax if he guessed rightly. He'd seen some uneasy looks as he'd entered and laughed to himself. From the whispering his sharp ears had caught, the landlord was expecting a delivery that night – and they were afraid that he would talk of what he'd seen.

He wouldn't talk. Ralph knew that his father's cellars often held a barrel or two of smuggled brandy and he didn't care – but he might come back and see what he could get from these rogues to keep his mouth shut. He laughed mockingly, angry that he was reduced to such stratagems. He was a Penrith. Damn it! They owned this place... or they had; he was owed his share of their illicit trade. Yet soon he would have no authority here – and the common folk would sneer at his family for throwing away their birthright.

'Gone... all gone...' he muttered and then cursed aloud. 'That bastard robbed us...'

The innkeeper looked startled. He whispered to the serving

girl and she approached Ralph nervously. ''Tis time for closing, sir...'

'Damn and blast you,' Ralph yelled. 'I'll go when I'm ready. Fetch me another brandy, wench.'

'I can't, sir – my mester said no more...'

Ralph swore and grabbed for her, but she jerked away and went off before he could get to his feet and catch her. His head swam and he almost fell, clutching at a chair back and sending it flying. 'Another brandy!'

'Sir Philip would have me out of here if I gave you more, sir,' the landlord told him. 'You go home and sleep it off, sir...'

'Keep your advice to yourself, rogue. I know what...' Ralph swore as the room swirled. He lurched towards the man, who avoided him. Profane words poured from him as he staggered towards the door, snatching a jug of something from a table and taking a long swig. It was just ale and he cursed, throwing it to the ground so that it smashed.

Seeing that he would get no more brandy here, Ralph barged his way out of the door into the cold night air. It hit him like a brick in the face and he nearly fell. Muttering and groaning, he lurched towards his horse; he'd left the poor beast, sweating and thirsty, as he drank the night away. He staggered a few steps, stumbling to his knees and getting up. He managed to reach the horse and untie the reins, but couldn't mount the beast.

'Here you!' he yelled at a man leaving the inn by the back door. 'I need your help to mount this bastard thing.'

The man came towards him, and, as he got closer, he saw it was Tor Hardy.

'You!' Ralph spat the word at him. 'You bloody thief... cheating us of a fortune.'

Tor looked at him in disgust. 'I cheated no one. Your father knew there could be mineral deposits elsewhere; I begged him to continue – but he didn't want to waste his money searching...'

'Bloody liar. You knew it was there – and now we're ruined...' He spat at Tor's feet. 'Get me up on this bloody thing... or are you too important to be what you are now? Bloody servant...'

Tor surveyed him coolly. 'I am none of those things you name me – and I'll not help you to kill yourself, Ralph. Sleep it off somewhere – and look after that horse. It looks half dead, poor thing... it needs water.' Tor went to the pump in the yard, filled a bucket and brought it back; the horse whinnied, bent its head and drank deeply.

Ralph glared at him, truculent and befuddled with strong drink. 'I know what you are – bloody smuggler, and thief. I'll have the law on this place. You see if I don't.'

'You'll have a hard time proving it,' Tor said. He walked on, mounted his own horse and rode off.

Ralph cursed him, spat on the ground, put his foot in the stirrup and, somehow, swung himself up. Perhaps it was his rage that made him successful, but this time he made it. He took hold of the reins and started to race after Tor. He would bloody teach him some manners.

Ralph had gone only a short distance when something loomed out of the darkness. It was as black as the night but solid, as his horse nearly collided with it, rearing on its hind legs, and throwing Ralph to the ground. The horse then went careering off into the night, its reins still entangled around Ralph's arm, dragging him over the rough ground.

* * *

The solid mass cursed loudly. 'That stupid fool has injured one of the ponies. We'll have to carry the load ourselves – and get rid of the poor beast. We can't lead it all the way back to the cave.'

'What was he doing here at this hour? No decent folk are about at this time of night,' another deep voice grunted.

'That was Sir Philip's son.' The worried landlord came out to them. 'Take the stuff to our secret cellar. I'd best see if I can find him... if he is alive.'

'Leave him,' the pack leader commanded. 'If he lives through the night, he'll be too sick to remember us. Bring him into the inn and he'll have the excisemen down on us. I heard what he said to Hardy...'

'Did you do it deliberately?' the landlord asked.

'The fool was drunk. I wouldn't have sacrificed a valuable pack pony for that weakling. I could have settled him another way. Nay, man. He brought it on himself. Now forget it – let someone else find him – and stick to your story. He got drunk and went off; you saw nothing after he left the inn.'

'Aye...' The landlord glanced in the direction Ralph Penrith's horse had gone, but it was too dark to see much. It wasn't his place to run after the beast – and he was too frightened of the man who led the pack horses to argue. In this business, you did what Red Tikka said or you disappeared for good...

* * *

It was Ike Hanson who brought the news that Sir Philip's son was missing two days later. When Tor heard, he swore beneath his breath and summoned the men from the mine.

'We have to look for him,' he told them. 'He may have gone off on his horse, but he could be lying injured – if he is alive. The work can be left for today. We search until we find him.' He looked at Ike. 'You say he has been missing two days?'

'That's the talk in the village…' Ike nodded. 'They say he quarrelled with his father and went off like the devil was after him – so the gardener says.'

'Then we'll split up and search for him. He may have taken the road through the mountains. I saw him drunk two nights ago but told him to sleep it off.'

The men looked from one to another doubtfully.

'You will be paid your day's work,' Tor said. 'We need to find him. Sir Philip may not be mester here now – but I am. I'll search down the valley towards Settle. I saw him drunk out that way when I was riding home.'

Tor mounted his horse and rode off, leaving the men to start a search. Ralph Penrith could be anywhere. Tor wouldn't put it past him to go nosing about down the mine, looking for what damage he could do. He knew well enough that it wouldn't suit that gentleman's pride to be brought low. Tor had no love for Sir Philip's arrogant son. Yet he prayed that he would find him alive, possibly drunk, and resentful, but in one piece.

* * *

It was the blacksmith who found Ralph. He and two others were bringing the shattered body back as Tor met them halfway to the inn, where he'd last seen him.

'Is he alive?' Tor asked, seeing their grave faces.

'Nay, he's gone,' Blacksmith Murray said. 'Dragged to his death I reckon, Tor. His neck was broken and he is cut and bruised all over. There's a deep gash across his forehead and his face is terrible bruised; the poor devil is hardly recognisable.'

'My God!' Tor stared at him in horror. 'What on earth happened to him?' He pulled back the blanket, glanced at the young man's face and recoiled. 'With injuries like that happen he's best dead. He looks as if he has been trampled.'

'Stamped on, I reckon. The horse was nearby with a broken leg. I had to put it out of its misery.'

'Just as well. Sir Philip would have shot it after this...'

'Aye, that's for certain.'

Tor turned his horse. 'I'll warn Sir Philip you are coming.'

* * *

Sir Philip came forward eagerly as he saw Tor striding towards him. 'They told me you'd instigated a search. Thank you – have you news?'

'News? Yes – but not what you'll want to hear, Philip. I am sorry. It seems Ralph was thrown and dragged, perhaps trampled, and... it is not a pretty sight. Your lady must not see it.'

'She isn't here, thank God.' Sir Philip swayed, but Tor was beside him, saving him from falling. 'I'd like to bury him here, in the family plot. He didn't want to leave, and now he never will. I'll tell his mother when it is over.'

'If there is anything I can do...'

'Thank you for helping to find him. There is nothing you or anyone can do now – but thank you...' Sir Philip's face was graven stone, all feeling suppressed by his grief.

'The mine...' Tor began uncertainly. 'I wasn't sure when I offered to take it off your hands...'

'I know.' Sir Philip lifted his weary eyes. 'It matters nothing. I neither hate you nor care for you, Tor. I doubt I will ever care for anything ever again.'

He left Tor standing there and went to the wagon in which his son was lying. Lifting the blanket, he looked down at Ralph for some seconds in silence, then nodded to the waiting grooms.

'Take him to his room. I shall do what must be done.'

With that, he walked away, a sad, broken man.

* * *

Three days after Ralph was buried, Sir Philip left Penrith for the last time. It was three weeks before they heard the news, brought by the carrier. He had spoken to his wife, quarrelled with her, then gone out to the stables and shot himself through the head.

A few in the valley nodded, clearly thinking it justice. He'd not always treated his people fairly. Others mourned him. Some wondered what their future would be now. Everyone spoke of little else but when the new owners of the estate would arrive, but there was no word – and no wages for the staff.

Mrs Briscoe decided to close the house. Emma was sent home with the other servants. She inquired for work at the vicarage but was told the vicar was now suited; he had a live-in housekeeper. There was nothing for Emma now but a job as a milkmaid or marriage to Tor Hardy.

11

Emma looked up from the cow she was milking. It was a humid morning in early June and the stink from the midden was disgusting to a girl used to service and the smell of lavender and beeswax. A fly buzzed about her face and she batted it away, feeling sweaty, her cheek smeared with dirt where she'd brushed it. She was slow and not good at her job, and expected to find the mistress glaring at her. Instead, she saw Mrs Briscoe for the first time in two weeks.

'I've been instructed to hire servants for the house,' she told Emma without preamble. 'Do you want to be the cook – or stay here?'

Emma's pail was filled at last. She stood up, with a weary sigh. 'You know the answer to that – but won't they bring their own with them?'

'Apparently not. I was sent for and glad of it – I've been at the miller's house, doing work I'd not have touched if Sir Philip had kept his word and given me the cottage and pension he promised.'

'I expect he forgot you. The poor man was out of his mind

with grief and I dare say he got no help from her ladyship,' Emma said, tipping her milk into the churn. 'When am I needed?'

'Next week. Do you have to give notice here?'

Emma laughed, the sound light and pretty. 'They will be glad to see the back of me. I am the worst milkmaid they ever had.'

'They should have hired you as their cook, Emma.'

'The mistress does that – and she's a good plain cook, but she can't make pastry for trying.'

'Don't let the master taste yours then, or they'll never let you go. You're to have four pounds a month, Emma. I told the man who came that we won't work for nothing – even though I was crossing my fingers behind my back. However, it seems the new master has instructed we're to be paid properly.'

'I wonder what the mistress is like,' Emma replied as she washed her hands in a pail of water she'd used to clean the cow's udders and then wiped them on her coarse apron.

'There's no mistress – just the young master. I reckon he's a bit of a devil, that's why I was hired to make things look respectable and get him some staff – but I'll not have my maids interfered with and I told the agent so.'

Emma goggled at her. 'What did he say to that?'

'He just shrugged and said it wasn't up to him. His lordship had instructed him to find servants and my new master was a lord's grandson and a respectable man – in most ways.' Mrs Briscoe grimaced as they walked outside into the fresh air, and wiped her shoes on the young fresh shoots of grass. Everything looked green now, the fields a patchwork of emerald, dotted with swathes of wild flowers that gave them a blue haze in the early morning when the mist was on them. 'That shed stinks! As for the new master, I've heard he's not to be trusted around women, so be careful, Emma.'

'There aren't that many men you can trust,' Emma replied ruefully, for her new master had a habit of pinching her bottom as he passed her in the cowsheds; then she smiled. 'Did you know I am to be wed in the autumn? We've settled on the last Saturday in September.' She hadn't rushed into her decision, but the more she'd seen of Tor, the more she'd come to like him, and their walks on a Sunday morning had continued, giving them both pleasure. Emma didn't yet feel as she had about Joe Davies, but she knew she felt safe and cared for with Tor and had decided it was what she wanted of life. 'I'll work for this new mester until then, but after we're wed, I'll never need to work for another again. I can look after my home and spend time with Ma when Tor is working.'

'I heard you were walking out with Tor Harvey,' Mrs Briscoe said. 'Even more reason to be careful – can you imagine what he'd do to the man that hurt you?'

Emma shuddered as fear shot through her. 'Don't. I think he would kill him. He does love me with a passion I'd not looked for. I doubted it at first, but it is true.'

'I don't know the man other than by sight,' Mrs Briscoe told her. 'But – well, I'm wondering if I should have offered you the job, Emma. You're young and pretty, and I've heard the new owner likes his women that way...'

'Well, I won't be one of them,' Emma replied confidently. 'I'd scream and fight if he tried anything – and leave at once.'

Mrs Briscoe nodded her approval.

'Right. I'll be at the house on Monday next – and we've got our work cut out to put it back in order. It has been empty nearly a month...'

Emma agreed. She knew she would need to help clean it, for

they'd never had enough maids and, until folk saw the new master, they might be reluctant to send their daughters to work at the house.

* * *

'So, he is to come at last,' Tor said as he met Emma that evening. It was his habit to walk her home from the farm, for she often worked until seven in the evening and he would not let her make the long walk home alone that late. During the day, she was safe enough, because Ike Hanson was at work in the mine. Tor knew that Ike envied him, his position in life, his house and money – though most of what he'd earned from the mine thus far went straight back into it. It had needed a great deal of money to make it safe for his men, and then he'd paid a hundred and fifty pounds' recompense to each of the men injured in the mine over the past three years, which was when the accidents had begun. When he was able, he would give them the same again, and continue to care for them into old age.

Tor had no desire to be rich beyond a man's dreams. He wanted a good life, with money to spend on his family, but he'd wanted the mine viable so that it would continue to give work to the folk who needed it. Despite the deathbed promise to his mother, Tor had liked Sir Philip; he would have told him of his beliefs that the mine held more minerals than they'd known if he'd been sure the mine was secure for the future. Now he was being proved right, and though he would take his due, he'd be a fair master.

Yet he was no saint. Tor had continued to buy contraband, and occasionally to help the smugglers that came in with their illicit loads from the coast near Whitby to unload – and he would cheerfully have beaten Ike into submission if the man had given him cause – but sly looks and sneering comments beneath his breath were not sufficient. Instinctively, Tor knew that Ike would harm him the only way he could – through Emma.

He'd wanted her himself and now that she smiled for Tor and ran to greet him with evident pleasure, Ike was seething with jealousy and a suppressed fury. Only his job kept him from taking his revenge on them both. So Tor made certain to walk her home; besides, it was a pleasure to him to have the extra time together. Just to talk to her and hear her laugh, for as she learned to trust him and like him, she opened up and all her joys, fears and dreams came tumbling out. She filled his heart with the sweet innocent love he had never known – for his parents had been bitter souls, demanding obedience but giving little warmth in return. The money they'd been given to keep silent about the murder of an innocent woman had done them little good, for it had soured their lives. Tor believed his father had been shamed, for though he'd never spoken of it, there was sometimes a look in his eyes.

Tor had thought Emma a suitable wife at the start, never realising that she would make him feel the way he did now, consumed by love and a fierce desire to protect her. He brought his thoughts back to Emma as she talked of her day.

'So Mrs Briscoe says.' Emma looked up at him, her face alight with mischief. 'She is like a new woman, fighting for our rights and warning them that she'll not put up with misconduct towards her maids.'

'He'd better not try his tricks on you,' Tor replied, a sudden glint in his eyes. 'If any man lays a finger on you and causes you grief, I'll kill him, Emma. I swear he won't live to regret it.'

'Oh, Tor, don't,' Emma said, for the look in his face frightened her then. 'I won't give him the chance. I promise I'll keep out of the young mester's way. Mrs Briscoe says he is a bit of a devil – but I'll make sure to stay in the kitchens until he's away on his horse – or his carriage, if he has one.'

'If he's a lord's son, he'll have several, maybe even one of those new automobiles,' Tor said, grimacing, for he had no time for the abomination that was the horseless carriage; they stank and made loud noises as they crawled along roads meant for horses. 'I'll stick to horses – those new-fangled machines are dangerous things I've heard. Though horses can be the very devil too, if you don't treat them right.'

'You're thinking of Master Ralph,' Emma said as she saw the look in his face. 'I think he was to blame – not the horse. He was so bitter when he left his father that day – I saw his face and he was mad with it.'

'Aye, and he drank himself into a worse state,' Tor said. 'I blame myself. I should have taken the horse from him, made him sober up before he could ride – but he made his feelings towards me clear, so I let him be. I regret that, for a good man died because of him.'

'You thought Sir Philip a good man?' Emma asked, gazing up at him.

'I think he was a man who tried to be good, decent at heart – but was betrayed by those around him, and too weak to do anything about it.'

'Yes…' Emma nodded. 'I believe you are right, Tor. He wasn't a bad man; he made the wrong choices.'

'Yes, he did – and a man has to live or die by what he does.' Tor smiled down at her. He tipped her chin up to look at him. 'I've chosen you, Emma, and I think I've been wise and lucky.' He bent his head and kissed her softly on the mouth. Emma swayed towards him. It was the first time he'd kissed her on the lips and she discovered that she liked it. Even more when he took her in his arms and held her pressed against him. 'Never think of leaving me, Emma,' he said hoarsely into her hair. 'I'll be good to you, I promise – but... I know that a devil lives inside me and it might take over if I had cause.'

Emma shivered then and the early-summer evening turned cool suddenly.

'You're cold,' Tor said. He took his jacket off and put it around her shoulders.

Emma couldn't speak. She'd forgotten the feeling she'd had when Tor first asked for her – a premonition that caring for him could bring only despair – and now it had returned. Yet even as she knew she was being warned, she also knew it was too late, because she was caught. Her innocent heart had reached out to him and she was his, for good or evil.

'No, I'm not cold,' she said and smiled up at him. 'I do like you, Tor – I care for you. I shall always try to be good to you and make you happy.'

'I love you with all my heart, Emma,' he said. 'All the rest is as nothing compared to what I feel for you.'

'Then we shall be happy,' she said and prayed that it would be so.

'I'd best get you home, my love. I don't want you to catch a chill. You'll be working hard for a time now, but we'll be married come the end of September and then I can keep you safe...'

* * *

Emma was on her way to work that next Monday when she saw something that gave her disquiet. She had almost reached the house when she noticed a man and a woman walking towards her in the mist of early morning. Even in summer, after a hot day previously, the mist would settle in the Dales, gradually clearing as the day wore on. The couple were unaware of her. They were obviously arguing and didn't notice her in the gloom. She heard their voices loud and clear as they quarrelled.

'I won't come again. If he knew, he would kill me!' the girl shouted.

'If you don't come, I'll tell him myself...'

Emma shivered as she heard that voice. It was Ike Hanson! She was almost certain that the woman was Sarah – now Joe Davies's wife of two months. What on earth was Sarah doing with Ike Hanson at this hour?

'I hate you!' the woman screamed. 'I won't come to you again. I swear it...'

'You'll come because I give you what you crave,' Ike sneered and laughed. 'And what would he do if he knew the brat you carry is mine?'

Emma shuddered and turned away, moving out of their eyeline. She did not want them to see her, nor did she wish to hear their quarrel, for she knew what it must mean. Joe Davies was a proud man and if Sarah was carrying Ike Hanson's child and not his...

Emma hurried on to the house and the work that awaited her. She could never speak of what had happened that morning, because she knew it would devastate Sarah's husband – a man Emma had once thought she loved. She knew now it had been merely a young girl's fancy, but she would still not hurt a man she respected. Besides, she could not be certain that the girl was Sarah Davies.

* * *

'You're nice and early,' Mrs Briscoe beamed at Emma when she arrived. 'I didn't expect you for another hour.'

'I came early to get a good start,' Emma said, wishing with all her heart that she had not, because then she would not have heard something that was meant to be private. 'Where do you want me to begin?'

'Would you take on the kitchen, please? I am going to begin with the master bedroom. The other girls will be here later – Ruby's younger sister is to be a kitchen maid, and a girl named Maria, from the Ribblehead, will be the parlourmaid and live in. They were all I could get for now – though the gardeners came back and there's a man for the stables, but I believe the new owner brings his grooms and his valet with him. Mebbe a butler, too.'

'A valet?' Emma gave a little giggle. Neither Sir Philip nor his son had ever bothered with a valet, at least in the country. 'Is it the Marquess of Salisbury then?' she teased. Robert Gascoyne-Cecil, the third marquess of Salisbury, was the present Prime Minister. Neither Mrs Briscoe nor Emma had ever seen, or would ever see, that august man, but they had seen a blurred picture of him in a paper brought from London on the train and delivered by Jem with the post.

'Aye, well, things will be different now,' Mrs Briscoe said, smiling at Emma's joke. 'No doubt we'll be entertaining often.' She nodded her satisfaction. 'I'll leave you to get on then, Emma.'

She left the room armed with dusters, polish and a broom. Emma laughed softly to herself. Mrs Briscoe would not have dreamed of such work in the old days, and it was likely that she would not do so once the full staff was in place. It wasn't her job, but she knew she had no choice for the moment, as it was difficult to get servants after what had happened. Once folk knew it was a settled household and they would get paid, then no doubt they'd have half the girls in the valley begging for a job, but not yet.

Emma rolled up her sleeves. She would scrub the large pine table first, then clean all the dresser shelves and the pantry. Only when that was all fresh and clean would she scrub the tiled floor. One of the gardeners had got the range going the previous day and banked it up overnight, so she was able to heat kettles of water, which was good since the floor was filthy.

* * *

Three hours later, her back aching, Emma heated water to make a pot of tea. Mrs Briscoe had provided fresh bread, butter, cheese and some pickle.

'They are bringing provisions for us this afternoon,' she told her new staff as they settled down with their lunch and a pot of tea. 'You'll be able to bake then, Emma. I got the bread from Mr Thiery's farm and the butter and cheese – but I had to send to Settle for our provisions for the store cupboard, though I understand some additional provisions will be coming from Fortnum and Mason's – a prestigious store in London. I was told the goods from Settle would come today, after noon. I'll need you to help me put everything away,' she said, looking at Maria. 'Nellie, you can carry on polishing furniture. You do that very nicely.'

'Ma likes her furniture polished hard,' Nellie said and grinned. 'Ruby said it was nice here and I'm glad to take her place. Ma is forever scolding. Ruby wrote and told us she was having a reet good time in her new place – her mistress is American and she does things different to us. Ruby gets a day off – and an afternoon. She gets things too – like scent bottles with some of the perfume left, scarves and a dress she and Cook have cut down to make herssen a blouse and skirt.'

'Yes, Ellie says it is a good place,' Emma told them. 'She is much happier there.'

'We'll be better off here now,' Mrs Briscoe said. 'Our Mr Rawlings intends to live well. It will take me the best part of the afternoon to put everything away. The wine arrived yesterday, and the cellar is full – but I hope he is bringing his butler with him because there is no one here that can do the job.'

'Well, we shall just have to wait and see...' Emma said, eyes sparkling. 'And now we need to get on. I want the work done so that I can spend some time this afternoon going through the stores and deciding what to cook for us tomorrow – and the new mester when he arrives...'

12

Tor arrived the following morning to discover his men clustered at the mouth of the mine; they were looking anxious and some were arguing, shaking their heads. His heart caught. Had there been a fall in the mine, injuring some men? Though all seemed to be there. Apart from Ike Hanson.

'What's wrong?' Tor asked, looking from one to another as they shuffled their feet uneasily, not meeting his eyes. 'Is it a fall?'

'Nay, sir.' One of the older men came forward. 'It's not the mine – but it is a bad thing, Mr Hardy. A very bad thing.'

'What has happened, Jacob?' Tor asked, an icy shiver at his spine. 'Are you afraid to tell me?'

'Nay, mester – though there's some mardy fools who think tha's at the back of it.' Jacob cleared his throat. 'Ike has been found dead – out in the dale, with his head broken open and his face smashed to a pulp. Joe farrier saw him brought in.'

'Ike is dead?' Tor felt a flood of something like relief, but then it changed to apprehension as he saw their faces and understood. 'You think I killed him? Why would you think that?

Stop havering and speak out then, lads. I swear I'll not hold it against you.'

'Ike were always on about how he hated you, Mr Hardy.' One of the younger men came forward now. 'He swore only yesterday that he'd get even with you – that he'd have the bitch you're courting and kill you. Begging pardon, mester, for the disrespectful words.'

'Nay, lad. I asked for the truth and I'll tell it.' Tor's flinty eyes narrowed. 'If Ike had laid a finger on Emma I would have killed him,' he said, speaking coldly and clearly. 'But he was nowt but threat and bluster. He hasn't been near her. I saw her on her way to work this morning and she smiled and waved to me.'

'I'm telling you what he said, as you asked, nowt more.'

'And I thank you for it, Evan,' Tor said and looked at their faces, which were still slightly suspicious and anxious. 'I give you my word that I didn't kill Ike, nor did I know he was dead. Damnation, he was one of my best workers and we need all the men we can get now the mine is producing.'

'If you give your word that is good enough for me,' Jacob said, raising his voice so that it carried to the cluster of men.

Evan agreed and then turned to the other men. 'It's time to get to work,' he told them. 'I told you I didn't believe it was Mr Hardy – despite what some think. He'd have killed in anger but not in cold blood, same as me – and most of you. Happen, any man worth his salt would kill for his woman and children. We all know that...'

There were nods of agreement, smiles and a general movement towards the mine entrance.

Tor touched Evan's arm. 'Care to tell me who suggested it might be me?'

'No, I don't,' Evan said. 'He's a man I've respected but...' He shook his head. 'Mebbe he had his reasons and that's all I'm saying.'

'So I've an enemy I don't know.' Tor nodded and let him pass. He went to greet Jonathan, who had emerged from the mine office – a wooden structure he used to test some materials and brew a pot of tea over his pot-bellied stove.

'What was that all about?' Jonathan asked, brows arched. 'They were arguing, nearly coming to blows a few of them, and refused to work. One of them said they wanted to talk to you, so I left them be...'

Tor nodded. 'Ike Hanson was murdered – last night, since he was at work yesterday – and they thought I might have done it.'

'Why would you?' Jonathan looked puzzled. 'He was surly, I know, but a good worker.'

'Aye, he'll be missed for that,' Tor replied and frowned. 'He was not to be trusted with the womenfolk, and I had occasion to thrash him with my whip once – he was trying to take a woman down against her will and I stopped him.'

'The bastard! I don't hold with that...'

'Nor I,' Tor admitted. 'I could have killed him cheerfully on more than one occasion – but he wouldn't give me provocation. I'm no murderer, Jonathan, though I'd kill if I had to.'

'Most of us would – though I wouldn't advise it,' Jonathan replied wryly. 'I paid dearly for my deed – but, in truth, I would do it again.'

'Aye, well, I didn't kill him – so who the hell did?' Tor asked. 'I have no idea, Jonathan, and it worries me. We have a murderer amongst us...'

'Yet it was Ike – not a woman or a bairn,' Jonathan said. 'He was a big man and strong. Whoever did it must bear the marks; Ike would have fought for his life.'

'Aye, he would,' Tor agreed. He nodded to himself. 'I have an idea – but it can wait. On to business. How are the figures for the past month?'

'Good, better than the one before.' Jonathan grinned. 'When you finally stop spending and giving your money away, Tor, you should make a profit.'

'Good.' Tor laughed. 'A mine works by the strength and good will of the men, and they need to know you will treat them well.'

'Aye, it's true – but still, they thought you capable of murder.'

'No doubt some would resent any master, but I'd wager most wouldn't. I hope that they will take my word for it now – and that we discover for ourselves who was guilty, before the law comes pushing its nose into our lives.'

* * *

Tor rode towards the farrier's when he left the mine an hour or so later. He'd checked figures with Jonathan, examined some new deposits, which Jonathan reckoned were richer than the first seam they'd found and therefore worth more, and been down the mine to look at a section of roof that might need more work before they could go further in. He authorised the repair and promised to order the new wood needed, then left. Ike Hanson's death played on his mind as he rode towards the farrier's stables. The glow of his forge told Tor he'd been working, though there was no sign of a horse or Joe.

As he dismounted, Joe came out of the stable, carrying a pair of tongs that held a red-hot iron horseshoe, which he laid on his anvil, a heavy hammer beside it. He picked up his hammer and beat at the shoe for a couple of minutes before glancing at Tor; then, apparently satisfied, he plunged the metal shoe into a bucket of cold water before looking up.

'Something wrong with your horse's shoes?' he asked.

Tor didn't answer immediately. He'd been watching the farrier work, noticing the red marks on the back of his hands, and now he saw dark bruising on Joe's face and swelling round his eye. As he put down his hammer and moved towards Tor, he walked with a slight limp.

'What happened to you?' Tor asked, one eyebrow raised. 'You look as if you walked into a barn door and came off worse.'

'I had an argument with a horse,' Joe muttered. 'Bloody great brute of a thing. Kicked me in the leg and sent me flying. Hit my face on the anvil...'

'Horses!' Tor said and laughed. 'Don't know which is more trouble – them or women.'

Joe stared at him, anger simmering in his eyes. 'What are you getting at, Hardy? If you've something to say, come out with it.'

Tor looked at him but said nothing for a moment. He knew what he'd seen of an early morning and at night, but he hadn't come here to taunt Joe about his wife. 'I was told you saw Ike Hanson brought in this morning. Who found him – and where?'

'Two lads from t'other end of the valley,' Joe replied, his earlier tension easing. 'Moby and Gavin Russell. They're a farmer's lads – brought him home on their father's hay wagon. Said it looked as if he'd fallen from the crag.'

'More than one crag round here,' Tor said. 'Bit vague, but I think I know where those lads live. I'll ride over and have a word with them.'

Joe looked at him oddly. 'Some folk might think you did for him, Hardy. I've heard Ike bad-mouthing you in the village – but when folk said you might have killed him, I didn't believe one word and so I told...'

'And who was it that thought I might?' Tor asked, frowning.

Joe hesitated, then. 'My Sarah's father. He was here getting his carthorse shod, damned brute.' He rubbed at his arm.

'Mullen is a decent man, Tor – but mighty suspicious. He didn't much like me wedding his daughter the way I did – but he got over it.'

'Aye, he might have it in for me,' Tor agreed. 'He told me once he'd be willing for me to wed Sarah, but I refused him – no insult to your Sarah intended, but she wasn't the girl for me.'

'I'd have fought you for her,' Joe said, a glint in his eyes. 'I knew the old bugger wanted better than me for his son-in-law – that's why I gave into Sarah. I'd have waited for our wedding night, but she said the only way was for me to get her with child. It worked an' all. Her father couldn't get the wedding arranged fast enough once we told him, though the look he gave me made me feel he'd rather have stuck a knife in me.' Joe laughed. 'I'd have gone off with her if I'd had to – she is the only one for me. I am a happy man.'

'Glad you're pleased with life,' Tor replied brusquely. 'I'll ride over to the Russells' farm and hear more from them.'

'Tom Constable reckons they'll decide he fell down from the crag, probably drunk, and leave it be.'

Tom Crawford was the police constable from Settle. He usually rode his horse when he visited the isolated farms and small hamlets in the Dales, which was once in a blue moon, since there was little trouble – apart from the smuggling. However, the excisemen were responsible for that and Tom Constable, as everyone called him, never got involved. He would find it difficult as he was often the recipient of a few bottles of French wine or some good Dutch cheese by way of a thank you for turning a blind eye.

'Well, he hasn't been labelled a murderer,' Tor replied and noted a flicker of something in Joe's eyes. 'I'd like to get to the bottom of it.' He nodded to Joe and rode off, his mind busy but disbelieving.

Joe had been in a fight recently. The bruises on his hands were from hitting someone in the face, and that bruise on his cheek – it could have happened in a fall, but the swelling round his eye? Tor doubted it. Joe had been in a fight. Not necessarily with Ike – but probably. Because Tor had seen Sarah hanging around Ike Hanson's neck, kissing him like she meant it – both before her wedding to Joe and since. It was mostly very early in the morning, though he'd seen them together at night before she was wed.

Shaking his head, for he would not presume a man guilty unless he knew more, Tor looked about him. Despite the heat of high summer, the Dales still looked green, with patches of meadow-sweet and white cow-parsley among the long grass. The slopes of gentle hills, divided here and there by limestone dry-walling, held small groups of sheep grazing on the rich grass; they were the lifeblood of these Dales, and to be seen all over. Further away, he noticed a few cattle, lying on the grass, which meant it might rain before nightfall, and further still in the distance, a couple of white horses raced carelessly after one another in their field. Beyond that, the land rose once more, and only a stand of silver ash trees, their trunks ghostly white, hid the gracious house that had once belonged to the Penriths. Like everyone else in the dale, Tor wondered what the new master would be like.

Shaking his head, his thoughts returned to the mystery of Ike's murder – who had wanted him out of the way?

* * *

'You know the crag well enough,' Moby Russell grinned at Tor. 'You visit it often. It's where the gentlemen pass by on their way to Highlands.' Highlands was the name of the inn where the smuggled goods were first delivered before being distributed throughout the Dales.

Tor nodded. It had been his first thought that Ike might have fallen foul of the gentlemen, as folk called the smugglers. He knew Red Tikka was a murderous brute who would kill a man as easily as he would swat a fly. When he'd heard where Ike had been found, he'd thought it might have been that Ike had come across the smugglers and fallen foul of them. He might even have joined them, but angered their leader. Tor had ceased to help them since he'd bought the mine, but he'd taken his leave amicably and still bought freely from them. They might have recruited other strong men to help them distribute the illicit goods.

Tor frowned. In his opinion, the days of the smugglers were all but over. With the railways opening up the land, and the introduction of the telegraph back in 1884, there was more chance of them being seen, and reported. Though they knew all the caves, nooks and crannies to hide in isolated areas deep within the Pennines, and usually moved only at night, it was a matter of time before they were caught. He'd told Red his opinion the last time they'd spoken, and the man had looked at him strangely, before nodding.

'Aye, you might be right,' he'd agreed. 'I've been thinking I'll not come this way again for a while at least.'

His thoughts returning to the present situation, Tor asked, 'You think Ike fell from the crag then?'

'Mebbe had a little help,' Moby said and looked slyly at Tor. Then, as he saw Tor's frown, 'Nay, not thissen, Mr Hardy. Ike Hanson wasn't popular. There's more than one father hereabouts has a score to settle with him.'

'You know that for certain?'

'Well, I know of three lasses that were taken down by him –

and all say it was against their will, but they would…' Moby shrugged. 'I've seen him with a few barmaids, as well as girls from the farms. Ike were nobbut wind and trousers – that's what my da says. Ma slaps his lug and tells him not to be crude, but Da said he'd kill our Rosie if she looked at him twice.'

'You'd best keep that to thissen,' Tor said. 'If Tom Constable comes calling, he might get ideas.'

'Ar, he has already been. We told him where we found Ike – and that it looked as if he'd fallen from the crag. He said we should have called him before moving the body, but we said we didn't know that – and he said we were gormless and wrote it all down in his notebook. He asked if we'd seen any strangers in the Dales – but we told him no. Da says turn your head when the gentlemen go by… 'Sides, they ain't been this month. Red says it has been getting a bit hot, so they're going somewhere else for a while until the law gets tired of looking for them and gives up.'

Tor nodded. He'd known there had been a couple of narrow escapes recently, when the smugglers had actually been fired on down the coast from Whitby. Red had told Tor that they might go elsewhere for a time – but he hadn't been sure until now that that had been the case, which seemed to rule out Red as the murderer.

'Would you show me exactly where you found Ike?'

'If you want,' Moby said and shouted to his brother, who was shovelling muck from the pig pen, that he'd be back in a while.

Tor dismounted and led his horse. They walked together but didn't say much until they reached the rugged outcrop, the rock scarred where it had been mined by ancient folk centuries earlier. Black crows were circling overhead, their loud caws disturbing the still air. In the distance, a flock of sheep was grazing lazily, undisturbed by whatever violence had taken place the night before, and a patch of wild flowers flourished among the rocks, despite the odds. At the old deserted iron mine, there was a sheer drop at one point where the earth had crumbled away, and it was there that Moby led him, pointing to the ground.

'His head was lying against that lump of fallen rock...'

Tor walked over to the large jagged stone that Moby had pointed out and examined it. It could certainly kill a man if he fell onto it from the overhanging ledge above. He looked carefully and at last found what he'd been looking for – but not enough. One tiny smear of blood. If Ike had cracked his head open here, there should surely have been more.

He turned to look at Moby, who was leaning against a large boulder, clearly uninterested, and picking his teeth with a bit of grass stalk. Tor examined the ground, then knelt down and snatched something up. He nodded and placed it in his pocket.

'Find something?' Moby asked, staring at him now.

'Yes,' Tor said and showed him a cigarette butt. 'Ike didn't smoke – but someone has been here who did. I shall take it to Tom Constable. He must have missed it.'

'He didn't even look on the ground,' Moby replied. 'Just glanced at the rock and said Ike must have fallen – then went off back home.'

'Well, I'll ride over and see him,' Tor said. 'It's not much of a clue, but it proves something.'

'What?' Toby clearly didn't understand.

'Ike wasn't here alone – and this butt has not been here long. It hasn't been rained on; it's quite fresh, probably last night.'

'Or mebbe this morning,' Moby said. 'Been a few folk wanting to look this morning – all gave me something for showing them where he was found.'

Tor took the hint and tossed him a florin. 'You could be right, but I'll give Tom Constable my opinion anyway.'

He mounted his horse, leaving the farm lad staring after him.

* * *

'That could've been left there at any time,' Tom Constable objected when he was shown the cigarette butt.

'Not that many folk round here smoke cigarettes,' Tor pointed out. They had only been introduced into the country in the past few years and were still mostly used by the gentry. Most folk either smoked a clay pipe or chewed a wad of tobacco. 'These look expensive – probably foreign.'

'Damn it, Tor! Do you think I don't know that?' Tom Constable said, a flicker of annoyance in his voice. 'If you want to upset the gentlemen, I don't – best just leave it that he fell.'

'What about the blood?'

'What blood? I didn't see any…'

'That's it – he didn't die there,' Tor said calmly. 'If he had there would be lots of it.'

'Not always,' Tom Constable retorted. 'Sometimes wounds bleed inwards. Anyway, I don't want trouble over this, Mr Hardy. If I report it as a murder, we'll have the militia snooping round. They've been hunting the smugglers for weeks now – and nearly had them a couple of months ago. We don't need them pushing their noses in here now, do we? Too many decent folks might get hurt.'

'Some folk might think I had a hand in Ike's murder. I'd rather expose the real culprit,' Tor replied. 'I'm no murderer, Tom Crawford, and I won't be called one.'

'I'll arrest anyone who says it and throw them in the cells for a night,' Tom promised. 'No sensible man would think it – I certainly don't. I think we both know how it happened, Mr

Hardy. Now, just go home and forget it. That's my advice to you, Tor.' The use of his given name told Tor their interview was over.

Tor stared at him, shrugged and left. There was no point in stirring up trouble, because he didn't know for sure, even though he suspected. Besides, he didn't particularly want someone he liked hung for murder. He'd made his point, spoken to the law, and hoped to be believed. After all, had it been Emma that Ike had taken down, Tor would have killed Ike without a flicker of guilt, but he would have done it openly, in front of witnesses – a fair fight. If Joe Davies had discovered that Ike had been meeting his wife – might even be the father of her unborn child – Tor could hardly blame him for wanting the man dead.

13

'You killed him, Joe. I know you did,' Sarah Davies cried, beating at her husband's chest with her fists. 'Why? You knew that it was over. I told you. I gave you my true promise.' She raised sullen eyes to his. 'Why did you have to do it? They will find out it was you and they will hang you – then what's to become of me and the babe?'

'Is that all you think of, Sarah?' Joe asked her wearily. 'Yourself and your child?'

'Your child, Joe!' Sarah's face flamed with angry colour. 'It is yours, no one else's. I swear.'

'Can I believe you?' Joe asked, eyes narrowed and hostile. 'You swore to me before that you'd stopped seeing him – that you never loved him and didn't want to see him again. Then I saw you with him, twice. I'd left early for work, but I came back for some tools I'd forgotten – and I saw you run to him.' He sighed. 'The second time I came back to watch what you did – and you went to him again... How can I trust you?'

'Because Ike made me,' Sarah cried. 'He threatened to kill you if I didn't meet him, but nothing happened. He tried to force me, but I kicked him where it hurts, and he swore at me and would have harmed me if I hadn't managed to outrun him. I swear it, Joe. I swear it on the life of our child.'

'Don't do that!' Joe cried. 'Don't risk the baby, for I love it whosoever's it may be – just as I love you despite what you've done to me. I love you, Sarah, but I don't trust you.'

'Suit yourself then,' Sarah yelled, angry now. She had a temper to match the flame of her hair. 'Shall I go home to my father and tell him you threw me out? You'll not get a penny of his money then – and I know that's why you started to court me, Joe Davies.'

'That's a lie!' Joe shouted, but his anger was muted, because at the start he'd been flattered that the beautiful daughter of Miller Mullens was making eyes at him. In the first instance, he'd thought about the money that might come his way one day if he married her, though, at the time, he'd been planning to ask another young woman to walk out with him. Emma Watts. She was a nice, decent girl and he'd noticed her. He'd been considering whether to ask her to attend the church fete with him – but Sarah had flirted with him, tantalising and teasing him, until he could think of nothing but her.

She'd been so beautiful in her yellow gingham dress and her cloud of red hair falling about her shoulders. He'd been fairly caught and had asked her to wed him. She'd said no, and then maybe. Then one night she'd come to his door in tears and told him that she loved him, but her father wanted her to marry a richer man. She'd told Joe that the only way for them to marry was if he got her pregnant. Joe had been startled, a little shocked, because he hadn't thought to take her until their wedding night. However, Sarah's tears had melted his heart, and God knew he'd wanted her! He'd wanted her to the point of madness and still did; she was a temptress, with her flashing eyes and her pouting mouth that invited kisses – and she always smelled of roses, sending his senses racing.

Within three weeks, she'd told him she was late with her monthlies and persuaded him to go with her to her father and confess their wicked secret. Miller Mullens had been furious, his fists balling at his sides, but after he'd calmed down a little – and after he'd called Joe all the filthy names he could conjure up – he had agreed to their wedding.

Of course everyone knew that Sarah was pregnant. The wedding was rushed and her father complained of it to everyone he knew, rather than trying to keep it a secret; it was almost as if he wanted his daughter's shame to be known. Joe had thought that strange, but perhaps he'd been protecting her name. How much worse it would have sounded had it been suspected that Sarah had first been with Ike Hanson. Joe had wondered why Miller Mullens hadn't taken a stick to him or driven him out of the house – and he'd wondered at how quickly the baby had started to swell Sarah's slim waist. Then he'd seen her meet Ike Hanson in the morning mist – and he'd remembered. Before they were wed, he'd seen them talking in the dale on more than one occasion when he'd been visiting the various farms to tend the horses there. Mostly on a Saturday or Sunday, which was when he often visited friends, farmers, who were too busy to come to him. True, Ike and Sarah had only been talking and she hadn't been his wife then, but still... the memory was enough to arouse his suspicions when he'd seen her meet Ike after their marriage.

Joe had questioned Sarah about her meetings with Ike. At first, she'd tried to lie, but then she'd come out with a story that had built such fierce anger inside him. Yes, it was true that Ike had forced her to lie with him before she'd wed Joe – but only once and months before she'd started courting Joe. After their marriage, he'd forced her to meet him again, threatening to tell Joe what had happened. She'd gone the first time and begged him to leave her alone, but he'd held her roughly and kissed her against her will. She'd told him she would never meet him again, but he'd waylaid her on her Sunday visit to her father and mother – and told her that he would not take her now while she was big with child but would come after her once it was born.

'He told me I was his and he would take me when he wanted me,' Sarah had confessed, her face wet with tears. 'I love you, Joe – but I am afraid of him. If I don't do as he wants, he might try to kill you... both of us.'

'He can try,' Joe had told her. 'I am as strong as he – and you are my wife. I'd fight any man for you.'

Joe had made Sarah promise never to meet Ike again, and to tell him if she was threatened. He hadn't asked if the child was his, but the thought that it might not be – that she and her father had tricked him – had built in his mind. Joe had tried hard to put it aside, to believe in the woman he loved, but it had been hard – and his hatred of Ike Hanson had grown to be an unbearable burden. There was another side to Joe, one he seldom showed, one born of ill treatment as a youngster, and that other side hid the anger that, if allowed to fester, could erupt into something he feared.

It was over now. Ike was dead. He could never threaten Sarah again, nor make another girl ashamed to tell her parents what she'd done. He was gone and he would soon be forgotten, like others of his kind. Joe would not grieve his death, nor would he feel guilt. The man was rotten to the core and deserved his fate. Whoever had killed Ike had done the community a service and that person did not need to be named nor to feel guilt, at least in Joe's mind.

The only niggling doubt left in Joe's thoughts was whether

his wife had lied to him over and over again. Had she lied when she said Ike had forced her? Had she lied when she came to him and told him that they had to make a child before they could marry – had that child already been growing inside Sarah when Joe first lay with her?

Sarah would never tell him if it was so and Joe wasn't sure he wanted to know. He wanted Sarah to love him and he longed for the child to be his – despite that he'd had the measles when young and the kindly old doctor had warned him he might not be able to father a child. His mother had told him it was nonsense – but she had loved him. God rest her soul! His father had died of a fever and his mother had followed six months later, unable to live without her beloved husband. Joe had been trained as a farrier by the man who had bought him from the parish orphanage – a hard cruel man Joe had learned to hate.

When he was old enough, he'd deserted his master and started up for himself. It was a new chapter and a new life and he never looked back. He told himself there was nothing to remember but much to look forward to. When Joe had thought Sarah loved him and he had a child of his own, it was as if the world had become brighter. Now, he wondered if the mist of his gloom would ever lift – or would his sins of long ago forever sour his life?

* * *

Ike's funeral was private, attended by his sister and elderly mother. Tor Hardy was there to show respect for a man who had worked for him, and two other men who had worked down the mine with Ike – one of whom, Nate Mesby, was courting Ike's sister, though so far, she'd refused his offer of marriage.

No one saw Sarah as she hung back in the trees that shaded

the churchyard. She had not dared to attend the service, nor was she wearing black, but she wept tears as she watched the coffin being lowered into the ground, and, later, when the small group of mourners had gone and the grave diggers had finished, she crept out and laid a single flower on the turned earth.

'I loved you, Ike,' she whispered, so low that none could hear her. 'Why wouldn't you wed me?'

No answer came. Ike would never give her an answer. He'd sworn that he loved her, that he would always love her, but when she asked if they would be wed, promising her father's wealth one day, he'd turned his head aside.

'Why not? Why not?' Sarah had plagued him, but Ike would never answer, until one day, he'd whirled on her.

'I have a reason, but I shall never tell you – now stop your teasing and kiss me. You'll always be mine. Wed another – whoever you choose – but come to me when you need me. You will always need me, Sarah, because you are mine in your heart.'

Sarah had been angry with him then and she'd left him. She'd wanted to catch Tor Hardy in her net, for he was an important man, but he would have none of her – and so she'd settled on Joe Davies, the next most important single man in the valley. Joe was a silent, introverted man, keeping himself to himself. He'd been easy to catch. She'd seen interest in his eyes when she'd teased him, flirting and retreating, but then she'd known she had to marry. It hadn't been easy to turn Joe from his steady ways, but she'd done it – and her father had played his part. She'd faced him with the truth, knowing his pride would not allow her to wed a man he considered beneath her. He'd wanted Tor Hardy for her, but Tor had refused his offer, too. Sarah hated Tor for that, but it hadn't mattered. Joe was easier to deceive than Tor Hardy would have been.

At least Sarah had thought so, until he'd accused her of

meeting Ike Hanson. Sarah had panicked then and told the first lies she could think of. Afterwards, she knew she'd chosen the wrong story, but then it was too late.

She was certain Joe had fought Ike and killed him. She'd seen him splashing cold water all over himself, washing off the blood in the scullery. He hadn't come to bed that night, but slept downstairs in the kitchen. Sarah hadn't dared to say anything – until she was told that Ike was dead. Then she'd accused Joe of killing him. He'd denied it. He would. Of course he would! Yet she had sensed something in him then, seen it in his eyes. Sarah knew then that she'd picked the wrong man. She'd thought Joe would be easy to manipulate. She'd thought she could control him – but there was a hidden side to Joe, something she could not even guess at, and she'd brought it to the fore – a snarling beast who might do anything.

Sarah dipped her head, pulling her shawl up over her so that her face was half hidden as she left the graveside. If Joe knew she'd been here – if he guessed that Ike was the man she'd loved – had always loved – he might kill her next.

A shudder went through her as she thought of the long years ahead. She didn't love her husband. She'd liked him, even cared for him a little at the start, thought him a gentle, soft man, but he wasn't. There was a hardness in Joe Davies she'd never seen before. She'd thought he would dance to her tune, but now she was a little afraid of him.

14

'The master arrived last night – near ten of the clock it was,' Mrs Briscoe complained when Emma arrived at work the next morning. 'He demanded supper and I had to give him cold meats and cheeses and the bread you'd made earlier. He wanted to know where his cook was and I told him you go home after you prepare the evening meal. He did scowl over that, Emma. Told me he expected his servants to live in so that they could provide what he wanted when he needed it...'

'Oh dear, did he?' Emma sighed. 'I do hope he won't insist on it, Mrs Briscoe. I really do not want to live in – if he complains, then you will have to advertise for another cook. It is only another two months or so to my wedding, so I could go back to milking until then...'

'We'll see what sort of a mood he is in this morning,' Mrs Briscoe said. 'I think he was drunk last night – and so were the three young men he brought with him. When they wake, what are you planning on giving them for their breakfast?'

'I cooked a ham and a joint of beef rib yesterday,' Emma said. 'I could do coddled eggs, bacon and warm scones with the home-made plum jam we made last year. Or the marmalade you ordered from that shop in York.' Some of the provisions the new master wanted had not been available at Thomas Clarke and sons in Settle, a fine big store established nearly forty years previously, so they'd had to send all the way to York for them.

'He will probably demand kedgeree or smoked salmon and cream cheese,' Mrs Briscoe lamented. 'The ingredients are on order but neither arrived – they told me the smoked salmon would come next week and the haddock was unavailable at the moment.'

'Well, I'll bake fresh bread and scones and serve what we have,' Emma told her. 'The mester has a stream filled with trout so he and his friends can go and catch some if they want fresh fish for their breakfasts.'

'Yes, that is what Sir Philip had it stocked for,' Mrs Briscoe reflected. 'He wasn't sure the fish we bought was truly fresh, so he stocked the stream and that deep pool on his estate with trout. They bring fresh fish to the market in Settle most weeks,' Mrs Briscoe went on thoughtfully. 'Sometimes a boat will come up to the coast from Cornwall to Whitby, and they will have crabs, or lobster and prawns. Now they are lovely… but, as a rule, I like a bit of fresh cod, if it can be found.' She nodded to herself. 'It's not all they bring north with them, so I've heard – but that is only a rumour and not to be repeated, Emma.'

'I wouldn't dare,' Emma said. 'I've never heard or seen the gentlemen, have you, Mrs Briscoe?'

'I've heard things – not seen,' Mrs Briscoe replied. 'Sounds in the night – in the cellars, but the voices were pure Yorkshire, not Cornish, so local lads are involved. That being the case, it is best to not look or listen. You know what they say of smugglers – "close your eyes when the gentlemen go by".'

'That's what my da used to say.' Emma laughed. 'I think he

went out to help them bring their loads through a few times – years ago. Ma says that when Sir Thomas was around, they stored contraband in the mine, in the disused tunnels, and he was a party to it.'

'I wouldn't put anything past him,' Mrs Briscoe agreed. 'It was before my time, but they whisper that, after a wild party here, a young man of gentle birth disappeared one night, never to be seen again. A search was set up for him. They went down the mine to search – but he was never found, nor heard of again. Rumour had it that he and Sir Thomas had fallen out over something and his body was dumped somewhere far from here – perhaps on the way back to Cornwall.'

'Mrs Briscoe!' Emma laughed at her. 'I've never heard that one – I am sure it isn't true.'

'I wouldn't be so sure about that...' The sound of the man's voice startled them and the two women spun round to see a tall young man dressed in a dark crimson robe, his feet bare, fair hair tousled and damp, curling about a handsome face. 'The tales I've heard of Sir Thomas would deem him perfectly capable of murdering anyone who thwarted him...'

Emma looked into the laughing blue eyes, a flush heating her cheeks as she saw his frank appraisal of her. 'We didn't realise you were up, sir. We were wondering what you would prefer for breakfast?'

'If you really want to please me, I'd like bacon, scrambled eggs, followed by toast and strawberry jam – or marmalade.'

'That's easy enough,' Emma replied. 'I could provide more variety if your guests would wish it.'

'Those idiots drank far too much last night. They won't make an appearance before luncheon.' He gave her a frank stare. 'You must be Emma Watts – my cook. Where were you last night when I arrived?'

'At home in bed,' Emma replied. 'Fast asleep, I should think. I start early in the morning and I finish at about seven in the evening when I've cooked the meal. Then I go home to help my mother.'

'Damn it! I often eat at nine in the evening…' he swore softly. 'Country hours. I suppose I can't persuade you to stay later for more money?'

'I can leave something ready that Mrs Briscoe could put in the oven – like a pie or similar,' Emma told him. 'Or I can cook a big luncheon, and do cold food that you can eat at any time, if you wish.'

'You won't live in for me…?' He gave her a smile that was calculated to soften the hardest of hearts.

'If you were holding a large party, sir. I could stay overnight – but not as a regular thing. I'll stay on as I am until you can find a new cook – but there's none in the valley. He or she will have to come from away…'

'Alphonse flatly refused. He is my grandfather's chef in London and could quite easily have spent time here, but he cannot be prised out of the city – and who can blame him? I came under protest and will return there as soon as I've served my penance. In other words, when my grandfather allows it.'

'You didn't wish to visit the country, sir?' Emma was astonished that he should be so frank to a servant.

'Not in the least,' he replied blithely. 'If truth be told, I've been sent to this godforsaken place to cool my heels while my grandfather airs his temper. I've been a naughty boy, Emma Watts.' He grinned at her, suddenly darted forward and swung her off her feet. 'Light as a feather!'

'Put her down, sir! Emma is a respectable girl and she is to be wed soon,' Mrs Briscoe said severely.

'Now that is a shame,' he replied but set Emma on her feet.

His twinkling eyes turned to Mrs Briscoe. 'I was told you were a martinet and I would have to behave. I apologise – but that doesn't mean I shan't do it again. My mother always said I was incorrigible; God bless her soul!' He made a little sign of the cross over his breast. 'Both my parents died when I was young. My grandfather says I am unmannerly, rude and impossible. I fear it is true – thus I am banished.' His laughter rang out, joyous and infectious. 'Shall I go away again, back whence I came?'

'Now then, sir,' Mrs Briscoe said, but Emma could see that his infectious charm was working on her. 'That would be silly. This is your home and you have work to do – tenants to see. Everyone will want to meet the new mester.'

'Alas, I am not my own master, so how can I be theirs?' he said in a mournful tone. 'Yet I must try because I wish to please my grandfather.'

'Why don't you go for a ride to clear your head, sir?' Mrs Briscoe said. 'Your breakfast can be cooked when you return.'

He saluted her, his eyes dancing with amusement. 'I shall do as you request, ma'am. Shall we say one hour – that should clear my head.' He looked at Emma. 'Convince me that I cannot do without you, Miss Watts.' And then he was gone.

Emma met Mrs Briscoe's startled eyes and then they both started to laugh. 'Well, I never! He is certainly different this morning. Last night I was on the brink of giving notice – a rowdy, rude and inconsiderate lot. However, thinking about it, he said the least last night and I wasn't even sure who he was until one of the others addressed him by name.' She looked at Emma. 'So what do you think of our Mr Rawlings?'

'Charming – perhaps dangerous,' Emma said and saw the housekeeper frown. 'I don't know him, Mrs Briscoe – but he seems too frank, too free and easy in his manners. Can that be true? He is a lord's grandson. I think him either a troublemaker, sent here to be out of his grandfather's way, as he confessed – or a deceiving schemer.'

'Emma! That is unkind. He was lovely to you – to both of us.'

'I know and perhaps I am unfair,' Emma replied. 'But remember what you told me before he came – you told me to be careful of him, and now I've met him, I shall.' There was just something that didn't ring true in his manner, at least in Emma's mind, though she had to admit he'd made her laugh.

15

Witnesses came forward at the inquest into Ike Hanson's death. He had been seen that night in the Highways Inn. Ike had been drinking until he could barely stand, then staggered out into the night swearing revenge on his enemies – and they were anyone in authority or those who tried to reason with him. It seemed that he hated everyone and most kept clear of him when he was in this mood. He'd been in a fight before he started drinking and was in a foul mood. No one had spoken to him, because of his black looks.

The magistrate listened to the witnesses, nodding wisely. He then gave it as his opinion that Ike Hanson had met with an accident after drinking excessively. Why he should have chosen that particular crag to climb in the middle of the night, or why he had not staggered home to bed, remained a mystery. However, the judgment was given, justice was done, and everyone went home feeling satisfied and nodding wisely, telling one another that they'd always known Ike Hanson would come to a bad end.

Two men went home in a different frame of mind. Tor felt

resentful and thwarted, because no one had looked beyond the end of their noses. Ike Hanson was a troublemaker. Ike Hanson was dead. He'd drunk too much and fallen while under the influence of too much rum. End of story. Most working men wondered how he could afford to drink so much. One man knew the truth of Ike's death and felt relieved that he'd got away with murder.

* * *

'Well, good thing that is over,' Jonathan said cheerfully when Tor returned and told him the verdict. 'We shall miss him in the mine, but I doubt anyone else will.'

'His mother and sister will,' Tor said with a frown. 'I've heard that Nora Hanson is a scold that would drive many a man to drink, but how she will live without Ike's money I can't think.' He sighed. 'I'd best visit her and see if I can help.'

'Do that and she'll likely think it hush money,' Jonathan warned. 'He wasn't killed in the mine, so you don't owe them anything.'

Tor frowned as he considered. His friend was right; it might seem as if he was offering money to cover his guilt. Yet he would do it for any other family whose sons and husbands worked in the mine.

'Mebbe I'll wait for a while then,' he said. 'I know Nate Mesby is courting the girl, so maybe he'll look after them.'

* * *

In thinking no one would miss Ike, Jonathan was wrong. Sarah missed him. Little as she liked to admit it, even to herself, she needed him. Joe was normally a gentle, tender lover, which was nice and comforting if you were old and had been married for years, but Sarah craved excitement and danger – and Ike had given her both. Now that he was dead, her life had become dull and boring. She washed dishes, made their bed and swept through their small house. She refused to wash sheets and took them to the widow in Butts Lane, who, for a small fee, did them instead. The rest of the day, she sat staring out of the window and wishing that she was in York or London. The child was causing her once-slim body to swell and look ugly and she felt like a lump of lead, her aching back the only thing that reminded her she was human. Yet the worst thing of all was that Joe hadn't made love to her since the day Ike had been brought back to Penrith on a farm cart and they'd quarrelled.

Sarah had apologised for accusing him of murder. She'd wept and told him over and over that she'd just been so worried that he might hang for it, but as yet he had not forgiven her. Her tears and pleas brought her nothing. His excuse was that it could hurt the child, but Sarah knew he was angry with her. He suspected the child was Ike's – and Sarah knew that he was right. She had lied to him, coerced him to wed her, because Ike had refused, and now since the change in Joe, she was suddenly afraid.

The strange thing was that the more Joe turned away from her, the more she wanted and needed him to smile at her again. She had thought he was just her dupe to use as she chose, but Joe had shown her that she was wrong. Sometimes now, when he looked at her, she felt a frisson of fear at her nape, yet perversely now that he ignored her, she craved the little loving attentions she had once scorned.

She went from feeling lethargic and wanting nothing more than to be left alone, hoping to die giving birth, to raging anger and determination to win Joe back. It was in one of her fits of rage that she set off to meet Joe as he made his way home at the end of a working day. Sarah had made up her mind to challenge him. She would tell him that unless he came back to her and started being her husband again, she would leave him and go home to her father. Sarah wasn't sure her father would have her in his house, but Joe wouldn't know that – and if he didn't give in, she would go. After the birth, she would go off to London or York. She'd had enough of this dull life. At that moment, Sarah cared nothing for her child. She would leave it for someone else to care for; her mother would take it. If something exciting didn't happen soon, she would go mad!

When she got to the forge where he worked, Joe wasn't there. Sarah could have screamed her annoyance. The long walk home alone was just too much, and the bright summer sunshine had gone, leaving the sky grey and threatening rain. Pulling her shawl up over her head, Sarah started for home, her rage and frustration urging her to run, though she was seven months gone with child.

The rain beating down on her head, her long hair beginning to straggle across her face, she ran, anxious now to get home. Joe would never believe that she had been to meet him and might hit her if he thought she had been meeting someone. His jealousy had turned him bitter and sometimes she thought he hated her now. So she ran faster and faster, until the pain struck, taking her breath and causing her to stumble and fall. She felt a blinding pain as she struck her head on a rock, half hidden by the long grasses, and then knew no more for several hours.

* * *

It was Stephen Rawlings who found her lying unconscious a mile or so from her home. He had taken his friends to the railway station in his chaise and was on his way home, regretting that he had not gone with them, back to the pleasure and gaiety of London. In the flickering light from his carriage lamps, he saw a body slumped in the grass by the side of the narrow road. He swore and stopped the horses, getting out instantly, for he could see it was a woman. Stephen might be a bit of a rogue where certain women were concerned, but he was also a gentleman. He could not pass by a woman in distress, even though she be but one of the farming folk by the look of her. She was, he supposed, one of his folk now, and he owed her a duty.

Kneeling at her side, he felt for a pulse and discovered she was alive. He also saw that she was heavily pregnant.

For a moment, he wondered what to do. The nearest house was some distance away, so he stood and then bent and lifted her, hauling her over his shoulder. He was a fit man, his hobbies boxing in town and hunting in the country, both of which kept him strong. The woman was very heavy but limp; she made no resistance as he lifted her into the chaise and let her flop back across the seat.

Retaking the driving box, Stephen drove home as quickly as he could without being reckless. He had no idea who the young goodwife was, so the only thing was to take her to the house and let Mrs Briscoe care for her.

It took fifteen minutes or so for him to accomplish the journey, driving his horses faster than he normally would at this hour of the night. As soon as he reached the front of his house, he jumped down from the chaise and rushed into the hall, calling loudly for help. Within seconds, his valet, butler and a footman appeared, followed more slowly by Mrs Briscoe. However, it was she who immediately took charge when she knew what was wrong, instructing his valet and the footman to go to the chaise and bring in the young woman. A maid was summoned and sent scurrying to pull back the bedcovers in one of the newly made beds, freshly changed after their visitors had left.

Stephen watched and said nothing until the patient vanished up the stairs. Then he turned to Mrs Briscoe. 'I should let her husband know, but I have no idea who she is...'

'That's Sarah Mullens as was – now wed to Joe Davies, the farrier, this past five months – but she looks more than seven months gone. We all knew that she was pregnant when she wed, of course, but Joe did the right thing by her. What on earth was she doing wandering at this hour? She should have been at home getting his supper.'

Stephen nodded. 'Where can I find him – and a doctor I suppose...?'

'Go for the doctor first, sir. He lives at the far end of the dale, towards Settle. Well, 'tis the next vale really, and he has a large house. Doctor Hayburn. You can ask at Highfields. Don't worry about Joe Davies. I'll send one of the gardeners for him. We need the doctor, for if I am not wrong, that child may be born this night or in the wee hours of the morning.'

Stephen blanched at the idea. The last thing he needed was to be in the house when a woman was giving birth. It would remind him too vividly of the reason he'd been banished here – and other harsher memories.

'I'll go for the doctor,' he said and vanished back out of the house.

Mrs Briscoe smiled as she heard him calling for grooms and fresh horses. It would probably be hours before Sarah's child was born, but she'd thought he might refuse to drive back all that way if she hadn't made it sound urgent.

* * *

Sarah woke later that evening to find herself lying in a clean bed in a beautifully furnished room. All pink and cream silks at the windows, and in the bed-curtains, the high ceilings were painted with cherubs and fluffy clouds. It was like something from her dreams and she sighed with content, inhaling the scent of lavender. It was the last time she was to smile that night, for the pain came suddenly, striking like a knife in her back, and she screamed for all she was worth.

The door opened almost immediately, and a woman she'd seen in the village a few times came in with a bowl in her hands; she was followed by a maid with a steaming kettle, and then, as she departed, Emma Watts entered, carrying towels and more sheets.

'Oh, Emma,' Sarah shrieked in relief at seeing a face she knew. 'Hold my hand, Emma, don't leave me. It hurts. It hurts so much...' She gave a sobbing cry. 'I think I am going to die.'

'Don't be daft, lass,' Mrs Briscoe said. 'The pain is natural and all mothers bear it. You'll be better soon enough.'

Emma moved to her side and held her hand, clasping it tightly as another spasm of pain gripped Sarah. 'I know it sounds cruel,' she whispered softly. 'But 'tis true. The pain will go when the babe is born – and then you'll be so happy thissen will forget it.'

'I'll never forget this and I'll never have another,' Sarah said through gritted teeth. 'And I damn the man who did this to me. I hope he rots in hell!'

'Now then, now then,' Mrs Briscoe said, looking shocked. 'Your husband is a good man, Sarah Davies, and it is only natural for him to love you. Having children is women's lot and we have to bear it – otherwise the human race would be finished.'

'As if I bloody care,' Sarah said fiercely. 'How would you know? You don't have children.'

'No, but I did – two of them,' Mrs Briscoe said, surprising Emma as well as Sarah. 'They and my husband all took a virulent fever and died. I was the only one left. I had to find a life, so I did the only thing I knew and became a housekeeper. It was a long time ago...' A shadow passed across her face at remembered grief.

'I am sorry for your loss,' Emma said, but Mrs Briscoe shook her head.

'How long does it take?' Sarah asked, oblivious to anyone's pain but her own. There were tears on her cheeks now as the pain struck yet again.

'Sometimes a few hours, sometimes longer,' Mrs Briscoe replied. 'Don't push like that, Sarah. Your waters haven't broken and until they do, baby isn't quite ready.'

'I can't help it... ahhh... bugger! I've wet myself.' Sarah screwed up her face in disgust. 'No one ever told me loving would lead to this...'

'It is a good thing your waters have broken.' Mrs Briscoe smiled. 'Baby is on his way now. Put your knees up, Sarah, and spread them wide. I'll look and see...'

Sarah obeyed and Mrs Briscoe looked. She turned to Emma.

'It looks as if the baby is almost here. Stay with me, in case I need help. I helped her ladyship when her daughter was born, but the cord was round the poor thing's neck and by the time the doctor got here, it had died. It shouldn't happen – but if it does, I'll need help to get it free. I won't see another babe die needlessly...'

Sarah gave an almighty scream and pushed hard, struggling as the pain hit her again and again, but then she felt something give and Mrs Briscoe gave a crow of pleasure.

'It's through, Sarah, the head is out. I am going to help you now – just one more push and it will be all over, you lucky girl.'

Sarah didn't feel lucky, but she did as she was urged and felt her body release her child into the world. Mrs Briscoe did the rest, and Emma took the baby, wrapping it in a towel and wiping a smear of blood and mucus from its nose and mouth. Then she brought the little bundle, which had started to scream, and placed it into Sarah's arms. It was a tiny scrap of a child, born before its time, but seemingly healthy. Sarah realised that she must have been pregnant some weeks before she'd realised. It might be fortunate that she'd had her accident, for otherwise Joe would have known he was not the father.

Sarah had been determined to hate this thing that had ruined her life, but the moment she looked into her child's blue eyes, she felt an overwhelming surge of love.

'It has got Joe's eyes,' she said, shocked to the core, because the baby couldn't be Joe's.

'Your baby is a little girl,' Emma told her. 'She is beautiful – and her eyes are lovely.'

'All babies have blue eyes,' Mrs Briscoe said. 'They will probably change in a while.'

'Is that true?' Emma asked. 'Ma says my eyes were always green, right from the moment I was born.'

'That means you're a witch,' Sarah told her and laughed in delight. 'I always knew you were, Emma.' She reached for her hand and squeezed it. 'Thank you – and you, Mrs Briscoe. You saved my life…'

'It was probably Mr Stephen who did that; he found you unconscious on the moors. If he hadn't, you would have died in the night, all alone and in your condition. It will be a wonder if you haven't caught your death of cold!' She stopped as they all heard voices outside the room; then the door opened and

Stephen Rawlings and the doctor entered. Mrs Briscoe hastily covered Sarah with a sheet.

'So you managed it without me, Mrs Davies.' The doctor smiled at her. 'Well done – but I may as well check you and the child over to make sure all is well. If you would leave, sir...' He looked pointedly at Stephen.

'Oh yes, of course...' He backed from the room, followed by Emma, who was carrying bloodstained cloths and a sheet. 'Did you help with the birth?' he asked Emma, looking dazed. 'I drove as fast as I could. We could hear her screams outside the house...'

'Well, she is over it and she wasn't in labour long,' Emma said. 'I did nothing much, just held her hand. Mrs Briscoe did it all.'

'Of course. Bravo, Mrs Briscoe – but I think I'd rather have you as my nurse, Emma. Will you promise to look after me if I get ill?'

'If it was my place, sir,' Emma replied and backed away nervously as she saw the gleam in his eyes. 'I am promised to be wed, sir. You know that...'

'Yes, to my sorrow,' he said, his mouth curving in a wicked smile of delight. 'I'm not as much of a rogue as you think me, Emma. I wouldn't hurt you... Oh, don't look like that! I know you've heard the stories, but I didn't care for either of them. They threw themselves at me – and I'm a man, Emma. I took what they offered. Now both are with child and claim it's mine – but I'd swear neither was a virgin...'

Emma flushed to the roots of her hair. 'Please do not,' she begged. 'Such things are not for me to judge – and I would not hear them if you please.'

'I only wish you to understand and not think me evil.'

Emma looked at him and thought him sincere, at least in

this. 'I do not think you evil – just a little dangerous for girls like me.'

'There are none,' he replied and then turned and walked away from her.

Emma took the dirty linen to the wash house at the end of the scullery and then walked back to the large kitchen. When she got there, she saw Joe Davies had arrived and Molly, the new parlourmaid, was giving him a cup of strong tea.

'I should think Mr Davies could do with a drop of the kitchen brandy,' Emma said and smiled. 'You've got a daughter, Joe; she is tiny, born before her time, but healthy – and her eyes are just like yours. I wasn't sure when Sarah said so, but now I look at you, I can see it is true.'

'She has my eyes?' Joe's eyes sought hers. 'You think it, Emma?'

Emma saw the appeal in his gaze and understood what he was asking. 'I would swear to it, Joe.'

'Oh God,' he muttered and dropped his head, covering his face with his hands. 'Forgive me. God, forgive me... I've been unkind and she might have lain there all night and died of a fever had she not been found.'

'Sarah will forgive you,' Emma said. 'Go up to her now, Joe. I can hear the doctor taking his leave, and she'll be asleep soon, for the pain was bad. Go quickly and tell her you love her – she needs to hear it.'

'Emma Watts, you are an angel,' Joe said and stood up. 'If I wasn't married to Sarah, I'd ask you tomorrow.'

Emma's eyes met his. 'There was a time I would have said yes,' she murmured. 'But now I am promised to Tor – and I love him. I love him with all of my heart.'

'Then I wish you well of him,' Joe said, 'and I promise you

this, Emma – if ever you should need my help, I will give it...' With that, he walked away from her and up the stairs.

Emma was not there to see the reconciliation, but Mrs Briscoe described it all in detail when she came down to the kitchen.

'Such a carry-on. The both of them kissing, hugging and crying. All she did was have a baby – you'd think no woman had ever done it before.'

'No woman has ever had Joe's baby,' Emma said and smiled, turning away to prepare the master's supper. She was going to be late home, but if she was lucky, Tor would be here soon to make sure she got there safely. He'd begun to call for her every night, now that she often worked later.

'You can leave if you want,' Tor had told her. 'I will look after your family. You know that, Emma.'

'I've given my promise to stay until summer's end. It won't be long, Tor – and then we'll be wed. It's less than two months.'

'Aye, but a lot can happen in that time,' he'd said. 'I wish I could wed you now, Emma. I promised your father I'd wait until the mine was making money – and that will be next month or the month after, so we'll call the banns then.'

Emma held the promise inside her. By the end of August, she would be sitting in church to hear the banns called, and then, three weeks later she would be wed. Before that, there would be the annual summer thanksgiving, when all the folk of the valley came together for a church service and then a feast of the good things they had grown. Emma had not been to the feast since her father was injured, because it could get a little riotous when the men drank too much beer. She could not go without an escort and she'd not wanted to leave her family at home. This year she would go with Tor...

* * *

In his study, Stephen Rawlings sat drinking brandy, his face thoughtful. The events of the night had made him vaguely uneasy, taking him back some years to his childhood.

As a very young boy, Stephen had been wild, forever in trouble, and he recalled having temper tantrums when he'd been thwarted: one in particular. His mother was carrying a child and had turned him away when he'd tried to crawl onto her lap; his nurse had been reprimanded and told to keep him in the nursery. He'd screamed and cried as he was carried away, but to no avail – and that was why he'd taken his mother's diamond necklace, to pay her back...

It was a beautiful single drop, large and lustrous on a fine chain. His mother had loved it – more than she'd loved him. One evening as she was preparing to go out, Stephen had wandered into her room, wanting to see her, hoping for a careless kiss or caress. No one was there, but the necklace lay on her dressing table. He'd taken it and hidden it where no one would find it.

The necklace had been hunted for, servants searched, their rooms turned upside down, a maid dismissed, but the necklace had never been found. His mother had died in childbed soon after... and Stephen had wondered if it was his fault. After that time, his father went away and Stephen was forgotten, unwanted, unloved – in the care of servants until he was sent off to school. He'd never seen his father alive again, only as a cold white statue in his coffin.

Now that he was a man, he knew he hadn't caused his mother's death, but he still had the necklace. He didn't want it. He'd never truly wanted it, but he couldn't sell it – because then his grandfather would know how wicked he had been. And his grandfather would die soon enough and leave him a fortune. For Stephen, that day could not come soon enough.

16

Life settled down for Emma over the next few weeks. Looking back in later times, she would think of it as a charmed period, the happiest of her life. It seemed to her that summer that the sun was almost always shining; the weather could be changeable, dark clouds sometimes spreading in from the purple haze at the top of the Pennines without warning. Not that year, or, if they did, Emma didn't notice, because she was happy. Even the sudden flurry of snow across the whole country in July only made her laugh when everyone else saw dire warnings in such a freak occurrence. Snow in July! Was the world about to end? Emma just laughed and scooped it up to throw snowballs. Tor was courting her, showing her his love and a softer side that no one else ever saw. His eyes would glow when they looked at her and her heart swelled with love and pride.

Emma was proud to be marrying one of the most important men in the dale. The mine was doing well now and a glow of prosperity had fallen over the valley, for Tor was a good mester. He paid his men normal rates, but when there was an exceptional find of a rare mineral that brought him more money, all of his men received a bonus – not forgetting those that were no longer able to work because of an injury at the mine. Zinc, witherite, bayes and fluorspar had all been found, as well as a small vein of silver. Jonathan spoke of the possibility of copper, but none had yet been discovered, though in some parts of the Lake District it was still being mined.

Tor was a popular man now and people smiled and tipped their caps to him – and if Emma was seen in the dale, folk would smile on her. She was Tor Hardy's chosen woman.

Her work at the house was easy. The mester disappeared for days, or even weeks, to York or London, with friends, often returning with three or four young men. When that happened, there was more work for his servants, including Emma, but not more than she could easily manage. She produced good home cooking with the occasional special sauce or a fancy pudding and everyone was satisfied.

Letters arrived from her friend Ellie regularly. She was well and enjoying her new life. Her mistress was easy-going, the master genial but hardly ever there, other than for his dinner and breakfast, though they entertained often.

I wish you were here, Emma, but I am happy you are to wed. Thank you for inviting me. I shall come if I can. Ruby is coming home soon, just for a few days. She has saved five pounds that she wants to spend on her family – and to give them the news that she is courting. We have an American butler here and he has taken a shine to her. He asked her to wed him and Ruby agreed. She will continue to work for the mistress but has been promoted to parlourmaid and we are looking for a kitchen girl to take her place. Ruby says her youngest sister might like to take the job, if her mother will let her.

I must finish now for the footman will take my letter to post for me if I am quick. I have a busy day as we have a large dinner party this evening.

I think of you often, Emma.

Your loving friend, Ellie XXX

So life was good for Emma; Ellie was happy, and Mrs Briscoe was content with her job. 'I think we were misled when folk said the young mester was a wild one,' she commented as she sat over her tea and cake one afternoon when the work was done. 'He hasn't troubled us at all, has he?'

'No, but do not tempt fate,' Emma said, laughing. 'Have you thought what you will do when I leave to marry?'

'Don't speak of it!' Mrs Briscoe told her. 'Oh, I wish you well, Emma – you know I do, but I'm sure we shan't find anyone half as good. I've been looking in the *Ladies Monthly* – but no one has advertised for a job in this area. All those that do ask for positions in London or York – but never here.'

'Perhaps if you advertised the position...' Emma suggested. 'I really think you should, Mrs Briscoe. A month soon passes – and Tor will post the banns next week. Three weeks after that, I'll be married.'

'Yes, you will.' Mrs Briscoe smiled. 'Well, I am sure you deserve your good fortune...'

'The mester has just arrived with a party of six young gentlemen.' Milly, their latest housemaid, came hurrying in, looking flustered. 'What am I to do, Mrs Briscoe? Only four of the guest bedchambers are freshly cleaned and the beds made up.'

'Find Ruth and make up two more,' Mrs Briscoe replied, frowning. 'Is there any food for them, Emma?'

'Yes, for a day or so – then we'll have to get supplies from the local farms. It will be plain fare, for nothing special has been ordered – unless the mester has brought some hampers himself.'

'We must hope he has or he'll settle for whatever the farms can supply...'

Mrs Briscoe bustled off to discover what she could. Emma busied herself making bread. It was the one thing she was short of for a large company, but she had plenty of flour and yeast, and dough was soon rising by the range fire. Her mind was occupied with her work and planning what to serve for dinner that night and she sang as she worked, in her light sweet voice,

My love... my love... oh, my love...
My love he was a fair true knight,
My love, my love... oh, my love...
He comes to me by candlelight...
And his kisses fill me with sweet delight...

My love, my love... oh, my love...
But when the dawn comes, he is gone, and
I know... I know... oh, I know...
He lies beneath the cold, cold, snow,
Never more to ride the high toll road
And I know... I know... oh, I know.
My love, my love... oh, my love lies dead
But, oh, when he comes to me by candlelight...

Emma's voice soared to the high notes, then a slight noise made her whirl round. Stephen Rawlings was standing just inside the door staring at her oddly, almost as if mesmerised by her song.

'That is a sad song – what is it called?'

'A lover's lament, I think,' she said. 'My father used to sing it when we went walking in the fells. He said it was about a highwayman and his lass.'

He nodded. 'You have a lovely voice, Emma.'

'Not as fine as my father's, sir. He can sing opera – and his voice fills the house or the church when he sings.' She sighed. 'He doesn't sing now, though.'

'He was injured, I know. I am sorry,' he said.

'You were not to blame, sir,' Emma said, wondering why he was staring at her still. 'I should get on – unless you wanted something, sir?'

'You are very beautiful when you work,' he said, a brooding look in his eyes.

'Oh, sir. I am said to be an attractive woman, but never beautiful.' Emma lowered her gaze hastily.

'You are to me,' he replied, bringing her head up sharply. His look just then was darker than she recalled seeing before. 'Congratulate me, Emma. My grandfather has chosen a bride for me. She is rich – and as ugly as sin...'

'That isn't kind, sir,' Emma chided. 'Why marry her if tha does not love her?' She blushed as she spoke, for it was not her place to say such things to her master. 'Forgive me, mester. I should not have spoken so.'

'I shall forgive you, Emma. And I will answer your question. She is rich; I am not – and she is prepared to have me, disreputable reputation notwithstanding.'

'But you don't love her...' Emma wished the words unspoken the moment they left her mouth.

A flame leapt in his eyes and he moved towards her, then stopped abruptly.

'As well her as anyone,' he muttered. 'She has money – and I can't have the only woman I want, because she loves another.' He looked at Emma with such intensity then that she took a step backwards. 'Don't look so frightened,' he said, holding up his hand in supplication. 'I'd never hurt you, Emma, never force you – but don't begrudge my loving you. I can't help myself.'

'Oh, sir. Oh, sir, please – you must not. I never meant to hurt thee...' Emma said, her heart catching. 'I do like you... but it would never do, even if I didn't love Tor.'

'If you didn't love him, the rest wouldn't matter.' The look of longing in his eyes shocked her. 'But you do – and I can't hurt you, because I love you. So a rich willing woman will do as well as any other.'

With that, he turned and walked abruptly from the kitchen.

Emma found that she was trembling. He had frightened her with his intensity – and his declaration had left her numb. How could a man love her that way when he didn't know her? It was strange and unsettling. Yet she sensed a deep loneliness, a darkness of the soul in him, and it made her shiver. He appeared light-hearted and good-natured, but there was more within that he did not often show.

Taking a long breath, Emma went back to her work of preparing the meal, scolding herself for being foolish, but Stephen Rawlings had not been joking. He was far too intense and serious for that...

For a moment, Emma considered leaving her work unfinished and returning to her home. Tor wouldn't mind; he'd told her she need not work – but Emma wasn't a quitter and it would make things awkward for Mrs Briscoe just when they had company. She shrugged off her feeling of apprehension. As soon as the housekeeper had found a new cook, she would leave – but if the master made the slightest attempt to touch her, she would go home and never return.

It was the summer feast that weekend and Emma was looking forward to it. She knew Tor was very busy at the mine and she didn't want to worry him, so she would say nothing. On Saturday, they would go to the feast together – and on Sunday they would sit in church and hear the banns read. There was nothing to fear, nothing to make her insides twist and clench the way they were.

Emma laughed at herself as Mrs Briscoe came bustling back into the kitchen carrying a small hamper. A footman followed, carrying a huge one, followed by yet another carried by Milly.

'We have our provisions then?' Emma said. 'That was thoughtful of the mester.'

'There are more to follow,' Mrs Briscoe replied. 'The mester has come for a few weeks this time – and I understand his bride-to-be and her father will visit in two weeks. She is coming to see what her home will be like, no doubt.'

'Is he to be married here then?'

'No, in York,' Mrs Briscoe informed her. 'Her father is a wealthy merchant, it seems. So we shall have a mistress again, Emma.'

'You had better advertise for your new cook then,' Emma reminded her. 'Unless you fancy adding the cooking to your work, Mrs Briscoe.'

'I shall send tomorrow morning, when Jem takes the post to Settle,' Mrs Briscoe replied. 'I must hope I can find someone, Emma. I suppose you wouldn't consider coming in for a while after you marry?'

'Oh, no,' Emma said quickly. 'I was thinking of leaving the week before my wedding – or sooner. I shall stay for another week or two but... well, you could always ask Sarah Davies to come and help you. I saw her the other day and she seems fine. She is over the birth, as healthy and lovely as ever. She would need to bring the baby, but Sarah is a good plain cook, so I've been told...'

'Do you think she might?' Mrs Briscoe looked hopeful. 'Just until I get a proper cook.'

Emma was thoughtful, then, 'I was talking to her last Sunday after church, and, though she loves her child, she said she gets bored just being at home all the time. So, yes, she might. Sarah likes pretty things and the extra money she'd earn would be hers to spend as she wished.'

'Do you think her husband would permit it?' Mrs Briscoe frowned.

'Considering that the mester helped to save her life, I don't think he could refuse,' Emma said with a smile. 'I shan't leave you in the lurch, unless I have to – but it would be sensible to ask her.'

'Yes, it would,' Mrs Briscoe agreed. 'I suppose she is well over the birth now. I was surprised she took no harm from her soaking that night.'

'Sarah is very strong.' Emma smiled. 'She was talking of visiting the summer feast with Joe. Her father told her to leave the babe with him for the night.'

Mrs Briscoe nodded. 'Yes, you young things deserve a little fun now and then, and there's nothing here – unless you make the journey into Settle. Well, I'd best see if all our young gentlemen are suited with their rooms, Emma.' She walked to the door and looked back. 'What are you going to serve for supper?'

'We'll have a clear soup to start, followed by trout Jem fished from the lake for us – and then roast beef, and a raspberry trifle to follow with some little meringues and a red currant compote.'

'That sounds wonderful,' Mrs Briscoe replied. 'Not what they might be used to in London – but a feast all the same.'

'You wait until they taste my puddings and gravy,' Emma said with a smile. 'I don't think they will regret their fancy French sauces for an instant...'

17

Emma dressed in a pale blue cotton dress with a pin-tucked bodice that fitted into her neat waist, caressed her slim hips and swirled about her ankles in little pleats. She and her mother had made it together, and the pleats had taken ages to get right, but they'd copied it from an old magazine that Lady Penrith had left behind, and it looked very well, the short, puffed sleeves just right for a summer feast.

'You look a reet treat, Emma,' her father said as she did a twirl for him so that he could see her in all her finery. Her little white buttoned-up ankle boots and her Sunday-best straw hat completed the outfit and she looked beautiful. Her mother had told her so and Tor's eyes did the same when he called for her. She went out to meet him, carrying a basket with some cakes and pastries she had baked for the feast. Every woman or girl attending would do the same, though she knew Tor had supplied some hams and a big rib of beef, which one of the farmers' wives had spent hours cooking.

A bonfire had been lit at a pleasant grassy spot near the little stream, with ancient trees to give some shade, that the villagers liked to use for their celebrations. The men had set up tables and benches, and quite a few folk had brought rugs and blankets to spread on the ground. There were jacket potatoes roasting in a fire pit and two great barrels of beer, beside lemon barley and other home-made fruit drinks for the women and children. Lots of children were running around on this summer afternoon, playing games of tag and cricket – a game some of the men would join in a bit later on. Emma's little brother and sister were here with some friends, for Emma's mother had insisted she and Tor did not want the bother of bairns.

'They can go with their friends and come home at dusk. You'll want to stop longer, Emma.'

For the moment, everyone was busy greeting newcomers, calling out and laughing. All were dressed in their finest clothes and, in a spirit of friendship and camaraderie, celebrated a rare holiday. The folk of Penrith did not have many feast days in the year; they were all normally hard at work, other than on a Sunday. Sunday was for church and quiet pursuits, like reading, walking, fishing, or embroidery, not the rumbustious fun and games the feast gave way to as the afternoon wore on, and the men relaxed with a few pints of beer tucked away.

A few women drank the beer but most stuck to their cordials, but that didn't stop their faces becoming flushed as the fiddler played and they danced. As the sun began to fade, the fiddler played faster and the dancing and fun became wilder. Shrieks of laughter were to be heard as young men chased and caught young women, kissing them and tugging them back to the dancing, though some crept away into the shadows, wanting to be alone with their chosen partner as blood heated and pulses quickened.

Emma's brother and sister came to say goodnight. She

hugged them and asked if they'd enjoyed themselves, but she could see the answer in their sun-kissed happy faces.

'Shall we find somewhere a little quieter?' Tor asked when the light from the fire was a brilliant glow in a blood-orange, sunset sky. 'I want to talk about our wedding, Emma.'

'Yes, let's go for a walk,' Emma said and took the hand he offered to pull her to her feet. She tucked her arm through his and they strolled away from the glow of the fire and the noise. 'It won't be long now. Ma is so excited. We've made her a new dress and she has been baking a cake for us...'

They were holding their reception where all the villagers did, in the church hall. Tor had invited various folk, including Sarah and Joe Davies, his partner Jonathan and some of the farming folk. He would supply some food and beer for his miners the evening before the wedding.

Emma had invited Mrs Briscoe and Ellie, who had promised to come the night before and would stay at Tor's house, because he had plenty of room. Ruby couldn't come at the same time as Ellie, so Emma hadn't invited her. But she'd asked the seamstress who had helped her make her wedding dress, and two of her mother's friends. Her father was to be carried to the hall on a stretcher and would be made comfortable on a sofa with pillows so that he could join in, but he could not sit in church to see her wed. It was sad for him and for Emma, but she would show him the dress before she left for church, and she'd asked an old friend of her father's to give her away.

The details had all been settled, but Emma knew Tor just wanted to make sure she had all she needed and to be alone with her for a while. They had seldom had the chance to be alone at this time in the evening, the walk to and from church their time for talking and a stolen kiss. Both of them led busy lives and, besides, there was nowhere to go in the evenings, other than the inn at Highways – and Emma's parents would never let her go there. In summer, some couples went for long walks just to be alone, but Emma seldom had time for much courting.

Before Christmas, there would be an evening get-together at the church hall, and she hoped to attend as a young wife, but for young folk there was nothing else, which was why most wed as soon as they could. They could be together in their own homes, though most couples spent the best part of their lives working. Life was hard in Penrith valley, which was why they so enjoyed their special feast days.

Walking now with Tor, Emma knew that she was happier than she'd ever been, and so when he turned to her and kissed her, passionately, almost fiercely, she responded with all her heart.

'I love you, Emma,' Tor told her. 'You are the only woman for me.'

'I love you, Tor,' she said quietly, pressing herself against his strong body. 'I wasn't sure at first, but then I began to know you – and now I wouldn't have anyone else.'

The softness of her lips, the smell of her clean hair and the pliant supplication of her body as she melted into him made Tor groan with longing. 'I wish we were wed and could go home to our bed,' he murmured in her ear.

'We can't go there, but...' Emma looked up at him, wanting, needing something she hardly understood, sensing his desire. 'I am yours,' she whispered. 'We'll be wed in another three weeks...'

Perhaps it was the magic of a warm summer night, the distant glow of the bonfire, and the sound of laughter and music, but as of one they went to the ground, which was dry, warmed by the heat of a hot day, the long grass settling around them. The smell of crushed grass and the warm earthy scent of the soil would remain in their minds forever, reminding them of this night when they became one: one heart, one love, one body, joined in the age-old way that gave pleasure and comfort, but could also bring pain. It would do all three in the future but neither thought of anything past that moment of glorious love, when Tor took the woman he adored with infinite care, so that Emma felt warmed and caressed, wrapped in his arms and safe from all harm.

Afterwards, when they lay talking and holding each other, he apologised. 'That should not have happened until our wedding night,' he told her as his fingers caressed her cheek, her throat and then played in her long hair. 'It was wonderful – I'll never forget it, but I'll make sure to be there for the banns to be read tomorrow. Will you forgive me, Emma, my love?'

'I was as ready to love as you were,' she said, giggled a little and curled closer to him. 'I wish now we'd married weeks ago – I didn't know what I was missing.'

'My own sweet love. Tha's a reet tyke, my Emma,' Tor said. The slang was an affectionate term for a true Yorkshire lass and Emma giggled, because Tor seldom used the humour of the Dales. 'What do thissen think?'

'Shy bairns get nowt,' she said, which meant if one didn't ask, they didn't get.

Tor laughed and clasped her to him, and they made love a second time, but by then it was growing dark and, as he helped her to her feet, they heard different sounds coming from the direction of the bonfire. Some shouting and a couple of screams.

'We'd best see what is happening,' Tor said, but Emma hung back. She was seized by a shivering fit, though the night was still warm.

'No, Tor. Take me home please. If there is trouble, I don't want us to be involved in it...'

Tor looked down and saw a flicker of fear in her eyes. 'It is probably just a couple of the lads got into a fight. I'll take you home first...' He caught her to him. 'Never forget how much I love you, Emma.'

'I shan't,' she said and held tightly to his hand as they walked home. As they got nearer to her house, her feeling of unease grew stronger. Then she saw the gig parked outside her home. 'I think something is wrong...' She let go of his arm and ran the last few steps to her house, just as the door opened and the doctor came out. 'Is it my father?' she gasped in fear.

Doctor Granby looked at her sadly. 'He has taken a turn for the worse, Emma. No, no, he isn't dead, but I fear it won't be long.'

Emma gave a little scream and ran into the house, leaving Tor to speak to the doctor, before following her in.

Her mother was sitting by the bed in the parlour, tears on her cheeks. She looked at Emma reproachfully. 'He asked for tha, lass. I sent someone to fetch you,' she said. 'They couldn't find you...'

'Tor and I went for a walk,' Emma replied. 'We were discussing the wedding...'

'If your father dies, tha'll have to put that back a bit,' her mother said, giving her a hard look. 'It wouldn't be respectable to have a wedding with your da...' She choked back a sob.

Emma went to the bed, bending over her father to kiss his brow. It was heated and wet with sweat, but his eyelids flickered. He opened them and looked up at her.

'My little lass,' he murmured. 'You've been a good girl, Emma – don't lose your happiness over me. Promise me you will marry Tor when the banns are read – even if I'm dead.'

'Don't,' she whispered against his hair. 'I am sorry I wasn't here sooner, Da. I was with Tor.'

'As you should be.' He squeezed her hand limply. 'I can die easy knowing you'll be his, Emma – and he will take care of you and your ma and the bairns.'

'Yes, Tor will look after us all,' Emma replied. 'He has plenty of room in his big house. They can move in with us if Ma likes...'

She heard her mother sobbing behind her but didn't look round. Her mother's harshness had been caused by grief and she understood. She stroked her father's head, then looked at her mother.

'I'll fetch some warm water to bathe his face, Ma – and say goodnight to Tor.'

'I'm sorry, Emma...'

Emma shook her head and went out, through to the kitchen. Tor was sitting in what had once been her father's chair, but he stood as she came to him and opened his arms to her.

'I am sorry, love,' Tor said gently. 'Is there anything I can do?'

'You might have to wait to have the banns called. If Da dies, we can't marry immediately.'

'Not for a few weeks – but he wouldn't want us to wait for long, Emma.'

'No. He thinks a lot of you, Tor. He says we'll be safe with you.'

'You and your family,' Tor promised. 'Shall I stay tonight? In case you need me?'

'Go home and sleep, Tor,' Emma told him. 'You can call early and see if I am able to walk to church with you...'

'I'll speak to the vicar first thing,' Tor said and kissed her softly. 'We'll put the wedding back a few weeks – your father may rally again.'

'The doctor thinks not,' Emma said, suppressing a sob of

grief for the father she adored. 'I must go and tend to him, Tor. 'Tis too much for my mother. She is broken with grief.'

'Tomorrow then,' Tor said and left her.

Emma poured water from the kettle on the range into a bowl, added a little cold from a jug, then picked up some cloths and went back to the bedroom. There was little she could do for her father, but she could at least make him comfortable and keep him clean. He needed to be changed, as did the bed sheets, and her mother could not do that alone.

Raising her head, she faced the truth that she would be needed at home to care for her father until he passed. She would send word in the morning that she could not return to her job. It would make things awkward for Mrs Briscoe, but perhaps Sarah Davies would step in and help. Emma regretted letting them down at the house – but her family came first.

18

Tor walked away from the cottage in Butts Lane, feeling sorrow for Emma's father, who was a good man and should have had many more years with his family. Men who worked the mines were always at risk of a rockfall, because sometimes gasses were released by the hammering and explosions could happen. More often, a fall was caused because maintenance had been neglected and that was the case in Emma's father's case. It would not happen on Tor's watch if he could prevent it!

His thoughts were diverted by the sounds of a fight, yelling and screaming. Tor wondered at it, for there had been something similar earlier; he'd ignored it then, for Emma had wanted to get home. Yet that was a woman screaming. He turned his steps in the direction of the sounds and saw two men fighting and a third struggling with a girl. Tor didn't recognise any of them at first, but as he approached at a run, he saw that one of the men was the young farmer's son, Moby, and the girl was his sister – the other two men were unknown to him but looked to be better dressed than the local lad.

'Leave the lass alone!' Tor cried as he saw the girl's dress had been ripped at the bodice. It was obvious what was happening. The two men had jostled and tried to interfere with the girl and Moby was fighting to protect her as best he could, but he couldn't take on two, for he was struggling as it was.

The man who had hold of young Rosie Russell looked at Tor for an instant, and in that moment, she bit his cheek and he yelled, letting go of her as he put his hand to his face, finding blood. 'Bloody vixen! She bit me...' he exclaimed as Tor reached him. 'I only wanted a kiss...'

'It serves you right,' Tor told him, watching as Rosie disappeared into the darkness, running for all she was worth. 'Don't touch our lasses unless they give you permission.'

'It was just a bit of fun...' The man's voice was sullen, defensive.

'Well, how do you like it?' Tor grabbed his right arm and twisted it up behind his back.

The man struggled but couldn't get free. He yelled at his friend, who turned to look at him. In that instant, Moby gave him a punch to his stomach, followed by a knee in his groin, which made him double over in pain and swear.

Tor forced the one he had in a grip of iron over to join the other stranger. 'Where are you from?' he demanded. 'If you're staying at the big house, you'd best get back where you belong. We don't take kindly to men molesting our lasses.'

'Who the hell do you think you are?' the man who had been fighting Moby demanded, his hands still pressed to his groin and in obvious agony. 'I am Ravenscroft – my father is Lord Ravenscroft, and you and your friend here will pay for this...'

Tor released the man he'd been holding, shoving him into his companion and almost knocking him down. 'I care not who you are, sir – you caused this affray and I'll bear witness to what

I saw. Get back to where you came from, both of you. You are not welcome here.'

'You don't own this valley, but I have a friend who does,' Ravenscroft leered at him. 'You'll find yourself turned out of your home and your farm by tomorrow night if I have my way.'

Tor looked at him and then laughed. 'Good luck with that, sir. My name is Tor Hardy. I'll bid you goodnight.'

He turned his back on them and walked over to Moby, who was glaring angrily at the men, while still trying to get his breath.

'Thanks, Tor. They set on us for no reason – just because Rosie refused to kiss them. You know what they would've done if she had...'

'Ay, I do. Get off home now thissen – make sure your sister is safe...'

'Ay... Watch out!'

Tor turned as Ravenscroft came at him from behind. He had picked up a large stone from somewhere and his arm was raised to strike Tor on the back of the head, but it didn't happen. Tor ducked, then reached out and grabbed his arm, forcing it back and twisting it hard. The crack was sharp as a bone was broken and a shrill scream issued from Ravenscroft's mouth. He swore terribly, turning away to nurse his broken arm, yelling and moaning. Then he swung round, his face blazing with fury. 'You'll go to prison for this – it is assault and you won't get away with it, you bastard.'

'You attacked me from behind and that is the way of a coward,' Tor replied. 'I merely stopped an unlawful attack on a young and innocent woman – but you chose to attack me. I have a witness...' He looked at Moby, who nodded.

'Aye, I saw it – and I'll stand in any court and say so...'

'You'll pay, Hardy. I'm warning you... Come on, Scott, let's get back to Penrith Manor. I need a doctor...'

Tor watched as they left, standing there until they were out of sight.

'He will make trouble for you,' Moby told Tor. 'Be careful. He is a nasty devil. They came to the feast after you left and were looking for a fight; there was a bit of a scrap, but then they cleared off. We thought they'd gone back to the Manor – but then as I was walking Rosie home, they suddenly appeared and started grabbing at her. I did my best, but I'm not much of a scrapper. If Gavin had been here, he would've half killed them... so thank you for what you did, Tor.'

'Just remember to stand for me in court if that one tries anything – but I doubt it is more than bluster.'

'Aye, he's full of pie-crust promises, drunk and may not remember – the both of them had been drinking before they came to the feast.'

'Rich and self-important,' Tor said. 'Get off after Rosie. Make sure she is all right.'

They parted then, Tor walking to his home, deep in thought. The fight was the least of his worries. He knew that he ought not to have used so much force, but he'd been attacked and a man was entitled to protect himself. No, his concern was more for Emma – and her father. With the wedding postponed, he could only pray that she had not quickened with his child. He would not have her the subject of gossip and common jests.

Tor cursed himself for giving way to his desires. Why had he broken his vow to himself that he would not lie with her until his wedding night? It wasn't the first time he'd longed for her, nor yet the first time the scent of her skin had made his pulses throb – why then had he chosen to take her this night of all nights? Now her father was ill and she would be worn down with grief when he passed; she must not be harmed whatever.

If the lord's son made trouble for Tor, he knew that he could face a trial – and imprisonment for a short period. He might be arrested and imprisoned until he could prove his innocence...

'Damn him! Damn him to Hell!' Tor cursed aloud. He was innocent, but that would only be proven in a court of law. It might delay their wedding for months.

Shaking his head, he went into his own house and settled down in his favourite chair. There would be no sleep for him that night. He must plan for a future that might hold fear for Emma and trouble for himself. Tor could face a prison sentence if he wasn't believed, because in an unfair world, the word of a lord's son would often be taken above a mere commoner. Jonathan would look after the mine, but it was Emma he worried for. He must find a way to make sure that she and her mother were safe if he could not look after them for a while.

19

Early the next morning, Tor visited Jonathan at his home, a small cottage he had rented from the Penrith estate. He handed him a document, which Jonathan read. Having scanned it once, he read it through again, then looked at Tor.

'I don't understand – you've made me a full partner in the mine. Why? I thought that was going to happen in a few years?'

'You've more than proved your worth,' Tor said with a smile. 'Besides, I may be going away for a while and I want to be sure that it is in your interests to look after things for me.'

Jonathan frowned. 'I would have anyway – but I see that this gives me authority to act on your behalf, Tor. I can tell you are worried – what's wrong?'

'I had an argument with a man – the son of a lord. Ravenscroft, he said his name was. I broke his arm and he swore to get even.'

'My God, Tor!' Jonathan exclaimed. 'I've heard of him – nasty sort, by all accounts. Friend of Mr Rawlings up at the Manor.' He looked at Tor anxiously. 'Why did you do that?'

Tor explained and Jonathan looked grave.

'And Moby was the only witness to Ravenscroft's attack on you?'

'Yes. I am afraid so,' Tor said. 'Unless he comes through for me, I could find myself in prison for a few months.'

'For assaulting a man with his influence, it could be a couple of years at least,' Jonathan told him. 'Why on earth did you break his arm – that is grievous bodily harm, Tor.'

'I'm not sure whether I just used too much force or whether I meant to hurt him,' Tor admitted. 'I used just enough to control the other one – his name was Scott. He had been roughly assaulting Rosie, that's Moby's sister.'

'Yes, I know her,' Jonathan replied. 'Pretty girl – a bit shy. She didn't encourage him, I'll wager.'

'She was screaming and Moby was fighting Ravenscroft – and losing, if truth be told. I had to stop it, but I did neither of them any harm – until he attacked me with a weapon. Surely a man is entitled to protect himself?'

'Of course you are, Tor – but can you prove he attacked you first? You only have Moby's word – and I wouldn't rely on him too much.'

'No.' Tor nodded, acknowledging the truth. 'He swore he would stand in court, but he's terrified of the law – and for good reason. I doubt he'd dare show his face there, which means I could be in trouble.'

'This other man – Scott – would he testify for you?'

'I doubt it. Ravenscroft is his friend – I doubt he'd go against him.'

Jonathan looked serious. 'I'll keep this paper safe, Tor, and I'll look after things for you – but what about Emma and the wedding?'

'Her father is ill. We've put the banns back. I will make sure Emma is all right. You'll have your work cut out; Rawlings would like to get his hands on the mine, no doubt. So would Sir Philip's widow, if she could. They may come after you and try to make trouble, so make sure you're ready – and keep within the law.'

'Yes, you needn't worry about me or the mine,' Jonathan said. 'It will still be here when you get back – but I will try to look out for Emma, if you wish?'

'Thank you. Do what you can for her.' Tor inclined his head. 'I've a letter here. It's to a friend of hers, who works in York. And I've two hundred pounds that I intend to give to Emma when I call at her house later – there's not much more I can do for now but be prepared.'

'Perhaps Ravenscroft will cool off when he's slept on it?'

Tor shook his head. 'He will make trouble for me one way or the other. Either he'll set the law on me, or he and some friends will come after me. I feel it in my bones, Jonathan. So I've done what I can – and I'll tell Emma. I'm going there now.'

'I shall always stand for you.' Jonathan offered his hand. 'That's my promise; I'll keep your interests safe – and if Emma needs help, I'll do anything I can, but, as you say, I'll have my work cut out at the mine.'

Tor thanked him, left and mounted his horse. He rode back across the Dales, towards Penrith Scar village, but he never reached Butts Lane, and he didn't give Emma the money he'd hidden in a money belt.

* * *

Emma's father was feverish and calling out for her. She was up with him all night and didn't sleep until her mother came to take her place when the church clock struck five on Sunday morning. So Emma went to lie down on her bed and fell asleep. It was past ten when she woke to hear a thunderous knocking on her door. She sat up in bed, blinking, her heart racing. Still fully dressed, she struggled to her feet, when suddenly she heard the sound of heavy feet coming up the stairs and the door to her room was flung open.

She stared at Tom Constable in astonishment. 'What do you want?' she demanded, shocked and angry. 'Don't you know my father is dying and I've been up half the night?'

'I'm sorry, Miss Watts,' Tom Constable said and looked ashamed. 'I wouldn't have come, for I knew he wouldn't be here – but the officer made me.'

'What are you talking about?' Emma asked, bewildered now. 'Who did you think might be in my bedroom?'

'Tor Hardy,' Tom replied, his cheeks red. 'I didn't – but they did. The excisemen. They've been hunting a gang of smugglers for months and someone told them that Tor is one of the leaders.'

'That is a lie!' Emma cried. 'Why would Tor run with the smugglers? He owns a rich mine and his house and small-holding – why would he want to break the law? He wouldn't do that...'

Tom looked at her uncomfortably. 'It's been reported, Emma. By a man of importance, what's got a broken arm to prove it. He swears that he and a friend – a Mr Scott, and well-to-do – stumbled across the smugglers after the feast last night. They don't know the area well and they'd strayed up the Dales and they saw the gentlemen leading a pack of ponies towards an inn – and they say Tor saw them and attacked them. It was a lord's son has got his arm broke – and that means trouble. 'Sides, the excisemen believe Tor is involved with the smugglers and they came after him; they fired at him, but he saw them and got away through the hills. They chased him; he evaded them, and I thank God for it – but they are asking, why would he run if it isn't true that he is involved?'

'What would you do if a man fired a gun at you?' Emma demanded, face pale, heart racing. 'Of course he tried to escape them – but he is innocent. He will return and the truth will be known.'

'How do you think he found the money to buy that mine?' Tom asked. 'If they get him, he'll hang. The smugglers have killed exciseman and there's a new officer who has sworn to hunt them down and see them all dead.'

'It isn't true. It can't be,' Emma cried, a queer pain clawing at her heart. 'We were to be married. Tor loves me. He wouldn't go without telling me. No, you're wrong. He will come back...'

'I hope he does, but I doubt he'll dare,' Tom replied. 'Because a second officer was killed last month by smugglers, and they say they'll hang all they catch – and they think Tor could be the leader; the one who shot the second officer.'

Emma gave a little moan and swayed, her head spinning as she felt a sharp pain, as if a knife had struck at her heart. 'Please, no,' she whispered. 'No. He has to come back. I love him so...'

'Emma!' Her mother came rushing into the room. 'There's men searching your father's room and him lying there near death...'

'I will come.' Emma ran from her bedroom and down the stairs to her father's room. He was tossing feverishly, calling her name as she went to the bed. 'I am here, dearest,' she said softly. She glared at the men who had finished searching the small room. 'Are you satisfied?' she asked, her voice ringing with scorn. 'My father is dying – must you come searching an innocent man's house? Tor has not been here – and he was not the leader of the smugglers.'

One of them mumbled an apology and left, but another stayed and looked at her. 'The smugglers are murderers and bandits, and we'll get them all – and they will all hang for their crimes. We know there's folk in this valley have helped them – and Tor Hardy's name has been mentioned a few times before this. Now we have the word of a respectable man, and a man that's been grievously wounded. You've seen the last of Tor Hardy. We'll get him and he'll hang...'

Emma's father suddenly sat bolt upright, his arm pointing towards the door. 'Get out of my house, you filth! If I were a fit man, I'd thrash you for upsetting my daughter...' Then he made a choking sound and fell back against the pillows.

Emma was too concerned for her father to notice the man leave. He was staring at her, clearly conscious as he reached for her hand and gripped it.

'Don't believe him,' he whispered harshly before another coughing fit took him. She gave him a sip of water and he smiled weakly. 'Tor will come for you, however long it takes. Believe that whatever they say, Emma...'

'Yes, Da, I will,' she said, smoothing his forehead with a cloth dipped in cool water. 'Rest now... rest and sleep...'

Her father gave a little cry, his eyes closing. His breathing was laboured as Emma's mother returned to the room.

'They've all gone now.' She bent over her husband and touched his face, then looked at Emma. 'Those wicked men – coming here with their guns and their lies...'

'Tor isn't the leader of the smugglers...'

'No. He dealt with them – but so do they up at the Manor,' her mother said. 'The vicar – everyone buys their goods. It has gone on for the past two hundred or more years, and will continue after we've gone, Emma.'

Emma looked down at her father, her heart catching. 'Ma – I think...'

Her mother looked at his face and gave a little cry. 'He's stopped breathing. Oh, Emma – your da is dead...'

'No! No...' Emma's tears started to trickle down her cheeks. 'Oh, Ma. I am so sorry. Those men... he tried to defend me... it's my fault. If I'd been here sooner...'

'Stop blaming yourself, Emma!' her mother said sharply. 'It was his time and now he's at peace. We have to think of the bairns now – and ourselves. Tor was there to protect us, Emma. Now he has gone, and even if he comes back, it will be a long time before things are sorted.' She stood up and bent to her husband, crossing his arms over his chest. 'I'm away to the vicar to have him blessed and arrange for his burial. Make him decent, Emma.'

'Yes, Ma,' Emma said, feeling empty, lost and alone. She loved all her family, but her father had been special to her. He'd gone – and Tor was gone too. It might be months, even years, before he returned. She shut out the thought that he might never return. She knew Tor hadn't killed anyone. They surely couldn't hang an innocent man...

* * *

Some days later, Emma stood beside her father's grave after the last mourners had gone. The whole of the village – every mine worker, every farmer, even Miller Mullens – had turned out to see him buried. Women were not encouraged at funerals, but Emma and her mother were there – and Sarah Davies. She stood with Joe in church and followed out to the burial. She was the last of the mourners to leave.

'I'm sorry for your loss, Emma,' Sarah said before she turned to join Joe. 'Your father was a good man – and you've other sorrows to bear.'

Emma looked at her. 'Thank you for your kindness, Sarah.'

'Mrs Briscoe wants you back as soon as you can manage it, Emma. She couldn't come but bid me tell you. The mester created something fierce when he heard you'd left us.'

'Don't you want my job?' Emma asked curiously.

'I'm to help out when the new mistress arrives and that will suit me better,' Sarah told her. 'Will I tell Mrs Briscoe you'll come back?'

'I'll need a few days to think,' Emma replied and turned back to the grave.

Her mother looked at her as Sarah walked away.

'You'll have to go back,' she said. 'There's no choice, Emma. Give it a few days and then go. We have nothing now – and the nest egg Tor gave your father won't last forever. Then what shall we do? Besides, Mr Rawlings can take the cottage now your father is dead. If he wants... Those in the miners' cottage are all right, for Tor bought them along with the mine and his right of way across the land. Unless the law confiscates it all now he's a wanted man.'

'Tor will come back and prove his innocence,' Emma said, her face bright with anger. 'Don't turn against Tor now, just because others do, Ma. He was good to us and I'll not believe evil of him.'

'Oh, Emma...' Her mother sighed. 'I am not against him. Never that, but he has little chance against the word of a lord's son; they will likely hang him, whether he be guilty or not.'

'No!' Emma shook her head wildly.

'Don't break your heart for him. You must live for us, Emma. Live for your family. It is what your da would want...'

'Leave me alone to grieve...' Emma said, and her mother turned away.

Emma stayed on by the graveside for several minutes, then

became aware that someone was behind her. She whirled round and saw Stephen Rawlings standing there, looking at her, his face full of sympathy.

'I had to come. Please do not resent it, Emma. I did not know your father – but I know how all this must hurt you.' Emma did not speak and he took a step towards her. 'If you will trust me, I shall try to help Hardy. I did not know him well, but we met and spoke about the mine. I told him I had no interest in it and wished him well of it. If you will permit me, I will try to talk to the magistrate who ordered his arrest. I do not believe that he was the smuggler's leader. It was spite on the part of one of my guests. I have requested him to leave and he will not be asked here again. Forgive me for bringing this sorrow to your door, Emma.'

She hesitated, hardly believing her ears, then she took a step towards him, her face suddenly alight with hope. 'Oh, sir. Can you truly help Tor?'

'Yes, I believe I may,' he told her, clasping her hands as she held them out in supplication. 'Do I have your permission to try?'

'Yes! Yes, please. If you could clear his name...' Emma was all eagerness. 'It would mean so much to me to have his name cleared...'

'Then it will be so,' Stephen promised and squeezed her hands once before letting them go. 'I promise I will use all my influence, Emma – and he will return to you soon.'

'Thank you. Thank you so much...'

'Will you return to us until Tor comes?' he asked hesitantly. 'I know this is so hard for you...'

'I need to work,' Emma replied, smiling at him though her tears. 'Yes, I shall return to the Manor until I can marry.'

'Yes, you will be my cook until you can marry,' he said.

Emma thought there was something odd in his tone, but when she looked up at him, he seemed serious and concerned for her.

'I must get back to my mother. Friends will call and we must give them cake and tea. It is expected...'

'I shall see you at the Manor and I will do all I can for the man you love. I swear it.' He turned and walked away.

Emma threw her wild flowers into the open grave. 'I shan't forget you, Da,' she murmured, and then she too walked away. Her heart was still sorrowing for her father, but at least now she had some hope for Tor.

20

'So,' Ravenscroft said, lifting his wineglass to taste the illicit French brandy, a look of sneering triumph on his face. His left arm was in a sling and evidently giving him pain. 'The bastard ran like the coward he is and you got the chance to play Sir Galahad. Did it work? Did she believe you meant to help her?'

'I doubt Hardy is a coward. Faced with half a dozen armed men, some of them firing at him, he had no choice. You made certain they thought him a desperate killer,' Stephen replied. Then, irritated by his leer, 'Stop grinning, Ravenscroft. You owed me fifteen thousand guineas, and even for you that is a large sum.'

'And now my debt to you is paid,' his companion snarled. 'When I agreed to help you, I didn't expect a broken arm. It hurts like hell. I would have had him for assault if you hadn't demanded that I pay my gambling debts by informing on Hardy to the excisemen.' He laughed wildly, already half drunk, though it was but lunchtime. 'They were so excited to have a clue that might lead them to the smuggling gang at last – and then the fools let him get away.'

'He knows the trails through the Dales as well as any man and they lost him, in the woods or one of the caves up at the scar. Not that it matters. He won't return for a while and by then it will be too late. Emma needs me now and I'll be there for her. In a little while, she'll forget him...'

'Is she worth fifteen thousand guineas?' Ravenscroft mocked. 'I wouldn't pay that for any woman. I can take what I want for free...'

Stephen looked at him in dislike. He wondered why he'd invited the fellow to stay, but Ravenscroft had been dining with Stephen's cousin, Jack Scott, and something had prompted him to extend the invitation to him, though he'd barely known him. However, he'd proved useful, his broken arm and angry threats against Tor Hardy showing Stephen how he could be rid of the man who stood in his way – but it was done now and Stephen wanted him gone.

'It's time you were leaving,' Stephen said bluntly. 'Scott left for York at first light – and, besides, I told Emma you were gone and would not be invited again, so be good enough to leave, Ravenscroft.'

'Served my purpose, have I?' Ravenscroft mocked him. 'You're a ruthless devil, Rawlings! Damned if there's anything to keep me here. The women are either ugly or too virtuous. So I'll return to London and you'll not hear from me again.'

'Thank you. I can't say it has been a pleasure.'

'If my arm wasn't broken, you'd pay for your insults!' Ravenscroft glared at him. 'You're a fool if you clear his name. Let him hang. If he returns, the girl will go back to him.'

'I think not,' Stephen said. 'Don't expect an invite to my wedding.'

'To the merchant's daughter?' Ravenscroft sneered.

'No, not to her; that was when I thought my cause lost – but I do expect to marry within the next year.' Stephen finished his drink and then threw the beautiful etched glass into the fireplace, where it smashed into pieces.

Ravenscroft laughed and followed suit, then turned and walked from the room.

He was seething inside as he called his valet. 'Is everything in the chaise?'

'Yes, sir.'

'We are leaving immediately.'

'Yes, sir. May I ask where we are going?'

'To York for a few days and then London,' Ravenscroft replied. 'I need money, Grably. I must sell a few trinkets I picked up at the card tables. If I go home and ask for a loan, my father will hit the roof. He has only just finished paying my last gambling debts...'

'I have a few guineas, sir,' Grably suggested in a flat, calm tone. It would not be the first time his master had borrowed money from him, but he always repaid it when he was in funds again; the valet found it satisfying to be the one to help out when Ravenscroft was in financial straits, besides being profitable, since he was paid interest at an extortionate rate of 20 per cent. 'The same terms as usual, sir.'

'Shyster!' Ravenscroft muttered but accepted the loan. His valet had helped him on more than one occasion. Although he would inherit a fortune, Ravenscroft had only what he considered a miserly ten thousand a year, and that soon went on his horses, his women and his gambling. Unless he hit a lucky streak soon, he would be in the suds again, and Lord Ravenscroft had threatened to see him in the debtor's prison next time he was in trouble over gambling.

Muttering to himself, he went out to his chaise; unable to drive, he was forced to watch as his groom took the reins and told him to let them go. 'I am in a hurry,' he said as the groom whipped up his horses so they started racing. They would be foaming at the mouth by the time he stopped for his dinner, but at that moment he couldn't care less, though they'd cost him a fortune.

* * *

Stephen stood at the window, frowning as he watched his unwelcome guest go. Had he been a fool to use Ravenscroft? He was the spiteful sort that would nurse a grudge and might use his knowledge against Stephen one day. Did he suspect that he had been cheated at cards, encouraged as he drank deeply to continue, even though he was losing large sums? He hadn't appeared to – but he was still an enemy now, someone to watch out for. Because if Emma ever discovered what he'd done, his chance with her would be gone. Ravenscroft had called him ruthless, but he didn't understand that Stephen was caught by an emotion he'd never thought to know. He loved Emma to the point of desperation. She was all he thought of, haunting his dreams. Had he a little more courage, he would have arranged an accident for Ravenscroft, but these things had a habit of coming back to bite one. Stephen put a hand to his throat. He didn't fancy the hangman's noose, so he'd simply sent Ravenscroft away, insulting him deliberately in the hope he would never come near again.

Stephen wasn't sure where the idea had come from. For some time now, he'd been hoping Tor Hardy would meet with an accident on his horse or at the mine, but the man was too careful. He never raced his horse and he always kept his mine in good order so that an accident would need to be arranged – but not underground. Stephen had held back on that – too many folk would be killed, and any hope he'd had of getting his hands on the mine gone.

It irked him that the mine belonged to Tor Hardy. Surely it ought to have been part of the estate? He'd consulted with his lawyers when he first came to Penrith Scar, hoping for a loophole whereby he could claim the land on which the mine stood and force Hardy to give him a share of the profits – but the contract had all been done properly. There was nothing he could do but appear not to be interested and greet Hardy as one would a man who was important, rich but not one's equal in birth. It was something he believed he'd managed perfectly. No one would suspect the anger and envy burning inside him – the hatred he felt for Hardy, because he had what Stephen wanted more than anything in the world.

Stephen had always taken what he wanted with no thought of the consequences. If frustrated, the anger and desire to own whatever he fancied would grow until it tormented him, and he would do almost anything to get what he wanted. And now he wanted a woman – Tor Hardy's woman.

Emma. He'd been amused by her when they'd first met, finding her practical Yorkshire manners refreshing, a change from the women who had fallen at his feet all his life. She didn't want him, was barely aware of him, other than as the new master. It had piqued his interest and he'd become determined to have her one way or the other – but then he'd found his feelings towards her changing and, for the first time in his life, he'd realised that he loved a woman deeply.

He'd watched her with Sarah Davies after the woman gave birth – and he'd been fairly caught. She had such tenderness, such loving warmth, and Stephen had never known that. His parents were both cold, selfish people who had left him to be brought up by the servants until he was old enough to be sent away to school. When he was very young, a pat on the head by his father and a cool kiss on the cheek from his mother had been all the affection he'd ever known, and after she died, he'd not had even that much attention – making him believe that love did not exist. Carnal pleasure was to be found in the arms of many young women, because he was the grandson of a lord and handsome, but he'd never cared for anyone, until he met Emma.

His feelings had become an obsession with him. He'd tried to charm her, but she loved Tor Hardy – that hulking brute of a man. Stephen could give her the finer things of life, and he would. Once he married, he would inherit his maternal grandmother's fortune and his grandfather couldn't control or stop it. It was the reason he'd decided to pretend he would take the rich merchant's daughter. He'd taunted Emma with it and seen sympathy and warmth in her eyes. Stephen knew he could turn those feelings to love if Hardy was out of the way – and now he was. Stephen did not intend that he would return. After a time had passed, he would tell Emma that Hardy's name had been cleared, making her grateful to him, but when Hardy didn't return, she would turn to him and she would be his. If Hardy came, then it would be too late – and Stephen hoped that his plans for keeping Hardy away long enough would work.

He would let Hardy be found and arrested and only after he'd spent some months languishing in prison would Stephen give his evidence to the magistrate. By then, Emma would be his...

Stephen smiled. He could, if needed, arrange for Hardy to meet with an accident away from here, yet he shied away from murder; there were other ways of ensuring that the man could not spoil his plans for the future. Hopefully, Tor Hardy would just keep on running, saving him the problem of what to do with him next.

* * *

Tor stabled his horse at a hostelry just outside York. It had taken him ten days to get here. He'd ridden by night, hiding by day, knowing he was hunted and not daring to chance the railway. It was a risk coming here, but he had funds in York and he wanted to leave money with Emma's friend; the kindly woman who had been cook up at the Manor. He would stay in York just long enough to complete his business and then ride on to the coast. If he stayed here, he would eventually be recognised and, in a few days, there might be wanted notices pinned to the town hall or another of the official buildings. So he would visit Ellie, leave the money with her and then move on. There was a place near Whitby he intended to visit before deciding what to do next.

Tor wasn't certain of his plans for the future. It was clear that someone had accused him of running with the smuggling gang, for it was the excisemen who had come for him. Several people might have known of his involvement, but who would have been malicious enough to betray him? Tor wondered who had cause to hate him. Ravenscroft had vowed to see him in prison, but that would have meant a visit from Tom Constable and not an armed arrest. The shots fired at Tor had told him that they wanted him dead or alive and didn't much care which. They hadn't even warned him, just fired at him on sight.

He must lie low for a while, at least until the heat died down. He wasn't sure how he could clear his name of the charge, for though he'd never been one of them, he had worked with the smugglers to dispose of their contraband. He might have proved his innocence against a charge of assault – but he couldn't when it was smuggling.

Ravenscroft had been clever. It was a fine and cruel revenge – yet how had a stranger known about the smugglers? Someone must have told him – someone who wished harm to Tor. Someone must hate him, but why? Tor could not understand it. He'd done no one harm – Ravenscroft apart, and that was in self-defence.

So what of the future? He could not return home, at least until he could find a way to clear his name. Tor could join the smugglers in their dangerous work. He knew where to find them, because some of them had been his friends and had told him more than they ought. Yet that way led only to prison or a grim death in the end, now that they were being hunted in earnest.

He toyed with the idea of seeking his fortune abroad. It was unlikely that he would ever be able to return to Penrith Scar and the mine. If Jonathan held true, and Tor believed he would, there would be money paid into an account in London for him. He could use it to begin his new life. At the moment, he had the two hundred pounds he intended for Emma, and another five hundred lodged in an account he'd set up long ago in York with a merchant. They'd had a business arrangement and Tor had left his credit with the merchant, always aware that if ill fortune ever struck, it was available money.

Tor needed to contact Emma, to ask her to come to him – perhaps in York or elsewhere. He would ask her friend Ellie to send her some of the money and a letter asking her to meet him. It was a risk, but not as great as if he went back for her himself.

Would Emma want to come to him now that he was a wanted man? Could she leave her sick father – was he still alive? Tor cursed himself for running, for it would seem to prove his guilt – but at least two shots had been fired at him. He knew that as a smuggler, he could be shot without trial, for who cared what happened to such men? So he'd made a bolt for it.

Tor felt the searing heat of regret. If Emma would have none of him, he'd lost what was most important in his life. If the mine was entirely lost to him, so be it. He was young enough to make a living – even his fortune, if he went abroad to lands where he'd heard you could find gold or even diamonds. Yet without Emma, what would any of it mean to him?

PART II

PENRITH SCAR, SEPTEMBER 1888

21

Mary Watts looked at the letter that had come for Emma. It was postmarked York and rather fat, though she knew the writing was Ellie's, the woman who had been the cook at the Manor. In later life, she would regret what she'd done, but at that time, just three weeks after her husband's death, she was consumed with grief and fear. She wondered if Ellie was hoping to return as cook once more and feared Emma might lose her job – and what would they do then, now that Tor Hardy was a wanted man with a reward of a hundred guineas offered for news of him?

She stared at the envelope, fear warring with her sense of what was right, then she opened it, discovering five one-pound notes and two letters. The first time a five-pound note had been used was in 1779: it had been issued by the Bank of England, because gold stocks were low, and people were suspicious of it; many still were. Mary stared at the notes, uncertain at first what they were, because her husband had always been paid in coins, and she'd never seen this much paper money. Tor Hardy had given her husband gold sovereigns as his compensation, most of which Mary had tucked away for an uncertain future. After examining the promissory notes, she realised what they represented and shook her head as her foreboding grew. Why would Ellie send Emma so much money?

Putting the notes into her apron pocket, she turned the letters over in her hand. She had no right to read her daughter's letters. Yet she was so afraid of what they might contain that she overcame her scruples and opened the single sheets of paper.

The first was from Ellie, the second from Tor Hardy. Ellie had written a kind letter, saying how sad she felt that Emma's father was so ill, but Tor's was an entreaty. He spoke of his love and sorrow for the trouble that had taken him from her, and he wanted Emma to join him. He was planning to leave the country for a while and he wanted her to go with him. His idea was to leave some money with Ellie – which Emma could ask for and would be sent to her, or she could meet him and Ellie would send the money to her family. It was all arranged, if Emma would trust him and know that he was innocent of the charges; though he admitted he had traded with the smugglers, he had not joined them at sea to bring in their illicit goods. Nor had he been involved in the shootings that had led to the death of excisemen.

Mary stared at the words as they blurred together. She wasn't a quick reader, but she could make out the sense of it and she knew that Emma was being asked to go with the fugitive Tor Hardy. A shiver of fear went through her and she was torn with anguish at the thought. Her Emma gone far away. She would never see her again. Tor had left money for them in York, but how long would that last? If he and Emma went abroad, they would never return and Mary would have to manage alone for the rest of her life. She wasn't a young woman and she'd never worked for a master, nor did she wish for it. If Emma stayed here, she would work and look after them. It was selfish to think of herself, but Mary had two young children to care for – and without Emma's help, she would feel lost. She did not want to lose her eldest daughter. But Emma need never know that Tor had sent for her!

Mary knew it must break her daughter's heart if she believed that Tor had deserted her, for she sincerely loved him – but it was the best for her and her family. She was young and pretty, and other men would come calling in time. Mary told herself that it was the right thing for Emma as she hid the money in her drawer and burned the letters. If Emma went with Tor, she would be a fugitive – and if he was arrested, her life would be ruined. Emma had a good job up at the big house now. They could manage as long as they stayed together. Hearts broke but they mended again. Mary felt guilt but she smothered it. She was doing it for Emma as much as herself. Of course she was! No mother would want her daughter wed to a man who might hang...

* * *

Tor visited the house in Micklegate again, to ask Ellie if there had been a reply to his letter. He'd been in York for more than three weeks now, hiding in a room above one of the butchers' shops in the Shambles; the whole street stank of raw meat and blood, filling his nostrils with the stench of bad offal that had been thrown out. However, the law rarely ventured into the area, for it was not a pleasant place, the deep gutters often littered with filth. The shop belonged to a good friend, and Tor knew he was safe there. Frustrated, and wanting to be away, he'd hoped that Emma would come to him, but driven at last to find out if there was news, he'd risked another visit to the prestigious house, where Ellie worked. She'd come to the back door herself to greet him, but shook her head in answer to his question.

'None, lad, and that is not like Emma. She hasn't even replied to my letter. Mayhap it went astray…'

'Nay, I have my answer,' Tor replied, a hint of anger mixed with the sorrow. 'Mebbe she's right to ignore me. I don't know what I can offer – though I'm off to make my fortune somehow, and who knows what hardships I'll face.'

'Will I write again and tell her you'll come back when the heat is off?' Ellie asked him, looking sad. 'It's a bitter thing for you both, Tor, and sorry I am.'

'Emma has made her choice. I'll not seek to change her mind, nor will I harm her. I've given you the two hundred pounds for her. It isn't enough. One day I'll return and then I'll give her more – but she is a strong lass and she will work. I dare say she will find another lad to wed – but I promised her da I'd look out for her, and I'll send more money when I can.'

'Will you ever return?' Ellie's face showed her concern for them both.

'Mebbe,' he said and then laughed mockingly. 'I'll return a rich and powerful man or I'll die trying.'

'Ar, lad, don't be reckless,' Ellie said. 'I don't believe Emma would just let you go without a word but…' She shrugged as she saw the disbelief in his eyes. 'Thissen must suit thyself, lad. If Emma comes, I'll tell her what you told me.'

'You're a good woman,' Tor replied. 'I'm away to the coast now – I'll not tell you whereabouts, but I've a mind to take work on a ship and I don't much care where I go – perhaps to America, where there's plenty of land and a man might be free to be himself.'

'God go with you, lad,' Ellie said, tears in her eyes. 'When I see Emma again, I'll have the truth of it.' She shook her head. 'It's sad that you lost everything just for doing what was right.'

'It must have been Ravenscroft went to the excisemen for revenge,' Tor told her. 'He was a mean bastard and I've no other enemies I know of.' Though there was a niggle at the back of his mind, for someone had raised his name when Ike Hanson was found dead. Yet he could not think who might hate him so much that he would try to destroy him.

'Well, good luck to thee, lad. It is not fair that you have to start again when you'd made the mine start to pay.'

'It's not the end of the world,' Tor said and grinned. 'I've a strong back and tha knows what we say in Yorkshire, lass – you never get nowt for nowt.'

'I know you, Tor Hardy. In future, if you do owt for nowt, do it for thissen.' Ellie laughed. She might not have been bred in Yorkshire, but she'd learned enough of their slang during her years of work in the Dales.

Tor nodded, smiled wryly and left her. He felt a surge of bitter resentment as he thought of all he'd lost. Jonathan would stay true, but it might be years before he could return and claim the money put aside for him. He would not have cared that he must be exiled for a few years, might never have bothered to return if Emma had chosen to come with him, but she had stayed for her family. Tor had feared that might be her choice and he could hardly blame her. It was wrong that he should have to break his word to wed her and flee for his life. If he could but get his hands on the devil who had brought this misfortune on him, he would cheerfully break his neck with his own hands.

Lost in his thoughts, Tor didn't see the man staring at him from inside a shop doorway. He was intent on reaching the river where he'd a boat moored. He would row himself upriver, past the back of the guildhall, to fetch his horse from the hostelry and be off for the coast. He did not look back as he strode off, otherwise he would have seen the man he hated most in the world burst from the tobacco shop near the tower and go rushing off to inform on him.

* * *

'I tell you he is a wanted man!' Ravenscroft swore angrily at the police officer who stared at him in a bored fashion. 'Are you a fool, man? Tor Hardy. There is a poster on the town noticeboard and should be one here... Yes, see, it is on your wall.'

'Happen it is, sir,' the constable replied calmly. 'I don't know what you expect me to do about it. I'll have to ask my Inspector – and he'll decide what's best. Never fret thissen, sir. If the man is what you say, he'll be taken. I've no orders and I can't leave the station to go chasing after a man who may or may not be a smuggler. It's not my job.'

Ravenscroft scowled. 'Damned fool!' he muttered as he flung away and went striding off down the street.

The police constable shook his head. 'Bloody foreigners!' Came from London and thought they owned the place. Londoners thought they were so clever, but true Yorkshire folk liked to make fun of them, though they never knew it. Baffled by phrases they didn't recognise, they usually went off in a huff, never understanding that they'd been deliberately bamboozled.

The constable knew well that a man named Tor Hardy was being hunted for being in league with a gang of smugglers – but that was best left to the coastguard and the excisemen, as they were still called hereabouts, though these days there was probably a new-fangled name for them – customs officers, if he recalled it rightly. It was their job to catch smugglers, not his – and he knew that a search was already being made, because Tor

Hardy was known here, and liked. Therefore, it stood to reason that he would be clever enough not to show his face here. He would be long gone, on his way south – or to the coast. Nobbut a fool would come here where he was likely to be recognised.

* * *

Unaware that he'd been seen and narrowly avoided a confrontation with his enemy, Tor left York in broad daylight. He was headed for Whitby, because he knew where he could find Red Tikka. He wanted to warn him not to return to Penrith Scar, and to ask if he knew of a ship headed for America. He was a mining man and the idea of making a fortune from gold appealed to him, but another place would do as well; men of enterprise had made fortunes in India, Spain, Portugal and the Far East. Tor had no real plans.

He'd collected his debt from the merchant who owed him five hundred pounds, though not in gold or paper notes.

'I've not got it by me just now,' Jake Harris had told him. 'I invested heavily in goods this past month, Tor – but come back in a month and I'll have it for you.'

'I need money now – how much can you give me?' Tor had insisted, but the merchant had shaken his head.

'Ten guineas, no more – but you could take these instead.' He'd produced what looked like two bits of stone from his waistcoat pocket. 'Uncut diamonds – or so I was told. I took them in payment of a debt – five hundred pounds they're supposed to be worth once cut. I dare say I was taken for a fool, but it's all I can offer.'

Tor had taken the stones, though he'd doubted their value. He'd thought Jake a friend, but if he was being cheated, there was not much he could do. 'If I find you've cheated me, I'll be back for my money,' he'd warned and walked away, holding his temper by a thread. It meant he had less money than he'd hoped, but what else could he do? He was angry, frustrated, his heart aching, because Emma had not chosen to come to him – and yet, in all honesty, how could he blame her? When he'd asked her to wed, he'd already owned a house, a smallholding and the mine – now he had a few guineas in his money belt and the stones that might be worth something hidden in his boot.

* * *

It was some days later that Tor reached his destination, a small cove a few miles down the coast from the picturesque harbour of Whitby. He knew there was an inn on the cliffs above, where Red Tikka could be reached, and he had written a curt message to the man. It would suit Tor to speak to him in person, because he wanted to know if Red had killed Ike Hanson in a fit of rage, but if he wasn't there, he would give the landlord the note and then go on to Whitby, where he hoped to find a ship he could take passage on. He might go to Ireland first and from there, wherever a ship was bound; it hardly mattered, for he was a man who could find work anywhere.

Tor knew that he must sell his horse before he left England. It would cause him grief to do so, for he loved the animal and would never have parted with it if this hadn't happened. He couldn't take the horse with him, so he must sell it to someone he trusted – perhaps at the inn he intended to visit.

It was nine in the evening when Tor walked in to the old inn, the oak-cased grandfather clock chiming the hour as he entered the gloomy public bar. Only a few oil lamps lit the dimness, set on small oak tables in front of hard wooden benches to either side of the empty fireplace; it was still warm, despite a fresh breeze from the sea. Inside, it smelled of stale ale and human sweat, the floor stained with filth and unwashed for many a day.

The few customers still drinking stared at him with hostility, because he was a stranger and they didn't trust strangers. It had been the same at Highways, he recalled with an inner smile. This was the inn he was looking for.

He approached the barman and nodded.

'Fine evening,' Tor said.

'Aye, fine enough,' the barman replied. 'Riding by then?'

'Mebbe,' Tor answered. 'I'll have a rum – and have one, thissen.'

'Yorkshire man then?'

'Aye, from thereabouts,' Tor answered and took the glass that was offered, tossing its contents back. He noticed the barman took his money for the extra drink but didn't pour himself a glass. 'I'll have another – and if you've bread and cheese, I'd appreciate it.'

'We've no rooms, if you were wanting to stay,' the barman told him plainly.

'No, I'll not stay,' Tor replied, keeping his voice steady despite the man's rudeness and obvious desire to get rid of him. 'I'll sit over there by the window. There's someone I need to see – Red Tikka. You know of him?'

'Nah, never heard of the man,' the barman replied, but his eyes flickered uneasily. 'I'll tell Poll to get you some bread and cheese – and more rum if you fancy it.'

'Ale will do,' Tor said and walked away to a table in the corner. He sat down and waited.

After a while, a girl in a grey dress, her hair lank and greasy beneath a limp mob cap, brought him cheese and bread, and a tankard of frothy beer. She smiled at him nervously and went away.

Tor ate his bread and cheese and drank some of his ale. The barman had gone through a door behind the bar. He reappeared with a rather stout, red-faced man, indicating Tor. The second man walked over to Tor, nodded at him, studying him for a moment.

'Mind if I sit?'

'Nay, suit thissen,' Tor replied. 'No need to fear me, lad. I'm not here to cause trouble. I came to warn someone. I know Red comes here, for he told me I could contact him. He is being hunted in earnest...' Tor slid a small piece of paper onto the table. 'It's written there. You can read it. Give it to him if he should happen to come by.'

The man sat down, took the paper and placed it in his pocket without looking at it. 'Travelling late?' he asked, eyes never leaving Tor's face.

'Aye, travelling late. I'm looking to take passage on a ship – the Americas, or the Far East, not fussed which. Might you know of anything leaving soon?'

'Running from the law then,' the other man said and grinned slyly. 'Well, you came to the right place, friend. Happen I know summat might interest you.' He summoned the barman. 'Bring us a bottle of the good stuff. This is a friend...' He winked at the other man.

Tor watched him warily. His manner had changed too quickly, but he needed help and he knew it. The coastguards would be on the lookout for a man who wanted a ship – any ship. Time enough had passed for them to have been informed of his appearance and his name. He should have kept going rather than waiting for Emma, left England before they could get the word out...

At the thought of all he'd left behind, a wave of such grief went through Tor that he lost his natural caution and drank the strong brandy he was offered at a toss. Another was placed in front of him and he tossed that down too; it stung his throat, but the warmth was easing him, dulling the bitterness... dulling his senses.

'So what can you do to help me?' Tor asked.

'Can you pay?' the other man questioned, and Tor nodded.

He drank another glass and then, suddenly, his head began to swim. He looked at the glass. It was strong stuff but no stronger than he was used to... Even as the suspicion entered his mind, he fell forwards, his head crashing onto the table and sending his empty glass flying.

'Daft as a brush,' the barman remarked when he ambled over to clear away the mess. 'Why trust strangers?'

'Desperate men...' the other replied. 'Good for us. We'll take what is in his pockets and then put him on a ship. There's always one looking for crew, no questions asked. I'll get paid twice for this night's work.'

'Might be a reward for him?'

'Inform on him? Nah, I hate the law worse than anyone. 'Sides, he might be a friend of Red's. Came here to warn him...'

'What you drug him for then?'

'Might be a ruse. Either way, he wanted to go abroad...' The man chuckled. 'Well, he'll get his wish. Mebbe not quite what he expected, but you've got to take the rough with the smooth...' He laughed heartily and the barman laughed too.

* * *

Tor woke to a sore head and feeling sick. He was lying on some sort of bed and the bed was moving. Jerking to the right, he vomited over the side of the bed to be greeted by a shout of anger.

'Look out you bloody fool!'

Tor focused on the pair of boots he had just emptied his stomach over and blinked warily. 'Where am I?' he asked. 'Is this a ship?'

'Too bloody right, mate,' the voice replied, but it wasn't so angry now. 'Bound for France we are – and you're with us all the way, like it or not.'

'Did I pay for my passage?' Tor asked. He ran his hands over himself; he was still wearing his clothes and boots, but his money belt had gone. That brandy had been drugged. Cursing himself for a fool, Tor shook his head.

'Mate, you're here as crew. You were blind drunk when they brought you aboard – and you slept two whole days. We were beginning to think you were a goner.'

'Hell,' Tor muttered. 'They took my money – I was at that blasted inn and they stole my money belt.'

'It happens,' the other man said with a shrug. He offered his hand to pull Tor to his feet. 'My name is Mack Hallidan. I am crew just like you – and broke just like you. I signed on with Red, because I couldn't get a decent job. I'm not long out of prison – I killed a man.'

'I haven't yet, but I intend to one day – if I ever get back to Yorkshire,' Tor said, gritting his teeth. 'Mayhap, more than one.' He held out his hand. 'Name is Tor Hardy. I know a murderer and he's my best friend – he killed his wife. He was going to kill her lover but never got the chance.'

Mack threw back his head and laughed, clasping Tor's hand firmly. 'I like that – and we'll be friends if you do your share. You'd best come now, because the captain is raging like a bull. We've been a man down because you were sick. Can you work or do you need to eat first?'

'I don't think I shall ever eat again,' Tor said as his stomach retched, but nothing came up. 'But I could do with a gallon of water.' He blinked hard as his head began to clear. 'Did you say this ship belonged to Red – Red Tikka?' Tor swore as the other man nodded his head. 'Bugger it! I was falsely named as being a smuggler – and now it looks like I'm about to become one.' He gave a harsh laugh. 'I suppose I might as well hang for something I did than for something I didn't...' He grimaced as the irony of it struck him. 'Bastards said they didn't know him...'

'They were going to put you on a ship for South Africa when Red turned up – so he took you himself.'

'Better the devil you know...' Suddenly seeing the humour of his situation, Tor laughed. 'I did wonder about joining them – but thought I might make a fortune elsewhere.'

Mack grinned. 'You'll do,' he said, clapping Tor on the back. 'I'll get you the water – and we'll talk. I'm thinking of jumping ship as soon as I can. Red Tikka is an evil devil.'

'Aye, he is,' Tor agreed. 'He won't let you just walk away. He would rather kill you than let you go free once you know too much – unless he trusts you.'

'I know – but I still hope to get away somehow.'

He walked off and Tor followed him up the ladder that led to the deck. The roll of the sea and the salty air nearly made Tor vomit again, but there was nothing left inside him, except an ache that he knew would never leave him.

He breathed deeply, feeling better for the air. This wasn't the way he'd planned his future, but the money in his belt wasn't all he had, and the rogues from the inn hadn't taken his boots. It was an irony that, if he'd been paid as he ought, all his money would be gone – but he still had the two diamonds, if diamonds they were, embedded in the heels of his boots. He would sell them for whatever they fetched when he was ready to start a new life – and he would rise again. Tor promised himself that his life would not end with Red Tikka and his cutthroats – he would part with them when he was ready, and on his own terms. For now, he must mind his tongue and do as he was told, because even though they had worked as equals in the past, Red was master of his ship and would treat Tor as any other crew member. He could expect no favours, nor would he ask. Tor might be new to the life, but he would learn.

'I'll get rich – and I'll get even,' he vowed, even as he heard the roar of an angry man.

'Get that bastard working or I'll lash him...' Red's voice blared out in a fury. Obviously intent on showing who was master here, he was making sure Tor knew his place.

Mack returned to Tor with a beaker of water. 'Get that down and come with me,' he said. 'I'll show you the ropes. We're on scrubbing duty today...'

Tor drank his water and pushed the beaker inside his coat. This was going to be hard, but no tougher than the mines, where he'd started at the age of thirteen. If Red Tikka thought it was a test of strength between them, he would find he'd met his match...

22

Emma woke to the dawn chorus, lying for a moment to listen to the birds, but then she felt the burn of vomit in her throat, jumped up and fetched the chamber pot from under her bed. She was sick twice, falling back against the feather pillows on her bed, feeling ill as she wiped her mouth with the back of her hand. What was wrong with her? She'd been sick yesterday and the day before, but no one up at the house had been ill, so she couldn't think it was anything she had eaten.

'Was that you being sick?' Emma's mother entered the bedroom, looking at her oddly. 'It's not the first time recently, is it?'

'No...' Emma pushed herself up against the pillows. 'I don't know what it is, Ma. You and the bairns are all reet – and there's nowt wrong with them up at the Manor.'

'Oh, Emma.' Her mother looked at her reproachfully. 'What have you done? If you've got thissen in trouble now... I don't know what we'll do.'

'What do you mean?' Emma looked at her mother, feeling puzzled, and then it came to her. In all her distress and torment, she hadn't given a thought to what had happened on the night of the summer feast. 'You think... I might be with child?' A flicker of fear went through her.

'You'd know that best, Emma.' Her mother's voice was hard and unforgiving. 'Don't tell me tha went with him...' She stared at Emma, and saw the realisation and the fear in her face. 'It was the night your da was took bad – that's why tha was late home and him calling for you – what were you doing but fornicating? You wicked girl! He thought you were his little girl who could do no wrong – and now you've brought shame and ruin on us!' She lashed out and slapped Emma's face in her anger and terror.

Emma's hand went to her cheek, feeling the sting of the blow. 'We were to be wed in three weeks,' she said in a voice barely above a whisper, for her mother had never struck her before. 'How could I know what would happen? Don't look at me like that, Ma. I'm not shamed for he loves me and we would have been wed soon.'

'Most girls in your trouble get wed quick,' her mother said, scorn and bitterness cutting at Emma. 'Who is going to marry you, Emma? How shall we live if you can't work? I can't do much... there's no work hereabouts for a woman like me. I'd scrub and wash, but who would pay me? I'd get a pittance at a farm, barely enough to feed myself. You were the one who had made a good life. I was relying on you to look after us until the bairns can work.'

'I shall work, up at the big house,' Emma said, though she felt hurt and shamed by her mother's bitterness. 'As much as I can – until someone notices and asks me to leave. Then we'll go away, mebbe to York. I can find work again after the child is born. You'll have to take it as your own, Ma – and I can work for us then.'

'It is easy for you to talk...' her mother accused, but her voice was less sharp now and there was a strange, half-shamed look in her eyes. 'If I'd known, mebbe...' She shook her head. 'You'll have to work – and we'll have to hide your condition as long as possible. There's a hundred pounds left from your da's compensation. It will tide us over when you can't work, I suppose... though I'd hoped to save that for my old age.' She shook her head. 'I'm glad your da passed; this would have hurt and shamed him something cruel.'

'Da would have understood,' Emma cried, tears starting to her eyes. 'Don't be harsh to me, Mother. It's not my fault everything went wrong. I've enough to bear without you turning on me – my da dead and Tor gone. I only wish he'd had time to fetch me. I'd have been away and none the wiser... We could have wed.'

Mary turned away. Then, with her back to Emma, she said, 'He's a fugitive, Emma. If he stays in this country, he'll be hunted and then hung. He'll likely go abroad somewhere – you wouldn't have wanted a life like that...'

'I'd have gone anywhere with him and gladly,' Emma replied. 'If he'd sent word... but I think he must have gone straight to a ship. I pray every night that he got away. It was the best thing for him, but I wish with all my heart he'd sent for me to go with him.'

'Well, he didn't,' her mother said harshly as she moved away, her voice coming back to Emma from the doorway. 'You'd best get to work, girl – and be careful no one discovers your secret, for you'll be turned off the minute they do.'

'If they do, I'll go to Ellie,' Emma said. 'She'll help me – and I'll send you money when I can, Ma. Perhaps Mr Crossly might help us. He might have news of Tor.'

'Stay away from him, Emma.' Mary's fear made her sharp. 'He's not from hereabouts and I don't trust him. Who's to say it wasn't him as betrayed Tor so he could get the mine from him? If you go asking questions, he might set the law on us.' Running through Mary's mind was the fear that if the man knew of Tor's whereabouts, he would tell Emma and she would go to him! Emma saw only the frightened look without understanding.

'Why would he do that?' Emma asked, puzzled. 'Surely it is worth trying?'

'We'll see what's best to do when it happens,' Mary muttered and went out, leaving Emma to sit on the bed and cry.

She cried because Tor wasn't there to put his arms around her and tell her he loved her and would take care of her and his son – because Emma knew he would hope for a son. She cried, because she knew she must leave her home and her friends – and she cried because her father would never see his grandchild.

After the storm of tears was over, Emma went to her wash-stand and poured water from the jug into the bowl. It was cold, but she welcomed the chill; it suited her mood and it helped her to think clearly. Crying and regretting would not help her. These past weeks she had hoped for a letter from Tor, but none had come. It was strange, but Ellie hadn't replied to her own letter telling her of her troubles. Emma thought that odd. She decided that she would write Ellie another letter and send it from the Manor with their post – the last might have gone astray, as might a letter from Ellie.

Emma would not give up hope just yet. She knew that Tor had not been caught, because she read all the newspapers that were brought to the Manor, after Mr Rawlings had done with them. He'd told her that until Tor was arrested and charged there wasn't much he could do, though he had been to the magistrate in Settle and told him that Ravenscroft had made his charge out of spite and it was his opinion it wasn't true. Tom

Constable had written it all down but told him that he believed Tor Hardy was no longer in the country.

'Nowt's been seen of him, sir,' he'd said. 'It is believed that he might have reached the coast and taken a ship, because his horse was sold and recognised by the ostler that bought it – though it wasn't Hardy as sold it to him but another man, who said he'd bought it from a stranger.'

Although Emma didn't know it, her master had been relieved that Hardy had gone abroad. It had saved him getting more involved in the murky business. Hardy couldn't wed Emma if he'd fled the country, which meant she would eventually turn to him, Stephen. She'd been so grateful when he'd told her that he'd spoken to the magistrate and the constable in Settle, thanking him several times for his kindness. It was just a matter of time before he could start to court her – when she understood that Hardy was never coming back. He would win her gradually, and then, once she was his wife, it wouldn't matter if Hardy was foolish enough to come back. He would have Emma and his grandmother's fortune; when he chose, he could go back to London, leave Emma here to care for his home, and visit her when he chose. It was a perfect solution to his problems. He might even take Emma to Paris to buy her some clothes, but she was a simple, undemanding girl and would be happy to live at home while he joined his friends in London.

Perhaps by then he'd have the mine, too. For the moment, Jonathan Crossly had thwarted any attempts to take it over, proving that he owned a half of it – so there was no point in trying to take it to court because he couldn't prove Hardy was a criminal – and, anyway, that would ruin his chances with the woman he wanted. Once things started to go wrong at the mine, and Jonathan Crossly was back on the drink, he would get it for nothing. Stephen would see if a few accidents could be arranged

– nothing that would kill folk, but enough to make Crossly want to be rid of it. Why would he hold on to it when he could be rich and go where he pleased? Stephen would get it somehow. He always got what he wanted in the end, one way or another. He would have Emma and he would have Hardy's mine.

Unaware of her master's thoughts and the fact that he'd caused Tor's flight, Emma had begun to trust and like the kind man she called mester. He was unfailingly polite and concerned when he spoke to her – to all of his servants. None of the maids had been molested, and Mrs Briscoe was inclined to believe the stories about him exaggerated out of all proportion.

'The mester is a true gentleman,' she'd told Emma one chilly autumn morning, when the leaves had begun to turn red and the fallen ones blew into doorways whenever the wind rushed down from the Pennines, rattling windows in the old house. 'He asked me if I was happy here and how long it was since I'd taken a holiday. Well, I told him I'd never had one for years, ever really – and he said that he would arrange for those of the staff that would like it to go to Whitby for a day – all expenses paid. He'll arrange for us to travel there and back on the train, to stay one night and return the next day – and it will all be free.'

'That is very generous of him,' Emma had replied and smiled at her. 'He is a kind man I think – but…' There was still a tiny voice in her head that warned her to be careful.

'Surely, you don't think he would harm you, Emma – after all he's done and the way he looks at you?' Mrs Briscoe had scolded. 'I know it isn't possible for you to wed him – the gap is too wide, for he's the grandson of a lord and you a miner's daughter – but I think he cares about you.' She'd frowned. 'It was strange the way he told us that the young lady he intended to wed had changed her mind… I don't understand that. She was only a merchant's daughter and should have been proud to wed nobility.' The girl had only her fortune to recommend her, and she'd turned down a fine gentleman. Not that he'd seemed distressed by it, more amused when she came to think on it, as if he had some secret plan of his own.

'Mebbe, he changed his mind,' Emma had suggested, and Mrs Briscoe had given her a worried look.

'Mebbe, he did...' Mrs Briscoe had hesitated, then with a shake of her head, 'He wouldn't be fool enough... his family would cut him off it he married his cook, Emma.'

'He comes into a fortune that his family cannot deny him when he weds,' Emma had told her. 'But don't worry, Mrs Briscoe – I have no desire to marry him.'

'It would be a mistake,' Mrs Briscoe had warned. 'You'd belong nowhere then, Emma. The gentry would look down on you and your friends would think you'd turned your back on them. Those sorts of marriages never work.'

'I told you; I have no thought of it,' Emma had replied. She knew it would never happen. Even if the mester liked her enough to ask – he would change his mind once Emma told him she was carrying Tor's child.

* * *

When Emma reached her work that morning, after the quarrel with her mother, her face was scrubbed clean of the tears she'd shed. She was feeling better and the smell of food as she cooked the master's breakfast did not turn her stomach, as she'd feared it might. Her sickness seemed to be on first waking and then, after eating a slice of dry toast, it had gone. Emma prayed it would stay that way. She needed to keep this job for as long as she could, but she had already written to Ellie and placed it with the letters on a silver tray in the hall of the Manor. She'd intended to give Jem the money for postage, but when she spoke to him, he said that the mester had seen it and franked it with his own stamp, so she need not pay him.

Emma did not see the mester that day, so was unable to offer to pay him the price of the postage. Nor did he mention it when he came to the kitchen to speak to her the next day. He merely told her that he was fairly sure that Tor Hardy had left the country – and that in the absence of any real evidence and his own testimony, already given, Tor's name had been cleared.

She thanked him, but the knowledge that Tor had fled, believing himself a fugitive, kept her awake several nights. She believed him gone, destined to a fugitive's life in some far-off land. Tears wet her pillow night after night and it began to show in her face. Her happy smile had gone; she no longer sang as she worked, and her despair made her thin, her eyes dark-shadowed and sad.

* * *

'You should stop this fretting over Tor,' Emma's mother told her some weeks later. The trees were bare of their leaves now, and the first frosts of winter sprinkled the moors and Dales, settling to a dense whiteness on the peaks. 'You're but three months gone and look tired to death, Emma – and you will be ill. If you carry on this way, you could lose the child.'

'You wouldn't care!' Emma accused.

To her surprise, her mother burst into tears, sitting down at the kitchen table as if her legs would give under her.

'Of course I'd care,' Mary Watts said when she had controlled her sobbing. 'I did it for the best, Emma – but I thought Tor would hang or take you away from me forever... now his name is cleared and I've done you terrible harm.'

'What do you mean?' Emma asked, bewildered. 'What did you do, Ma?'

Mary took a letter from her pocket and handed it to Emma. 'This came this morning. I burned the last one – but you need to see this; then you can hate me but stop fretting thissen.'

Emma took the envelope. Inside were five one-pound notes and a letter from Ellie. She read it through several times in disbelief, then looked at her mother, eyes widening in horror.

'Ellie says she sent me Tor's letter asking me to go to him in York. He waited two weeks for my reply and then he left – he was going abroad. He left two hundred pounds, which he told Ellie to give us, and promised to send more when he could... She says he didn't blame me because I chose my family instead of him, but she doesn't think he intends to return... he vowed he would make a fortune abroad, but told her he forgave me for choosing my family.'

Mary could not meet Emma's accusing stare. She lowered her head. 'Forgive me. I thought it best – I couldn't bear the idea of you being a fugitive and ending up the other side of the world, mayhap starving. I didn't know about the bairn then or I'd have given you his letter...'

'Oh, Ma...' Emma stared at her, the tears running down her cheeks. Tor had asked for her, waited for her – and then gone believing she had chosen her family over him. The pain that swept over her made her ill with loss and grief for the love she was denied. 'How could you do that to me? You knew I loved him – and Tor had left money for you... he would have sent more when he could.'

'It wouldn't be enough,' her mother said. 'It will help us, yes, but you'll still have to work, Emma.'

'You mean that you might have had to work, but why shouldn't you?' Emma said, and now the accusation was in her voice. 'You were just being selfish. I would have been happy. I could have been with Tor, married – and we'd have found work wherever he went...'

Mary's face paled. 'I admit I was selfish – but I've never worked for a mester, Emma. I helped my mother at home and then I wed your father. I was afraid of a future without you to look after us...'

Emma thrust the money at her. 'Take it. I don't need it. I hate you for what you've done to me...' She turned and walked out of the house, making her way back over the rise to the Manor, the tears trickling down her cheeks. It was freezing cold and her nose felt icy, as did her hands and feet. Worst of all was the feeling of despair – the knowledge that Tor thought she hadn't loved him enough to go with him. He would believe that she'd been willing to marry him just for what he'd had... and that hurt her, because her love had grown strong and true and she'd broken her heart because she'd thought he'd left with no word for her. And her mother had done that to her!

* * *

Mrs Briscoe looked at her when she walked into the kitchen. 'Good lord, Emma!' she cried. 'You're shivering, girl. Why are you back here tonight? Is there something wrong at home?'

Emma sat down at the kitchen table and bent her head. 'I quarrelled with my mother,' she said as the tears came faster. 'There was a letter from Tor asking me to go to him... weeks ago. She destroyed it...'

'Oh, Emma! I am so sorry,' Mrs Briscoe said, looking at her anxiously. 'That is heartbreaking for you. There is no chance you could contact him? Will he come back now that his name is cleared?'

'Nay, he's gone abroad. He told Ellie – he waited for me a while, but I didn't go to him, nor answer Ellie's letter or his. So he told her he was going abroad – and the mester told me his horse was sold. He loved that animal and wouldn't have sold it if he hadn't intended to leave the country.'

'Then he's gone,' Mrs Briscoe said, looking at her with sympathy. 'Mebbe it is as well, Emma. Have you thought what it will be like for him? Unless he returns here, he'll have little money and no friends. It will take him years to get on his feet again. I've no doubt he was a proud man and it would go hard with him to go cap in hand to a master...'

'I only know that I love him...' Tears were running unchecked down Emma's cheeks.

'Aye, there's no doubt – but you've little choice but to live without him, lass. It hurts now, but in a year or two you'll feel better – you'll find another to love.'

Emma was silent. Mrs Briscoe couldn't understand, because Emma couldn't tell her that she was carrying Tor's child. She would be shocked and angry and, like as not, she'd dismiss her – because she was a bad example to the other young females who worked at the Manor.

Emma wiped her eyes. 'I don't want to go home tonight. Can I have one of the maid's rooms? They aren't all full, are they?'

'No, they aren't,' Mrs Briscoe replied. 'You've nothing with you, but I can lend you some things... Do you want to stay for just one night, Emma?'

'No. I shall live in now,' Emma replied. 'I can't speak to my mother the way I used to. I'll go home once a month and take her half my wages, but I'll not go home every night.'

'Haway, lass.' Mrs Briscoe dropped into the local tongue, though she normally tried to speak like her employers, because it gave her more authority. 'Tha's seething for the moment, but that will ease. You can't shut tha's mother and siblings out of tha life, Emma – they need you, and tha'll discover you need them when tha cools down.'

'Mayhap I shall,' Emma admitted, because she was already realising that she would need someone when her baby was born. 'But I'm so angry and hurt... that she could do something like that to me.'

'Aye, it was wrong of her,' Mrs Briscoe replied, then more briskly. 'These things sting, Emma, but we survive and we go on. I wanted to die when my little ones died, but I didn't – and I found a new life, new friends. You will do the same. Mayhap you'll never forget Tor – but you'll move on, lass.'

Emma nodded but didn't speak.

'You can pick the room you fancy. You know where the linen is...'

Emma went out into the hall. She used the back stairs to the servants' rooms in the attic, then, when her bed was ready, came down to the kitchen. Mrs Briscoe had made a pot of tea and they were drinking it when the mester entered.

'Ah, the very thing,' Stephen said, nodding at the big brown pot. 'May I share it with you?'

'I'll bring tea to the study, sir,' Mrs Briscoe offered, but he shook his head and sat at the table with them. His gaze sought Emma. 'You are late this evening.'

'Emma is staying the night,' Mrs Briscoe told him. 'Her mother thinks the bairns may be sickening for something – so she doesn't want Emma to catch it too.'

'Ah, very sensible,' Stephen said, but Emma sensed that he didn't believe it. She blushed as he looked at her but said nothing. It had been an impulse to come here. She'd been so angry, she'd felt she wouldn't care if she never saw her mother again, but now her temper had cooled and she knew she couldn't just desert her family. Her father would have chided her – and, God knew, she must have disappointed him enough as it was. If he was looking down at her from Heaven, he would know she had shamed his name, and that made Emma want to cry again.

It was with difficulty that she held back her tears. Yet she knew she had to be strong. Self-pity wouldn't solve her problems. She needed to keep herself well and healthy, because she would have to find work when they left Penrith Scar village. Her savings would be small, and even with what Tor had left for her, she would need to work. She had her mother, her brother and sister, whom she loved, and Tor's child growing inside her.

Emma believed that she would not marry. No man she'd want would take her with another man's child in tow; they chose young girls who had no past and no baggage to carry. An older man might take her, but she did not want that sort of marriage; it must be love or nothing. So she had to work hard and take care of her family, all of them, for as long as she lived. A small selfish voice in her head said that perhaps she would die in childbed – but she dismissed it. She was needed; she had a duty, and she must fulfil it as best she could.

Emma nodded. She would go home in a day or two and make up her quarrel with her mother – but she hadn't forgiven her. She was not certain she ever could...

* * *

Stephen went to his bed that night in a fever of anticipation and desire. She was here, sleeping in his house – just a few rooms away, so close that he could sense her, and his mind raced with pictures of her... undressing... lying soft with sleep in his bed. It took all his strength of will not to go to her, to stop himself declaring his love and taking her in his arms. Imagining the scent of her flesh as he buried his face against her feminine sweetness and the taste of her. He could have groaned with the need to have her – but if he did, she would flee from him and he would lose her. He must play the long game, win her to him, because she was chaste and beautiful, and he wanted all of her, not just her body. Any slut on the street could give him the brief pleasure men craved from them, but he wanted Emma in all her innocent joy. He wanted her to reach out for him, to beg for his love so that they were joined as one.

So he left her to sleep alone and endured the torments that kept him awake half the night.

23

Tor felt the force of the wind as they battled the first real storm at sea of his experience. The waves were mountainous, crashing against the bows as if determined to crush this feeble thing that had dared to venture so deep into its world. He laughed in defiance, refusing to be beaten as he battled the elements, hauling on the ropes as they fought to secure the cargo, which was sheeted under tarpaulins. Over the past weeks, they'd fished, selling their catch of fish, crabs and lobsters in Antwerp, and taken on a different cargo, always keeping a lookout for the Revenue vessels, though Red boasted they couldn't catch his ship. He had, after a few days, given Tor a nod of approval; they'd reached an understanding, and since then he'd been treated as if he were his second in command.

They had taken goods on board in Amsterdam, Boulogne and other ports, and the ship was heavy in the water. Had they been under sail, Tor did not think they could have survived such a storm, but their vessel was powered by the new coal-fired steam engines. Red Tikka was a rich and powerful man, and he had a good stout ship – one that could outrun most others if it came to a pursuit.

When in Cornwall, Red was respected as the owner of a popular inn, and his ship was used for fishing, ostensibly its true purpose – but the real money came from the illicit runs to bring in contraband. Taxes on luxury goods were high, and the people who bought from him were happy to pay much less than they would if the goods passed through customs.

'It has gone on in Cornwall and Devon for centuries,' Red had told Tor as they sat together over a flask of rough red wine in a French inn. 'My father bought the inn with his earnings, but now I have this ship – the *Fair Mermaid* – she will outrun anything the customs has. We're never in danger at sea. It's when we take the goods across country that we run risks, Tor. Are you ready to risk your life for a share of the profits?'

'You'll give me a share – how much?' Tor had asked, not crediting the offer.

'I'll give you 10 per cent. My first mate gets that – the others get a wage and split 20 per cent of the profits.'

'Why would you give me some of your profit?' Tor had asked, and Red had grinned, managing to look more evil than normal, his eyes sly and amused, because he knew he'd met his match in Tor Hardy.

'Because you left me warning not to return to Penrith. I was offered good money to take a cargo to the Manor – but your note made me hold back... I think it was a trap. So I'll give you a share. I trust you – and I know you'll give me loyalty in return. Some of these bastards will jump ship at the first chance.' He'd jerked his head at members of the crew, who were rapidly getting drunk at another table. 'I'll have to kick them aboard in the morning.'

'I dare say...' Tor had nodded, thoughtfully. 'I'll work with you, and give you my loyalty for what you offer – but, one day, I'll walk away. I will do it with your blessing and I'll never reveal anything you tell me.' He'd offered his hand.

Red had spat on his own and they'd clasped hands.

Now, cursing the storm, Tor prayed that they would land their cargo safely and not end in the turmoil of the surf at the cove they were destined for. He wanted the profits he'd been promised so that he could begin to build his new life. When he had enough, he would find something legitimate to invest in – and he would earn back the fortune he'd been cheated of: his father's house and smallholding, his mine, the horse he'd trained from a wild colt, and the woman he loved.

The thought of Emma was a constant ache, always at the back of his mind. He understood that her father was ill, but if she'd sent word he would have waited for her... somehow, he would have remained hidden until she could come.

The ship was riding out the storm and Tor blessed its master for investing in modern engines, for sails would have been torn to shreds by now. The job of stoking the engines was hard, hot and dirty work, and Tor had been given his share of it at the start. Red Tikka was a hard man and his crew had a healthy respect for him, but although he'd been angry that Tor was unconscious for two days, making him short-handed in his crew, he'd known that Tor was not a man to be broken by bullying, and he'd soon accepted him.

This cargo was a rich one, the money invested several hundred pounds, and after they'd spoken in the French inn, and their bargain was struck, Red had put Tor in charge of it.

'The bastards are all thieves.' He'd spoken scornfully of his crew. 'Keep an eye out, Tor – remember it's your profits, too. Some of the buggers would get in those casks and drink themselves into a stupor if we don't watch them.'

Tor had smiled to himself then, understanding why, after thinking about it, Red had singled him out. He was the only one he could trust not to steal and it was better to give a percentage of his profits than lose it to scoundrels.

'I'll stand no pilfering,' Red had roared at his crew. 'If any man steals from my cargo, I'll give him a hundred lashes – or keelhaul him.' Tor knew that the sheeted cargo was worth a great deal of money – and a temptation to men who loved to drink. Everyone received a measure of rum each day as part of their wages, but these crates contained bottles of rare cognac and expensive wines, and men like these would have risked much to get their hands on it.

Tor had ignored the threats; the lashes were possible, of course, but keelhauling – the practice of dragging a man beneath the ship for the time it took from bow to stern – would lead to resentment, because it was torture and murder, as a man would not survive such barbaric practice. Once common enough on the high seas, the old punishments inflicted on many a crew were forbidden now. Red was a hard man and would kill if he was cornered, but even he could not sail without a crew. So his punishments would stop short of murder, for otherwise he'd find himself with a ship and no crew next time he needed them.

Tor warned Mack to be careful. 'He is a hard man,' he had said when Mack had suggested that they might steal some smaller items from the captain's cabin.

'He won't know who took his precious diamonds,' Mack had whispered to him as they were patrolling the deck together, keeping a watchful eye for any ship that might belong to the excisemen. 'We could take them when we enter harbour and be away across the sands while they unload the cargo. We'll be gone afore he knows what he's lost.'

'I won't be a thief,' Tor had told him. 'I don't know how you found out about the diamonds, but I'd not like to be in your shoes if he catches you trying to rob him. He would kill you – and I think he could be cruel.'

Mack had regarded him, eyes narrowed in suspicion. 'I thought you were a friend...'

'I am,' Tor had replied. 'I shan't tell him – but if I were you, I'd take my wages and then disappear when we get back.'

Mack had looked at him tight-lipped, angry and distrustful now. A self-confessed murderer, Mack was still a man Tor could like, but he thought him foolish to try to steal from Red Tikka.

'I didn't intend murder,' Mack had confided to Tor one night as they took the dawn watch together. 'I was just so angry at what that devil had done to my sister that I kept on hitting his head against the wall. I served nine years for it and should have done more, but I stopped a riot at the prison, and the governor was so relieved that he had me put on parole.'

'Are you allowed to leave the country?' Tor had asked, raising his brow.

Mack's laughter had disturbed him, because there was a wildness to it. 'Why do you think I'm on this ship? I'd be arrested for breaking my parole if I went back, but I don't intend to return for long. I'm seeking a new life – and I've heard there's gold to be had in America, if you're willing to work and to fight for it. I intend to take passage for the New World – but I needed some money so I signed on for Red...'

'Surely the land will all have been staked and claimed now?' Tor had asked, because the first gold strike had been reported some years earlier, though more might have been found recently.

'There's always a way,' Mack had said, grinning. 'Some will have found nothing and gone elsewhere, others will have money to throw around in a card game – and there's always the chance of finding gold where it has been found before. I've heard of more recent digs where there's lots of it. Anyway, you don't have to dig for it to end up with it…'

'I'm no thief,' Tor had protested.

'I'm a good card player…' Mack had winked at him. 'I've won and lost – but mostly I win.'

'I'm not a gambler either – I want property. A trading store or just land where I can farm or raise cattle, but like you I need to earn money.'

'We'll both earn money from this run – more if I can steal it.' Mack had looked at him hard. 'I'm going to America – why don't you come, too?'

Tor had been thoughtful. Despite his anger at being drugged, robbed and carried on board without his knowledge, he'd found the challenge of life at sea exhilarating; it had helped to ease the bitterness of having the life he'd planned with Emma stolen from him. At first, he'd been hurt that she hadn't come to him, but then he'd thought it over and realised that she couldn't leave her sick father and her family to fend for themselves. The money he'd been able to leave for them wasn't enough. He ought to have arranged for Jonathan to give Emma a share of the profits from the mine, but he'd had to think fast. If he stayed in Cornwall with Red and his men, he could earn good money – and he would send some of it to Emma's friend, who would pass it on. Yes, he could trust Ellie to do that…

'Nay,' he'd said. 'I'll stay with Red for a while, until I'm ready – but I wish you good fortune.' He'd offered his hand to Mack, who had hesitated, then taken it.

'You'll not betray me?'

'You have my word,' Tor had replied. He knew that he could go with Mack if he wished, take ship for a new land, as he'd intended, but he'd changed his mind. He would stay in Cornwall for a while, see how things went, because he knew what he truly wanted – and that was in Penrith village.

Tor knew Mack wasn't happy with his refusal. He'd hardly spoken to him since that night, but Tor's decision was made.

He raised his face to the sky now, welcoming the fierce bite of the wind as it howled about him, fighting to keep upright on the raging sea, and he laughed, tossing back his head, daring fate to dash him down.

Emma was the only woman he'd loved and there would be no other to take her place. Perhaps, if he could find a way, he might persuade her to come to him – and then they would go away, somewhere they could make a good life.

Pushing the hard thoughts to a corner of his mind, Tor went back to checking the ropes were secure on the cargo. The storm was easing at last, the wind blowing itself out. In another day or so, they would sail into the small cove where Red and his men unloaded their contraband. The trip had been long, several weeks at sea, but straightforward, no sign of pursuit.

Tor smiled as he thought of the profits he would share. The next step would be to find something he could invest in – something that he could build on... something that would help him win back the fortune he'd lost, and then he would go back for Emma.

24

Emma's back was aching. She had been working hard, cooking cakes, puddings and all manner of treats for the coming festivities. In another few days, it would be Christmas, and Emma knew she would not be here for the celebrations her master was planning – parties at the house, and also one for the villagers. She suspected he had suggested it to please her, because she could not fail to notice his special smiles and the small gifts that had come her way – a box of bon-bons for her brother and sister, a chicken to take home for her mother, and extra money in her wages. It was obvious the master was paying her attention. Even Mrs Briscoe had noticed and warned Emma to be careful once more.

Smiling inwardly, Emma had thought it the least of her worries. She would not be here at Christmas. Her condition was not noticeable for the moment, though she had put on weight, and in her nightgown, it was easy to see the small swell of her belly, but she wore stays under her gown for work and she had let out the seams. However, she would not be able to hide it for much longer, so she had decided that she would make all the preparations for Christmas and then slip away quietly, leaving a note for the housekeeper. She would have to lie, of course, but if she was careful, perhaps no one need know the shameful truth.

Emma had resolved her quarrel with her mother. It was not the same between them as it had once been, but they spoke to each other in careful, polite tones. Mary had said she would go with Emma when she left the village, but Emma told her that it would be best if she went alone.

'I shall go to Ellie and ask if she knows of work – perhaps in a tavern where they won't bother about my condition as long as I can work,' Emma told her mother that morning before she left for work. She explained what she planned for the future, which was to take any work she could until after the baby was born. She would not use her own name, nor apply for a job as a cook or lady's maid until she had regained her strength.

'And what of the babe?' Mary asked. 'Will you keep it or ask the nuns to take it in?'

'Of course I shall keep my baby,' Emma said, passion in her eyes. She gave her mother a fierce look, defying her to gainsay her, for no words would change her. 'Nothing would make me part with Tor's son... or daughter.'

'I could look after it for you...' Mary suggested, and Emma frowned. It was the sensible way, but, after some thought, she shook her head. She could no longer trust her mother. She might return from work one day to find the baby gone, given away to the nuns or a family that wanted a child.

'I can find someone – a widow, who would be prepared to care for the child while I work. I shall say that I am a widow too...' A flush stained her cheeks. 'Had Tor not been forced to run, I should have been his wife... and his widow if he'd died.' Her features twisted with the grief of not knowing whether he lived or was already dead, perhaps killed by one of the men searching for him, though the master had told her that his name was cleared and he could return a free man – but how would Tor know that? He had gone across the sea and there was no way she could reach him. 'I can get a brass ring in York...'

'I'll give you your grandmother's wedding ring,' Mary replied, her eyes begging for forgiveness. 'It is silver and if you say you are a widow, you may find it easier to get work – many folk need cooks, Emma. You should use your skills – it will be easier than scrubbing floors, which is what you'll most likely be offered; it is all I could get if I tried.'

But you haven't tried, Emma thought, a little flash of resentment making her turn away. If her mother had not been so selfish, Emma might have been with Tor now.

She thanked her for the gift of the ring, and her advice, but still felt it best that her mother remain in her cottage. Truthfully, she did not want her to go with her when she went to York, because she could not yet forgive her.

'That's why I think you should stay here, Ma, with the children. Here, you have friends, folk who will help you, bring you food from their gardens – and the bairns are happy with their friends. Who knows where I shall have to live until I find a decent home? I shall afford but one small room...'

'What will I tell folks?' Mary complained. 'Let me come with you, Emma. I know you hate me, but I can help you...'

'I don't hate you.' Emma paused, then, 'Try to understand, Ma. I shan't earn much for a start, but Ellie will send you some of Tor's money – and then, when the child is born, you can perhaps join me, if you wish.'

'I wish you could forgive me, Emma,' her mother said. 'I did what I thought right – but I hurt you more than I expected, and I regret it.'

'It is forgiven but cannot be forgot,' Emma replied. Her heart had been torn apart by her mother's cruel action in burning the only letter she'd ever had from Tor – and denying her the choice of whether to go to him. It was not only the pain of losing him, but also her mother's heartless deceit that felt like hot pins, torturing her when she lay restless at night.

'Then why not let us come with you?' her mother asked, a begging note in her voice now. 'You'll need help when the babe comes, Emma.'

'Ellie will help me – or I'll go to the Infirmary for the birth,' Emma replied, but, in her heart, she knew it was true that she might need her mother when the time came.

'If you go into the workhouse or the nuns, they might not let you keep the babe,' Mary warned. 'Don't let pride or anger stand between us, Emma.'

'We'll see when the time comes – mayhap you could come to me for the birth.' Emma was close to tears, her heart breaking once more as she thought of the future – a future that did not include Tor.

Mary nodded, then said, 'And if they turn me out of the cottage? What are we to do then? The only reason we are allowed to stay is because you work at the Manor.'

'Then we shall have to find lodgings for us all in York,' Emma cried in frustration. 'Can't you see, Ma? It's going to be hard for me. It is all I can do to go on – and if I can't find decent lodgings or work, you'd be better here where folk know you and would help if that happened. Why can't you see it would be better if I went alone and then sent for you when I'm able?'

Mary was silenced then, but she looked at Emma reproachfully, making her feel guilty. Emma knew her mother feared for the future and felt it would be better to stay together, but she was afraid too – and sometimes she hardly knew how to go on. It had been hard enough to believe that Tor had left the country without her, but to know that her mother had destroyed her one chance to be with him was a bitter pill. So the tension between them had not eased, for both reproached the other.

* * *

Later, at work, thinking about the argument with her mother, Emma felt unwell. It was no use. She would have to sit down! Emma's determination had sustained her while she worked, but her latest batch of marzipan fancies were setting in the larder and her cakes were in the oven. In a few minutes, Emma would need to make a start on the lunch needed for her master and three gentlemen friends he had staying for the weekend.

Sitting at the table, it suddenly all became too much for Emma. She was tired and her back ached – but not so much as her heart. At that moment, she wondered if her life was worth the candle. Her future could be nothing but work. She was only eighteen, but she had no hope of a home of her own, no hope of love – of seeing the man she loved ever again. It seemed impossible now that she had once doubted whether she wished to marry Tor. Now, when every fibre of her being cried out for him, and she felt as if she were being torn apart inside.

Salty tears ran down her cheeks as she struggled to contain the sobs, her shoulders shaking with the effort to control her emotions. Emma felt drained and empty, for nothing seemed to remain of all her hopes and dreams.

'Forgive me for disturbing you at your work...' It was her master's voice, but Emma could not find the energy to put on a smile, and, as she looked up, her misery must have shown in her face. 'Are you unwell, Emma? Have you been working too hard? You look drained... ill...'

Emma shook her head, forcing herself to rise. 'No, sir. 'Tis not the work...' She caught back a sob. 'I was just taking a rest and my thoughts...'

'Were for that rascal who left you without a word,' Stephen said. He was looking at her strangely, and Emma realised that she was standing with her skirt caught against her by the table, which must show the curve of her belly. At three and a bit months, it was not yet enough to notice beneath her heavy apron, but with her dress caught back like that...

She moved away hastily, letting it fall so that she was no longer exposed, but his eyes followed her and she saw something in his face – a look of what... horror, disgust, anger? Emma wasn't certain.

The silence seemed to last an eternity, then, in a voice that was strangely cold, he said, 'Emma – look at me.'

Emma turned reluctantly. 'You needed something, sir? Shall I make you some tea?' She waited for what she imagined would be instant dismissal. Raising her head at last, she looked towards him. He was angry, she could see that, but it was not the righteous indignation of an employer whose servant had fallen beneath his standards. Such a hurt in his eyes and anger – the look a betrayed husband might give his wife, rather than the disgust of a disappointed employer.

'Are you carrying Tor Hardy's child, Emma? Please, tell me the truth?'

Emma lifted her chin, pride coming to her rescue; there was no point in lying. 'Yes, I am – and I am not ashamed. I was to have been his wife and...' She shook her head. There was no need to explain to anyone. 'I have almost finished the preparations for your Christmas celebrations. My intention was to leave at the end of the week...'

'Before your condition was noticed?' He was still staring at her, still hurt, as if she had betrayed him. Emma's heart caught, because she did not know why he should look that way – as if she had let him down.

'Had I married I would have left before now,' Emma replied with dignity. 'Mrs Briscoe will ask Sarah Davies to help out – and she will advertise for a cook. I dare say she will find one far more skilled than I...' She took a deep breath. 'If you wish, I can leave now.'

He did not speak, so she went past him and out of the kitchen, her heart racing. She would go upstairs and collect her things from the room she used now and then when the master was giving a dinner party and she would not walk home after dark alone. Her wages for the past month had just been paid. She had enough for her fare to York and a little to spare – and there was the money from Ellie. She would manage: she had to.

Emma bit her lip as she packed her few belongings into the small carpet bag. She wondered how long it would take for her to find work; the thought of going to a strange town alone was daunting, but at least she had a friend there. Ellie would give her advice, help her to get settled...

Emma was pushing the last of her things into her bag when she heard a noise behind her and turned, expecting to see Mrs Briscoe. 'I am sorry but I have to leave...' She broke off as she saw Stephen Rawlings standing there.

'You can't leave me,' he said in a strangled voice. 'I don't want you to go...'

'Sir, I must,' Emma said, her throat catching with fright as she looked into his eyes and saw the untrammelled passion blazing there. 'My mother will be shamed if I stay in the village and folk know I am with child. I shall leave now, as soon as I can, and she will come to me when I am settled. I beg you will allow her to stay in the cottage...'

'No!' He moved towards her, gripping her arms with his long, strong fingers. 'You shall not go, Emma. You are mine. You should always have been mine. I know that brute forced you. You shall stay here and be mine – and the child, if it lives, will be mine too. No one must know it is not my child, Emma. My wife will not be scorned...'

'Sir!' Emma pulled back from him in shock. 'You do not know what you are saying. I am not yours – I cannot be your wife...' Her head was whirling. Could he truly have just offered her marriage? It wasn't possible. Surely, he must see that? She was a servant; he was the grandson of a lord. Besides, everyone would know that the child was Tor's and they would laugh and snigger at him for taking another man's leavings. If she was foolish enough to accept, because of her fears, he would grow to hate her and the child that was not his own.

Emma managed to pull away from him. She picked up her small bag.

'I thank you for your kindness, sir – now please allow me to pass...'

'Did you not hear me, Emma? You will be my wife – your child mine.' He smiled. 'You think people will gossip – but we'll go away from here. We'll live in London for a while. You will like that, Emma. We'll say you are the daughter of a vicar – that's respectable. No one has to know anything...' He reached for her again, taking her by the shoulders and giving her a little shake. He was smiling now, his eyes bright with hope and his plans. 'You know that I love you, Emma. I've never loved another person as I love you. I've never loved anyone else, even my parents and certainly not my grandfather – the old devil.' He laughed, but to Emma's ears, his words seemed foolish and his look dangerous, uncontrolled. She wondered if he were a little drunk.

'Oh, sir,' she said, trying to move away, but discovering she was held fast. 'You are good and kind – but I cannot wed you. It wouldn't be right...'

'I shan't let you go ever...' he said, ignoring her.

Emma raised her head then. He was offering her a good life, a way out of her troubles, but she did not love him, and she did not want to be his wife. Sometimes there was an intensity in him that frightened her – and he was frightening her now.

'Sir, please let me go. I do not wish to marry you. I love Tor and – and I believe he will return for me one day...'

He stared at her blindly for a moment, then her words seemed to sink in. 'You would refuse me? You still prefer that great lout to me – when I've offered you marriage? You insult me thus... After all I did to get you...'

Emma felt chilled. All he'd done to get her? She was a bright girl and she knew that could only mean one thing – it was he who had betrayed Tor. It had been a masquerade; the kindness, smiles, offers of help to clear Tor's name when he knew it would be too late. It had all been a trap to ensnare her. She wrenched herself free as anger flared in her.

'You said it was your friend that betrayed Tor to the customs men...'

Stephen laughed harshly. 'Ravenscroft hadn't the wit to see it for himself. He wanted to get even – but there were witnesses that he had attacked a girl and then Tor after he stopped him deflowering her...' His eyes were very bright, strangely so, as if he had lost all control, all sense of what was right or wrong. 'Yes, it was my idea. I had to get rid of him so that you would turn to me because I wanted to wed you... but you're just a little slut like all the others...' Suddenly, he lashed out at Emma, hitting her across the face. She recoiled and tried to get free, but he had her fast about the waist now, and he was forcing her backwards in the direction of the bed. 'Well, now you can give me what you gave him, you slut. I'll teach you to insult your betters...'

'I never meant to insult you...' Emma cried desperately. 'You always knew I was his...'

Her pleas were useless. He was going to rape her. Emma struggled helplessly in his arms, but he was so strong. She knew that he would take her down and there was no way she could stop him. Her eyes moved feverishly about the room and then she saw the iron poker leaning against the grate. To reach the bed, they must pass the fireplace. It was a desperate hope, but Emma allowed herself to go limp so that he was able to force her backwards. Her hand went behind her back and she caught the solid poker, bringing her arm up sharply and hitting him in one fluid movement. He gave a cry but then fell, hitting the side of his head against the cast-iron overmantle as he went down.

Emma stared at him. Blood was seeping from the wound to the back of his head where he'd hit it, his eyes were shut and he was not moving. She had killed him! A shudder of terror went through her. She had meant only to stun him, but the blow to the back of his head as he fell had done the rest. He was dead and she was a murderer.

'What have you done?' Mrs Briscoe spoke from the doorway. 'Oh, Emma – you've killed him...'

'He tried to force me...' Emma whispered. 'I was defending myself.'

'You'd best go quickly,' Mrs Briscoe said, looking at her in horror. 'I didn't see this... I'll let someone else find him later. Take your things and go, Emma. Leave the village – go to London, a big city where they won't know you. They won't think to look for you there.' She pulled some coins from her pocket. 'I was meaning to pay the carter – but I'll get more. This will help you – run, Emma. Run for your life, because they will hang you for this if they catch you...'

Emma took the money and threw it into her carpet bag. 'Thank you. I shan't forget,' she said in a choked voice, and then she was going from the room and down the stairs, out of the house. No one saw her leave. They were all busy, all working elsewhere, decorating the house with holly and ivy for the Christmas celebrations their master had planned. Emma had cooked and prepared for weeks and it was an irony that it would not now be enjoyed, for with her master's death all entertainment would be cancelled.

Once outside the house, Emma started to walk down the hill. Despite what Mrs Briscoe said, she wouldn't run. She wouldn't draw attention to herself, because she had to get home and warn her mother they must leave. Everything had changed now. Emma's mother couldn't stay in the village after what Emma had done. People would spit at her and she would never hold her head up again. They must leave Penrith now, walk to Settle and take a train. It hardly mattered where they went; Emma simply had to get away while she could.

25

'Oh, Emma! That wicked man,' Mary cried when Emma told her that her former master had tried to rape her. 'But you should not have killed him.' Her hand went to her throat in fright. 'You must take all you can carry and go... Go now, before they send someone after you.'

'You must come too, Ma,' Emma said. 'Don't you see, they will take the cottage from you – and people may turn against you because of what I did...'

'I would slow you down – and the bairns are at school.' Mary shook her head. 'Go alone, and when you are settled, send word through Ellie – and I'll join you. If I come with you, it might seem as if we planned it...' She went to the vase on the mantle and took out a few coins. 'It is all there is left of the five pounds Tor sent for you the first time. I spent the rest on shoes and clothes for the bairns.'

'Keep it, Ma. I have my wages for the month, and Mrs Briscoe gave me a bit more. You will need it, for it might be months before I can send for you...'

'I've a bit in the drawer upstairs that was your da's – Tor gave him compensation. Some of it was spent on the children. I was keeping the rest for a rainy day – well, now it is pouring.' She thrust the coins into Emma's hand. 'You'll need it more, my girl – take it and go.' Her eyes met Emma's. 'I owe it to you. It is I who brought this on you, Emma. I'm sorry – but I know that won't help you now.'

Emma went up to her room, thrusting a few more items of clothes into her bag, but she could not take any of the sentimental items given her over the years by her father, for she could only carry one bag. Going back down the stairs, she looked at her mother and then went to hug her; it might well be the last time they spoke. 'I'm sorry, Ma. I know you didn't mean to hurt me – and I do love you.'

'Oh, my Emma,' Mary cried, tears springing from her eyes. 'It is sorry I am for what I did to you. If I'd given you that letter, you'd be safe now... If anything happens to you, it's me that's to blame.'

'No. It's him,' Emma denied. 'I think he's strange in the head, Ma – I never gave him cause to think I'd welcome his attentions. I might be his servant, but he'd no cause to act the way he did... and I only meant to stun him.'

'Aye, I know that – but the law won't listen. He's a lord's grandson and you're a miner's daughter, what ought to be grateful for anything she's given,' Mary said sadly. 'Folks will blame you, lass. Now go – and take care of thissen.'

'You too – and the bairns. I'll write when I can...'

'Don't send me your address. Write to Ellie and let her send it on,' her mother warned. 'Be careful, lass – they will be searching for you once it is known that you've done murder...'

Emma nodded. She hugged her mother again, picked up her bag and went out. Hardly a soul was about as Emma walked past the cottages, her heart fluttering. She felt that at any moment someone might shout at her and come after her and she would be taken away to prison, but no one noticed her or called out.

It was half an hour or so later that she heard the sound of a wagon on the road behind her. Pulling her shawl over her head so that it covered her face, she stepped off the road to let the wagon by, but it pulled up beside her.

'Emma.' A voice she knew well spoke urgently. 'I've heard a tale that you might be in trouble for an attack on the master up at the house... Nay don't look afeared, lass. I've come to take you into Settle. If you walk, someone may come after and catch you. I'll have you there and none the wiser...' Joe Davies leaned down and offered her his hand. 'Up you come, lass.'

She hesitated and then took his hand, sitting beside him on the box seat. 'Who told you?' she asked, her stomach clenching.

'Jem, the stable lad, was sent to fetch the doctor,' Joe said. 'I was getting my wagon ready – I'm going to Settle for supplies. Jem called out as he passed me, something about you killing Stephen Rawlings...'

'He attacked me,' Emma whispered. 'He was going to...' She swallowed hard. 'I hit him with a poker and he went down hard, struck his head on the iron mantle... I never meant to kill him, but he was going to hurt me...'

Joe looked grave. 'That's bad, Emma. I know you did it in self-defence, but the law is harsh on murder – and who knows if they'll believe you?' He turned his head to study her. 'Where are you making for – York?' Emma hesitated. 'Not one word will pass my lips...'

'I have a friend in York – but folk know that; they might look for me there. I thought London, for a while... I don't know...'

He nodded, a thoughtful expression in his eyes. 'A big city is probably best for you, lass. No one takes notice of a stranger there. If you stay round here, folk will be suspicious of a lass alone. York is a big place – but if they come looking, your friend, if you go to her, could be in trouble for helping you.'

Emma bit her lip. She felt sick inside. Her hopes of going to Ellie for help seemed too dangerous now. Mrs Briscoe was right. She needed to go where no one would think to look for her. In London, she would be safer – but would she be able to find work?

Her mind was busy with all the risks and problems she now faced. 'Perhaps I should go back – take my chance with the law,' Emma said, because did it really matter if she lived or died?

'Nay, lass,' Joe told her firmly. 'I know you've had it hard since Tor was forced to run, but if I know him, he won't forget you, Emma. You may think you've nothing to live for, but life is good. I once did something foolish and for a time I was forced to hide. I've told no one else, Emma. I too wondered if life was worth the living – but then I found a place I could work and live and I made a good life. You'll find something one day – and then...' He broke off as tears welled in her eyes. 'Nay, don't cry then, lass.'

'I'm carrying Tor's child,' Emma told him. 'The mester guessed and that's what changed him; he wanted me to wed him, said we'd go away and no one would know it wasn't his – but I was frightened. I didn't want him. I love Tor. When I told him so, he attacked me – called me a slut like all the rest.'

'He's one of them – the gentry...' Joe said, his mouth sour. 'They think they're entitled and you hurt his pride, Emma. He had no right...' He smiled at her. 'Tor can come back now his name has been cleared. If he comes, I'll tell him what happened, Emma. He will come looking for you and the babe. So keep in touch with your friend. There's no way Tor would have left if he'd known.'

'It was too soon...' She blushed. 'It was... the summer feast...'

Joe nodded. 'He could not have known then. Well, there's no use crying over it, Emma. You're a strong lass, and you'll manage.' He was quiet for a moment, then, 'You'll need to buy a ticket for Leeds, and then to York, but speak to your friend and stay only one night there – then go wherever you think is best, but I don't believe you can stay in the Dales, for they would find you.'

'Thanks, Joe,' Emma said, tears stinging her eyes again. 'I shan't forget you helped me.'

'You helped my Sarah – and me...' Joe shook his head. 'Don't be worrying about your ma. I'll speak to Tor's man up at the mine. He's had a fight on his hands to keep the mine going; there have been rumours about Tor being wanted for murder. Some of the men walked off, saying as they wouldn't work for him. Crossly had to bring in new men – and he had lawyers after him, trying to say the mine wasn't his, but he was a match for them. I know his intention was to visit you once things settled; he will see as your family is all right for money, I reckon – and if Rawlings' family turn her out, there's mayhap a chance of a miner's cottage.'

'Oh, Joe...' Emma sniffed, because his kindness had made her realise how much she would miss folk, not just her mother but village people – and Mrs Briscoe. Mr Crossly had known she was still working and thought her able to cope, which she would have been had the master not discovered that she was with child. Now it had all suddenly changed. The Dales had been her life, but it was going to be very different now...

* * *

Emma had to wait for a train for an hour when she got to Settle. After leaving Joe, she spent a little time looking round the small town. Set on a steep hill, there were fine buildings here, and she ventured into the Golden Lion Inn, where her father had once stood outside and listened to a concert in the rain. She bought herself a glass of lemonade, sitting in a corner of the ancient building with its dark beams and inglenook fireplace, staring into an uncertain future. The old market square was thronged with folk about their business and Emma felt a kind of homesickness, knowing that she could never return, never be a part of the gentle, friendly way of life that went on in the Dales, and it made her heart ache for all she had lost.

Making her way back to the buff-bricked station house a little later, she bought a ticket for Leeds. A train was leaving in the opposite direction for Carlisle. To get on, Emma would have needed to climb steep steps and cross over to the other platform, and she wondered for a moment if she would have been better to go that way, but her ticket was purchased, and she longed to see Ellie, because her friend was all that she had left now – all that she could trust.

The journey seemed to take forever, though the view from her window was lovely, but the changing scenery of rolling hills and limestone walls enclosing small fields, occupied by sheep, with steeper dark hills in the distance, made her heart ache. This was her home and she was leaving it forever. Tears blurred her eyes as they passed station after station, all of them neat; the buildings the same soft buff stone, still new and clean for they had been built by the railway only a few years previously. Tubs of bright chrysanthemums, the small bright flower of winter, stood outside the station houses, carefully nurtured and protected from the frosts by devoted stationmasters, for the heavy snows had not yet fallen over the Dales, and the maroon-painted lamp posts all looked the same, becoming a blur as her heart grew heavier.

Leeds station was so big and noisy that it frightened Emma. It was so much bigger than any of the Dales' railway stations. Dirty and smelly, with people rushing from one platform to another, it made her aware of her vulnerability and the tears were very close. At first, she did not know what to do or where to go to get her train, but then she heard an announcement and realised that she was close to the platform she needed; she hurried there, though her train did not come for several minutes.

Once on board the train, Emma closed her eyes against the tears that threatened. It was all so strange and difficult and she wished with all her heart that she had never killed her master. She had thought only to stun him, to give herself time to escape, but, of course, she had not truly thought at all. Now she was feeling the horror of what she had done. Perhaps she should have stayed and let them punish her – yet what of her innocent unborn child?

Gradually, Emma's feelings calmed. She lifted her head, forcing herself to think clearly. It was not her fault. After what Stephen Rawlings had done to harm her, he deserved a sore head – if only that were all. She'd thought him dead for she'd struck hard and he hadn't moved. Emma breathed deeply, because it did not sit well with her to have taken a man's life, even though he'd brought it on himself.

The journey from Leeds was much shorter than the one from Settle, and sooner than she'd thought, Emma heard the announcement. She stood up, gathered her bag and shawl and followed the other passengers.

Descending from the train in York, she stood for a while looking around her as people rushed about the platforms, in a hurry to catch their trains. She jumped as she heard a loudspeaker telling folk that a train was about to leave for London in five minutes. For a moment, she considered getting on it, but then she turned and followed others leaving the station. She handed in her ticket and then stood wondering which way to go. There were cabs with horses waiting in the lamplight for a fare and Emma debated whether to take one to the house where Ellie worked. She decided against it, because she would need all her money; even with the extra that Mrs Briscoe had given her, she didn't have much in her purse; just a few pounds and some coins, which would soon be gone if she didn't find work quickly.

She began to walk along the street, looking around with interest, because apart from the Manor, she'd never seen such fine buildings, though it was too dark to see clearly, shadows falling, adding mystery and apprehension. Some of them were grand – far bigger than the house she'd worked in. Emma remembered what Sarah had said about York Minster – that it looked like a palace, and so it did.

Emma knew Ellie's address by heart but, after she'd been walking for a while, she became lost in the wonder of what she saw – shops and hotels, restaurants with people going in and out, all busy as life flowed about her. This was a town, like nothing she'd ever seen, the shop windows filled with Christmas goodies and treasures beyond imagination; she'd been told how grand York was, but the reality exceeded her dreams.

She heard a loud popping sound and a bang, jumping in fright only to see that the noise had come from one of those new motor vehicles – a man with a red flag walking in front of it to warn folks. It was all so different from the lonely sweep of the moors and Dales, where all you could hear was birdsong and the croaking of a cricket. Her head seemed to spin as she wandered, lost both in spirit and in truth, for she had no idea where she went.

She stopped at last and asked someone the way to Ellie's

house. The first person she asked wasn't sure but just pointed vaguely to the left.

'It's down there somewhere,' she said and hurried off.

Emma walked in the direction she'd pointed, but after a few minutes she stopped again and asked a baker's boy. He was carrying a basket of freshly baked bread and the smell of it made her feel hungry. This time she was lucky, because he delivered to the area and was able to direct her.

'It's down that street over there – past that row of shops, ma'am.'

Emma wondered why he'd called her that, then recalled she was wearing her grandmother's silver wedding ring. She had forgotten – and she hadn't decided what she would call herself either. Her thoughts whirled for a moment. She couldn't use her mother's maiden name or Tor's second name, because either might give her away if the authorities came looking for her.

She would use her own first name, she decided, because otherwise she might not realise when someone was talking to her – so what should it be? Emma Watson... No, too close to her real name. Emma Robinson... It came from nowhere, but it was as good as any.

Emma's wandering thoughts came to an abrupt halt as she realised that she had reached Micklegate Bar, a location with impressive houses that Ellie had told her had been built almost four centuries earlier.

'Some of them are draughty places too,' she'd written in one of her earlier letters, 'but ours has been restored and made comfier, Emma – and the mistress likes a good fire. She finds Yorkshire cold, even in our summer. In the south of America, she says it is much warmer.'

Emma saw that she was now outside the house where Ellie worked. She would have gone round to the back but could see no way to reach it, since the houses were built close together, and the only passageway had a locked gate. So she stepped up and knocked at the front door. It seemed an age to Emma before she heard the lock being turned and her stomach clenched as she tried to steady her nerves, but when it opened, she saw the maid dressed in a neat black gown and white apron and cap was Ruby.

Ruby stared at her for a moment, then her face broke into a smile. 'Why, if it isn't Emma,' she cried. 'Does Cook know you are coming?'

'No. It was a sudden decision,' Emma replied. 'Is she here?'

'In the kitchen, where else would she be?' Ruby said, chuckling. 'You're in luck, Emma – the mistress and mester have gone off to London for the week. There's only me, Cook and the scullery maid in the house. They took the butler and secretary with them – and she's got a new maid to dress her. Martin wasn't pleased they left me here, but his hints went unheard.' Ruby pouted. 'I could have helped her dress as well as that French woman she took a fancy for...'

Ruby indicated that she should follow, and Emma went with her down a long hall and then some stairs at the back, which led to the kitchen and servants hall in the basement.

Ellie was busy at the stove and she asked who was at the door without turning.

'You'll never guess...' Ruby said, giggling, and Ellie turned her head sharply. She gave a cry of wonder and delight, put down her spoon and hurried to embrace Emma.

'Lord have mercy!' Ellie cried. 'Is it thissen, Emma Watts?'

'Aye, it is,' Emma replied. 'I ought not to have come, Ellie – but I needed to see you...' She glanced at Ruby and something in her face must have warned Ellie, for she sent the girl off to make up a fresh bed in the attics.

'Because Emma will stay for a day or two...' When Ruby had gone, she motioned to Emma to sit, then said, 'Summat is wrong – badly wrong, Emma. I know it, for why else would you have come without warning?'

Emma sniffed, choking back her tears as she told Ellie the whole truth, leaving nothing out; how she was having Tor's child, how her mother had destroyed Tor's letter, and her master had guessed about the babe and attacked her.

'If they find me, I'll go to prison,' she said. 'If he dies, I could hang – but even for grievous assault, I'll be in prison for years. I had to get away and I'm going further. I can't stay in York. They will know about you, Ellie – and they will come and ask if you've seen me.'

'They'll get nowt from me, Emma,' Ellie said. 'Ruby won't tell if I say not to – and the scullery girl is a daftie. She'll do as I tell her.' Ellie frowned. 'I'd tell you to stay here, but there's folk visit from time to time – people that might know your master...'

'I won't bring trouble on you,' Emma said, blowing her nose on the big handkerchief Ellie gave her. 'I just wanted to see you – and to ask for a little of the money Tor left for us.'

'Take it all, love. I've kept it safe for you, Emma – and he promised to send more when he could, but there's no telling when that might be – probably years.'

'I must work for myself. I know that – I will take five pounds, but can you send Ma some every now and then, because I'm not sure when I will be able to...'

'She wouldn't come with you?'

'She wanted to – but I'm a fugitive, Ellie. I told her to stay in the village where she has friends. I shan't write to her – but when I am settled, I'll write to you, and if you could let my mother know... If she wants to come to me, she will then.'

Ellie looked at her. 'Tor wanted you to have the money – and after what Mary Watts did to you, she doesn't deserve it.'

'Don't say that, Ellie,' Emma begged. 'I was angry and I hated her for a time, but she is my mother – and there are the bairns. If they starved, I'd not forgive myself.'

'Aye, for their sakes I'll do as you ask, Emma – but if you need help, you must let me know. In time, perhaps you could return to York. If that devil lives, you will be forgotten in time. I'd like it if you were nearby. I could help you – and I've no other friend like you, Emma.'

'I wish I could stay. It was my plan to find work in York and be near you when the baby was born – but everything changed when I struck my master. You know they will arrest me if they catch me. Even if he lives, it will be assault.'

'Aye, for his word will be taken above yours, Emma. It is unfair, but it is the way of things...'

Emma raised her head, her tears gone now. 'I will manage somehow. I'm strong and I can work – but I shall miss you and my family. I must disappear for a while, but if he lives, as you said, perhaps in time it will be forgotten. I can never return to Penrith, but if I change my name, I could come to York in time...'

Ellie nodded. 'Promise me you will not give up hope, Emma – and keep in touch with me always.'

'I shall try,' Emma said. She hesitated, then, 'Did you mean that I could stay for tonight? I will go in the morning...'

'You'll stay tonight, for it is dark out and I would not have you sleep on the streets. No decent house will open their door to a stranger after dark and lord knows where you might end up. In the morning, I'll give you breakfast and food for the journey, wherever you go...' She sighed. 'It is little enough, Emma, but I can do no more; it isn't safe for you to stay here longer, because they will come looking, once they know you've run.'

'Running made me look guilty, but Mrs Briscoe told me to go – and I know I should be in prison this night if I'd stayed. I think he was dying, but even if he lives, he will hate me and want me arrested.'

'You hurt his pride and men don't like that,' Ellie agreed. 'Hush now – someone is coming...'

The door opened and a girl entered. She was a tiny little thing with fair hair and dazed blue eyes.

'Ah, there you are, Daisy. Have you finished your chores for the day?'

'Yes, Cook. I've done all the bedrooms, same as you said. Can I have me dinner now afore I go home? And can I have a bit of that cake you was cooking?'

'The cake is for Christmas Day, Daisy, like the puddings and the cinnamon biscuits. Dinner will be another half an hour...' She noticed that the little maid was staring at Emma. 'This is my niece, Joyce. She's come to York for the Christmas shopping. Say hello to her and then go out and fetch me some water from the pump in the yard.'

'The water bucket is full, Cook.'

'Then take this jug,' Ellie said. 'Go on, be a good girl...'

Daisy took the jug and went off obediently, just as Ruby entered.

'Ah, Ruby, take our friend up to her room and let her rest for a while. We'll all talk later, after Daisy has had her dinner and gone home...'

Emma nodded, feeling tired and drained. Already, the lies and deceit had begun, for Cook had lied to the little scullery maid. It would be nothing but lies from now on – her whole life would be a lie.

She followed Ruby up the back stairs to the maids' rooms in the attic. It was a tiny room, but there was a bed, a chair and a chest with a jug and basin on top – more than she needed for her brief stay.

'It's not as nice as my room,' Ruby told her. 'But it is the only one not used. Daisy would have it, but she lives not far from here with her grandmother and she won't live in. Says the old lady can't look after herself at nights.'

'I don't blame her. I'd go home too if I could...'

Ruby looked at her oddly, but Emma didn't enlighten her. Cook would tell her what she needed to know.

'I'll leave you to rest like Cook said...' Ruby murmured and then went back the way they'd come.

Emma lay down on the bed, curled up in a ball and closed her eyes. She felt safe in this little attic room, at least for the moment. If only she could stay here in York with her friends, life could be easy again – but it was impossible. Ellie could be in trouble for helping her – particularly if she had committed murder. If her employers returned from visiting London, Ellie might lose her job. Especially if they discovered what Emma had done.

The thought filled her with horror. She – Emma Watts – had stolen a man's life. It was true she'd been frightened of his anger and what he'd meant to do – but murder was a terrible sin. She had not thought about the consequences when she'd grabbed that poker – only her desire to stop him forcing himself on her. Now he was dead or lying close to it and he did not deserve it, for he was not a wicked man. Emma thought that he had truly loved her and felt himself betrayed and she wished that she could go back... tell him that she did not wish for marriage in a different way. She'd hurt his pride and that was why he'd flared into anger. Emma hadn't meant to hurt him – or kill him – but his disparaging of Tor and his betrayal of the man she loved had made her angry too. Betwixt fear and anger, she had done something she would regret for the rest of her life...

26

Ruby woke Emma when Daisy had eaten her dinner and gone home. 'Cook has saved some for you,' she said, watching in concern as Emma rubbed the sleep from her eyes and got to her feet. 'It is sorry I am for your trouble, Emma – and I'll not tell a soul that you came here.'

'Thank you,' Emma said. 'It might get Cook into bother and you wouldn't want that, Ruby.'

'No, nor would I want you in prison for hitting a man that tried to take you down against your will,' Ruby said stoutly. 'You were kind to me, Emma. I'll never forget that.'

Emma thanked her and followed her back down to the kitchen. Ellie gave her a plate of lamb hotpot with cabbage and turnips, and she ate every scrap. She hadn't realised how hungry she was until the plate was put in front of her and its tantalising smell aroused her need for food. She must remember that she was eating for two and her child required nourishment.

After she had eaten, the three of them sat and talked about the old times, then Ruby went up to bed, because she wanted to curl her hair in rags so that it looked nice when her fiancé returned the next day. Ellie and Emma sat talking for longer, going over and over what might suit her best.

'You can't try for work as a private cook, because they will ask for a reference,' Ellie said. 'I think you should approach the inns and public houses wherever you go. Once you work for them, you can show others you are a cook – and then perhaps you'll get a better job.' She paused. 'What about when the child comes? You can't manage that on your own...'

'I must find an infirmary where they will help me...'

'If they suspect you aren't married, they will take the child from you...' Ellie thought and then nodded to herself. 'When the time is near, I'll take my holiday and come to you. Don't forget, Emma. You let me know where you're staying and I'll come. Your mother would wish to, but she can't leave the bairns – and she might be followed, but they won't suspect me. If they come here once, that's all they'll bother with...'

'Oh, Ellie, thank you,' Emma said. She was close to tears again, but she held them back. Crying made her feel weaker and she needed to be strong, not just in body but in mind.

Ellie hugged her and they parted, each to their own rooms. Emma slept, though for a start she lay listening and worrying, but then she became so weary that she just fell asleep. She was up early in the morning and had cooked breakfast for herself, Ellie and Ruby. Ellie smiled sadly.

'I wish you could stay, Emma lass. I should enjoy being waited on once in a while.' She shook her head sadly. 'I've a load of work to do when my mistress returns, for she'll be entertaining friends at Christmas.'

Emma smiled but said nothing, but she wished that she could stay, feeling sad that she would have no one to spend Christmas with this year. There had been little money for gifts and special foods in the Watts' family household, but they had still managed to make it special. In future, she would spend it alone, because the next part of her life was unknown and frightening.

Emma took her leave soon after. She hugged both her friends and said goodbye, for in truth she did not know if they would meet again. A night's sleep and talking with Ellie had helped her, and her first fears had eased for a while.

* * *

The platform at York station was busy, for there were several people waiting to board the London train, and no one noticed her. Why would they? She was just an ordinary woman and who could know what she had done? As yet, the hue and cry had hardly started. In Penrith Scar, everyone would know, but the news might not have reached York yet. The wheels of justice were oft-times slow but once turning were unstoppable. The newspapers would write about it for a while, because murder was a heinous crime and she was sure her master had been dead after that fearful blow to the back of his head. Emma would be looked for – but not yet, and perhaps not in London.

Emma boarded the train with others and found herself a window seat. Two smart gentlemen in suits and bowler hats entered and sat down opposite her, and then a woman and a young girl came and sat beside her. The woman nodded but said nothing. The little girl stared at her and then started to suck her thumb.

Feeling the jolt of the train as it started, Emma turned her head to look out of the window. She had never been to York before and had seen only a small part of it. Now she was on her way to London – a place that might have been the moon as far as Emma was concerned. Her fears of the previous day returned and she wondered what life held for her. The world seemed big and unfriendly to a girl who had never before left her beloved Dales and was now alone.

The man sitting opposite her had a newspaper and he started to read it. Emma looked at the headlines, but there was nothing concerning her – her name did not jump out of the page at her. She tucked her hands in her lap, forcing herself to be calm. Even if she had been named as a murderess, no one could know it was her – there were no images of her. She'd never had her likeness taken and her description could fit a hundred girls of her age.

After half an hour or so, the train stopped and the man with the newspaper got off, leaving his paper discarded on the seat. Emma waited, but when no one moved to retrieve it, she asked the gentleman still sitting there if she might read it. He looked down his nose at her but handed it over. She took it and read steadily for the remainder of the journey. Then she saw it – just one small paragraph.

> Servant being sought after a disgusting attack on her master. Mr Stephen Rawlings was violently attacked at his home in Penrith Manor by a young woman he had employed as his cook. At the moment, Mr Rawlings lies desperately ill at his home, attended by doctors and his devoted housekeeper. The reason for the attack is not known. Doctors gave it as their opinion that he is unlikely to recover…

Emma gave a little gasp and folded the paper. She had not been named in this first report, but no doubt she would be as the search widened. Her employer was still alive, but if he died, as the reporter seemed to think inevitable, the search for her would intensify. It was a good thing that she had spent only one night in York, for they were bound to discover she had been there. The man in the ticket office in Settle would remember her. He did not know Emma, but he would recall that a young woman of her description had bought a ticket for Leeds, because he'd asked her if she was going to find work. She'd told him she had family there... her first lie. There would be so many more once she got to London.

A little shiver went through her. She was truly alone now. It was a strange feeling and not one she relished, but, once again, she pushed the thought from her. She would manage. She would survive somehow. She had to, if only for the sake of her child.

Tor's child was inside her. For the first time, she was aware of something that felt like a kick. It made her smile. Of course she wasn't alone. As long as her baby lived, she had a part of Tor with her.

Her head went up and, all at once, her natural confidence flowed back. She would live and work, and make a home for her and her child – and perhaps one day she could have her family back...

* * *

It was the noise of the big city that hit Emma when she emerged from the dimness of the railway station to the busy street in London. Immediately, the sounds of voices, harsh to her ears, the clatter of hooves from dray horses, and the horn of an automobile together with a loud popping sound assailed her. Emma had thought York big and noisy, but compared to this street in London, it had been quiet and peaceful, its old buildings graceful and charming. The pavements here looked dirty and greasy after a downpour of icy rain and the skies were dull with clouds. In York, there had been an atmosphere of celebration as Christmas approached, but in these dark London streets, there was nothing. No tantalising smells of chestnuts roasting, nor the sound of young voices singing carols. She saw one man carrying a small fir tree, but otherwise there was nothing to speak of Christmas cheer. She shivered, feeling cold, alone and lost. Where in all this endless maze of buildings, many of them admittedly imposing, would she find a place to live – and, even more importantly, work?

A barrow piled with oranges and apples stood near the entrance to the station. The young lad standing beside it was calling out to passers-by, offering his wares. Emma watched him for a while, deciding that he often smiled as he spoke to the folk who bought from him and might therefore be safe to speak to. She approached him hesitantly.

'Beg pardon, sir,' she said. 'I am new come to London, and look for a place to stay. Thissen knows of a cheap but decent house with rooms to let?'

The lad looked at her for a moment, eyes narrowed. 'Yer from up north, ain't yer?' he said.

Emma nodded, because her accent had betrayed her, though she had tried hard to speak properly, the way the gentry did. She must be more careful in future, for the authorities might look for a woman with a Yorkshire accent newly arrived in London.

'I might,' the lad said after a moment's thought. 'Peg said she was looking for a lodger.' He looked at her consideringly. 'Can you read, miss?'

'Aye, I can read,' Emma replied.

He nodded, took out a little notebook and wrote an address on it.

'Is it far?'

'It's a good walk from here,' the lad said. 'There's a cab over there – he'll charge you a shillin' ter take yer – might be best, seein' yer new to the city. Yer don't want ter get lost, not wiv that devil stalking the streets. It ain't safe fer a woman at night, not even wiv them vigilantes on patrol. Yer can go that way...' He pointed down the street. 'Turn left at the corner and keep on walkin', but yer might get lost. Better to ask the cab – but don't let 'im cheat yer. It's a shillin', no more.'

Emma wondered what he meant by saying it wasn't safe, then she remembered hearing something about several murders of women in London, and she shivered. At home in the Dales, it had seemed so far away that she hadn't taken much notice, but now she was in London.

'Oh, thank you, I shall,' Emma said, giving him an uncertain smile. 'You are very kind.'

'You tell Peg Robbie sent yer. She'll look after yer and 'elp yer get started. You'll be needin' a job – unless yer already 'ave one?'

'No, I don't,' Emma replied. 'I... I'm a widow and I was turned from my cottage, for the mester wanted it for another.' Emma cursed herself for the slip. By speaking of her mester, it might trigger the fact that she was a servant – and a servant from Yorkshire was wanted for murder. 'Thank you so much, Robbie.'

He nodded, turning away from her as a customer approached, then called after her, 'Be careful no one snatches yer bag, missus.'

Emma walked away, holding tighter to her bag, and asked the cab driver if he could take her to the address Robbie had given her in Whitechapel. He nodded and held out his hand. Whitechapel... there was something about that word that rang a bell, but she didn't know what, or why she'd heard it spoken of.

'Two shillin's...' The cabbie held out his hand.

'Nay, the fare is a shilling,' Emma said, her eyes sparking. 'I'm not a daftie.'

The cabbie looked at her and nodded. 'In advance then,' he said.

Emma agreed and placed the coin in his hand. She tried not to think of how much food that would have bought for her family – and how few coins she had left in her purse after she'd paid her fares to get here. Ellie had wanted her to take more of the money Tor had left for her, but she'd told her that it was for her mother and the children.

'I can work,' she'd said firmly. 'Ma has the children to care for and she's never worked for a mester, for she helped at home on the farm until she was wed.'

Ellie had muttered something but Emma hadn't heard, nor had she wanted to. It was true that her mother might find work helping the mistress on one of the farms, for she was strong enough to scrub or to churn butter, but would anyone want her – the mother of a murderess? Even if the master didn't die, folk would still see it as a wicked crime. She might be shunned and spat on, for folk could be unkind.

Sitting in the cab, looking at the buildings as they passed, she felt a return of her fear; the shops, their windows dark and uninviting, the market traders, a tall church steeple, other run-down buildings, public houses, fancy restaurants, these at least had lanterns outside, banks... so much to see and take in that Emma felt bewildered. How would she manage here? It was so big, so... busy, with never-ending noise. The cab had to slow down once to avoid the spilled load from a wagon. Barrels had rolled off and one had split open, and the stink of its contents was foul. Emma glanced out of the cab window and saw what looked like bones and offal scattered on the ground, but it was already nearly dark. She heard the cab driver swear, but then he was past and, a little further on, he finally came to a halt.

'It's just down the road, the house yer want,' he told her as she hesitated to get out, for it was not a pleasant area from what Emma could see. The houses were terraced; their bricks looked grey and grimy, as did the pavements. Some buildings at the end of the road appeared to be warehouses and there were no shops or market traders, only a child playing and a dog hunting in the filthy gutters.

Emma got out and looked at him. She checked her paper. 'This isn't the address I gave you.'

'Walk to the end of the street – it's just round the corner. I ain't goin' there fer a shillin'...'

With that, he gave a jerk on his horse's reins and Emma had to step back or get knocked over. She felt like weeping as she looked about her. What an awful place to live! Butts Lane with all its faults had been a king to this!

Blinking back her tears, Emma walked to the end of the street and looked. She saw a sign above a narrow alley. Bakers Lane. Emma's heart sank. It looked even worse than the street she was in, but she had no real choice. As far as she could see, there were no cabs anywhere, nor could she afford to go elsewhere. It was here or nowhere, at least until she could find work; then, once she began to find her way about, she could look elsewhere.

Taking a deep breath, Emma walked towards the narrow lane. She'd been given the number 2 as Peg's house and it was almost at the end of the lane. There were no signs here that Christmas was near, its run-down poverty uninviting. The back of her neck prickled as she walked along the cobbled road, feeling certain that eyes were watching her from behind grimy lace curtains, but she saw no one; every door and window was shut against the night. Ma would be ashamed to live in a place like this, and Emma was suddenly glad she was alone.

She knocked at the door of number 2 Bakers Lane, and, after

a moment, a woman answered the door. She was taller than Emma, thin and heavily pregnant, her fair hair long and caught up in her nape. From behind her came the indignant cry of an infant left on its own.

'Wot yer want then?' the woman demanded, pushing back a wisp of greasy hair; her dress looked clean but old and worn.

'I'm looking for a lodging,' Emma said. 'If you are Peg, Robbie said you might have a room to let.'

'Cheeky bugger!' the woman muttered, but her frown eased. 'Well, you look decent…' She glanced at Emma's hand and then at her face. 'You'd best come in. It's not safe on these streets after dark.' Peg glanced down the lane and gave a little shiver.

Emma stepped hurriedly inside. 'Why isn't it safe?' she asked, feeling ice at her nape.

'Ain't yer 'eard of Jack the Ripper – wot kills women?' Peg asked.

Emma suddenly remembered why the name Whitechapel had seemed so familiar. 'I did read something once,' she said, shocked that she had come to such a dangerous location. 'I think two women had been killed.'

'He's struck again. I reckon it's five now, mebbe more. You won't catch me going on the streets after dark.'

'Why does he kill women? I think the newspaper said one was… well, a woman of ill repute?'

'Prostitutes,' Peg replied. 'Got a grudge against 'em, ain't he?' She sniffed and looked at Emma's hand again. 'It's just you – no husband?'

'I am a widow. Mrs Emma Robinson,' Emma told her. 'I need work too…'

'I'll show you the room…' Peg stood back and allowed her to enter.

The room they stepped into was clearly the parlour, and to

Emma's surprise it was as neat and clean as a new pin. A staircase ran from one corner of the room and Peg led her up to the small landing above. Although only a narrow, terraced house, Emma could see that it extended out to the back.

Peg opened the door at the end of the landing. It was tiny, space only for a single bed, a chest of drawers and a chair beside the bed. The furniture was dark mahogany wood, but it shone with polish and the room smelled of lavender. On the bed was a pale blue and white counterpane and a pillow with a white pillowcase.

'Well,' Peg said belligerently. 'Yes or no.'

'Oh yes, please,' Emma said, then faltered, 'How much is the rent please?'

'Two shillin' fer the room per week – more if yer want feedin'.'

'I will take the room,' Emma said eagerly. She had been nervous about what kind of room she would find that she could afford, but this was clean and neat and perfect for her needs. She thought herself lucky to find it, but perhaps not many women alone would choose to live here, because of the terrible murders. 'I can pay in advance for a month – but I'm not sure about food. I-I don't have much money until I find work.'

'There's a factory hiring round the corner,' Peg told her. 'They make biscuits. It's five shillings a week until yer know what yer doin' – then six if yer do the job proper.'

'Oh – yes, that would suit me fine,' Emma said. It was more than she'd earned as maid to Lady Penrith, but much less than she could earn as a cook. She would have three shillings a week to feed and clothe herself – but nothing to save or send home. She could not manage on that wage forever, but in time, once the child was born, she might be able to find better work. Emma really wanted to go back to being either a cook or a lady's maid, but that wasn't likely to happen, because she had no references to offer a new employer and, without them, she could not apply for such a post. However, in time, she might find a job as a cook in a restaurant or a public house.

Peg held out her hand for the money. 'I'll give yer a bit of toast fer yer tea, Mrs Robinson. I know what it is like to be without a man to bring home his wages – and you're with child by the look of yer.'

Emma looked at her sharply. 'How did you guess? I didn't think it showed yet.'

'It's in yer face – yer eyes,' Peg told her and nodded as Emma counted the eight shillings into her hand, paying her a month in advance. 'I've had five kids and I've still got two; the others died – and this one.' She indicated the unborn baby and sniffed. 'Fred cleared orf and left me after the first three – I've had a couple of blokes since, but once there's a kid involved, they don't want ter know. I worked at the factory until last week, but the old woman what looked after my youngest went and died of a fever. Typhoid, I reckon. So I had to stay home and I need extra coming in... Robbie gives me four bob for his room and board, but it ain't enough...'

'Thank you for taking me in,' Emma said. 'I could pay you two shillings a week – for a bit of toast and a cup of tea at night, if that would help?'

Peg grinned at her. 'It would and all,' she said and held out her hand for another eight shillings. 'I'll give yer toast and marge fer yer breakfast and a mug of tea, and the same when yer come home at night. They let yer have broken biscuits cheap at the factory, but everyone wants 'em, so yer can't alus get any – if yer do, bring 'em back and I'll do a bit of egg or dripping on yer toast fer 'em. The kids like 'em...'

'Oh yes, my brother and sister liked any sweet treats I brought home...'

'Worked at a factory afore then?'

'No, in a cake shop. I helped bake them...' Emma lied, but she dared not tell the truth.

'If yer can cook, yer might get a better job,' Peg said with a nod. 'They're wantin' someone at the Cock and Bull for the Christmas trade – it's just two streets away. I'll take yer there in the mornin' if yer like. I know the landlord. Pete is all right – and he'll give yer a chance if he knows yer stoppin' wiv me.' Peg gave her a cheeky grin. 'Robbie might walk yer home nights when you've done work, to protect yer. If yer earn extra, yer can pay me more fer yer tea...'

Emma thanked her and Peg left her to settle the child who was screaming her head off. Emma still didn't much care for the situation of her lodgings, but her sensible side told her she was lucky. Peg seemed honest and friendly, and she could have done much worse. It might be that they would become friends, for both were women on their own and both had a child on the way. Peg's would be born sooner than Emma's, but it might be a bond between them. If she could make friends, life wouldn't be so bad. Besides, she didn't have much choice until she earned some money and could look for somewhere in a better area.

As Emma unpacked her bag and put the contents away in the chest of drawers, she knew that she must be satisfied with her lot. Life in the Dales had been very different, but she was wanted for murder now – or attempted murder at the very least – and she did not believe that she could ever go home. Perhaps one day she could find a place for her and her family to live and be happy again, but it would take years to get enough money together to even think of renting a home of her own. Until then, she must do whatever she needed to survive.

27

Just as Tor had feared, Mack was caught as he tried to steal from Red's cabin. After weeks at sea, they had slid into the tiny cove under cover of darkness, and the order to unload the small boats onto the beach was given. In all the bustle and noise, Mack had taken the chance to slip down to the captain's cabin and was caught trying to force the lock of Red's sea-chest. He'd been seen and Red had followed him. Mack started to bluster, but his words died as he saw his fate in the other man's eyes.

'I don't like thieves,' Red said, his voice low and dangerous. 'You'll wish you were never born when I've...' Before he'd finished speaking, Mack lunged at him in desperation, ducking under his arm as Red swung a heavy baton at him. Red roared in anger, but Mack was swift; scrambling up the narrow ladder, through the hatch, he ran across the deck and jumped into the sea.

Tor saw his desperate leap and knew what had happened, cursing the foolish man for what would possibly be a terrible end to his life. Not many could survive in the icy seas like this, for the surf was high and the tide strong, and it was bitterly cold, the salty air stinging flesh and turning noses and fingers red. He turned as Red came up to him.

He'd followed Mack on deck at a slower pace, for he'd known there was no escape for the would-be thief. He stood watching the man swim away. 'If anyone sees that bugger again, I want him,' Red roared his anger at Mack's escape. 'He's a dead man if I get him.'

'Shall I shoot him?' one of the smugglers asked him, raising his rifle and aiming it in the direction of Mack's head, bobbing up and down in the surf as it crashed against the shore.

'Do you want to bring the law down on us?' Red muttered. 'He didn't take anything. I saw him go down and followed. I knew he would try something, for I never trusted the bugger.'

Watching the scene as he supervised the unloading of precious casks, Tor could only be glad that Mack had got away. He hadn't been paid so he had no money and must wait in hiding until he could get a ship – one bound for America, if he followed his dream of finding gold. He'd been a fool to try to steal from Red, and Tor was glad he hadn't agreed to throw in his luck with the man he'd once thought might become a friend. Mack couldn't show his face here again. If he survived the pull of these rough seas, he would need to run for his life, as Red would surely kill him if he caught him. On a day like this, his chances were next to nil.

When all the cargo was unloaded, Tor walked across to Red, who was glaring at the men on the beach as they loaded his cargo onto pack-ponies and led them towards a secret cave, which was where the contraband was stored before its journey to wherever Red decided to sell it. Until then, armed men would guard it day and night.

'What now?' Tor asked as the other man turned to look at him, his frown easing slightly.

'You'll be paid wages tonight at my inn, as will the others,' Red told him. 'You'll wait for your profits until we've sold the cargo.'

'You'll not take it to the Dales?'

'Nay, I'll keep clear for a while, mebbe for good,' Red said. 'I've plenty of willing customers nearer. Stay close and I'll send for you when we're ready to transport it. It has become too dangerous to trade further afield in these modern times.'

'Aye – but what do I do in the meantime?'

Red shrugged. 'Please yourself – there might be work at the mine. It belongs to a man named Sir Robert Helman, but his foreman is a devil. I'd tell him you were a cousin, but then he'd tell you to go to Hell!' Red roared with laughter. 'You're a man, find your place here, Tor – but if you want your profits stay near until I need you.'

Tor's hands balled at his sides. He longed to strike the other man, but held his temper. He would be paid first and then decide what he wanted to do next. Depending on what profit he made, he would try to send something to Ellie and ask if she'd had word of Emma – but he would need to find somewhere he could safely have letters delivered. He was still a wanted man, as far as he knew, for the excisemen must still be looking for the smugglers.

Looking about him, he could see little but the cliffs and a small village clustered above them. He would be known for a stranger here, but he had scant choice but to do as he was told – for the moment.

* * *

Tor found lodgings with one of the crew's mother, a sharp-tongued woman who berated her son for bringing a stranger to her house, but gave him a mug of ale and a bowl of stew with a chunk of fresh bread. He paid her with a florin the next morning but thought that he would try to find pleasanter lodgings when he could.

After walking round the small village, and discovering there was little here but the inn and a few cottages, apart from the big house set in walled grounds with high gates, he realised how important Red was to the people here. There was no employment apart from the mine, and Red's ship. A handful of men worked for him when the ship went sea-fishing, the others up at the mine, though he'd been told that most of the miners lived further along the coast from Beam Head, as the rugged cove was named, in a larger village, and walked the five miles each way every day. The money earned from smuggling might mean the difference between a comfortable life with a few luxuries, like butter, or a bit of meat, and starvation for these families, unless they left their homes and found work in one of the bigger towns, like Truro or Penzance.

Talking to some of the older men he discovered sitting on the beach mending nets, Tor learned that there were three other large houses in the district, and a few farms, but the villagers relied on its mine and Red Tikka for their employment. One or two men and a few girls gained employment at the houses, and there was a blacksmith and a farrier, as in most villages, but they employed only one man each.

Tor realised there was nothing for him here, unless he was taken on at the mine, but if the mine foreman hated Red Tikka, he was hardly likely to take on one of his men, or to grant him leave when he was needed to help transport the contraband. He walked the five miles into the next village, discovering there were two inns: the Risley Arms and the King's Head, the latter having a room to hire; one small shop that sold everything, from a bar of carbolic soap to fisherman's boots, a cobbler, a dress-maker and a market once a week.

Risley village reminded Tor of his home, though Penrith Scar did not boast a shop, and he decided to take the room, paying six shillings in advance, which was a large chunk of the ten guineas he'd been paid for his work on board ship. With so little in his pocket, it was imperative that Tor found work swiftly, and he cursed the men who had stolen his money belt. The stones in his boot might or might not be diamonds; he had no idea of their value or where he could have them appraised. Jonathan would have known – but that life was behind him. If he wrote to him, it could bring the law on Tor here. To have the stones cut, if they were diamonds, would cost money, but when he had it, perhaps he would take a trip to London.

* * *

The following morning, Tor presented himself at the mine office and asked if they were hiring. A tall, thickset man, almost his own height, stared him in the eyes for a few seconds, then shook his head.

'I've no work here for a stranger,' Gar Willaby grunted. 'Why should I take you when there are other, local men looking for work?'

'I've worked in a mine before…' Tor had thought his story out before he came, remembering his friend's stories. 'In America – and up north for a while.'

The other man stared at him a moment longer, then shook

his head. 'You don't look like a miner – and there's no work to be had...' he began, but even as he spoke, there was an ominous rumble from the mine and, as both men turned their heads to look, a cloud of dust belched from the mine entrance.

'You've had a fall,' Tor said and, not waiting for approval, started to run towards the mine.

'Where the hell do you think you're going?' Gar Willaby called after him.

'There will be men trapped,' Tor muttered but didn't turn his head. He reached the mine entrance just as two men came stumbling out, choking and gasping. 'Are men trapped?' Tor demanded of them, because he knew the importance of getting to the men as quickly as possible.

'Aye, at least ten...' one of them choked. 'Some of the others are trying to clear the blockage, but I came for help... I'll show you.'

'Come on then,' Tor said and grabbed a pick lying at the feet of the other survivor, who was gasping for breath. 'Let's see how many we can save.'

'Jack...' the man said his name. 'My brother Bob is still down there.'

'Tor...' Tor said, forgetting he'd meant to give a false name, but there was no time now to regret or worry about the past. Men's lives were at stake, and he was at heart a miner. When an accident happened, there was only one thing that mattered.

* * *

Tor staggered from the mine some five hours later, his face blackened, hands bruised and bleeding, but even as he collapsed on the ground outside, exhausted by the choking fumes of gases released in the fall, and the hard physical work, he was triumphant. They had worked as a team, with Tor directing the men, warning them to take care, because they couldn't afford another fall and he could see the roof was unstable; it was the old problem, no proper maintenance.

Somehow, the men had recognised authority and experience and they'd done as he suggested, working in single file, with him at the head, passing the debris back down the line from hand to hand. It had taken all Tor's strength to break some of the huge rocks with the pick, and then move them, but gradually, piece by piece, they'd managed to make a hole that a man could wriggle through, and one by one, all the miners had emerged. Three were badly hurt and needed to be pushed and pulled, then carried over a colleague's shoulder out of the fetid, choking air. The rest were relatively unhurt, though coughing and spluttering as they emerged.

It was several minutes before Tor realised that most of the village women had gathered round. As he came back to himself, recovering his breath and his strength, he could hear the cries of relief from the women as they went to their men, blessing God for their deliverance. Then, suddenly, a man's voice said, 'It ain't God you should be thanking – but this man, though I know not his name...'

Tor was too busy breathing the clean sea air to realise that everyone was staring at him, then, as he raised his head and looked about him, he saw that everyone's gaze was centred on him.

'What?' he asked, pushing himself to his feet. 'It was working together that saved your men.'

'Aye, lad, we knows that,' one of the older men said, grinning at him. 'But you led the way and showed us how to do it safely. The last time we had a fall, it was twelve hours or more afore they got to them and they were dead – three good men. All because he did nothing until it was too late...' His gaze went to the mine manager, accusing and angry.

There was a murmur of agreement from all round, and their eyes turned in the direction of their foreman.

Gar looked at them, muttering something no one could hear, then said, 'There will be no work until we can make that tunnel safe again... so you may as well go home.'

'You need better maintenance work.' Tor spoke without hesitation. 'That roof wasn't properly supported – if you're having too many rockfalls, it will be the problem.'

'Explosions can happen at any time,' Gar said, his cheeks red with suppressed fury.

'Aye, they can,' Tor agreed. 'But if the mine is in good repair, you've more chance of getting to your men – and this wasn't an explosion. I could see where the wood had rotted and given way...'

'Why don't you clear off, back where you came from?' Gar snarled. 'We don't want interference from strangers...'

Tor stood looking at him for a moment, scorn on his face. 'On your head be it next time you cause a man to lose his life for your carelessness...' he said and began to walk away, but then another voice – a voice of authority – rang out.

'Hold a moment, sir. I would have a word with you, if you will spare me your time – and I would offer you food and drink up at the house – and any of you men that need a drink or medical attention. Please follow me now and my housekeeper will see to your needs.'

Tor noticed that those men wearing caps took them from their heads and bowed, and the women curtsied respectfully to the man on the black horse. It was evidently the mine owner, Sir Robert Helman.

Sir Robert brought his gaze back to Tor. 'Will you come, sir?

And you'd better come too, Gar. There can be no work here until the problem is solved and I need to discover the truth of these falls; there have been too many for comfort.'

'I will come,' Tor said, meeting his eyes. 'And my name is Tor Hardy...'

28

Peg's baby was coming. It was past midnight and she'd been in pain for hours. Emma had found her screaming on the kitchen floor when she got back from work that evening. Emma's luck had been in when she'd turned up at Peg's front door six weeks previously, and she'd found work at the pub just two streets away, as a cook. Hired for the Christmas period, she'd been kept on afterwards because the customers liked her food. It was simple fare, fresh bread, pies, tarts and stews or soups – working men's food; the kind she'd learned to cook at her mother's knee.

So, she was grateful to Peg, and when she'd found her in pain, Emma had helped the other woman upstairs to her bed. She'd placed old papers and torn sheets under her, ready for when Peg's waters broke and the babe came, and then she'd gone down to heat water and fetch towels and linen for the child. Peg's brother, Robbie, had been sent for the midwife, but as yet he hadn't returned with either the doctor or the midwife.

All Emma knew of childbearing she'd witnessed as her mother gave birth to her little sister, and later at Sarah Davies' side. She'd helped the midwife bring her sister into the world, for it had been a breach birth and Mary Watts had been in a lot of pain. Emma had done what the midwife told her, holding her mother's hand, encouraging her to breathe and then push when the time was right. It was little enough and Emma had no idea what she would do if this was a breach birth, for, though she'd seen the midwife manipulate her mother's babe, Emma wasn't sure she could do it.

However, just as the clock struck one of the morning, Robbie returned with the midwife, who grumbled at being brought from her bed, but soon settled once she was given a mug of porter and saw that Peg was close to giving birth.

After another few hours of encouraging the mother, the baby was finally brought forth and obligingly screamed its head off until wrapped in warm, clean towels and placed in its mother's arms, where it immediately nuzzled at Peg's breasts.

'You've got another girl,' the midwife told her when she'd finished her work and seen both mother and baby comfortable and settled. 'That makes three – time you called a halt, especially with no man to call yer own, Peg.'

Peg sniffed and ignored her, but nodded to Emma, who paid the midwife in coin and then gave her another glass of porter. She drank it down and wished them goodnight, vanishing into the murky alley as abruptly as she'd come.

Robbie told them then that she'd not wanted to come, because it was dark and she feared to walk in Whitechapel, but he'd promised to protect her and in the end she'd agreed. It was nearly dawn when she left and the evil man who stalked the dark alleys by night would surely not strike in daylight. No one could say for certain that they'd seen him; it was thought he used disguises, because the vigilantes that patrolled the area had not seen anyone suspicious, and yet another woman had lost her life in the cruel manner that was Jack the Ripper's trademark.

Emma fetched warm water and washed both Peg and her baby, dressing Peg in clean nightclothes and the baby in a soft white gown she had made for it herself. Peg looked at her baby fondly.

'It was a good day for me when you came to my door, Emma,' she said and smiled. 'Thank you. I think I might have died this time if you hadn't found me.'

'Not a chance,' Emma said. 'Thissen's as healthy as a milk cow...'

Peg went into a peal of laughter. 'You say such funny things, Emma. I reckon they must all be rare-humoured where you come from...'

'Aye, we like a little joke,' Emma agreed, feeling a pang of regret for the folk she'd known. It was three months since she'd arrived in London and her life had been much better than she could have hoped for – mainly because of Peg and her brother.

Robbie brought them fruit home each evening. Most of it was either bruised or too ripe to be sold. Rejected by customers, it made a tasty fruit pie or crumble for their teas. Peg wasn't much of a cook and she'd soon made use of the fact that Emma's cooking was both tasty and economical. So Emma cooked their tea before going to work at the pub and Peg let her share the fruit and anything else the family had. Meat was expensive and there was little of it in the stewing pot, but Emma made sure even a bit of offal or scrag end was tasty. In return, Peg took just the two shillings for her room and nothing for the food. Peg sometimes disappeared for an hour or two during the afternoon and always came back either with money in her pocket or some food. Emma didn't ask where she went or what she did, but accepted the task of caring for Peg's two little girls while she was out as a part of her keep.

Emma couldn't afford to buy newspapers, but she sometimes found one left behind at the pub, and occasionally Robbie would bring home an evening paper. She read them from cover to cover, but had never found another article about Mr Rawlings or herself. It was as if it had never happened, and as weeks and then months passed, Emma began to relax. She hadn't meant to hit her master that hard and perhaps he had recovered. Emma prayed he had, because she didn't want to have the shadow of murder hanging over her all her life. Life was busy and hard, but bearable.

* * *

After the birth of her child, Peg had taken to Emma even more, treating her as one of the family. Emma went to work every evening, continuing though her back ached and her body grew large and ungainly, but they spent much of the day together, talking and becoming friends. Gradually, Emma had settled to her new life. She did not forget those she cared for and wrote to Ellie twice with messages for her family, and she thought often of Tor, but her working life was much as it had always been. At least she had made friends, for she was appreciated at her place of employment. And when, at the beginning of May, Emma's child was born, Peg fetched the midwife to her, cooing over her son when he came kicking and wailing into the world. He was a big baby and caused Emma terrible pain but came quickly so that she was able to smile when he was placed in her arms, exhausted but happy.

'Ain't you the lucky one?' Peg asked with a grin. 'He's a fine big lad and will be a handsome man, I'll swear.'

'He has Tor's eyes,' Emma replied, cradling her child to her breast. She'd suffered to give birth, but it was over and her heart was filled with love. Now she had someone of her own to love and care for – and the babe was the image of his father.

Emma had settled well into her new life. She returned to work four days after the baby's birth and she was strong again, her employer glad to have her back, for his customers had done nothing but complain in her absence, and he was more interested in profits than morals. Peg cared for the babe while Emma was working at night, and she cared for Peg's children when she went out each afternoon. It was convenient for them both and they managed well enough.

Her routine of long hours at work, with her child to care for, washing and cleaning, was hard and exhausting, and Emma struggled to realise how many months had fled since she was forced to leave home. Despite the frightening news of several horrific murders in the surrounding streets, the women killed by having their throats slit and their private parts mutilated, Emma had continued to work and walk home late at night with Robbie as her escort. She had seen nothing sinister, other than the extreme poverty of the area, which had shocked her. Her mother had considered they were poor, but no one in Penrith Scar had lived in such squalor as Emma witnessed here. This part of the city teemed with people, many Irish immigrants, crowded five or six into a single room. The women were shabby, the children had no shoes, and their pinched grey faces made Emma's eyes sting with tears, as she thought of the family she'd left behind, and prayed that they were not starving as were so many of these poor families.

Her heart still ached for all she'd lost, but, over the past months, she'd come to realise that many people lived far worse lives. She'd written to Ellie again after the birth of her son, with news that she was well, and had a letter in return, but of late she had been too busy to send more news and none came her way either.

Peg was fond of saying that Emma was her lucky charm and so it was a shock, when on a certain summer day of 1889, Peg came home from one of her mysterious outings and gave her a strange look. She didn't say anything at first, then, when they'd eaten their meal, and Emma was about to leave for work, she suddenly stood up and threw her arms around her. Hugging her to her ample bosom, she gave a little cry of despair.

'You mustn't go tonight,' she said in sudden passion. 'I was told by someone – he's traced you to London, Emma... the man you nearly killed. He's had agents looking for you for months and now they know you are here. They went to the Cock and Bull, asking questions, and they are going there for you this evening... you'll be arrested.'

Emma's face went white with shock. She sat down, her knees suddenly weak. 'How do you know this?' she asked, too stunned to lie or pretend she didn't understand. 'Who told you?'

Peg looked down, her cheeks red. 'You must have wondered where I go in the afternoons?' Emma nodded but didn't speak. 'Well, he's a man of the law – but he likes me and I give him what his wife won't,' Peg said a little shame-faced as she met Emma's gaze. 'He gives me money and it saves me from going on the streets, and I daresn't do that no more... and the last babe is his, but he doesn't acknowledge it, for he dare not, though he knows it to be true.'

'Oh, Peg. I am sorry. I didn't know,' Emma said, her heart catching with pity for the woman she'd come to love as a friend. 'You should have told me if you couldn't manage. I would have tried to pay you more...'

'You've done your share,' Peg told her. 'My friend is a decent man – he just married the wrong woman. I am happy enough; it is much better than going with any who will pay, especially now.' Peg shivered and averted her eyes from Emma's sympathetic look. 'It's how I live, Emma. I'm not the only one...'

'I know...' Emma shuddered, because if it hadn't been for Peg, it might have happened to her when she had first arrived with little money left in her purse, no home and no prospect of work. Alone on the street, she might have become one of the Ripper's victims, her belly slashed and her child ripped out. She smiled and reached for Peg's hand. 'This friend – he told you my story?'

'What he knew of it,' Peg confirmed. 'Because that man didn't die; the official word is that you are wanted for assault but not murder – but your master wants to find you. He has hired private investigators to trace you and they have now, to the pub, but they don't know you live here. Your friends haven't betrayed you.' Tears trickled down Peg's cheeks. 'You have to leave, Emma – go now before they discover where you are staying.'

'Your friend hasn't told them?'

'No, because he wanted to protect me – and himself. He can't be seen to know me – but he gave me warning.' Peg sniffed hard. 'I don't want you to go, Emma. But you can't stay here... they might arrest me, too.'

'Yes, they might,' Emma said regretfully. 'I'd best leave at once... before someone tells them where I am.'

'Have you got any money?'

'I've saved a pound or two,' Emma replied, her eyes smarting with the tears she was fighting. Her wage at the pub had been more than twice what she'd been offered at the factory, and despite giving Peg extra sometimes, she had more now than when she'd arrived in London.

'Where will you go?' Peg asked. 'I swear I won't tell, Emma.'

'I can't tell you because I don't know...' Emma felt a wave of helplessness sweep over her. If her former master was so determined to find her, he would do so wherever she went – which meant it was only a matter of time before she was found and arrested. She'd used a false name and told no one where she'd come from, but somehow his clever agents had traced her. Emma supposed that her Yorkshire accent had betrayed her. The agents couldn't be sure until they caught her, but then, once they had her, she would be identified, tried and imprisoned. She would lose her child and her liberty, perhaps even her life.

'Why don't you go to that friend in York?' Peg asked her. 'They won't think you'd do that – and if they ask me, I'll tell them you spoke of visiting Liverpool.'

'You might get in trouble when they discover you lied...' Emma said, looking worriedly at her.

'Nah, I shall only say you spoke of it – they can't prove I lied. I'll make them drag it out of me.' Peg wiped her face on her sleeve. 'I shall miss you, Emma – but you have to leave now. If they ask at the Cock and Bull, someone will send them here...'

Emma nodded, then turned and ran upstairs. She hurriedly packed her belongings into the bag she'd arrived with, but had to fill another small one with her son's things. She slung one over her shoulder and the other over her back, and then took her son into her arms.

Emma left the house by the front door. Peg stood there and watched her walk away, then closed the door and went back inside. Tears almost blinded Emma as she walked swiftly away. She had thought herself lucky to find a home, and now she had to run again. London was no longer safe for her. Nowhere was. Eventually, they would find her, so she might as well return to Ellie and York. Yes, if it was inevitable that she would be found, she would go to York. At least she had a friend there... perhaps Ellie would look after her son if she was arrested.

Her mind made up, Emma reached the railway station. Despite her fears, no one had followed her. Her arms were aching from carrying the weight of her child combined with the bundles on her back. However, she bought a ticket for York, waited for some minutes for the train to arrive and then boarded. No one called out or came after her – but she knew she would only be safe for a time. At least she could spend that time close to someone she cared for...

* * *

Once safe in York, Emma found herself a room not far from the railway station in a small hotel that catered for folk who came to spend a few days sightseeing and wanted a hotel close to the railway that would carry them up as far as Carlisle. It was very different from the first time she'd visited York; then she'd felt lost and unsure, but now she was used to the noise of busy streets and knew that she could find work. She would have to change her name again, but lying came more easily now. Her head raised, Emma knew that she would not run again. If she was traced and arrested, she would ask Ellie to take her son, at least until her mother could. Then she would stand in court and tell her story. Surely, someone would believe her! It would break her heart to part with her beautiful son, for she loved him with all of her heart, but at least he would be safe with Ellie.

She had called him after her lover and father, but his full name would be Torquil James Hardy, for she had decided to take Tor's name. She would not hang her head in shame; had it not been for another's perfidy, she would now be Tor's wife. It was her right and her pride to use Tor's name.

She gave her name at the hotel as Emma Hardy. Paid a night's rent in advance and, leaving her possessions in the room, went in search of her friend Ellie. When she reached the fine house in Micklegate, she discovered that the knocker was off the door and it looked as if it was closed, with all the blinds drawn. She knocked at the door, getting no answer, but as she was turning away, a man spoke to her.

'They've gone back to America,' he said. 'The house is empty until it is let again.'

'Oh... thank you.' Emma's heart sank. 'Do you know if their servants went with them?'

'No idea, ma'am,' he said, tipped his cap to her and walked on.

Emma turned away sadly. She had been counting on Ellie to help her find work, but there was nothing she could do now but search for employment herself – and, importantly, someone who might look after her son while she worked. The prospect no longer frightened her; in London, she had found work easily. It could surely not be too hard here, for there was none of the grinding poverty she had seen in Whitechapel.

Returning to the hotel, Emma fed and changed her son; then, strapping him into a shawl that she wore tied across her breast, she went out and purchased an evening paper. It was an expense she could do without, but it might have advertisements of jobs on offer in York. She couldn't afford to eat meals at the hotel and she would have to look for a cheap room elsewhere soon, but her most pressing need was work. She bought some chips and a portion of peas for her supper and ate them on her way back to the hotel. When in her room again, with Torquil sleeping on the bed beside her, she sat and turned to the newspaper columns advertising work. The months she had spent in

London had made Emma stronger and given her valuable experience.

She discovered that the firm of Terrys, who made fine chocolates in York, was asking for women to work in their factory. It said that applicants must be clean and honest, and Emma nodded to herself. Even when she lived in the Dales, she'd heard that the owners were good people who paid their workers well. It was there she would try first for work – it just left the question of who would look after her son...

* * *

The next morning, Emma joined the small queue of women wanting to apply for jobs at the factory. She was one of the first and was fortunate enough to be taken on at a wage of just less than she'd earned as a cook in London – her wage as a quality controller would pay her eight shillings a week. It was enough for Emma to find a little home of her own, if she was lucky enough to discover one for rent – and then perhaps to send for her mother to come to her. That was a risk and she would have to consider it – but if her mother was careful, it could be done. Mary could buy a ticket for Settle and get off there, then buy another ticket for Leeds. If people still looked for Emma, they might be confused by the little subterfuge.

It was as she was walking away, pleased that she had found a job so easily, she heard her name called and for a moment her blood ran cold. Her heart raced, for who could know her – and would they betray her? Then she noticed a woman standing almost at the end of the queue and her eyes watered as she saw it was Ellie.

Emma went to her at once, smiling and crying as they embraced. 'I called at the house, but it was closed...'

'Aye. The master and mistress were recalled to America, because of family problems. They asked me to go with them, Emma, but I refused – that's why you see me here in this queue...'

'Are you looking for work?' Emma asked. 'I think I got one of the last jobs – they aren't paying what you're used to, Ellie...'

'I know that, lass, but needs must. I haven't been able to find a cook's job,' Ellie told her. She left the queue. 'I'll try elsewhere another day.' She smiled at Emma. 'Where are you staying? Come home with me and tell me, Emma...'

Emma went with her. They spoke carefully until they reached the small terraced house by the river; it was central, not far from the boundary wall and the Lenton Tower. Although nothing much outside, within, it smelled of beeswax and was clean, recently decorated with flock wallpaper, and as neat as a pin. 'Do you live here? Is it expensive?' Emma asked, looking about her with pleasure at the feeling of home it gave her. 'I need something like this...'

'It is six shillings a week,' Ellie said. 'That is why I need to find work quickly...'

'How many bedrooms does it have?' Emma asked as she went into the small kitchen. It was much nicer and the rooms were bigger than those at Peg's. Peg had kept her parlour neat, but the rest of the house had been untidy, but with three children's washing hanging around the kitchen, that wasn't surprising.

'Two decent ones and a boxroom. I only use the one – Ruby went with the mistress...'

'She always wanted a different life,' Emma said. 'I say good luck to her.'

'And what of you, Emma? Did you write to me these past three months? I would have written, but I must have lost your address when I left my employ, for I could not recall nor find it, and, of course, your letters would not reach me once my employer's house was closed.'

'No – not since I told you I had a son,' Emma replied with a smile. 'I was lucky and found a friend, Ellie – but life was so busy, and then I had to leave quickly. Mr Rawlings has people searching for me.'

'I heard he'd recovered and was back in the Dales,' Ellie told her, looking anxious. 'I am sorry you were forced to leave your good friend, though I am glad you no longer live in that terrible place, Emma. I worried for you – all those wicked murders. How many now? I have lost count...'

'I'm not sure. Some folk say that it couldn't be just one man – but I know that more than eleven murders of women have happened in just over a year, and they were so terrible, Ellie. Peg knew someone who had witnessed one of the bodies – a police officer – and he said it made him vomit, for he had never seen the like. Whoever this man is, he must be evil.'

'I pray to God he will be caught,' Ellie said, shaking her head. 'Those poor women...'

'Aye, it must have been awful for those he killed.' Emma shuddered at the thought of their suffering. 'Please, do not speak of it, Ellie. Peg and I preferred to try to forget it.'

Ellie looked at her pale face. 'As long as you are well and here, we can forget such horrors, my love – but will you be safe here?'

'I am hoping they will waste time looking for me in London and elsewhere,' Emma replied, then lifted her head proudly. 'If they do come for me, I shan't run again, Ellie. You would take my little one if need be?'

'Yes, Emma, I would – and be glad to care for him.' Ellie was silent for a moment, then, 'Your mother writes to me now and then and asks if I've heard anything of you.'

'She is still in her cottage? He hasn't forced her to leave?'

'She says he calls and asks her if she has heard from you, but she says no – for 'tis true. You have not written to her, Emma. She writes you must have been mistaken in his meaning, for he is kind and says he wants to help you – and no, he has not turned her from her cottage. She complains that you do not write to her, Emma.'

'For her sake and mine. My letters might have been traced. I could not be sure she would still be in the cottage.'

'She's there – but she works now. The vicar's housekeeper left and she has taken on cooking his meals and a bit of cleaning.' Ellie looked at her then. 'Mary said I should keep Tor's money for you and your child. Apparently, Mr Crossly gave her some money and told her to go to him if she needed anything. I think she might marry again.'

'Ma – marry?' Emma stared in astonishment. 'I never thought she would do that... Who does she think of wedding?'

'The vicar, I believe,' Ellie told her. 'Mary says he is tired of his housekeepers leaving and has offered her a permanent home as his wife. I think your sister is to live with them – but your brother is to be sent to boarding school.'

'Pete won't like that,' Emma said. 'I was going to ask if they wanted to live with me, if I could find a house here, but it would be better for Ma to be his wife. She wouldn't have to worry...'

'Aye, there's that – and you're no longer hunted as a murderer, Emma. I was going to write and tell you, but I've been doing whatever work I could find, scrubbing and the like, while I tried to find a decent job, and, as I told you, I lost your address somehow. Apparently, the case against you has been dropped for lack of evidence.'

'I ran away. Is that not evidence enough?' Emma looked at her in surprise. 'Did Mr Rawlings not accuse me?'

'I don't know, Emma. I did see a short notice in the paper to say you were no longer looked for, but I've seen nothing more.'

'If the case has been closed – why does he still hunt me?' Emma asked, frowning. 'I was warned he had men looking for me and I was to be arrested that night.'

Ellie frowned. 'Not by the law, Emma. Yet he might have his own plans for you – I fear what he might do to you if he caught you.' Ellie looked at her anxiously. 'I suspect he means revenge...'

'Why would he seek to harm me? He must know it was his own fault for trying to force me.'

'Mayhap, he has his reasons,' Ellie replied and shook her head. 'Tell me, what of your son – where is he?'

'The wife of the hotelier where I am staying told me she would care for him while I sought work.' Emma nodded. 'I must go and fetch him for she will weary of looking after him. May I return later with him?'

'You do not have to ask...' Ellie hesitated, then, 'Why don't you bring all your things and move in with me, Emma? The rent is easy for two – and I'll find better work soon.'

Emma's face lit up. 'Do you mean it? Can I really live here with you? That would be wonderful...'

'It would be,' Ellie said and reached for her hands. 'When you left York, I feared we might never meet again, and I've missed you, Emma. I think we can have a good life, sharing our home. I've no one of my own and you are more than just a friend to me; I see you as the daughter I might have had.'

'Oh, Ellie, yes! My dearest friend. I would love to make my home with you. I'll go now to fetch my son,' Emma said and hugged her. 'Thank you! It looks as if my luck is turning, Ellie. I just have to hope Mr Rawling's agents do not trace me here...'

'Don't you worry, I'll not let them near you. If he wants to see you, he must come here himself. If there's no case against you, he can't harm you, Emma. If he tries force, I'll take my broom to him.'

Emma laughed, feeling free for the first time in months. She was not a murderer after all. Why her former master had not pressed charges for assault against her, she did not know, but could only be relieved that her life was improving.

* * *

Emma moved in with Ellie that afternoon and the hotelier refused to take the shilling she owed for another night. The hotel keeper's wife smiled at her. 'Tha needs it more than we do, lass. Keep it and good luck to the pair of you.' Tears stung her eyes, for the friendliness of the folk here made her feel she was home again. London had been an experience, but she was glad to be back where she belonged.

'We are moving in with a friend,' Emma told her. 'And I got the job, Mrs Tomas. Thank you so much for looking after Torquil for me...'

'That's such a big name for a little boy,' the kindly woman laughed.

'Oh, we'll call him Torrie for short,' Emma replied, 'after his father.'

She smiled as she walked away, carrying her possessions and her child. At last, she had a settled home and a decent job. Perhaps she would be safe now and could stop looking over her shoulder...

29

Stephen awoke from the terrifying dream. He was soaked in sweat and for a moment as he lay there, the scene that had woken him remained vivid in his mind. A woman was lying dead at his feet and her blood was on his hands. Her throat was slashed, her belly cut open and her entrails lying on her shoulder. As he stared at his victim, he saw that she had a face he knew – Emma Watts.

'No!' he screamed in fear at what he had done. He was the Ripper and he'd killed the only woman he'd ever loved. 'I didn't want to...' he wept, but then his head began to clear and he realised that it was all a terrible dream. He was lying in his own bed in Penrith Manor and he'd killed no one.

Why was he haunted by these dreams? Dreams that were sometimes so real that he believed he had done those terrible murders that the whole country spoke of. Women were frightened to walk the streets of London alone, and vigilantes now patrolled them – yet still the Ripper had managed to kill eleven women... if one man had killed them all. Some people thought that improbable – that some were copycat murders. Despite letters to the press from someone claiming to be the Ripper, no one had a clue who he was; there were rumours and whispers, but no one knew.

Stephen thought the authorities looked in the wrong place, among the poor Irish immigrants and others of ill repute. The Ripper was surely an educated, clever man – a man with some knowledge of anatomy and disguise. He must adopt other disguises, for how else would he escape them? The vigilantes were stopping suspicious-looking men and questioning them – but would they question a young lordling out for a night of pleasure, or a man of politics?

Stephen threw off his nightmare. He could not be the Ripper, even though he became him in his dreams; he had not even been in London for half of the murders... and yet in his mind, increasingly hazy since that bitch hit him, he sometimes seemed to remember things so ghastly they turned his stomach.

Dousing his head with cold water from the jug on his washstand, Stephen began to think clearly. It was just another of his nightmares, brought on by lurid newspaper reports – and his thoughts of what he would do to Emma when he got her. His agents were searching for her and would bring her to him secretly once they had captured her – as they would.

Stephen's fingers curled as he glanced at his reflection in the mirror. The scars of the wound she'd inflicted were not all, for he'd had a slight stroke as he lay ill and his mouth had twisted to one side, his eyelid drawn tight. She had disfigured him, the bitch, and he could not wait to get his hands on her – he would make her suffer.

* * *

'You found her and then let her slip through your fingers? Damn you for your incompetence, man! I told you to be careful. I want her brought back to me – alive and unharmed.' Stephen Rawlings glared at the man who cringed before him later that morning.

'I was careful, sir,' the dejected agent replied. 'I knew where she worked and I was waiting that evening with a cab ready to drug her and bring her back here – but, somehow, she found out. Someone told her and she slipped away. By the time I learned where she lived, she had gone – to Liverpool so the woman she'd stayed with said...'

'That will be a lie,' Stephen snapped, his face suffused with anger. Over his right eye, there was a dark scar where the poker had cut his flesh deeply and there was another at the back of his head; his hair had refused to grow back over it and his mouth and eye revolted him, for they were ugly. His extreme good looks had gone for good, and Emma Watts had done that to him.

His love for her – if ever it had been love – had completely gone and in its place was a cold hatred. He wanted to find Emma and make her suffer. He'd survived and, when questioned about why Emma had attacked him, Stephen had lied, but Mrs Briscoe had told them that Emma had fought back in self-defence and the magistrate, who was a friend of Lord Rawlings, had had the case dropped.

As he'd explained to Stephen, 'If it came out that you had tried to rape the girl, there would be a scandal, and your grandfather particularly wants to avoid that, sir. He still has hopes of a good marriage for you – and lurid stories in the newspaper wouldn't help that now, would they, sir?'

Stephen had cursed but been forced to agree. His grandfather's letter made it clear that he wanted no more scandal and a marriage had been arranged to another merchant's daughter. It was to go ahead very shortly and Stephen's anger grew as the day of his wedding approached. He spent most of his time drunk or close to it these days, his temper on a short rein; often, he lost hours at a time and could not recall where he'd been or what he'd done. The girl he was supposed to marry wasn't ugly and she seemed a decent person, but he cared nothing for her. In fact, all Stephen felt these days was rage. It burned inside him, and dismissing his housekeeper, because she'd spoken against him, had done little to put out the flames of his anger. It seethed within him. He wanted Emma back and he craved his revenge.

All his problems were because of Emma Watts. If he got his hands on her again, he would make her pay. He would take his pleasure and then... he would leave her scarred for life. He would burn her face with a red-hot poker... then set her free to earn her living in the gutter where she belonged. Or maybe he'd do to Emma what the Ripper did to his victims. Stephen's plans grew ever more cruel and bitter as the months passed and she evaded him.

An evil smile touched Steven's lips. Yes, he would make her pay once he got her... He always got what he wanted in the end. If in a saner corner of his mind he knew that once he had his revenge it would turn to ashes, he ignored it. He wanted her. She had hit him with a poker rather than give in to his lusts – so she must suffer. Right and wrong did not enter into it. He wanted Emma in his hands... to see the life drain out of her. Had someone told him that he still cared for her, he would have dismissed them as fools – but there was no one to tell him. Stephen's so-called friends had deserted him, driven away by his temper and sudden rages.

He looked at his agent. 'It's my belief that she will have come home to Yorkshire,' he said, a queer blind look in his eyes as he saw in his mind the face of the woman he craved to punish. 'She has a friend in York. Go and find her – and if you want your wages, make sure that this time you do…'

A tap at the door made Stephen turn as a young woman entered. Sarah Davies. At the moment, she was acting as cook-housekeeper and getting paid well for it. His frown eased, because she was a beautiful woman and she never failed to give him her special smile. A cold smile touched his mouth as he realised that here was a woman he could have for the asking; she cared nothing for his looks, the bitch. He knew her type and she wanted money – like all the sluts. He despised them all. Only Emma had ever touched his heart – she could have saved him with her love, but she'd insulted him.

'Yes, Sarah,' he said, and his voice softened to a caress. 'What was it you wanted?'

'Your lunch is ready, sir. Should we lay two places?'

A hopeful look appeared on the face of his agent, but Stephen dismissed it with a shake of his head. 'I am dining alone today. This gentleman has work to do in York…'

'Very well, sir.' Sarah's eyes met his and the invitation was there.

Stephen felt better than he had in a while. He would wait until the agent had gone and then he would seek out his new housekeeper in the kitchen…

* * *

Sarah's heart beat rapidly. She'd seen the answering glow in her master's eyes and knew he wanted her. Joe would kill her if he ever discovered what she was planning, but Sarah was bored with her life – she wanted pretty things and the money to live as she pleased. If she could persuade Stephen Rawlings to give her some expensive jewellery, she could go to York and sell it – and then she could live as she wished. She would leave the Dales and go somewhere there was some life and excitement, leave her dull husband and the brat she'd borne.

Sarah knew that her husband would never be enough for her. She craved passion and laughter, and Joe was dull. In a town, Sarah would find men who would pay her for what she could give them. For a while, Joe had frightened her when he'd been angry, accusing her of carrying Ike Hanson's child, but after her daughter was born, he had seemed to forget his accusations. Joe doted on the child and was always fussing over her if she caught a chill or had a little cough. He hadn't wanted Sarah to work at Penrith Manor, but she'd reminded him that she might have died if the master hadn't found her – and told him that she would save the money so that they could have a better life, so she left the child with her mother and went to work each day.

'You are an important man, Joe. You should have a big house,' she'd told her husband between kisses. 'If I work for a while, just until the master can hire a new housekeeper and cook, then we can afford lots of nice things.'

Sarah had no intention of spending her wages on a new house in this godforsaken place. She wanted the excitement of York – or perhaps even London. She'd heard a whisper that Emma Watts had gone to London and she envied her.

So she'd smiled at the master, given him that special look that men always understood – and this time he had responded. Sarah was happy as she served the dinner for the housemaid to take into the dining parlour. Sooner or later, he would come asking and she knew what her answer would be...

* * *

Sarah lay beside her husband that night, her heart thudding. She had feared that Joe would want to make love to her and she was so tender that she could not have borne it. Stephen Rawlings had taken without asking. He'd come to her after he'd eaten and he'd just reached for her, locking the kitchen door so that no one could enter. He'd taken her there on the floor and he'd been brutal.

Sarah had revelled in his desire and his prowess. Even Ike had not made her feel the way her master had; the wild, rough loving was just what she craved and she'd bitten back her screams of pleasure, for fear one of the other servants should hear. Stephen had laughed, his eyes bright with desire and pleasure as he took her, not once but twice. Afterwards, he'd given her ten guineas.

'I pay for what I take,' he'd told her coldly. 'Even though you loved it, you bitch.'

Sarah was frightened by his sudden violence. Ike had never hit her, but she had a feeling that this man would if she defied him. Too late, Sarah realised what she had gotten into and regret came like a searing pain. Joe would never forgive this – and she wouldn't put it past this man to tell him, just for the pleasure of hurting Joe and her. Supposing she fell for another child? No, it wouldn't happen! It mustn't!

Once again, Sarah's desire for excitement had led her astray, but this time she did not think it would end with Joe forgiving her – nor did she truly wish it. She would simply have to hoard whatever valuables she could get from her master, and then leave Penrith Scar. She could go to London, where Queen Victoria lived in a big palace and there were lots of rich people, and she would find a way to become rich. Sarah would run away, just as Emma had.

30

Emma was feeling terrible when she returned from work that Friday evening. She'd had a headache for most of the day and the sweet smell of the chocolate had seemed to make it worse, but as she walked home to her son and Ellie, she had begun to feel feverish and dizzy, her throat hurting her so much, she could barely swallow her saliva.

Ellie took one look at her and sent her straight to bed. 'You've caught some kind of a fever, lass,' she said. 'It's a good thing it is the weekend; you can stay in bed and hopefully you will be better by Monday. If not, I'll let them know at the factory.'

Emma protested weakly but knew that she had no choice. She could hardly keep her head up and was glad to just lie in bed and close her eyes. Never in her life had she felt this ill, not even when she'd had the measles as a small child.

'I'll be better soon,' she told Ellie. 'I am so glad you're here – look after Torrie for me, please.'

'Aye, I will, lass,' Ellie promised and brought a warm drink for Emma to swallow, but she could not manage more than a few sips.

'My throat hurts,' she whispered. 'I think I've taken something nasty.'

''Tis just a chill,' Ellie told her to comfort her. 'You'll be better soon.'

Emma nodded and tried to smile, but she was too ill.

So ill did she become that the next day, Ellie sent for the doctor, though they could hardly afford his fees. He took one look at Emma and placed a handkerchief to his mouth and nose, backing away from the bed in horror.

'What is it?' Ellie asked, heart racing in fear as she saw his expression.

'I think it may be diphtheria,' the doctor told her. 'Be careful how you nurse her, madam. Wear a scarf over your face, wash your hands with carbolic and boil everything she touches. If she has it, I doubt you can save her – but keep yourself safe and do not spread it by going out. I will see that soup is sent into you each day. My nurse will leave it at the door.'

'But can you do nothing for her?' Ellie cried, anger and desperation making her voice sharp.

'She is in God's hands now,' he replied piously. 'I can do nothing and must protect myself, for I have many patients. I wish you well, madam, and if God wishes, your friend may recover...'

With that, he took his leave. Ellie stared after him. He had been in such a hurry to leave that he had not demanded a fee – just as well, for he would have had a tongue lashing if he'd had the cheek after giving them no help whatsoever.

Ellie went back to Emma's bedside. Her friend was burning up with fever and complaining of a sore throat, but her words were slurred and barely discernible. Wiping tears from her cheeks, Ellie rolled up her sleeves. She had once nursed a kitchen maid through a fever and seen her recover. If this was the diphtheria, Emma would likely die, but in the meantime, Ellie would do all she could for her. She loved Emma as the daughter she would never have and her heart was heavy.

Looking down at the girl's flushed face, Ellie made a vow. If Emma died, she would take her son as her own – but she would fight with all her strength to save her and she would pray.

* * *

Mary Watts read the letter from York twice. Ellie had told her that her daughter was sick and like to die of it.

> *If you would see Emma once more, you must come as soon as you receive this. I fear even then it may be too late, though your grandson does not take it. I am finding it hard to manage alone, though I will never desert her, and I beg you to come to her if you can.*
>
> *Your friend Ellie.*

Mary's eyes were wet with tears. She had always feared this. Her Emma would die and she would never see her again...

Hearing her husband's voice in the next room, Mary hastily thrust the letter into the kitchen fire. How she wished she had never married him! He was a cold, selfish man and she'd been a fool, driven by her constant fear of being alone. She had done her daughter great harm by burning the letter from Tor Hardy, and now she was being punished for her sin.

Mary could never tell him that she'd had this letter. He would be angry that Ellie had written to her of Emma – he thought her a sinful girl and had forbidden Mary to have anything more to do with her. Mary had learned to her cost that he was an unforgiving man. She'd thought that marriage would bring her security, but he treated her little better than a servant and she had no rights or say in her life.

Her husband would never give her the fare to York in such a cause. Mary had nothing of her own, for her husband had taken what little she had when they wed, telling her she had no need of money for he would take care of her and the children. But he was mean and tight with his money – and uncaring. He'd sent her son to Leeds to a boarding school, despite her pleas, and her youngest child lived in fear of his scolds. Too late, she'd realised that this marriage meant she was an unpaid servant rather than having a comfortable life with someone who cared for her. She wished with all her heart that she had been brave enough to leave the village and go to York; there she might have found work and been paid for it.

'Mary – did you not hear me call you?' Her husband stood in the doorway glaring at her.

'Forgive me, Henry,' Mary said meekly. 'I was busy and did not hear you.'

'Very well, I shall pardon you,' he said, though his eyes did not soften. 'I trust that my dinner is ready?'

'Oh yes, Henry,' Mary replied meekly. 'I shall serve it at once.'

'Good.' He looked around. 'Where is the child? Not out playing, I hope?'

'No. She did her homework and then went to bed.'

He nodded his approval. 'You heard her prayers, Mary?'

'Yes, Henry. I think she sleeps.'

'That is as it should be...' He looked thoughtful. 'I will keep her with us another year – and then she must be sent into service.'

'She is only seven, Henry.'

'I dare say a place can be found for her. I believe the school mistress needs a girl – We shall see. If she is good and obedient, I may keep her longer – but she will go into service as soon as she is able...'

'Yes, Henry.'

Turning away to serve his supper, Mary blinked away her tears. Her one hope of leaving Penrith had been if Emma sent for her, but she was dying and Mary could not even go to her to say goodbye...

31

'You are certain you've found zinc?' Sir Robert looked at Tor with respect and new hope in his eyes. 'This could make the world of difference, Hardy. When you told me you suspected it was there after the rockfall, I wasn't sure you were right. We've mined tin and copper here since my grandfather's day, but Gar Willaby told me it was almost finished – and I feared for the local men. There is so little work for them here.'

'I caught a glimpse of something I thought might be zinc when I started to clear the rock away,' Tor told him with a smile. Sir Robert had made him his mine manager after sacking Gar, because he'd been horrified at the neglect of safety work in his mine.

'What happened to the money I paid for that work to be done?' he'd demanded from his former manager, and the look in his eyes as he shot a glance of hatred at Tor for exposing him had told Sir Robert all he needed to know. He'd dismissed the man, telling him, when he'd started to bluster and make excuses, that he was lucky to escape being arrested for theft.

'He hadn't been down the mine for years,' Tor said now. 'The men told me he was frightened of it, because he'd once been trapped – yet how he could neglect the safety of others, knowing, as he must, how it felt to be trapped…?' He shook his head. 'I'll not let you down, sir. I've learned much from my partner Jonathan about minerals, and we might also find arsenic and even silver if we look for them. Besides, there is still enough copper in the eastern tunnels to last a few years, and we'll start exploring other possibilities when we have enough men. We'll need to take more men on…'

Sir Robert was aware of Tor's past, including his recent trip with Red Tikka. Tor had decided to be honest with him when he was offered the job as mine manager. At first, Sir Robert had looked at him strangely, but when he understood the truth, he'd not hesitated.

'I know Red well,' he'd told Tor. 'Indeed, I know that some winters folk round here might well have starved, had it not been for the extra money they earned with him.' He'd given Tor a wry smile. 'I'm a justice of the peace – but when it comes to smuggling, I turn a blind eye, unless I am forced to act. I can't tolerate murder, but Red has stopped short of that, to my knowledge. The smuggling has gone on for centuries past, and my grandfather went out with them himself as a young man. I fear it becomes more dangerous in these modern times. The railway means the excisemen can move quickly, and the telegraph can tell men miles away where the smugglers are to be found. If Red continues, he will be caught and hung.'

Tor had agreed with him, for he too believed the days of smuggling were over – at least the old ways, though there were other ways, less risky.

'Red needs me to help transport his goods,' Tor had told him then. 'I'll get nothing if I refuse, and I could do with the money if I want to fight for justice – to clear my name, if it be possible.'

Sir Robert's eyes had twinkled at that. 'I dare say I might be able to pull a few strings,' he'd told Tor. 'In the matter of the contraband, I'll let Red know that I'll take all his brandy and wines – silks, too, if he has them. My daughter Jane is to be wed in the spring to the son of a lord – and a pretty penny that will cost me.' He'd winked. 'Some free traders wine and brandy will help with the wedding and Jane will need her silks. She is in London now with her aunt, buying new gowns and meeting his relations.' The smile had gone from his eyes then. 'My dear wife died last year. I shall need a housekeeper once Jane is wed, for she saw to the servants and kept house for me...'

'I am sorry you lost your wife, sir. It is hard to lose the one you love.'

Sir Robert had looked at him then. 'You think of the girl you were forced to abandon. Will you marry her – if your name is cleared?'

'If she will have me,' Tor had replied.

'She'll have you if she loved you,' Sir Robert had affirmed. 'Will you go back to your mine and your Dales if we can clear this slur from your name – and I doubt not it can be done.'

Tor had hesitated a moment, then, 'Perhaps not, Sir Robert. Jonathan does not need me to run our mine – and I would stay here, at least until we have you in profit again. Give you time to find a new man you can trust.'

'Would you stay for good if I made you my partner?'

'A partner?' Tor had met his serious eyes. 'Nay, sir. You've no cause to do that – I'll see things right for thissen afore I leave thee.'

'I have no son, though hope of a grandson,' Sir Robert had replied. 'I like you, Tor Hardy. Your honesty appeals to me – and your way of getting things done. As for the mine, it is but a part of my fortune and I run it for the sake of the folk who would starve without the work. I would count it a favour if you'll accept my offer – and have the papers drawn up straight away.'

'Then I thank you and I accept.' Tor had offered his hand and they'd shaken on it. 'You are a good man, Sir Robert, and I would gladly be your partner. I swear you won't regret it.'

'You'll be rich with two mines,' Sir Robert had said, and the humour showed in his eyes. 'Let me sort this little nuisance out for you, Tor, and then you can return to Penrith with your head held high. Marry your lady and bring her back to us...'

'I shall – and thank you for it all my days,' Tor had told him. He smiled at a sudden thought. 'I might just be able to help with the little matter of your housekeeper, too, sir. Emma's friend is the best cook you'll find anywhere, including London.'

'Get her for me and I'll be a happy man.'

* * *

Red roared with laughter when he heard what Sir Robert had said about the contraband. 'Aye, it will save him some guineas on the wedding.' He looked at Tor speculatively. 'Mine manager and partner no less – so you'll not be bothering with smuggling again?'

'It was never my intention, as you know,' Tor replied. 'I'll trade with you and keep your secrets. Don't fear, I won't betray you; it was an experience I enjoyed, but I have other plans.'

'I am changing my own plans as it happens,' Red said, lowering his voice so none could overhear. 'The days of running goods overland are done, for it is too dangerous and we've come close to being caught. I may bring a few barrels for my friends locally – but diamonds are more lucrative and harder to find. I shall make a fortune from them – and, even if they search my ship, they'll not discover them.' He chuckled.

'It is the way of the future – I would share if you would throw in your lot with me. There will always be those who are willing to smuggle, though the nature of the goods may change.'

'If it were not for Sir Robert's offer, I would have taken your hand on it,' Tor admitted. 'But I have a future here with him and it suits me to take it.'

'And what of them up the coast that put you aboard my ship? Will you look for revenge?'

'I want my horse back,' Tor told him. 'I might throw a few punches, but it was my own fault for being a fool.'

Red grinned. 'You'll find your horse at the Bridge Hostelry outside York, where you have oft stabled him – if they haven't got rid of the brute. It was I who sold him – no one else could handle him – and it so happened I had business with the owner, who had journeyed to Whitby to meet me.' He took a purse from inside his jerkin and counted out a hundred guineas. 'Fifty for your horse and the rest is your profit, as I promised.'

Tor accepted the gold and placed it inside his coat. 'I won't thank you,' he said grimly. 'But I won't cross you either.'

'Then we'll part as friends,' Red said and slapped him on the back. 'Now that you're in charge of the mine, can I store goods there if need be?'

'I'll think about it,' Tor replied. 'We're planning further exploration, and it may be dangerous, so at the moment it wouldn't be a good idea. We will talk again when things settle.'

'Aye, we'll talk again, if need be.' He grinned and patted his jerkin, where the smuggled diamonds lived since he'd come ashore. 'Running brandy is a dangerous game and the real money lies elsewhere. If these fetch what I hope, there will be empty cellars in the future.'

'I think the time has come for you to turn your talents in

other directions,' Tor agreed. 'If you continue, they will hang you one day, Red.'

'I've outrun them for years,' Red said, scowling. 'But I've heard they have new ships that might match mine.' He smiled slyly and nodded to himself. 'If they catch me, it might be they'll find only fish next time.' He patted his jerkin again. 'I'll hide these where none will think to look.' For a moment, he frowned. 'The thief who sailed with us had no chance to steal them – but he paid his price in that icy sea. I doubt he could live in a tide like that... and woe betide him if he did.'

'If Mack was lucky enough to survive, we may never know, for I doubt he'll show his face hereabouts. No, he'll be long gone – off to America.'

'He'd best not show his face here, for I don't forgive betrayal!'

'Nor I – but we have dealt well together. I wish you good fortune and prosperity,' Tor said, and they shook hands once more.

* * *

It was on a cold day in January 1890 that Sir Robert gave Tor the news he'd been waiting for. 'The charges against you have been cleared for some months, my friend,' he announced when Tor visited for their daily meeting at the house. 'It took me longer to discover it than I expected, because no proper records had been kept, and there were still notices in York that you were wanted for an unnamed crime, despite the original charge having been dropped for lack of evidence. I was told in confidence that the accusation was laid out of spite by Lord Ravenscroft's son.' He frowned, looking troubled. 'I told you Jane was to marry the son of a lord – but I did not tell you his name. It is Charles Ravenscroft – the man who harmed you, Tor.'

Tor met his eyes. 'Does this compromise our partnership?'

'Nay, for they will not live here – but you must perforce meet on amicable terms at times. Do I ask too much of you, Tor?'

'Nay. If I am bothered it is for your daughter – you cannot persuade her to look elsewhere, sir?'

'She would tell me I was prejudiced against him and it would cause a breach – which would break my heart. I must let her have her way, but if he hurts her – I'll kill him.' He smiled oddly. 'Jane tells me she knows that he used to be wild, but apparently love has tamed him. I suppose it may be true – I pray it is.'

'Then I wish her well of her marriage.'

'And you can accept what he did without thought of revenge?'

'I suspected it,' Tor replied, looking at him thoughtfully. 'I knew that he would try to harm me because I stopped him molesting a young woman when drunk – and when he came at me from behind, I broke his arm.'

'So he thought he'd get you hanged as a rogue?' Sir Robert looked grim. 'I would say keep clear of the man if I thought you needed a warning, Tor – but I know you won't be caught out twice.'

'He deserves that I should break his neck,' Tor said savagely.

'He might – but we don't want you in prison for murder. Nor my daughter a widow too soon.'

Tor laughed. 'I have no intention of it, sir. He meant me harm, but as it happens, he did me a favour, in some ways at least. I still have my property in Penrith Scar. I wrote to my partner Jonathan Crossly and told him I was living in England and trying to clear my name. He could not reply, for I thought it safer to withhold my location.' A frown creased his brow. 'Whether or not Ravenscroft did me serious harm remains to be seen. Jonathan would have spoken to Emma when he received my letter. I hope and believe that Emma may have waited for me, despite that she would not join me when I was a fugitive.'

'Perhaps she never received your letter?'

'I have wondered, for I have sent money to Ellie for her on two occasions since I began working for you, but have heard nothing from her – or Emma.' He met the other man's eyes. 'I count it good fortune to have met you, sir – and believe luck is with me.'

'Aye, you'll have two mines now.' His friend and partner laughed. 'Thank you. I was concerned that you might wish revenge on Ravenscroft and for my daughter's sake I would not have it so.'

'I would not make trouble for you, sir – nor harm your Jane.'

'You should call me, Robert,' his friend told him. 'You are becoming the son to me that I never had, Tor. You should go back to Penrith, find Emma and wed her – then return, just in time for my Jane's wedding.'

Tor laughed, because Jane was a lovely girl with an infectious smile, very like her father, and her wedding would be the biggest event the local folk had ever seen. 'I'd like that, Robert...' He hesitated, then, 'You wouldn't happen to know the name of a good jeweller – one that can cut diamonds?'

Sir Robert's eyebrows went up as Tor produced the two stones he'd transferred from the heel of his boot to his inner jacket pocket. 'I've not seen an uncut diamond before – how did you come by them?'

'They were taken in payment of a debt,' Tor admitted. 'Five hundred pounds were owed – but they are probably worth less. I needed money in a hurry.'

'Yes, I see – well, good luck with them.' Sir Robert thought for a moment and then wrote a name down. 'I've heard this man in London is the jeweller for cutting gems. Try him. I know him to be honest. I once bought a necklace for my wife from him.'

'Thank you. I shall go first to London, ask at the bank Jonathan invests our money with, get these stones cut and go up to York, then Penrith Scar with a special licence in my pocket. I hope to return in less than three weeks – and my new foreman Able will see things are right at the mine here, while I'm away.'

'The miracle of the modern railway,' Sir Robert replied with a smile. 'Such a journey would have taken much longer by stage in the old days. Take care of yourself, Tor – and remember that revenge isn't worth it. You have a good life here and I need you – and not just as a manager for the mine.'

Tor gave him his hand and gripped his. 'You are a good friend to me, Robert. My father was a surly man, my mother showed little affection to either of us – but here I feel I have found a friend for life.'

'Then come back to us soon…'

* * *

Tor's business in London took him longer than he'd imagined. His first visit was to the bank the mine used for their funds, but an inquiry for his account found it empty.

'There was fifteen thousand pounds in it last month, but it was withdrawn… three days ago, sir.' The teller looked at him in concern. 'Is something wrong, Mr Hardy?'

'I have no idea,' Tor replied, 'but I intend to find out very soon.'

He left the bank torn between anger and doubt. He would have sworn Jonathan was to be trusted – but what could have caused him to withdraw all the money they'd had in the mine account? Tor had sent him a telegram to say he would be returning soon. Was that the reason behind the sudden withdrawal? What would Tor find when he reached Penrith Scar? His face hardened because he would not stand being cheated of his share. Yes, he had prospects now – but that didn't mean he was a weak fool to stand by while a man he'd trusted stole what was rightfully his. Yet why would Jonathan do such a thing?

He would find out very soon – but first, and perhaps even more importantly now, was the matter of the stones that were supposed to be uncut diamonds.

* * *

Jacob Reiner was a working jeweller in Hatton Garden, London, but he was busy and Tor had to kick his heels for a week before he could cut the stones, though he'd confirmed at once that they were diamonds. However, when he returned to the small workshop that was in the basement of another much larger building, the news was good. This time, he was invited inside with smiles and respect.

'Ah, Mr Hardy,' Jacob said. 'You've come for your diamonds – I think you will be pleased with them.'

He drew out a small velvet box, opened it, and there, lying on black velvet, were two perfect diamonds that flashed in the light of the lamps illuminating the tiny workshop. One was oval and large, the other pear-shaped and a little smaller.

'They are beautiful,' Tor said, picking each one up in turn. 'Thank you. I didn't realise that what was inside those stones would look like this…'

'Very fine they are, too, almost flawless,' Jacob told him. 'Do you want to sell them? I could find a customer for you if you wish.'

'What are they worth?' Tor asked thoughtfully.

'The oval one will fetch near enough a thousand pounds,' Jacob informed him. 'I would need a small commission – but the pear-shaped diamond had a tiny flaw and the colour isn't as pure – perhaps five hundred pounds.'

'I will sell the oval one,' Tor replied. 'I should like the second one made into a pendant...'

'Ah, for a lady?' Jacob nodded. 'I will do that for you, Mr Hardy – and I will pay you the thousand pounds. If you call tomorrow morning...'

They shook hands and Tor left the shop, frustrated that he must spend another night in London, but delighted with the outcome. He'd gained a huge sum of money by accepting the stones in lieu of payment of his five hundred pounds, and knew that his merchant friend in York had had no idea of their value. It was Tor's good luck and he was smiling as he walked towards his hotel.

His pleasant thoughts were rudely interrupted as he noticed a smartly dressed young man being set on by thugs just ahead of him. Tor saw them kicking and punching the man, who was clearly wealthy; he saw them steal a gold watch, but before they could go through their unconscious victim's pockets, Tor was on them. He knocked one to the ground and turned, grabbing the arm of the second as he tried to hit him with a cudgel, breaking a bone with one twist of his hands. The ruffian screamed in pain, dropped the gold watch and the pair of them ran off down the street for all they were worth.

'Oh, good for you, sir,' a well-dressed lady said, coming up to him.

As Tor bent to discover if the victim was still breathing, which he was, though unconscious, a small crowd had gathered. A shopkeeper came out and invited Tor to bring the injured man into his shop, and the lady fluttered round them as he did so, offering smelling salts.

With all the confusion, it wasn't until he had the unconscious man lying on a small sofa inside what had turned out to be a furniture shop that Tor realised who he had assisted. For a moment, he thought that if he'd known, he would have left the rogues to it, but then he dismissed it – Ravenscroft might be his enemy, but Tor would not stand by and see him robbed and beaten, especially now. A tiny smile gleamed in his eyes at the irony of life.

At that moment, Ravenscroft opened his eyes; the lids flickered and closed, and then he groaned. When he opened them again, they focused on Tor and he muttered, 'Why am I always in pain when you're around? You bastard!'

'Sir!' the fashionable woman reprimanded. 'This man just saved you from being beaten to death – and your gold watch…' She held it out to him. 'You should be thanking him for your life.'

Ravenscroft took the watch, smothered a groan, then, 'Go away, madam, I beg you…'

'Well, I never!' she exclaimed in high indignation. 'The manners of the young these days…' Turning, she stormed off, her long skirts sweeping the ground. Her sniff of disgust as she left the shop brought an unexpected laugh from Ravenscroft.

He sat up gingerly and looked at Tor, who was turning away. 'Don't go yet, Hardy. I owe you thanks – and an apology.'

'I need no thanks for what I did this day,' Tor said, but halted and looked at him. 'But an apology is due. Why did you go to the revenue officers with that story? I too should apologise for breaking your arm. I don't always realise my own strength – but you did attack me.'

'I was drunk,' Ravenscroft told him. 'I was drunk most of the time back then – and that's why Rawlings fleeced me of fifteen thousand pounds at the card table. It was his suggestion that I should tell my story to the revenue men. It was my way of paying my debt to him, and I took it. If you want the truth, he needed you out of the way so that he could have that girl in his kitchens... wanted to marry her.' Ravenscroft gave a wry smile. 'He is a ruthless bastard and I've taken care not to go near him since. I thought him a fool then for giving up the money for a woman – but that was before I found love.' He got to his feet a little unsteadily and offered his hand. 'I am a changed man – and will be married to the love of my life very soon.'

'Aye, I know it,' Tor remarked, giving him a wry look. 'It's the reason I don't finish off what they started. You are to marry Jane, the daughter of Sir Robert – who happens to be a good friend. He was very wary of letting you have his daughter because you had something of a reputation – but she loves you and he could not deny her.'

'Well, I'll be damned!' Ravenscroft started to laugh, then stopped as it hurt. 'Will you come and have a drink with me? Shake hands just to show that no grudges are held on either side?'

Tor looked at him for a moment and then grinned. 'It wasn't your intention, but you did me something of a favour, Ravenscroft – though you may have lost me the woman I love. I'll be at your wedding, so we'd best be at least on nodding terms.'

'Sounds like you've a story to tell,' Ravenscroft said. 'Come, we'll lunch at my club... unless you have something better to do?'

'A thousand things,' Tor replied. 'Yet I shall come, for I must remain in town until the morrow...'

32

Tor reached York two days later, having travelled from London on the steam train. He went straight to the hostelry he had often used before and asked for the owner, Eddie Stoat. When Eddie came, he stared at Tor as if seeing a ghost and then a broad grin spread over his face.

'Tor Hardy as I live and breathe! I knew you'd be back for the horse – never believed you'd sold it to those rogues. Cost me sixty guineas that brute did – and its stabling since.'

'You've not sold him then?' Tor asked, his heart giving a leap of hope. 'Eddie – you have Lad still?' He'd thought his horse likely sold long since but had called on the off-chance it might be recovered.

'Aye, eating his head off and frightening all the other horses,' Eddie said. 'Blasted thing. No one would buy it if I'd wanted to sell it – it has kicked every stable lad that dared to come near. Had to care for it myself.'

'Then I'll buy him back from you,' Tor said. 'What do I owe you?'

'Sixty guineas and his keep, but I'll not charge you for that...' He winked at Tor. 'A barrel of brandy will settle it.'

'I've no brandy left,' Tor said and handed him eighty gold coins. 'Thank you.' They shook hands, both well pleased with their deal. His horse, when they were reunited, was sleek and well fed, restive and eager to go once it recognised its rightful master. Tor asked Eddie to care for him until he returned the next day, for he must stay in York overnight.

After leaving the hostelry, Tor went looking for Ellie. He wanted news of Emma, and to ask if Ellie was suited in her work. If not, he could offer her a job more to her liking. However, when he knocked at the house in Micklegate, it was opened by a young maidservant and he was told that the previous occupants had returned to America, and no one knew what had happened to the cook.

'I did hear as one of the maids went with the family, sir, though I don't think it was the cook. She must have found work elsewhere – but I'm afraid I know nothing more,' the girl told him.

Frustrated and not sure where to look, Tor found himself a place to eat and then a bed for the night. He'd thought to see Ellie and offer her what could be a place for the rest of her life if she chose to take it, but Emma might know where she was living.

His thoughts of Emma were mixed, for he longed to see her with all his heart, but knew that he might find her wed. He ought to have written to her once he became the mine manager at Hallen's mine, but he'd thought himself still a wanted man so he'd waited until he knew he could ask Emma to be his wife as a free man. He had, however, sent money to the house in Micklegate on two occasions after he'd begun to earn wages, with letters promising to come for Emma when he could, and wondered now if they had ever reached her. A frown creased his brow as he realised they could not have done.

Tor decided to go on to Penrith Scar the next morning, instead of wasting time looking for Ellie in York. He would ride rather than take the train, for he wanted to visit more than one place in the Dales. He would take food to last him for the journey, resting his horse overnight at an inn he'd used in the past. Lad would appreciate his own stable, rather than being left in York once more, and, besides, Tor had an uneasy feeling in his guts that made him impatient to be in Penrith Scar.

More than a year had passed since he was forced to flee. Emma might have grown tired of waiting for a man she might never see again and married another. Supposing... But surely, she had not quickened with his child for they had only lain together twice? The thought had crossed his mind more than once, but he'd dismissed it, because he was powerless to do anything for her until his name was cleared. As soon as Sir Robert had given him the good news, he'd set out to find his true love. Now he was seized with the fear that she would spurn him. Perhaps she had not come to York when he'd asked, because she did not truly love him – but that could not be true, for his Emma had given herself to him so sweetly.

Fear that something was wrong had begun to grow in his mind since his visit to the house in Micklegate. He'd sent money twice to Ellie, asking her to pass it on and to tell Emma that he was safe and would come to her if he could – but had she ever received the letters? It seemed probable that she had not. Tor cursed himself. He should have written to Emma and asked her to come to him... He'd waited until he was sure he could claim her as a free man, but had he waited too long? The fear that he was somehow too late niggled at him, making him impatient to see Emma and learn from her lips if she still cared.

Ravenscroft's story of lies and deceit had sent his thoughts into a spiral of doubt and uncertainty. Could it be true that the new master of Penrith Manor had lusted after his Emma to such a degree that he would have plotted the death of her promised husband? It was only by the grace of God that Tor still lived and was on the way to building his fortune again. He might have been killed in the pursuit, for he'd been fired at more than once during his escape. Then he'd been drugged, robbed and might have been put on a ship bound for the other side of the world. Only good fortune had found him as part of Red's crew – and then his own actions at the Hallen Mine had led to his new and promising life.

It was Stephen Rawlings' intention to see him dead or ruined so that he could have Emma! Instead of moving against him openly, Rawlings had used another man to do his work. He was a coward!

Anger against the man who had tried to destroy him built as Tor rode through countryside he'd thought he might never see again. He was frustrated that the money owed him had disappeared, though unwilling to accuse his friend Jonathan of theft. But his guts churned as he imagined what might have happened in his absence. Had his mine been confiscated? Had Jonathan been tricked out of the money? Should he have written and told Emma he was coming? Had she grown tired of waiting? Would the lure of being the wife of a lord's grandson have turned her from him? So many questions and he could answer none, but the fear churned in his guts.

No, not his Emma! She would not be turned by promises of wealth. Tor tamped down his anguished thoughts. She'd loved him; he was sure of it – and she was his by rights... She was his woman.

His thoughts in turmoil, Tor went first to his own house,

leading Lad into his stable, only to find that another horse was already there. It belonged to Jonathan – so his partner had taken over his home. What more had he taken?

Tor let himself into the house. A brief glance round told him that it was occupied, though when he looked, he discovered that his own room had not been touched. He nodded. It was reasonable that Jonathan should have moved in; the house was empty, better to live in it than let it go to rack and ruin, for no one had expected Tor to return. Yet still it rankled, stoking the fires of resentment building inside him.

Tor found bread and cheese in the pantry and helped himself, washing it down with some ale. He found the mine ledgers where they'd always been kept and sat down to read them, his mouth tightening as he saw the profits for the past year or so had been very high. The mine was doing well – so why had the money been withdrawn?

Replacing the books at last, he went out to the stable, making sure that Lad was comfortable and had both food and water. Then he took the other horse and set out for the mine. As he rode through the village, Tor was aware of heads turning, but he didn't stop, neither did he speak. He felt as tight as a drum, nerves stretched as he battled his anger. What had been going on in his absence? Had he been a fool to trust Jonathan? Was he betrayed on all sides?

He dismounted and walked towards the mine office, pausing for a moment to gain control before entering. Jonathan was working at his bench and didn't immediately turn, then, 'Yes, what is it? I'm busy...'

'I can see that...' Tor replied, and Jonathan whirled round, shock and then delight in his face.

'By heaven, it is you!' he cried and came forward at once, his hands outstretched. 'Tor! I am so glad to see you! You know your name has been cleared? I would have told you, but you gave me no location. We thought you gone abroad until I had word.'

'It was my intention,' Tor said, some of his tenseness draining away. 'I got shanghaied on to a ship – but I'm back now. So, how are things here?'

'Good,' Jonathan said, then his smile faded. 'The mine was making a lot of money until the last month or so, but then the zinc just ran out. We're making searches, but I doubt we'll find another huge deposit... bits here and there. I think it might really be finished this time...' He took a deep breath and looked at Tor. 'That's why I sold it to Rawlings last month, though the contract went through just five days ago. He has been plaguing the life out of me since you left, so now he owns it. I am just finishing up here before I leave for good...'

'You what?' Tor glared at him in disbelief and shock. 'You sold my mine to that devil. Damn you... don't you know what he did?'

'Well, I know he tried to force Emma to lie with him, but she hit him with the poker and ran away, He was close to death for weeks, but then recovered, more's the pity,' Jonathan said, then hesitated as he saw the thunderclouds in Tor's face. 'I am not sure what you've heard...'

'None of that,' Tor replied, and the fear began to wriggle inside him as he watched the expressions reflected in the other man's face. 'I think you need to explain.'

'What he did to Emma was one of the reasons I sold him the mine,' Jonathan said frankly. 'It's truly finished this time, Tor, but he doesn't know that yet. There's enough zinc to last a few months, but then it's done. I wanted to pay him back – and Mary told me that Emma said it was Rawlings who got you arrested...'

'Aye, that bit is right,' Tor grunted. 'He'll pay for that if I get near him.'

'I think we've got our revenge already,' Jonathan chortled with glee. 'Don't you see, Tor? He has been after that mine ever since he came here, tried all sorts after you were forced to flee – and I sold it to him. I took all his farms and his land; we own all of it from the far side of the stream all the way up to Highways, land, mineral rights – everything he owned. I gave him the mineral rights at the mine, same as you had – and I had to pay him a bit of cash...'

'You mean the fifteen thousand pounds you took from our account?' Tor's eyes were like flint.

'Nay, only five thousand. I told him that was all we had – but I used part of the rest to buy more land... land Sir Philip sold when he left... So we own all the valley, apart from the big house and its grounds, the mine and Penrith Scar village.'

Tor ran a hand over his thick dark hair, bewildered. 'You've bought all the land in the dale? I don't understand – why would you do that?'

'Because I've found zinc and other minerals further up the valley, and we'll need to own the land, and to buy new equipment, because Rawlings demanded ours was included in the sale. I moved the eight thousand pounds remaining into a new bank account that paid more interest... but we'll need most of it, because we want new equipment, as ours was old. I intend to build new cottages for our workers and a hall the men can use as a club...' He paused as Tor was silent. 'Say I've done right, Tor... Don't you see? He has nothing worth anything left... I did it for you, for Emma...'

Tor stared at him as he thought about what Jonathan had done. 'You mean you own the whole valley? You've taken his land and farms – in return for a played-out mine?'

'We own the valley – the deeds are in both names, with me able to sign – or you – the way you did it when you left...'

Jonathan frowned. 'Did you think I would cheat you? After what you've done for me?'

'It crossed my mind, for you couldn't know if I'd ever be back – or did you think to give my share of the money to Emma? Have you given her anything?' Tor groaned. 'Tell me she hasn't wed another…'

'That I can't answer,' Jonathan said. 'I know little of Emma since she ran away, but I gave her mother a bit of money, before she wed – and I heard a rumour…' Jonathan looked grave. 'If it be true you'll not care for what I've done, but it is only hearsay…'

'Out with it, man!' Tor was aflame with fear and anxiety.

'I heard she took a virulent fever after her child was born, and died – but I don't know if it is true.' Jonathan saw Tor stagger as if he'd been hit by a ton weight. 'It was Mary Watts that told me. She said Emma's friend had written and said she was dying, but…'

Jonathan got no further, because Tor turned and strode from the office without a word.

'Mary married the vicar – she'll be there…' Jonathan called after him.

Tor registered his words, but they made no sense to him. Nothing made sense any longer. His mind whirled as he tried to absorb all Jonathan had told him. He'd exchanged the mine for the farms and moorland… used their money to buy more land because he thought he'd found minerals elsewhere. It sounded like madness to Tor, but none of that mattered – it didn't matter because Emma was gone. Either disappeared or dead… dead… dead… dead…

The word echoed in his head, going round and round as he walked away. All he'd ever wanted was within his grasp and more than he could ever have expected – but what good was it? What good was anything if his Emma was dead?

Tor didn't go to the vicarage immediately. He walked and walked until it was dusk, and by then he was at the place he'd so often gone to when his thoughts were black. Hardy's Tor. It was his special place, but as he stood there buffeted by icy winds and freezing with cold, his thoughts burned like a fire in his head.

One man had caused this agony. Stephen Rawlings. It was he who had tried to have Tor arrested... Jonathan said he'd wanted Emma. He'd been willing to see Tor dead to have her... but even after he'd fled, Emma had rebuffed him. She'd hit him and fled. His Emma had been a fugitive because she would not have that man – his enemy.

His eyes closed and he felt the sting of hot salty tears on his icy skin. His Emma – she had stayed true to him, but now she was dead. Tor was so distraught that he could hardly think. Rawlings had tried to rape her; she'd hit him and run away... Was that what Jonathan had said? Yes, yes, but there was more... After the birth of her child, she'd died.

It was as if he was in a fever of despair, his mind unable to cope with the grief and pain of his loss. Emma had died after her child was born...

'Who was the father?' Tor cried the words aloud, but only the cawing of ravens answered.

His child – or Rawlings? It would drive him mad until he knew... yet what did it matter? What could anything matter ever again? In his terrible grief, he forgot his promise to Sir Robert and the life that awaited him. He forgot the rich farmland that was now his and Jonathan's – and even the prospect of a new mine. What could any of that mean to him now? He laughed wildly as he realised what his friend had done. By taking the rich farmlands and land in return for a mine that was nearly finished, he had ruined Stephen Rawlings. When the fool realised, he would probably sell his fine house... Tor smiled wryly. It could be his house if he wished it… but what need had he of any of it? No one would buy it without the land. Let the accursed place lie empty and rot – as its owner would in the ground.

Rawlings had to die. Tor knew that if he took a life, he would forfeit his own, but it meant nothing to him now. He'd intended to give Rawlings a beating, but now nothing but his life would do. Tor would kill him and then they could do what they liked with him. He didn't care. Without Emma, his life wasn't worth the candle.

Stiff with cold and numbed with grief, Tor climbed down from his high perch. He would ask Mary what had happened to Emma, if she was truly dead, and then, if she confirmed what Jonathan had told him, he would kill Stephen Rawlings – break his neck with his own hands…

* * *

'Tor Hardy!' Mary stood in the vicarage doorway and stared at him in disbelief. Then she burst into tears and sank to her knees before him, the storm of grief overcoming her. 'Forgive me…'

'Now then, lass,' Tor said, moved even in his stony anger by her sorrow. He bent and picked her up, carrying her into the house. In the kitchen, he set her down in a chair and stood looking at her. 'Nay then, I'm not blaming you, Mary – just tell me if Emma lives?'

'It was me that stopped her coming to you,' Mary said at last, raising her head to look him in the face. 'I didn't know she carried your child until it was too late. I was afraid that I could not manage without her, so I kept the money you sent and destroyed your letter.'

'Emma never knew I had asked for her?' Tor stared at her, this latest revelation almost beyond belief.

'Ellie told her later, but by then you'd gone.' Mary took a handkerchief and wiped her face. 'I caused you both great pain and grief and I've regretted it – and it's my fault she's gone...'

'Gone?' Tor gripped her by the shoulder. 'Emma is dead?'

'Ellie begged me to go to her, but I couldn't – my husband thought her a wicked girl and forbade me. I had no money for the fare...' Mary sobbed once more. 'I am repaid for the evil I have done and must bear my penance.'

Tor reached in his pocket and took out ten golden guineas. 'Take this and go where you will – if you choose,' he said gruffly.

He turned and walked blindly from the room, not hearing Mary call his name.

Emma was gone. Emma was dead. There was nothing left for Tor but revenge.

33

Tor rode up to the house on the hill, murder in his heart. Before this day was out, Stephen Rawlings would lie dead – or Tor would himself be dead. His loud knocking at the imposing black door brought, after several minutes, a young, scared-looking girl, but his demands for the master were met with a shake of the head.

'The mester be out, sir – and the housekeeper didn't come this morning. There's only me to answer the door, for most of the staff left days ago when the master beat his valet half to death. In a fearful rage he was and they all upped and left, all the London servants, swearing they would not serve such a mester – for he is always drunk or in a rage these days.' She finished breathlessly, clearly distressed.

Her hurried words hardly registered with Tor. In his head, two words echoed over and over. *Emma dead. Emma dead...*

'Where is your master, girl?'

She shook her head tearfully. 'He might be at the mine. 'Twas all he spoke of, on an' on about how he wanted it and would have it, so Sarah said – but she hasn't come today... I don't know what to do... What should I do, sir?'

Tor stared at her, then, 'Go home to your mother,' he muttered and turned on his heel. He left her staring after him, tears on her face, and mounted his horse. A thin smile curved his mouth as he rode in the direction of the mine. It was fitting that it should happen there.

As Tor drew closer to the mine, he saw a man riding just ahead of him and pushed his horse harder so that they arrived at almost the same time.

'Joe – Joe Davies?' Tor called, driven by some sudden instinct, and the man turned to look at him with such a queer blind look that he recognised a fellow sufferer. 'What's wrong, Joe? Trouble at the mine?'

'There will be shortly,' Joe answered, tying his horse to a post and coming to greet him. 'I heard you were back. Have you come for revenge? If so, then you'll have to wait your turn, Tor. That bugger Rawlings is mine. I'll kill him...' He showed Tor the heavy hammer he carried in his belt. 'He'll not live five minutes when I find him.'

'I intend to kill Rawlings for what he did to Emma and to me...' Tor said angrily, ready to fight Joe for the privilege if he had to.

'She hurt him more than he hurt her,' Joe said and cursed. 'He took my Sarah and he used her, used her like a prostitute – and now she's dead. Rawlings has to die at my hands... Get in my way and I'll kill you, too.' The two men glared at each other and then Joe gave a muffled sob. 'Go to Emma in York and forget him, Tor. I'll do for him; that's my word on it. I've nothing left to live for, but you have a son and Emma. Go to her and let me pay the price for his murder.'

Tor stared at him in sudden hope. 'They told me Emma was dead of the fever...'

'Then they lied or knew not the truth,' Joe replied. 'Emma was alive three days ago when I visited York, for I saw her and I spoke to her...'

Tor took two steps towards him. 'You spoke to Emma – but they said she died...' Tor felt as if he'd been swept up in a maelstrom of conflicting feelings, pulled this way and that until he hardly knew where he was.

'She was ill, but Ellie nursed her. She and the boy live with Ellie now.'

'Where...'

'A house near the river – terraced houses...' Joe began when they heard a terrible rumbling sound.

'That's the mine...' Tor said and started to run. 'Come on, Joe. We have to get the men out...'

Tor didn't look back to see if Joe followed. Choking dust was coming from the mine entrance as he reached it and three men came staggering out.

'Is it a bad fall?' Tor asked, and one of the men nodded. 'Can you tell me where? How many men are trapped?'

'Four or five, including the mester,' the man replied, and Tor recognised him as Nate Mesby. 'Is that you, Tor? We thought you were gone for good...'

'So did a few others, but I'm not that easy to get rid of,' Tor said. 'How did it happen – was it a blowout or maintenance?'

'Neither,' one of the other three said. 'It was his fault – bloody Rawlings. We warned him the old tunnel wasn't safe. It hadn't been maintained because we'd closed it off after a part of it collapsed, but he wouldn't listen. He was convinced we were hiding something and forced us to open it up. We worked slowly, but he was impatient. He tugged at one of the broken supports and suddenly it all gave way.'

'Right,' Tor said. 'We have to get our lads out. I'll go and see what I can do – can you organise a chain if there's a way to get to them?'

'Aye, we'll do it for the men, though if it was just him, I'd leave him to rot.'

'Bad master, is he?' Tor nodded but took off his jacket. Jonathan had come from the office, carrying a satchel of his tools. 'Nothing you can do – but organise food and drink for the men.' He nodded to some of the other men who had emerged from the mine, as they always did when there was an emergency elsewhere. 'Follow me – we'll see if we can get to them...'

'I'll help,' Joe said. 'Just tell me what you want me to do, Tor.'

'Look after the survivors.' Tor led the way inside the mine. It sounded as if it might be a bad fall and he cursed, because now that devil Stephen Rawlings had even more to answer for.

* * *

It was hours before they got close enough to hear a faint cry from the trapped men. They'd had to stop for food and drink and to rest once or twice, but Tor wouldn't give up his place at the head of the line. The space they worked in was cramped and the air was poor, but he kept working, removing the fallen rock piece by piece until at last they heard a cry from inside the tunnel.

'We're here...'

'How many?' Tor asked.

'Four men and the mester – he's hurt bad.'

'What about the rest of you?'

'We're all right – hungry and thirsty; the air is bad. You need to get us out quick.'

'We're nearly through. Is it safe for you to work your side?'

'Aye, we've been carting a bit back down the line – but the air is bad. We can't breathe...' He started to cough.

'Good man. Same here. We'll be through soon.'

'Thank God for that...'

Tor turned to the man behind him. 'Most of the men are unhurt – exhausted and thirsty but all right. Rawlings is hurt bad.' He heard grunts but sensed the mood was against the man that had caused the fall.

Carefully, piece by piece, Tor widened the gap big enough for the first man to crawl through, then the second and third, and finally the last of the miners pushed the top half of Rawlings' body through.

'I think he's nearly done for, but I'll not leave even him to the rats,' he muttered, and Tor lifted the body of his enemy over his shoulder to the next man.

'Good to see you, sir,' the last man out said. 'I never expected we'd get out alive.'

'You were lucky we were here,' Tor said. 'I think otherwise no rescue could have come for much longer.'

'By then we'd be dead,' the man acknowledged. He was passed over Tor to the next man and then they all turned where they stood and walked out in single file, until every man was in the fresh air.

Tor was the last out. He gasped the air into his lungs, flopping down on the cold hard ground to get some rest, closing his eyes, then rolling on his side to bring up some choking bile caused by the dust and the foul air in the tunnel.

'Are you all right, Tor?' Joe Davies asked and, after a moment, he opened his eyes, nodding. His head was pounding and his mouth tasted foul, but he was breathing.

As Tor sat up, he saw the men clustered around a body lying on the ground. They were all just standing there shaking their heads. 'He needs to be taken home and a doctor summoned...'

'Too late for that now, sir,' Jacob said. 'He's dead. Looks as if he caught a rock on his head when the roof caved in.'

'He was alive a while back,' one of the others said. He looked to Tor. 'What do we do now, sir?'

'You still need to get him home – and someone must get the doctor and Tom Constable. He has a family somewhere and they will need to be told.'

'What shall we do, sir?' one of the men asked him. 'Do we open the mine, investigate the old tunnels? The mester wanted the old tunnels open, because we told him the zinc was nearly done. He was furious, cursing and saying as he'd been cheated...'

'The mine doesn't belong to me now. I think it ought to be closed – until someone comes to take charge of his estate...'

'We'll have no work...' some of the men cried, but Jonathan came forward then.

'This was my last day here. I was collecting my own tools – but I'll be hiring soon. Come and see me at Tor's house in the morning, all of you. I'll see you right. You three, get a wagon and take Rawlings home – and you, Noah, you go for the doctor. You can ride into Settle, Jem. Tell Tom Constable what happened here – all of it, mind.'

'Are you going to stay now, Mr Hardy?' one of the men asked.

'The answer to that is I don't know,' Tor replied. 'I'm going to York now to find someone – and it will be she who will decide. Jonathan will be here, though, and he'll give you work as long as his new mine produces.' He arched his brows at his friend. 'You didn't tell me where that mine is to be?'

Jonathan laughed. 'At Hardy's Tor, of course – the old iron mine. After you'd gone, I went there a lot and there had been a rockfall. I saw traces of something and I tested it – zinc. So I found the old entrance, tore the boards down and went in – there are rich sources of minerals all over. The ancient folk who took the iron centuries ago either didn't recognise them or didn't want them – and no one had thought to look since.'

Tor stared at him and then threw back his head and laughed. He laughed until his cheeks were wet with tears. 'And I call myself a miner,' he said. 'All those years I haunted the place and never thought to look...' He stopped laughing at last and looked around. 'Jonathan will treat you all to a drink at Highways, on me – I'll be in touch.' His eyes met Jonathan's and they both nodded, before Tor walked away and mounted his horse. 'Joe...' he called as he saw the farrier standing looking lost. 'Will you ride with me for a bit?'

Joe hesitated, then nodded and mounted his horse. They rode in silence until the forge was reached, then both dismounted.

'Thank you for your help, Joe,' Tor said and offered his hand. 'The mine was not your concern, but you did all you could for the men.'

'As any man would,' Joe replied, and there was a glint in his eyes.

Tor frowned. 'Did you tell me Sarah was dead?' He'd been in too much of a rage to take it in earlier.

Joe looked him straight in the eyes. 'She is – I killed her, as I've killed him. I made sure he banged his head hard on the way out...'

'Joe! I care not about Rawlings. He got what he deserved – but Sarah?'

'Sarah betrayed me with him. He'd given her money and a diamond necklace; she was leaving me.' Joe looked cold, hard, defiant. 'I killed her. She cared nothing for me or her child... And, if you're still wondering, I killed Ike because she went with him. You knew that anyway...'

'I guessed it,' Tor agreed.

'But said nothing – that's why I helped you in the mine.' Joe shrugged. 'I hardly cared if I died there.'

'But your child?'

'The child was Ike's. She trapped me...' Joe sounded bitter. 'Her father can take it – the girl is with her grandmother now. I'll leave before they find Sarah's body... If they catch me, they'll hang me, but I don't care much either way.'

'Then I'll wish you good luck.' The two men shook hands and Tor rode away. He did not look back.

34

'I should write to my mother, send her some money,' Emma said, looking at her friend as Ellie fed little Torrie his boiled egg. The child was growing strong and healthy and every day looked more like his father. 'She probably thinks I died of that fever.'

'Why bother?' Ellie said wrathfully. 'I wrote and begged her to come, but she didn't even answer my letter. She is married now and has forgot you.'

'Supposing she didn't get the letter?' Emma replied, reaching out to wipe her son's egg-smeared mouth. 'Or she might have been ill herself...'

'Mebbe,' Ellie replied but looked unconvinced. 'When I think of all the money we sent her, Emma – and you having to work, even though it took ages before you could.'

'I know you hate where you work,' Emma said, because Ellie had found a job at a pub, cooking for the customers, and disliked it. However, Emma had been unable to work for two whole months and had lost her job at the factory. She was now scrubbing floors at a hotel and doing the work of a chambermaid, because it was all she could find. 'I am sure one of us will find better work soon.' She looked thoughtful. 'If Ma didn't get that letter, she might have written to your old place of work... She'll be wondering why there's no answer.'

'Mebbe,' Ellie said, but still believed that Mary had simply ignored her plea for help. 'I'll go there this evening on my way to work – ask if there are any letters for me. I haven't given them a forwarding address, because that devil Rawlings might still be after you.'

'I've been in York nearly five months now,' Emma pointed out. 'He hasn't come near, nor has anyone inquired for me that I know of. I think he just gave up looking for me. Why would he bother after what I did?'

'I thought he was out for revenge,' Ellie said and looked at the clock on the wall. 'You'd best get to work, Emma. It's past seven...'

'Oh, no, is it!' Emma jumped to her feet, making Torrie wail. 'I'm sorry, I'll have to go. If I am late again, they will give me the sack...'

Emma kissed her son's eggy face, smiled at Ellie and grabbed her coat, because it was bitterly cold. She ran all the way to the hotel where she worked, feeling worried. It wasn't a job she liked, but she couldn't afford to lose it and she was going to be late. She had been warned twice, but there was always so much to do and the work was so tiring that sometimes Emma felt like weeping. Yet she knew she had to keep going. Neither she nor Ellie earned much and they were both terrified of losing their jobs, because it was so hard to find another – especially if you'd been let go by your last employer.

If only she could be back in her beloved Dales. If she could be with Tor as his wife. If things could just get better...

Shaking her head, Emma rushed into the back of the large hotel, taking her coat off in the cloakroom provided and putting on her apron. She was in the store cupboard, getting her brooms and dusters, when she heard a sniff behind her and turned to see the housekeeper.

'Late again, Mrs Hardy?' she said. 'I think I've warned you of what will happen if this continues?'

'Yes, Mrs Summers. I am truly sorry...'

'Sorry isn't good enough. Get on with your work. I'll speak to the manager and he'll decide – but there are plenty of girls out there who would love your job and make sure they were here on time.'

Emma didn't answer her. She couldn't. She was fighting her tears. It was all so unfair.

* * *

Ellie called at the house she'd been employed at when she arrived in York. She was invited to enter and then a woman who seemed to be the housekeeper came to greet her.

'Ah, this is most opportune, Miss Blake,' she said, beaming. 'A gentleman has been to the house inquiring after you twice – and I gave him your letters only yesterday. He said that he would give them to you and seemed very anxious to learn where you were living. You did not leave your address, but I understand you live near the Lenton Tower?'

Ellie looked at her warily. 'You gave him my letters? Did he give you his name?' If that devil Rawlings was after Emma...

'His name... Oh yes, Mr Tor Hardy. Such a pleasant man... He gave me a guinea for my trouble.'

'Tor Hardy was here asking? You gave the letters to him?' Ellie stared at her in wonder.

'Yes, I did – and told him where I thought he might find you. Was that all right?'

'Yes, oh yes. It was very much all right,' Ellie said, and it was all she could do not to hug her. 'He didn't say where he was staying, I suppose?'

'Yes, he has taken rooms at one of the best hotels and asked me to let him know if I could give him more information.' She handed Ellie a scrap of paper – and Ellie saw it was the biggest hotel in York. Tor must have come into money.

Ellie could scarcely contain her excitement. She thanked the woman and took her leave, setting off to the imposing red-brick building Tor had given as his address. She chuckled to herself as she walked, because it looked as if her old friend had done all right for himself.

Ellie was hardly dressed for such a fine hotel, but she entered with her head high and approached the reception desk. When the snooty girl behind the desk looked down at her and told her the trade entrance was at the back, she bit her tongue.

'I'm here to inquire after one of your guests, my girl, so none of your lip. I'd like to know if Mr Tor Hardy is staying here?'

'Mr Hardy?' The girl stared at her as if she would deny her, but then her eyes lit up and she said, 'Oh, Mr Hardy – there is a person here asking after you...'

Ellie whirled round and there he was, and by the look on his face, it was hard to know who was the most surprised and pleased.

'Ellie, by God! I've been looking all over for you,' Tor cried. 'I found your house, but there was no one there – is Emma living with you?'

'Emma is at work and I've been to the Micklegate house to see if any post had been sent there...' Ellie went to him and he swept her up, swirling her around in his exuberance. 'Put me down, you daft lad. I'm that glad to see you...'

'Come into the lounge,' Tor invited, glancing over his

shoulder at the reception. 'Bring tea and toast and something stronger for me...'

'You shouldn't waste your money,' Ellie scolded. 'I could get you a bit of toast at mine...'

'I can afford to waste a little,' Tor told her, his grin a mile wide and growing. 'You've just given me the best news of my life. Tell me, is Emma well – and what of the child?'

'Torrie is with my neighbour,' Ellie said. 'She dotes on the lad and offered to look after him while I was out. Your son is a fine boy, Tor, and looks just like you.'

'My son, Ellie?'

'Aye, of course. Did you doubt it?'

'I heard about Stephen Rawlings...'

'He tried, but she would have none of him. He offered her marriage, even though she told him she carried your child. When she refused, he got angry and tried to abuse her. She hit him with a poker and fled the Dales. I couldn't help her then, so she went to London – but she'll tell you her story when she gets home at two.'

'I've heard some of it,' Tor said, his expression grave. 'I meant to kill Rawlings – but there was a rockfall at the mine; he was trapped and he died...' He saw her inquiring look. 'Aye, there's a tale to tell, but not here.'

A maid brought their tea and toast on a tray and a glass of rum for Tor. He tossed it back and sat watching Ellie as she drank tea and ate her toast. They talked for a while, then Tor walked home with her and he told her the full story.

'Well, I can't say I'm sorry he is dead. That man would never have let Emma be if he'd lived. He'd had agents searching for her for months...' She explained how Emma had gone to London but returned to York when she was close to being arrested. 'She came here and took your name, Tor. She said if she was to be arrested then she might as well be the wife she would have been had they not plotted against you.'

'It has been hard for her then,' Tor said, his face twisting with grief and sorrow. 'Do you think she can forgive me?'

'Haway, lad. When was it your fault?' Ellie asked, then heard noises from outside. 'That sounds like Emma now...' She got to her feet as the door opened. 'Emma – there's someone here to see you...'

Emma was staring across the room. It was clear that she'd seen Tor by the surprise, delight and tears that burst from her. He took three steps towards her and she flung herself into his arms, crying his name over and over again, as he held and kissed her.

'Hush, my love,' Tor said, his lips against her hair. His strong arms closed around her as he held her pressed to his heart. 'Hush, my Emma. I'm here and if you will have me, I'll never leave your side again...'

Ellie slipped from the room as Emma mumbled something incoherent. She went next door to her neighbour and sat with her for a few minutes, giving them time together before she took Torrie to meet his father. She hadn't collected the boy, because it was Emma's privilege to show Tor her son, not Ellie's, but she couldn't stop smiling as she thought of the two people she cared for most in the world. Ellie was going to miss her friend when she left, but she was glad that at last Emma would be happy.

When Ellie decided to take Torrie home, she discovered them sitting on her sofa, looking into each other's eyes and talking eagerly, their faces a proper picture that told it all.

'Emma – perhaps Tor would like to meet this lad...'

Emma jumped up and came to take the child, kissing him and carrying him to Tor. 'This is your da,' she told him. 'He's been away, but now he's home and he'll be with us always...' Her eyes went to Tor's.

Both women felt their eyes glisten as they saw the look in the proud father's face.

'My lad...' Tor said in a gravelly voice that told of his emotion. 'My son...'

Emma took him to his father and Tor held him in his arms, lifting him high so that the child looked down on him and smiled, blowing bubbles. For a long moment, Tor could look only at his son, then, at last with a sigh, he turned to her. 'And so we'll be wed...' he said, and Emma smiled.

'Aye, we'll be wed – and then we'll go to your home, Tor.'

'Back to Penrith Scar?' Ellie asked, but Tor shook his head.

'I've a new home now, Ellie, as I told you – and Emma only wants to visit her mother. We'll take the children if they're not happy; Mary too if she wants... but we'll be wed in the Dales.'

'Tor has a new mine there, as well as a share of one in Cornwall... Oh, there is much to tell,' Emma cried. 'He gave me the choice, but I don't want to go back, even though Mr Rawlings is dead. I'd rather go with Tor wherever he chooses.'

'Jonathan can look after my interests in the Dales,' Tor said. 'I have friends in Cornwall and I'm needed there – so that's where we'll head once we're married.'

'Aye, and I'm glad of it,' Ellie said, bravely hiding her sorrow at the parting. 'I'll miss you all...'

'No, you won't,' Emma cried, her eyes alight with joy. 'That's what is so wonderful, Ellie. Tor says Sir Robert, his partner in the mine, needs a live-in housekeeper now his daughter is to marry. You can come with us, Ellie – please say you will...'

Ellie stared at her, dawning hope in her eyes. 'I'll come and be glad of it,' she said. 'There's nowt to keep me here now, is there?'

35

Emma decided that she would be married in the church in the Dales, where she'd been christened. Mary persuaded her husband to conduct the service by giving him a good meal, and hints that if he refused, she would leave and go off with her youngest daughter to live near Emma and Tor. Accustomed to his comforts, he grudgingly gave in, though had he known that Mary had been asked to go with them and refused, he might have been less amenable.

Tor had settled his affairs in Penrith Scar. Jonathan would continue in charge of the new mine, which he was already setting men on to shore up and make safe before work commenced.

'I want nothing more to do with that family at the Manor, nor those that came after,' Tor said when Jonathan asked if he wanted his father's old house. 'I will not often be here, so it is your choice, my friend.'

Tor had found himself lodgings at Highways, while Emma and Ellie moved into his house until the banns were called. It was one Sunday morning after the second asking that Tor and Emma left the church just as a coach and horses went by.

'That will be someone about Rawlings' estate,' Tor said with a frown. 'I doubt they will sell it easily.'

'I did what I did, because I had to,' Emma sadly. 'But I did not hate him and I am sad for his family.'

'Aye, death for a young man is a sad thing – though I had sworn to kill him when I thought you dead.'

'Oh, Tor my love,' Emma said. 'The fever was not his fault...'

'No – but he caused you to flee and I blamed him, but it would have been murder...'

'Instead you tried to save him, along with the others.'

Tor nodded thoughtfully. 'Perhaps I should go up to the house. Whoever it is may need to hear the truth of the story.'

'Are you sure?' Emma asked anxiously.

'Aye, it's best.'

Emma watched him walk off, a tingle of fear at the nape of her neck. Once before she'd been about to wed the man she loved, but fate had broken her heart. Perhaps she should have been married in York, as Ellie had suggested...

* * *

Tor arrived to a scene of some confusion. The occupant of the coach was still sitting inside it, and though a man was banging on the door of the house, no one had answered.

'You'll get no answer,' Tor addressed the man who had been knocking uselessly. 'Most of the servants left weeks ago. In the end, there was just a young maid, but she was frightened to be there alone – and she left after Stephen Rawlings died in the mine.'

'You, sir!' a voice called from the coach, and Tor went to it.

The owner of the voice was an elderly man, clearly a gentleman with stern features. Once handsome and strong, he looked fatigued and worn down by grief and Tor immediately felt sympathy. This must be Stephen Rawlings' grandfather, who had bought the estate for his grandson in the belief it would be the making of him and stop his dissolute ways.

'I fear you've had a wasted journey,' Tor told him. 'The house was closed after Mr Rawlings died. There is nowhere fitting for you to stay here, sir – you will need to return to Settle.'

The coach door opened and the occupant got out. He was almost as tall as Tor but much slighter. He looked at Tor wearily. 'I must see to my grandson's effects. I care nothing for the house or what may be left of the estate – I was told he sold his land to purchase the mine, though why in God's name…' He shook his head. 'You seem to be a man of authority, sir. May I ask your name?'

'Tor Hardy, sir…' Tor offered his hand and it was taken in a soft but firm grip. 'I was not here at the time of the sale, but Jonathan says he'd been after the mine for some time – and in the end they did some kind of a deal.'

'I've been told of it. I am Lord Rolfe of Rawlings, and Stephen my only grandson.' He shook his head. 'He would have been a wealthy man soon enough… What possessed him to buy a mine and go down it, I have no idea…'

'No, nor I,' Tor replied, for the only reason he could fathom was jealousy or hatred. 'It makes no sense, sir, and I am sorry for your loss. If I can be of any assistance. I might be able to find someone to come and make the place habitable.'

'No. No. I just need to get in to collect some of my grandson's personal items and then I shall send someone to close the house, though I see it already is.'

'I can get in and open it for you,' Tor offered.

'That would be a kindness. My man will look after me – we brought a hamper with us. The people in Settle were kind and spoke well of Stephen, for he visited with his friends... I dined last night at the Golden Lion...'

'I know it well, sir,' Tor replied. 'Wait a moment and I'll open the front door for you.'

He walked round to the back of the house, found the cellar door and the key to it, under a large stone, where it had always been hidden, and let himself into the house. Within a few minutes, he was standing in the open doorway at the front of the house, brushing cobwebs from his coat.

'You obviously know the house well,' Lord Rolfe remarked wryly as his man carried a hamper in.

'It belonged to my half-brother,' Tor told him. 'I know it as well as any man now.'

Lord Rolfe looked him in the eyes. 'You are the man who got them out of that hellish place, aren't you?' Tor nodded and saw his eyes water. 'Tell me, was he still alive then?'

'Barely, sir,' Tor told him. 'He was struck on the head when the roof caved in and I think he could not have lived for long after that... He was unconscious and could not have suffered after the first blow.'

Lord Rolfe closed his eyes briefly. 'Thank you. That was kind...'

'I shall be in the village if you need anything.'

'Thank you, but it is to be a brief visit. I shall return to Settle when I have what I came for – a few precious items, sentimental really. After that... well, the lawyers may deal with it, though from what I've seen, they will find it hard to sell this place without the land.' He looked weary. 'What that grandson of mine was thinking to exchange his land for a mine, I shall never know...'

They shook hands once more and Tor walked away, back to the village. He would never tell that noble old man what his grandson had truly been like and he hoped that no one else would either. The jealousy, greed and terrible rage that had lived inside Stephen Rawlings was something he could not fathom, nor wished to. Yet the grandfather was a decent man and did not need to know of his grandson's drunkenness and his darker side. He had enough grief to bear without learning of the wild behaviour and the rages that Jonathan and others had witnessed after Emma ran off. Whatever the cause, Stephen Rawlings had descended into something near madness by the sound of it, but he did not wish to inflict that on a tired old man who had come to mourn his kin.

36

Emma married Tor in the church in the dale in which she had been christened. She wore a pretty blue dress and a white bonnet, with a white shawl and white kid boots, and she carried a Bible of white leather and a posy of blue violets. Tor wore a dark suit and a starched white shirt with a frilled cravat, and was very uncomfortable. He looked handsome and strong, a man of some importance, as he now was, for he was part owner of two mines and almost the whole valley.

Emma held her head proudly as she walked into church on Jonathan's arm that Saturday morning. Ellie had Tor's son in her arms as she sat in the front pew and watched her dearest friend marry. Jinny was Emma's only attendant and received her Bible and flowers proudly as the shining gold ring was placed on Emma's finger, and she smiled up at Tor as he kissed his bride. Her heart swelled with love and pride as they went out into a blustery day, the wind sweeping down from the hills, to be met with cheers and a shower of rice and dried rose petals.

It seemed that the whole village had turned out to greet

them, and they all crowded into the church hall for the feast Tor had provided. For an hour or so, Emma was kissed and greeted by friends who all said they had missed her and wished her well. No one was prepared to admit that they had condemned her or laughed and thought her well served to flee for her life after striking her master. No one wanted to speak of the late Stephen Rawlings or his wild behaviour after his attack on Emma. It was as if he had never existed.

It was a new beginning. The villagers had heard of the change of ownership of most of the dale, and, in time, it would be accepted and the Penrith family and those that came after would be forgot.

After the cake was cut and the toasts made, Emma took her leave of her mother and sister. 'You can come to us whenever you wish if you're unhappy,' Emma told her mother and hugged her, for she'd guessed that her mother's life was not all it should be.

'I will if I feel the need,' Mary promised and kissed her. 'Your sister may come to you soon rather than late, though I'll keep her with me for now. I can bring her to you, because your husband gave me the means – but I've made my bed and I'll bide, for now at least. Tor has made an impression on Henry, so perhaps he'll treat me better now I'm mother-in-law to the man who owns the roof over his head.'

Taking their leave of the valley, Tor helped Emma up into the hired chaise and then scooped up the reins as he sat beside her. Lad was tied to the back, tossing his head in disgust to be led rather than ridden, but with silver coins thrown for the children, and her flowers tossed to be caught by one of the village girls, they were finally away.

At Settle, they would stay for one night. Ellie would travel on the train to Lord Robert's estate in Cornwall alone. Their baggage had already been sent on ahead when they left York. Sir Robert was eagerly awaiting her arrival, for his daughter's wedding was imminent.

Tor and Emma had decided to travel at a slower pace, using the journey as their wedding trip and staying at pleasant hotels each night. Tor needed his horse in Cornwall and by using the posting inns, which were now gradually dying out because of the railways, it was a fond farewell to an old way of life. The future belonged to the steam engine, and other types of engines were now being invented, which would change the lives of everyone in the country eventually.

'We'll not know ourselves in a few years,' Tor had told Emma as they drove though the Dales at a steady pace, stopping when and as they pleased, to rest and feed the horses, enjoying the pleasure of simply being together.

'I pray the Dales won't change too much,' Emma said, looking about her, for already there were new houses being built close to the railway that had opened up the Dales to curious eyes.

'The land will stay the same, but there will be more folk, I reckon,' Tor said, glancing at her. 'Not regretting your choice, Emma?'

'Nay, my love,' she answered, smiling up at him. 'It is a new life for us – a new future. Penrith Scar holds too many memories, some good – but others best forgot.'

'Aye, we're needed where we go, Emma. Jonathan has plans for his mine and the folk there, so I leave with an easy heart – but I want you to be happy, my love.'

Emma gave her hand to him and smiled. 'Do you doubt my love for you?'

Tor shook his head, because they were well matched in

loving and in life. Emma had come to his arms on their wedding night with as much innocent sweetness as the first time they'd loved. As he'd known for a long time, much longer than she, Emma was his woman and could never have been anyone else's.

'Know that I would go anywhere you asked,' Emma told him. 'I took thee for richer or poorer, Tor – and I would follow you if you had nowt and were forced to wander.'

'I trust it will not happen again,' Tor replied, and a frown took the smile from his eyes. 'Though others might not be as lucky.'

'You think of Joe Davies?' Emma asked, for the whole valley had been shocked when Sarah's broken body had been found, her neck bruised and her face purple. The child had been left at its grandfather's without explanation and the valley was awash with rumours. Why would a father abandon his own daughter? Or mayhap it wasn't his? No one knew, but there were whispers. When Joe was discovered to be missing, the rumours and speculation grew, but Tor had not spoken, though he knew Joe's story.

'I pity him,' Tor replied. 'She betrayed him, Emma. She broke his heart – but he should not have killed her. He would have killed Rawlings as he did Ike Hanson, had the mine not done it for him.'

'Sarah went to his bed?' Emma was shocked. 'I knew she went to Ike, but I thought once their child was born, she and Joe were happy.'

'Joe said Rawlings had given her money and she was planning to leave him but didn't want the child.'

'Not want her child?' Emma was shocked. She would never have given Tor's son up even if she'd been close to starving.

'So Joe told me. I know he's done wrong,' Tor said, glancing at her. 'But I hope they don't catch him. He has suffered for her unkindness.'

Thinking about it, Emma agreed. Joe had done wrong, but Sarah had betrayed him not once but twice. 'It is tragic,' she said. Then she looked at him. 'I would never betray you, Tor.'

He smiled down at her. 'I know…' he said. 'Look, there's an inn I've used. We'll stay for the night and go on in the morning…'

EPILOGUE

It was the day of Sir Robert's daughter's wedding. They had been in their new home but a few days and Emma had decided to wear her own wedding dress for the occasion. She had almost finished dressing and was singing her favourite song.

> My love, my love... oh, my love...
> My love was a fair true knight
> And he comes to me by candlelight
> My love, my love... oh, my love...
> His kisses fill me with such sweet delight...
> My love, my love... oh, my love.
>
> When the dawn comes, he is gone...
> And I know, I know, oh I know...

'That is a sad song, Emma. Are you unhappy?'

Emma whirled round to see Tor watching her.

'No. I am very happy – and the song is not sad to me. My

father sang it when we walked the Dales together. I was a small girl and he carried me on his shoulders and he told me the story. It is about a highwayman and his lover – and in the end she dies too and they bury her with him.'

'I know the story,' Tor said. 'It is of Tom Hathaway and his lass Bess – and his horse. After she died, it was said that the pair of them could be seen riding the high toll road together on moonlit nights. The mare's eyes were said to glow like rubies and her hooves strike fire...'

'Da said it was a story of undying love. He said that a love like that was worth dying for.' Emma brushed away some wetness from her eyes. 'He would be happy to see us now, Tor, for he believed in you – as I do.'

'You look beautiful, my Emma.'

'Nay, Tor. I'm well enough, but I was never a beauty.'

'To me you are,' Tor said and handed her a blue velvet box. 'I had this made for you, my love.'

Opening it, Emma saw a sparkling diamond in the shape of a pear drop and as big as her thumbnail, set on a fine gold chain. She gave a gasp of surprise as Tor took it and fastened it about her neck. 'Oh, Tor, it is beautiful – but it must be so valuable. Too good for me...'

'Nay, lass. Nothing is too good for my Emma. It is just the start – one day you'll have pearls, and emeralds to match your eyes...'

Emma looked down at the pendant. It set well on her, but she meant it when she glanced up at him. 'All I truly want is you and my son... and the others that may come.'

'Love is more important than wealth,' Tor agreed, bending his head to kiss her. 'When I thought you lost to me, I knew that life held nothing of value for me – but now that you are my wife, I will give you all that comes my way – and I am going to be rich,

Emma. Both mines are producing well – and this came today...' He held out a letter for her to read.

'What does it say?' Emma asked.

'Lord Rolfe died soon after he returned home, but he gave instructions to his lawyers that have been honoured, for he has only a daughter to succeed him. He has thanked me for trying to save his grandson – and he left me Penrith Manor and the old mine – with the provision that it stays closed, which it will, for no one wishes to work it now that we have the new one.'

'He left you that house?' Emma stared in amazement. 'Why?'

'Apparently, he told his lawyers it was owed to me. I think he may have discovered some of what Rawlings did to harm me – and you.'

Emma looked at him thoughtfully. 'Does it change things? You could live in the house that belonged to your father's family...'

'Nay. I'll not live there. I want no reminders of the Penrith family. Philip and his son are dead and I had no time for her ladyship, wherever she might be, for I know she must resent me. My first thought was to let the house go to rack and ruin, but that is a waste. I'll sell it if I can and give Jonathan the money to help the local people. He'll know what's best to do...'

'Oh, Tor. I am so glad,' Emma cried and went to throw her arms around him. 'I am happy here in our home and could never be in that house.'

'I know,' he said simply and kissed her on the lips. 'And now, Mrs Hardy, we have an important wedding to attend...'

* * *

MORE FROM ROSIE CLARKE

ABOUT THE AUTHOR

Rosie Clarke is a #1 bestselling saga writer whose books include *Welcome to Harpers Emporium* and The Mulberry Lane series. She has written over 100 novels under different pseudonyms and is a RNA Award winner. She lives in Cambridgeshire.

Download your exclusive bonus content from Rosie Clarke here:

Visit Rosie's website: www.lindasole.co.uk

Follow Rosie on social media here:

facebook.com/Rosie-clarke-119457351778432
x.com/AnneHerries
bookbub.com/authors/rosie-clarke

ALSO BY ROSIE CLARKE

Welcome to Harpers Emporium Series

The Shop Girls of Harpers

Love and Marriage at Harpers

Rainy Days for the Harpers Girls

Harpers Heroes

Wartime Blues for the Harpers Girls

Victory Bells For The Harpers Girls

Changing Times at Harpers

Heartbreak at Harpers

Troubled Times at Harpers

Duty and Dreams at Harpers

The Mulberry Lane Series

A Reunion at Mulberry Lane

Stormy Days On Mulberry Lane

A New Dawn Over Mulberry Lane

Life and Love at Mulberry Lane

Last Orders at Mulberry Lane

Blackberry Farm Series

War Clouds Over Blackberry Farm

Heartache at Blackberry Farm

Love and Duty at Blackberry Farm

Family Matters at Blackberry Farm

Tears and Fears at Blackberry Farm

The Trenwith Trilogy

Sarah's Choice

Louise's War

Rose's Fight

Dressmakers' Alley

Dangerous Times on Dressmakers' Alley

Dark Secrets on Dressmakers' Alley

Better Days on Dressmakers' Alley

The Family Feud Series

A Family at War

A Family Secret

A Family Fortune

Yorkshire Dales Series

Wild Hearts on the Pennine Moors

Standalone Novels

Nellie's Heartbreak

A Mother's Shame

A Sister's Destiny

The House of Secrets and Lies

Printed in Dunstable, United Kingdom

80996236R10207

Hans J. Kleinsteuber

Reisejournalismus

Hans J. Kleinsteuber

Reisejournalismus

Eine Einführung

Unter Mitarbeit von

Diana Lühmann
sowie
Johannes Broermann, Doris Ehrhardt, Niokolas Fentrop, Katharina Griese, Achim Griesel, Frank Höfer, Undine Kayser, Astrid Kusser, Peter Linden, Sabine Neumann, Michael Pahl, Dagmar Rößler, Martin Sonnleitner, Marina Tischer, Kia Vahland, Sonja Valentin, Kathrin Voss, Alex Weck, Sonja Wielow, Verena Wolff

Westdeutscher Verlag

Der Westdeutsche Verlag ist ein Unternehmen der Bertelsmann Fachinformation GmbH.

http://www.westdeutschervlg.de

Gedruckt auf säurefreiem Papier
Umschlaggestaltung: Horst Dieter Bürkle, Darmstadt
Titelbild: Privatphoto „Philippinen"
Druck und buchbinderische Verarbeitung: Druckerei Hubert & Co., Göttingen
Printed in Germany

ISBN 3-531-13049-8

Inhalt

Vorwort

Reisejournalismus - das ist ein alles andere als gesicherter Begriff. Ein Blick in die verfügbare deutschsprachige Literatur bestätigt, daß es wenig fundierte Informationen zum Thema gibt. Teils wohl, weil die Reiseberichterstattung als redaktionelle Aufgabe nicht gerade höchste Achtung genießt. Wenn man die Rahmenbedingungen mancher gesponsorter Reportagen bedenkt, sicherlich zu Recht. Andererseits, die Tourismusbranche boomt, die Umsätze der Veranstalter steigen. Ebenso steigt das Bedürfnis nach den kleinen Fluchten aus dem Alltag und sei es auch nur eine 'Traumreise', die auf dem Kanapee beginnt und endet. Unbezweifelbar nimmt auch die Nachfrage nach Reiseberichten zu, sowohl in den allgemeinen Publikumsmedien, aber ganz besonders in Form spezialisierter Reisezeitschriften. Unverkennbar ist das ungebrochen starke Interesse daran, dem kalten, industrialisierten und dichtbevölkerten Mitteleuropa zu entgehen, die Paradiese in der Ferne zu suchen. Der Reisejournalismus bietet hier Startrampen an, für reale wie virtuelle Abflüge in die weite Welt.

Mit diesem Handbuch wird der Versuch unternommen, in das gesamte Themenfeld des Reisejournalismus einzuführen. Damit wollen wir einerseits dem aktiv schreibenden Praktiker zur Hand zu gehen, zum anderen auch den interessierten, aber nur passiv konsumierenden Leser umfassend informieren[1]. Zumal, da festzustellen ist, daß beide Zielgruppen so streng nicht zu trennen sind, denn gerade in diesem Metier sind Grenzüberschreitungen nicht selten. Das zeigt die allgemein hohe Zahl von frei tätigen Reisejournalisten, die ihren Broterwerb auch, aber nicht allein als Schreibende bestreiten.

Das Anliegen des Buches mag so umrissen werden: Es sollen Grundlagen vermittelt werden, es werden aber auch weiterführende Kenntnisse in den für Reisejournalismus typischen Gebieten präsentiert. Die Darstellung beginnt mit einem Abriß der langen Geschichte der Reiseberichterstattung. Darauf

---

1 Wir wissen um die Zweigeschlechtlichkeit der Welt und respektieren sie. Lediglich um der Lesbarkeit willen beschränken wir uns auf die männliche Form. Die weibliche ist mitgedacht.

widmen sich zwei Kapitel den handwerklichen Fertigkeiten rund um die Reisedarstellung in Wort und Bild. Da geht es z.B. um die Geheimnisse der Reportage oder den sinnvollen Einsatz von Bildern. In den zwei folgenden Kapiteln wird ein Überblick über Reisemedien und -ressort gegeben, wobei im Mittelpunkt der Berichterstattung Hamburger Redaktionen stehen - denn hier entstand das Buch. Die Kommentierungen befragter Redakteure werden darauf 'quer' verwertet, um halbwegs repräsentative Antworten der Praktiker auf typische Fragen zu erhalten. Weitere Abschnitte beschäftigen sich mit den Märkten für Reisemedien, mit den Fußangeln der Werbeabhängigkeit, mit den Schäden die der unerfahrene Umgang mit Stereotypen und dem Fremden hinterlassen können. Das wirft Fragen nach einer Ethik der Reiseberichterstattung auf. Schließlich interessiert uns die Zukunft der Reiseinformation unter dem Diktat von Digitalisierung und Interaktivierung. Die Darstellung besteht nicht allein aus einer 'Textwüste'. Eingestreute Zitate, Beispiele, Tabellen und Zitate sollen für etwas Abwechslung sorgen. Wo die Grenzen der Darstellung erreicht sind, wird auf weitere Quellen verwiesen.

Das Handbuch beruht auf einer Besonderheit. Es wurde nicht nur von dem einen Autor verfaßt, der auf dem Titelblatt steht. Viele Einzelautoren waren daran beteiligt, was seinen Grund an der ungewöhnlichen Entstehungsgeschichte hat. Die Ursprünge liegen in zwei Universitätsseminaren im Rahmen des Hamburger Teilstudiengangs Journalistik. Die beteiligten Studierenden zeigten ein ungewöhnlich hohes Interesse am Thema, ausgelöst wohl von der Reiseleidenschaft der Beteiligten. Es stellte sich zudem heraus, daß viele Teilnehmer auch praktische Erfahrungen im Metier vorzuweisen hatten - als freie, in einzelnen Fällen auch als feste Redakteure in einem der zahlreichen Reiseressorts Hamburgs, vereinzelt auch anderswo. So nebenbei stellten wir fest, daß Hamburg - das ist nicht als Beitrag zur hier sattsam gepflegten Standortwerbung gemeint - sicherlich das Zentrum der deutschen Reisepublizistik darstellt. Es lag also nahe, daß Studierende ausschwärmten und mit den Redakteuren vor Ort sprachen, um dann deren Medien und Meinungen zu porträtieren. Nicht selten war es die eigene Redaktion. In jedem Fall haben viele an diesem Buch mitgewirkt, die aus praktischer Erfahrung zu berichten wissen - bis hin zur Expeditionen fast ans Ende der Welt, um Filme für ein TV-Reisemagazin zu drehen.

Eine weitere Besonderheit der Hamburger Journalistik kam dieser Darstellung zugute. Sie wird als erweitertes Nebenfach studiert, das Hauptfach wird aus dem traditionellen Kanon der Universität gewählt. So konnte ich Literaturwissenschaftler bitten, etwa über die Geschichte der Reiseberichte zu schreiben, während sich Sozialwissenschaftler eher über den Redaktionsalltag hermachten. Die studentische Mitarbeit enthebt den Initiator und Hauptautor dieses Handbuchs nicht seiner Verantwortung. Auch die von anderen Autoren verfaßten und gezeichneten Abschnitte sind von ihm gegengelesen und redigiert, mitunter auch mitgeschrieben worden. So hat er die Verantwortung für das Gesamtwerk zu übernehmen, und für Schwächen hat er geradezustehen.

Der Unterzeichnende dankt allen, die an diesem Buch mitgearbeitet haben. Ihre Namen finden sich am jeweiligen Abschnitt, Biographische Hinweise bietet das Autorenverzeichnis. Mein besonderer Dank gilt Diana Lühmann, welche die organisatorische und technische Betreuung der Bucherstellung übernahm und das Projekt zu einem guten Erfolg führte.

Hamburg, im Juli 1997 Hans J. Kleinsteuber

1 Einleitung: Die Widersprüche des Reisejournalismus

Hans J. Kleinsteuber

„**Reisen**, zu verschiedenen Zwecken (hauptsächlich zu solchen des Erwerbs, der Entdeckung und Erforschung, der Belehrung, des Vergnügens, der Heilung oder Besserung Kranker, sowie aus religiösem Eifer) unternommene Bewegung nach entfernten Orten."
(Definition nach: Brockhaus Konversations-Lexikon, Leipzig 1903)

Die Arbeit dessen, der professionell über das Reisen berichtet, also die eines Reisejournalisten, wird immer widersprüchlich bleiben. Dabei sieht auf der Oberfläche alles einfach aus: **Gegenstand der Reiseberichterstattung** sind offensichtlich **Weg und Ziel einer Reise**. Die Reise besteht folglich aus zweierlei: Einerseits der 'Anreise', andererseits dem 'Reiseziel'. Letzteres ist „an einem entfernten Ort", also niemals mit dem Wohnort des Reisenden identisch. Damit ist die leitende Perspektive jeder Reiseberichterstattung bereits umrissen, die über das 'Fremde' berichtet. Über den Journalisten sagt dies noch nichts, er kann durchaus jemand sein, der vor Ort lebt; seine Aufgabe ist es dann, in die Rolle des ortsunkundigen Besuchers zu schlüpfen.

In der Regel wird die Reise, wie sie Gegenstand journalistischer Berichterstattung ist, nicht aus geschäftlichen oder weiteren, z.B. familiären Gründen angetreten. Die hier in Rede stehende Reise dient dem 'Vergnügen', ist eine Reise zur **Zerstreuung, Unterhaltung oder auch Bildung**. Das muß freilich nicht sein, es gibt auch andere Zielgruppen für Reiseberichte, etwa die Zeitschrift für den Vielflieger *Business Traveller* - aber das sind kleine Ausnahmen.

Legt man das zentrale Muster zugrunde, so erscheint die Rolle des Journalisten klar abgesteckt zu sein. Er reist dem Leser des Reiseberichts voraus, wie ein Pfadfinder oder Scout, ist sozusagen Auge und Ohr dessen, der ein zumindest potentielles Interesse an dieser Reise hat. Fast könnte man (in freier Interpretation eines Bildes von Marshall McLuhan) den **Reisejournalisten als Verlängerung menschlicher Sinnesorgane** interpretieren. In diesem Bild berichtet der reisende Journalist von entfernten Orten im Auftrag und unter Beachtung der Interessen seiner Leser, der dann in Abwägung der geschilderten Vor- und Nachteile sich selbst auf die Reise macht.

Was so plausibel klingt, ist ein sicherer Weg, den Reisejournalismus nicht zu verstehen und den Leser falsch zu bedienen. Sicherlich gibt es Situationen, bei denen der lesende Kunde sich mental gerade an dem Punkt seiner gedanklichen Erwägungen befindet, da er eine Reise plant, bereits bestimmte Ziele in die nähere Wahl einbezogen hat und sich gezielt informieren will. Dann mag er auf der Titelseite von *GEO* oder *Merian* entdecken, daß 'sein' Ziel Thema ist und das Heft daraufhin erwerben. Aber meist ist er dann schon in die Phase gerückt, in der er eher zum Reiseführer in Buchform greift. Und die sind zwar eng mit der Reiseberichterstattung verknüpft (welche als Vorform zum Buch interpretiert werden kann), aber für ihre Erstellung gelten andere handwerkliche Regeln.

Nehmen wir also die Realitäten zur Kenntnis: Die Reisemagazine werden vor allem im Abonnement bezogen, also gilt das **Interesse den fremden Welten allgemein** und nicht spezifischen Zielen. Und die Reiseseiten der Tageszeitungen oder Reisefilme im Fernsehen erscheinen in schöner Regelmäßigkeit, sind also nicht gezielt nach Interesse abrufbar. Trotz aller damit verbundenen Streuverluste sind Reiseberichte aber bei den Lesern populär. Also muß es andere Gründe für die Motivation zum regelmäßigen Lesen geben.

Der große Reiseschriftsteller Sommerset Maugham schrieb einst: „Der kluge Mann reist nur in Gedanken". Und er setzt noch eines drauf, indem er behauptet: „Die Reisen, die man vor seinem eigenen Kamin unternimmt, sind wahrscheinlich die schönsten; denn dabei büßt man keine Illusionen ein." (Maugham 1951: 215f) Tatsächlich ist jeder Reisejournalist gut beraten, wenn er davon ausgeht, daß die Mehrzahl seiner Leser kein oder höchstens ein vages Interesse am geschilderten Reiseziel hat. Dann erscheint das Studium der Reportage nicht als Vorbereitung der Reise zu einem konkreten Ziel, sondern eher als deren Ersatz, **die Reportage wird zum Reise-Surrogat**. Ein wenig vergleichbar den großen Vergnügungsparks, wo der Besuch von Papp-Kulissen, von Burgen, Urwäldern und Schatzinseln im Stile von Disneyland die Suggestion ferner Welten ohne deren Gefahren und Unbill liefert. Dabei wird die Mühsal der Abenteuerreise erspart, weil man familienfreundlich aus dem dazugehörenden Hotelkomplex in die Pseudo-Fremde abtauchen kann. Der Reisejournalist muß wissen: Häufig wird er für einen Leser schreiben, der 'Ohrensessel-Reisender' ist.

Die hohe Bedeutung, die der **Bebilderung** zukommt, nährt diese Einschätzung. Heute werden fast alle Reisberichte von - inzwischen fast immer farbigen - Abbildungen begleitet, die als 'Eyecatcher' den ersten Blickkontakt mit dem Leser herstellen. Entsprechend reizvoll müssen diese Bilder sein, fast immer zeigen sie das Reiseziel in freundlichem Licht, oft kommen die Vorlagen geradewegs aus den Schubladen von Touristikzentralen oder PR-Agenturen. Unsere Träume bestehen vor allem aus Bildern, folglich werden Reiseträume mit Reisebildern beginnen. Richtete sich unser Interesse vor allem auf handfeste Informationen aus dem Reisegebiet, so wären Bilder von geringem Wert, denn die Sehenswürdigkeiten können wir mit viel mehr Genuß selbst in Augenschein nehmen. Bilder - die immer nur reduzierte und konstruierte Abbildungen der Realität darstellen - haben so vor allem eine Aufgabe, dem Leser und seinem Auge den Besuch des entfernten Ortes zu ersetzen.

Ein Ethnologe und Schriftsteller reflektiert über das Reisen:

„Im Grunde sind äußere Reisen nicht von ganz anderer Art als innere, imaginäre Reisen. Nur der Aufprall des Fremden wirkt handgreiflicher, sichtbarer. Alles, was einer in der Fremde erlebt, kann er, im Prinzip, auch zu Hause erleben; oder anders gesagt: er wird in der Fremde nur das erfahren, was in ihm (für das Erlebnis) bereit ist. Nur hindert ihn in der eigenen Kultur allzuoft das Eingespielte des Alltagslebens daran, sich für Anderes zu öffnen. Der Zugang zu vielen Erlebnissen in ihm ist erschwert und verstellt.

Er benötigt einen veränderten Standpunkt, einen Ortswechsel. Manchmal geht einer nur von hier nach dort und fühlt sich schon wie ein neuer Mensch. Es ist der alte, aber belebt und zugänglich für den Austausch an Energien, für die Spannung zwischen den Dingen und den übergestülpten Bildern.

Keine Erfahrung - so gewöhnlich sie auch sein mag - nimmt nur das auf, was im Augenblick an diesem Ort im eigenen Gesichtsfeld erscheint, sondern ist überlagert und geprägt von eigenen und von kollektiven früheren Erfahrungen, von Traditionen, Symbolen und Klischees.

(Heinrichs 1993: 19f)

Vielfach erweisen sich Reiseberichte tatsächlich als „Fluchthilfe ins Paradies“ (Luger). Häufig sollen sie an unser Gefühl appellieren, das uns auf vergangenen - und hoffentlich zukünftigen - Reisen umfängt, und das hier mit Begriffen umschrieben werden soll, wie wir sie sattsam aus den Prospekten der Reiseveranstalter kennen. Die fabulieren gern vom 'Urlaub vom Alltag' oder der 'Freiheit ohne Zwang'. Was hier als gefühlige Stimmung vermittelt wird, ist gleichwohl real: Seit Jahrhunderten leben wir mit der Erfahrung, daß wir oft erst auf Reisen wir selbst sind. Wir finden sie z. B. in der literarischen Reise wieder, etwa wenn der Italien-Reisende Goethe (1786-1788) in Briefen ans kalte Weimar schwärmt vom „freyeren Leben, höherer Existenz, Leichtigkeit und Grazie". Kein erfolgreicher Reiseautor wird ohne Appell an diese Gefühle auskommen. Das impliziert, daß ihm der im Geiste reisende Leser wichtiger sein sollte, als der, der ständig um den Globus jettet. Denn letzterer wird vor allem an handfesten Informationen interessiert, zudem häufig gar nicht im Aktionsradius heimischer Medien unterwegs und damit für sie erreichbar sein. Eher sollte man vom **Typ des Ohrensessel-Reisenden** ausgehen, der brav daheim auf das spirituelle Abheben zu neuen Abenteuern wartet und dem Schreiber genau deswegen nicht davonläuft. Es ist wie mit dem Sex im Fernsehen: Will man ihn kommerziell ausbeuten, so muß man immer davon reden, aber füglich dafür sorgen, daß er nicht quotenfeindlich praktiziert wird. Zugegeben ein wackeliges Argument, denn der Reiseautor hat den Vergleich mit den Porno-Geschäftemachern nicht verdient.

Legen wir die These zugrunde, daß Reiseberichte oft in Räume der Imagination führen, die von heimatlicher Sicherheit aus durchflogen werden. Nimmt man diese Ausgangssituation ernst, so ergibt sich eine Reihe vielleicht ungewohnt klingender, gleichwohl plausibler Konsequenzen. Zuerst einmal erwartet der Leser wohl oft nicht die Realitäten über das geschilderte Reiseziel, will von **Schönheiten und Exotik** lesen und **nichts von der düsteren Kehrseite** erfahren. Eine idealisierte, auf freundliche Stereotypen reduzierte Sichtweise wird ihm wohl am ehesten als Startrampe aus dem unbefriedigenden Alltag hinaus dienen. Nicht zufällig finden sich die Reiseteile der Tageszeitungen in der Wochenendausgabe. Die Gründe für die Nutzung der Reiseberichte zur Phantasiearbeit sind wahrscheinlich mannigfaltig: Die Neugier auf das Fremde zählt dazu, gepaart mit Angst vor den Gefährdungen der Reise, schlichte Bequemlichkeit oder auch mangelnde Kaufkraft. Jedenfalls entspricht die so in rosaroten Farben geschilderte Ferne in einer spezifischen Weise den Interessen der Tourismusindustrie, die gern in genau diesem Sinne auf die Berichterstattung Einfluß zu nehmen versucht. Folglich bietet sie Journalisten großzügig und mit Hintergedanken die Finanzierung von Reisen an, für die sie Gegenleistungen im Form von Jubelberichten erwarten. Dazu kommen die mit der Werbung verknüpften Zwänge: Wer wird schon in einem journalistischen Umfeld werben wollen, in dem von Enttäuschungen und Katastrophen die Rede ist? Wir wollen hier keiner kritiklosen Schreibe das Wort reden, aber so sieht die Praxis aus. In diesem Band wollen wir Hinweise geben, wie man verantwortungsbewußt und ethisch mit dem Fremden umgeht.

Offensichtlich möchte der Lesende in seiner Reiseträumerei aber ernst genommen werden. Er möchte als nur virtuell Reisender nicht ertappt werden, weil er sogleich die eigene Enge zugeben müßte. Auch im bequemen Sessel möchte er als Globetrotter angesprochen werden. Deshalb erwartet er eine zwar das Träumen bestärkende Darstellung in der Reportage, aber allzu auffällig darf es nicht werden. Die Berichterstattung muß seriös und verläßlich sein - oder ihm zumindest als solche erscheinen. Die Reportage darf keine Unwahrheiten enthalten - für getürkte Berichte haben sich Chefredakteure schon in aller Form entschuldigt und die Schuldigen demonstrativ gefeuert. Der **Ernsthaftigkeit der Reise-Schreibe** dienen auch die begleitenden Service-Informationen über Anreisemöglichkeiten, die schönsten Hotels und die ungewöhnlichsten Restaurants. Manchem Leser werden sie den Abschied von seinen Illusionen leichter machen, denn fast immer werden dabei die Preise der edlen Hotels und der Luxusrestaurants genannt. Das mag dem Leser, da er als zahlungskräftig angesprochen wird, zwar schmeicheln, gleichwohl wird er es oft nicht zahlen können. Gebrochene Botschaften also auch hier.

Eine weitere Beobachtung ist unverkennbar: Im Reisejournalismus - vielleicht Glossen ausgenommen - gibt es das nicht, was den organisierten Tourismus auszeichnet, die Massenreise. Berichtet wird nach dem Prinzip ‘Die Lemminge sind die anderen’. Ich (der Journalist) und Du (der Leser) begeben sich quasi in ein **gemeinsames Komplott gegen den gemeinsam gering geschätzten Massentourismus**. Da werden ‘Geheimtips’ verbreitet, da werden noch unentdeckte Ziele so beschrieben, als harrten sie geradewegs der Entdeckung durch den einen Leser. Die Widersprüchlichkeit ist offensichtlich: Massenmedien eignen sich per definitionem nicht für interne Information. Der Tip hört in dem Moment auf, ein geheimer zu sein, da er die Zeilen eines Mediums erreicht, das sich an ein disperses Publikum wendet. Im Ernst: Welcher Journalist wird seinen ganz persönlichen Urlaubsunterschlupf solange öffentlich propagieren, bis er von den eigenen Lesern überlaufen wird?

Seit Jahrhunderten werden die reisenden Mitbürger in ‘bessere Reisende’ und ‘blind folgende Lemminge’ aufgeteilt. Der Tourismussoziologe Christoph Hennig stellt fest: „Das negative Image des Tourismus ist fast so alt wie der Tourismus selbst.“ (Hennig 1995) Schon immer ist über **stupide und desinteressierte Reisende** geklagt worden. Normalerweise von den Aristokraten, die ihre Vergnügungs- und Bildungsreisen für sich behalten wollten. Tourismus wurde aber über die Jahrzehnte immer mehr ‘demokratisiert’, neue, ‘niedrigere’ Bevölkerungsschichten schlossen sich an. Dazu kommt, daß vor der Sehenswürdigkeit alle gleich sind, der soziale Unterschied unterwegs verblaßt. Dies um so mehr, da heute die Rucksackreisenden mit Niedrigbudget weit mehr zu sehen bekommen, als der verwöhnte Luxustourist. Der Reisejournalist kann diese Dispositionen nicht ändern. Will er sie nicht thematisieren, so wird er sich einpassen müssen. Seinen Lesern wird er dann suggerieren, daß - solange sie ihm folgen - ein Abfall ins Lemminge-Dasein nicht zu befürchten ist.

Christoph Hennig über den 'Anti-Tourismus als Denkblokade':

Alle reisen, doch niemand möchte Tourist sein. Touristen, das sind die anderen. Dem massenhaften Reisen unserer Zeit haftet im öffentliche Bewußtsein ein zwar unbestimmter, doch unbestreitbarer Makel an. (...) Man hört von *ausgetretenen Touristenpfaden*, von *Touristenfallen* und *Touristenspektakel*. Dem stehen positiv die *ganz unhistorischen*, die *unverdorbenen* Orte gegenüber. Die Urlauber, so heißt es, lassen sich auf fremde Länder nicht ein, schauen nie richtig hin, bekommen das Wesentliche nicht mit und suchen noch in der Fremde Komfort, deutschen Kaffee und Sicherheit. (...)

Die anti-touristischen Haltungen erscheinen vor allem im Alltagsbewußtsein und in journalistischen oder literarischen Texten. Aber immer wieder kommen sie auch in der theoretischen Diskussion zur Geltung. Sie lasten gleichsam als historisches Gewicht auf der Reflexion über den Fremdenverkehr. Das ist nicht verwunderlich. Die Intellektuellen, die über den Tourismus nachgedacht haben, gehören mehrheitlich den Mittelschichten an, in denen die Geringschätzung der Urlauber und die Betonung der eigenen Reise-Originalität besonders verbreitet sind. Man versteht sich hier nicht als Normaltourist, sondern reist engagierter. Von der Insider-Position des Kenners fremder Sprachen und Länder können die Erfahrungen der Massen an spanischen Stränden und österreichischen Skiliften nur als oberflächlich und irrelevant erscheinen: schlimmstenfalls als Folge von Manipulation und Verblödung, bestenfalls als pervertierter Ausdruck des Wunsches nach einem besseren Leben.

(Hennig 1977: 13, 23)

Der immer wieder erhobene Anspruch auf Exklusivität kollidiert zudem mit dem häufig kommerziellen Hintergrund der Berichterstattung. Die **Reiseveranstalter und Öffentlichkeitsarbeiter**, die dem Journalisten die Feder zu führen suchen, vertreten eine aufs Geldverdienen ausgerichtete Industrie, die vor allem eines im Visier hat, nämlich noch mehr Reisende heranzuholen. Es gibt kluge Reisende, die allein deswegen ein Ziel meiden, weil es gerade in einem auflagenstarken Medium als einzigartig angepriesen wurde, um dem erwarteten und gewollten Run zu entgehen. Und die Qualität eines Restaurant wird automatisch nachlassen, wenn es feststellt, daß ihm die Journaille die neugierigen Esser in großer Zahl vorbeischickt. Vielleicht wird man in Zukunft die Reiseseiten vor allem konsultieren, um festzustellen, welche Ziele nicht mehr besuchbar sind.

Ohne zynisch werden zu wollen: Es scheint, daß der Reise-interessierte Leser ein wenig betrogen sein will. Andererseits weiß er aus Erfahrung, daß hinter vielen kumpelhaften Empfehlungen schnöde kommerzielle Interessen stehen. Und daß dieselben Empfehlungen von Zehntausenden seiner Mitbürger zum selben Zeitpunkt gelesen werden, die vielleicht derselbe Impuls packt, dort bald vorbeizufahren. Aber er möchte seine eigene Widerspüchlichkeit nicht noch vorgehalten bekommen, will als Individualist behandelt werden. Auch wenn weder das **Massenmedium** noch der **Massentourismus** dies de facto tun - und beide von derselben Produktion für die große Zahl leben und profitieren.

Die Doppelbödigkeit geht weiter. Es gilt als weltbeflissen, wenn wir uns in anderen Teilen des Globus auskennen. Kenntnisse von anderen Völkern, Besuche in entfernten Winkeln der Welt schmücken den Bürger, heben ihn aus der Masse der (mehr oder minder) Daheimgebliebenen hervor. Aber was bedeutet Reisen heute schon? Wer einige Wochen am Strand von Tunesien oder Jamaika verbracht hat, kennt deshalb noch nichts von - um diese abgedroschene Formel einmal zu benutzen - Land und Leuten. Will es wohl auch nicht. Andererseits will er nicht als Urlauber im Hotel-Getto dastehen, also entwickelt er ein Maß an Neugierde über das Gastland, das wiederum der Journalist aufgreifen sollte. Die Versuchung dabei ist groß, in die eigenen oder zumindest die dem Leser **vertraute Kiste von Stereotypen** zu greifen und dabei Klischees und Plattheiten zu verbreiten, die uns alle über andere Teile der Welt bekannt sind. Eine andere Herangehensweise ist es, mit der Differenz vom Eigenen und Fremden zu spielen und die Karte der Exotik zu ziehen. Da wird geschildert wie andersartig, befremdlich, aber auch anziehend oder abstoßend das Leben da draußen sei. So schufen sich die Deutschen ihre imaginär 'edlen' Indianer in Amerika in derselben Epoche, da sie andere 'Edle', die Hottentotten in Afrika, real abschlachteten. Unser großer Ohrensessel-Schreiber Karl May war ein Meister darin, unsere Innenwelten auf ferne Kontinente zu projizieren. Das konnte er um so besser, da er selbst die Kulissen seiner Abenteurerromane nicht zu Gesicht bekommen hatte. Gerade weil uns viele seiner Phantasien so vertraut schienen, waren sie konstruiert und falsch. May und seine Leser schufen sich Außenwelten, die ihnen als willkommene Flucht vor den komplexen Realitäten anderer Kulturen und unserem Umgang mit ihnen dienten. Jeder Reisejournalist wird den Karl May in sich immer neu bekämpfen müssen.

Viele dieser sich aus früher Sozialisation speisenden und um verquaste Fremden-Gefühlen gestärkten Emotionen haben die Reisejournalisten nicht zu verantworten und werden sie auch nicht aus der Welt schaffen können. Allerdings dürfen sie diese nicht noch verstärken. Arbeitet der Autor mit Stereotypen, so muß er sich bewußt bleiben, daß sie schnell in diffamierende Vorurteile umkippen können. Dabei sind sie wahrscheinlich - wie der Wortschöpfer und Journalistenkollege Walter Lippmann schon argumentierte - unausrottbar. Bleibt nur, verantwortlich mit ihnen umzugehen, sie spielerisch einzusetzen und gleichzeitig zu relativieren, die Reise zu nutzen, um ihrem Wahrheitsgehalt auf die Spur zu kommen. Ähnlich gilt für das **Fremde**: Weder leben die da draußen genauso wie wir, noch ist alles gänzlich anders. Diese Einsicht macht die Welt vielleicht weniger aufregend, aber die Berichterstattung ehrlicher. Darum sollte der Journalist seinen Leser auf eine Reise zu den Originalschauplätzen (z.B. der May'schen Abenteuerromane) mitnehmen, die Neigung zum Romantisieren weder ganz ignorieren, noch verstärken, sondern die Zusammenhänge auf ihren rationalen Kern reduzieren.

Wer von dem verantwortlichen Umgang mit dem Reisethema spricht, wird erläutern müssen, was er damit meint. Damit ist angesprochen, daß sich jeder im Reisemetier tätige Journalist der Sitten und damit auch dem Sittlichen seiner Arbeit bewußt sein muß. In der Wissenschaft werden diese Fragen als praktische Ethik behandelt. Es ist keine Frage, die Sitten im Reisejournalismus sind rauh und vielfach verlottert. Die Klage darüber, daß Beiträge von der Tourismusindustrie erkauft werden, hilft freilich allein wenig. Dies um so mehr, wenn es Usus für manche Verleger und Chefredaktion ist, den Beitrag möglichst günstig einzukaufen. Wissend, daß ein Dritter ihn faktisch gesponsort hat, ohne daß dies dem Leser deutlich wird. Gibt es überhaupt Möglichkeiten für den Reisejournalisten, sich gegen diese übermächtigen Marktkräfte zu wehren? Wir glauben schon und diskutieren **Prinzipien der journalistischen Ethik** und was sie konkret für den Reisebereich bedeuten. Schließlich informieren wir den aufgeweckten Leser gern, was in diesem nicht immer sauberen Gewerbe möglich ist. Es ist in seinem Interesse, daß er fair informiert wird. Schmuddelige Verwischung von redaktioneller Arbeit, Werbung und PR belasten Journalist und Leser gleichermaßen. Nur wenn sie offen angesprochen werden, haben wir die Chance, gemeinsam über Besserung nachzudenken. Wir machen es hier vor allem auch orientiert an Erfahrungen im Ur-Land der journalistischen Ethik, den USA.

2 Die lange Geschichte der Reiseberichterstattung

Traveller - Postboy.	Reisender und Postillon.
T. Postilion, drive slowly.	Postillon (Schwager), fahren Sie langsam.
T. Take care you do not upset us.	Geben Sie Acht, dasz Sie uns nicht umwerfen.
T. The coachman (postilion) is - drunk - impertinent - follhardy.	Der Kutscher (Postillon) ist - betrunken - impertinent - tollkühn.
T. The carriage is near the precipice.	Der Wagen ist ganz nah dem Abgrund.
T. One of the wheels is off.	Ein Rad ist losgegangen.
T. Oh, dear! The postilion has been thrown (off) down.	O weh! Der Postillon ist herunter gefallen.

Aus: Murray´s Handbook of Travel-Talk 1874, einem Handbuch für britische Reisende im Ausland (zit. Newby 1985: 18).

2.1 Einleitung

Hans J. Kleinsteuber

Reisen ist eine uralte Menschheitsbetätigung, die sich in grauer Vorgeschichte verliert. Man denke nur an die Ausbreitung des Homo Sapiens über die gesamte Welt, die Wanderung der indianischen Urahnen von Asien nach Amerika, die antiken Seefahrer, die Völkerwanderung, die koloniale Eroberung - alles nur Vorläufer dessen, was heute den Kern multikultureller Gesellschaften ausmacht. Über Erlebnisse auf diesen Reisen ist wahrscheinlich schon immer berichtet worden, lange bevor es irgendwelche schriftlichen Quellen gab. Später, als Worte niedergeschrieben wurden, gab es viele Variationen, wie die Erfahrung der Ferne festgehalten wurde. Zahlreiche Reisebeschreibungen transportierten vor allem Mythen, es ging also nicht um eine tatsächliche Fortbewegung, sondern - zumindest im Vordergrund - um die uralten Menschheitsprobleme wie Leben und Tod, Religiosität, Sexualität etc. **Homers** großes Epos *Odyssee* ist ein gutes Beispiel dafür. Oder: Immer wieder wanderte die antike Sehnsucht in die Ferne, wo die legendäre Stadt Atlantis versunken sein sollte.

Aber in der Antike begann auch die sachliche Beschreibung von Reiseerfahrungen, für die mehr als jeder andere der Grieche **Herodot** (geb. 490 v. Chr.) steht. Es zog ihn bis nach Babylon und dem Ägypten der Pharaone. Seine Kultur- und Länderberichte wurden begeistert von den Daheimgebliebenen aufgenommen, wenn er seine Eindrücke 'zusammentrug' und 'zurückbrachte'. Genau diese Bedeutung des Heimbringens steckt in dem lateinischen Wort 'reportare', womit wir dann direkt in den Quellen der modernen Reise-'Reportage' wären. Michael Haller, der sicherlich fundierteste Autor zum Thema, beginnt seine Darstellung zu den Geheimnissen der modernen Reportage folgerichtig mit besagtem Geschichtenerzähler Herodot. (Haller 1987: 20ff) Halten wir fest, daß eine ganz zentrale, vielleicht sogar die wichtigste Quelle für das, was wir modernen Journalismus nennen, die Berichterstattung über die Fremde war.

Die **Sehnsucht nach der Ferne** wurde immer schon begleitet von der Angst vor dem Andersartigen, vor den Belastungen und Gefährdungen der Reise. Als **Marco Polo** aus dem chinesischen 'Reich der Mitte' zurückkehrte, hielt man ihn für einen Aufschneider; seine berühmten Erinnerungen mußte er im Gefängnis diktieren. Die eigene Selbstzufriedenheit ließ man sich nur ungern durch Konfrontation mit dem gänzlich Anderen verunsichern. Andererseits: Seit Herodot hat die Berichterstattung Erstaunliches und Erschreckliches von außerhalb in die Heimat zurückgetragen, und das hat immer seinen Marktwert gehabt, ließ sich die Reiseerfahrung wegen der Neugier der Zurückgebliebenen wohlfeil versilbern. Ganz weit weg, so lehren es viele Religionen, gibt es ein Paradies, aus dem die Menschen einst vertrieben wurden. Der Reisende ist immer auf dessen Suche und der Zurückgebliebene will wissen, ob es wiedergefunden wurde. Da die Realitäten in der Ferne naturgemäß oft recht ernüchternd waren, wurde gern dazugedichtet. Die phantastischen Ausschmückungen dienten der eigenen Selbsterhöhung zum wagemutigen Abenteurer. Oder sie wurden zur Vermarktung eingesetzt, um dem aufgeregten Zuhörer seine Vorurteile zu bestätigen und ihm Schauer über den Rücken laufen zu lassen.

Dies alles darf nicht so verstanden werden, als sei in der Vergangenheit das Reisen gefahrlos gewesen. Im Gegenteil: Wer sich im Zeitalter der Renaissance auf Reisen begab, - sofern er nicht ein ganz junger Mensch war - pflegte vorher sein Testament zu machen (Richter 1991: 100). Die **Gefähr-**

dungen durch Naturgewalten, durch Not, durch Räuber oder Piraten, durch feindseelige Völker war absolut real. Es waren diese tatsächlichen Gefahren, die als solche aber auch mythisch überhöht wurden: Skylla, das von Homer beschriebene sechsköpfige Meeresungeheuer, bedrohte zusammen mit seinem Gegenüber Charybdis die vorbeifahrenden Seefahrer. Reisejournalisten neigen mitunter dazu, moderne Versionen dieser uralten Reisemythen unter die Leserschaft zu bringen.

Werbung eines Atlantik-Überquerers, insbesondere für Auswanderer

— 319 —

Norddeutscher Lloyd.

Regelmäßige Post-Dampfschifffahrt

Bremen und Newyork,

Southampton anlaufend:

Von Bremen:	Von Newyork:	Von Bremen:	Von Newyork:
D. **Union**, 14. März.	9. April.	D. **Hansa**, 28. März.	23. April.
D. **Deutschland**, 21. März.	16. Apr.	D. **Bremen**, 4. April.	30. April.

ferner von Bremen jeden Sonnabend, von Southampton jeden Dienstag, von Newyork jeden Donnerstag.

Passage-Preise: Bis auf Weiteres: Erste Cajüte 165 Thaler, zweite Cajüte 100 Thaler, Zwischendeck 50 Thaler Courant incl. Beköstigung. Kinder unter 10 Jahren auf allen Plätzen die Hälfte. Säuglinge 3 Thaler.

Fracht: ermäßigt auf *l.* 2. mit 15% Primage pr. 40 Cubikfuß Bremer Maaße.

BREMEN und **BALTIMORE**

Southampton anlaufend.

Von Bremen:	Von Baltimore:	Von Bremen:	Von Baltimore:
D. **Baltimore** 1 März.	1. April.	D. **Baltimore** 1. Mai.	1. Juni.
D. **Berlin** 1. April.	1. Mai.	D. **Berlin** 1. Juni	1. Juli.

ferner von Bremen u. Baltimore jeden Ersten, von Southampton jeden Vierten des Monats

Passage-Preise bis auf Weiteres: Cajüte 120 Thaler, Zwischendeck 50 Thaler Crt., Kinder unter 10 Jahren auf allen Plätzen die Hälfte, Säuglinge 3 Thaler.

Fracht bis auf Weiteres: *l.* 2 mit 15 % Primage per 40 Cubikfuß Bremer Maaße. Nähere Auskunft ertheilen sämmtliche Passagier-Expedienten in Bremen und deren inländische Agenten, sowie

Die Direction des Norddeutschen Lloyd.

Crüsemann, Director. ***H. Peters,*** Procurant.

Quelle: Fürstlich lipperales Regierungs- und Anzeigen-Blatt; 7. März 1868

Das **Wechselverhältnis** zwischen dem aus der Ferne zurückkehrenden und dem **Daheimgebliebenen** prägte, das wird hier sehr deutlich, schon immer jede Art von Reiseberichterstattung. Man kann über Reiseerlebnisse nur schreiben, indem man sich ständig an demjenigen orientiert, der zurückblieb und deshalb am Konsum der Berichte zu interessieren ist. Der Marktwert eines **Reiseschreibers** richtet sich folglich entscheidend nach seiner Fähigkeit, den unausgesprochenen Erwartungen des Gegenübers entgegenzukommen. Früher gingen politisch-faktische und kulturell-impressionistische Berichte über andere Länder oft noch Hand in Hand. Man war froh, überhaupt Kunde von einem anderen Erdteil erhalten zu können. Heute bedienen dagegen die Nachrichtenagenturen den Markt der politischen und wirtschaftlichen Informationen aus aller Welt, auf die viele schon beruflich angewiesen sind. Diese Nachrichten, auch wenn sie trocken und spröde sind, müssen gelesen werden. Anders bei der modernen Reiseberichterstattung, deren Themen heute die Freizeit bereichern. Die Reisemedien finden sich zwischen Sport- und Hobbyzeitschriften am Kiosk oder auf den Wochenendseiten der Zeitung. Der Autor derartiger Berichte wird immer um den Leser werben müssen, dem reichlich andere Möglichkeiten zur Verfügung stehen, seine freie Stunden erlebnisreich zu gestalten. Ihm muß es gelingen, seinen Leser auf eine fiktive Reise mitzunehmen, ohne ihn zu bevormunden oder zu überfordern. Aber ähnliche Probleme, das sollte hier deutlich werden, hatte schon Herodot zu lösen.

Hermann Bausinger, Kulturwissenschaftler an der Universität Tübingen über Motive zum Reisen:

Mit der Urlaubsreise sucht der Mensch Gegenwelten: sonnige Landschaften, freie Natur, rustikale Umgebung und so weiter. Aber das bedeutet nicht unbedingt die radikale Abkehr von der eigenen Welt, von der man vieles im Gepäck mit sich führt - im wirklichen Gepäck, vor allem aber auch im übertragenen Sinn. Im Urlaub wird eine Vervollkommnung oder Verbesserung dessen angestrebt, was daheim nur unvollkommen gelingt. Als der Campingurlaub sich ausbreitete, wurde darüber meist aus romantischer Perspektive berichtet - freies Leben in freier Natur. Die aus solcher Naturbegeisterung entstandene Massierung von Zelten und Wohnwagen gilt allenthalben als ironische Pointe: Die Touristen werden wieder einmal eingeholt vom unvermeidlichen Massenauftrieb. Tatsächlich aber suchen die meisten Camper durchaus die Möglichkeit engen Kontakts mit Gleichgesinnten. Auch für andere Urlauber sind Kontakte wichtig, Formen unbeschwerter Geselligkeit - unbeschwert nicht zuletzt wegen ihrer Unverbindlichkeit. „Bis zum nächsten Jahr!“ heißt es am Ende des Urlaubs; und da die meisten Urlauber Jahr für Jahr das Reiseziel wechseln, stimmt oft nicht einmal das.

(Bausinger 1996:31)

Reisen und die Berichte darüber standen in ihrer langen und eindrucksvollen Geschichte immer in engem Wechselverhältnis zueinander. Zur Wiedergabe des Erfahrenen bediente sich der Autor der ihm jeweils zur Verfügung stehenden Techniken für Speicherung und Weiterverbreitung von Informationen. Im Altertum bis zum Ende des Mittelalters waren es die handschriftlich weitergegebenen Berichte, mit dem Buchdruck (ca. 1450 eingeführt) hatten alsbald Bücher über fremde Welten Konjunktur, die ersten gedruckten Periodika kamen im 17. Jahrhundert auf (erste Zeitungen ab ca. 1620), und Nachrichten über ferne Länder wurden zu deren festem Bestandteil. Schwieriger ist es schon, die Anfänge eines eigenständigen Reisejournalismus zu benennen. Wohl erstmals im 18. Jahrhundert, parallel zum Anstieg des europäischen Tourismus, finden sich erste Reiseartikel in der hier zugrundegelegten Bedeutung. Seitdem hat sich der Reisejournalismus beständig ausgebreitet und diversifiziert. Heute haben wir Mühe, Periodika zu finden, die nicht auch irgendwann Reiseberichte aufnehmen - und sei es zur Fußballmetropole in der Sportillustrierten oder zum Silicon Valley in der Computergazette.

Wegen der langen Geschichte der Reiseberichterstattung widmen wir ihr ein ganzes Kapitel. Darin findet der Leser **Hinweise auf Autoren und Quellen, Reisziele und kurze Charakterisierungen des Inhalts**. Breit ist das Spektrum der vorgestellten Autoren: Literaten und Abenteurer, Forschungsreisende und Entdecker. Ihre Beiträge sind aus mehreren Gründen von großer Bedeutung. Zum einen gibt es für jede Weltregion historische Reiseberichte, Klassiker also, die sich für aktuelle Einstiege eignen (vgl. dazu etwa: Märtin 1987, Newby 1985). Nun ist es keineswegs mehr sehr originell, zum hundertsten Male mit Johann Wolfgang von Goethe nach Italien zu reisen oder mit Theodor Fontane durch die Mark Brandenburg zu wandern. Andererseits ist das Wissen über deren Eindrücke oft schon Bestandteil unseres kollektiven Gedächtnisses geworden, sehen wir Reiseziele nicht zuletzt durch ihre Augen. Auch heute gilt, daß eine Reportage durch den Hinweis auf das belebt wird, was der Reisende 'damals' als wichtig empfand, was sich inzwischen geändert hat oder gleich geblieben ist. Im Sinne von Service am Leser stellen wir hier Hintergrundinformationen zur Verfügung, verbinden wir den historischen Abriß mit einem Verzeichnis vieler Klassiker einschließlich ihrer Reisziele. Zudem hängen wir einige typische Textpassagen an. Schließlich sollte nicht übersehen werden, daß damals wie heute die **Verbindung zwischen den Reiseredakteuren und den Reiseliteraten** fließend ist. Manch einer der heute gefeierten Reiseliteraten begann als Journalist, wie etwa Graham Greene und Bruce Chatwin bei der *Times*. Oder nehmen wir einen der international erfolgreichsten Bestseller-Autoren, Michael Crichton (Jurassic Parc), der erste Schreiberfahrungen mit Reisereportagen sammelte, inzwischen unter dem Titel 'Travels' (1989) erschienen. Seit Jahrhunderten treffen wir auf Autoren, die sowohl mit kurzen Artikeln journalistisch tätig sind, als auch umfängliche Folianten verfassen. Aus der Perspektive eines Autors und seines Überlebensinteresses gibt das auch Sinn: Oft bietet es sich an, ein Reisegebiet, das man sich mühsam erarbeitet hat, mehrfach zu vermarkten, also in Reportagen, in einem Reiseführer und/oder als literarisches Reisewerk. Offensichtlich ist nichts an diesen Verwertungsstrategien wirklich neu.

2.2 Überblick

Sonja Wielow

„Man ziehe den Rock des Landes an, das man besucht,
und bewahre den Rock des Landes auf, aus dem man stammt."
(Denis Diderot, 1713-1784)

Wenn einer eine Reise tut ... Und das taten schon die alten Griechen. Darüber erzählt und geschrieben haben sie auch. Die journalistische Reisereportage, wie wir sie heute in Magazinen, Zeitschriften und im Reiseteil der Tageszeitung finden, ist das Ergebnis einer literaturgeschichtlichen Entwicklung, die bis in die Antike zurückgeht. Dabei haben sich, abhängig von Reisemotiv und Schreibenden, fast unzählig viele verschiedene Arten der Reisebeschreibung herausgebildet: Da gab es die **Pilger des Mittelalters**, die **Entdecker Amerikas**, die **Bildungsreisenden des 18. Jahrhunderts**. Und alle hatten einen ungestümen Drang, andere am Erlebten teilhaben zu lassen. Schließlich gab es so viel Neues, Fremdes, Exotisches, über das sich zu schreiben lohnte. Heute, im Zeitalter des *homo last minuticus*, macht sich das Unbekannte rar. Denn Reisen ist bequem und billig geworden. Mit eigenen Augen kann man sich von dem überzeugen, was früher einigen wenigen vorbehalten war. Zwar ist auch das *arm-chair-travelling*, das Reisen im Kopf, beliebt. Doch immer häufiger liest man über Länder, von denen man aus persönlichen Gesprächen schon gehört hat, in denen man selbst schon gewesen ist oder die für den nächsten Urlaub als Ziel vorgemerkt sind. Eine harte Zukunft also für alle, die sich der Reiseberichterstattung verschrieben haben. Da heißt es, sich entweder mit ausgetretenen Pfaden zufrieden zu geben und dort immer wieder Neues zu entdecken - oder vielleicht die Fahrt zum Mond zu wagen...

Tröstlich dabei, daß zumindest die 'Artenvielfalt' innerhalb der Reiseliteratur groß ist. Reiseliteratur ist ein dehnbarer Begriff. Von **Reiseführern** und **Handbüchern**, mit sachlichen Informationen, über **wissenschaftliche Reisebeschreibungen** bis hin zu dichterisch ausgestalteten Reiseschilderungen, die entweder tatsächliche Erlebnisse wiedergeben oder von imaginären Gefahren und spannenden Abenteuern in der Fremde erzählen (**Reiseromane**), zählt alles dazu. Im folgenden Kapitel werden die wichtigsten literaturhistorischen Strömungen und Entwicklungsstufen der Reiseberichterstattung skizziert. Aus der schier unerschöpflichen Fülle an Primärliteratur wurden jeweils genretypische Autoren und Werke, vorwiegend aus dem deutschen und angelsächsischen Raum, ausgewählt.

2.3 Reiseliteratur von der Antike bis zur Romantik

Sonja Valentin

Seit dem **3. Jahrhundert v. Chr.** verfaßten die **Periegeten** ('antike Fremdenführer', von gr. periegesis = 'herumführen') Beschreibungen von Städten, Ländern und Sehenswürdigkeiten, die als die eigentlichen Vorläufer der modernen Reisehandbücher gelten. Der **Baedeker** ist nicht das Ei der Reiseliteratur!

2.3.1 Die Väter des literarischen Reiseberichts

Der literarische Reisebericht als traditioneller Vorläufer für die moderne journalistische Reisereportage hat viele berühmte Väter, deren 'Zeugungsanteil' heute allerdings umstritten ist. Als frühestes episches Muster gilt **Homers** *Odyssee* (ca. 850 v. Chr.), in der wir noch die dichterische Einheit von Reiseschilderungen und Abenteuern erkennen können. Es folgen die griechischen Reisebeschreibungen von **Skylax** aus Karyanda, der die persisch-arabische Küste von Indien bis Suez erforschte (um 516 v. Chr.) und von **Pytheas** von Massilia, dessen Bericht über seine Reise zu den Shetland- und Orkney-Inseln um 325 v. Chr. erschien. Eine erste Verbindung von erotischen und phantastischen Elementen, die später besonders in mittelalterlichen und Barockromanen mit stark exotischem Einschlag aufgegriffen wurden, finden wir in **Heliodors** *Aithiopika* (Ende 3. Jh.). In journalistischen

Handbüchern wird häufig **Herodot** (490-425), bedeutender Chronist und Volkskundler des hellenischen Altertums, als erster Reise- und Länderberichterstatter angeführt. Auf seinen Reisen von Kleinasien nach Ägypten, Griechenland und Italien erhob er die damals übliche Erzählform der Logoi zur literarischen Kunstform (gr. Lógos, 'das Sprechen'; menschliche Rede; Wort; Vernunft): kurze, in sich geschlossene Berichte mit Anekdoten und spannenden Geschichten über die Kulturen und Lebensweisen fremder Völker. Bereits in Herodots Logoi finden wir das Urelement jeder modernen Reisereportage: die Absicht, das Fremde und Andersartige dem Vertrauten gegenüberzustellen. Dabei nimmt der gute Erzähler dem Fremden das Befremdliche, läßt Vergangenes für die Leser gegenwärtig werden und vermittelt ihnen durch lebendige, sinnliche Schilderung der Erlebnisse das Gefühl, als begleiteten sie den Reisenden auf seinen Wegen.

Ein anderer namhafter Vater der modernen Reisereportage ist **Gajus Cacilius Plinius (der Jüngere)**. Mit seiner Schilderung vom Ausbruch des Vesuvs um Jahre 79 n. Chr. gelingt ihm ein spannender, eindrucksvoll sinnlicher Augenzeugenbericht, der heute noch als Glanzleistung des Altertums zitiert wird. Plinius schlüpft in die Rolle des Beobachters einer Naturkatastrophe und kommt mit seinem Anliegen, ein möglichst realistisches Bild der Ereignisse zu liefern, der ursprünglichen Bedeutung des lateinischen Begriffs reportare ('zusammentragen, überbringen') sehr nahe.

2.3.2 Reisebeschreibungen im Mittelalter

Als frühestes Beispiel einer literarischen Reisebeschreibung aus dem Mittelalter gilt **Marco Polos** Bericht *Il millione* (verfaßt 1298/99, dt. 1477 unter dem Titel *Die Reisen des Venezianers Marco Polo*) über die Mongolei. Im **15. und 16. Jahrhundert** entsteht eine wahre Flut an Reiseschilderungen von Pilgern, sogenannte **Pilgerführer**, die mit ihren Vorläufen bis ins 12. Jahrhundert zurückreichen und innerhalb der Literaturwissenschaft eine eigene literarische Gattung bilden. Aus der Fülle der Pilgerberichte sei ein Titel herausgegriffen: *Die heyligen reyssen gen Jherusalem* des **Bernhard von Breydenbach** (1486). Im Wortlaut des lateinischen Originals, *Peregrinationes in Terrram Sanctam*, finden wir bereits das charakteristische Merkmal einer guten Reisebeschreibung: Das Wort peregrinus bedeutet 'der Fremde' und bezieht sich im Kontext der Pilgerreisen auf denjenigen, der in der Fremde sein Heil sucht. In der biblischen Überlieferung gilt Abraham als der erste Pilger, da er auszog, um das verheißene Land zu finden.

2.3.3 Reiseliteraten der frühen Neuzeit

Mit Beginn der **Neuzeit** und der Epoche der Eroberungskriege, Seereisen und Expeditionen verwandelt sich der klassische Reisebericht mehr in eine Abenteuergeschichte, die **Vorurteile gegenüber fremden Kulturen** bestärkt und häufig eher zum Zeugnis abendländischer Arroganz und Habgier wird, als der Aufklärung zu dienen. Die Entdeckung neuer Länder führt aber auch zur Verlegung utopischer Staatsromane in ferne Gebiete und regt Autoren wie **Grimmelshausen** (*Der Fliegende Wandersmann nach dem Mond*, 1650, *Simplicissimus*, 1669) oder **Reuter** (*Schelmuffskys Warhaftig Curiöse und sehr gefährliche Reisebeschreibung zu Wasser und Lande*, 1669/70) zu phantastischen und parodistischen Reisebeschreibungen an.

In der frühen Neuzeit wächst die Reiselust - und mit ihr ein ganzer Bücherwald von Veröffentlichungen. Unter den verschiedenen Formen der Reiseliteratur sind die im 16. Jahrhundert auftauchenden **Apodemiken** besonders hervorzuheben. Sie beschäftigen sich weniger mit der Beschreibung von Reiserouten oder Sehenswürdigkeiten als mit dem theoretischen Konzept des Reisens als Kunst und Wissenschaft. Ursprünglich in lateinischer Sprache abgefaßt, beinhalten apodemische Handbücher philosophische Erörterungen über die Nützlichkeit (und die Schädlichkeit) des Reisens und geben Empfehlungen für das richtige (christlich-moralische) Verhalten des Reisenden in der Fremde. Vor allem im Zusammenhang mit der Verbürgerlichung der *grand tour* junger Adliger liefern Apodemiken wichtige Informationen für die (Bildungs-) Reisekultur der Zeit.

2.3.4 Reiseliteratur zwischen Aufklärung, Romantik und Sturm und Drang

Seit **Mitte des 18. Jahrhunderts** beginnt sich der kritische Diskurs über Sinn und Zweck des Reisens in die für die **Aufklärung** exemplarischen Zeitschriften und Journale zu verlagern, und aus den Apodemiken entwickelt sich das Reisehandbuch im modernen Sinne.

In Deutschland gelangt der Reisebericht als literarische Gattung erst mit dem Niedergang der höfischen Barockdichtung im 17. Jahrhundert zu neuer Blüte und erfreut sich vor allem bei den Dichtern des **Sturm und Drang** (ca. 1765-1785) großer Beliebtheit, da sie in ihm eine vom Zwang zur Authentizität und Überprüfbarkeit weitgehend befreite Gefühlsschilderung sehen. Für den kometenhaften Aufstieg des **empfindsamen Reiseromans** in Deutschland gibt **Laurence Sterne** mit *A sentimental journey through France and*

Italy (1768, dt. *Yoricks empfindsame Reise durch Frankreich und Italien*) den entscheidenden Impuls. In seiner direkten Nachfolge steht zum Beispiel *Sophiens Reise von Memel nach Sachsen* (1769-73) von **Johann Timotheus Hermes**. **Novalis'** *Heinrich von Ofterdingen* (1802) gilt als Musterbeispiel für den frühromantischen Reiseroman. Natürlich darf an dieser Stelle der 'Klassiker' der deutschen Reiseliteratur nicht fehlen: **Goethes** *Italienische Reise* (1829), eine Zusammenstellung von Briefen und Tagebuchaufzeichnungen des Dichters, markiert den Höhepunkt und zugleich einen neuen, vom Korsett des einheitlichen Handlungsstranges befreiten Typus der Reiseberichterstattung.

Nach den Pilgerreisen des Mittelalters und der frühen Neuzeit, den Kavalierstouren des Barocks, den Handelsreisen der Kaufleute und den Wanderungen des Theaterleute von Hof zu Hof begeben sich seit Mitte des 18. Jahrhunderts vor allem bildungsbeflissene Bürger auf die Reise.

Getrieben von botanischen, archäologischen, literarischen, kunsthistorischen und ökonomischen Interessen, erobern deutsche Reisende im Jahrhundert der Aufklärung Italien, Griechenland, die Schweiz und die britischen Inseln. Vor allem England gehört dank seiner vorbildlichen sozialen und politischen Verhältnisse bald zum unverzichtbaren Bestandteil der **bürgerlichen Bildungsreise**. London wird zum Anziehungspunkt für anglophile Reisende aus Deutschland, die in der pulsierenden Metropole Abenteuer und Erfahrungsmöglichkeiten suchen, die ihnen die verschlafene Heimat nicht bieten kann. Die Faszination der Großstadt - mit London und Paris als Zentren - schlägt sich in einer Vielzahl von Veröffentlichungen nieder.

Neben Tagebüchern, Briefen, Apodemiken, Naturbeobachtungen, politischen und pädagogischen Reiseberichten entsteht im 18. Jahrhundert eine neues Genre der Reiseliteratur: die **Stadtbeschreibung**. Paris und London besitzen für den modernen, 'säkularisierten Pilger' eine ähnliche Anziehungskraft wie Rom und Jerusalem für seine mittelalterlichen Vorfahren. In seinen *Englischen Fragmenten* begrüßt **Heinrich Heine** (1797-1856) England als das Land der Freiheit, und er formuliert eine neues Programm des Reisens, bei dem es nicht darum geht, die Fremde nur zu beschreiben, sondern sie im Hinblick auf die politischen und kulturellen Verhältnisse in der Heimat darzustellen. (Ein ähnliches Ziel verfolgte übrigens schon der römische Historiker **Publius Cornelius Tacitus**, als er 98 n. Chr. seine ethnographische Studie über die Germanen verfaßte: *Germania*).

Die Anglophilie der Aufklärer läßt **England** in das Zentrum europäischer Interessen rücken, und deutlicher noch als andere Reiseberichte prägen Englandbeschreibungen die Verständigung des Bürgertums über eigene Werte.

Man kann sogar annehmen, daß sich das moderne Selbstbild einer deutschen Nation nicht ohne Auseinandersetzung mit der englischen entwickelte hätte. **Friedrich Engels** Bericht über *Die Lage der arbeitenden Klasse in England* (1845) gehört zwar nicht zum klassischen Repertoire des Reiseliteratur, doch für moderne Englandfahrer bietet die Lektüre interessante Vergleichsmöglichkeiten.

Der österreichische Kommunikationswissenschaftler Kurt Luger zu den Grundmustern des literarischen Reiseberichts:

Der literarische Reisebericht, der als Genre auf eine große Tradition verweisen kann, gibt dem 'Ich' wesentlich mehr Spielraum. Mehrere Grundtypen lassen sich unterscheiden. Ob sich der Schriftsteller auf eine überwiegend biographische Auffassung vom Dort-Sein festlegt oder auf eine abenteuerliche, eine beobachtende oder reflektierende, er bestimmt damit ein bekenntnishaftes Verfahren, das er im Text zum Ausdruck bringt. Das Grundmuster - Ich war dort - teilt er mit dem Ethnologen, aber im Unterschied zu diesem wird das 'Ich' wichtiger: Es wird zu einem Filter, das dem öffentlichen Räsonnieren eine andere Richtung gibt. Selbst in der Reflexion drückt sich diese gewollte Subjektivität aus, der Leser soll nachvollziehen können, was der Reisende empfunden hat, soll an dessen Interpretationen teilhaben können, ohne einen Kulturwechsel, eine Perspektivenänderung vornehmen zu müssen. Über die Länder, in die die Reise führte, erfährt man allerdings in vielen dieser literarischen Erkundungen fast gar nichts, über den Autor dafür fast alles.

(Luger 1994: 9)

2.3.5 Reisebeschreibungen im 19. Jahrhundert

Die Form des **feuilletonistischen Reiseberichts** wie wir sie aus Magazinen und Tageszeitungen des **19. Jahrhunderts** kenne, gewinnt unter dem Einfluß **Heinrich Heines** und des *Jungen Deutschland* neu an Popularität. Vor allem Heine (*Harzreise*, 1826) gelingt es, Natur- und Landschaftsschilderungen mit kritischer Gesellschaftssatire zu verbinden, ohne das literarische Genre zu wechseln. In zahlreichen Werken der Romantik (1789-1832) spiegeln sich Abenteuer- und Reiselust (z.B. in **Joseph von Eichendorffs** Novelle *Aus dem Leben eine Taugenichts*, 1826), begleitet von einem charakteristischen Reisemotiv des 19. und 20. Jahrhunderts: der Sehnsucht in die Ferne von Raum und Zeit.

2.4 Die angelsächsische Tradition

Sonja Wielow

2.4.1 Die britische Reiseliteratur

Kurios, aber wahr: Die Geschichte der britischen Reiseliteratur nimmt ihren Lauf im deutschen Heidenheim. In ihrem Kämmerlein schreibt eine Nonne - anonym - über den angeblich ersten reisenden 'Englishman' Willibald, der 718 n. Chr. mit seiner Familie nach Rom aufbricht. Doch erst einige Jahrhunderte später, **um 1500**, boomt der Markt der Reiseliteratur auf der britischen Insel dann zum ersten Mal so richtig. Mit der in Mode kommenden **Pilgerreise** tauchen unzählige *guide-books* auf, die über Wegstrecken und Reiseziele informieren.

Doch nicht nur beflissene Schreiberlinge wittern ein Geschäft. An den Pilgerstätten machen sich Souvenierverkäufer breit, kleine Reisebüros öffnen ihre Pforten. Sie locken auch damals schon mit *all-in package tours*: England - Santiago de Compostela hin und zurück, achttägige Schiffsreise, Unterkunft, Verpflegung, Eselsritt inklusive. Bekanntestes Zeugnis einer Pilgerreise dieser Zeit dürften wohl **Geoffrey Chaucers** *Canterbury Tales* (ca. 1380) sein. Und schon 1357 verfaßt **Sir John Mandeville** seine *Travels*. Allerdings werden hier Fakten und phantastische Ausschweifungen munter miteinander vermischt, geographische Angaben über die verschiedenen Teile der Erde bleiben geradezu bemerkenswert vage.

Der Markt der Reiseliteratur wächst ständig; besonders ab dem **16. Jahrhundert** werden Publikationen über fremde Länder zahlreicher. Denn die Briten wagen sich immer weiter vor in der Welt. Sie machen sich auf in die Kontinente, sind von der Karibik bis in den Fernen Osten unterwegs. So ziemlich alles wird erforscht, was sich nur irgendwie untersuchen läßt. In den *Principal Navigations, Voiages, and Discoveries of the English Nation* (1598) von **Richard Hakluyt** ist nachzulesen, was die Insulaner über Menschen, Flora und Fauna in fremden Ländern erfahren haben.

Zu den *Discoveries* gehören aber nicht nur theoretische Erkenntnisse. Die Entdecker bringen ihre Funde den Daheimgebliebenen auf ganz praktische Art und Weise nahe: Im Park von St. James in London kann der erstaunte Spaziergänger 1623 einige friedlich grasende Kamele bewundern.

Neben denen, die ihre Forschungsergebnisse zu Papier bringen, greifen auch die zur Feder, die in diplomatischer, kirchlicher oder militärischer Mission unterwegs sind. Selbst Kolonisten und Piraten auf Kaperfahrt lassen es sich nicht nehmen, die Öffentlichkeit - in einer oftmals haarsträubenden

Orthographie - mit ihren Beschreibungen zu beglücken. Diese haben vorwiegend faktologischen Charakter - Übertreibungen und kleine Phantastereien allerdings eingeschlossen.

Die Laienschreiber treten in den Hintergrund, als sich ein Großer der professionell schreibenden Zunft der Sache annimmt: Der Journalist **Daniel Defoe** schafft mit einem fiktiven Werk - dem Roman *The Life and Strange Surprising Adventures of Robinson Crusoe* (1719) - einen literarischen Evergreen und Bestseller. In aller Welt wird das Buch über den nach einem Schiffbruch auf einer exotischen einsamen Insel gestrandeten Robinson begeistert gelesen. Das Reiseabenteuer soll noch Jahrhunderte später in sogenannten 'Robinsonaden' zahllose Nachahmer finden.

Doch nicht nur Abschweifungen in große Ferne kommen beim Lesepublikum gut an. Auch die schriftlichen Belege der *home travels* erfreuen sich großer Beliebtheit. Gleichzeitig ist das **18. Jahrhundert** aber auch das Jahrhundert der Bildungsreise auf dem Kontinent. Auf der sogenannten *grand tour* sollen adelige Jünglinge einen Teil ihrer höfischen Erziehung genießen. *Journals* und *diaries* überschwemmen den Buchmarkt. Ihre Verfasser preisen die Vorzüge eines Aufenthalts in Frankreich und Italien und brandmarken den Daheimgebliebenen als gesellschaftliche Unperson - wie zum Beispiel **Lady Mary Wortley Montague**, die als Frau eines Diplomaten den Kontinent bereist und ihre Erlebnisse in Briefform festhält. So widmen sich auch die großen Autoren des 18. Jahrhunderts dem Topos: von **Tobias George Smollett** bis **Laurence Sterne**, von **James Boswell** bis **Henry Fielding**. Im Zusammenhang mit dieser Epoche darf auch **Johnathan Swift** nicht unerwähnt bleiben, der mit *Travels into Several Remote Nations of the World* (1726) - besser bekannt als *Gullivers Reisen* - eine utopisch-satirische Reisebeschreibung geschaffen hat, die den Leser in ein Zwergenland und das Reich der Riesen entführt.

Das **19. Jahrhundert** ist dann durch eine eher realistische Art der Reiseschilderungen gekennzeichnet. Autoren machen es sich zum Ziel, über Menschen, Länder und Ereignisse unvoreingenommen zu berichten. **Charles Dickens** ist - mit seinen *Pictures from Italy* (1846) zum Beispiel - einer der Verfechter dieser realistischen Darstellungsweise, die sich bis ins 20. Jahrhundert fortsetzen soll.

2.4.2 Die amerikanische Reiseliteratur

Rund 800 Jahre nachdem die Heidenheimer Nonne am Schreibpult ihr kleines Werk vollendet hat, setzt **Edward Haie** 1593 den Grundstein der nordamerikanischen Reiseliteratur. Er erzählt von der Fahrt des Engländers Sir Humphrey Gilbert zu den Ufern des knapp hundert Jahre zuvor entdeckten Kontinents. Das '*New-found-land*' bleibt bis ins 19. Jahrhundert das beherrschende Thema der Reiseliteratur. Es bietet so viel Unbekanntes, daß den Reisenden - und Schreibenden - kaum Zeit bleibt, sich mit anderen Zielen in der Welt zu beschäftigen. Die Schreiber sind keine Literaten, sondern zunächst „nur" englische Seefahrer. Wie **Captain John Smith**, der Virginia erforscht und in der Schrift mit dem bemerkenswerten Titel *A True Relation of such Occurences and Accidents of Note as hath hapned in Virginia since the first planting of that Colony* (1608) über die erste Kolonie in Nordamerika berichtet. Auf die Entdeckung des Kontinents folgen Niederlassung, Ausbeutung und Kolonisation, und nun sind es die Grund- und Bodenmakler, die, um potentielle Käufer zu locken, sich über Landschaften und Klima ausbreiten.

Ganz nebenbei, und unfreiwillig, entstehen weitere **Reisedarstellungen von Laien**. Bei Streifzügen durch den Kontinent werden viele Siedler von Indianern überfallen und gefangengenommen. Einige, die ein solches Abenteuer überleben, schreiben ihre Erfahrungen auf. **Mary Rowlandson** verfaßt 1682 das erste bekannte Werk dieser Art. Im selben Jahrhundert kommen auch die Quäker ins Land und hinterlassen unzählige Berichte, Reisebeschreibungen und Pamphlete über die Neue Welt, geschrieben von Frauen und Männern gleichermaßen. Als erster Freizeit- und Vergnügungsreisender geht dann **Alexander Hamilton** 1744 mit den Ausführungen über seine Reise von Annapolis nach Portsmouth in New Hampshire in die nordamerikanische Literaturgeschichte ein.

Das Interesse an geographischen Gegebenheiten, Naturwundern, Flora und Fauna wächst. Auf Expeditionen, die diese Neugier mit neugewonnenen Erkenntnissen stillen soll, ist auch immer ein Chronist mit von der Partie. Manchmal greifen die **Anführer der Forschungsreisen** sogar selbst zur Feder, wie **Jonathan Carver** oder **William Bartram**. Letzterer hält seine Beobachtungen in einem *journal*, einem Reisetagebuch, fest.

Diese und andere auf ähnliche Art entstandenen Berichte finden in der alten Welt beim britischen Publikum wenig Anklang. So wenig, daß **Sydney Smith** im *Edinburgh Review* vom Januar 1820 schreibt: „In the four quarters of the globe, who reads an American book?" Einen solchen Affront kann und will man nicht einfach auf sich sitzen lassen. Und so nehmen sich endlich hauptberufliche Schreiber der Darstellung ihres Landes an: **James Fenimore Cooper** und **Washington Irving**. Mit ihren Werken, wie *The Wept of Wish-ton-Wish* (1829, Cooper) oder *Astoria, or Anecdotes of an Enterprise beyond the Rocky Mountains* (1836, Irving), überzeugen sie die skeptischen Leser auf der britischen Insel, daß auch fern von der alten Welt 'echte' Literaten Zuhause sind.

Nachdem das einmal klargestellt ist, wenden sich die Amerikaner wieder den wirklich wichtigen Dingen des Lebens zu: nämlich der weiteren Erforschung 'ihres' Landes. Einzelne Landstriche und Streckenabschnitte werden zum Gegenstand zeitgenössischer Literatur. Der *Santa Fé Trail* führt Reisende - und Schreibende - nach Texas, Arizona und New Mexiko. Der *Oregon Trail* bringt sie nach Kalifornien und in die Rocky Mountains. Noch heute findet sich in vielen Bibliotheken der USA ein Standardwerk zu diesem Thema, **Thomas Jefferson Farnhams** *Travels in the Great Western Prairies, the Anahuac and the Rocky Mountains and the Oregon Territory* (1843).

Im Schlepptau der Entdecker befinden sich auch Missionare und Mormonen, die ihrerseits über ihre Erlebnisse schreiben. Professioneller geht ein erfolgloser Bergarbeiter zu Werke. Zunächst Journalist, wird er Autor von Weltklasse: **Mark Twain** - bekannt durch Tom Sawyers und Huckleberry Finns Abenteuer - verfaßt auch Geschichten, die sich ausschließlich mit dem Reisen beschäftigen. Sein Lieblingsthema ist dabei immer wieder das Leben an und auf dem Mississippi.

Weder Mittel- noch Südamerika bleiben vom Forschungsdrang der Nordamerikaner verschont. Die entsprechende Reiseliteratur entsteht. Der Goldrausch zieht die Verstreuten in die Heimat zurück. Wieder wird eine Welle der Reisebeschreibungen ausgelöst. Genauso ist es, als die Planungen für die *Pacific Railway* beginnen. Und nachdem sich auch Scouts und Jäger zur schriftlichen Niederlegung ihrer Erlebnisse entschlossen haben und *Cowboy-Poets* zu Ruhm gelangt sind, haben die Amerikaner endlich wieder Zeit, sich dem Rest der Welt zuzuwenden. Sie bereisen Asien, den Orient, die Südsee, die Weltmeere. Man denke hier nur an **Herman Melvilles** *Moby Dick* (1926). Kaum ist Alaska im Besitz der USA, zieht es die schreibenden Reisenden auch dorthin.

2.5 Moderne Reiseberichterstattung

Sonja Valentin / Sonja Wielow

2.5.1 Britische Reiseliteratur

Im 20. Jahrhundert überschneidet sich der Kanon bedeutender Reisedarstellungen oft mit dem bekannter Autoren. Viele britische Schriftsteller widmen sich neben anderen Themen auch dem des Reisens, wie **D.H. Lawrence**, **Aldous Huxley**, **Evelyn Waugh** und **E. M. Forster**. Der versteht seine *Passage to India* (1924) als Antwort auf **Rudyard Kiplings** verklärte Hommage an die ehemalige britische Kronkolonie.

In den **dreißiger Jahren** scheint das intellektuelle Leben im britischen Traditionalismus zu ersticken. Unter den Schriftstellern bricht das große Reisefieber aus. Berlin. Paris. Moskau. Der Ferne Osten. Sie locken die Insulaner auf den Kontinent. Der Reisebericht avanciert kurzfristig zur dominanten literarischen Gattung. Von der Aufbruchsstimmung läßt sich auch **Peter Fleming** - ein Bruder des *James Bond*-Erfinders **Ian Fleming** - anstekken. Der exzentrische Weltenbummler unternimmt eine 6 000 Kilometer lange Reise von Peking bis nach Indien. Während dieser Zeit macht er eine zentrale - und enttäuschende - Erfahrung der Zeit: Die anderen sind immer schon vor ihm dagewesen. Davon läßt sich **Graham Greene**, Zeitgenosse Flemings, nicht entmutigen: Über Jahrzehnte fällt er dem Laster des Reisens anheim, das ihn von Liberia bis nach Südamerika lockt.

In den **fünfziger Jahren** dann findet selbst **Daniel Defoe** noch einen späten Nachahmer: **William Golding** schreibt seine - moderne - Robinsonade *The Lord of the Flies* (1954), in der es gleich eine ganze Gruppe 'flugzeugbrüchiger' Kinder auf eine einsame Insel verschlägt. Weniger dramatisch geht es in **Bruce Chatwins** und **Neal Aschertons** Reiseromanen zu, die dem Interessierten heute auf der Suche nach Lesestoff über die Ferne in die Hände fallen. Dabei steht Ascherton wieder ganz in der Herodotschen Tradition: Als Reporter ist der schottische Historiker in der ganzen Welt unterwegs.

2.5.2 Amerikanische Reiseliteratur

Auch amerikanische Schriftsteller zeigen sich in unserem Jahrhundert immer noch reiselustig. **Ernest Hemingway** und **John Steinbeck** arbeiteten für die

Reiseressorts großer Zeitungen und verbanden den journalistischen Reportagestil mit literarischen Elementen. Sie waren so Vorbilder für die *new journalists* der **sechziger Jahre**.

Paul Theroux ist ein Name, der seit 25 Jahren eine wesentliche Rolle in der amerikanischen Reiseliteratur spielt. Er sucht nicht nach exotischen Abenteuern, sondern spürt neugierig den kleinen Begebenheiten des Alltags nach, für die man in vertrauter Umgebung so schnell den Sinn verliert. Er berichtet über Land und Leute, fängt aber gleichzeitig auch das Lebensgefühl des Reisens ein.

Diese Gabe ist den angelsächsischen Schriftstellern bis heute nicht verloren gegangen, während deutsche das Schreiben über das Reisen verlernt zu haben scheinen. In Großbritannien und den USA füllen Reiseromane die Regale ganzer 'Travel-Sections' in den Buchhandlungen. In deutschen Landen sucht man dagegen vergeblich nach einer solchen Abteilung.

Literarische Reiseliteratur hat in angelsächsischen Ländern eine lange Tradition. Bei uns führt sie häufig ein Schattendasein.

Berlin: Ein junger Mann betritt eine Buchhandlung. Er erkundigt sich nach Reiseliteratur. Die Verkäuferin fragt, wo er denn hin will, um ihn auf das entsprechende Sortiment an Reiseführern verweisen zu können: Kunst-Reiseführer, Abenteuer-Reiseführer, Individual-Reiseführer, Reisen-mit-Kind-Reiseführer. Der Mann will aber gar nicht verreisen. Er will lesen.

London: Die Frage nach Reiseliteratur führt zu einem Regal, dessen Bücher nicht nach Ländern, sondern nach Autoren geordnet sind: Bruce Chatwin, James Fenton, Norman Lewis, Jan Morris, Eric Newby, Jonathan Raban, Paul Theroux etc.

Im Gegensatz zu Deutschland wird in Großbritannien der zweite Teil des Begriffs '*Reiseliteratur*' ernst genommen. Nicht daß es hierzulande keine guten Reiseberichte gäbe, es kennt sie nur kaum einer. Zugegeben, daß Goethe in Italien war, ist allgemein bekannt. Auch Heinrich Böll hätte Irland als Thema der diesjährigen Frankfurter Buchmesse nicht gebraucht. Ob Alfred Andersch, der über Spitzbergen geschrieben hat, mit Norwegen geholfen wäre, ist schon eher wahrscheinlich. Das 'Verzeichnis lieferbarer Bücher' vermerkt lapidar: „Andersch, Alfred, 'Hohe Breitengrade'. Letzte Auflage 1989, z. Zt. Vergriffen, Datum der Neuauflage unbestimmt."

(Hager 1997)

2.5.3 *Deutsche Reiseliteratur*

Das Feld der modernen deutschen Reiseliteratur ist in der Tat alles andere als weit. Kommerzielle Reiseführer und Spezialzeitschriften dominieren den Markt und werden zur wichtigsten Bezugsquelle für den modernen Touristen.

Mit der Veröffentlichung des ersten praktischen Reisehandbuchs von **Karl Baedeker** im Jahr 1835 (*Rheinreise von Straßburg nach Rotterdamm*) vollzieht sich ein entscheidender **Wandel von der literarischen Reisebeschreibung zum zweckorientierten, schematischen Reiseführer**. Statt den Leser in die fremde Welt zu entführen und ihm eine ästhetisch-sinnliche Reiseerfahrung (wenn auch nur in der Imagination) anzubieten, geht es im Zeitalter des modernen Massentourismus um schnelle, praktische Information, die die Reiseplanung erleichtert und das Programm der Sehenswürdigkeiten vorgibt. Natürlich gibt es Ausnahmen und Mischformen auch unter den Reiseführern: 1948 erscheint im Verlag *Hoffmann und Campe* die erste Ausgabe des Reise- und Kulturmagazin *Merian*, das bis heute unverändert jeden Monat pro Heft eine Stadt, eine Landschaft oder eine Region der Erde vorstellt. Hier verknüpfen sich in vorbildlicher Manier traditionelle, literarische, geschichtliche und sinnliche Aspekte der Reisebeschreibung mit praktischen Informationen (vergl. Abschnitt 5.11).

Zurück zur **literarischen Reisebeschreibung im 20. Jahrhundert**. Die **Weimarer Republik** ist eine Zeit der kurzen Form: Tagebuchnotizen, Skizzen, kulturkritische Essays und Reportagen spiegeln die Reiseerfahrungen des modernen Wanderers, den es allerdings nicht mehr - wie seinen romantischen Vorgänger - in die unbehauste Natur zieht, sondern in die Großstadt. Die **Stadt** wird zum prägendsten Erlebnisraum aller modernen Reiseerfahrung. Vor allem in den zwanziger und dreißiger Jahren unseres Jahrhunderts avanciert die fremde Metropole zum Hauptanziehungspunkt für Journalisten, Schriftsteller, Künstler. In den Berichten der Zeit spiegelt sich die Mischung aus Faszination und Beklemmung, mit der die Reisenden dem 'Mythos Stadt' begegnen. Während **Ludwig Börne** sich bei seinen Spaziergängen durch Paris noch der müßigen Betrachtung seiner Umgebung widmen kann, wird der moderne Großstadtreisende in den Strom der Lichter, Autos- und Menschenmassen gerissen.

Besonders spektakulär scheint allen Reiseliteraten dabei die amerikanische Metropole **New York**. War Jerusalem das Mekka des Pilgerreisenden im Mittelalter, so wird New York zum Eldorado des modernen Flaneurs und Freizeitmenschen. Wolkenkratzer, Verkehrslärm, Leuchtreklamen und Straßenlabyrinthe beherrschen die touristischen Impressionen - und ihre literarische Umsetzung. In fast hymnischen Beschwörungsformeln drückt zum Beispiel **Alfred Kerr** seine Begeisterung für das *Yankee-Land* und dessen urbane Zentren aus (1925). **Egon Erwin Kisch** steht dem Reiseerlebnis Amerika weniger enthusiastisch gegenüber und versucht, in seinen Reportagen auch die soziale Realität im Land der unbegrenzten Möglichkeiten wiederzugeben (*Paradies Amerika*, 1930).

Neben New York zieht vor allem **Moskau** viele Reisende an, die in der Stadt den Beginn eines neuen (ideologischen) Zeitalters suchen. **Ernst Toller** (*Russische Reisebilder*, 1926) ist hier ebenso zu nennen wie **Walter Benjamin** (*Moskau*, 1927) und **Heinrich Vogeler** (Reise durch Rußland, 1925).

Das **Dritte Reich** und der **Zweite Weltkrieg** bringen einen massiven Einschnitt in die deutsche Reiseliteratur, und mit Ausnahme der literarischen Umsetzung von Exilerfahrung gibt es zwischen 1930 und 1950 keine nennenswerten Reisebeschreibungen.

In der Reiseliteratur **nach 1945** läßt sich eine Wendung zu nichtfiktionalen, reflektierenden und autobiographischen Formen erkennen. Ein charakteristisches, trotz aller Stereotypen vielzitiertes Beispiel ist **Heinrich Bölls** *Irisches Tagebuch* (1957). Zu den fiktionalen Entdeckungen neuer Welten gehören *Die Stimme aus Marrakesch* von **Elias Canettis** (1967) und **Peter Handkes** Amerika-Erzählung *Der kurze Brief zum langen Abschied* (1972).

Da Phantasie und Wirklichkeit sich gerade beim 'Abenteuer Reisen' nicht immer trennen lassen, hat **Kurt Tucholsky** recht, wenn er sagt: „Es kommt freilich nicht darauf an, wo man seine Koffer hinträgt; es kommt darauf an, was man nach Hause bringt - im Kopf." (*Das Zeltdorf*, 1932)

2.6 Lektürehinweise: Reiseliteratur

2.6.1 Britische Reiseliteratur

Geoffrey Chaucer	*Canterbury Tales* (ca. 1380)
John Mandeville	*Travels* (1357) (verschiedene Erdteile)
Richard Hayklut	*Principal Navigations, Voiages, and Discoveries of the English Nation* (1598) (verschiedene Erdteile)
Daniel Defoe	*The Life and Strange Surprising Adventures of Robinson Crusoe, of York, Mariner* (1719) (Engl., Brasilien, Afrika, Südamerika)

Mary Wortley Montague	*Embassy Letters* (1763) (Türkei)
Tobias George Smollett	*Humphrey Clinker* (1771) (Badereise durch England und Schottland) *Travels through France and Italy* (1766)
Laurence Sterne	*A Sentimental Journey through France and Ital* (1768)
James Boswell	*An Account of Corsica* (1768) *Journal of a Tour to the Hebrides* (1785)
Henry Fielding	*The Journal of a Voyage to Lisbon* (1755)
Jonathan Swift	*Travels into Several Remote Nations of the World* (1726)
Charles Dickens	*Sketches by Boz* (1839) (London) *American Notes* (1842) *Pictures from Italy* (1846)
David Herbert Lawrence	*Sea and Sardinia* (1923)
Aldous Huxley	*Across the Mexique Bay* (1934)
Evelyn Waugh	*When the Going was Good* (1946) (verschiedene Erdteile)
E. M. Forster	*A Passage to India* (1924)
Rudyard Kipling	*Plain Tales from the Hill* (1888) (Indien)
Peter Fleming	*Brazilian Adventure* (1933) *News from Tartary* (1936) (Reise von Peking nach Indien)
Graham Greene	*Journey without Maps* (1936) (Liberia) *Lawless Roads* (1939) (Mexiko) *Travels with my Aunt* (1969) (Europa, Südamerika)
William Golding	*Lord of the Flies* (1954)
Bruce Chatwin	*In Patagonia* (1978) *The Songlines* (1987) (Australien) *What am I doing here* (1989) (verschiedene Erdteile)
Neal Ascherson	*Black Sea* (1995)

2.6.2 Amerikanische Reiseliteratur

John Smith	*A True Relation of such Occurences and Accidents of Note as hath hapned in Virginia since the first planting of that Colony* (1608) *The True Travels, Adventures, and Observations of Captain John Smith in Europe, Asia, Africa, and America, from ... 1593 to 1629...* (1630)
Mary Rowlandson	*A Narrative of the Captivity and Removes of Mrs. Mary Rowlandson* (1682) (Nordamerika, Ostküste)
Jonathan Carver	*Travels through the Interior Parts of North America* (1778)
William Bartram	*Travels through North and South Carolina, Georgia, East.and West Florida, the Cherokee Country, the Extensive.Territories of the Muscogulges or Creek Confederacy, and the Country of the Chactaws* (1791)
James Fenimore Cooper	*The Red Rover* (1827) (Nordamerika) *The Wept of Wish-ton-Wish* (1829) (Nordamerika) *The Water Witch* (1830) (Nordamerika)
Washington Irving	*A Tour of the Prairies* (1835) (Nordamerika) *Astoria, or Anecdotes of an Enterprise beyond the Rocky Mountains* (1836)
Thomas Jefferson Farnham	*Travels in the Great Western Prairies, the Anahuac and the Rocky Mountains and the Oregon Territory* (1843) *Life, Adventures and Travels in California* (1849)
Mark Twain	*Life on the Mississippi* (1883) *Letter to the Californian Pioneers* (1911)
Herman Melville	*Moby Dick* (1926) (Atlantik, Antarktis)
Ernest Hemingway	*Dateline: Toronto* (Reportagen aus den Jahren 1920-24, Europa)
John Steinbeck	*Travels with Charley. In Search of America* (1926)
Paul Theroux	*The Great Railway Bazaar* (1975) *The Old Patagonian Express* (1979) *The Happy Isles of Oceania - Paddling the Pacific* (1992) *The Pillars of Hercules* (1995) (Mittelmeerraum)

2.6.3 Textanhang: Das Erdbeben von Pompeji (Gajus Cacilius Plinius d. J.)

Als sein Onkel 79 n. Chr. beim Erdbeben von Pompeji ums Leben kam, war Gajus Cacilius Plinius 18 Jahre alt. Über die Katastrophe und den Tod seines Onkels hat Plinius dem Historiker Tacitus detailliert in Briefen berichtet:

Bericht über das Erdbeben von Pompeji

An Tacitus
(79 n. Chr.)

Der Brief, den ich Dir auf Dein Verlangen über den Tod meines Oheims geschrieben, hat Dich, wie Du sagst, begierig gemacht, auch zu wissen, was ich zu Misenum, wo ich geblieben war - denn da hatte ich meine Erzählung abgebrochen -, für Unruhen und Gefahren ausgestanden.

Bebt mir gleich, es denkend, das Herz -
Dennoch beginn ich -

Nachdem mein Oheim abgereist war, wandte ich die übrige Zeit aufs Studieren; denn deshalb war ich zurückgeblieben. Späterhin badete ich, aß zu Nacht, legte mich nieder und hatte darauf einen kurzen und unruhigen Schlaf. Viele Tage vorher war ein Erdbeben gewesen, das, als etwas Gewöhnliches in Campanien, uns nicht sehr erschreckte. In derselben Nacht aber wurde es so heftig, daß alles nicht erschütterte, sondern umgekehrt zu werden schien. Meine Mutter stürzte in meine Kammer, als ich eben aufstand, um sie zu wecken, wenn sie noch schlafen sollte. Wir setzten uns in den Hof, der das Meer von dem Haus durch einen kleinen Raum trennte. Ich weiß nicht, ob ich es Standhaftigkeit oder Unbedachtsamkeit nennen soll; denn ich war erst achtzehn Jahre alt. Ich ließ mir den T. Livius geben und las ihn gleichsam zum Zeitvertreib; ich machte sogar Auszüge, wie ich schon angefangen hatte. Ein Freund meines Oheims, der neulich aus Spanien zu ihm gekommen war, kam dazu. Da er mich und meine Mutter sitzen und mich noch dazu lesen sahe, verwies er ihr ihre Gelassenheit und mir meine Sorglosigkeit; dessen ungeachtet blieb ich auf mein Buch geheftet.

Es war schon sieben Uhr des Morgens, und noch schien nur ein dämmerndes und mattes Licht; schon waren die umliegenden Häuser zerrüttet und also an einem zwar freien, aber engen Orte die Gefahre des Einsturzes groß und gewiß. Nun erst fiel uns ein, aus der Stadt zu gehen. Das bestürzte

Volk folgte nach und - was bei Furcht den Anschein von Klugheit hat - zieht fremden Rat dem seinigem vor; es drückt und drängt haufenweise die Wegeilenden. Nachdem wir zur Stadt hinaus sind, bleiben wir stehen. Hier erfahren wir neue Wunder, neue Angst. Die Wagen, die wir hinaus hatten fahren lassen, wurden obgleich auf flachem Felde, so hin und her geworfen, daß sie nicht einmal, von Steinen unterstützt, auf einem Flecke stehenblieben. Überdies schien das Meer sich selbst einzuschlürfen und durch die Erderschütterung vom Ufer gleichsam zurückgetrieben zu werden. Wenigstens hatte sich das Ufer erweitert, und viele Seetiere waren auf dem trockenen Sande sitzengeblieben. Auf der anderen Seite spaltete sich eine schwarze furchtbare Wolke, durch mannigfaltig verschlungene und geschwungene Feuerströme zerrissen, in langen Flammengestalten; ähnlich den Blitzen, jedoch größer. Darauf wurde ebenderselbe Freund aus Spanien noch ernstlicher und dringender. Wenn dein Bruder, wenn dein Oheim, sagte er, noch lebt, so wünscht er euch gerettet zu sehen; ist er tot, so war sein Wunsch, daß ihr überleben möchtet. Was zaudert ihr also und entflieht nicht? Wir würden, antworteten wir, an unsere Rettung nicht denken, solange wir der seinigen wegen in Ungewißheit wären. Ohne länger zu verweilen, eilte er davon und entriß sich im schnellsten Laufe der Gefahr.

Nicht lange hernach stieg diese Wolke zur Erde herab und bedeckte das Meer. Sie umhüllte und verbarg die Insel Careã und entzog das Vorgebirge Misenum unseren Augen. Darauf bat, ermahnte, befahl meine Mutter mir, zu entfliehen, wie ich könnte: denn ich sei noch jung, sie als eine alte und schwere Person sei es nicht vermögend und wollte gern sterben, wenn sie nicht Ursache an meinem Tode wäre. Ich wollte nicht anders, versetzte ich, als mit ihr zugleich gerettet sein; darauf ergriff ich ihre Hand und nötigte sie, fortzueilen; sie folgte mit Mühe und machte sich Vorwürfe, daß sie mich aufhielt. Schon fiel Asche auf uns, doch noch wenig; ich sehe mich um; ein dicker schwarzer Dampf gerade hinter uns ergoß sich wie ein Strom auf die Erde und folgt uns nach. Laßt uns auf die Seite gehen, sagte ich, da wir noch sehen, damit wir nicht auf der Straße von der zudrängenden Menge in der Dunkelheit zertreten werden. Wir hatten uns kaum entfernt, als eine Finsternis einbrach, nicht wie die einer bewölkten oder nicht vom Mond erhellten Nacht, sondern wie in einem verschlossenen Zimmer, wann das Licht ausgelöscht ist. Man hörte nichts als das Heulen der Weiber, Winseln der Kinder, Geschrei der Männer; einige schrien nach ihren Eltern, andere nach ihren Kindern, andere nach ihren Weibern; und erkannten sich nur am Schreien. Einige beklagten ihr eigenes Schicksal, andere das Schicksal ihrer Verwandten. Verschiedene wünschten sich den Tod aus Furcht vor dem Tode. Viele flehten den Beistand der Götter an, noch mehrere glaubten, daß keine Götter mehr wären, und hielten diese Nacht für die letzte und ewige Nacht der Welt. Andere vermehrten die wirkliche Gefahr durch eingebildete und erlogene Schrecken: sie brachten die falsche Nachricht, die aber doch Glauben fand, ein Teil von Misenum sei eingestürzt, ein anderer stehe in Flammen. Es ward ein wenig helle; aber dies schien uns nicht den Tag, sondern das herbeinahende Feuer, welches jedoch in der Entfernung blieb, zu verkündigen. Die Dunkelheit kam wieder, und viele und dicke Asche fiel herab, die uns oft aufzustehen und sie abzuschütteln nötigte, sonst wären wir zugedeckt und von der Last erdrückt worden. Ich könnte mich rühmen, daß bei so schrecklicher Gefahr mir kein Seufzer, kein zaghaftes Wort entfallen, wenn ich nicht geglaubt hätte - zwar ein elender, aber doch großer Trost für den armen Sterblichen -, daß alles mit mir zugleich unterginge.

Endlich zerstreute sich diese dicke Finsternis und verschwand gleichsam in Rauch und Nebel. Bald erschien der Tag und auch die Sonne, aber nur gelblich, wie bei einer Finsternis. Den noch zitternden Augen stellten sich alle Gegenstände verändert dar und mit Haufen Asche, wie mit Schnee, überdeckt. Wir kehrten nach Misenum zurück, und nachdem wir uns erholt, so gut wir konnten, brachten wir die Nacht zwischen Furcht und Hoffnung zu; wiewohl die Furcht die Oberhand behielt. Denn das Erdbeben dauerte noch fort, und halb wahnsinnige Leute vermehrten durch Unglücksweissagungen ihre und anderer Furcht. Ob wir nun gleich so viel Gefahr ausgestanden und noch vor uns sahen; so kam uns doch der Gedanke nicht ein, wegzugehen bis wir Nachricht von meinem Oheim hätten. Du wirst diese Nachricht lesen, ohne Gebrauch davon in der Geschichte zu machen, deren sie nicht würdig ist; und Du mußt es Dir selbst zuschreiben und Deiner Wißbegierde, wenn Du findest, daß sie nicht einmal eines Briefes wert ist. Lebe wohl.

2.6.4 Textanhang: Life on the Mississippi- Stadtansichten (Mark Twain)

44. Kapitel: Stadtansichten

(1883)

Das alte französische Viertel von New Orleans - früher das spanische Viertel - hat keinerlei Ähnlichkeit mit dem amerikanischen Teil der Stadt: dem amerikanischen Teil jenseits des dazwischenliegenden Geschäftszentrums aus

Backstein. Die Häuser stehen in Blocks zusammengedrängt, sie sind von strenger Einfachheit, würdevoll, einheitlich in der Bauart mit hier und da einer angenehm wirkenden Abweichung; alle sind außen mit Putz versehen, und fast alle haben lange, von Eisengittern umgebene Veranden, die sich an den verschiedenen Stockwerken entlangziehen. Ihre größte Schönheit liegt in der satten, warmen, mehrfarbigen Tönung, die mit der Zeit und Witterung den Putz bereichert haben. Sie harmoniert mit der gesamten Umgebung und sieht aus, als gehöre sie auf eine so natürliche Weise dorthin wie das Rot der Wolken zum Sonnenuntergang. Diese reizende Zierde läßt sich nicht erfolgreich nachahmen und ist auch sonst nirgends in Amerika zu finden.

Auch die Eisengitter sind eine Besonderheit. Ihr Muster ist oft überaus zierlich und anmutig, beschwingt und leicht - mit einer großen Zahl oder einem Monogramm in der Mitte -, ein zartes Spinngewebe von verwirrenden, verschlungenen Formen aus Schmiedeeisen. Die alten Gitter sind handgearbeitet, jetzt verhältnismäßig selten und dementsprechend kostbar. Sie sind zu Antiquitäten geworden.

Die Reisegesellschaft hatte das Vorrecht, zusammen mit dem feinsinnigsten literarischen Genius des Südens, dem Autor der „Grandissimes", durch diese alten Viertel von New Orleans zu streifen. In ihm hat der Süden einen meisterhaften Schilderer seines Innenlebens und seiner Vergangenheit gefunden. Die Erfahrung hat mich gelehrt, daß das ungeübte Auge und das unbeschriebene Gemüt den Süden tatsächlich in seinen Büchern besser kennenlernen und ihn mit größerem Gewinn betrachten und beurteilen kann als durch persönliche Bemühungen. [...]

Wir besuchten auch die ehrwürdige Kathedrale und den hübschen Platz davor - die eine dämmrig in geistlichem Licht, der andere strahlend in dem der weltlichen Art und lieblich mit Orangenbäumen und blühenden Sträuchern geschmückt; dann fuhren wir in der heißen Sonne durch das Häuserdickicht und in die weite leere Ebene dahinter, mit den Landhäusern und den Wasserrädern zur Entwässerung der Stadt und den Gemeindewiesen, die von Kühen und Kindern bevölkert sind, vorbei an einen alten Friedhof, wo, wie man uns sagte, die Asche eines Piraten der alten Zeit liegt, aber wir glaubten es ihm und besuchten ihn nicht. [...]

Von dort aus fuhren wir ein paar Meilen durch einen Sumpf, über eine erhöhte Straße mit Muschelschalendecke, die auf der einen Seite von einem Kanal, auf der anderen von einem dichten Wald gesäumt war, und hier und dort ragte in der Ferne mit winkeligen Ästen und Moosbärten eine zottige Zypressenspitze empor und hob sich scharf gegen den Himmel ab, so wunderlich geformt wie die Apfelbäume auf japanischen Bildern. Das war unser

Weg und seine Umgebung. Gelegentlich sahen wir einen gemütlich im Kanal dahinschwimmenden Alligator und gelegentlich malerisch am Ufer einen Farbigen, dessen statuenhaft starre Gestalt sich im stillen Wasser spiegelte und der darauf wartete, daß ein Fisch anbiß.

2.6.5 Textanhang: Sketches by Boz - Die Straßen am Morgen (Charles Dickens)

Erstes Kapitel

Die Straßen am Morgen

(1839)

Das Aussehen der Londoner Straße vor Sonnenaufgang an einem Sommermorgen fällt sogar den wenigen in einem hohen Maße auf, die, weil sie bei ihren Vergnügungen oder ihren Geschäftsunternehmungen unglücklich waren, sehr wohl damit vertraut sind. Es macht einen ganz besonderen Eindruck, die geräuschlosen Straßen, die wir gewohnt sind zu anderen Zeiten von einer geschäftigen, wogenden Menschenmenge gefüllt zu sehen, so nüchtern, einsam und verödet und die Häuser so still und dicht verschlossen zu schauen, die bei Tage einen so äußerst belebten Anblick bieten.

Der letzte Zechbruder, der noch im Dunkeln seinen Weg nach Hause fand, ist soeben mit schweren Gliedern, von Zeit zu Zeit den Refrain eines Trinkliedes der durchschwärmten Nacht grölend, entlanggetaumelt; der letzte obdachlose Herumstreicher, den Armut und die Polizei in den Straßen gelassen, hat sich verklommen in einen gepflasterten Winkel gedrückt, um von Speisen und Trank und einem wärmenden Kamin oder Bett zu träumen. Die Trunkenbolde, Wüstlinge und Heimatlosen sind verschwunden, die nüchternen und ordentlichen Leute zu ihren Tagesgeschäften noch nicht erwacht, und in den Straßen herrscht die Stille des Todes, der ihnen sogar seine Farbe mitgeteilt zu haben scheint, so kalt und leblos sehen sie in der bleichen, grauen Morgendämmerung aus. Die Mietkutschenstände in den größeren Straßen sind verlassen, die „Nachthäuser" geschlossen, die Tummelplätze der Ausschweifungen und des Elends leer.

Hier und da sieht man einen Polizisten an einer Straßenecke stehen und gedankenlos die verödete Straße hinunterschauen; und dann und wann schleicht ein loses Kätzchen quer hinüber und verliert sich in seinem eigenen Revier, zuerst auf die Wassertonne, dann auf das Kehrichtloch und endlich auf die Steinplatten so vorsichtig und listig hinunterspringend, als ob es meinte, sein guter Ruf hinge davon ab, daß seine Galanterie der entschwundenen Nacht unbemerkt bliebe. Hier und da steht ein Schlafzimmerfenster halb offen und deutet hin auf die Schwüle der Luft und den unruhigen Schlummer so manchen Schläfers, und der matte Schimmer seines Nachtlichtes hinter den Fenstervorhängen bezeichnet ein Krankenzimmer. Von diesen wenigen Ausnahmen abgesehen, bieten die Straßen kein Zeichen des Lebens, die Häuser keine Spur, daß sie bewohnt sind.

Eine Stunde schleicht hin. Die Kirchtürme und die Dächer der vornehmsten Gebäude werden vom Licht der aufgehenden Sonne schwach gefärbt, und die Straßen beginnen fast unmerklich wieder belebt zu werden. Marktkarren rumpeln langsam daher; der schläfrige Fuhrmann treibt ungeduldig seine müden Pferde an oder bemüht sich vergeblich, den Knaben aufzuwekken, der, auf dem üppigen Lager der Gemüsekörbe ausgestreckt, süß träumend seine lange gehegte Neugier vergißt, die Wunder Londons zu schauen.

2.7 Geschichte des Reisejournalismus

Hans J. Kleinsteuber

> In der Wirthsstube fand ich lauter Leben und Bewegung. Studenten von verschiedenen Universitäten. Die Einen sind kurz vorher angekommen und restaurieren sich, andere bereiten sich zum Abmarsch, schnüren ihre Ranzen, schreiben ihre Namen ins Gedächtnisbuch, erhalten Blumensträuße von den Hausmädchen; da wird in die Wangen gekniffen, gesungen, gesprungen, gejohlt, man fragt, man antwortet, gut Wetter, Fußweg, Prosit, Adieu. Einige der Abgehenden sind auch etwas angesoffen und diese haben von der schönen Aussicht einen doppelten Genuß, da ein Betrunkener Alles doppelt sieht.
>
> (Heinrich Heine über das Brockenhaus, Harz)

2.7.1 Zu den Wurzeln des Reisejournalismus

Aus den Entwicklungen des Buchdrucks entstand die Idee der regelmäßigen Publikation von Druckwerken - zuerst die Zeitungen, später die Magazine. Aus der Verbindung der **Berichte über fremde Länder** mit der **Journaille**, entstand der **Reisejournalismus**. Journalismus zeichnet sich schon definitorisch dadurch aus, daß seine Produkte regelmäßig publiziert (*jour* = *Tag*) werden. Ein Blick in Reiseberichte der Vergangenheit wie der Gegenwart verdeutlicht allerdings, wie gleitend die Übergänge zwischen Buch und Periodikum sind. Viele Buchautoren waren vorher, nachher oder auch währenddessen Artikelschreiber - was deren literarischer Qualität zugute kam. Oft sorgte der Journalismus überhaupt erst dafür, daß der Autor reisen konnte und dabei die Muße fand, auch Werke von Bucheslänge zu schreiben.

2.7.2 Das 18. Jahrhundert: Beginn der modernen Reiseberichterstattung

Während die Entwicklung der langen Reiseberichte seit Herodot und Homer recht präzise belegt werden kann, ist der **Beginn der aktuellen Reiseberichterstattung** nur schwierig auszumachen. Er liegt, so die Ergebnisse der wenigen Untersuchungen, die vorliegen, im 18. Jahrhundert, als zuerst belehrende, darauf auch unterhaltsame Berichte über andere Länder zum regelmäßigen Inventar von Periodika wurden. (Für diese Darstellung, vgl.: Schmitz-Forte 1995: 23-32) Deren Zielsetzung lag vor allem darin, über andere Länder 'aufzuklären', also zu bilden, aber auch die Neugierde auf alles Fremde in jenen Jahren der europäischen Welteroberung zu befriedigen. Viele dieser Berichte wollten nicht zum Nachreisen animieren, dazu war die Fortbewegung viel zu teuer und zu beschwerlich, es waren schon damals Anleitungen zum Träumen von der Ferne. In der Art der Darstellung wurde bereits früh experimentiert, in Wielands Weimarer Monatsschrift *Der teutsche Merkur* erscheint der Rest der Welt häufig in Form fortlaufender Briefe beschrieben, was - dem Stile von Briefen folgend - eine intimere und subjektivere Darstellung ermöglichte. Die Reiseberichte folgten jeweils dem Trend und den Moden der Epoche; in der Romantik wurden die Darstellungen insgesamt gemütvoller und wärmer, persönliche Eindrücke gewannen an Bedeutung.

In jenen Jahren gab es bereits einen bescheidenen Tourismus, zumindest für eine kleine Minderheit von Adeligen oder auch für religiöse Pilger. Für diese Klientel bedurfte es praktischer Informationen, wie sie in der Form von **Reisebüchern** bereits eine beachtliche Tradition hatten. Das älteste war bereits 1563 in Augsburg erschienen, Jörg Gails *Ein neuwes nützliches Raißbüchlein der fürnemesten Land und Stett.* (Mehr dazu: Krohn 1987: 315ff) Es fällt nicht schwer, von diesem Büchlein eine direkte Verbindung zu dem Klassiker Baedeker (sein erster Führer zu den Rheinlanden erschien in der 1830ern) zur Unzahl moderner Reiseführer zu ziehen. So entstanden auch

Reiseartikel, in denen **Ratschläge für das Fortkommen** unterwegs im Vordergrund stehen, oft auch zur Aktualisierung der Standard-Informationen, die in den weit verbreiteten Reisebüchern zu finden waren.

> Wilmont Haake hat viel zum Feuilleton geschrieben. Das Reisefeuilleton sieht er als Kommunikationsmittel eigener Art:
>
> 1. Sinn und Zweck des Reisefeuilletons
>
> Der Reiz des Reisefeuilletons liegt darin, daß es aus dem Milieu entführt, in dem man lebt, liebt, mit Kindern um sich herum von neuem aufwächst und abermals Augenblicke lang glaubt, jung zu sein. Es vermag den Menschen sogar von seinem Arbeitsplatz in der Fabrik, im Büro, im Hör- oder Lesesaal wie unter Zauberkraft entschwinden zu lassen. Durch Reisefeuilleton wird man gewissermaßen seiner Umgebung entrückt.
>
> Vor- und Nachgeschmack möglicher Reisegenüsse bietet es in Fülle. Zunächst freilich kaum mehr als dies, denn will man die notierten Genüsse wirklich kosten, gilt es, dem Reiserat zu folgen. Dann tue man sich selbst fern von Gewohnheit und Gewühl um, mag das in Badenweiler oder bei Positano, auf Sylt oder zu Dubrownik geschehen!
>
> Was erwartet den Lesenden allen Ortes? Gewissermaßen im voraus in eine andere Szenerie des Welttheaters. Auf dem Hintergrunde herrlicher Landschaften, vor anderen Stadtkulissen und in anderen Kostümen werden überall zwar ewig wechselnde, im Kern allerdings zumeist gleichartige Szenen gespielt. Ihnen nur zuzuschauen bereitet schon Freude. Nur allzu gern sind die Menschen bereit, an ihnen indessen nicht nur als passives Publikum, sondern als agierende Komparsen teilzunehmen und, dank der in den Reisefeuilletons ausgesprochenen Einladung, mitzuspielen.
>
> Gut geschriebene Reisefeuilletons stellen Versprechungen auf noch nicht Erfahrenes, noch nicht Geschehenes, noch nie Erlebtes dar. Sie wecken Neugierde - und damit verlocken sie zum Abenteuer.
>
> Aus solchen vorweggenommenen Umschreibungen des Reisefeuilletons geht nebenbei hervor, daß sie für Länder und Landschaften, Städte und Stadtschaften, Theater und Museen, Kurorte und Ausflugsziele, Dampfschiffe und Schwimmbäder werben.
>
> Demnach stehen sie im Dienste einer optimistischen und heiteren Publizistik. Sie ist so menschenfreundlich und liebenswürdig, daß sie es nicht ablehnt, Verliebte darüber zu beraten, wo sie ihr Glück im Winkel (es muß nicht immer Reit in Oberbayern sein) finden können.
>
> (Haacke 1967: 306f)

Es wird berichtet, daß bereits 1782 in Hamburg eine Zeitschrift mit dem Titel *Der Reisende* erschienen sei, sicherlich eine der ersten ihrer Art und eine Ausnahme. Der klassische Art des **Reiseberichts** fand im **Feuilleton** der Zeitungen statt. Eine Auswertung der *Berliner Vossischen Zeitung* ergab, daß dort im April 1852 der Reise-bezogene Anteil an den Artikeln des Feuilletons 14,1 % betrug, bei der *Spenerschen Zeitung* waren es 6,8 %. (Becker 1938, zit. Schmitz- Forte 1995: 28f) Mit beginnender Reaktion nach 1848 wurde die kritische politische Berichterstattung erschwert, statt dessen wuchs das Reisefeuilleton an, aber wohl nur an Umfang, nicht an Gehalt.

2.7.3 Erste Reisebeilagen in den Zeitungen des 19. Jahrhunderts

Sehr früh erkannten die Verleger auch die kommerzielle Bedeutung des Reiseberichts. Von dem Urvater der Gesellschaftsreise und Begründer erster Reisebüros **Thomas Cook** wird berichtet, er habe die (britische) Reisezeitschrift *Excursionist* gegründet. Reisen erfährt im 19. Jahrhundert einen ungeheuren Aufschwung; im Mittelpunkt stand meist die Eisenbahn, manchmal das Schiff. Der begüterte Teil des an Bedeutung wachsenden Bürgertums genießt die neue Mobilität.

In der Zeit vor dem Ersten Weltkrieg wandert die Reiseberichterstattung erstmals aus dem Feuilleton aus und es entstehen abgetrennte **Reisebeilagen**, etwa bei der *Leipziger Zeitung* unter dem Titel *Aus Bädern und Sommerfrischen.* Darin sind manche der redaktionell daherkommenden Berichte nunmehr auf Waschzettelniveau, dazu sind sie von Reklamen umgeben. Ein reisejournalistischer Sonderteil ist bei der *Vossischen Zeitung* 1904 belegt, genannt *Für Reisen und Wandern.* Insgesamt waren vor dem Ersten Weltkrieg wohl schon 50 Zeitungen mit Reisebeilagen ausgestattet. (Wagner 1962, zit. Schmitz-Forte 1995; 30) Längst waren der Reiseteil und die reisebezogene Werbung eine enge Allianz eingegangen.

2.7.4 Die Reiseberichterstattung seit dem Ersten Weltkrieg

Die Nähe von Umfang und Erscheinungsbild der Reiseberichterstattung zur politischen 'Großwetterlage' ist unverkennbar. Der erste große Krieg erstickte die Möglichkeiten für 'Lustreisen', nun nutzte das Militär die Verkehrsverbindungen. In der frühen **Weimarer Republik** hatten die Bürger andere Probleme. Eine eigene, pervertierte Form der Reiseschreiberei entstand im **Dritten Reich**, in dem staatlich organisiertes Reisen im Stile von 'Kraft durch Freude' zum festen Bestandteil der nationalsozialistischen Propaganda wurde. Dabei wurde das Reisen nicht nur im Stile von 'Zuckerbrot und Peitsche' zur Lockung der skeptischen Massen genutzt, der Urlaub selbst wurde zum Kalkül in der Politik des Größenwahns. Adolf Hitler dazu: „Ich will, daß dem Arbeiter ein ausreichender Urlaub gewährt wird und daß alles geschieht, um ihm diesen Urlaub ... zu einer wahren Erholung werden zu lassen. Ich wünsche das, weil ich ein nervenstarkes Volk will, denn nur allein mit einem Volk, das seine Nerven behält, kann man wahrhaft große Politik machen.“ (angeblicher Führerbefehl, zit.: Spode 1996: 18) Interessanterweise wurde im Dritten Reich der Reisejournalismus selbst erstmals zum Thema wissenschaftlicher Durchleuchtung, widerspiegelnd das große Interesse der Diktatoren an Kommunikation. Ernst Groth promovierte 1941 zu dem Thema „Die Zeitung im Dienste des Fremdenverkehrs“. Die Reisebeilage der Tageszeitungen und ihre ‘politische Aufgabe’. Der Autor zählte 1939 bereits 395 Tageszeitungen, die Reisebeilagen enthielten. Er begrüßte, daß der Fremdenverkehr im neuen Reich mit ganz anderen Augen gesehen werde, da er nun mit nationalsozialistischen Grundsätzen und Lebensanschauungen verwoben sei (Groth 1941, zit. Schmitz-Forte 1995: 30f). Was den glühenden Nazi-Propagandagist offensichtlich nicht störte, war die von ihm beschriebene unheilvolle Indienststellung der Presse durch die Fremdenverkehrsförderung - solange sie nur unter NS-Vorzeichen erfolgt.

Der **Zweite Weltkrieg** führte zur nächsten Zäsur im Gewerbe der Reiseschreiberei. Erst mit dem beginnenden ‘Wirtschaftswunder’ ab Währungsreform und **Gründung der Bundesrepublik** 1949 konnten die Westdeutschen wieder an Ausflüge denken. Die deutschen Konsumenten holten nach, der ‘Freßwelle’ folgte die **‘Reisewelle’.** Die *Süddeutsche Zeitung* begann 1949 mit ihrer ersten Reisebeilage, der *Kölner Stadt-Anzeiger* 1950 (wie Schmitz-Forte in seiner sorgfältig erarbeiteten Dissertation darlegt). Die inhaltsanalytischen Studien ergaben, daß die Reiseberichterstattung im Volumen stark zunahm, zudem sich die Themen mit den veränderten Reisegewohnheiten änderten. Gleichwohl gab es auch Konstanten, etwa indem viele Reiseziele mit recht unwandelbaren Etiketten versehen wurden, der Deutsche ließ sich seine Stereotype nicht nehmen.

Unverkennbar ist weiterhin, daß der Reisejournalismus zunehmend dem **‘System Tourismus’** unterworfen wurde, das er zu stabilisieren angetreten war. „Für die Zeitung als Wirtschaftsbetrieb ist der Verkauf von Anzeigenraum die wichtigste Einnahmequelle. Touristikanzeigen sind ein lukrativer Teilbereich des **Anzeigengeschäfts**. Die Reisebeilagen bieten den Inserenten einen Rahmen, innerhalb dessen sie ihre Anzeigen um so wirkungsvoller plazieren können.“ (Schmitz-Forte 1995: 395)

In dieser Darstellung sollte deutlich geworden sein, welch lange Geschichte hinter der aktuellen Reiseberichterstattung steht, wie differenziert sie auf gesellschaftliche Großtrends reagierte, wie Erwartungen der Touristikindustrie und Gewohnheiten der Leser sie veränderte. Selbst die Annoncenabhängigkeit der Reiseberichte hat ihre Geschichte - bleibt zu hoffen, daß die so bombardierten Konsumenten über die Jahre angesichts immer neuer und immer raffinierterer PR-Bemühungen kaltblütig und nüchtern abwägend geworden sind und gelernt haben, die fundierte Reportage vom bestellten Jubelbericht sorgsam zu trennen.

Abb. rechts: Diese kurze Darstellung der Wandlungen in der Reiseberichterstattung einer überregionalen Tageszeitung erschien in der Jubiläumsausgabe der Süddeutschen Zeitung.

Für Bergsteiger und Skifahrer – Alpines in der SZ

Die Erstbezwingung des 13. Achttausenders, das Bergfilm-Festival in Trient, Expeditionsberichte von Prominenten und 1961 die Tragödie am Montblanc waren seit 1949 ebenso „Thema“ wie der Meinungsstreit um Holz- oder Metallski, Piste oder Tiefschnee und die Wedeltechnik

Von Gert Kreyssig

Am 7. Mai 1949 standen auf der Seite 4 der SZ „Grüße an die Bergsteiger“ – von Kultusminister Alois Hundhammer, Oberbürgermeister Thomas Wimmer und Albert Heizer, dem Vorsitzenden der Landesarbeitsgemeinschaft Bayern des Alpenvereins. Die Sektion München und damit der *Deutsche Alpenverein* (der offiziell von den Alliierten noch verboten war) wurden 80 Jahre alt. Zufall oder nicht, jedenfalls gibt es von da an nach alter Münchner Zeitungstradition eine alpine Seite in der *Süddeutschen Zeitung*.

„Die Throne der Götter sind besetzt“: Seit diesem halb resignativen Resümee von 1960 anläßlich der Erstbesteigung des Dhaulagiri hat sich der Aktionsradius von Bergfexen auf den Luftraum über allen Gipfeln ausgeweitet (hier: bei Westendorf in Tirol).

Photo: Regina Schmeken

„Holz oder Metall?“

„Berghütten in Vorarlberg warten auf deutsche Touristen“, ist da zu lesen. Oder: „Helft mit zum Aufbau des Alpinen Museums!“ Auf den nächsten Seiten „Alpines“ geht es um Wanderungen im Karwendel, es wird an Hans Dülfer, den „großen Lehrmeister der modernen Klettertechnik“, erinnert, und es wird berichtet, daß man für Bergseile neuerdings auch die Nylonfaser verarbeitet. Antrag im bayerischen Landtag: In Verbindung mit der Militärregierung soll erreicht werden, daß Jugendlichen in den Sommerferien Bergfahrten in benachbarte Alpenländer ermöglicht werden. In einem SZ-Gespräch entpuppt sich die Liesl Karlstadt als „waschechte Alpinistin“, die auf dem Totenkirchl und auf der Wildspitze war (während der Valentin darüber die Hände überm Kopf zusammenschlug). „Bergsteigen als Lebensform“, heißt die Festschrift der Alpenvereinssektion *Bayerland* zum 50jährigen Bestehen, erschienen 1949. Vergangenheit und neue Zeit. Unvorstellbar, daß es jemals so etwas wie Wettklettern an künstlichen Wänden oder gar Mountainbikes geben würde.

In den fünfziger und frühen sechziger Jahren herrscht Hochstimmung in den Bergen der Welt. Expeditionsfieber ist ausgebrochen. Im Himalaja wird ein Achttausender nach dem anderen bezwungen, Anapurna, Mount Everest, Nanga Parbat ... „Die Throne der Götter sind besetzt“, resümiert die SZ 1960 nach der Erstbesteigung des 13. Achttausenders, des Dhaulagiri. Der 14. und mit 8013 Metern letzte in der Rangliste liegt in Tibet; die Shisha Pangma wird 1964 von einer chinesischen Expedition erstiegen.

Auf den Seiten „Für den Bergsteiger“ finden sich Expeditionsberichte etwa aus dem Karakorum (von Hias Rebitsch) oder aus den Kordilleren (von Fritz März, später Alpenvereins-Vorsitzender). Das Bergfilm-Festival in Trient, über das die SZ immer wieder berichtet, wurde zu einem Treffen der Bergsteiger und Bergsteigerinnen, die alpine Geschichte geschrieben haben.

Viele große Namen in dieser Zeit. Zumal auch in den Alpen Spektakuläres geschieht. Winterbesteigungen sind angesagt: Eiger-Nordwand, Matterhorn-Nordwand, Große-Zinne-Nordwand-Direttissima. Ferner die Erstbegehung der Westwand der Drus („das allerletzte Problem der Alpen“) und ihres Südwestpfeilers („Bonatti-Pfeiler“) und schließlich die Tragödie am Frêney-Zentralpfeiler (Montblanc), wo 1961 von sieben erprobten, berühmten Bergsteigern vier ums Leben kommen. Die SZ-Bergsteigerseite berichtete.

Auf den Seiten „Für den Skifahrer“ geht's bunt her. Parsenn, Cevedale, Roter Kogel, Sonnblick, Große Reib'n, Schinderkar, Marmolada und viele andere Tourenvorschläge werden geboten, und es zeigen sich die Veränderungen in der Skifahrerei. Überschriften in den fünfziger Jahren: „Holz oder Metall – das ist die Skifrage“ – „Schußfahrt auf Plastiksohlen. Das Skiwachseln einst und jetzt.“ – „Der Ski aus Plastik, die Hose aus Elastik.“ – „Der weite Weg zur Sicherheitsbindung.“ – „Hie Marker, hie Lusser.“ – Schöne Worte im Meinungsstreit um Piste oder Tiefschnee: „Beides sollte man beherrschen, den Pisten- und den Tourenskilauf.“ – Und dann: „Wedeln hin, wedeln her – für und wider die neue Skilauftechnik.“ Das war 1957. Ein Jahr später steht auf der Seite 3 der SZ: „Die ganze Welt will wedeln.“ Übrigens entsteht in diesen Jahren auch eine Doktorarbeit über die Skifahrerei. Verfasser ist der Diplom-Kaufmann Franz Benk aus Isny im Allgäu. Das Alpine hat sich in der SZ nicht nur wacker gehalten, sondern weiter entwickelt – zu *Berg-Journal* und *Ski-Journal* mit festen Erscheinungszeiten.

(Süddeutsche Zeitung vom 6. Oktober1995, S. J. 73)

3 Handwerkszeug des Reisejournalisten: Der Text

3.1 Einleitung

Hans J. Kleinsteuber

Wir schlagen den Reiseteil einer gleichermaßen hypothetischen wie typischen Zeitung auf, nehmen uns die Wochenendausgabe einer regionalen Kaufzeitung mit überregionaler Verbreitung vor. Noch konkreter: Wir blättern die *Frankfurter Rundschau* auf. Dort wendet sich die Abteilung *Magazin* gezielt an den 'samstäglich-sonntäglich' gestimmten Leser und beginnt mit insgesamt sechs Seiten zu *Reise und Erholung*, fährt darauf mit *Freizeit und Familie, Fernsehen und Funk* und anverwandten Themengebieten fort. Der Einstieg in diesen Teil *Magazin,* der unverkennbar eine Nähe zu wochenendlicher Entspannung und Zerstreuung markiert, erfolgt mit einer großflächigen, bunt bebilderten Reisereportage. Was sonst könnte den Kontrast zu Alltag und Berufstätigkeit besser signalisieren? Auf den weiteren Reiseseiten werden die Artikel kürzer, Teile bleiben der Werbung vorbehalten, die fast ausschließlich Reiseleistungen anpreist. Ein volle Seite bietet die Vorschau auf Leserreisen im kommenden Jahr (mit der *Frankfurter Rundschau* zum chinesischen Neujahr nach Hongkong oder zur Tulpenblüte nach Amsterdam). Die mit der Werbung verknüpften Probleme werden, da außerhalb der journalistischen Verantwortung stehend, in Kapitel 8 bearbeitet.

Konzentrieren wir uns darauf, wie die Redakteure und Autoren der *FR* die Reiseseiten 'inszenieren'. Es fallen bestimmte handwerkliche Regeln der Präsentation auf, die so ein hohes Maß an Allgemeingültigkeit verkörpern. Die erste Seite hat unverkennbar zwei Aufgaben zu erfüllen, sie soll dem flüchtig schauenden Leser signalisieren, daß hier Freizeitbedürfnisse befriedigt werden, zum anderen wird hier großzügig in Farbe und Text (und ohne Werbung) der Einstieg in das Reise-Ressort zelebriert: Eine besonders umfängliche **Reisereportage,** garniert mit einladend bunter **Bebilderung** beherrscht die Seite. Daneben finden wir den **Serviceteil** zu dieser Reportage, überschrieben mit *Tips für ...* der ergänzende Angaben zu Reisezeit, Anreise, Unterkunft etc enthält. Unten auf der Seite ist mittig unter der Rubrik *Unter-*

wegs ein kürzerer Beitrag 'Kunde Hund' eingefügt. Es geht dabei um die Nöte der reisenden Hundebesitzer und das Angebot des größten Veranstalters für Reisende mit Hunden in Deutschland. Ein Bericht mit ernsten Passagen, aber doch überwindend als **Glosse** verfaßt.

Auf der zweiten Seite (und ähnlich auch auf den Folgeseiten) finden wir, nun nur noch schwarz-weiß bebildert, in der unteren Häfte Reisewerbung, meist recht kleinformatig und häufig als Kleinanzeigen in Gruppen zusammengefaßt, etwa regional gegliedert (Rhön - Odenwald - Ostsee) oder auch nach Zielgruppen (Kegelausflüge). Darüber ist links ein längerer **Bericht** plaziert, der sich mit Duty Free-Shops beschäftigt und in dem es vor allem um Fakten geht (die Institution wurde 50 Jahre alt), aber am Rande auch um Stimmungen (man geht nicht nur zum Sparen hinein). Rechts finden sich, abgeteilt unter dem Rubrum *Die neue Saison*, kürzere Mitteilungen über Neuigkeiten bei den großen Veranstaltern (Neckermann Reisen, SuperSoccer Fußballschule mit Rudi Völler). Wir nennen sie zweckmäßigerweise **Nachrichten.** Auf der folgenden dritten Seite finden wir Leserreisen-Werbung. Auf den Seiten 4 bis 6 erscheint jeweils in der oberen Hälfte eine Reportage, kürzer und weniger bebildert als auf der Titelseite, wiederum begleitet von *Tips über...* Die kürzeste der Reportagen wird rechts von einer Spalte mit der Überschrift *Kurzstrecke* ergänzt, wo aktuelle Reise-News präsentiert werden (Nachrichten über den Touristenansturm in der Dominikanischen Republik oder eine neue reiserechtliche Entscheidung mitsamt Aktenzeichen).

Dieser Abriß eines in keiner Weise außergewöhnlichen Reiseteils soll verdeutlichen, mit welchen Darstellungsformen der Reisejournalist in seinem Alltag arbeitet.

- Vor jedem Schreiben steht die gründliche Materialsammlung, die **Recherche**. Sie wird je nach Aufgabe sehr unterschiedlich ausfallen. Bei den langen Darstellungsformen, insbesondere der Reportage, ist sie vorab von höchster Bedeutung. Sonst droht der Autor bei der darauffolgenden Reise kenntnislos in der Fremde zu stehen, abgeschnitten von den vertrauten Materialquellen. Im Reisebereich tauchen spezifische Probleme auf, genannt seien Sprachbarriere, kulturelle Differenzen, Hindernisse beim direkten Zugang. Für die Nachricht reichen dagegen meist der Agenturticker oder anderes Informationsmaterial aus.

- Im Zentrum, sozusagen als Krönung des Reiseschreibens steht sicherlich die **Reportage**, also eine auf persönlichem Augenschein aufbauende, subjektiv gehaltene Darstellung von Ziel und Durchführung der Reise.

Hier gilt es, Standardwissen und allgemeine Regeln zur Reportage als zentrale journalistische Darstellungsform zu vermitteln, wobei zu beachten ist, daß Reisedarstellungen immer schon zum Kernbereich der Reportage zählten. Dazu kommt, daß es spezifische Anforderungen an die **Reportage mit Reiseinhalt** gibt, die gleichfalls zu erörtern sind.

- Reisereportagen folgen einer eigenen 'Dramaturgie'. Sie schildern meist nicht ein spezielles Ereignis, sondern reihen Eindrücke aneinander, ein wenig wie ein Mosaik. Dazu ist das Eingehen auf das Zielpublikum von größter Bedeutung. All das erfordert besondere Reflexion über handwerkliche Fertigkeiten, die so nur bei Reiseberichten gefordert sind. Schließlich geben wir einige Tips für Reportagen, die nicht ausgetretenen Bahnen folgen und damit ein wenig 'Pfiff' in die Schreibe bringen sollen.

- Neben der Reportage steht, deutlich von ihr getrennt und doch gleichermaßen wichtig, der **Serviceteil**, der ergänzende praktische Informationen enthält. Große journalistische Anforderungen stellt er nicht, bei der Abfassung stehen Recherche vor Ort oder daheim im Vordergrund. Es ist häufig zweckmäßig, den Serviceteil gleich mit der Reportage abzufassen, andernfalls muß er in der Redaktion nachgetragen werden. So unscheinbar dieser Serviceteil ist, so wichtig ist doch seine ergänzende und informierende Funktion. Zudem entlastet er die Reportage von störenden Fakten.

- Neben der Reportage steht, in Bedeutung und Länge gegenüber dieser nachgeordnet, der **Bericht**. Er bezieht sich, wie andere Berichte auch, auf fremde Quellen, z.B. Agenturmeldungen oder Pressemitteilungen von Veranstaltern. Der Bericht vermittelt nicht primär eigene Eindrücke, er informiert den Leser in differenzierter Form über reise-bezogene Fakten und Themen. Nicht selten dienen vorbereitete Bericht recht schlicht dazu, als Lückenfüller zu dienen. Dennoch sind sie überall zu finden und sollten ernstgenommen werden.

- Eine Zeitung bezieht ihr Selbstverständnis daraus, ein aktuelles Medium zu sein. Dazu gehört auch, daß in sachlicher Form über laufende Ereignisse berichtet wird. Dabei handelt es sich um Einzelinformationen, die 'kurz und knackig' übermittelt werden sollen. Die zentrale Darstellungsform dafür stellt die **Nachricht** dar.

- Reisejournalismus, wir haben es anderswo ausgeführt, soll vor allem freudig stimmen, angenehme Reiserlebnisse vorwegnehmen oder sie ersetzen. Echte Reisen sind dagegen nicht immer erfreulich, der Leser weiß dies meist aus eigener Erfahrung. Besonders bei seinen Ohrensessel-Exkursionen wird er davon wenig lesen wollen. Wenn Mißgeschicke oder Probleme thematisiert werden, dann meist nicht in der Reportage, sondern in einer davon deutlich getrennten ironischen Darstellung, der **Glosse**. Sie ist nicht gerade häufig, aber wir haben sie als eigene Darstellungsform aufgenommen, zumal sie oft ehrlicher ist als der übrige Reisejournalismus.

3.2 Die Recherche

Michael Pahl

Das Reiseziel steht fest? Ebenso existiert eine ungefähre Vorstellung davon, was der Reisebericht zum Inhalt haben soll? Dennoch wäre es verfrüht, sofort den nächsten Flieger zu buchen (sei es auf eigene Kosten oder auf 'Einladung' eines Veranstalters...).

Dieser Abschnitt beschäftigt sich mit der Recherche, die der Reise vorangehen, sie begleiten und abrunden sollte

3.2.1 Die Vorbereitung

Sich 'auf gut Glück' und ohne jede Vorbereitung in ein fremdes Land zu begeben, ist nicht nur töricht, sondern auch unverantwortlich - nicht zuletzt dem späteren Leser des Berichts gegenüber.

All die Eindrücke, die auf dern Journalisten warten, die Erlebnisse und alltäglichen Vorgänge im zu bereisenden Land - wie will der Reporter die Eindrücke einordnen und später darüber kompetent schreiben können, wenn er weder mit der Geschichte, noch der Kultur oder dem aktuellen Geschehen im Lande vertraut ist? Er sollte sich auf jeden Fall über die Region, in die er reisen und über die er berichten will, vorab kundig machen.

Es gibt viele Möglichkeiten, sich eingehend zu informieren: Nachschlagewerke, Bibliotheken, bereits über die Region erschienene Artikel oder Bücher sowie Archive oder Behörden. Besonders gut strukturierte Informationen bieten **Reiseführer in Buchform**. Aber Vorsicht: Sind sie noch aktuell? Und helfen sie, das Reiseziel mit den Augen der Leser zu sehen? Oft sind die Informationen zu speziell, als daß sie sich für einen ersten Einstieg in Reportageform eignen. Leider ist es keine Seltenheit, die Servicetips aus diesen Büchern abzuschreiben. Fast immer sind die aber nicht mehr 'up-to-date', Preise und Konditionen haben sich inzwischen geändert. Für Anregungen sind sie aber allemal gut, die mit aktueller Recherche vor Ort zu ergänzen sind.

Besonders wertvoll sind **Informanten,** die bereits in der Region bzw. dem Land waren, und den Journalisten mit Hintergrundinformationen und '**Insider-Tips**' versorgen können. Sie können Fragen zum alltäglichen Leben beantworten und den Reporter für bestimmte kulturelle Besonderheiten oder eventuell auftretende Probleme sensibilisieren.

Um noch einmal kurz auf das Thema **Stereotypen** zu sprechen zu kommen: Auch sie sollten Teil der Vorbereitung auf eine Reise sein. Wir haben sicherlich zu fast jedem Land, das wir bereisen wollen, bestimmte klischeehafte Bilder in unseren Köpfen. Es gilt, diese zu sammeln und sich mit ihnen bewußt auseinanderzusetzen; vor, während und nach der Reise. Wir können Ihnen gegebenenfalls nachrecherchieren (Beispiel: rothaarige Iren), sie dann später entweder widerlegen oder sie auf andere Weise in unseren Bericht miteinfließen lassen - vielleicht sogar spielerisch mit ihnen umgehen.

Auch hier sind Informanten, die jahrelange Erfahrungen gesammelt haben, von großem Wert. Das wird helfen, ein differenzierteres Bild zu entwerfen als jenes, das vor der Ankunft im entsprechenden Land in unserem Kopf war.

Bei allen Recherchen, die wir durchführen, ist die Zeit begrenzt. Vor der Reise vielleicht weniger, während der Reise bestimmt und nach der Reise sicherlich auch (will doch der Chefredakteur oder gar der Reisesponsor möglichst schnell Resultate sehen). In der Praxis wird dadurch eine eingehende Recherche oft nicht möglich.

Die Frage, die sich aufwirft, ist, welche Ansprüche der Journalist an seinen Bericht stellt. Wenn eine eingehende Recherche nicht möglich war, so kann es passieren, daß auch der Bericht nicht besonders tiefschürfend, vielleicht sogar ungenau ausfällt. Eine Lösung kann es in vielen Fällen leider kaum geben. Zeit ist in diesem Metier tatsächlich oft bares Geld. Wer allerdings die Wichtigkeit der Recherche verkennt und auf sie teilweise oder ganz verzichtet, darf für sich sicherlich nicht in Anspruch nehmen, anspruchsvolle Reiseberichterstattung zu betreiben.

3.2.2 Die vorbereitende Recherche

Der Journalist sollte sich über die **Geschichte und aktuelle Begebenheiten** des zu bereisenden Landes informieren. Solches Wissen kann helfen, die Mentalität der Menschen und ihre Kultur besser einzuordnen. Wieder sollten das Wissen hier nicht nur aus Büchern, sondern auch aus allen anderen uns zugänglichen Quellen stammen (zur Recherche im Serviceteil vgl. auch Kap. 3.9).

Das Bild, das der Journalist im voraus von einem **Land und seiner Bevölkerung** entwirft, wird vor Ort mit eigenen Erlebnissen und Erfahrungen bereichert und fügt sich hoffentlich zu einem differenzierten Ganzen zusammen. Ohne fundierte Vorkenntnisse wird man kaum in der Lage sein, dem Bericht ein **stimmiges Gesamtbild** zu geben, wobei 'stimmig' bitte nicht mit 'harmonisch' oder 'idyllisch' gleichgesetzt werden soll. Es sollte sich von selbst verstehen, daß Probleme, Widersprüche und Unstimmigkeiten in der Berichterstattung nicht unter den Tisch fallen.

In der Praxis kann das allerdings oft anders aussehen, denn gerade hier taucht das Problem der **Reisesponsoren** auf: Die Reise wurde mit Hilfe eines Reiseveranstalters finanziert. Dessen Erwartungshaltung in bezug auf eine möglichst positive Berichterstattung ist natürlich groß. Abwägen hieße, bei einem negativ ausfallenden Bericht zukünftige Reisemöglichkeiten aufs Spiel zu setzen oder gar alle finanziellen Hilfsquellen ein für allemal versiegen zu lassen. Und wieviele Journalisten würden sich ihre eigene Lebensgrundlage entziehen wollen?

Denen, die gerade über Krisengebiete berichten oder diese bereisen wollen, sei natürlich besonders ans Herz gelegt, sich im Vorfeld der Reise gründlichst zu informieren und abzuschätzen, ob das Risiko einer solchen Reise nicht doch zu groß ist.

- Wie steht es um die **Wirtschaft** meines als Reiseziel gewählten Landes?
- Wie ist die aktuelle **politische Lage**?
- Was weiß ich über die **Mentalität** der Leute dort, ihre **Lebensart**?
- Wie steht es um die **soziale Struktur**, die **Infrastruktur**, das **Klima**?
- Gibt es vielleicht **Besonderheiten**, auf die ich gefaßt sein muß, z.B. den Brauch des Bakschisch-Gebens bei jeder Gelegenheit?

All das sind Fragen, mit denen der Journalist sich beschäftigen sollte. Zur Vorbereitung einer Reise bzw. zur vorbereitenden Recherche gehören aber auch Fragen wie diese:

- Habe ich ein gültiges **Visum**?
- Muß ich evtl. eine spezielle **Einreise- oder Arbeitserlaubnis** beantragen?
- Ist eine **Impfung** nötig?
- Wie sind die Möglichkeiten der **Unterbringung**, **Fortbewegung**, **Kommunikation** etc. vor Ort?
- Wenn ich **Photos** machen will, benötige ich dafür eine spezielle Genehmigung?

Es ist fast überflüssig, zu erwähnen, daß man sich vor allem auch über die **Landessprache** Gedanken machen sollte. Wenn man diese beherrscht, wird es einfacher fallen, mit den Einheimischen Kontakt aufzunehmen, mit ihnen ins Gespräch und so an Informationen zu kommen. Der Journalist wird sich leichter zurechtfinden und muß sich keine Sorgen um grobe Mißverständnisse machen. Die Beherrschung der einheimischen Sprache wird außerdem die Recherche vor Ort enorm erleichtern. Ein unsicheres Gefühl wird immer bleiben, wenn man sich ausschließlich auf einen **Dolmetscher** verlassen muß. Und was, wenn dieser gerade einmal nicht verfügbar ist? Interessieren nicht auch die täglichen Nachrichten, das Radioprogramm, die lokalen Zeitungen? Oder das sprichwörtliche 'was die Leute so reden'?

Wenn der Journalist der Landessprache nicht mächtig ist: Welche andere Sprache, die er beherrscht, wird außerdem von einem Großteil der Bevölkerung gesprochen (z.B. Englisch, Französisch)? Diese könnte ihm zumindest in entscheidenden Situationen weiterhelfen, ein vollwertiger Ersatz wird sie dennoch nicht sein.

Verfügt der Reporter über keine derartigen Fremdsprachenkenntnisse, wird er gezwungen sein, sich einen Dolmetscher zu besorgen, dem er vertrauen kann - und der ist oft schwer zu finden. Die Kontaktaufnahme mit der Bevölkerung, Behörden usw. wird das sicherlich kaum erleichtern.

Wer sich optimal vorbereitet, wird mehr Spaß an seiner Reise haben, sich während seiner Reise sicherer fühlen und seine Leser bzw. Zuschauer später mit einer kompetenten und interessanten Berichterstattung versorgen können. Eines sollte man sich dennoch vor Augen halten: So sehr man sich auch vorbereitet, so sehr man auch mental auf das zu bereisende Land eingestellt ist - es wird sich nicht vermeiden lassen, daß einem trotzdem noch vieles fremd vorkommt. Schon die ersten Eindrücke können vieles, was der Journalist sich 'angelesen' hat, auf den Kopf stellen. Oft taucht man in eine völlig unbekannte Welt ein, deren Sitten und Bräuche man nicht genau kennt und in der man sich unsicher bewegt. Doch gerade dieses Fremde macht ja auch den

Reiz des Ganzen aus. Und ein gewisses Vorwissen wird es eventuell erleichtern, vieles zu verstehen und darüber später in angemessener Form zu schreiben.

3.2.3 Die Recherche während der Reise

Wesentliches Merkmal vieler Reiseberichte sind gerade die **persönlichen Erlebnisse**, die der Autor schildert, welche dann zusammen mit Hintergrund-Informationen dem Rezipienten ein möglichst lebendiges Bild von einem Land bieten sollen. Das 'Sich-treiben-lassen', das 'Auf-sich-zukommen-lassen' ist oft wesentlicher Bestandteil einer Reise, macht den Reiz des ganzen Unternehmens aus. Daher wird nicht jeder Berichterstatter während seiner Reise in Dokumenten recherchieren müssen bzw. wollen.

Wenn doch, dann gilt es herauszufinden, welche Hilfsmittel zur Verfügung stehen - fast unabdinglich ist in so einem Fall die Kenntnis der Landessprache, denn nur sie öffnet uns die Türen zu den zur Verfügung stehenden Informationsquellen, die zum größten Teil die gleichen sein werden wie die bereits weiter oben genannten.

Wenn der Journalist sich an **Behörden** wendet, sollte er sich vorher informieren, ob sie ähnlich wie in Deutschland einer gewissen Auskunftspflicht gegenüber den Medien unterliegen, und ob von dieser Auskunftspflicht auch Ausländer Gebrauch machen können.

Es seien an dieser Stelle auch sehr aktuelle Medien angesprochen, die dienen können - wer sich einen Laptop inklusive **Internet**-Anschluß leisten kann, dem stehen sicherlich besonders viele Möglichkeiten der Information zur Verfügung. Nicht zuletzt kann er so schnell mit der Heimat in Verbindung treten und wichtige Informationen auch per e-mail austauschen. Das Internet als schier unerschöpfliche Quelle der Information und Recherche kann für den reisenden Berichterstatter - auch schon vor Antritt der Reise - von enormer Bedeutung sein. Stadtpläne und Landkarten, 'Insider-Tips', Berichte von 'schon-Dagewesenen', andere Medien im Internet (Zeitungen etc.), Bibliotheken online, Flug- und sonstige Reisepläne, Reisebuchung per Tastendruck - alles keine Zukunftsmusik mehr.

Wer schon vor der Reise absehen kann, daß er in dem zu bereisenden Land Recherchen durchführen will, sollte sich rechtzeitig über seine Möglichkeiten informieren: Wo finde ich meine Quellen, seien es Behörden, Bibliotheken, Informanten? Ist der Zugang zu ihnen gesichert? Was für Probleme könnten auftreten und bin ich auf sie entsprechend vorbereitet?

3.2.4 Die nachbereitende Recherche

Wieder zu Hause angekommen, gilt es, das gesammelte Material zu sichten, zu ordnen und auszuwerten. Die neuen, während der Reise gewonnen Informationen müssen eventuell vertieft und noch einmal gründlich recherchiert werden. Oft tauchen dann Fragen auf, die während der Reise noch nicht gestellt wurden. Diesen Fragen sollte so genau wie möglich auf den Grund gegangen werden - **falsche Informationen** im späteren Bericht sind nicht nur peinlich, sie werden einem Anspruch auf kompetente Berichterstattung nicht gerecht. Oder können sogar den Job kosten.

Wenn trotz eingehender Nachrecherche eine Frage nicht eindeutig geklärt werden konnte, sollte das im Bericht erwähnt, oder aber der betreffende Themenbereich außen vor gelassen werden.

Die zur Verfügung stehenden Hilfsmittel sind die gleichen wie bei der Vorrecherche. Vielleicht kann der Journalist ja auch auf Informanten zurückgreifen, die er während seiner Reise kennengelernt hat. Die Nachrecherche sollte im Idealfall jeden Reisebericht abrunden. Sie garantiert, daß der Bericht keine falschen Informationen enthält, und sorgt dafür, daß neu gewonnene Eindrücke und Informationen richtig eingeordnet und angemessen verarbeitet werden.

Wer sich eingehender mit den allgemeinen Methoden des Recherchierens beschäftigen möchte, dem sei das Standardwerk von Michael Haller (Haller 1991) empfohlen. So wichtig die Recherche im Reisejournalismus auch ist, so karg bleibt die Quellenlage. Weiterführende Angaben und Ratschläge bleiben schwierig.

3.3 Die Reportage

Diana Lühmann

Die Reportage ist die 'krönende' Darstellungsform der journalistischen Berichterstattung und nimmt auch im Reisejournalismus die führende Rolle zwischen den anderen Textgattungen ein. Sie gilt als „besondere, aber auch als besonders schwierige Darstellungsform“ (Haller 1995: 48): Sie ist „gekennzeichnet durch Nähe zur objektiven und dokumentarisch nachprüfbaren Wirklichkeit und leidenschaftslos sachliche Schilderung des Details ohne einseitige Tendenz, allenfalls aus der Perspektive des Berichters“ (Wilpert 1964: 575), zugleich gestaltet der Reporter in ihr aber „ein plastisches Bild von Menschen und Ereignissen, das geprägt ist von seinem Erleben, seiner inneren Anteilnahme und seiner Wertung“ (Autorenkollektiv 1988: 176).

3.3.1 Die Funktion der Reportage: teilnehmen lassen

Was macht eigentlich den Reiz, das besondere der Reportage inmitten der verschiedenen journalistischen Textgattungen aus, die uns tagtäglich in Zeitungen und Zeitschriften begegnen? Was fesselt Rezipient wie Journalist gerade an dieser Art der Berichterstattung? Der Blick auf das Wesen, den Zweck eines als Reportage verfaßten Artikels erklärt, was diese Form journalistischen Schreibens zur ‘Königsdisziplin’ hat werden lassen.

Wesentlich ist, daß es sich um eine **subjektive Darstellungsform** handelt, die den Leser durch authentisches Erzählen an Ereignissen teilhaben lassen will, welche der Journalist als Beobachter selbst vor Ort erlebt hat. Die recherchierten Geschichten werden so an den Leser herangetragen, daß dieser unmittelbar - wie durch die Augen des Journalisten blickend - ein individuelles, ganz besonderes Geschehnis „miterlebt“. Der Reporter handelt hier also getreu der Bedeutung des lateinischen Verbs ‘reportare’: er trägt seine Eindrücke zusammen und überbringt sie - bildlich gesprochen - den Lesern seines Artikels. „So ist die Reportage mit ihrer Konkretheit und Nacherlebbarkeit besonders geeignet, wesentliche Erfahrungen aus allen Gebieten des Lebens aufzugreifen und sie anschaulich darzustellen“ (Autorenkollektiv 1988: 176). Der Reporter überwindet anstelle des Lesers Hindernisse wie beispielsweise soziale Barrieren und räumliche Distanzen, so daß dieser über die Vermittlungsfunktion des Journalisten miterleben kann, was ihm sonst alltags aufgrund mangelnder Gelegenheiten und Möglichkeiten verschlossen bleiben würde.

Das Ziel, den Leser an einem Ereignis teilnehmen zu lassen, unterscheidet die Reportage von anderen Textgattungen wie beispielsweise dem tatsachenbetonenden Bericht. Darin geht es allein um die Vermittlung von konkreten Informationen und aktuellen Neuigkeiten, nicht aber um detaillierte Erlebnisbeschreibungen eines Journalisten, welche in Reportagen zudem meist ‘nur’ mittelbare Aktualität besitzen.

Dieser Vergleich macht das besondere einer Reportage deutlich: Sie geht über einen bloßen Nachrichtencharakter hinaus. Sie will dabei aber weder abstrakte Themenzusammenhänge veranschaulichen und ‘trockene’ Nachrichten aufbereiten wie bei einem als Feature verfaßten Bericht, noch, wie etwa in Magazingeschichten und Hintergrundberichten, Entwicklungstendenzen aktueller Geschehnisse aufdecken und Sachverhalte erklären. Auf den Punkt gebracht: „Der Bericht ist eine einfache fotografische Aufnahme, die Reportage ist ein Röntgenbild, oder, noch präziser ausgedrückt, ein Röntgen-Film“ (Frei 1934: 4). Denn in einer Reportage geht es vor allem um das authentisch erzählte Ereignis selbst, sie taucht in das Wesen der geschilderten Personen, Verhältnisse, Dinge und Sinneseindrücke ein. Weitläufige Hintergründe oder Bedeutung für aktuelles Zeitgeschehen stehen nicht im Vordergrund einer Reportage, sie sind - wenn im thematischen Zusammenhang überhaupt erwähnenswert - nur Ausschmückungen am Rande.

Während die beschriebenen Personen in anderen journalistischen Stilformen wie dem Feature oder der Magazingeschichte meist nur typische Illustration und somit austauschbar sind, lebt die Reportage von ihren real existierenden Akteuren, ihren ‘echten’ Geschichten und Handlungsverläufen, die sich vor allem durch eines auszeichnen: den stark subjektiven Zugang des Autors. Durch die **authentische Schilderung** und die **Individualität der Handelnden** vermittelt die Reportage ihren charakteristischen „Eindruck, daß die Akteure gerade nicht austauschbar und die Ereignisse einmalig, mithin unwiederbringlich sind“ (Haller 1995: 79/80).

3.3.2 Was sind Reportagethemen?

Welche Themen werden den reportagetypischen Forderungen nach Individualität und Erlebnischarakter gerecht? Das Primat des Besonderen eröffnet dem Journalisten in dieser Frage vielfältige Perspektiven. So können Reportagen von Menschen mit besonders interessanten Lebensläufen, Berufen, Hobbys und Ansichten handeln, Geschichten aus anderen Ländern und Kulturen berichten, hinter die Kulissen von Politik, Kultur und Gesellschaft blicken, von einer Reise erzählen, aber auch im alltäglichen Geschehen neue Perspektiven durch besondere Betrachtungen, Blickrichtungen und Fragestellungen eröffnen.

3.3.3 Stilistische Besonderheiten

Um den Leser an diesen Geschichten authentisch teilhaben zu lassen, muß die Reportage ihrer Funktion auch stilistisch angepaßt sein. Eine derartige Nähe zwischen Leser und Text kann nur durch einen farbigen und fesselnden Schreibstil erreicht werden: Der Journalist schildert seine Erlebnisse und

Eindrücke vor Ort so lebensnah, daß der Rezipient sich die beschriebenen Szenen vor dem geistigen Auge vorstellen kann. Allerdings sollte nicht das wortschöpferische Talent des Journalisten, sondern das Geschilderte selbst für Sinnlichkeit und Witz des Textes sorgen: „Die Reportage ist weder Feuilleton noch Glosse“ (LaRoche 1991: 139).

Schon der Einstieg einer Reportage sollte in der Lage sein, den Leser einzufangen, ihn zur weiteren Lektüre einzuladen. Daher beginnen die meisten Reportagen mit einem szenischen Einstieg, der ganz gezielt die für jede Reportage einzigartige Atmosphäre entstehen läßt. Ebenso kann der Journalist dem Erzählfaden seines Textes durch Rahmengeschichten, einen Spannungsbogen von interessanten und unerwarteten Szenen- oder Perspektivenwechseln sowie die Einführung neuer Aspekte packende Wendungen verleihen. In der Dramaturgie seiner inhaltlichen und stilistischen Mittel sind der Phantasie des Autoren einer Reportage keine Grenzen gesetzt, um der Erzählung eine gewisse Spannung und Eigendynamik einzuhauchen.

3.3.4 Reportagen über Reisen: Den Leser mit in die Ferne nehmen

Um ihre Leser in die Welt des Reisens zu entführen, ihnen ferne wie fremde Kulturen und Landschaften zu eröffnen, ist die Reportage sowohl in Zeitungen als auch Hochglanzmagazinen wie *GEO* die zentrale Darstellungsform des Reisejournalismus. Schließlich zählten Reisedarstellungen immer schon zum Kernbereich der Reportage (Kap. 2): Die Art, wie einst vier Jahrhunderte vor Christus der griechische Volkskundler und Chronist Herodot seine Reisen nach Ägypten und Persien schilderte, gilt noch heute als „eine Urform der Reportage“ (Haller 1995: 18).

Dennoch unterscheidet sich die Reisereportage von Reportagen, die zum Beispiel ein bestimmtes Ereignis schildern oder sozialkritische Milieustudien vornehmen. Oft ähnelt eine Reportage mit Reiseinhalt dramaturgisch einem Kaleidoskop wechselnder Bilder und Themen. Dabei ist „eine gute Reisereportage (...) ja selten nur Protokoll einer konkreten Reise, sondern fast immer ein Komprimat sämtlicher Erlebnisse und Erkenntnisse“ (Guilino 1995: S. 5): Die Schönheit der Landschaft und die Lebensart Einheimischer werden ebenso stimmungsvoll inszeniert wie mit der Reise verbundene Probleme, die Hotelsituation, örtliche Gastronomie und manchmal auch politische Verhältnisse eines Urlaubziels. Diese vielfältigen und bunt wechselnden Bilder wollen dabei weniger das Besondere, sondern eher das Typische illustrieren.

Das Schreiben einer Reisereportage bedeutet für ihren Autor nicht nur das Überwinden räumlicher Distanzen, oftmals entpuppt dieser sich als Pionier in vielerlei Hinsicht. So kann eine Reisereportage neben illustrer Darstellung geographischer und klimatischer Begebenheiten zum Botschafter fremder Kultur und Lebensart werden. Allerdings sollte ein guter Reisejournalist, wenn er mehr als ein der Reiseindustrie genehmes 'Sonne, Strand und Cocktails'-Bild bieten möchte, über ein plumpes Rezitieren von allseits verbreiteten Stereotypen oder - schlimmer sogar - Vorurteilen hinausgehen. Authentizität und der subjektive, gut recherchierte Eindruck des Journalisten sind auch in Reportagen mit Reiseinhalt oberstes Gebot.

Im Reisejournalismus **orientieren sich Reportagen vornehmlich an dem Interesse der Leser**, fremde Regionen, Länder und Kulturen kennenzulernen. Aber auch, wenn eine Reportage 'rund um´s Reisen' geht: Thematisch erschließt sich dem Reisejournalisten eine Vielfalt an Variationen. Ein entscheidender Faktor in der Wahl des Themas ist das Medium, in dem der Text erscheinen und seine Leser faszinieren soll. So setzen die einzelnen Redaktionen ihren Mitarbeitern klare Maßstäbe: Während in den Wochenendausgaben von Lokalzeitungen neben Reisezielen der 'großen weiten Welt' auch die Sehenswürdigkeiten der unmittelbaren Nachbarschaft vertreten sind, konzentrieren sich überregional erscheinende Publikationen auf die großen nationalen und internationalen 'Reise-Highlights'. Daß dieser Journalismus dabei in hohem Maße zielgruppenorientiert ist, zeigt sich vor allem auf dem Zeitschriften-Markt. So thematisieren Reisereportagen in Frauenzeitschriften meist entweder attraktive Single-Reisen für die junge unternehmungslustige Frau oder den perfekten Familienurlaub für verheiratete Mütter mittleren Alters.

Ein typisches Beispiel für eine auf die Freizeitinteressen des Lesepublikums abgestimmte Reiseberichterstattung sind Special-Interest-Magazine zum Thema Sport und Lebensart. Hier finden sich Reportagen über Surfen, Angeln und Bergsteigen oder auch Wohnkultur, Historie und Gastronomie in fernen Ländern - entsprechend den Interessen der jeweiligen Leserschaft.

Doch damit sind die Möglichkeiten der Reisereportage bei weitem noch nicht ausgeschöpft: Das Reisen selbst kann anstelle eines bestimmten Zielortes in den Mittelpunkt einer Reportage rücken - wie beispielsweise die Schilderung einer Fahrt mit der Transsibirischen Eisenbahn oder einer Kreuzfahrt auf einem Luxus-Liner. Oder das Reisen auf den Spuren großer Dichter, Seefahrer und Feldherren.

Bei all dieser Themenvielfalt sollte sich der Autor einer Reisereportage auf jeden Fall folgende Fragen stellen: Fordere ich meine Leser dazu auf, mir nachzureisen, oder schreibe ich für den 'Geist, der in die Ferne schweift'? Sind für mich gesellschaftliche Begebenheiten von Interesse, die über den Dunstkreis der Tourismusbranche eines Landes oder einer Region hinausgehen; wenn ja: wird in meiner Darstellung auch 'die andere Seite' der sozialen Mißstände und Probleme Eingang finden, die es ja selbst in unserem Land gibt? Und schließlich: Wie gehe ich überhaupt mit dem Fremden, dem Andersartigem um, welches mir während meiner Recherche begegnet und auf mich gleichermaßen faszinierend wie erschreckend wirken kann?

Diese und andere ethisch relevante Fragen gelten für den Autor einer Reisereportage in ganz besonderer Weise: Durch ihn erfahren die Leser etwas von der **Atmosphäre eines Landes**; er trifft die Auswahl der Eindrücke, die das Bild der Leser von einem Staat, einer Region nachhaltig prägen und diese nicht zuletzt dazu animieren können, die vermittelte Szenerie in natura nacherleben zu wollen. Eine für einen Reisejournalisten schwierige Verantwortung: Preise ich die Ursprünglichkeit der Amazonasregion an - auch auf die Gefahr hin, daß die dort lebenden Indianer neben Goldsuchern und Missionaren nun auch von Touristenschwärmen heimgesucht werden? Schildere ich nur die tunesische Sonnenseite, oder lenke ich die Blicke meiner Leser auch auf das Leben der Menschen abseits umzäunter Touristenstrände?

Oftmals steht die Sparte der Reisejournalisten in Verruf, sich diese Entscheidungen nur zu gern von der ansässigen Touristenbranche abnehmen zu lassen. Ein Vorwurf, der wiederum besonders die **Glaubwürdigkeit** von Reisereportagen im allgemeinen betrifft. Doch seriöse Zeitungen und Zeitschriften - allen voran *GEO* - zeigen, daß sie auch im Ressort 'Reise' zu finden ist: die verantwortungsvoll und journalistisch professionell geschriebene Reportage.

3.4 Das Schreiben einer Reisereportage

Diana Lühmann

> „Eine Reisereportage soll mehr sein als Gebrauchsanweisung, mehr als spannender Lesestoff. Sie kann gleichsam nebenbei Wissen und Verständnis vermitteln, wenn sie Typisches aufgreift, Wesentliches erklärt - gerade indem sich ihr roter Faden locker und vermeintlich absichtslos um Beobachtungen und Erfahrungen des vor-reisenden Journalisten schlingt."
>
> (Guilino 1995: 5).

An Reisereportagen werden Ansprüche gestellt: Es gilt, die Zielgruppe des Mediums, an das der Text verkauft werden soll, zu beachten, eine möglichst allumfassende Recherche durchzuführen und die gewonnenen Eindrücke und Einblicke sprachlich sowohl sinnlich-fesselnd als auch sachlich-informierend in eine durchstrukturierte, pointierte Reportage umzusetzen.

Zwar werden Kriterien wie 'Talent' und 'Inividualität' von vielen Journalisten hochgehalten. Im Zeitalter harten Konkurrenzkampfes unter den Medien, voranschreitender Spezialisierung des Zeitschriftenmarktes und immer genauer erforschten **Zielpublikums** ist das jedoch nur die halbe Wahrheit journalistischen Schreibens. Und so wandern in vielen Redaktionen eingesandte Manuskripte zurück an den Absender oder schlicht in den Papierkorb, weil sie bestenfalls schreiberisches Können aufweisen, jedoch keinesfalls an stilistische und inhaltliche Vorgaben des **anvisierten Mediums** angepaßt sind. Besonders im Ressort Reise, das in vielen Zeitungen und Zeitschriften vorwiegend von Texten freier Mitarbeiter lebt, ist die Konkurrenz groß. Deshalb sollten Autoren von Reisereportagen besonders umsichtig in der Vorbereitung und Gestaltung ihres 'Produktes' sein.

Während sich deutsche Handbücher über journalistische Textgattungen und (Reise-) Journalismus hinsichtlich der **kommerziellen Seite** journalistischen Schreibens meist zurückhalten und sich eher **sprachlich-ästhetischen Gesichtspunkten** zuwenden, finden sich auf amerikanischer Seite regelrechte Wegweiser, wie (Reise-) Journalisten ihre Zeilen erfolgreich in bare Münze verwandeln können. So verraten schon die Untertitel der Bücher *The Travel Writer's Handbook: How to Write and Sell your own Travel Experiences* von Louise Purwin Zobel (1992) und *Travel Writing: A Guide to Research, Writing and Selling* von L. Peat O'Neil (1996), daß im Beruf des Reisejournalisten mehr als 'bloß' journalistisch-handwerkliche Bewanderung vonnöten ist, wenn ein Text verkauft und gedruckt werden soll.

Die amerikanischen Ratschläge können zwar nicht uneingeschränkt auf den deutschen Markt angewendet werden, dennoch sind sie erwähnenswert. Aus ihnen und den Tips deutscher Autoren läßt sich eine Liste von Anhaltspunkten aufstellen, nach denen sich - frei von irgendeinem Schema - Reisereportagen durchaus beurteilen und erfolgreich kreieren lassen.

3.4.1 Für wen schreibe ich?

Mit dem Thema Reisen beschäftigen sich in der deutschen Presselandschaft recht unterschiedliche Medien: Fast alle Tages-, Sonntags- und Wochenzeitungen sowie zahlreiche Frauenzeitschriften und sogenannte Special-interest-Magazine haben ihre Reise-Ressorts. Daneben stehen Zeitschriften, die sich ausschließlich dem Thema Reisen widmen: die Hochglanz-Reisemagazine. Den Autoren von Reisereportagen bietet sich ein umfangreicher, jedoch hochgradig differenzierter 'Absatzmarkt'.

Reisereportagen werden in vielen Redaktionen von freien Mitarbeitern bezogen. Dabei haben besonders die großen Reisemagazine ihre sogenannten festen Freien, die gezielt für ausgesuchte Themen beauftragt werden. So auch beim Reisemagazin *GLOBO*:

> „Eine Handvoll Stammautoren wird vor der Jahresplanung nach Wunschthemen befragt. Üblicher Vorlauf der Reportagen ist ein Jahr - schon damit die Fotos zur Jahreszeit passen. Die Heftplanung reicht etwa eineinhalb bis zwei Jahre in die Zukunft. Schon lange vor der Reise sind Autor und Redaktion im Dialog; viele Themen und Routen werden gemeinsam entwickelt. Weitere Gespräche klären die Richtung der Reportage, die Schwerpunkte und deren Umsetzung."
>
> (Benedikt 1995: 20.)

Stammautoren von aufwendig produzierten Hochglanz-Reisemagazinen sind meist namenhafte Journalisten und/oder Buchautoren, Künstler und Kenner vor (Reise-) Ort. Sie kommen oft sogar „aus den anspruchsvollen Nischen bei Hörfunk und Fernsehen, aus der Theaterwelt oder dem Feuilleton sowie natürlich auch aus dem klassischen Reportage-Genre" (Benedikt 1995: 20).

Das Prinzip der festen Freien im Reisejournalismus ist auch in den Reise-Ressorts von Zeitungen und Zeitschriften anderer Sparten ein Phänomen. In kleineren Lokalzeitungen existiert ein solches Ressort oft gar nicht: Texte mit Reiseinhalt werden 'nebenbei' von den Redakteuren erstellt; oft werfen die eigenen Urlaubserfahrungen genug Stoff dafür ab.

Will man also Reportagen mit Reiseinhalt schreiben und verkaufen, muß man seine Texte auf die Bedürfnisse der einzelnen Medien abstimmen, um in der Flut von Manuskripten nicht unterzugehen - das gilt besonders für 'Neulinge' im Geschäft. **Interessen und Geldbeutel der Leser** stehen im Mittelpunkt einer Reisereportage: Schreibe ich für junge Singles, Camper-Familien, Sportler, wohlhabene Intelektuelle oder mittellose Studenten? Profile der Zielgruppen werden durch Leserbefragungen ständig präzisiert. Reisejournalismus orientiert sich außerdem in hohem Maße an den **aktuellen Reise-Trends**. „Die Grundlage bildet natürlich das übliche Instrumentarium eines spezialisierten Journalisten der Publikumspresse: Lektüre der Fachpresse, Studium der neuen Kataloge (und der Pressemitteilungen dazu), Besuch der Messen (deren wichtigste die Internationale Tourismus-Börse *ITB* in Berlin ist)." (Benedikt 1995: 18)

3.4.2 *Worüber schreibe ich?*

Sind Trends und Zielgruppe umrissen, gilt es, darauf abgestimmt ein interessantes, möglichst originelles Thema zu finden: „Tatsächlich beginnt das Reportageschreiben nicht mit dem Schreiben, nicht mit der Materialbeschaffung und nicht mit der Verabredung am Ort des Geschehens, sondern mit der sorgfältigen Herrichtung des Themas." (Haller 1995: 99) Eine Reisereportage zielt in der Regel auf einen bestimmten Typ Reisenden ab. Abgestimmt auf dessen Freizeitverhalten können bestimmte Angebote am Zielort vorgestellt werden, z.B. Strände, Sportanlagen, Nachtleben, Kultur oder Gastronomie. Auch kann eine interessante Methode des Reisens im Mittelpunkt stehen: Mit dem Fahrrad durch Europa, Touren von Jugendherberge zu Jugendherberge oder zu Fuß durch Südafrika.

Auch die Leser, die eine Reisereportage in der Ohrensessel-Perspektive genießen, gilt es in Anlehnung an ihre persönlichen Vorlieben und Interessen zu fesseln. Sie wollen fremde Orte im Geiste erkunden, sie so in Erinnerung behalten, als ob sie selbst dort gewesen sind. Diesen Effekt kann der Journalist mit einer besonders sinnlichen und umfassenden Darstellung erreichen: Athmosphäre und Hintergrundbeschreibungen stehen im Mittelpunkt (Zobel 1992: 275-277).

3.4.3 *Wie bereite ich mich vor?*

Eine **umfassende Recherche** ist für die Reportage mit Reiseinhalt wie für andere Reportageformen grundlegend. Denn „erst diese Erkenntnisse - in der Regel zum kleineren Teil vor Ort gewonnen, zum überwiegenden Teil vor der Reise recherchiert - versetzen den Journalisten in die Lage, Erlebtes zu gewichten und einzuordnen: Man sieht nur, was man weiß." (Guilino 1995: 5) Der Reisejournalist muß sich für das Schreiben einer Reportage fundierte Kenntnisse erwerben, ob über Reiseindustrie und Hotellerie, politische, gesellschaftliche und wirtschaftliche Begebenheiten eines Landes, Landschaft und Kultur, Sitten und religiöses Brauchtum. Der Reisejournalist reist dem Leser als Scout voraus, gilt als Kompetenz vor Ort. Er wählt die Informationen aus, die das Bild des Lesers von dem beschriebenen Land, der geschilderten Region prägen. Diesen Vorsprung an Wissen, die Basis seiner Auswahl an Informationen muß sich der Autor einer Reisereportage erarbeiten - es sei denn, er lebt vor Ort und schreibt als Korrespondent. Aber das ist die Ausnahme.

3.4.4 Wie schreibe ich eine Reisereportage?

Die Recherche ist abgeschlossen, das Material ist sortiert, nun kann drauflos geschrieben werden? Falsch - es sei denn, an dem Autor ist ein literarisches Genie verlorengegangen. An der Komposition einer Reisereportage kann und sollte viel gefeilt und perfektioniert werden:

Was ist die Kernaussage der Reportage?

Die Amerikanerin Louise Purwin Zobel rät jedem Reisereportagen-Autor: „Write a **'Capsule Sentence'**" (Zobel 1992: 196). Bevor man auch nur eine Zeile einer Reportage aufs Papier bringt, sollte man in der Lage sein, die Kernaussage, die Idee des Artikels präzise zu formulieren - und zwar in einem einzigen Satz. Die Reportage ist eine Botschaft an den Leser, deren Sinn von diesem auch verstanden werden soll. Der Kernsatz muß dem Leser frühzeitig in der Reisereportage deutlich gemacht werden und sollte sich als „roter Faden" durch den Text ziehen. (Z.B.: „Wenn Sie London besuchen, müssen Sie auf jeden Fall bei Madame Tussot gewesen sein." oder „Im Ozeanographischen Institut in Monaco kann man spannende Entdeckungen machen.") Die Botschaft darf allerding nicht zu generell („Machen Sie Urlaub in Australien.") oder zu eng („Nehmen Sie am 14. Juni die Fähre Hamburg-Harwich.") formuliert werden.

Wie ist eine Reisereportage aufgebaut?

Bevor es an das Formulieren geht, muß der Aufbau des Artikels festgelegt werden, und der sollte bei Reisereportagen stets sehr bedacht sein. Die Erzählungen einer Reportage folgen einer gewissen **Dramaturgie**. Nicht der strenge Aufbau - wie bei Nachricht oder Bericht gefordert - ist gefragt, es gilt nicht das Prinzip abnehmender Wichtigkeit bei voranschreitender Zeilenanzahl. Weiter gibt es oft keine vorgeschriebene Chronologie der Ereignisse. Der Journalist nimmt den Leser seiner Geschichte mit auf einen Rundgang sinnlicher Wahrnehmungen, bewegter Szenen und bunter Geschichten.

„Damit erinnert die Reportage ein wenig an einen Film, dessen Bilder in der Phantasie des Lesers gleichsam entwickelt werden." (Gerhardt 1996: 151)

Besonders bei Reisereportagen ist die Gliederung des Stoffes sehr wichtig, denn an den Leser sollen sowohl Stimmungsbilder als auch „harte Fakten" herangetragen werden (O'Neil 1996: 78/79). Gewöhnlich behandelt eine Reportage mit Reiseinhalt nicht die chrononologisch-detaillierte Nacherzählung der vom Journalisten selbst absolvierten Reise. Meist ist die Vorstellung eines Ferienzieles, einer Route oder einer Reiseart ein **'offenes Thema'**, das erst in 'Form' geschrieben werden muß. Sind die schönsten Elemente und die wichtigsten Informationen ausgewählt, besteht die Schwierigkeit darin, „den Stoff so auf die Reihe zu bringen, daß die Episoden und Beobachtungen plausibel verknüpft sind und sich am Ende das vom Reporter gewollte Stimmungsbild bei den Lesern einstellt" (Haller 1995: 137).

Um dem Leser überhaupt einen Anreiz zu bieten, seine Zeit zu 'opfern' und sich einen langen Text wie eine Reportage durchzulesen, muß der Reporter einen packenden **Einstieg** finden: „Er sollte szenisch sein und die Leser wenn möglich mitten ins Geschehen stellen; nicht unbedingt ins Zentrum, aber doch dorthin, wo sich etwas Erzählenswertes ereignet." (Haller 1995: 141) Doch wie sollte ein solcher Lead aussehen? Möglichst bildhaft wie z.B. die Beschreibung einer Szene, einer Landschaft, eines Menschen. Der Auftakt einer Reisereportage sollte die Phantasie und Vorstellungskraft des Lesers wecken, ihn 'mit auf die Reise nehmen' in ferne Länder, zu fremden Kulturen oder in vergangene Zeiten. Auch Zitate oder Fragen können ein gelungener Auftakt sein - Hauptsache, die Stimmung und Tonart des folgenden Textes ist eingefangen.

Da so viel vom Einstieg, vom ersten Satz einer Reportage abhängt, sind besondere Formulierungssorgfalt und Sprachgefühl gefragt. Deshalb sollte der Reporter schon bei seiner Recherche vor Ort mit Argusaugen nach geeigneten Momenten Ausschau halten und später am Schreibtisch sorgsam auswählen.

Um den Leser 'bei der Stange zu halten', müssen dem Lead weitere spannende Momente folgen. Die Reportage „wird also nicht nach dem Prinzip abnehmender Wichtigkeit gegliedert, sondern in der Abfolge der Szenen so, daß auch in der Mitte und am Schluß noch Höhepunkte kommen" (LaRoche 1991: 139). Abwechslung ist gefragt - insbesondere für Reportagen mit Reiseinhalt bedeutet das ein **kontrastreicher Wechsel der Perspektiven**, der beschriebenen Stimmungen, Orte, Menschen und Hintergrundinformationen. Reisereportagen gleichen selbst einer Reise, folgen einer eigenen Dramaturgie.

Die Amerikanerin L. Peat O'Neil empfiehlt in ihrem Handbuch über *Travel Writing*, sich beim Aufstellen einer Struktur für eine Reisereportage an folgenden (für journalistische Texte traditionellen) Fragen zu orientieren:

- WO - der Ort, die geographischen Gegebenheiten
- WANN - Jahreszeit (und damit die klimatischen Gegebenheiten)
- WER - der Augenschein des Reporters, seine Eindrücke
- WARUM - Motivation, weshalb gerade dieses Reisziel / -erlebnis
- WIE - das Reisen / die Urlaubsgestaltung selbst
- WAS - detaillierte Schilderungen, Anekdoten und Fakten.

(O'Neil 1996: 88/89)

Eine Reisereportage ähnelt einem Kaleidoskop an Eindrücken und Ansichten. Ist der geistige Blick des Lesers in einem Absatz noch auf die Romantik einer kleinen, verwinkelten Gasse gelenkt, informieren die nächsten Abschnitte über die Historie des Landes, die Qualität der ansässigen Gastronomie und die wirtschaftliche Lage der hiesigen Weinbauern - um dann wieder in die Athmosphäre vor Ort zurückzuschwenken.

Episoden und Momentaufnahmen werden durch einen **Erzählfaden** zusammengehalten und sollten so angeordnet sein, daß ein **Spannungsbogen** erzeugt wird. Dynamik erhält die Reisereportage z.B. durch eine zu Beginn eingebaute Rahmengeschichte, die nach und nach fortgesetzt wird, aber auch durch die Einführung neuer, interessanter Aspekte. „Neben dem Stimmungsbild bietet eine gute Reportage möglichst viele Informationen. Nur müssen sie so eingefügt sein, daß beim Leser nie das Gefühl aufkommt, der Handlungsfluß werde gerade angehalten, damit er nun belehrt werde." (Gerhardt 1996: 179) Das gilt bei der Reisereportage z.B. für Informationen über Einwohnerzahlen, Bildungsstand der Bevölkerung, Fangmethoden dort lebender Fischer oder historische Rückblicke.

Wichtig ist auch der **Schluß** einer Reisereportage, denn er beeinflußt wesentlich den Gesamteindruck des Textes auf den Leser. Deshalb sollte das Ende einer Reportage möglichst pointiert sein und die ganz eigene Stimmung des Textes nachklingen lassen. Eine 'runde Sache' ist beispielsweise das Aufgreifen und Abschließen einer zuvor begonnenen Rahmengeschichte oder ein sich aus der Botschaft der Reportage ergebender Ausblick in die Zukunft.

Sprachlich-ästhetische Aspekte

> „Reportagen und Features haben eines gemeinsam: Sie müssen stilistisch so durchgefeilt sein, daß sie Kabinettstücke sind, farbige Steine, die aus der Druckerschwärze einer Zeitung herausleuchten."
>
> (Gerhardt 1996: 161)

Wortgewandtheit und Gefühl für Sprache gelten auch - oder ganz besonders - für Reisereportagen. Wie sollte die Sprache in einer Reisereportage sein? Gibt es trotz des (notwendigen) **individuellen Stils** eines jeden Autors allgemeine Grundsätze?

„So konkret und anschaulich wie möglich" (LaRoche 1991: 136) ist eine Anforderung an die Reportage. Reportagen sollen die Vorstellungskraft des Lesers anregen und Bilder in seinem Kopf erzeugen. Und das geht nicht mit Allgemeinplätzen, sondern nur mit **detaillierten Schilderungen** von dem, was der Reporter selbst gesehen und erlebt hat. Allerdings sollte diese Möglichkeit, eine Reportage farbiger zu gestalten, in Maßen angewandt werden.

„Show, Don't Tell" fordert Louise Purwin Zobel als Anleitung zum Reportageschreiben: **Aktive Verben und präzise Nomen** sprechen den Leser an - Adjektive und Adverben und anderer 'passiver Ballast' sind dagegen sparsam zu verwenden. Ebenso sollte man Klischees und Umgangssprache vermeiden. (Zobel 1992: 206/207)

Zitate hauchen der Reportage mehr Leben ein: „Sie sollten immer dann eingestreut werden, wenn andere authentischer, glaubwürdiger sprechen als der Reporter selbst." (Gerhardt 1996: 180)

Spannung kann in einer Reportage mit einem **Wechsel des Sprachduktus** erzeugt werden: „Kühle, faktizierende Sprache für raffende Abschnitte; sinnliche, bilderreiche Sprache für episodale Schilderungen; distanzierender und erwägender Sprachduktus für das Räsonnement; unbegriffliche, metaphernreiche Alltagssprache für die Akteure in den Zitaten." (Haller 1995: 143) Dabei sollte der Reporter beachten, daß die Reportage durch die Verwendung raumgreifender, schillernder Sprache zu lang geraten kann: Wenige bunte Episoden und Detailschilderungen anstelle einer Masse von aneinandergereihten Geschichten sind effizienter. Außerdem ist es ratsam, das Erzähltempo gegen Ende der Reportage zu beschleunigen, damit der Leser seine Lektüre nicht doch noch vorzeitig gelangweilt abbricht.

Umstritten ist (zumindest in Deutschland), ob sich der Autor als **'Ich'** in eine Reisereportage einbringen sollte. Während Reisereportagen in amerikanischen Reisemagazinen fast ausschließlich als Erlebnisberichte in der ersten Person Singular (oder, wenn der Reporter mit Familie unterwegs war, auch in der ersten Person Plural) verfaßt sind, ist das 'Ich' in deutschen Pressetexten sehr selten zu finden. Zwar heißt es bei Walther von LaRoche: „Das ehrliche 'ich' für die Person des Reporters ist mir sympatischer als das pseudoobjektive, angeblich Bescheidenheit ausdrückende 'wir'" (LaRoche 1991: 140), dennoch stellt in Deutschland das subjektive 'ich' in Reportagen mit Reiseinhalt eine Rarität dar. Eine Reportage ensteht aus der subjektven Beobachtung des Journalisten, und in bestimmten Fällen ist die erste Person Singular durchaus angebracht, trotzdem „sollte man mit dem 'Ich' sparsam umgehen und es dem Leser nicht auf Schitt und Tritt um die Ohren hauen." (Gerhardt 1996: 193)

3.4.5 Redigieren, redigieren

Ist eine Reportage frisch geschrieben, ist der Journalist noch viel zu nahe an seinem Text, an seinen Formulierungen. Er muß **Abstand** zu seinem 'Produkt' gewinnen. Erst dann sieht er unpräzise Formulierungen und überflüssige Füllwörter und kann den Text inhaltlich verbessern wie sprachlich straffen. Jeder Satz sollte kontrolliert werden:

- Wie kann ich dasselbe noch knapper sagen?
- Wie kann ich es noch genauer sagen?
- Wie kann ich es noch anschaulicher sagen?
- Wie kann ich es noch interessanter sagen?

(Haller 1995: 166)

Effektiv ist es auch, die Reportage von Dritten gegenlesen zu lassen, um Widersprüche und Ungenauigkeiten auszumerzen, die der Autor des Textes übersieht, weil er einfach zu sehr in der Materie steckt. So kann überflüssiger Phrasen-Ballast eliminiert werden, gewinnt die Reportage an **Prägnanz**.

3.5 Anleitung für die 'etwas andere' Reisereportage

Hans J. Kleinsteuber

Eine erschreckende Anzahl von Reisereportagen lebt aus ihrer Normalität, um nicht zu sagen **Banalität** heraus: Anreise zu einem Ziel, der Aufenthalt vor Ort, die Schönheit der Landschaft, die Buntheit der Folklore, die Freundlichkeit der Menschen, Essen und Schlafen. Zum Abschluß muß leider tränenreich von paradiesischer Umgebung wieder Abschied genommen werden. Bleiben Wünsche offen, so helfen die Ratschläge im Serviceteil. Das alles wird dem Leser als Geheimtip verkauft, den der offensichtlich konspirativ reisende Journalist mir - dem geschätzten Reisekenner - ganz speziell zuteil werden läßt. Über Sponsoren und deren Interessen erfahren wir nichts. So oder ähnlich hat es die Touristikindustrie wohl gern, und so kommen leider auch viele Reisereportagen daher. Diese **Schlichtheit** langweilt, oft ist sie peinlich in ihrer Klischeehaftigkeit. Schlechter Reisejournalismus lebt auch von beliebigen Versatzstücken. Im Extremfall könnte man einen Baukasten entwerfen, aus dem sich jeder im Sinne einer 'public domain' bedienen kann, dem nichts mehr zu seinem Thema einfällt. Nehmen wir einmal diesen Beginn einer Reportage:

> „Jede Stadt hat ihre magischen Orte. Wo ihr Herz schlägt, wo der Besucher ihren Rhythmus und ihre Seele spürt, wo sie sich ihm zeigt in all ihrer Schönheit oder Verdorbenheit, wo er sie lieben oder hassen lernt."
>
> (*stern* Nr. 8 1997: 103 - Reisesonderteil)

Für den Autor mag es der Vorteil eines derartigen Allgemeinplatzes zu sein, daß er universell einsetzbar ist. Aus der Schublade zu ziehen, wenn ihm nichts spezifisches einfällt. Aber Qualität entsteht so nicht. Es handelt sich übrigens um Sydney, Australien - wären Sie darauf gekommen?

Hier werden einige Beispiele vorgestellt, wie man sich äußerer Thematik und innerer Dramaturgie einer **Reisereportage einmal ganz anders** nähert. Es handelt sich dabei um bereits gelaufene Projekte, gleichwohl soll nicht das Abkupfern unterstützt werden. Vielmehr geht es um eine andere Herangehensweise, bei der eine Reportage herauskommt, die eingefahrene Bahnen verläßt, unkonventionell und für den Leser überraschend.

3.5.1 Das 'verlorene Paradies'

Die Vorstellung eines Paradieses ist eng mit der Ferne verbunden. Seit der Vertreibung von Adam und Eva liegt dieses Paradies der Christen immer woanders. Paradiese gibt es in vielen Religionen und Mythen rund um die Welt. Eine Erklärung dafür mag sein, daß tief im kollektiven Gedächnis des Homo Sapiens die Erinnerung an die eigene Herkunft bewahrt ist: Ein Land von mildem Klima und harmonischer Natur - so wie die Wiege der Menschheit in der Savannenlandschaft des afrikanischen Hochlandes aussah (Zimmer 1991). Zurückkehrende Weltreisende haben in der Vergangenheit oft behauptet, sie hätten das Paradies gefunden - etwa in Amerika oder der Südsee. Gerade in schlechten Reportagen taucht das Etikett paradiesisch besonders häufig auf.

Längst ist das **Paradies kommerzialisiert**, in den Reiseprospekten ist der Begriff abonniert, der Garten Eden führt geradewegs zum Eden Hotel. Wer auf derartige Versprechungen hereinfällt, nun, dem ist nicht zu helfen. Die *ZEIT* machte sich einen Spaß daraus, unter dem Titel 'Paradise Island' den ganzen Schmus der schreibenden Reisebranche in eine geschlossene Darstellung zu bringen. Fündig wurden die Autoren in Zeitungen von A bis Z von *Abenteuer & Reisen* bis zu *ZEIT*-Artikeln im eigenen Haus. Eine Kostprobe:„Fröhliche Menschen singen und tanzen, legen frische Blütenkränze auf fremde Schultern. Die sanfteste aller Weisen erklingt, das Lied von der Dankbarkeit, hier leben zu dürfen. Geformt wie ein Schmetterling, liegt die Insel inmitten der blauen Weite des Ozeans. Sie wirkt so unberührt, so glückstrunken, wirklich wie ein zurückgeholtes Paradies." (Loppow/Krohn 1995)

Wieviel intelligenter erscheint es da, die Trauer um das **unwiederbringlich verlorene Paradies** ironisch zu brechen und ganz neu aufzuarbeiten. In einer Reportage von *GEO SAISON* zum Thema 'Die Suche nach dem Paradies' wurden in den USA alle 19 Orte aufgesucht, die auf den Namen 'Paradise' hören (Shnayerson 1996). Dabei handelt es sich um mehr oder weniger vergessene Ansiedlungen in der Weite des Landes, irgendwo zwischen Texas und Washington State. In dieser 'wahrhaft biblischen Mission' von Autor und Fotograf wird nicht eine Anleitung zum Nachreisen gegeben, dazu sind die Nester viel zu sehr über den ganzen Kontinent verstreut. Vor allem wird ein Einblick in tiefste Provinzialität eröffnet, werden Menschen beleuchtet, die in das 'Paradies' einzogen, und denen es nicht anders geht als uns. Ironisch wird so die Trauer aufgearbeitet, daß viele Einwanderer einst in Amerika das Paradies suchten und in öder Provinzialität strandeten.

3.5.2 Reisen als Fortbewegung

Wer in die Wortgenese der **Begrifflichkeit vom 'Reisen' und 'Wandern'** einsteigt, der wird feststellen, daß hier viel deutsch-germanisches enthalten ist, ohne Entsprechung in anderen Sprachräumen. Auf jeden Fall verweisen die Begriffe auf **Ortswechsel und Unterwegssein**, aus einer Zeit stammend, da Pauschaltourismus und Sonnenbaden noch gänzlich unbekannt waren.

Historisch gesehen ist Reisen immer Arbeit gewesen, das englische 'travel' ist mit dem französischen 'travail' für Arbeit verwandt. Auch neuere Begrifflichkeiten, etwa die des Tourismus, seit ca. 1800 im Englischen belegt, betonen die Tour, also die Bewegung in Form eines Rundgangs oder einer Wanderung. Erst Begriffe wie Urlaub und Ferien lösen die Reise von der Anstrengung, knüpfen an die Freistellung vom Dienst (Urlaub) oder meinen die schulfreie Zeit (Ferien). In dieser modernen Bedeutung ist jeder Bezug zu Fortbewegung geschwunden. Nun wird der 'Urlaub auf dem eigenen Balkon' möglich, die Reise dagegen nicht (Zur Begrifflichkeit: Opaschowski 1989: 11-28).

Die wirkliche Reise ist immer mit einer Ortsveränderung verbunden. Reisen bildet bekanntlich, danach sind wir 'be-wandert' und 'er-fahren'. Auch uns erscheint das ständige Unterwegssein meist noch als Krönung der Reisetätigkeit, der Pauschaltourist wird belächelt. Eine ganze Kategorie von Berichten widmet sich dem Metier der **Fortbewegung**. Eine Sondernummer des *ZEIT-Magazins* steht unter dem Motto „Man reist ja nicht, um anzukommen" (Unterwegs sein 1995: 6ff). Deutlich wird dabei, daß weit mehr möglich ist als Charter-Flieger und Mietauto. Vorgeschlagen werden Eisenbahnreisen quer über sämtliche Kontinente, Frachtschiffrouten, Segelyacht-Törns, Reisen mit einem PS (also auf dem Pferderücken), Abenteuer mit Heißluftballon und Schlittenhunden. In konkreten Reports geht es um Skiwandern zwischen Dörfern in Lappland, eine Fahrt auf dem Mekong - 4900 km von der Quelle in Tibet bis zur Mündung in Vietnam, mit der U-Bahn um die Welt (geht nur virtuell im Computer), mit dem Fahrrad nach Rom oder einfach zu Fuß durch die Dolomiten.

Die Welt vom Verkehrsweg aus betrachtet, das schafft eine ganz neue Perspektive. Zumal die Fortbewegung auch die Art bestimmt, wie wir die vorbeigleitende Landschaft aufnehmen. Eine stimmungsvolle Reportage muß diese Eindrücke einfangen und wiedergeben können. Schon in der Postkutsche unterhielten sich die Reisenden über das Er-fahrene. „Angenehme Gesellschaft und gutes Wetter sind die vorzüglichsten Bedingungen einer vergnüglichen Reise", so wird ein Bericht von 1810 zitiert (Beyrer 1991: 138). Oft wird das **Verkehrsmittel** zum Selbstzweck. Dann kann man selbst dem allerweltlichen Automobil noch neue Seiten abgewinnen: „Die Reise als Roadmovie" (Unterwegs sein 1995: 7). Zum Stereotyp ist es dann nicht mehr weit. Vielen Ausländern fällt bei den Deutschen vor allem deren Neigung zur Raserei auf den letzten Highways ohne Geschwindigkeitsbegrenzung auf. „The brainchild of Adolf Hitler ... have long been the envy of petrolheads in the Western World." Und zum (angeblichen) deutschen Nationalsport, des

Staus:"...you can be Michael Schumacher in a red Ferrari and drive as fast as your tiny Trabant will take you." So sah es zumindest ein Autor in der *Travel Section* des *Australian* aus Sydney (17. Aug. 1996).

3.5.3 Literatur nachreisen

Wie oft ist schon der Versuch gemacht worden, **auf Goethes Spuren nach und durch Italien** zu reisen? Sehr originell ist das nicht mehr, zumal auch manch ein Reisender im Deutschen-Traumland Italien den Goethe schon im Original mitnimmt. Aber die Eindrücke von früheren Reiseberichten einzubeziehen, das verleiht einer Reportage doch einen Hauch von Klassik und Exklusivität. Bereits im ersten Kapitel dieses Buches haben wir einen Überblick gegeben und viele historische Darstellungen mit konkreten Hinweisen der besuchten Orte versehen. Das soll nicht wiederholt werden, hier geht es um zeitgenössische Autoren und deren Bezug zum Reisethema.

Wer mit dem Mietwagen in den USA unterwegs ist, dem sei angeraten, **Jack Kerouac** zu lesen, dessen 'On the Road' von 1957 Furore machte, erst in Amerika, inzwischen auch bei uns. Wie kein anderer lebte er die Unruhe und Entwurzelung vieler Amerikaner aus und raste wie ein Bessesener kreuz und quer durch die USA, immer auf der Suche nach Abenteuer und Freiheit und Rausch und Gott und dem wahren Geist Amerikas (wie es in einer *ZEIT*-Reportage heißt). Auf seiner Spur die USA neu zu entdecken, das kann nicht danebengehen. Zumal, wenn gerade auch noch eine neue Verfilmung von Kerouacs bekanntestem Opus herausgekommen ist. Kerouac ist heute schon ein Klassiker in den USA, und Bars, Motels und Restaurants entlang seiner Piste - darunter die notorische Route 66 - bekennen sich inzwischen stolz zu ihm. In San Francisco gibt es eine Kerouac Lane. Viele andere literarische Vorlagen eignen sich für ein ähnliches Unterfangen.

Wer kommt schon darauf, daß sich ein berühmter Kriminalroman von **Friedrich Dürrenmatt** als ideale Besuchsanleitung für die Region Bielersee in der Schweiz entpuppt. Von 'Der Richter und sein Henker' heißt es: „So kann man mit dem Roman als Wander- und Reiseführer in der Hand auf Tour gehen." (Schaefer 1996) Offensichtlich ließ Dürrenmatt seine Schurken vor einer Bilderbuchkulisse agieren, die gegenüber vielen anderen Krimis den Vorteil hat, auch real zu existieren. So viele Synergie-Effekte wirken sich auf den Service-Teil aus: Dort wird nicht nur der Verkehrsverbund Biel-Seeland-Bielersee genannt, es gibt auch Verweise auf das zugrundeliegende Buch und dessen Verfilmung.

Ein ähnliches Bild entwirft die Reportage „Die mörderische Eifel". Darin wird eine Einführung in das recht neue Phänomen des Eifel-Krimis gegeben. Begleitet von einer Karte mit Hinweisen auf die Stätten des grausigen Tuns. In der Umgebung von Bitburg heißt es **„Bitte ein Mord"** (so auch ein Krimi-Titel). Wir erfahren, daß hier nicht nur die geruhsame Provinz gebietet, sondern den Urlauber auch eine brisante Mischung übler Gestalten erwartet: "Im Bundeswehrdepot wimmelt es von Spionen; Kölner Loddel mit Spitznamen wie Koks-Frenzi und Dom-Bomber fallen ein, Dorftresen werden zu konspirativen Treffs von Agenten des BND, der CIA und des KGB; in Provinzdiskotheken geben sich Ecstasykuriere die Klinke in die Hand..." (Kieffer 1997). Die meisten Sommerfrischler nutzen die Ferien, um zu lesen. Warum also nicht die Lektüre mit der bereisten Nahwelt korrespondieren lassen? Ist das Wetter gut, werden die Tatorte erkundet, ist es schlecht, wird geschmökert. Bleibt man ganz daheim, hat man zumindest gute Lesetips erhalten.

3.5.4 Die politische Reise

Bei erster Annäherung scheint der Reisejournalismus unpolitisch zu sein. Die harten, oft bedrückenden Fakten aus den anderen Teilen der Welt werden in den Ressorts Politik und Wirtschaft 'verwaltet', die Reise zählt zur Freizeit, von ihr wird geradezu verlangt, daß sie ein ablenkendes, die Phantasie beflügelndes Bild der Welt entwirft. Das 'garstige Lied' der Politik wirkt da völlig deplaziert. Man könnte es so sehen. Dennoch: Welche Berichterstattung ist schon unpolitisch? Weder das Kleinschreiben der ökologischen Zerstörungen durch den Tourismus ist es, noch das Ignorieren des Elends und der Ungerechtigkeiten in vielen Zielländern. Schon in der Auswahl der Reisegebiete werden Präferenzen deutlich. Derzeit wissen die Chefs, daß z.B. Hefte zu den Schönheiten der USA, Kanadas und Australiens Selbstgänger sind. Alles auch politisch stabile Länder

Für den Journalisten stellt sich immer neu die Frage, ob er ausgetretenen Pfaden folgen soll, oder ob er das Experiment suchen will und die Reise politisch kritische, aber genau deshalb auch interessante Gebiete propagieren soll. Hier werden Widersprüche des Konsumenten von Tourismus deutlich. Er will den Massenbetrieb von Mallorca vermeiden, gleichwohl sollen vertraute Ruhe und Berechenbarkeit am Zielort garantiert sein. Vieles von den daheim verlorenen Welten - unverfälschte Ursprünglichkeit und Distanz von westlicher Zivilisation - finden wir zudem gerade in politisch heiklen Gebieten. Wo ist Asien noch ursprünglicher als im von den Militärs unter Verschluß gehaltenen Burma/Myanmar? Wo läßt sich islamischer Alltag besser studieren als im Iran der Ayatollahs?

Der Journalist wird immer dafür verantwortlich sein, was er empfiehlt: Sind **Diktaturen** darunter, Länder in denen Frauen und Kinder gegen Geld verkauft werden, in denen sich kleine Oligarchien am Geld der Touristen bereichern, in denen die Natur vernichtet wird? Der Journalist ist bereits bei der Auswahl des Ziele ein - wie es der Kommunikationswissenschaftler nennen würde - klassischer Gatekeeper, der selektiert und bestimmt, welche Gebiete überhaupt ins Bewußtsein der Reiseinteressierten gerückt werden. Aber seine Aufgabe muß auch sein, eingefahrene Vorurteile auszuräumen, etwa deutlich zu machen, daß der einstige 'Kriegsgegner' des Westens, Vietnam, heute ein wunderschönes Reiseland abgibt.

Jenseits der **theoretischen Unmöglichkeit, unpolitische Reportagen zu schreiben**, tritt ein zweites Moment. Immer wieder entstand in der Geschichte der Berichterstattung über eigene Reisen das Bedürfnis, Sozialkritik einfließen zu lassen. So eine Faszination ging früher z.B. vom politischen Frankreich aus, nachlesbar in den Berichten zur französischen Revolution von Joachim Heinrich Campe (1790) oder Gerhard Anton von Halem (1791). Später sandten Heinrich Heine und Ludwig Börne ihre Korrespondenzen und Briefe aus Paris in die Heimat (Wuthenow 1980). Dabei wurde nicht nur kritisch durchleuchtet, was am Zielort geschah, die Botschaft richtete sich ja an die Daheimgebliebenen und war auf sie gemünzt. Diese Praxis, in der Fremde das Eigene kritisch zu beleuchten, wandte übrigens schon der römische Schreiber Tacitus in seinem Bericht über die Germanen an, deren erster Triumpf über die imperiale Militärmaschine er mit germanischer Sittentreue begründete - römische Dekandenz gegen germanische Unverdorbenheit.

Aus alledem ergibt sich, daß Ausflüge in die Politik nicht nur geboten sind, um das Bild von der Welt abzurunden. Sie geben vielen Reportagen erst Farbe und Aktualität.

Hier einige Beispiele:

- **Machtwechsel in Hongkong:** Es ist Tatsache, daß die touristischen Buchungen in der Kronkolonie vor der Übernahme durch die Volksrepublik China 1997 noch einmal Rekordhöhe erreichten. Wie sehen die Jahre des Übergangs aus? Wie bereitet sich die Stadt auf die neue Situation vor? Was ist von den neuen Machthabern zu erwarten und wie sichtbar werden sie sein? (*DIE ZEIT*: Schon regiert China mit).

- **Militärs in New Mexico, USA**: Eine grandiose Landschaft, kaum besiedelt, aber auch das traditionelle Terrain des US-Militärs mit riesigen Manövergebieten, wo immer noch - geheimnisvoll, gleichwohl für den interessierten Touristen mitunter sichtbar - neue Waffensysteme erprobt werden. Militäranlagen wurden in Museen verwandelt, Überbleibsel der Nuklearrüstung bereiten ökologisches Kopfzerbrechen (*taz*: Ein Road Movie für Pazifisten durch New Mexico).

- **Panzerfahren in der Ukraine**: Ein ehemaliger Hamburger Klempner hat sich mit seiner *ARO X-TREME Travel Agency* selbständig gemacht. Mit offensichtlich finanziell klammen Generälen in Kiew sprach er ab, Panzerfahrten mit Nachtschießen und MiG-Fliegen im Überschall anzubieten. Die 3-Tages-Reise kostet so um DM 10.000. (*FAZ*: Panzer fahren total und Nachtschießen im Urlaub).

- **Wiederaufbau nach dem Hurrikan**: Mitte 1994 fegte mit 200 Miles-Per-Hour ein Hurrikan über die karibische Insel St. Thomas hinweg und hinterließ eine Spur der Zerstörung. Die gutbetuchte Touristen-Klientel buchte kurzerhand auf die unversehrten Nachbarinseln um. Was tun die Verantwortlichen für den Wiederaufbau und die Belebung des Geschäfts? (*USA Today*: Stormy Road Back to St. Thomas).

- **Burma, eine Diktatur als Touristenziel**: Hier gilt es, die Sirenengesänge der Reisebranche mit den Realitäten der Menschenrechtsverletzungen zu konfrontieren. Man wird nachdenken müssen über die wohl einzigartige Ursprünglichkeit dieses asiatischsten aller Länder, dessen touristischer Reiz vielleicht auch der harten Faust der machthabenden Militärs gschuldet ist. (*ZEIT-Magazin*: Nach Burma reist man nicht im Zustand der Unschuld.)

- **Die Südsee als Paradies und letzte Kolonie**: „Nirgends ist der Südpazifik schöner als im französischen Polynesien. Der Sonnenuntergang (...) ist tatsächlich ein unvergeßliches Ereignis". Dennoch: Hier wird auch ein hartes Kolonialregime durch Deutschlands engsten Verbündeten Frankreich aufrechterhalten, finden Großmachtspiele mit der Atombombe statt, werden Kritiker wie Greenpeace vom Geheimdienst weggebombt. (*DIE ZEIT*: Mururoa ... war da nicht was?)

3.5.5 Das Spiel mit Stereotypen

An anderer Stelle haben wir beschrieben, in welchem Umfang Stereotypen den Reisejournalismus durchdringen (Kap. 7). Hier soll einmal nicht vor **Klischees** gewarnt, sondern deren spielerischer Einsatz beschrieben werden. Mitte der 90er Jahre tauchte in den Reiseregalen der Buchhandlungen ein neuer Typ von Schrift auf. Die Serie stammt vom Fischer Taschenbuch Verlag und wirbt mit dem eingängigen Spruch: „Kaum etwas verbindet die Menschen mehr als die Bestätigung insgeheim gepflegter Vorurteile.“ Neben dem Namen der jeweils karikierten Nation prangt deutlich der Stempel 'pauschal' auf dem Titelblatt. Der Band zu 'Die Amerikaner pauschal' beginnt wie folgt: „Amerikaner sind wie Kinder: Laut und vorwitzig, unfähig, ein Geheimnis für sich zu behalten, ohne Gespür für Zwischentöne und mit einem gewissen Hang, sich danebenzubenehmen. Hat man jedoch erst einmal diese grundsätzlich etwas pubertäre Art der Amerikaner akzeptiert, bereitet der Umgang mit ihnen keine weiteren Schwierigkeiten mehr...“ (Faul 1997: 9). Würde dies ein Politiker absondern, so wäre wohl eine Regierungskrise fällig. Aber die Autorin Stephanie Faul ist selbst Amerikanerin, womit sich das Dargestellte als Autostereotyp entlarvt und akzeptabel ist.

Stereotypen können, richtig eingesetzt, aus einer faden und farblosen Beschreibung einen lebendigen, ja sogar schrill überzeichneten Text werden lassen. Das Geheimnis liegt im offenen und unverkrampften Umgang mit ihnen, in der **Übertreibung und Selbstironie**. „Amerika: O´zapft is in Tschortscha“ beginnt im *stern* der Bericht über das ehemalige Holzfällerdorf Alpine Helen in der Nähe von Atlanta/Georgia, dessen Bürgermeister einst aus finanzieller Not auf die bayerische Masche verfallen war. Nun hängen an den mit ausladenden Holzbalkonen geschmückten Berghütten blauweiße Fahnen. Oans-Zwoa-Kapellen mit Namen wie 'Lorelei und Schatzi' oder 'The Sauerkrauts' spielen zum Verzehr von Knackwürsten und Superbrez´n auf. Ganz nebenbei erfährt der Leser, daß die Umgebung dieses Stein gewordenen Stereotyps wunderschön ist (Fiedler 1997). Zum Schmunzeln über diese gelungene Glosse mischt sich die Erkenntnis, daß wir alle verfangen sind. Unsere Südsee-Idylle im Badeparadies nebenan folgt im Prinzip denselben Regeln.

Man kann den Spieß auch herumdrehen. Nichts ist aufschlußreicher, als einen **aufmerksamen Ausländer** zu bitten, über seine **Eindrücke in Deutschland** zu berichten. Der brasilianische Journalist und Schriftsteller Joao Ubaldo Ribeiro zeigte sich - wären Sie darauf gekommen - besonders von den nackten Deutschen an unseren Badestränden fasziniert. Immerhin kommt dieser Gast aus dem Land, das uns die Copacabana und den Tanga gab und oft als erotischste aller Weltecken beschrieben wird. Ribeiro: „Hier gibt es keinen Sex, nur Nackte." Und zu seiner Reaktion: „Ich hätte nie gedacht, daß ich ein so erstaunliches Verblassen der Libido erleben (und daran teilhaben) würde." Wie so oft sagt der pauschaul Urteilende eigentlich mehr über sich und den eigenen Hintergrund als über die Deutschen. Ribeiro aus dem inflationserfahrenen Lateinamerika schaut sich auch sonst interessiert um und erstaunt über deutsche Zahlteller und die Selbstverständlichkeit fester Preise. Ihn verwundert das Stehenbleiben der Menschen bei roten Ampeln und das Auftreten von Radfahrern in Horden. „Wenn es etwas Heiligeres gibt als den Zahlteller, dann ist es der Radweg..." (Ibeiro 1991). Wirklichkeiten sind immer konstruiert, und sie basieren auf subjektiven Vorerfahrungen, das wird hier bestens demonstriert.

Stereotypen selbst zum Gegenstand der Berichterstattung zu machen, das ist sicherlich ein legitimes Stilmittel. Es kann allerdings auch unbeholfen daherkommen. *GEO SAISON* brachte es nicht über sich, eine Irland-Reportage ohne das Konterfei einer rotbehaarten Person zu illustrieren. In der Bildunterschrift wurde dann ganz ernsthaft betont, daß es ein Irrglaube sei, **Iren** generell für das zu halten; was man gerade im Bild zeige, nämlich **Rotschöpfe**. Stereotypen sind nicht dazu da, seriös dementiert zu werden. Sie müssen für sich selbst sprechen und in der Konfrontation mit der Realität ironisch diese erst herstellen können. Sonst ist etwas daneben gegangen.

Abb. auf den folgenden Seiten: Es folgen zwei Beispielreportagen. Die GEO-Reportage wurde uns mehrfach und nicht nur seitens der GEO-Redaktion als besonders gelungen empfohlen. Sie gehört auch in dieses Buch, da in ihr Reiseberichterstattung thematisiert wird. Zudem verweisen wir auf das Interview mit dem Autor Alexander Smoltczyk in Kap. 6.9. Aus technischen Gründen wird hier nur ein Teil der (hervorragenden) ganzseitigen Fotos reproduziert. Die Reportage ist auch vorbildlich, was die Bilddramaturgie anbetrifft, was hier leider nur teilweise erkennbar wird. (GEO EXTRA Fotografie Nr.2/96, S. 30-42)
Die Brigitte-Reportage der Autorin Monika Held wurde uns von der Redaktion empfohlen. Sie zeichnet sich dadurch aus, daß in ihr intensiv persönliche Erfahrung und 'orientalische' Stimmung (auf dem Rücken eines Kamels) transportiert werden. Aus technischen Gründen fehlen die begleitenden, sehr stimmungsvollen Fotos. (Brigitte Nr. 20/96, S. 84-94)

Fotografieren im Regenwald. Das bedeutet: schlechtes Licht, angelaufene Objektive, wenig Schlaf und jede Menge Selbstzweifel. George Steinmetz war für GEO sechs Wochen lang unterwegs in Irian Jaya, dem Westteil Neuguineas. Er litt unter Moskitos, Stammesfehden und Schlamm – und einem Autor, der sich ständig Notizen machte: Wie entstehen eigentlich Bilder für GEO? Hier wird es beschrieben

DER BLUES DES JÄGERS

VON ALEXANDER SMOLTCZYK

Fotoreporter sind nette Menschen. Außer bei der Arbeit. Dann werden sie unausstehlich. Dann ähneln sie heliotropen Pflanzen, deren Gemütszustand vom Lichteinfall geregelt wird: Zwei Lux zuwenig, und die Mundwinkel hängen welk herunter. Yves zum Beispiel. Bevor es über ihn kam und er Fotoreporter wurde, hatte er Medizin studiert. Yves ist von angenehmster Wesensart, jeder würde sich von ihm eine Niere herausnehmen lassen oder auch beide.

Doch als wir drei Wochen lang für GEO durch den Iran reisten, saß da plötzlich ein Mr. Hyde neben mir, der unansprechbar wurde, jähzornig und tyrannisch, sobald er etwas witterte, was er *une double* nannte – eine Doppelseite. Dann war Yves auf Fährte. Bei dem jährlichen Pferderennen eines turkmenischen Reitervolkes am Kaspischen Meer kletterte er gegen alle Warnungen so lange in der Startmaschine herum, bis er den Favoriten zum Fehlstart trieb. Wir mußten die Rennbahn unter Polizeischutz verlassen. Nur einer in dem Getümmel lächelte, still und in sich gekehrt: Yves hatte seine Doppelseite.

Jene Besessenheit, die nette Menschen ergreift, sobald sie graue Khakiwesten mit vielen Taschen überstreifen, erstaunt uns Laien, irritiert wie Stierkampf, Boxen oder schlechte Manieren. Zumal ich nie verstanden habe, weshalb Reportagefotografie so schwierig sein sollte. Schließlich geht es lediglich darum, eine tolle Kamera an jenen Ort zu schaffen, wo die tollen Bilder herumliegen. Wo ist das Problem? Aber dann lernte ich George kennen.

In GEO Nr. 1/1996 wurden 22 Bilder veröffentlicht, die George Steinmetz, ein 38jähriger, in Beverly Hills wohnender Fotograf, aus einem unzugänglichen Teil Neuguineas mitgebracht hatte. Es waren Bilder über das Leben der Korowai, eines Stammes, der in Baumhäusern wohnt und weder Kleidung noch Eisenwerkzeuge kennt. 22 Fotos, das sind insgesamt rund 0,22 Sekunden – eine gute Fünftelsekunde, in der die Blende offenstand und einen Blick auf die

Welt erschnappte. Aber nicht weniger als 22 Monate und jede Menge Besessenheit waren nötig, um an jenen Punkt zu gelangen, wo die Bilder waren. Hier ist die Geschichte hinter den Bildern.

Am 7. Juli 1995 steht George Steinmetz auf der Dschungelpiste der Missionsstation Yaniruma, allein mit sich und einigen tausend Quadratkilometern Regenwald. Ein langer, magerer Kerl mit offenem Gesicht und schütterem Haar unter einem australischen Rangerhut. Das jedenfalls sieht man. Unsichtbar ist die Kette aus Straußenei-Plättchen, die er von den Dinka im Sudan eingetauscht hat und seit 15 Jahren tagtäglich um den Bauch trägt: „Erinnert mich an den Bruch mit der Achtstundentag-Welt, die ich auf jedem Trip hinter mir lasse. Wenn ich einen Anzug trage, ist sie eine Art Talisman, um den Glauben zu behalten, daß es noch eine andere Art von Existenz gibt.“ Die Kette läßt sich nicht ablegen.

Es war auf einer früheren Fotoreise durch Irian Jaya, als Steinmetz beim Pinkeln etwas abseits im Wald plötzlich einen nackten Mann auf sich zurennen sah, schreiend und mit gespanntem Bogen: „Ich hatte den Kopf voll von den üblichen Stories über Steinzeitmenschen und Kannibalismus. Ich glaubte nicht recht dran. Und mit einem Mal war ich mitten drin.“ Er entkam, mietete für fünf Stunden eine Cessna von der Missionars-Flugbereitschaft und entdeckte etwas, was er noch nie gesehen hatte und was ihn seither als Bild verfolgte: Baumhäuser, die 30 Meter über dem Boden auf den Wipfeln balancierten und offenbar von Clans bewohnt waren, die nie Kontakt mit der Außenwelt gehabt hatten.

Er mußte wiederkommen und die Bilder machen. Beim Pentagon beschaffte er sich Fliegerkarten des Terrains, kaufte sich John Barkers „Praktischen Sprachführer Indonesisch“ und lernte ihn auswendig. Das heißt, die Wörter „Taube“, „Butter“ und „Tankstelle“ lernte er nicht. Er würde ohnehin nur einen einzigen Begriff brauchen: *rumah tinggi-tinggi* – sehr hohes Haus. Steinmetz flog für seine Geschichte nach Washington und nach Paris, Amsterdam und Hamburg. Er band sich eine Fliege um und ging in die Büros der Chefredakteure.

Allen erzählte er von seinem Traum: „Eine einmalige Chance. Es wird vielleicht das letzte Mal sein, daß ein unberührtes Leben dokumentiert werden kann. So viele Kulturen sind verschwunden, weil niemand sie zumindest in Fotos dokumentiert hat. Zum ersten- und letztenmal können wir mit unserer heutigen Sensibilität die Erfahrung von Kolumbus machen! Bevor die Goldsucher, Ölprospektoren, Händler oder Soldaten kommen."

Aufbruch in den Urwald mit 293 Kilo Gepäck

Die Redaktionen in Washington wollten die Geschichte nicht. Unentdeckte-Völker-Geschichten sind ein heikles Thema, zumal wenn mit Kannibalismus etwas im Spiel ist, das es eigentlich gar nicht geben darf… – „Sorry, George."

Steinmetz ging in die Bibliotheken und las alles, was es über die Region zu lesen gab, kopierte Aufsätze über rituelle Bräuche und Heilwesen. Er vertelefonierte 1200 Dollar, dann hatte er im niederländischen Groningen Gerrit van Enk und Johannes Veldhuizen aufgetrieben, die einzigen Weißen mit Korowai-Sprachkenntnissen. Sie hatten als Missionare im Korowai-Gebiet gearbeitet, und nachdem er die beiden zur Mitreise hatte gewinnen können, nickte in Hamburg ein Chefredakteur.

22 Monate Vorbereitung. Und jetzt ist das Schlimmste passiert, was einem Traum passieren kann: Er ist erfüllt worden. Jetzt ist George 10 000 Meilen von allen Bildredakteurinnen entfernt, mit 293 Kilo Gepäck auf dem schlammigen Rollfeld von Yaniruma, über ihm ein leerer Himmel ohne Licht. Jetzt liegt es nur noch an ihm, ob die Story etwas wird.

Und am Licht. Und an den Korowai. Und an der Crew. Und an den eigenen Nerven.

Das verlassene Missionshaus dient als Basislager. Auf der Veranda hocken 20 Träger. Die Männer sind zur Sechs-Wochen-Expedition mit je einer Turnhose, einem Hemd und einem Netz aus Borkenfaser erschienen, in dem ein Klumpen Sagopalm-Mehl und etwas Tabak liegen. Nur ihr Chef hat als Insignien noch ein zweites T-Shirt und einen Taschenspiegel dabei.

Die Träger beobachten, was die Weißhäuter in den Wald geschleppt haben: sich selbst aufblasende Luftmatratzen samt Flickzeug, Seilrollen, Kerosinlampen, eine indonesische Bibel und einen Weltempfänger; einen rotweißen Regenschirm, wie ihn Golfer verwenden („Ich reise in den Tropen nie ohne ihn", sagt George, „weil man im Regen oft zu guten Bildern kommt") und eine Armbrust, um Kletterseile in die Baumwipfel zu schießen.

Da sind vier Kameragehäuse, zwei Dutzend Angelhaken als Gastgeschenke, Instant-Nudelsuppen, Milchpulver und Cornedbeef-Dosen, ein Vogelbestimmungsbuch für Neuguinea, eine Buschapotheke samt Augenklappe und Skalpell, 300 Filme, zwei Säcke Reis, Öl, Beutel mit Salz, Macheten, Erdnußbutter, Marmelade und Kaffeepulver, Regenplane und Klopapier. Diverse Fläschchen mit Zitronell-Öl gegen die Mücken und einige Meter elastischer Intubationsschlauch, wie er in Krankenhäusern verwendet wird – auf Dschungeltrips das ideale Allzweck-Allwetter-Festbindemittel. Eine Klemmschraube, mit der die Kamera an Bäumen zu befestigen ist: „So kann ich Fotos aus der Baumperspektive machen, ohne daß die Eingeborenen auf den Fotografen starren."

Und weil es die nächsten Wochen nichts geben wird außer Schlamm und Wald und krabbelnder, stechender, saugender Biomasse, keine Ärzte und Notrufsäulen, liegt in einer Tonne ein Kurzwellensender, um notfalls mit der „Freeport Indonesia"-Bergbaugesellschaft Kontakt aufnehmen zu können – Steinmetz ist studierter Geologe und hatte sich mit dem Chefprospektor von Freeport angefreundet.

Zwischen Äxten und ausgeklügeltem Positionscomputer, zwischen diesem in wasserdichte Traglasten verpackten Substrat von Zivilisation sehen die Träger, wie ein athletischer Jüngling mit einer Art Grubenlampe an der Stirn und einem Batteriekasten am Hinterkopf von Tonne zu Tonne irrlichtert. Das ist Neeld Messler. Ein Outdoor-Maniak, der einen Großteil seines Lebens in Zelten und Höhlen verbracht hat und sich ausschließlich von Kraftriegeln, Haferflocken und Vitaminpillen ernährt.

»Bisher hattest du immer Glück. Diesmal schaffst du es nicht«

Messler ist Verpackungskünstler und hat eine paramilitärische Leidenschaft für Logistik. Zu seinen Spezialitäten gehört es, in unzugänglichen Regionen Plattformen in Baumwipfeln zu installieren. Deswegen hat Steinmetz ihn mitgebracht in das Missionshaus von Yaniruma. „Anybody's got the tape handy?" fragt Neeld jetzt in einem Akzent,

Der Kletterpfahl zu den Baumhäusern ist nicht für weiße, dazu noch mit Kameras behängte Menschen ausgelegt. Ein Fehltritt ist gefährlich: Die aus Rattan und Ästen zusammengebundenen Wipfelhütten der Korowai schweben in 20, 30 Meter Höhe über dem Boden. Damit sie geschützt sind vor Getier, Geistern und anderen Angreifern

der den Trägern aus „Dallas“ bekannt vorkommen würde, wenn sie die texanische Serie kennten beziehungsweise wüßten, was Fernsehen ist, beziehungsweise überhaupt jemals von der Existenz eines Kontinents namens Amerika gehört hätten.

Des weiteren sind zu sehen: zwei Missionare, denen der Jet-lag an der Laune zerrt, sowie als besonderer Ballast ein Schreiber, dem jede Form von Camping stets zuwider war. Etwas anderes entzieht sich dem Blick der Träger. Das schwerste Gepäckstück liegt nicht auf dem Boden des Missionshauses.

Es steckt, ganz klein zusammengefaltet, irgendwo unter dem Zwerchfell des Fotoreporters. Die Angst, diese Eiseskälte im Magen bei dem Gedanken: Du schaffst es nicht. Diesmal nicht. Bisher hattest du immer Glück, aber diesmal merken sie, daß es immer nur Glück war. Dieser Anruf nach Hamburg: „Hi, it's George. I'm pissed. Got no story. Sorry.“ Das ist der Blues der Jäger, und keiner, der ihn nicht hätte. „Okay“, sagt George. „Los jetzt. Let's go!“

Stopp.

Die Missionare möchten einige Tage in dem Dorf bleiben, das sie einst gegründet haben: „Man kann auch hier schöne Fotos machen ...“ – „Wie bitte? Hier sind keine Bilder. Die Typen haben dreckige T-Shirts an und sitzen herum wie in einer Busstation in Idaho. Wir müssen in den Wald.“ Keine Zeit verlieren, bloß nicht. Zumal jeder Tag tausend Dollar kostet. Und die späteren Etappen werden noch mehr Wartezeit mit sich bringen. Los, endlich los jetzt! Der Jäger hat die Witterung aufgenommen.

Auf dem Marsch zu den Bildern gibt es alle nur denkbaren Plagen und nur einen Trost: Es gibt sie nicht alle auf einmal. Mal sind es Moskitos, mal ist es ein Hornissennest und dann eine einstündige Schlammpassage durch einen Dornensumpf. Bis zur Hüfte im Trüben, hält Steinmetz es für angebracht, von einer Reportage im Kongo zu berichten: „Ich wurde von einer Fliege gestochen. Nach sechs Monaten, als ich meine Freundin zur Arbeit brachte, blickte ich in den Rückspiegel, schaute näher hin und sah, wie sich etwas in meiner Pupille schlängelte. Ein Loa-Loa-Wurm.“ Die Ärzte hätten das Tier mit irgendwelchen Pillen aus seinem Auge vertreiben können.

Bei einem der ersten Stopps erkundigt Steinmetz sich nach einem Gegenstand seines Traums. Da war doch, an der Biegung des Flusses, jenes unglaublich hohe Baumhaus: „Gerrit, frage die Träger, ob dieses sehr hohe Baumhaus bei Mangghé noch steht.“

„Sie sagen ja. Sie kennen es ...“

„Great! Gehen wir!“

„... sie sagen, sie kennen es, weil dorthin immer die Touristen geführt werden.“

Der kalte Knoten im Magen zurrt sich ein wenig enger. Touristen? So ist es. Was beim letzten Besuch noch das Jenseits der bekannten Welt war, kann inzwischen bei einem bayerischen Abenteuer-Reisebüro gebucht werden? Und daß George vielleicht, ohne es zu wissen, der Pfadfinder dafür war, macht es nicht besser: „Ich habe zwei Jahre lang darauf gewartet, zurückzukommen. Und jetzt höre ich, daß man die Korowai mit Kreditkarte bezahlen kann?“ Ringsum knarren die Baumfrösche. Was machen wir hier eigentlich noch?

Es gibt zwei Spezies unter Reportern: Autoren und Fotografen. Die einen sind meist Sammler, die anderen immer Jäger. Der Schreiber kann sich das Flanieren leisten, ihm bleibt auch im Scheitern der Trost, noch das Scheitern beschreiben zu können. Der Fotograf muß sein Bild jetzt machen, weil es sonst niemals gemacht wird. Er muß alles andere hintanstellen. Jeder Gedanke, jede Geste ist auf die Beute ausgerichtet, und die Gegenwart ist nur Hindernis auf dem Weg zum Bild. George hat angefangen zu rauchen, um leichter Zugang zu seinen Sujets zu finden. Der Fotoreporter muß sich tarnen, seinem Gegenstand anpassen bis zum Verschwinden, sich gemein machen bis zur Selbstaufgabe. Denn es gilt nur ein Gesetz: „Magazine drucken Fotos, keine Ausreden" – das war die Maxime von Georges erstem Boss bei „National Geographic".

„Los jetzt. Tiefer in den Wald hinein. Let's go!"

Der Fotoreporter Steinmetz läuft durch diesen Dschungel wie eine Laus im Broccoli. Ohne die Träger würde er sich nach drei Schritten verirren. Er spricht die Sprache jener Menschen nicht, die hier irgendwo leben und von denen er nur weiß, daß sie bisher jeden Kontakt mit der Außenwelt vermieden haben. Sie sind unsichtbar, aber er soll sie fotografieren. Und das wird er auch.

George hat sich seine Strecke schon zurechtgelegt, er braucht nur die Augen zu schließen, um die Bilder zu sehen.

Ein Motiv wie ein Traum. Und dann ein Schwitzfleck im Objektiv

Da ist der Aufmacher: ein spektakulär hohes Baumhaus, auf Wipfelhöhe fotografiert. Auf der nächsten Seite: nackte Menschen mit Steinbeilen, ein Familienleben in der Steinzeit, mit diesem weichen Streulicht, das jeden Muskel hervorhebt, als wäre er mit Öl eingerieben; dann ein Sago-Maden-Fest, vielleicht ein Begräbnis, auf alle Fälle eine Jagdszene, mit Pfeilen und Bögen, am besten eine Pirsch auf Paradiesvögel, wenn möglich Spuren von Kannibalismus: Köpfe an einen Baum gebunden, mit dem 50er oder 85er, daß der Hintergrund tonig unscharf wird… George hat die Doppelseiten irgendwo in seinem Hinterhauptslappen eingebrannt, und er wird so lange durch diesen Schlamm laufen, bis etwas da draußen vor der Netzhaut mit dem Bild in Übereinstimmung gebracht wird. Alles weitere ist Reflex: Scharfstellen. Schießen.

Nach einer Woche hat Steinmetz nur fünf Filme belichtet. Er hat sich um Packlasten und um die Auswahl der Einbäume gekümmert, hat mit den Trägern um jeden Dollar gefeilscht, und als sie nach Zigarettenpapier fragten, hat er es ihnen verboten: „Ich will nicht überall Kippen herumliegen haben. Das Foto eines unberührten Stammes, wo Kippen herumliegen? Sorry, sie sollen Pflanzenblätter nehmen." Der Jäger überläßt nichts dem Wird-schon-werden, jedes noch so lächerlich erscheinende Detail muß kontrolliert werden, weil ein gutes Bild an einem Detail scheitern kann.

Aber es gibt kein Bild. Jedenfalls kein gutes. Manchmal ist ein T-Shirt im Weg, manchmal „ein Gesicht nicht gut". Und George hält sich an die Philosophie des Jägers: Nur schießen, wenn etwas wirklich gut ist.

Mit jedem Schritt zieht der Wald sich enger zusammen. Ein Bote wird ausgesandt, um Kontakte zu suchen. Ein Tag Warten, zwei Tage. Der Bote kommt nicht wieder. „Vielleicht war es der falsche Mann", sagt Gerrit van Enk und setzt an zu einem Vortrag über die Dominanz mutterseitiger Verwandtschaftssysteme bei den Korowai. „Vielleicht hatte er schlechte familiäre Beziehungen? Ich werde selber gehen."

Steinmetz bleibt gefaßt und übt mit Neeld Messler Klettertechnik. Warten. Steinmetz lernt Indonesisch und studiert in dem Bestimmungsbuch das Balzverhalten des Laubenvogels: „Man muß das natürliche Umfeld genau kennen, um die Leute zu verstehen, die in ihm leben." Warten. Für tausend Dollar am Tag. Nach zwei Tagen kommt Pastor van Enk zurück: „Es war der falsche Mann. Sein Bruder wird von den Wallohatum der Hexerei beschuldigt. Er hat sich nicht getraut, es uns zu sagen und ist lieber verschwunden."

„Great guy. Und nun?"

„Hier sind wir unerwünscht. Sie drohen uns anzugreifen, falls wir weitergehen. Wir müssen es woanders probieren."

George versucht, gefaßt zu sein. Der Anruf in Hamburg.

„Let's go."

Und dann, nach sehr viel Warten und tabakrauchender Diplomatie öffnet sich der Regenwald plötzlich wie ein Portfolio. Wie eine Doppel-, wie eine Ausklapp-Panoramaseite, und George sieht den World Press Award. Zehn Korowai-Männer balancieren nackt wie antike Olympioniken auf einem Gerüst und binden ein Biwak zusammen. Die Raumaufteilung ist gemäß den Regeln des goldenen Schnitts, der Hintergrund gleichmäßig, die Körper wie aus der Parfümreklame, kein T-Shirt weit und breit!, das Licht warm und gestreut, die Kamera bereit, geladen, jetzt nur noch visieren, scharfstellen und ...

„Fuck."

Ein Schwitzfleck im Objektiv. Einige Milligramm Wasser, die, noch kalt von der Nacht, nun plötzlich außerhalb der Kameratasche Tropen spielen müssen. Es ist zum Verzweifeln ... – „Neeld? Kannst du diesen Baum da kletterfertig machen?"

Vom Intubationsschlauch bis zur Blitzanlage liegt alles in Steinmetz' Rüstkammer bereit. Jeder Fotograf trägt mit den Jahren sein eigenes Expeditions-Arsenal zusammen. Eine Menge Aufwand für jene Hundertstelsekunde, die letztlich zählt

Weiter probieren, keine Pause. Eine 250stel Sekunde genügt, um *das* Bild zu machen. Aber wann kommt sie? Es ist wie bei dem Messias der Kabbala: In jedem Moment kann er erscheinen. Also muß der Fotograf jede Sekunde bereit sein. Kein Nachlassen, keine Schwäche.

Abends um zehn, wenn jeder froh ist, die nassen Stiefel, die schlammdurchtränkten Thermosocken los zu sein, wenn Reis-mit-Cornedbeef-und-Ameisen den Bauch füllt und jeder nur noch für ein paar Stunden Schlaf vergessen möchte, daß der nächste Morgen genauso trostlos sein wird wie der letzte – dann schnarrt diese „Hier spricht ihr Käpt'n"-Stimme durchs Biwak: „Gerrit, ich weiß es, du hast es schon getan: Aber könntest du noch einmal fragen, ob Fenélun nicht einen Cousin hat ..."

Auf Reportage gibt es nur das Jetzt. Keine Vergangenheit. Jeder Teil des eigenen Lebens, der nicht zu dem Job gehört, ist weggepackt, die Wohnungstür abgeschlossen, in der Gewißheit, die nächsten sechs Wochen bist du in einer anderen Welt. Sechs Wochen ohne Telefon, Mahnungen und die Schlange im Supermarkt. Sechs Wochen im Mittelpunkt stehen. Manch einer wird süchtig nach dieser Freiheit.

Der Vollmond steht über dem Baumhaus. Der Schreiber sitzt teetrinkend im Biwak und diskutiert mit Veldhuizen über den Gedanken der Mission bei Calvin. Der Fotograf Steinmetz hängt von Moskitos umsurrt an einem Brotfruchtbaum, die Kameratasche zieht mit 20 Kilo am Gürtel, der Klettergurt reißt am Gesäß, irgendein Nachtzeug flattert am Mund. Das Baumhaus wird durchs Lagerfeuer schwach von innen beleuchtet.

Wunderbar! Eine Doppelseite! Aber die Kamera sieht das anders: 20 Sekunden Belichtungszeit. An einem Baum pendelnd schlicht unmöglich. Man könnte die Korowai bitten, mehr Holz aufzulegen, aber dann würde die ganze Hütte abbrennen. Also: „Neeld! Könntest du den Blitz ins Baumhaus bringen ...?" Später im Heft sieht es aus wie echt.

Ist das Lüge? Verrät es die Realität? „Es gibt keine Realität", sagt Steinmetz. „Es gibt nur Heisenbergs Theorem: Wenn wir etwas sehen, hat es sich durch unser Sehen schon verändert. Ich bin hier, um zu zeigen, wie diese Leute lebten, bevor wir auftauchten ... Also muß der Fotograf irgendwie eingreifen. Wozu ist er sonst da?"

Es ist eine Geschichte über Baumhaus-Bewohner. Also muß es ein Bild geben, auf dem zu sehen ist, mit welcher Behendigkeit ein Korowai sich auf Bäumen bewegt, zugleich muß auch die schwindelerregende Höhe sichtbar gemacht werden. Ohne Manipulation geht das nicht: „Vom Boden aus sieht es nach gar nichts aus. Das Foto muß in den Wipfeln gemacht werden. Aber diese Jungs klettern blitzschnell auf Bäume, wo unsereins sich zwei Stunden emporseilen muß. Spontan ist das Bild nicht zu machen." Ganz abgesehen davon, daß die Korowai gar nicht daran denken, auf Bäume zu steigen, solange fünf Weißhäuter mit drolligen Dingen für Unterhaltung sorgen. Es widerstrebt George, eine Situation auszulösen. Aber hier muß er es tun. Und er tut es.

Doch wie umgehen mit dem T-Shirt-Dilemma? Bei jeder Reise ins Wahre-Schöne-Gute vorindustrieller Länder gibt es einen Begleiter, der nicht in der Honorarliste erscheint. Das ist „Dirty-T-Shirt-Man". Jeder Fotoreporter kennt ihn. Er ist immer da. Wenn endlich ein Initiationsritus in authentischen Kostümen gefunden ist, wenn die Leute den Fotografen vergessen haben – dann steht Dirty-T-Shirt-Man irgendwo im Sucherfeld herum.

Wenn im Vordergrund die Tänzer stampfen und die Farben sprühen – dann lehnt da ein Typ im schmutzigen T-Shirt am Langhaus und starrt in die Kamera. Er ist ein Merkposten, ein Vergißmeinnicht der Zivilisation. Auch im Korowai-Wald gibt es den Dirty-T-Shirt-Man: „Ich kann ihn nicht bitten, das Hemd auszuziehen. Das ist gegen jede Ethik. Also muß ich warten, bis alle T-Shirts außerhalb des Bildes sind."

Nichts ist einfach, alles ist zähes Ringen. 200 Meter entfernt vom Biwak ste-

»Der vierte von rechts bin ich.« Steinmetz mit Yali-Männern vor dem Missionshaus in Walley. Wegen der Eiweißarmut ihrer Kost bleiben die Yali klein

hen in diesem Moment, vom Dickicht verborgen, drei Doppelseiten im Wald: spektakulär hohe und bewohnte Baumhäuser und kein T-Shirt weit und breit.

Steinmetz weiß nichts von ihnen. Die Träger schon, und sie wissen auch, daß dort Clans leben, die beim Anblick eines weißen Geistes sofort schießen würden. So sagen die Träger dem Jäger nichts. Sie wissen, daß er dann losziehen wird und daß er schon zu lange Matsch getreten hat, um noch auf ihre Warnungen zu hören.

Und zu Hause, über dem Leuchttisch sind plötzlich die Bilder da

Als George später davon erfährt, möchte er alle Träger wegen Illoyalität entlassen. Für die Missionare dagegen ist deren Verhalten völlig rational: „Sie können sich nicht leisten, ihre Stammesbrüder zu verraten. Wir verlassen den Wald in einigen Wochen. Sie müssen hier weiterleben."

Okay, okay. Doch in sein Tagebuch schreibt Steinmetz an diesem Abend: „Der Trip war zuerst schwierig. Dann wurde er schlimm. Jetzt scheint er zum Desaster zu werden. Ich war Diplomat und Psychologe und habe Polaroids verteilt wie Konfetti. Aber meine ganze Zähigkeit scheitert an der Furcht der Korowai vor der Außenwelt. Es war naiv zu glauben, wir könnten hier einfach durchlaufen. Ich beiße mir die Zähne aus. Vielleicht bin ich in meinem Wunsch, das Leben der Korowai zu dokumentieren, genauso selbstgerecht wie die Missionare mit ihrer Religion. Eine unverhoffte Verwandtschaft... Aber eines ist klar: Keiner von uns macht hier irgendwelche Konvertiten."

Und weil der kalte Knoten unterm Magen sich regt und weil die Wunde am Handgelenk eitert und der Schweiß juckt und die Moskitos beißen, packt er das für Prachtschüsse und Katastrophen reservierte Notschlückchen aus.

„Fuck."

Es gibt keinen Fotografen, der nach einem Auftrag glücklich ins Flugzeug steigt. Die meisten lassen sich von der Stewardess zwei Whiskey-Fläschchen geben und erklären, daß das ihr letzter Job gewesen sei, daß die Zeiten für Fotojournalismus vorbei und Bildredakteurinnen sowieso keine Ahnung hätten. Und zwei Wochen später rufen sie an, nette, entspannte Menschen, krähend vor Zufriedenheit: „Laß uns ein Buch aus dem Material machen!"

Aber vorher ist der Blues da, und er packt jeden Fotoreporter mindestens einmal auf jedem Trip. Meistens ist es abends, etwa in einem schäbigen Devisenhotel in Magnitogorsk, wenn das Licht verschwunden ist und die Ahnung dämmert, daß das Leben nicht aus Doppelseiten besteht. Da war Hans, ein anderer Jäger, einer der besten deutschen Fotoreporter, der seine Fotos quasi mit dem Körper machte, unter vollem Einsatz seiner Person. Aber eines Tages, irgendwo im malaysischen Regenwald, schaute er durch den Sucher und merkte, daß er nichts sah. Daß das Feld viel zu begrenzt war für das Licht, die Geräusche, die Erinnerungen, die plötzlich in ihm waren. Er packte die Kamera ein und hat seither kein einziges Foto mehr gemacht.

George kennt den Blues der Jäger. Aber wie er nie ohne Kompaß in der Kameratasche losziehen würde, so hat er auch eine Antwort für den Sinnotstand dabei, einfach und effizient: „Diese Welt verschwindet. Ich bin hier, um etwas von ihr festzuhalten. Und ich muß es so gut tun, wie ich kann."

Let's go. George macht weiter, am nächsten Morgen und am übernächsten auch. Und vielleicht weil zwei Missionare dabei sind oder weil es Gerechtigkeit gibt oder weil Besessenheit dem Scheitern schlicht keine Chance läßt – auf alle Fälle sind plötzlich die Bilder da.

Nach fast zwei Jahren Vorbereitung, nach sechs Wochen Strapazen hat Steinmetz 7704 Bilder belichtet und durch alle Kontrollen und Röntgen-Checks sicher nach Hause gebracht. Doch erst über dem Leuchttisch, zu Hause in Beverly Hills, sieht er endlich jene Bilder, von denen er geträumt hat.

22 von ihnen sind erschienen. Und wenn sie sich aus der allgemeinen Bilderflut womöglich herausheben, wenn ihre Verfallszeit weniger kurz ist, sie sich auf die Netzhaut des Betrachters ein wenig einbrennen – dann ist hiermit beschrieben, weshalb. □

GEO-Autor **Alexander Smoltczyk**, 37, hatte mit **George Steinmetz**, 38, schon in Französisch-Guyana zusammengearbeitet. Doch erst im Regenwald der Korowai lernte er die Zähigkeit seines Kollegen an der Kamera richtig kennen – und schätzen.

VOM HIMMEL IN

REISE-REPORTAGE

In ein paar Stunden nach MAROKKO fliegen und dann im Tempo der Kamele durch die Sahara ziehen. Nicht an gestern denken, nicht an morgen. Mit dem Herzen sehen lernen, die Sonne fragen. Eine Trekking-Tour durch den Süden des Landes

DIE WÜSTE

d

EIN BERICHT VON MONIKA HELD (OBEN)
MIT FOTOS VON KNUT MÜLLER

Du hast die Welt gewechselt in weniger als einem Tag. Du bist vom Himmel mitten in die Wüste gefallen. Der größte Teil von dir ist noch zu Hause, und das merkt man auch. Du kommst aus der Welt der tausend Wichtigkeiten und wirkst wie jemand, der gleichzeitig überreizt und ausgehungert ist. Du plapperst wie ein Wasserfall, wer du bist und was du kannst, und wirkst gleichzeitig wie ein Hund, der eine neue Fährte wittert. Du steckst deine Nase in jede Blüte. Du breitest die Arme aus, als wolltest du so die Fläche vergrößern, auf der du den Wind spüren kannst. Du zerkrümelst Blätter und Kräuter und steckst sie dir in die Nase, um dich aufzufüllen mit ihrem Duft. Noch ahnst du nicht, in welchem Ausmaß die Wüste ein Gehirn auf den Kopf stellen kann – mit nichts als Himmel und Sand, Steinen und Wind.

Wann immer du aufwachst, Basaid ist schon wach. Halt die Augen geschlossen, du kannst ihn hören. Sein Kleid raschelt, seine Hände brechen dünnes Holz für das erste kleine Feuer am Morgen. Er stopft in die bauchige Kanne grünen Tee und frische Minze und bricht vom Zuckerhut einen kräftigen Brocken ab, das macht den Tee so süß wie Sirup. Den ersten Tee kocht Basaid immer in dem unwirklichen Licht zwischen Nacht und Tag. Während hinter seinem Rücken ein blasser Mond verschwindet, schiebt sich vor ihm eine große rote Sonne über die Erde. Wenn Basaid merkt, daß du wach bist, dann schenkt er ein nach altem Brauch. Mit viel Abstand zwischen Kanne und Glas. Auf dem Tee muß Schaum sein, wenn er ihn serviert. Er bringt dir dein Glas auf einem Messingtablett an den Schlafsack. Es ist noch früh – so zwischen fünf und sechs. Bonjour, sagt Basaid. Der Tag fängt gut an.

Vier Stunden gehen wir am Tag, fünf Stunden, manchmal sechs. Oben die Sonne und unter den Stiefeln die Steine. Schwarze Brocken bis zum Horizont. Neun Millionen Quadratkilometer. Bahr bela ma – Meer ohne Wasser. Die Sahara ist die größte Wüste der Welt. Aber nur zehn Prozent sind Bilderbuchwüste, gelber Sand, haushoch und weich wie ein Kissen. Träum nicht in die Landschaft beim Gehen, sonst wirst du stolpern. Schau auf deine Schuhe und die Steine vor dir, die sind kantig und spitz.

Wer durch die Wüste geht, geht nicht spazieren, der bewegt sich im Tempo der Kamele, legt fünf Kilometer pro Stunde zurück oder mehr. Wozu? Das fragst du dich, wenn du erschöpft bist und

Manchmal siehst du Menschen in der unendlichen Einsamkeit und bist verblüfft: Woher kommen die?

MAROKKO

keuchst und neidisch wirst auf jede Heuschrecke, die bewegungslos im Schatten döst. Für dich sind diese Schatten viel zu klein. Steine werfen solche Schatten und die Blätter kleiner Blumen. Wie lange noch, fragst du den Reiseleiter. Wo rasten wir? Wo werden wir das Nachtlager aufschlagen? Der grinst und zeigt dir den Horizont. Und wenn er es gut mit dir meint, dann sagt er: Zwei Stündchen, vielleicht drei, und verspricht dir eine lange Rast. Noch weißt du nicht, daß Ausruhen und Nichtstun gekonnt sein will, wenn über dir die Mittagssonne steht. Du lernst die erste Lektion: Bind die Uhr ab, frag nicht nach dem, was vor dir liegt, setz geduldig einen Fuß vor den anderen, finde den eigenen Rhythmus. Mach es wie die Kamele: Geh und geh und geh und geh. Und sauf nicht so gierig deinen Wasservorrat leer, teil ihn dir ein. Wasser ist das Kostbarste, was du hast.

W

Wer geht mit wem durch die Wüste? Lektion zwei: Das ist keine Frage der Sympathie. Die Starken, die Trainierten, die Schnellen – die sind die Spitze der Karawane, immer. Die anderen keuchen hinterher, mit großem Abstand. Erst am Abend, wenn es darum geht, wer sich neben wem in den Schlafsack rollt, sortiert sich die Gruppe um. In der Nacht geht es nicht um Kraft, sondern um Zuneigung. Da liegen die Körper nebeneinander, die sich mögen.

Lektion drei: Die Bilder im Kopf, die du mitgebracht hast von zu Hause, die von der Arbeit und der Stadt und den Menschen, die bleicht die Sonne aus. Und die heimischen Gedanken bläst der Wind davon. Der Kopf wird leer, und du machst dir ernsthaft Sorgen. Wirst du vielleicht blöd in der Wüste? So schnell geht das? Aber hatte der leidenschaftliche Wüstengeher Otl Aicher nicht behauptet, die Wüste sei eine Denklandschaft? Und beim Gehen beginne der Kopf so munter zu werden wie die Beine? Und wer durch die Wüste gehe, lasse das Denken von der Kette los? Bist du schon so weit, nur weil du dich fragst, warum eine kleine Blume in der Wüste so leuchten kann, als wäre Licht in ihr? Haben sich deine Sinne schon erholt von der heimischen Lärmverschmutzung? Vielleicht. Du hörst deinen Schritten zu, dem Wind und dem leisen Rascheln einer flüchtenden Echse. Die Augen lernen sehen. Sie saugen sich an Winzigkeiten fest. An einem Käfer, einer Ameise. An der gelben Blume, die neben deinem Stiefel wächst.

Die Menschen bei dir zu Hause, sagte der kleine Prinz, züchten fünftausend Rosen in ein und demselben Garten...und doch finden sie dort nicht, was sie suchen.
Sie finden es nicht, antwortete ich.
Und dabei kann man das, was sie suchen, in einer einzigen Rose oder in einem bißchen Wasser finden.
Ganz gewiß, antwortete ich.
Und der kleine Prinz fügte hinzu:
Aber die Augen sind blind. Man muß mit dem Herzen suchen.
(Antoine de Saint-Exupéry: Der kleine Prinz)

Kamele stöhnen, wenn sie sich hinlegen sollen. Sie schreien, wenn sie aufstehen müssen, und wenn sie beladen werden mit den großen Taschen voller Gepäck und Wasserkanistern und Proviant, dann seufzen sie. Erst wenn die Karawane aufbricht – dann ist Frieden. Kamele, so scheint es, fühlen sich erst richtig wohl, wenn sie gehen dürfen, auch wenn sie dich noch hinter ihrem Höcker auf dem Rücken tragen.

Stundenlang siehst du von deinem Kamel nichts als den braunen, lockigen Hinterkopf, der sich bewegt wie ein Ball auf den Wellen. Zwei flauschige Ohren und sehr lange Wimpern. Und von dem Kamel, das vor dir geht, siehst du den Schwanz, die langen, strammen Schenkel, die Füße mit den dicken Hornschwielen.

Rechtes Vorderbein, rechtes Hinterbein, linkes Vorderbein, linkes Hinterbein. Weich gehen sie, wie auf Puschen. Kamele sind Paßgänger, das teilt sich der Wirbelsäule mit bei jedem Schritt. Seegang im Steinmeer. Auf langen Reisen verlieren Kamele bis zu einem Drittel ihres Körpergewichts – dafür können sie innerhalb einer Viertelstunde zweihundert Liter Wasser saufen. Ein Mensch von sechzig Kilo würde am Ende einer solchen Reise nur noch zwanzig wiegen. Der Kamelkot, der vor dir auf die Erde fällt, ist hart und klein wie der von Hasen. Kamele haben Zellen, die dem Kot die Feuchtigkeit entziehen, um sie im Körper zu speichern. Du kannst ihn einsammeln, er brennt so gut wie ein Brikett. Du trägst ein Tuch auf dem Kopf gegen die Sonne und ziehst dir die langen Enden vor den Mund gegen Wind und Sand. ▶

Das hast du den Beduinen abgeguckt. Und vielleicht haben die ihre Weisheit von den Kamelen. Die haben in der Nase einen Muskel, der sich bei Sandsturm schließt. Die Beduinen tragen Djellabas, weite Kleider, unter denen sich die Hitze nicht stauen kann. Ein Kamel, das Durst hat, produziert bei großer Hitze künstlich Fieber. Seine Körpertemperatur steigt auf 42 Grad an. So schwitzt es nicht mehr und verliert auch kein Wasser.

Deine Phantasie kreist um die Menschen, die die Kamele an langen Stricken führen. Wie die durch die Wüste gehen! Anders als du in deinen klobigen Stiefeln. Ihre nackten Füße stecken in Sandalen. Nie würde dir zu dieser Art, sich fortzubewegen, das Wort „wandern" einfallen. Die schlurfen, die huschen federleicht über den steinigen Boden. Aus zwei Meter Höhe schaust du auf sie herunter, siehst sie von hinten. Den geraden Rücken, die Hornhaut unter den Hacken. Und wenn sie sich, um den Rücken zu entlasten, einen Stock über die Schultern halten, siehst du ihre Hände. Vorgestern die kleinen, praktischen von Abdellah. Gestern die von Ramdan, die so zart aussehen, als würde er mit ihnen nur in Büchern blättern. Und heute die von Basaid, dem Afrikaner, der so guten Tee kocht, so wenig spricht und so sanft lächeln kann. Beide Hände sind verkrüppelt. Von ihm erfährst du nichts – es sind die anderen, die dir ganz sparsam seine Geschichte erzählen. Sie sagen, er sei als Sklave geboren. Habe mit zehn Jahren die Familie, für die er arbeiten mußte, bestohlen. Sie sagen, dafür hätten sie ihm die Hand, die sich verging, abhacken dürfen. Sie sagen, es sei eine vergleichsweise milde, wenn auch makabre Strafe gewesen, daß sie seine Hände „nur" ins Feuer gehalten hätten. Immer, wenn er vor dir geht, wenn du auf ihn schaust, auf diese Hände, dann tun dir oben auf deinem Kamel die eigenen Hände weh.

Manchmal siehst du Menschen in der Wüste und bist verblüfft: Woher kommen die? Die sind so plötzlich da, als seien sie aus dem Boden gewachsen. Du schaust dich um. Der Rücken des Kamels ist wie ein Aussichtsturm. Irgendwo zwischen den schwarzen Steinen siehst du Ziegen, vier in die Erde gerammte Stöcke, eine Plane – das mobile Zuhause einer Nomadenfamilie. Basaid zeigt auf einen dunklen Punkt in der Wüste. Bäume. Akazien. Schattenspender. Die Sonne steht senkrecht über der Karawane. Dort werden wir rasten.

Steine wegräumen, die alten Teppiche ausbreiten, die Sättel der Kamele sind ein guter Windschutz. Du fällst auf das Lager wie ein Sack, schläfst, döst, ißt und trinkst. Heißen, süßen Tee und frischen Salat und wieder Tee. Du fragst: Wie lange bleiben wir hier? Drei Stunden, vielleicht vier, sagt der Reiseleiter, legt seinen Kopf in den Schatten und schläft. Vier Stunden – so lange? Die Pausen bremsen den Alltag aus, den du noch immer in dir hast.

Einer sagt: Das ist ein Gefühl wie früher. Wenn deine Eltern Besuche machten, und dir war's so entsetzlich langweilig. Dös weiter. Oder steh auf, setz dich unter die nächste Akazie, vielleicht ist es dort anders. Oder hilf beim Salatschneiden. Keine Lust. Längst hat dich die Sonne schlapp und faul gemacht – aber das Stückchen Hektik in dir, das du mitgebracht hast von zu Hause, das treibt dich um. Du und deine zivilisierten Kumpane – ihr wirkt in der Wüste wie eine kleine Bande, die etwas anstellen möchte. Aber was nur, hier ist ja nichts? Ihr wartet, daß etwas passiert. Ihr lauert auf ein Ereignis, ihr lungert herum. Du lernst eine neue Lektion über Ruhe und Geduld. Hier bestimmt nicht der Mensch das Tempo. Wann geht es weiter? Quengle nicht und frag vor allem nicht deinen Reiseleiter, der schläft noch immer. Frag die Sonne, wann sie dich aufbrechen läßt. Frag den Wind, frag die Kamele. Frag die Wüste.

Und wenn du wissen möchtest, ob die Wüste so bleiben darf, wie sie ist, dann frag Abdellah. Du siehst vier lehmgelbe Mauern, die eine große Akazie einschließen. Ein wunderbarer Rastplatz in der Nähe einer Oase, Grabstätte eines heiligen Mannes, eines Marabu. Dich erinnert die Anlage an ein Fort, und dein auf Tourismus geschultes Auge sieht hier schon voller Furcht die Grundmauern für ein Hotel und dicke, weiße Waden in bunten Shorts, ein bißchen Abenteuer mit viel Komfort. Kann das passieren? Abdellah schüttelt so energisch den Kopf, daß du beruhigt bist. Die Wüste ist kein Niemandsland, sagt er, die Wüste gehört vielen

Wann immer du aufwachst, Basaid ist schon wach. Den ersten Tee kocht er im Licht der vergehenden Nacht

MAROKKO

Oben die Sonne, unten Steine und Sand bis zum Horizont. Neun Millionen Quadratkilometer Meer ohne Wasser

MAROKKO

Klans. Und ein vereinzeltes, geschäftstüchtiges Familienmitglied würde den Zorn aller auf sich ziehen mit einer solchen Idee. Du erzählst ihm, was du gelesen hast in den glänzenden Werbeprospekten des marokkanischen Fremdenverkehrsamtes. Wie man ein Land zum Produkt machen will auf dem europäischen Markt durch ausgefuchste Medienstrategien. Fernseh- und Anzeigenkampagnen in großen Zeitschriften, der Fachpresse. Das funktioniert in den Städten, sagt er. Massentourismus in der Wüste – das ist ein Widerspruch in sich.

Und das, was wir tun, ist das nicht auch absurd für ihn als Nomaden? Uns begleiten auf einer Tour durch die Wüste ohne den Sinn und Zweck, den es jahrhundertelang für seine Familie hatte? Wir verkaufen keine Kamele, wir treiben keinen Handel, wir bessern nicht einmal versandete Brunnen aus – wir gehen um des Gehens willen. Nein, sagt er, das sei in Ordnung, schön sogar, auch für ihn. So lerne er seine Wüste von einer ganz neuen Seite kennen.

Bis du merkst, daß deine Augen nicht mehr den Horizont absuchen nach dem großen Ereignis, ist die Reise fast zu Ende. Noch eine Lektion: Das große Ereignis ist immer neben dir. Warum haben die Akazien hier keine Blätter? Weil sie schlau sind. Je kleiner die Blattoberfläche, desto geringer die Verdunstung. Als du die große Sanddüne hochstürmst, außer Rand und Band geraten von so viel Schönheit, und dir die Hitze den Atem nimmt, siehst du den kleinen schwarzen Käfer neben dir. Sechs flinke Beine. Lern vom Käfer. Nimm deine Hände dazu, dann hast du vier Beine und kannst krabbeln wie er. Wieso verdurstet der nicht? Weil er schlau ist. Der krabbelt in der Nacht auf den Grat einer Düne. Dort macht er Kopfstand und fängt den feuchten Nebel auf, den der Wind vom Meer mitbringt. Das Wasser kondensiert auf seinem harten Panzer, rinnt ihm über den Kopf in den Mund. In einer Nebelnacht nimmt der kleine Schwarzkäfer vierzig Prozent seines eigenen Körpergewichts an Wasser auf. Stell dir vor, du wachst auf und bist am Morgen um die Hälfte schwerer als am Abend.

Hast du schon einmal in der Wüste geschlafen? Mach das, die Erfahrung kann dir keiner mehr nehmen. Du schläfst wie ein Tier. Flach und leicht, immer bereit zu reagieren. Du hörst den Atem deines Nachbarn, du hörst den Wind. Du machst die Augen auf und siehst eine Sternschnuppe vom Himmel fallen.

In der Wüste kannst du mondsüchtig werden. In deiner Häuserschachtel zu Hause siehst du ihn nur, wenn er dir ins Fenster scheint. Hier ist er über dir die ganze Nacht. Es ist wie ein Spiel. Du machst die Augen auf, und er steht über deinen Knien. Du schläfst, wachst auf, und er scheint dir auf den Bauch. Dann mitten ins Gesicht. Beim nächsten Mal mußt du den Kopf schon in den Nacken legen, um ihn zu sehen. Und wenn du aufwachst, mußt du dich nach ihm umdrehen. Dann ist er blaß geworden und gibt dich an die Sonne ab.

Bevor die Reise zu Ende geht, fängst du an, gierig die Bilder in dich hinein zu schaufeln, die du mitnehmen möchtest. Beim letzten Ritt auf dem Kamel schneidest du dir ganz bescheiden ein Stück Wüste aus der Landschaft und pflanzt es dir ein. Sie ist groß genug, die Wüste, das fällt niemandem auf.

Die Wüste ist eine Denklandschaft, sagt Otl Aicher. Der Weg zur Macht, sagt ein arabisches Sprichwort, führt durch die Paläste. Der Weg zum Reichtum durch die Basare. Der Weg zur Weisheit aber führt durch die Wüste. Du auf deinem Kamel sagst dir: Damit hat es diesmal nicht geklappt. Verzage nicht. Geh zurück in deine eitle, hektische Welt. Übe dort. In dem Stück Wüste, das du dir mitgebracht hast.

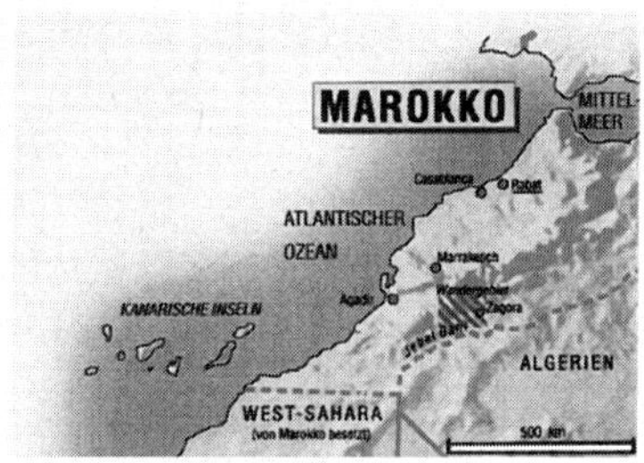

Karte: Harald Blanck

TOUREN IN DIE WÜSTE

Pauschale: Die beschriebene 15-Tage-Reise bietet Trekking Tours M. Hoffmann an (Wolferskamp 27, 22559 Hamburg, Tel. 040/ 81 18 63, Fax 81 24 70). Termine: von Oktober bis April. Preis: ca. 3000 DM, inklusive Flug ab Frankfurt. Die Teilnehmer sollten etwas sportlich sein, da sie vier bis sechs Stunden am Tag auf ihrem Kamel reiten oder, wenn sie Lust haben, wandern. Geschlafen wird unterm Sternenhimmel im Freien. Wer im Zelt übernachten möchte, muß sein eigenes mitbringen. Die Verpflegung ist einfach, aber gut: Morgens backen die Beduinen in der Glut des Lagerfeuers Fladenbrot, mittags gibt es Salat und Obst, abends Couscous, Lammeintopf oder Gemüse mit Reis.

Klima: tagsüber 18 bis 32 Grad. Die Passatwinde machen die Mittagshitze erträglich. Nachts wird es sehr kalt, in manchen Winternächten werden Minustemperaturen gemessen.

Ausrüstung: Das wichtigste sind gute Wanderschuhe. Sie sollten eingelaufen sein und immer mit dicken Socken getragen werden. Gegen die Sonne schützen ein Hut und ein langer Schal, den man sich um den Kopf bindet (am besten in Marokko kaufen). Außerdem unentbehrlich: Sonnenmilch mit hohem Lichschutzfaktor, eine gute Sonnenbrille, weite Hosen und weite, langärmelige T-Shirts aus Baumwolle.

Literatur: Zur Einstimmung „Sandmeere" von Isabelle Eberhardt (Rowohlt, zwei Bände je 14,80 DM), „Himmel über der Wüste" von Paul Bowles (Goldmann-Verlag, 15 DM) und die Bücher von Antoine de Saint-Exupéry „Der kleine Prinz" (8,80 DM), „Wind, Sand und Sterne" (14,80 DM) und „Die Stadt in der Wüste" (48,80 DM), alle im Rauch-Verlag erschienen.

Reiseführer: Vor allem Individualreisende spricht der Band „Marokko" aus der Reihe Reise Know-How an (44,80 DM); aktuell und hervorragend bebildert: der Nelles-Guide „Marokko" (26,80 DM).

3.6 Der Bericht

Nikolas Fentrop

Der Bericht findet in der Literatur viele Beschreibungen: „Zwillingsbruder der Nachricht, aber größer geraten und auch schon ein wenig reifer" (LaRoche 1992: 131), „kausal ordnende Mitteilung" (Traub 1992: 16), oder sehr plastisch, „das Gerippe Nachricht mit Fleisch" (Marquart 1992: 15). Dort, wo die Nachricht wegen ihrer Kürze an ihre inhaltlichen Grenzen stößt, kann der Bericht anknüpfen. In einem Bericht hat der Journalist Raum, mehrere Einzelereignisse miteinander in Verbindung zu bringen. Er informiert zum Beispiel über unterschiedliche Reiseziele, Ausflüge, Unterkünfte, Extraservice und Preise. Alternativ kann der Journalist auch mehr Informationen zu einem Ereignis zusammentragen, als es in einer Nachricht möglich ist. Der 'einfache' Bericht, oft nur wenig länger als eine Nachricht, ist wie diese eine **informative Darstellungsform**.

Der Bericht hat vor allem die Funktion, komplexe **Hintergrundinformationen** zu geben und Ursachen aufzuzeigen. Wenn die Zielsetzung des Journalisten über die rein faktische Darstellung hinausgeht, sollte er versuchen, dem Publikum Synthese, Analyse und Interpretation anzubieten. Die Einbeziehung von subjektiven, interpretierenden Komponenten führt zur Erweiterung des 'einfachen' Berichts. Dieser Typus Bericht, der über die reine Aufzählung von extern gewonnenen Sachinformationen hinausgeht, wird deshalb gemeinsam mit der Reportage als 'interpretierend' bezeichnet.

3.6.1 Die Auswahl der Informationen

Das Material für einen Bericht läßt sich typischerweise nicht am Ort des Geschehens finden, denn die Informationen beruhen nicht wie bei der Reportage auf dem Erleben des Journalisten. Sachverhalte, die in einem Bericht dargestellt werden, müssen überprüfbar sein (Haller 1995: 93) und **Allgemeingültigkeit** besitzen. So ist die gründliche Recherche der beste Garant für einen Bericht. Besonders viele kurze Berichte werden von **Agenturen** geliefert und in der Redaktion passend zum Stil des Mediums bearbeitet. Das ist kein Problem, solange die Agenturen journalistisch seriös arbeiten und sich um **Objektivität** bemühen. Im Gegensatz dazu sind in der Praxis des Reiseressorts besonders in Tageszeitungen die Mehrzahl der Nachrichten und kurzen Berichte **Public Relations** von Veranstaltern und Fremdenverkehrsämtern. Sie werden von den Journalisten häufig ungeprüft und unkritisch übernommen.

Grundsätzlich ist es ein Kennzeichen des Berichts, daß der Journalist vorrangig in Dokumenten recherchieren muß. Das unterscheidet den Bericht von der Reportage. Dabei besteht besonders im Reisejournalismus die Gefahr, die vorbereiteten Informationspakete der Veranstalter als ungeprüfte Vorlagen für den Artikel einzusetzen und sich die aufwendige Recherche zu ersparen. Wer dies tut, wird schnell als 'Schönschreiber' für Veranstalter auffallen. Viele Leser, Hörer und Zuschauer erwarten etwas Nützliches, das über einseitige Informationen der Hochglanzprospekte der Reisebranche hinausgeht. Journalisten sollen das touristische Angebot transparent machen, sie sollen die Vorschläge der Reiseindustrie mit Sachverstand kritisch beurteilen (Ganser 1995: 32/33).

3.6.2 Der Aufbau

Der Aufbau eines Berichts beginnt mit dem Lead. Der **kurze Sachbericht** wird in den folgenden Absätzen weitere Einzelheiten nennen und diese nach abnehmender Wichtigkeit ordnen. Damit unterscheidet sich der Aufbau eines kurzen Sachberichts kaum von dem einer längeren Nachricht - der Übergang ist fließend. Die oft tagesaktuellen Berichte, deren Material in der Regel von Agenturen geliefert wird, werden häufiger im Reiseteil der Tages- und Wochenzeitungen veröffentlicht, als in Reisemagazinen oder in gehefteten Reisebeilagen der Wochenzeitungen.

Dagegen ist der **längere Sachbericht**, der meist über die Darlegung der Fakten hinausgeht, im Aufbau variabler. Die Absätze nach dem Lead können das Geschehen zum Beispiel in chronologischer Reihenfolge wiedergeben, oder das 'Für und Wider' kann absatzweise wechselnd dargestellt sein. Am Schluß steht ein Ausblick auf die Zukunft, es wird eine kurze Interpretation der Inhalte gegeben, und ein praktischer Reisetip schließt sich an. In Reisemagazinen dominieren die Berichte, deren Nachrichtenwert im Publikumsinteresse liegt. Der Aufbau solcher Berichte ist besonders vielfältig.

Das **Feature** oder der **'angefietscherte' Bericht** garniert die sachliche Information mit anschaulichen, bildhaften Beschreibungen und handelnden Menschen. Der Lead in einem angefietscherten Bericht kann beispielsweise aus einem Zitat bestehen. Es sollte charakterisierend für den Inhalt sein. Hier der Einstieg eines Berichts über den Bau und den Betrieb des kanadischen Eisenbahnnetz: „Da wir die Landschaft nicht in die Städte bringen können, müssen wir die Städter in die Wildnis bringen", sinnierte William von Thorne vor mehr als hundert Jahren ..." (*GLOBO* Sonderheft Kanada 1996: 56). Ein Bericht kann auch mit einer Frage oder einem ungewöhnlichen, rätselhaften Zusammenhang beginnen. Der Leser soll so gespannt sein, daß er nicht mehr 'abschalten' kann: „Sie sprechen eine Fremdsprache? Würden Sie sich an die Paßkontrolle eines deutschen Flughafens stellen, um Ankommenden mit Verständigungsschwierigkeiten bei der Bewältigung etwaiger Probleme zu helfen?" (*GEO SAISON*, März 1996: 12). Die Frage wird gestellt, weil genau diese Hilfe in Daytona Beach am Flughafen geboten wird.

Auch das Negative, das Schlechte dieser Welt kann ein zumindest aufsehenerregender Einstieg in einen Reiseartikel sein. Hier über Paris: „Atombombentests, Terroristenbomben und die alles lahmlegenden Generalstreiks - es sieht so aus, als könne all das unsere ewige Liebesbeziehung zu Paris nicht schwächen" (King 1996: 1).

Am **Ende** vieler Berichte im Reiseteil stehen eine oder mehrere Kontaktadressen, unter denen Veranstalter oder Fremdenverkehrsämter erreicht werden können. Hier kann auch weiterführende Literatur zu dem behandelten Thema empfohlen werden. Einen Teil der Informationen, die der Journalist zusammengestellt hat, wird er jedoch außerhalb seines Berichts im sogenannten Serviceteil, auf der Infoseite oder in der Infobox unterbringen.

3.6.3 Die Auswahl der Themen

Der Bericht über Reiseziele kann die **allgemeinen Aspekte** eines Landes oder Ortes zum Inhalt haben. Zum Beispiel Informationen über den Osten Kanadas oder Wissenswertes über 'sanften Tourismus' auf Fidschi.

Statt für ein unspezifisches Reisepublikum ausschließlich allgemeine Aspekte zu erwähnen, kann der Bericht die Reiseziele auch aus einem **speziellen Blickwinkel** heraus betrachten. Als Themen bieten sich an: Gourmetreise, Geschäftsreise, Bildungsreise, Campingreise, Gesundheitsreise, Abenteuerreise oder die Reise mit Kindern.

Andererseits kann ein Bericht über ein Reiseziel auch nur **einzelne Facetten** vorstellen und sich zum Beispiel Museen in Venedig oder Lebensart auf Zypern widmen. Oder aber über das Streichelverbot für Koalas in Australien berichten, das eingeführt wurde, weil die Beutler dadurch zu sehr gestreßt werden.

Eine ideale Form für Berichte im Reisejournalismus sind **Zusammenfassungen**. Der Bericht gibt einen zusammenfassenden Überblick über unterschiedlicher Reiseziele, Reisewege, Reisearten mit einem gemeinsamen Aspekt. Journalisten können bei dieser Art des Berichts ihre Fähigkeit zur Synthese und Analyse beweisen. Sie stellen Vergleiche an, arbeiten Unterschiede heraus und ziehen ein Resümee. Zu möglichen Themen zählen Naturschutzgebiete, Campingurlaub in Europa, Urlaubsziele mit Kindern, Urlaub auf dem Bauernhof in Schleswig-Holstein, Eisenbahnfahrten in historischen Zügen, Schiffsfahrten auf der Elbe oder Pauschalreisen in Afrika.

Als **Reiseratgeber** kann der Bericht auf ein besonders breites Themenspektrum zurückgreifen: Gesundheit auf Reisen, Versicherungen und Sicherheit, Einkaufen auf Flugplätzen, Auto mieten in den USA, Sitten und Gebräuche des Gastlandes, die Geschäftsreise nach Fernost, Sparen auf Reisen, Reisen mit Kindern oder Reisen mit Behinderten. So berichtet „Auf du und du mit der Natur“ über das ökologisch korrekte Campen und die Aktivitäten in Parks, über die zweckmäßige Ausrüstung, außerdem wie die Gesundheit zu erhalten ist und was das ganze kostet (Stein, 1996).

3.7 Die Nachricht

Nikolas Fentrop

3.7.1 Die Aufgaben der Nachricht

Die Nachricht ist eine faire und verständliche Information über Tatsachen, die für das Publikum neu und entweder wichtig oder interessant ist (Schneider/Raue 1996: 54).

Der Begriff 'fair' bedeutet, daß eine Nachricht den Leser, Zuschauer oder den Hörer möglichst wirklichkeitsnah unterrichten soll - bei Auseinandersetzungen unter Berücksichtigung der unterschiedlichen Standpunkte der Kontrahenten.

Heute ist es eine allgemeine Übereinkunft unter den Journalisten, daß eine Nachricht zu den **informativen** und **referierenden** Darstellungsformen zählt. Sie ist **tatsachenbetont**. Interpretationen und Werturteile sollen demnach nicht Teil einer Nachricht sein. In der Praxis werden Interpretationen angeboten, wenn der Inhalt einer Nachricht allein keinen Sinn ergeben würde. Solange die Interpretation klar als solche kenntlich ist, ist dagegen nichts einzuwenden. Michael Haller reiht die Nachricht zur Abgrenzung von anderen Darstellungsformen zwischen objektiv und subjektiv ein. Für ihn ist die Nachricht die objektivierte Form des Tatsachenberichts. Sie wird verwendet, wenn ausschließlich unstrittige Ereignisinformationen weitergegeben werden sollen (Haller 1995: 90-93).

Auch wenn in der Nachricht keine interpretierende oder wertende Bemerkung zu finden ist, stellt bereits ihre Auswahl und ihre Plazierung eine Wertung dar. Gerade auf den Reiseseiten ist das von besonderer Bedeutung: Veranstalter von häufig und ausführlich präsentierten Reisezielen werden ihre Leistungen besser verkaufen können.

3.7.2 Der Nachrichtenwert: aktuell - wichtig - interessant

„Die Nachricht von heute ist prima, die von morgen wäre besser", hat mancher Redakteur schon scherzhaft gesagt. Bei den Tageszeitungen steht die Tagesaktualität im Vordergrund. Die Wochenzeitungen und Monatsmagazine müssen ihre **Aktualität** meist anders definieren. Im Ressort Reise geht es nur selten um die tagesaktuelle Meldung. Die 'schwebende Aktualität' tritt an die Stelle der Tagesaktualität und betrifft z.B. Themen, die 'in' sind.

Eine weitere 'Alternative' zur tagesaktuellen Berichterstattung sind am Schreibtisch erdachte Themen. Ihnen wird beispielsweise mit dem Einleitungsatz „Immer mehr Deutsche ..." eine 'Schein-Aktualität' verliehen (Schneider/Raue 1996: 57-58). „Baden in klaren Gewässern. Wandern durch malerische, unzerstörte Natur. Wohnen in umweltfreundlich orientierten Hotels. Das wünschen sich immer mehr Deutsche für die Ferienzeit ..." (in der *Funk Uhr* 1996).

Wichtig ist alles, wonach sich das Publikum richten muß oder richten könnte. Im Ressort Reise gehören dazu Nachrichten über Sperrungen von Alpenpässen, Einreisebestimmungen in Urlaubsländer, die Rationierung von Benzingutscheinen und die Androhung von Bombenattentaten in Ferienzielen.

Wichtig sind außerdem Hintergrundinformationen, die es dem Publikum erlauben, sich und ihr Handeln oder das Handeln anderer in einen Zusammenhang zu stellen.

Ob eine Meldung interessant ist, hängt vom Geschmack des Publikums ab. Der ewige Ostsee Urlauber in Damp 2000 wird sich brennend für die erste private UV-Meßstation direkt am Strand interessieren. Dem Tramper in Südamerika ist das egal, und erst recht demjenigen, der den Urlaub in seinem eigenen Rosengarten daheim verbringt.

Die Nachrichtenforschung hat sich seit den fünfziger Jahren sehr detailliert damit beschäftigt, **nach welchen Kriterien Journalisten Nachrichten**

auswählen. Das Informationsangebot ist auch für den Journalisten fast unüberschaubar groß. Es ist für jeden Redakteur eine vorrangige Aufgabe zu entscheiden, welche Meldungen er dem Publikum präsentiert. Praktiker werden einwenden, daß sie im Gefühl haben, welche Nachricht es verdient, publiziert zu werden. Es ist fraglich, ob dieses Gefühl immer richtig ist. In der Regel sollte es sachlich überprüft werden. Bedenklich ist, daß die Kriterien und deren Gewichtung für den sogenannten Nachrichtenwert oft davon abhängen, welche persönlichen Erfahrungen und Erwartungen die Journalisten haben, was die Kollegen und Vorgesetzten für einen hohen Nachrichtenwert halten, welche organisatorischen und technischen Zwänge in einer Redaktion herrschen, wie die redaktionelle (verlegerische) 'Linie' aussieht und was die Agenturen anbieten.

Der Kommunikationswissenschaftler Siegfried Weischenberg hat eine Liste mit Merkmalen erstellt - den Nachrichtenfaktoren -, die in ihrer Summe den **Nachrichtenwert** ergeben (Weischenberg 1988: 17ff). Er hat die unterschiedlichen Nachrichtenfaktoren zwei Kategorien zugeordnet: Erstens der **Bedeutung** der Nachricht und zweitens dem **Publikumsinteresse** an der Nachricht.

Die Bedeutung einer Nachricht kann entweder das Ausmaß oder die Konsequenz eines Ereignisses sein. „Hundert tote Muslime bei einem Hotelbrand in Indien" - dieses Ereignis hat ein großes Ausmaß. Die Auswirkung ist für uns gering. Demgegenüber ist die Kürzung des Urlaubsgeldes für uns von großer Konsequenz.

Der Nachrichtenwert unterschiedlicher Meldungen muß in der Redaktion gegeneinander abgewogen werden. Die für den Außenstehenden makaber scheinende Frage „Nehmen wir nun die 100 Toten oder die Urlaubsgeldkürzung?" ist journalistischer Alltag. Im Ressort Reise ist das Publikumsinteresse häufiger als die oben genannte Bedeutung der Grund, weshalb Journalisten ihre Nachrichten, Berichte, Reportagen und Glossen schreiben.

Das Publikumsinteresse kann von weiteren Nachrichtenfaktoren abhängen:

- **psychologische Nähe**: „Kreuzfahrt für Behinderte. Eine achttägige Vier-Flüsse-Kreuzfahrt veranstaltet der Verein Deutsches Behindertenschiff vom ..." (*Süddeutsche Zeitung* v. 9. 7. 1996: 34). Hier werden alle Behinderten und deren Angehörige angesprochen.

- **Prominenz**: „Pilgern zu Luther. Das Bayerische Pilgerbüro veranstaltet vom 3. bis 9. August eine Studienreise auf den Spuren Martin Luthers:

Die berühmte Wartburg, auf der Luther das Neue Testament übersetzte, und weitere Stätten des Wirkens des Reformators (...) gehören zur Reiseroute." (*Süddeutsche Zeitung* v. 9. 7. 1996: 34). Allein die Berühmtheit Martin Luthers reicht aus, um diese Nachricht unter vielen Reiseangeboten auszuwählen.

- **Aufgeschlossenheit des Publikums**: „Ruhe Bitte! Wie stark der Straßenverkehr die Entwicklung eines Urlaubsortes beeinflußt, zeigt eine Untersuchung des Innsbrucker Tourismusinstituts. Danach erreichen Orte, die den Verkehr aus ihren Zentren verbannen (wie Zermatt, Saas-Fee, Serfaus, Ischgl), deutlich höhere Gästezahlen. Die Hälfte aller Gäste besteht auf ruhiger Unterkunft ..." (*Hamburger Abendblatt* v. 3./4. 8. 1996: 105). Diese Nachricht trifft auf ein Publikum, daß für die Themen Lärmbelästigung und Umweltschutz im allgemeinen sensibilisiert ist.

- **Human-Interest-Element:** Hier stehen menschliche Aspekte im Vordergrund. Die typischen Komponenten des Human-Interest-Elements sind Kuriosität, Konflikt, Liebe und Romantik, Sex, Humor, Wissenschaft und Fortschritt, Spannung und das Ungewisse, Abenteuer und Risiko, Tragödie, Sympathie, Alter und Tiere (Weischenberg 1988: 21ff).

3.7.3 Inhalt einer Nachricht

Die Nachricht bildet ein enges Korsett. Der Journalist wird gezwungen, das Wichtigste herauszufiltern, zu ordnen, es kurz und präzise, verständlich und interessant auszudrücken. Das 'richtige' Verfassen einer Nachricht kann jeder lernen. „Die Nachricht ist das Darstellungsmittel aktueller Berichterstattung, das am wenigsten mit Kunst und am meisten mit Handwerk zu tun hat" (Weischenberg 1988: 11). Die einfache Regel für den vollständigen **Inhalt** einer Nachricht lautet: Möglichst viele '**W-Fragen**' beantworten! (Wer?, Was?, Wann?, Wo?, Wie?, Warum?)

Der Versuch, möglichst viele Information in einer Nachricht mitzuteilen, findet seine Grenze in der Kürze einer Nachricht. Die ersten vier W-Fragen sind meist einfach zu beantworten; die Fragen 'Wie' und 'Warum' dagegen erfordern höheren Aufwand. Dieser Aufwand ist nötig, denn gerade wenn Nachrichten nicht beantworten, wie oder warum etwas geschehen ist, verlieren sie beim täglichen Bombardement mit Informationen leicht ihre Relevanz.

Zwei weitere Aspekte, die Antwort auf 'wer meldet', also auf die Frage nach der Quelle der Information und auf die Frage 'wem nützt die Information' werden zunehmend wichtig.

Besonders in der Reiseberichterstattung wollen Leser oder Hörer Rückschlüsse auf die **Intention und Verläßlichkeit einer Meldung** ziehen können. Es ist ein großer Unterschied, ob die Information „traumhafte Strände" aus einer Pressemitteilung des Fremdenverkehrsamts oder von einem Journalisten vor Ort stammt.

Die Nachrichtenagentur *dpa* sieht den Sinn einer Nachricht darin, „daß man sich nach ihr richten kann" und fordert: „Sie muß die Informationen liefern, die wir brauchen, ehe wir uns entscheiden." (Weischenberg 1988: 50) Aus diesem Grund kann je nach 'Redaktionssitte' der sonst streng sachliche Inhalt einer Nachricht um eine Interpretation ergänzt werden. Dies ist angebracht, wenn dem Leser die Wiedergabe von Einzelinformationen kein verständliches Bild ergeben würde.

3.7.4 Aufbau einer Nachricht

Das Wichtigste zuerst! Die wichtigsten Informationen einer Nachricht tauchen im Vorspann, dem sogenannten **Lead** auf. Er kann aus einem oder mehreren Sätzen bestehen. Wenn der Lead besonders spannend ist, hat er eine weitere Funktion erfüllt: Er hat Anreize zum Weiterlesen geboten. In den anschließenden Sätzen der Nachricht folgen weitere Einzelheiten, wie erläuternde Informationen, die nach **abnehmender Wichtigkeit** geordnet sind.

Damit hängt die Reihenfolge der Antworten auf die W-Fragen vom Nachrichtenwert der Meldung ab. Liegt er in der Kuriosität eines Ereignisses - „Ein Golfplatz erstreckt sich über eine vielbefahrene Straße" - dann wird das 'Was' zunächst beantwortet. Ist die Frage nach dem 'Wer' am wichtigsten - „Berühmter Golfspieler lädt zum Golfwochenende"- wird sein Name ganz am Anfang genannt. Wenn ein Hotel in der Nebensaison mit Sonderangeboten lockt, werden das 'Was' (Geld sparen) und das 'Wo' zuerst erwähnt. Der Lead soll möglichst viele, aber nur wichtige W-Fragen beantworten. Trotzdem soll er leicht lesbar sein und verständlich bleiben.

Längere Nachrichten können im ersten Satz oder Absatz eine Zusammenfassung der wichtigsten Inhalte geben. Die W-Fragen werden in den darauf folgenden Sätzen noch einmal, jetzt aber detaillierter beantwortet.

3.7.5 Der Stil

Eine Nachricht soll **verständlich** sein. Die Verständlichkeit hängt vom Aufbau und vor allem vom Stil, von der Sprache des Autors ab. Nachrichtenschreiben verlangt **Direktheit, Kürze, Prägnanz, Einfachheit und Klarheit der Sprache**. Die Nachricht soll aus schlichten, geläufigen, unmißverständlichen Wörtern in unverschachtelten, durchsichtigen Sätzen bestehen (Schneider/Raue 1996: 69). Wer sich in einer Nachricht mit 'schönen' Worten schmückt, wird seinen Leser und seine Leserin schwer erreichen. Elitäre Fachsprache muß ebenfalls verschwinden, Floskeln sind zu vermeiden: Aus 'Niederschlägen' wird 'Regen' oder 'Schnee' und aus 'Vakzinen' 'Impfstoffe'. Aus dem Modewort 'Befindlichkeit' wird vielleicht 'Laune'. Aus den Verschleierungswörtern 'viele' oder 'breite Masse' sollte besser eine konkrete Zahl werden.

Mancher meint, Schachtelsätze zeugten von Intelligenz. Dem Leser tut ein Journalist damit keinen Gefallen! Schachtelsätze hemmen den Lesefluß erheblich und sollten immer in **kürzere Sätze** zerlegt werden. Dabei gehört in den Hauptsatz die Hauptsache, in den Nebensatz die Nebensache. Prägnante Hauptsätze sind die kraftvollste Form der Mitteilung. In einem Satz sollte nicht mehr als ein Thema behandelt werden. Wer abwechselnd kurze Hauptsätze und Haupt-Nebensatz-Kombinationen wählt, gestaltet seinen Text außerdem interessanter.

Wenn Satzanfang und Satzende zu weit auseinander stehen, muß sich der Leser zuviel merken. Das gleiche gilt für alle zusammengesetzten Verben, für Subjekt und Prädikat und für Substantive mit dem dazugehörigen Artikel (Schneider/Raue, 1996: 181).

Neben der **einfachen und klaren Satzkonstruktion** macht eine **anschauliche Sprache** eine Nachricht interessant. Konkret geht vor Abstrakt! Statt allgemeine Begriffe wie 'schöne Aussicht' zu verwenden, sollten Journalisten z.B. von den 'weiten grünen Tälern', den 'schroffen, verwitterten Felswänden' und den 'kreisenden Adlern' berichten.

Der Journalist ist Nachrichtenübermittler, daher muß er die Aussagen anderer **zitieren**. Dabei kann sowohl direkte Rede als auch indirekte Rede verwendet werden. Die direkte Rede in 'Gänsefüßchen' eignet sich für Aussagen, die besonders hervorgehoben werden sollen. Sie sollte allerdings spärlich verwendet werden, denn sonst nutzt sich ihre Wirkung ab.

3.8 Die Glosse

Verena Wolff

Wenn man die Reisezeitschriften aufschlägt, findet man eine Menge witzig geschriebener Artikel, die ballastfrei daherkommen und dem Leser gerne ein Lächeln abgewinnen, aber wirkliche Glossen oder bissiges Schreibwerk ist selten darunter. Das mag daran liegen, daß die Glosse eine der schwersten Aufgaben für einen Journalisten darstellt, aber auch daran, einen Grat zu finden, wo der witzig geschriebene Artikel aufhört und die satirische und manchmal auch zynische Glosse anfängt.

Traut man einer der zahlreichen Definitionen einer Glosse, so soll sie „Argumente auf die Spitze [treiben], ironisch übertreiben, entlarven, verspotten, witzig sein und endet in einer Schlußpointe", außerdem ist sie „gefühlsbetont und subjektiv“. Die Glosse „spielt mit den Mitteln der Sprache, verwendet originelle Formulierungen, die Umgangssprache [und] den Dialekt“ (Mast 1994: 190/191).

Dabei böte es sich gerade im Reisejournalismus an, über die verschiedensten **Themen** Glossen zu verfassen, denn es gibt viel kritisch zu beleuchten: den **gemeinen Urlauber**, **das Reiseziel** (natürlich immer mit dem nötigen Respekt) und den **Reisejournalisten** an sich. Der Mangel an Glossen scheint aber auch ein Resultat der fehlenden Unabhängigkeit der Reisejournalisten zu sein, denn wer als ‘Freier’ seinen Sponsor auf die Schippe nimmt, wird diesen Sponsor nicht mehr lange haben. Außerdem kommt es auf die Auffassung der Publikation von sich selbst an, ob sie sich als praktisches Medium sieht, das die Reisen schon mal für die Urlauber ‘vorreist’, oder ob man sich als Wohnzimmermedium auffaßt, quasi vom Ohrensessel aus in fremde Länder führt.

Bei ersterem hat der Journalist mehr Möglichkeiten, die Reise glossierend zu beschreiben, denn er kann den Urlauber, bestimmte Sitten oder auch sich selbst mit einer reichlichen Portion Ironie oder Zynismus betrachten und beschreiben.

Es ist auch nicht immer einfach, ein Thema so aufzubereiten, daß es für den Durchschnittsleser so überspitzt ist, daß es witzig zu lesen ist und nicht nur für eine kleine Insidergruppe. Ferner hat auch die witzigste Glosse ein Ziel, nämlich einen Mißstand oder eine Situation aufzudecken und zu kommentieren. Wichtig ist, daß beim Leser das kleine Schmunzeln erreicht wird und nicht das große Schenkelklopfen, er aber gleichzeitig über das aufgegriffene Problem nachdenkt.

Der Schreiber darf sich alles erlauben, er darf alles kritisieren, solange er nicht dem Leser, also auch dem potentiellen Touristen, zu nahe tritt. Es ist immer besser, über ein allgemeines aber stark begrenztes Thema zu schreiben als über ein zu spezielles; so wird ein breiteres Publikum erreicht (Zobel 1992: 255-287).

Wenn also das Thema 'Beschweren-nach-dem-Urlaub-und-so-wieder-das-Geld-eintreiben' behandelt wird, ist das interessant für einen großen Teil der Leserschaft, denn jeder hat sich im Urlaub schon einmal über Baulärm oder ähnliches geärgert. Würde sich die Glosse mit schwimmendem Altholz vor der Küste Corralejos auf Fuerteventura beschäftigen, wäre sie für weitaus weniger Menschen interessant, denn darüber ärgern sich nur die Urlauber, die tatsächlich jetzt Splitter in den Füßen aus ihrem letzten Urlaub auf Fuerteventura haben.

Setzt man sich damit auseinander, daß es auch im Urlaub immer wieder kleinere Probleme gibt, die einem den Urlaub vermiesen, so ist das ein Thema, das weder auf ein bestimmtes Urlaubsgebiet noch auf eine bestimmte Art der Spezies Urlauber zugeschnitten ist.

Hier kann man von Leuten berichten, die alles hinnehmen, aber auch von solchen, die man ständig mit Fotoapparat und Zollstock antrifft, damit sie auch alles schön dokumentieren können und vielleicht für null Prozent Spaß im Urlaub drei Prozent der Reisepreises zurückerstattet bekommen:

„Hier einige Tips für alle, denen gute Beschwerden ein ernstes Anliegen sind:

- Nehmen Sie einen Zollstock, ein Tonbandgerät und Ihren Anwalt mit in den Urlaub. Lassen Sie zur Not Taucherbrille, Bücher und Kinder zu Hause.
- Verhindern Sie den Abflug Ihres Flugzeugs (acht Stunden Verspätung können 120 Mark bringen).
- Falls Sie am Urlaubsort keinen Grund zur Klage finden, belauschen Sie die Gespräche an den Nebentischen. Irgend jemand ist immer unzufrieden.
- Locken Sie mittels einer Marmeladenspur Ameisen an Ihr Bett (kann bis zu 20 Prozent Reisekostenerstattung bringen).
- Haben Sie vier Kakerlaken im Zimmer, so besorgen Sie sich noch zwei zusätzliche (ab sechs Kakerlaken ebenfalls 20 Prozent). Aber:
- Aufpassen! Sollte ein Gecko in Ihrem Zimmer wohnen, schmeißen Sie ihn schnell raus. Der Insektenfresser könnte Ihnen die 20 Prozent schnell wieder zunichte machen.
- Verlangen Sie einfach, daß alles so wie zu Hause ist.
- Wenn alles so wie zu Hause ist, bestehen Sie einfach darauf, daß alles exotisch sein muß.
- Seien Sie am Urlaubsort 24 Stunden auf den Beinen, um Mängel zu finden. Schlafen können Sie daheim."

(Pursche 1996: 87)

So kann es gehen auf Reisen. Um aber Erlebtes verarbeiten zu können, muß erstmal eine Zeit vergehen, und die Wogen müssen sich glätten, bevor etwas witzig und 'glossentauglich' ist. Während der Reise sind vielleicht unangenehme Dinge passiert, die aber im Nachhinein doch noch ein Schmunzeln hervorrufen, warum also dieses Schmunzeln nicht zur Glosse aufbereiten und andere daran teilhaben lassen?!

3.9 Der Serviceteil

Verena Wolff

3.9.1 Der Serviceteil in Zeitschriften

Dies ist wohl der Teil, in dem sich die Reisemedien am meisten und auch wiederum gar nicht unterscheiden. Die Aufmachung der Serviceteile und auch ihre Plazierung differiert von Zeitschrift zu Zeitschrift. Der Serviceteil ist immer möglichst bunt und vielfältig und umfaßt alles, was man vor Reisebeginn und während der Reise wissen muß. Außerdem wird oft eine Gratwanderung zwischen Werbung oder Sponsoring und einer ausschließlich selbst recherchierten Arbeit unternommen.

Wie der Serviceteil konkret gemacht ist, hängt vom **Stil der Publikation** ab, eines ist jedoch allen gleich: Die Reisejournalisten sind ein recyclebegeistertes Völkchen. Es gibt keine Information, die nicht noch mal verwertet werden kann, und es gibt wenig Hotels oder Restaurants, die nicht schon früher in Reiseführern erwähnt worden sind. Weshalb sie nicht schlecht sein müssen...

Manchen Redakteuren fehlt die Zeit und manchen Zeitschriften schlicht das Budget, alle Hotels und Restaurants durchzutesten oder so viele Leute zu treffen, daß über alles eine Bewertung aus eigener Erfahrung erfolgen kann.

Die meisten Serviceteile folgen einem **ähnlichen Schema**. In Kurzform wird die Lage des Landes dargestellt. Eine Klimatabelle und einige andere Grafiken (z.B. eine Währungs- bzw. Umrechnungstabelle) erlauben eine erste Orientierung über das Reiseziel. *Holiday* bewertet die Reiseziele nach diversen Gesichtspunkten, allerdings sollten diese Bewertungen mit Vorsicht genossen werden. In einigen Serviceteilen ist ein Kurzporträt der betreffenden Orte vorangestellt. Die wichtigsten Kategorien in den Serviceteilen sind - wie im richtigen Leben - **Essen und Schlafen**.

Bei den Hotelvorstellungen gibt es mehr und weniger übersichtliche und sinnvolle Darstellungen. *GLOBO* zum Beispiel kategorisiert die Hotels nach Preisen und Sternen, so kann der Reisende schnell die richtige Unterkunft für seinen Geldbeutel finden. Die Unterkünfte werden kurz beschrieben, manchmal befinden sich Kartenausschnitte neben den Beschreibungen, die deren Lage verdeutlichen.

Fast ebenso wichtig wie Übernachtungsmöglichkeiten sind die Restaurantvorstellungen, Tips für die Freizeit und für Nachtschwärmer. Meist wird darauf wert gelegt, möglichst viele verschiedene Tips zu geben. Das *ADAC reisemagazin* hat pro Ausgabe mehrere Prominente, die an dem jeweiligen Ort leben, nach deren 'Insidertips' befragt. Nur steht zu bezweifeln, ob die Promis dort auch tatsächlich anzutreffen sind. Weiterhin werden Anreisetips (meist mit Preisen und Fluggesellschaften) gegeben, dem Leser Vorschläge zu Ausflügen unterbreitet. Ging es in dem Artikel um ein bestimmtes Thema werden es dazu nähere Informationen präsentiert. Normalerweise werden die Fremdenverkehrsämter erwähnt und der Leser bekommt Literaturtips, die eine vertiefte Vorbereitung auf die Reise ermöglichen.

Es gibt zwei unterschiedliche Möglichkeiten der Plazierung von Serviceteilen. *GEO SAISON*, *GLOBO*, *abenteuer & reisen* und *tours* schalten die Serviceteile gleich hinter den verfaßten Artikel, *GEO Special* und *holiday* haben den Serviceteil komprimiert am Ende der jeweiligen Ausgabe.

Welche dieser Plazierungen sinnvoller ist, sei dahingestellt, die ausführlichsten Darstellungen kann man aber sicherlich in der *GEO Special* finden. Der Serviceteil nimmt dort ca. ein Fünftel der jeweiligen Ausgabe ein, man kann sich detailliert informieren und auch auf Probleme (z. B. mangelhafte Straßen) im Reiseland wird hingewiesen. Für diese Serviceteile ist in der Regel ein Autor verantwortlich, der am 'Reiseziel' lebt oder gelebt hat und sich entsprechend gut dort auskennt. Außerdem werden Aufträge an Redakteure vergeben, und die Journalisten in der *GEO*-Redaktion tragen zusammen, was sie selber wissen und erlebt haben. Auch in Reiseführer wird gerne mal ein Auge geworfen, wieviel 'recyclet' wird, ist unterschiedlich.

Ferner ist zu beobachten, daß sich auch im Serviceteil der *GEO Special* **Kleinanzeigen von Reiseveranstaltern** häufen, die organisierte Reisen in das 'behandelte' Land anbieten. Man kann sich darüber streiten, ob das journalistisch anstößig ist, für den Leser, den das Ziel interessiert, tut sich hier die - sehr bequeme - Möglichkeit auf, sich gleich einen Überblick über die Reiseveranstalter zu verschaffen und sich über die Preise einer solchen Reise zu informieren.

3.9.2 Der Serviceteil in Zeitungen

Aber nicht nur Special interest-Magazine informieren ein relativ breites Publikum über die große weite Welt, auch die meisten Tageszeitungen bieten dem Leser einen Reiseteil, meist recht ausführlich und in der Wochenendausgabe. Allerdings ist das Angebot an Reisezielen und deren journalistischer Darstellung häufig etwas begrenzt, es handelt sich vor allem um Reportagen. Oft hat man auch den Eindruck, der verreiste Redakteur hat aus einer Reise so viele unterschiedliche Artikel machen wollen (oder müssen) wie nur möglich.

Bei diesen Zeitungsartikeln hat man es zumeist mit recht langen Reportagen und recht kurzem Service zu tun, auch die Photos kommen in der Regel aus derselben Quelle. Mitunter drehen sich die Reportagen um ein (touristisches) Ereignis in einem Land, manchmal wird eine Stadt oder eine Region vorgestellt, um im Anschluß des Artikels auf eine Leserreise dorthin zu verweisen.

3.9.3 CD ROM als Reise-Service

Neben diesen 'herkömmlichen' Serviceteilen der Reisezeitschriften gibt es die neueren Formen des Services, sowohl über CD ROM als auch über das Internet abrufbar. Bei dieser Art der Information unterscheiden sich die verschiedenen Anbieter sehr wohl voneinander. Die ausführlichsten und wahrscheinlich auch abwechslungsreichsten Darstellungen eines Reiseziels sind auf CD ROM möglich. Per Mausklick kann man sich z. B. auf einen imaginären Spaziergang durch den New Yorker Central Park begeben, der zuvor als kommentierte Diashow ('slide show') auf die CD gespeist wurde. In einem Stadtführer auf CD ROM werden Hotels und Restaurants kategorisiert, um das Abrufen zu erleichtern. Die CD ROM bietet eine viel größere Speicherkapazität als eine Zeitschrift, außerdem sind die Bilder interessanter, weil sie 'laufen' gelernt haben. Allerdings ist so eine CD als Reisebegleiter etwas unpraktisch, denn wer trägt auf einem Stadtrundgang schon gerne seinen Labtop unter dem Arm, oder eine Mappe mit lauter losen ausgedruckten DIN A4 Zetteln? Außerdem sind die Produktionskosten für einen solchen 'Silberling' natürlich sehr viel höher als für ein Printprodukt, so wird der Reisende sich überlegen, zehn Mark für eine Zeitschrift oder das Zehnfache für eine CD ROM zu den Reisekosten zu addieren.

3.9.4 Reiseinformationen über das Internet

Die modernste Form der Reiseinformation ist mit Sicherheit das Internet. Wo sonst bekommt man die Dreitagesprognose der Wetters in Hong Kong oder den tagesaktuellen Wechselkurs des Rubel mit einem Mausklick in Sekundenschnelle? Es gibt inzwischen eigene Internet-Medien, die sehr zielgruppenorientiert und speziell angelegt sind. Ein großer Reiz besteht darin, sich unmittelbar hintereinander in die unterschiedlichsten Medien einzuklinken oder alle Informationen zu einem bestimmten Thema abzurufen. So verfügt man jederzeit über eine aktuelle Riesentüte voller Informationen. Auch wenn die herkömmlichen Reisezeitschriften noch nicht alle vertreten sind, kann man sich sehr genau über mögliche Reiseziele informieren. Durch die unterschiedlichsten Links besteht die Möglichkeit, sich sein ganz spezielles Reiseprogramm zusammenzustellen.

Eine Reiseplanungssitzung vor dem Computer kann man sich ungefähr so vorstellen: Als Reiseziel ist New York geplant, dort soll im nächsten Sommer ein möglichst günstiger und abwechslungsreicher Urlaub verbracht werden. Praktischerweise beginnt man die Reise bei einer Suchmaschine, z.B. *http://www.dino-online.de*, und ruft sich eine Flugverkehrsliste auf den Bildschirm. Denn zunächst muß man ja mal hinkommen nach New York! Die Suchmaschine verweist auf ein virtuelles Reisediscount-Center (*http://www.www-discount.de/reisecenter/*). Dort gibt es Unmengen von Möglichkeiten, der Heimat zu entfliehen. Um das eigene Ziel zu verfolgen, kann man die Möglichkeiten eingrenzen mit der Eingabe von Abflugdatum und Abflugort und schon geht's los mit den Angeboten.

Das Ganze geht natürlich auch direkt, indem man sich in eine Fluggesellschaft 'einbeamt' (z.B. *http://www.condor.de, http://www.lufthansa.de*). Die *Condor* bietet sowohl die Möglichkeit einer Flugreservierung als auch Informationen zu den Reisezielen. Zum Thema 'Hinkommen und wohnen' gibt es ein Online-Reisebüro (*http://www.traxxx.de/reisebuero/welcome.html*), in dem eine wachsende Zahl von Anbietern ihre Angebote darstellt. Hier bekommt man alles: Kurz- und Städtereisen, Trips rund um die Welt und Pauschalreisen nach Mallorca. Man kann gleich buchen, und als Service stehen Flug- und Hotelbeschreibungen sowie ein Länder-Informationsdienst zu Verfügung. In einem dieser Angebote findet man mit Sicherheit einen günstigen Flug nach New York.

Nun geht es um die Reiseplanung 'vor Ort' aus 5000 Kilometern Entfernung. Erstmal klicken wir uns in die virtuelle Touristeninformation ein, um einen Überblick zu Hotel- und Freizeitangeboten zu erhalten. By the way:

Wie steht eigentlich der Dollarkurs im Moment? Die Antwort gibt *http://www.lgbank.de/trading/waehrung.html*. Das erleichtert das weitere Vorgehen, denn man wird nun häufig mit Dollars rechnen müssen. Einige Hotels sind inzwischen in die engere Wahl gekommen (*http://www.web-hotel.com/namerica/usa/newyork.html*) nun wäre ein Auto nicht schlecht, um die Umgebung von Downtown New York erkunden zu können. Kein Problem, auch hier sind mehrere Rent-A-Car-Anbieter im Netz, z.B. *http://www.avis.com*, *http://sixt.de*. Natürlich muß man wissen, was los ist in der Urlaubszeit in New York. Also schauen wir kurz in eine der virtuellen Reisezeitschriften, ob es schon Tips für den nächsten Sommer gibt: *http://www.traxxx.de, http://www.travmag.de*. Ganz nebenbei konnte man auch in Erfahrung bringen, wo die billigsten Rollerblades für eine Tour im Central Park auszuleihen sind und wie das Wetter im Sommer normalerweise ist: *http://www.dwd.de*. Sollten bei der virtuellen Reise durchs Internet noch Fragen jedweder Art offengeblieben sein, kann man sich immer 'verlinken' mit einem 'Macher', der alles zu einem Thema sammelt und diese Sammlung den Internet-Surfern zur Verfügung stellt.

So auch zu dem Thema New York: *http://www.uwefreund.com/newyork/*. Was sich da auf dem Bildschirm aufbaut, kann getrost als allumfassender, mit anderen Angeboten verknüpfter Reiseführer bezeichnet werden. Nach ausgiebiger Lektüre sind bestimmt alle Fragen geklärt. Das alles ist hyperinteressant und bunt, das Medium Internet stößt jedoch immer da an seine Grenzen, wo es um die Konkretisierung von Plänen geht. Das 'Cybercash' ist noch nicht wirklich erfunden, man kann keine Unterschriften per PC leisten, und mag auch seine Kreditkartennummer nicht aller Welt zur Verfügung stellen. Deswegen sind konkrete Buchungen noch immer mit einem Risiko verbunden.

Ein weiterer Nachteil ist der 'Mißbrauch' des Mediums als reiner Werbeträger. Viele der Reisezeitschriften benutzen das Internet als einen solchen, um die Internet-Surfer anzuregen, noch mal ein bißchen auf Papier zu lesen (vgl. dazu Kap. 9). Es werden Geschichten angerissen oder extrem leserunfreundlich präsentiert, um am Ende den Hinweis auf das aktuelle Heft loszuwerden. Dazu kommt, daß die Anbieter immer daran denken müssen, wie viele User sie eigentlich über das Internet erreichen können, denn viele Menschen sind zu Hause nicht 'total vernetzt'. Sie nutzen das Internet-Angebot an der Arbeitsstelle oder an der Universität, wo sie auf bestimmte Zeitkontingente angewiesen sind.

4 Handwerkszeug des Reisejournalisten: Das Bild

4.1 Einleitung

Hans J. Kleinsteuber

Reiseberichterstattung ist in unserem visuellen Zeitalter ohne **Bilder** nicht mehr denkbar. Diese Bilder ziehen den Leser in den Reiseteil hinein, sie sollen in den Sekundenbruchteilen eines 'Augenblicks' wie eine Chiffre Ort und Inhalt der Berichterstattung signalisieren. Zudem haben sie die Aufgabe, das vom Text gelangweilte Auge mit thematisch begleitenden Fotos zu unterhalten. Vom Inhalt her gehen sie eher in Richtung Urlaubsromantik, Exotik, visuelle Stereotype, selten handelt es sich um provozierende oder nachdenklich stimmende Fotos.

Sicherlich ist die Auswahl dieser Bilder von zentraler Bedeutung, die einerseits den Text illustrieren, zum anderen auch aus sich heraus wirken sollen. Häufig finden wir eigene Bilddramaturgien in Größe, Farbigkeit und inhaltlicher Abfolge.

Diese Darstellung beginnt mit Fragen des Bild-Layout, fragt nach Bild-Auswahl und -bearbeitung und schildert speziell interessante Gestaltungsmittel bei Reisefotos. Weiterhin werden Hinweise zur Bildbeschaffung gegeben und Tips für die Betextung von Bildern präsentiert.

Bis zu diesem Punkt haben wir so argumentiert, als sei Reisejournalismus nur ein Thema der Printmedien. Reisen kamen und kommen natürlich auch in den Funkmedien Radio und Fernsehen vor. Ein ehrwürdiges Alter hat z. B. das Funk-Reisemagazin des *NDR Zwischen Hamburg und Haiti.* Auch das **Fernsehen** hat sich des Reise-Themas angenommen, etwa im Rahmen von Ratgeber-Serien oder auch eigenen Reise-Magazinen. Was wir über die Stilformen sagten (Reportage, Bericht, Nachricht, Glosse) findet sich auch im Fernsehen wieder, ebenso Service-Darstellungen. Dennoch hat die Reise längst ganz spezifische Formen der Darstellung im bewegten Bild gefunden, die wir getrennt erörtern.

Die Universität ist ein vielgestaltiger und kommunikativer Ort. Unter den am Projekt mitarbeitenden Studierenden fiel einer durch höchste Sachkenntnis auf. Er war nach Jahren praktischer Tätigkeit als Reisejournalist an die Universität zurückgekehrt. So ist er Berichtender und Beteiligter zugleich, Analyse und Erfahrung verweben sich ineinander. Sein Beitrag zur Reiseberichterstattung im Fernsehen (Kap. 4.5) gewinnt dadurch besondere Qualität. Allerdings werden hier Zusammenhänge geschildert (wie: Boom der TV-Reiseberichterstattung, der 'ideale' TV-Reisejournalist), eigentlich in nachfolgende Kapitel gehören. Aber der Zusammenhang ist hier so innig, die Distanz zum sonst im Mittelpunkt stehenden Printbereich so eindeutig, daß wir die Geschlossenheit der Darstellung nicht zerreißen wollten.

4.2 Bild-Layout

Marina Tischer

Für viele Journalisten und für viele Leser ist die Reisefotografie ein spannendes und beeindruckendes Thema. Reisefotos können einen Einblick in fremde Kulturen und Landschaften geben, vermitteln aber auch Eindrücke von anderen Leben und Gebräuchen. Gut fotografierte Reisebilder sollen einen Betrachter durchaus zum Träumen bringen und für einen Augenblick dem Alltag entfliehen lassen.

Im Bereich der Reisefotografie ist es daher besonders wichtig, daß der Fotojournalist einen **sehr guten Blick für alles fotogene** hat. Dazu muß er Reaktionsschnelligkeit besitzen, denn faszinierende Erlebnisse sind oft einzigartig. Seine Aufgabe ist es, beeindruckende Landschaften, exotische Tiere oder einmalige Momente mit seiner Kamera bildlich festzuhalten. In Reisemagazinen haben Fotos die Funktion, Lust zu verbreiten, in jenes Land zu reisen und dortige Kulturen kennenzulernen. In der Regel werden nur die schönsten Fotos veröffentlicht.

Die Motive auf den Bildern werden meist noch **retuschiert** und sehen somit noch schöner aus als in der Wirklichkeit. Es kann daher vorkommen, daß ein Urlauber von einem Foto sehr fasziniert ist, von der Gegend in natura aber enttäuscht.

In der Publizistik haben Fotos einen nicht zu unterschätzenden Wert. Damit sie entsprechend ihrer journalistischen Wirkung auch zur Geltung kommen, sind verschiedene Kriterien zu beachten, die in diesem Abschnitt näher erläutert werden. Voraussetzung für die Arbeit eines Fotojournalisten ist natürlich eine gute und komplette Fotoausrüstung.

4.2.1 Die verschiedenen Funktionen von Fotos

Fotos illustrieren einen Text und **veranschaulichen** das Geschriebene, dienen aber auch zur **Auflockerung** einer gesamten Seite. Sie verhindern, daß eine langweilige 'Bleiwüste' entsteht. Schwer zu verstehende Textpassagen können durch die Verwendung von Fotos verständlicher gemacht werden. Textzusammenhänge werden durch die Bebilderung dokumentiert, und mit Hilfe von Fotos wird einem Beitrag **Authentizität** verliehen. Aufgrund ihrer enormen Wirkung auf die Leserschaft sollten Fotos auf jeden Fall so plaziert werden, daß ein Artikel bzw. eine Geschichte zum Lesen reizt.

4.2.2 Bildauswahl und Bildbearbeitung

Studien haben ergeben, daß Leser als erstes über Fotos in eine Seite einsteigen, als nächstes auf die **Bildunterschrift** blicken, dann die Schlagzeile bzw. Überschrift zur Kenntnis nehmen und als letztes den Artikel lesen. (Poynter Studie von Dr. Mario Garcia und Dr. Pegie Stark vom Institut for Media Studies in St. Petersburg/Florida 1990). Deshalb ist es wichtig, daß bestimmte Aspekte bei der Bildbearbeitung berücksichtigt werden, sonst könnte es sein, daß die schönsten oder bewegendsten Bildmotive bei den Lesern keine Beachtung finden. **Plazierung** von Fotos, aber auch **Dimensionierung**, **Ausschnitt-Wahl** und **Beschnitt** von Fotos sind ebenfalls wichtige Bearbeitungsmethoden, um Fotos optimal zur Wirkung kommen zu lassen. Zum Thema Bildbearbeitung formulierte der deutsch-amerikanische Zeitungsdesigner Rolf Rehe folgende Überlegungen, die ein Bildredakteur unbedingt berücksichtigen sollte:

- Welche Elemente sind wichtig, um das Gesamtbild wiederzugeben?
- Welche Elemente sind überflüssig?
- Wie kann der dramatischste, interessanteste Effekt erzielt werden?
- Welches Foto besitzt die größte Klarheit, den besten Kontrast?
- Kann ein einziges Foto das Gesamtbild wiedergeben, oder sollten mehrere Bilder verwendet werden?

(Blum1995: 34/35)

Nachdem eine Bildauswahl getroffen wurde, sollte zunächst das Format eines oder mehrerer Fotos festgelegt und gegebenenfalls ein Bildausschnitt, der den wesentlichen Inhalt einer Aufnahme betont, bestimmt werden. Denn nicht selten kommt es vor, daß nur eine einzige Szene auf einem Foto von Bedeutung ist. In solch einem Fall wird also nur ein Ausschnitt auf dem Foto hervorgehoben. Überflüssige Details würden den Blick des Betrachters nur unnötig umherschweifen lassen und von der eigentlichen Aussage des Bildmotivs ablenken.

Für die **Hervorhebung einer Szene** gibt es verschiedene Methoden. Entweder wird die Fotovorlage mit Transparentpapier abgedeckt und darauf der gewünschte Bildausschnitt markiert, oder das Foto wird eingescannt und am Bildschirm elektronisch bearbeitet. Ein weiteres Verfahren bei der Bildbearbeitung ist das Kontern eines Fotos. Hierbei wird die Aufnahme spiegelbildlich wiedergegeben, d.h. seitenverkehrt reproduziert. Eine Reproduktion wird zum Beispiel angewandt, wenn eine Bewegung auf einem Foto den Blick des Betrachters aus der Seite hinauslenkt. Eine andere Technik bei der Bildbearbeitung ist das Ausschneiden. Porträtfotos können am Kopf an einer oder mehreren Seiten angeschnitten werden, so gewinnen sie an Nähe zum Betrachter, bekommen mehr Aussagekraft und wirken dramatischer.

Fällt die Bildauswahl auf **mehrere Fotos**, sollte beachtet werden, daß die Fotos nicht alle dasselbe Format haben, sondern abwechselnd als Hoch- und Querformate in unterschiedlichen Größen plaziert werden. Das Seiten-Layout ist dadurch vielseitiger gestaltet, ist kontrastreich und läßt eine Seite nicht langweilig erscheinen. Das größte Foto sollte dabei den optischen Schwerpunkt bilden und im oberen Drittel angeordnet werden.

Bei Foto-Reportagen müssen drei Bildelemente vorhanden sein: Totale, Halbtotale und Details. Das Bildelement mit der Totalen dient als Eröffnungsfoto, es fängt die gesamte Szene ein und dient außerdem zur Orientierung des Betrachters. Die Halbtotale gibt eine Annäherung an das Szenarium, Detail-Aufnahmen geben Einzelinformationen und können zusätzliche Eindrücke des Ganzen vermitteln.

4.2.3 Die Reisefotografie

Bild-Layout alleine ist nicht ausreichend, um Fotos wirkungsvoll zur Geltung kommen zu lassen. Weitere entscheidende Kriterien für gute Fotos sind die Motive, allerdings unter Berücksichtigung wichtiger **Gestaltungsmittel** wie z.B. Licht, Farben, Kompositionsregeln, Schärfe und Unschärfe sowie Brennweite. Die entscheidende Frage ist jedoch, welche Motive sollen abgelichtet werden? Sobald man seine vertraute Umgebung verläßt und in fernen Ländern auf neue Kulturkreise trifft, kann man anfänglich so begeistert und beeindruckt sein, daß man alles fotografieren möchte, was einem gerade vor die Linse kommt. Damit nicht einfach wahllos drauflos geknipst wird, und dabei das Bizarre und Besondere eines Landes nicht erkannt wird, sollte ein Reisejournalist zunächst einmal Eindrücke von dem Land sammeln und das Leben der Menschen, die fremden Sitten und Gebräuche kennenlernen.

Die Aufgabe, die Reisefotografie erfüllen sollte, ist, **Charakteristisches** und **Typisches** eines Landes, wie z.B. das Feilschen auf Märkten, das Leben und die Mentalität der Menschen zu dokumentieren. Um dieser Pflicht nachzukommen, ist es am sinnvollsten, eine neue Umgebung mit all ihren Eigenheiten in sich aufzunehmen, und zu überlegen, worin die charakteristische, unverwechselbare Atmosphäre eines Ortes liegen könnte.

Obwohl Reisefotos zum Reisen anregen sollen, sollte die Reisefotografie den Anspruch haben, nicht nur heile Welt zu zeigen. Traumhaft schöne, weiße Sandstrände, strahlend blauer Himmel und türkisfarbenes, sauberes Meer, gehören zwar in Reisemagazine. Aber schreibt man über ein Land eine Reisereportage, sollten ebenfalls Fotos von zehnjährigen Mädchen in Manila, die auf den Strich gehen, um ihre Familie zu unterstützen, oder das Elend in den Slums und andere soziale Probleme fotografiert werden. Reisefotografie sollte den Vorsatz haben, die Augen vor der Wirklichkeit nicht zu verschließen, und Armut, Umweltverschmutzung sowie andere Probleme eines Landes darzustellen.

Reisefotos sollen einen möglichst realistischen und umfassenden Einblick in das bereiste Land und deren Bevölkerung geben, und nicht schöne persönliche Erinnerungen festhalten. 'Alibifotos'- Beweisfotos einer teuren Fernreise - gehören nicht in die professionelle Reisefotografie, sondern in das private Fotoalbum.

4.2.4 Was sind gute Fotos?

Es gibt **kein allgemeingültiges Rezept** für gute Fotos. Viele verschiedene Kriterien spielen eine Rolle: Ästhetik, dokumentarischer Nutzen, Nachrichten-Bedeutsamkeit, Erinnerungswert, emotionale Wirkung. Wie bereits erwähnt, wäre das Erkennen eines Motivs - Ungewöhnliches,Einzigartiges oder ausgefallenes einer Situation, Landschaft oder eines Gebäudes -, der richtige Weg zu einem guten Foto. Vor allem bei professioneller Reisefotografie sollten außerdem einige Gestaltungsmittel berücksichtigt werden.

4.2.5 Licht als Gestaltungsmittel

Licht erzeugt Stimmungen und Atmosphäre, es erzeugt die **Illusion von Räumlichkeit**. Licht ist aber nicht gleich Licht, sondern Licht hat viele Gesichter: Morgen-, Mittag-, Abendlicht; Licht von vorne, von hinten oder von der Seite; Licht vor oder nach einem Unwetter.

Jede Lichtrichtung hat ihre Eigenschaften und Auswirkungen auf das Bild, jedes Tageslicht seinen Charakter. Zum Beispiel suggeriert ein feuerroter Sonnenuntergang Wärme, ruft eine romantische gefühlvolle Bildstimmung hervor. Während Aufnahmen im Gewitter einem Bild eine gewisse Dramatik verleihen. Lichtverhältnisse sind nur einer der Faktoren, die gewollte Bildstimmungen inszenieren oder den Eindruck einer Gegend beeinflussen können.

Der Fotograf Gerd Ludwig und der Photoeditor Tom Kennedy, beide von *National Geographic*, über die Zusammenarbeit von Autoren und Fotografen:

Wie eng arbeiten Fotografen mit den Autoren zusammen?

Gerd Ludwig: Unterschiedlich. Der Fotograf sucht nach den 'Beweisen' vor Ort, nach den Bildern, die ein bestimmtes Thema transportieren. Sehr oft finden Fotograf und Autor ihre 'Beweise' aber an ganz verschiedenen Orten. Wichtig ist vor allem der gegenseitige Respekt: Der Autor ist nicht dazu da, mir die Bildunterschriften zu liefern, und ich bin nicht dazu da, den Standpunkt des Autors zu illustrieren.

Aber diese 'Illustration' ist das, was in den meisten Zeitschriften stattfindet. Das Foto dient nur als Beleg.

Tom Kennedy: Ich bin immer schockiert, wie wenige Redakteure die Macht des Pressefotos begreifen. Fotografie ist eine Echt-Zeit-Angelegenheit. Der Fotograf muß am Ort sein, wenn ein Ereignis stattfindet, und nicht zehn Minuten später. Im Nachhinein ist nichts zu machen. Ein Autor hingegen macht ein Interview und vermittelt dem Leser das Gefühl, er sei selbst dagewesen.

(Arbeit im Paradies 1996: 64)

4.2.6 Farbe als Gestaltungsmittel

Gelb, Orange und Rot haben etwas Warmes, Ausgeglichenes und Harmonisches. Kontrast- oder Komplementärfarben, wie zum Beispiel Blau und Gelb, oder Rot und Grün, können dagegen provokativ und aggressiv wirken. Farbe und Licht darf man aber nicht getrennt betrachten, sie stehen im engen Zusammenhang zueinander. Zum Beispiel wirken Farben im Tageslicht manchmal kalt und bläulich, während sie in der Abenddämmerung warm und romantisch erscheinen.

4.2.7 Unschärfe als Gestaltungsmittel

Fotografen, die mit Unschärfe experimentieren, möchten nur bestimmte Details eines Motivs hervorheben. Der Betrachter eines Fotos soll direkt auf das Wesentliche eines Bildes aufmerksam gemacht werden. Überflüssige bzw. unwichtige Vorder- oder Hintergründe versinken dann meist in Unschärfe.

4.2.8 Wie fotografiert man Charakteristisches eines Landes?

Typisches, Touristenattraktionen und klassische Sehenswürdigkeiten scheinen manchmal ihren fotogenen Reiz verloren zu haben, weil sie zu oft fotografiert wurden, bzw. auf jeder Ansichtskarte zu sehen sind. Trotzdem können solche Motive interessant dargestellt werden, da mit Sicherheit nicht alle Aspekte von Gebäuden, Landschaften und sonstigen Objekten ausgeschöpft wurden.

Es gibt diverse Möglichkeiten ein und dasselbe Motiv anders erscheinen zu lassen. Die zuvor erwähnten Gestaltungsmittel sind ein Faktor. Dazu kommt noch die Fotoausrüstung mit Weitwinkel-, Normal- und Teleobjektiv, aber noch wichtiger sind **Phantasie und Einfallsreichtum des Fotografen**.

Ein gefundenes Objekt sollte von allen Seiten betrachtet werden, von nah und von fern, vom Boden aus, aber auch aus der Vogelperspektive. Altvertraute Ansichten erscheinen somit frisch und neu.

Auch müssen Reisefotos nicht immer farbig sein, einige Motive kommen per Schwarzweißaufnahme viel besser zur Geltung, können eine Atmosphäre wirkungsvoller ausdrücken, wie zum Beispiel die Aufnahme eines kleinen verschlafenen Örtchens im Morgennebel. In Schwarzweiß erscheint es noch viel verschlafener und geheimnisvoller als womöglich in greller Farbaufnahme. Ebenso ist es mit Motiven, bei denen Strukturen, Formkontraste und

Umrisse hervorgehoben werden sollen. Genau wie ein Mensch haben Orte, Landschaften Gebäude u.ä. ihre Launen und persönlichen Gesichter. Die vielen Gesichter einer Landschaft sind weitgehend abhängig von der Tages- und Jahreszeit. Außerdem werden Landschaften oft nur in der Totalansicht dargestellt, dabei haben gerade die Details eines Objekts ihren ganz speziellen Reiz. Eine Nahaufnahme von einem Stein einer alten Mauer, kann durchaus den Charakter eines Ortes eindrucksvoll wiedergeben und die Altertümlichkeit unterstreichen.

Reisefotografie ist also ein breitgefächertes interessantes Thema. Mit dem Auge der Kamera können die Welt neu entdeckt und ihre unendlich verschiedenen Eigenarten dokumentiert werden.

4.3 Die Beschaffung von Reisefotos

Frank Höfer

Das Thema Bildbeschaffung wird im folgenden von zwei Seiten beleuchtet: Zum einen aus der **Sicht des Bildredakteurs**, der über verschiedene Kanäle zu Bildern kommt, und zum anderen aus der **Sicht des Fotografen**, ohne den diese Quellen trocken lägen. Beide Seiten stehen in gegenseitiger Abhängigkeit. Da zu diesem Thema keine spezielle Literatur existiert, basieren die Ausführungen auf Berichten in der Foto-Presse, Gesprächen mit Praktikern und den persönlichen Erfahrungen des Autors.

4.3.1 Bildbeschaffung aus Sicht des Bildredakteurs

Große Zeitungen, Zeitschriften und Magazine beschäftigen einen oder mehrere Bildredakteure, die für die Bildbeschaffung und -auswahl zuständig sind.

Bei *GEO* beispielsweise sind fünf Bildredakteurinnen tätig, eine weitere Bildredakteurin arbeitet für *GEO* in Frankreich. Zum Vergleich: *GEO* beschäftigt zwölf Textredakteure. *GEO SAISON*, ein monatliches Reisemagazin mit hohem Nutzwertcharakter, hat vier Bildredakteurinnen unter Vertrag.

Die Frauenzeitschrift *Brigitte*, in der regelmäßig große Reisestrecken erscheinen, beschäftigt zwei Bildredakteurinnen und einen festangestellten Fotografen. Auffällig ist, daß die Stellen der Bildbeschaffung bei den genannten Publikationen ausnahmslos weiblich besetzt sind.

Zur eigentlichen Bildbeschaffung: Es lassen sich vier Wege unterscheiden:

- Freie Fotografen bieten brieflich fertiges Material an. Meist kommen die Anbieter aber persönlich in die Redaktion, um sich und ihre Arbeit zu präsentieren. In diesem Fall liegen die Chancen (nach Aussage einer Bildredakteurin) deutlich höher, Fotos 'loszuwerden'.

- Fremdenverkehrsämter senden den Redaktionen - auf Anfrage oder unaufgefordert - Bildmaterial zu. Diese Fotos dienen der Werbung und sind honorarfrei.

- Jede Redaktion, die mit Freien arbeitet, hat einen festen Kreis an Fotografen. In der Regel bekommen nur Mitglieder dieses Kreises Aufträge, sie werden nach Tageshonorar bezahlt. Oft scheitern solche Auftragsarbeiten am Geld, die Verlage müssen sparen. Bei den renommierten Zeitschriften liegt das Tageshonorar für Fotografen zwischen 600 und 800 Mark. Unterkunft und Spesen werden in den meisten Fällen übernommen.

- Der Bildredakteur wendet sich an ein Archiv, eine Agentur. Mitte der 90er Jahre sind fünf Agenturen/Archive auf dem deutschen Zeitschriftenmarkt führend: *Bilderberg*, *Transglobe*, *Focus*, *Das Fotoarchiv* und *Look*.

Als weltweit führende **Agentur** gilt *Magnum*. Zur Zeit ist nur ein Deutscher bei *Magnum* beschäftigt. Die Agentur *Focus* vertreibt *Magnum*-Fotos in Deutschland. Im Yellow-Bereich (Regenbogenpresse, z.B. *Neue Revue*, *Frau im Spiegel*, *Die Bunte*) ist *Action Press* tonangebend. Alle der genannten Agenturen gehören anteilig den Fotografen selbst oder wurden von ihnen gegründet. Zum Teil kooperieren die fünf 'Großen' mit kleineren Partner-Agenturen. Große Verlage besitzen eigene Agenturen, die sogenannten Syndications. Fotos, die in einer der Publikationen des Verlags bereits erschienen sind, werden über die Syndications zweitverwertet, das heißt an andere Verlage verkauft. Dadurch versucht man, die hohen Kosten für eigenproduzierte Reportagen wieder 'hereinzuholen'. Voraussetzung ist, daß der Fotograf dem Verlag zuvor sämtliche Verwertungsrechte überlassen hat.

Freie Reportagefotografen beziehen ein Drittel bis die Hälfte ihrer gesamten Einnahmen aus dem Archivverkauf. Wird ein Archivfoto veröffentlicht, bekommt der Fotograf die Hälfte des Honorars, die Agentur die andere.

Vermittelt die Agentur einen Auftrag an den Fotografen, gibt dieser 20 Prozent des Honorars an die Agentur ab.

Hier die Adressen führender Agenturen:

Action Press:
Pressebild-Archiv
Kollaustr. 64-66
22529 Hamburg
Tel.: (040) 554 90 00
FAX: (040) 58 08 88

Bilderberg GmbH:
Archiv der Fotografen
Schulterblatt 120
20357 Hamburg
Tel.: (040) 432 84 40
FAX: (040) 420 78 76

Das Fotoarchiv:
Kortumstr. 61a
45130 Essen
Tel.: (0201) 78 24 48
FAX: (0201) 78 11 28

FOCUS GmbH:
Photo- und Presseagentur
Moorweidenstr. 34
20146 Hamburg
Tel.: (040) 450 22 30

Look:
Die Bildagentur der Fotografen
Kapuzinerstr. 9
80337 München
Tel.: (089) 54 42 33-0
FAX: (089) 54 42 33-22

Transglobe:
Foto-Presse-Produktion GmbH
Eimsbütteler Chaussee 21/23
20259 Hamburg
Tel.: (040) 44 50 01
FAX: (040) 44 72 22

Visum Fotoreportagen GmbH:
Lange Reihe 29
20099 Hamburg
Tel.: (040) 280 13 83
FAX: (040) 280 18 52

4.3.2 Bildbeschaffung aus Sicht des Fotografen

Als Fotograf in den Kreis der Top-Five-Agenturen aufgenommen zu werden, ist sehr schwer. Die Konkurrenz ist groß und nimmt ständig zu. Das liegt nicht immer nur an den Fotografen selbst. Die **Verlage** müssen aufgrund der allgemeinen wirtschaftlichen Lage sparen und versuchen, die **Bildrechte zu**

immer geringeren Preisen zu erwerben. „Das verdirbt den Markt", sagt die Bildredakteurin eines Zeitschriftenverlages.

Auch die Zeitschriftenverlage drängen die Fotografen mit verstärkter Konsequenz auf die Überlassung aller Rechte am Bild. Erstaufträge bekommen Fotografen häufig nur noch, wenn alle Rechte beim Verlag bleiben. Hier gilt das Gleiche wie bei den Buchfotografen: Verträge dieser Art werden nicht selten aus Unerfahrenheit oder schlichter Geldnot unterschrieben. Nur renommierte Fotografen können es sich noch leisten, auf solche Aufträge zu verzichten. Einige Verlage sind kompromißbereit. Veröffentlichte Dias werden für immer einbehalten, nichtveröffentlichte gehen nach einem halben Jahr zurück an den Fotografen.

4.3.3 Beispiele aus der Praxis

Ein Hamburger Verlag produziert seit einigen Jahren eine sogenannte 'Billigreihe' - Reisebücher mit hohem Bildanteil zu bestimmten Regionen Deutschlands für 19,80 Mark. Anfangs kassierte der Fotograf 53 Pfennig pro Buch für die erste Auflage, danach 50 Pfennig. Die Reihe verkaufte sich gut, für die Fotografen aber verschlechterten sich die Konditionen. Sie bekommen jetzt nur noch 40 Pfennig pro Buch. Das bedeutet bei einer Erstauflage von 15.000 Stück, daß der Fotograf seine kompletten Reise-, Film- und Unterkunftskosten von 6.000 Mark bestreiten muß. Er erhält nur noch 2,16 Prozent des Nettoverkaufspreises - früher waren es 5 Prozent.

Anderes Beispiel: Ein Verlag im Südwesten Deutschlands plant die Produktion eines Kleinstführers mit 64 Seiten und 100 Fotos. Ein Fotograf bewirbt sich und erhält folgendes Angebot. „Für die Bebilderung bieten wir ihnen ein einmaliges Pauschalhonorar von 1.500 Mark. Sie übertragen dem Verlag für alle Ausgaben und Auflagen sämtliche ausschließlichen Verlagsrechte an diesen Fotos. Der Verlag ist berechtigt, Sonderausgaben, Buchclub-Ausgaben, Taschenbuchausgaben zu veranstalten, bzw. die Rechte für diese Ausgaben sowie die verlagsüblichen Nebenrechte im Rahmen dieses Buches weiter zu übertragen." 1.500 Mark für 100 Fotos: Das macht 15 Mark pro Foto. Zum Vergleich: Bei einer Tageszeitung mit einer Auflage bis 10.000 beträgt das tarifliche Bildhonorar für schwarz-weiße Fotos 56,20 Mark (Erstdruckrecht).

Durch den hohen Konkurrenzdruck gibt es jedoch genügend Fotografen, die auf solche Angebote eingehen. Gerade junge Fotografen haben häufig keine andere Wahl, wollen sie in dem Markt Fuß fassen. Oder sie unterschreiben aus Unwissenheit.

> Klagen über tiefgreifende Veränderungen im Fotojournalismus:
>
> Vorbei sind die Tage, in denen Blätter wie *GEO*, *GEO SAISON* oder der *stern* die Kollegen sechs Wochen lang auf Reportagereisen schickte, wenige Aufnahmen mal ausgeklammert. Vier Wochen am Thema war fast die Regel, drei Wochen galt als knapp. Heute wird der Fotograf angehalten, den Job in zwei Wochen zu erledigen, sogar einwöchige Jobs für große Reportagen hat es in letzter Zeit schon gegeben.
>
> Die frühere Großzügigkeit diente nicht der Reiselust der Fotografen und Schreiber, sie galt dem Qualitätsanspruch und der Authentizität. Man wollte Unverwechselbares, keine Wiederholungen. Man wollte eine besondere Optik, das Markenzeichen dieser Magazine. Diese Tugenden haben heute nur noch eingeschränkten Wert.
>
> Dabei ist gerade Zeit einer der wichtigsten Faktoren für Qualität in der Fotografie. Daß man einem Land oder einer Situation nicht im Schweinsgalopp gerecht werden kann, sollte eigentlich jedem einleuchten. Zypern in einer Woche? Natürlich können so nur Klischees aneinandergereiht werden, man kann nicht einmal formal solide arbeiten, weil keine Zeit fürs Warten auf das beste Licht bleibt. Aber will denn heute außer uns Fotografen überhaupt noch jemand Qualität?
>
> (Nobel 1997: 6)

4.3.4 Fachzeitschriften zum Thema

Zum Thema Bildbeschaffung erscheinen folgende **drei deutschsprachige Publikationen**:

- *Visuell*, eine Fachzeitschrift für Bildverbraucher und Bildanbieter im gesamten publizistischen Bereich erscheint seit 22 Jahren und ist weltweit das führende Fachmagazin der Branche. *Visuell* als deutschsprachige Gesamtausgabe erscheint jährlich sechsmal. Im gleichen Verlag erscheint auch die englischsprachige Gesamtausgabe *Visuell International*. Anschrift: *Verlag Presse Informations Agentur GmbH* (*PIAG*), Stefanienstraße 25, 76530 Baden-Baden.

- *FreeLens* wird vom *Verein der Fotojournalistinnen und Fotojournalisten e.V. Hamburg* herausgegeben. Es wird von der Redaktion vor allem als Diskussionsforum verstanden. Anschrift: Markusstraße 9, 20355 Hamburg.

- Die *Red Box* ist das größte Adressenverzeichnis für Medienschaffende in Deutschland. Anschrift: Abteistraße 49, 20149 Hamburg.

4.4 Betextung von Bildern

Alex Weck

„Bildjournalisten sind für die Presse heute noch wichtiger als vor der Einführung des Fernsehens. Das Publikum ist optisch verwöhnt und anspruchsvoll geworden; es erwartet auch bei der Lektüre Zusatzinformationen und Auflockerung durch gute Bilder" (LaRoche 1991: 44). Ein Zitat aus der *Einführung in den praktischen Journalismus*, das den 'Nagel auf den Kopf' trifft, aber leider so nicht vollständig ist. Walther von LaRoche fährt daher damit fort, daß „auch der Fotoreporter recherchieren und texten muß, z.B. die Facts für die an Stelle eines Berichts festgelegte, erweiterte **Bildunterschrift** bzw. die Bildunterschrift selbst" (LaRoche 1991: 44). Also, das Urteil 'ein Bild sagt mehr als tausend Worte' ist für manchen so vielleicht richtig, aber journalistisch gesehen falsch - auch im Ressort 'Reise'. Denn „nach dem ersten Blick setzt normalerweise die Verstandestätigkeit ein, die das Bild verorten möchte. Man liest die Bildunterschrift. Man stellt einen Zusammenhang her. Man orientiert sich" (Sichtermann 1995: 30).

Ein ausdrucksstarkes oder einfach wunderschönes Bildmotiv ist deshalb ohne einen Textzusatz nur die Hälfte wert, aufgrund des fehlenden Bezugsrahmens und weil sonst ja keinerlei **gerichtete Information** enthalten wäre. Konkret umrissen sind die Aufgaben einer Bildunterschrift, dem Betrachter zu verdeutlichen, worum es in dem Bild geht, neugierig auf Bild und Artikel zu machen, über Wichtiges, auf dem Bild aber nicht Sichtbares zu informieren, Emotionen zu wecken und einen Überblick über den Inhalt des Artikels zu geben, falls der Leser sich nur kurz informieren möchte.

Mehrere Bildunterschriften zusammen ergeben am besten eine Mini-Geschichte. „Die Bildunterschrift ist der Apéritif des Beitrags, sie macht Appetit auf das ganze Menü. Geben Sie präzise Informationen: (...) Jubeln Sie in der Bildunterschrift nichts hoch, was der Lauftext wieder zurücknimmt" (Hamburger Journalistenschule - Der Bildtext: 11).

Es gilt also festzuhalten: Bildtexte sind die meist gelesenen Texte in der Presse; sie bilden den '**Einstieg**' in den Artikel. Fotos sind der **'Blickfang'** einer Zeitungsseite. Deshalb kommt auch der Bildunterschrift eine exponierte Bedeutung zu. „Ist sie dürr und nichtssagend, wird der Leser häufig auch den Text überspringen, zu dem das Bild gehört. Die Unterschrift muß deshalb 'sitzen' und zum Weiterlesen anregen" (Hamburger Journalistenschule - Der Bildtext: 13). „Das ist also eine Feststellung: 'Jedes Bild braucht einen Text.' Weiter: 'Ein Bild ist nur so gut wie die dazugehörige Bildunterschrift'" (Waller 1984: 193). Eine gewagte These? Offensichtlich nicht, denn ein Bild ohne Bildunterschrift wird man in der Presselandschaft lange suchen, selbst in visuell dominierten, optisch attraktiv gestalteten Reise-Publikationen. „Ganz wichtig: Stimmen Sie die Bildunterschrift und Textüberschrift aufeinander ab und vermeiden Sie Wiederholungen. Die Bildunterschrift sollte immer zusätzliche Informationen enthalten und nie das, was schon in der Überschrift steht" (Hamburger Journalistenschule - Der Bildtext: 13).

Im Idealfall, der hier gleichzeitig auch die Mindestanforderung bedeutet, sind **Bild und Bildunterschrift eine Einheit**, ergänzen sich also. Leider läßt sich dieser Idealfall beim Blick durch den 'Blätterwald' nur vereinzelt feststellen. Das liegt einerseits daran, daß „Fotojournalisten oft nicht in der Lage (oder willens) sind, ihre Bilder selbst zu betexten" (Waller 1984: 193). In der Regel ist für Reise-Redaktionen aber heutzutage ohnehin die freiberufliche 'Hybridform' des 'fotografierenden Schreibers' unterwegs. In jedem Fall müssen bei Reiseberichten, die in Personalunion Bild und Text liefern, qualitative Abstriche hingenommen werden. Außer spezifischen Reise-Fachjournalen (z.B. *GLOBO*) oder finanziell gut gepolsterten Zeitschriften (z.B. *stern*) leistet sich kaum noch eine Reise-Redaktion ein Team aus Schreiber und Fotograf unterwegs. „Entgegen anderen Meinungen sind für das Texten einer guten Bildunterschrift gewisse (lernbare) Fertigkeiten vonnöten. Genauso, wie man es als schreibender Journalist auch lernen muß, komplexe Sachverhalte in wenigen Nachrichten-Zeilen zu vermitteln" (Waller 1984: 193).

Wie sieht er nun im Einzelnen aus, der **gelungene Bildtext**? Er korrespondiert, wie bereits angesprochen, generell und auch im Detail mit dem dazugehörigen Artikel; nimmt Bezug auf die Thematik ohne dabei die bildeigene Information einfach nur zu beschreiben; animiert in Verbindung mit dem Bild zum Weiterlesen; vermittelt wenn nötig aber auch in Zusammenhang mit dem Bild wesentliche Zusatzinformationen für eilige Leser. Er besteht aus „kurzen prägnanten Sätzen, die erstens dem Charakter einer Kurzinformation entsprechen, zweitens aber auch das Hin- und Herspringen zwischen Bild und Text ermöglichen." Und: „Je länger der Bildtext ausfällt, um so größer wird die Gefahr, daß der Texter Abweichungen oder gar Widersprüche zwischen Bildtext und Artikel produziert" (Waller 1984: 195).

Die Funktion der Einheit Bild/Bildunterschrift variiert zuweilen in bezug auf formale Aspekte. Sie kann als Bildnachricht, also als eigenständige, unabhängige Info-Komponente vorkommen, die den Artikel mit zusätzlichen Informationen aufwertet. Eine andere formale Variante der Bildunterschrift steht im Einklang mit der illustrativen Funktion des dazugehörigen Fotos. Die Bildunterschrift kann „über Aphorismen oder gaghafte Texte bis zur ausführlichen „Bild-Betrachtung" reichen. (Was schnell zum Schwafeln geraten kann). Hier sind „Formulierungskünstler" gefragt" (Waller 1984: 198). Eine weitere stilistische Variante ist der Einsatz von Zitaten als Bildunterschrift. Das jedoch funktioniert wirklich nur, wenn eine nahezu vollkommene Verzahnung aller Elemente des Artikels erreicht werden kann. Zitate, die weder mit dem Bild, noch in Verbindung mit dem Bild, mit dem Artikel korrespondieren, sind allerdings tunlichst zu vermeiden. Ähnliches gilt für Zitate, die von Personen stammen, die ihrerseits selbst erst vorgestellt werden müßten.

Um welche stilistische Form es sich bei der jeweiligen Bildunterschrift auch immer handelt, **einige Grundsätze** sind generell gültig:

- Der Text muß gut zu verstehen und leicht zu lesen sein.
- Zu viele Adjektive sind zu vermeiden.
- Alle wichtigen Informationen müssen enthalten sein.
- Verhaltensweisen oder hineininterpretierte Eigenschaften von abgelichteten Personen sollten vermieden werden.
- Das Gleiche gilt für das ‘in-den-Mund-legen’ von Aussagen und die Zuschreibung von Emotionen, Stimmungen und Empfindungen und andere Prinzipien, die aber auch zum generellen ‘Form-Kodex’ journalistischer Arbeit gehören.

Insgesamt muß natürlich auch die Vielfalt der verschiedenen Publikationen mit ausschließlichem oder rubrikalem, reisejournalistischem Inhalt bedacht werden. Die Übergänge zwischen informativen Aufgaben und offensichtlichem Unterhaltungswert der Artikel im Ressort ‘Reise’ sind fließend. Dennoch: Was im 'seriösen' Zeitungs- oder Zeitschriftenmarkt als Todsünde gilt, ist in Gazetten oder der 'Yellow Press' manchmal durchaus üblich. Generell zu kritisieren ist die Manipulation des Bildmaterials durch falsche Bildunterschriften. Ein Strand mit Palmen, aufgenommen in der Karibik, aber betextet als ‘verstecktes Juwel einer Südseeinsel’ ist leider keine Seltenheit. Ob nun aus Nachlässigkeit oder vorsätzlich ist dabei am Ende fast unerheblich. Der Betrug am Leser ist in solchen Fällen nicht mehr rückgängig zu machen. Zum Glück für die Verantwortlichen fliegen solche Manipulationen selten auf, weil sie für den Betrachter kaum nachvollziehbar sind.

Seit 1888 geht *National Geographic* auf 'Entdeckungsreise'. Das traditionsreiche Blatt gilt als das beste seiner Gattung.

Weltweit betreibt keine Zeitschrift Journalismus mit so hohem Aufwand und solcher Akribie wie das *National Geographic*. So gibt es zum Beispiel eine eigene Abteilung für Bildunterschriften, die die Angaben der Fotografen zusammenstellt und überprüft. Um das Thema 'Wolle' vorzubereiten, las Fotografin Cary Wollinsky 65 Bücher und kontaktete 160 Personen in elf Ländern. Die Produktionszeit für ein Thema beträgt in der Regel allein für die Fotografie ein halbes Jahr. Dabei werden oft über tausend Filme belichtet. Insgesamt lieferten im Jahr 1993 alle *National Geographic*-Fotografen 46.769 Filmrollen ab - das sind 1.683.600 Dias. Veröffentlicht wurden im gleichen Jahr 1.048 Fotos, im Durchschnitt also etwa jedes Tausendzweihundertste.

(Scharnberg 1996: 62)

„Zusammenfassend ist zu sagen: **Bild und Bildunterschrift sind eine untrennbare Einheit** und sollten als zwei sich ergänzende Bestandteile mit derselben Sorgfalt hergestellt werden. Wo es sich (aus welchen Gründen auch immer) nicht bewerkstelligen läßt, daß beide Elemente von derselben Person angefertigt werden, sollte eine möglichst nahe Zusammenarbeit angestrebt werden. Vom Fotografen ist in jedem Fall zu verlangen, daß er alle wichtigen Fakten über das Bild weitergibt, vom Bildtexter, daß er sich um noch fehlende Zeilen einer Bildunterschrift bemüht.

Je mehr Hintergrundwissen hinter den wenigen Zeilen einer Bildunterschrift steht, desto informativer und wertvoller wird sie für den Leser sein" (Waller 1984: 199). Eine Aufgabe, die anspruchsvoll und verantwortungsvoll zugleich ist, bedenkt man den bereits geschilderten Effekt, den Bildtexte haben: „Die Bildunterschrift soll zum Lasso werden, das die Leser hineinzieht in die Geschichte: Sie hat eine ähnliche Funktion wie Titel und Vorspann" (Meyer 1995: 54). In einer vollendeten Symbiose von Bild/Artikel - das ist sicher unstrittig - ist deshalb auch in Zukunft die Bildunterschrift ein elementares Bindeglied.

4.5 Reiseberichterstattung im Fernsehen

Alex Weck

„Wie denn der 'berufliche Abenteuer-Urlaub' gewesen sei?", fragten mich Freunde, Bekannte und neidvoll-interessierte Kollegen nach der Rückkehr von den letzten Dreharbeiten für einen deutschen Privatsender. Sicher, das Team (Autor, Kameramann, Assistent) war fast neun Wochen in exotischen Südsee-Gebieten (West-Samoa und Tonga) sowie in Neuseeland unterwegs gewesen und hatte viel erlebt. Vielleicht waren sogar einige Abenteuer dabei, aber Urlaub, in welcher Form auch immer, war es sicher nicht. Im Gegenteil, was am Ende dabei herauskommen sollte, bedurfte harter Arbeit.

4.5.1 Der Alltag des Fernsehjournalisten

Wie sieht er denn nun wirklich aus, der Alltag des Fernseh-Reisejournalisten unterwegs? Die Drehtage beginnen früh, oft vor Sonnenaufgang, und enden meist erst bei Sonnenuntergang. Beides sind unverzichtbare Zeiträume für atmosphärische Bilder und müssen genutzt werden. Was sich bei Tageslicht abspielt, steht in teilweise traumatischer Abhängigkeit von unverrückbaren, nicht zu beeinflußenden Faktoren. **Budget-Druck** schreibt einen **festen Zeitrahmen** für den Drehablauf vor. Meist ist dieser aber trotz eingeplanter 'Puffertage' bereits schnell völlig überholt. Wettereinbrüche können gleich mehrere Drehtage kosten. Wartezeit auf mögliche Besserung der Bedingungen ist entweder nicht kalkulierbar oder von vornherein illusorisch. Tiere, die seit Jahren an der gleichen Stelle regelmäßig auftauchten, sind trotz perfektem Timing bei den Dreharbeiten plötzlich verschwunden. Flugverbindungen fallen aus, Straßen sind gesperrt und so weiter und so weiter.

Dinge, die der Reisejournalist für Print-Medien und Hörfunk noch aufgrund seiner Eindrücke beschreiben kann und mit einzelnen, ergänzenden Bildern (nach Qualität sogar punktuell selektiert) flankieren kann, sind für den Reiseberichterstatter im Fernsehen oft verloren, weil aus verschiedensten Gründen nicht in bewegten Sequenzen abbildbar. Wo das Reporterauge und auch die Fotokamera unter ungünstigen Bedingungen weiterbetrachten können, ist für die Film- und Videokamera aus technischen Gründen, Einsatz- oder Handhabungsproblematiken und anderen mediumspezifischen Schwierigkeiten ein Totalausfall oft unvermeidbar.

In Hast (aber unbedingt ohne Panik) ist Ersatz für Entgangenes zu finden. Der 'Doppelpaß' mit der Spontaneität auf Drehreisen muß ständig gespielt werden, um im Rennen zu bleiben, denn nicht nur die Natur hält **laufend Überraschungen** parat, die das Produkt in seiner ursprünglichen Form gefährden können. Interviewpartner oder Protagonisten erscheinen nicht oder stellen plötzlich unerfüllbare Forderungen. Manchmal verliert man sogar eine Geschichte, weil der Tod schneller vor Ort war oder andere Fernseh-Teams 'verbrannte Erde' hinterlassen haben. Behörden blockieren trotz Absprachen und Genehmigungen bestimmte Dreharbeiten. Technisches Gerät versagt regelmäßig, wonach in aufwendigen Aktionen Ersatz beschafft werden muß. Kameraleute, Assistenten oder Autoren verletzen sich oder werden krank. Fernsehproduktionen sind mit Beginn der Dreharbeiten absolutes Teamwork. Fallen Teile des Teams aus, so lahmt das gesamte Projekt und das wiederum kann in schlimmen Fällen sogar zum Abbruch führen.

Die Liste der möglichen, realistischen Pannen läßt sich endlos fortsetzen. Was sich hier wie ein bewußt überspitztes Horrorszenario anhört, ist leider (vielleicht nicht immer in dieser akkumulierten Form, so doch in seinen Facetten) Teil des reisejournalistischen Alltags im Fernsehen.

4.5.2 Ohne perfekte Planung geht nichts

Wer jetzt aber glaubt, bei diesen potentiellen Desastern ohne konkrete Planung oder gar Konzept auf Reisen gehen zu können, weil all dies ohnehin nichts bringt, hat sich getäuscht. Dabei spielt - neben der eigenen, gezielten Vorbereitung - der **Einsatz von sogenannten 'Stringern'** eine entscheidende Rolle, als Bindeglied zwischen den Reisejournalisten und der Zielregion. Dies sind in der Regel „einheimische freie Mitarbeiter (...), die ihnen Informationen beschaffen, Kontakte vermitteln, Assistentenarbeit verrichten und als Dolmetscher behilflich sein können" (Buchholz/Schult1990: 267).

Stringer kennen zudem die Parameter einer Reise im betreffenden Land am besten, können Transportzeiten kalkulieren, Mentalitäten einschätzen, zentrale Koordinationsstelle während der Drehreise sein und 'Feuerwehr' bei Problemen jedweder Art. Sie sind es, die das Konzept mit dem Autor auf Machbarkeit hin überprüfen, erfahrungsbedingt sinnvolle Änderungs- oder Ersatzvorschläge machen und das Resultat zeitlich so komfortabel, wie es das jeweilige Budget erlaubt und logistisch so effizient wie möglich mit dem Film-Team planen.

Das ist die Grundlage, um dem Schrecken der möglichen Pannen auf einer Drehreise, mit Hilfe einer konzeptionellen 'Sicher-heitsleine', überhaupt eine Struktur entgegenzusetzen.

Kurz: Kann Plan A nicht ausgeführt werden, tritt zumindest theoretisch sofort Plan B in Kraft, bevor möglicherweise tatsächlich frei improvisiert gedreht werden muß.

4.5.3 Die 'post-production' und der Schein der Leichtigkeit

In unserem Fall waren interessante Reportagen, Feature-Beiträge, Kurz-Dokus und Profile repräsentativer Persönlichkeiten schließlich die vorzeigbare Ausbeute des 'beruflichen Abenteuer-Urlaubs'.

Die 'post-production', also die **Nachbearbeitung des Rohmaterials**, bescherte uns dann ein Produkt, bei dessen Betrachtung die ersten Zuschauer des Werkes im engen Familienkreis, sogar den Zusatz 'beruflich' vor 'Abenteuer-Urlaub' zuweilen vergaßen. Alles sah so spannend, so leicht, so schön, ja sogar teilweise traumhaft aus. Selbst wir als 'Macher', konnten uns der Faszination unserer eigenen Bilder (hier noch ohne Sprachaufnahme, nur mit Original-Ton und unterlegter Musik) nicht entziehen.

Das 'Klischee' des sich sonnenden, Abenteuer erlebenden oder zumindest sein eigenes Fernweh stillenden Reisejournalisten, hatten wir indirekt durch unsere eigenen Bilder paradoxerweise selbst bestätigt. Eine Katastrophe? Ja und Nein, denn einerseits war es ja genau so nicht gewesen, andererseits hatten wir mit diesem Produkt, meiner Ansicht nach, unsere Aufgabe voll erfüllt.

Der 'Zuschauer-Traum' von geheimnisvoller, exotischer Kultur, atemberaubender Naturschönheit, spannungsgeladener Action oder Begegnungen mit leibhaftigen 'Südsee-Prinzen' und anderen faszinierenden 'Charakter-Köpfen' der Destination, war in unseren Filmbeiträgen materialisierte Realität geworden. Aber war es denn auch Wirklichkeit oder gar Wahrheit, was dort abgebildet wurde? Tatsache ist, daß 14 -18 Stunden täglich an dieser Realität gearbeitet, sie oft sogar 'zurechtgezimmert' werden mußte, was gegenüber den Abgebildeten vielfach manch sanftes Drängen zur Eile beinhaltete.

Auch nicht die Frustration über Schlechtwetterperioden, die nicht nur den Drehplan durcheinanderwarfen, sondern auch wertvolle Zeit kosteten. Regen in der Südsee will schließlich niemand sehen, zumindest keiner, der ein Reisemagazin mit dem Thema Südsee einschaltet. Ein Holzschnitzer, der mit der Ausführung seiner Arbeit für die Filmaufnahmen warten muß, weil es regnet und wir ihn (aus diversen Gründen) lieber bei Sonnenschein sehen, ist zwar am Ende filmische Realität geworden, ist aber sicher kein Abbild von Wirklichkeit und schon gar nicht Wahrheit. Daran ändert auch die Tatsache nichts, daß er zweifelsohne hin und wieder den gleichen Arbeitsablauf bei Sonnenschein absolvieren dürfte.

4.5.4 Bildsprache, Stil und Aussagekraft

Wie sieht sie nun aus, die gelungene Reiseberichterstattung im Fernsehen, ihre Bildsprache, ihr Stil, ihre Aussagekraft? Es gibt, wie in den meisten Bereichen des Journalismus, dafür kein Patentrezept. Zu unterschiedlich sind die Darstellungsformen im Ressort 'Reise', um generalisieren zu können. Es gibt die sogenannten **News- oder Info-Blöcke** in Reisesendungen. Hier kommt es vor allem darauf an, mit Hilfe der Bilder in kurzer Zeit möglichst viel auszusagen, Neuigkeiten oder informative Übersichten von Zielgebieten und anderen Themen aus der Reisebranche komprimiert zu vermitteln. Die Devise, das einzelne Bild ist die News, steht im Mittelpunkt. Ganz anders das Stilmittel **Reportage**, egal ob mit oder ohne Protagonisten. Hier lautet die Devise 'dranbleiben', also verstärkter Einsatz bewegter oder auch subjektiver Kamera, um das 'Mit-dabei-sein-Gefühl' beim Zuschauer zu wecken, eine Atmosphäre zu erzeugen. Features sind eine Art Hintergrundberichterstattung, mit durchaus subjektiven Zügen, also aus dem Autoren-Blickwinkel betrachtet. **Dokumentarische Beiträge** oder ganze Sendungen leben von der möglichst korrekten Wiedergabe von Wirklichkeit mittels filmischer Realität. Das heißt, ein thematischer Gesamtzusammenhang muß geschickt mittels Bildsprache auf das zur Verfügung stehende Sendevolumen 'getrimmt' werden, ohne das Darzustellende inhaltlich zu verfälschen. **Mischformen aus Reportage und Dokumentation** sind deshalb besonders anspruchsvoll, da oft Personen im Mittelpunkt stehen und wertneutrale Darstellung unweigerlich mit Emotionen und Atmosphäre durcheinandergerät. Manche Kollegen schwören auf diesen Effekt, formalistischen Puristen ist allein der Gedanke daran schon ein Greuel. Insgesamt gelten bei der Produktion für Reisesendungen aber die gleichen stilistischen und technischen Richtlinien wie auch in anderen Fernseh-Ressorts. Tips wie: schon beim Drehen an den Schnitt denken -, also nicht wahllos jagen und sammeln, reichlich neutralen Ton aufzeichnen usw., sind in anderen umfangreicheren Einführungen bereits ausreichend beschrieben worden.

Neben stilistischen Mitteln ist für die Ausdruckskraft vor allem der **Ablaufplan einer reisejournalistischen Fernsehsendung** entscheidend. Ist sie moderiert oder nicht, monothematisch oder in unzusammenhängende Themenkomplexe gegliedert, serviceorientiert mit festen Informationseinheiten oder eher appetitanregend durch verträumte 'Bildspaziergänge' oder Mini-Features. Diese Kriterien beziehen sich wohlgemerkt auf eine Magazin-Sendung. Ist aber die gut gemachte Reportage oder Dokumentation im Rahmen von 30 bis 45 Minuten nicht auch eine Form des Reisejournalismus im

Fernsehen? Ich meine ja, denn schließlich geht es vor allem darum, die Welt dem Zuschauer näherzubringen, in ihm Interesse zu wecken für die dargestellte Zielregion, ihre Natur, ihre Kultur, ihre Menschen und alles, was sonst noch dazugehört. Mein Kollege Jürgen Drensek, fast 6 Monate im Jahr unterwegs, unter anderem für die 30-minütige Reihe *Traumziele/Erlebnisreisen* (*WDR*), unterscheidet lediglich in 'nicht-formatierte Träumereien auf Film' (z.B. Traumziele) und 'nachvollziehbare Reisen' (z.B. Erlebnisreisen). Beiden Formen gemeinsam ist aber sozusagen, die weite Welt zu Hause auf dem Bildschirm zu erzeugen.

Wer kann - das zeigt die Position der Deutschen als „Reiseweltmeister" deutlich - fährt selber hin. Damit wächst kollektiv natürlich auch die Urteilskraft dem Medium Fernsehen gegenüber. „Die 'erste' Realität wird immer bewegender bleiben, (...). Den zweidimensionalen, geruchlosen Fernsehbildern ist ihre Herkunft aus einem Sender, also aus einer 'zweiten', reflektierten Realität, sofort anzumerke" (Sichtermann 1995: 30).

4.5.5 Der Boom der Fernseh-Reiseberichterstattung

Daß, ungeachtet von formalen Unterschieden, die **Reiseberichterstattung im Fernsehen** dennoch einen wahren **Boom** verzeichnet, verdeutlicht allein die Anzahl der Sendungen. Da ist zunächst der bereits angesprochene *ARD-Ratgeber-Reise*, die nachweislich beliebteste Ratgeber-Sendung im Ersten (1995: 16% Marktanteil/Quelle: Südwestfunk-Statistik 1995), welche außerdem in überarbeiteter/gekürzter Fassung alle 14 Tage im Wechsel mit *Unterwegs* (*SWF*) im *ARD-Kurzratgeber-Reise* für das *ARD/ZDF*-Vormittagsprogramm aufbereitet wird. Die Dritten Programme haben mit Sendungen wie *nix wie raus ...* (*Hessen 3*); *NORDtour* (*N3*); *Telejournal* (*Südwest 3*); *Ticket* (*WDR*); *on tour* (*BR*) ihre eigenen Reisemagazine, die teilweise (*Ticket*, *Unterwegs*) wiederum zusammen mit den Magazinen des Österreichischen und Schweizer Fernsehens, sowie dem *ZDF*-Magazin *Reiselust* auf *3SAT* in Wiederholung ausgestrahlt werden.

Hinzu kommt der immer stärker expandierende, private Fernsehmarkt im Ressort 'Reise'. Der Nachrichtensender *n-tv* bietet wöchentlich sein Magazin *reise* an, das Vollprogramm *VOX* leistet sich mit *Voxtours* und *Wolkenlos* inzwischen sogar zwei Reisemagazine im Programmablauf, wobei ersteres sich als ein journalistisches Reportagemagazin versteht, bei dem der Service-Gedanke weiter hinten steht, wogegen letzteres - genau umgekehrt - den Service-Gedanken im Mittelpunkt sieht. Ein Beispiel, wie verschiedene Philosophien von Reisemagazinen auf dem gleichen Kanal koexistieren und sich ergänzen können. Selbst Regional- bzw. Lokalsender wie *puls tv* in Berlin/Brandenburg (*Traumreisen*), *Hamburg 1* (*Relax*) u.a. sind mittlerweile auf den 'Reisezug' aufgesprungen. Eigene Spartenkanäle zum Thema werden folgen. Den Anfang machte bereits der Wetter- und Reisekanal aus Düsseldorf, der täglich Reise-Infos im Programmablauf führt und dieses Segment noch erweitern wird. In Vorbereitung befinden sich kompakte Dokumentationen über Reiseziele, Reise- und Urlaubsmagazine, u.a. (Quelle: Wetter und Reise Television, Factsheet 4/2.3, Stand 11/96).

4.5.6 Der 'ideale' Fernseh-Reisejournalist

Welche Qualitäten braucht also der ideale Reisejournalist beim Fernsehen? Wieder **kein pauschales Patentrezept**, aber Anhaltspunkte. Jürgen Drensek beschreibt ihn als „sprachensicher, souverän im Umgang mit schwierigen Aufnahmesituationen, möglichst nicht introvertiert, geschult in allen Spielarten des Bildjournalismus, mit reiseerfahrener Persönlichkeit und gutem Nervenkostüm". Ich würde noch extreme Belastbarkeit und die Fähigkeit zur Diplomatie hinzufügen. Zusammenfassend wird aber deutlich, daß Reisejournalismus im Fernsehen keine Aufgabe für 'Newcomer' oder absolute Einsteiger ist, was in den mannigfaltigen Zusatzbelastungen neben den normalen journalistischen Aufgabenfeldern begründet liegt. Erst Erfahrung und Sicherheit auf diesen grundlegenden handwerklichen Gebieten schaffen Reserven für das zwangsläufige 'Krisenmanagement' auf Reisen.

Außerdem wiegt auf Auslandsreisen ein Fehler doppelt schwer. Die Chance einen 'Patzer' notfalls irgendwie wieder auszubügeln, ist gleich Null. „Darüber hinaus fordert Gottfried Aigner von kritischen, urteilsfähigen Reisejournalisten außer einem steifen Rückgrat: Einfühlungsvermögen (...) in die Situation der Bereisten; Kenntnisse der Geschichte und Kultur der Reiseziele, über Wirtschaft und Sozialprodukt, Religion und Sitten, Geographie und Vegetation, Regierungssystem, Menschenrechte" (Guilino 1996: 16). Ist man dann unter den beschriebenen Voraussetzungen schließlich dabei, wird man natürlich auch die Vorteile des Berufsstandes genießen können. Wer darf schon als Normalsterblicher den Kronprinzen von Tonga durch einen seiner Tage geleiten? Ein treffendes Argument, aber es beinhaltet auch die eingangs geschilderte Problematik der Subjektivität in Reiseberichten. Subjektivität, die meist dem „Nachreisenden" weder in der technisch manipulierbaren Pracht des Films begegnen wird, noch im exklusiven Erlebnis des im journalistischen Auftrag Reisenden insgesamt. Ist dies deutlich als solches kenntlich gemacht, ist es ein vertretbares Stilmittel, doch selbst dann hat der Autor die ethische und moralische Verpflichtung, zumindest den Versuch zu unternehmen, die filmische Realität so nah wie möglich an die erlebte Wirklichkeit heranzurücken. Vor allem, wenn man die **unbestreitbare Machtposition des Mediums Fernsehen** bedenkt. „Das Fernsehen schlägt alle anderen Medien so leicht aus dem Feld, weil es ein Bildmedium ist. Das gedruckte Wort, die Töne aus dem Radio - sie entwickeln nie die suggestive Magie des bewegten Bildes“ (Sichtermann 1995: 28).

Eben weil der Zuschauer die bewegten Bildsequenzen oft für Wirklichkeit hält, trägt der Fernsehjournalist eine besondere Verantwortung. Die Dargestellten haben es nicht verdient, als etwas porträtiert zu werden, was sie nicht sind und dann auch noch darüber im Unklaren gelassen zu werden. Den Dargestellten muß die Chance gegeben werden zu erfahren, was wir mit den von ihnen erzeugten Bildern anstellen. Das gilt besonders für klischee- oder vorurteilsbeladene Völker und Kulturen. **Ein hohes Maß an Achtung für die Bereisten** sollte demnach also vor allem dem Fernseh-Reisejournalisten zueigen sein, denn er bringt von einer Reise an materiellen Ergebnissen schließlich mehr visualisierte, angebliche Wirklichkeit mit als jede andere journalistische Darstellungsform.

4.5.7 Qualitätsunterschiede der Fernseh-Reiseberichterstattung

Der Qualitätsstandard der Reiseberichterstattung - auch im Fernsehen - ist höchst unterschiedlich. „Der durchschnittliche Reisebericht stutzt ein Reiseland auf touristisch Anziehendes zurecht. Der Autor zählt auf, was ‘lohnend, reizvoll, paradiesisch, typisch, urig, preiswert’ ist, reichert den Steckbrief mit einschlägigen Stimmungsbildern (...) an und liefert manchmal mehr Verklärung als Aufklärung“ (Guilino 1996: 18). Das gilt natürlich auch für die eingangs geschilderte Produktion unserer Südsee-Sendungen. Sicher, dramaturgisch haben wir versucht, auch in sechs bis sieben Minuten jeweils einen Spannungsbogen aufzubauen; in zweidimensionale Bilder die Illusion räumlicher Tiefe hineinzubringen; durch Lichtgestaltung Charakteristika von Umgebung und Personen hervorzuheben usw. Doch all diese Maßnahmen, wie auch der **permanente Wechsel der Stilformen** innerhalb eines Beitrags oder gezielter Einsatz von **Musik** haben im Grunde nur ein Ziel: den **Zuschauer vor dem Gerät zu fesseln**, sein Interesse ständig aufs Neue zu wecken und seine Aufmerksamkeit zu lenken. Also Manipulation im klassischen Sinne.

Was im fiktionalen Fernsehbereich als gelungen eingesetztes Handwerkszeug gelten würde, wirkt im non-fiktionalen Beitrag manchmal verwerflich deplaziert. Daß es dennoch so und nicht anders läuft, ist eine Folge des sich schleichend auch auf alle anderen Fernsehbereiche ausbreitenden **Virus 'Traumfabrik'**. Und wo paßt dieser Ausdruck im non-fiktionalen Fernsehen schließlich besser als bei der Reiseberichterstattung.

Reisemagazine im deutschen Fernsehen (Stand Frühjahr 1997)

Titel	Sender	Sendelänge
ARD-Ratgeber Reise	*Saarländischer Rundfunk (SR), Mitteldeutscher Rundfunk (MDR)*	30 Min.
Björns Welt	*VOX*	60 Min.
Erlebnisreisen/Traumziele	*Westdeutscher Rundfunk (WDR)*	30 Min.
nix wie raus ...	*Hessischer Rundfunk (Hessen 3)*	30 Min.
NORDtour	*Norddeutscher Rundfunk (N3)*	15 Min.
on tour	*Bayerischer Rundfunk (BR)*	25 Min.
reise	*n-tv*	30 Min.
Reiselust	*ZDF*	30 Min.
ServiceZeit Reisen	*Westdeutscher Rundfunk (WDR)*	30 Min.
Telejournal	*Südwestfunk (Südwest 3)*	30 Min.
Ticket	*Westdeutscher Rundfunk (WDR)*	30 Min.
tips&trends reisen	*3sat*	25 Min.
Travel Xpress	*NBC*	20 Min
Unterwegs	*Südwestfunk-Fernsehen(SWF)*	25 Min.
VOXTOURS	*VOX*	60 Min.
Wolkenlos	*VOX*	35 Min.

5 Reisejournalismus: Bestandsaufnahme der Medien

„Jeder ist Nomade. Wenn nicht mit den Beinen, dann im Kopf. Die Entdekkungslust öffnet uns weite Horizonte. Neue Erfahrungen schüren die Neugier, noch weiter zu gehen, mehr zu sehen, mehr zu begreifen. *GEO* ist eine Entdeckungsreise ohne Grenzen. Journalismus, der nicht beim Bekannten aufhört. Ein Abenteuer, das Sie begeistern wird."

(aus der Eigenwerbung von *GEO*)

5.1 Einleitung

Hans J. Kleinsteuber

Wie ist der Reisejournalismus in Deutschland organisiert, wie sieht eine typische Redaktion aus? Und was denken die Journalisten über ihre eigene Arbeit? Was zeichnet eine wirklich gute Reportage aus? Die beiden Kapitel 5 und 6 stellen in vieler Hinsicht das Herzstück dieses Buches dar. Hier geht es um die Interna und den **Alltag eines 'real praktizierten' Reisejournalismus**. In **Kapitel 5** werden **typische Reisemedien** vorgestellt, basierend auf Besuchen in der Redaktion und damit verbundenen Gesprächen mit den verantwortlichen Journalisten. Um ein Minimum vergleichbarer Informationen zu sichern, wurde bei diesen Befragungen mit einem einfachen, standardisierten Fragebogen gearbeitet.

Einen darauf bauenden Verarbeitungsschritt findet sich in **Kapitel 6.** Dort wurden die eingeholten Antworten 'querverarbeitet', will sagen, die Antworten wurden gebündelt und gezielt ausgewertet. So konnten die **Stellungnahmen der Befragten nach Themenkomplexen geordnet** werden. Dabei wurden oft ähnlich klingende Antworten gegeben - ein Indiz dafür, daß sich inzwischen so etwas wie gemeinsame handwerkliche Standards herausbilden.

In diesem Teil des vorliegenden Bandes wird besonders deutlich, welche Vorteile in einer **gemeinsam mit Studierenden erarbeiteten Untersuchung** liegen. Ein einzelner Autor wäre kaum in der Lage, alle wesentlichen Reiseredaktionen und -ressorts in Hamburg 'abzuklappern', es gibt einfach zu viele davon. Ist diese Person dann auch noch ein Professor, so würde sich bei manchen Gesprächspartnern sicherlich Beklemmung oder Abwehr breitmachen. Will der uns etwa ausforschen? Wird er von der Konkurrenz geschickt? Bei den Fragen der netten jungen Leute gab es dagegen nur selten Probleme, oft wurde quasi schulterklopfend guter Ratschlag an die Novizen gegeben. Dabei wurde nichts vorgetäuscht, die Gesprächspartner wußten, daß mitgeschrieben (oder aufgezeichnet) wurde und Aussagen eventuell veröffentlicht werden.

Dieser spezifischen Herangehensweise ist es geschuldet, daß - wovon sich der Leser ein Bild machen kann - oft sehr plastische und eingängige Antworten gegeben wurden, die das Innenleben des Reisejournalismus auszuleuchten vermögen. (Kap. 5.3)

Für denjenigen Leser, den unsere **Methode** genauer interessiert, wird sie hier noch einmal im Zusammenhang geschildert: Die Recherche wurde im Rahmen einer Seminarveranstaltung in der Hamburger Journalistik im Sommersemster 1996 vorbereitet. Ausgangsbeobachtung war, daß Hamburg über eine einzigartige Dichte an Reiseredaktionen verfügt, seien dies klassische Reisemagazine wie *GEO* oder *Merian,* bedeutende Wochenzeitungen und Zeitschriften wie *DIE ZEIT* oder *Brigitte* oder auch Special interest- und Fachzeitschriften.

Im Bereich von Tageszeitungen ist die Stadt - seit langem eine Hochburg des Springer-Verlags - leider weniger gesegnet, so daß wir hier auch Redaktionen außerhalb der Medienmetropole hinzugezogen haben. Dazu kam, daß in einzelnen Fällen Reiseverantwortliche in den Redaktionen reagierten, als wollten wir Geheimnisse ausforschen und eine konstruktive Zusammenarbeit nicht zustande kam. Aber das blieb die Ausnahme. In fast allen Fällen wurden wir bestens unterstützt und den beteiligten Journalisten - deren Namen wir nicht nennen - sei für die gute Zusammenarbeit gedankt.

Im Seminar hatten wir besprochen, was in den Redaktionen erhoben werden sollte. Es ging um **zentrale Informationen** wie **Anzahl der Publikation: Selbstverständnis, Zielgruppen, Konzept, Mitarbeiter, Finanzierung** etc. Darüber hinaus wurde keine Vereinheitlichung angestrebt, statt dessen sollte die Eigensicht der Verlage im Vordergrund stehen. Auf dieser Grundlage wurden die kurzen Porträts der verschiedenen Reiseredaktionen im Kapitel 5 erstellt. Manche Zahlen, wie etwa die Auflagenhöhe, stehen bereits in vereinheitlichter Form zur Verfügung (IVW-Zahlen). In einem Abschnitt zum **Markt für Reisemedien** werden sie vorab präsentiert. Dieser Abschnitt verklammert sozusagen die folgenden Einzeldarstellungen.(Kap. 5.2)

Vereinheitlicht waren die **Fragen**, die allen auskunftsbereiten Redakteuren gestellt wurden:

- Wie wurden Sie Reisejournalist?

- Wie sehen Sie den optimalen Einstieg für einen Reisejournalisten? Wie sind die Auswahlkriterien in Ihrer Redaktion?

- Wie sieht der Alltag eines Reisejournalisten aus?
  - Wie war Ihr Tagesablauf während des letzten Monats?
  - Wieviel wird tatsächlich vor Ort recherchiert?
  - Was war Ihr aufregendstes Erlebnis?

- Organisation der Redaktion
  - Wieviele Mitarbeiter haben Sie im Reiseressort?
  - Wie ist das Verhältnis feste / freie Mitarbeiter?
  - Wie groß ist der Jahresetat Ihrer Reiseredaktion?
  - Wie läuft die Finanzierung von Reisen?

- Auswahlprozesse in der Redaktion
  - Nach welchen Kriterien werden Themen / Länder ausgewählt?
  - Nach welchen Kriterien werden Texte ausgewählt?
  - Wie ist das Verhältnis eigen- und fremdproduzierter Texte?
  - Nach welchen Kriterien werden Bilder ausgewählt?
  - Wie ist das Verhältnis eigen- und fremdproduzierter Bilder?
  - Mit welcher Intention entstehen bei Ihnen Bildunterschriften?
  - Wie wird der Serviceteils zusammengestellt?

- Was ist guter Reisejournalismus? Wie sieht die ideale Reisereportage aus?

- Welches Anliegen hat ein Reisejournalist?
  - Welche Funktion soll der Text haben? (zum Nachreisen / Träumen)
  - Welche Leser sollen angesprochen werden?

- Ethische Aspekte
  - Wie gehen Sie mit dem Fremden um?
  - Wie begegnen Sie Stereotypen?

- Die Zukunft des Reisejournalismus
  - Ist Reisejournalismus ein Wachstumsfeld?
  - Gibt es neue Trends in der Darstellung?
  - Gibt es schon online-Aktivitäten Ihrer Redaktion?
  - Hat Reisejournalismus online eine Chance?

Die Fragen waren vorab im Seminar besprochen worden. Ihre Gesamtzahl sollte kurz und überschaubar gehalten werden, um deutliche Assoziationen und aussagekräftige Antworten zu provozieren. Die Fragen wurden zwischen dem Spätsommer 1996 und dem Frühjahr 1997 an die gestellt, die sich in der Redaktion als Reisejournalisten zur Verfügung stellten. In den meisten Fällen konnten sich die Fragenden ihre Gesprächspartner nicht aussuchen; alle aber waren hauptberuflich in der Berichterstattung über Reisen tätig. In den monothematischen Reisemagazinen ist jeweils eine (kleine) Redaktion verantwortlich, bei den anderen Medien ist zumeist nur ein Redakteur mit der Koordinierung der Reiseseiten betraut. Manche Redakteure bekundeten Zeitnot, und unsere Fragesteller waren froh, überhaupt Antworten zu erhalten. Die **Fragen beantwortete** eine Auswahl von **Chefredakteuren, Ressortleitern** (diese oft ohne Unterbau) und ganz **'normalen' Redakteuren.** Was bei dieser Herangehensweise sicherlich zu kurz kam, sind die freien Mitarbeiter; sie sind auf diese Weise nicht zu erreichen.

Andererseits sind einige der studierenden Autoren selbst als **Freie** im Reisesektor tätig, so daß auch hier für Kompetenz gesorgt ist. In einigen Fällen schreiben sie über 'ihre' Redaktion, mit der sie Erfahrung hatten, in anderen Fällen haben sie sich bewußt andere Publikationen vorgenommen, um Interessenkollisionen zu vermeiden. Will man die Herangehensweise methodisch zuordnen, so kann man von einer - zugegeben - etwas ungewöhnlichen Melange von Experteninterviews, teilnehmender Beobachtung und Selbstreflexion ausgehen.

Der geschilderten Herangehensweise ist auch geschuldet, daß sich die meisten Kurzportraits ein wenig wie PR-Selbstdarstellungen lesen. Das liegt wohl in der Natur der Sache, wenn die Berichterstatter mit (Chef-) Redakteuren sprechen, die natürlich die Stärken und Vorzüge gerade ihres Blattes im Kopf haben. Bei dieser Art der Recherche ging ein wenig die kritische Distanz verloren. Im Kapitel 5 soll vor allem die Stimmung herübergebracht werden, die in den und um die jeweiligen Publikationen herrscht. Während hier die subjektive Sicht der 'Macher' im Vordergrund steht, versuchen wir ab Kapitel 7 den objektiven Blick von außen zu präsentieren.

Zum Abschluß dieses Kapitels dokumentieren wir noch erste Ergebnisse zweier Studien, die auf der Befragung der Reiseressorts deutscher Zeitungen sowie von Touristikveranstaltern und Fremdenverkehrsvereinen beruhen. Die erste Studie gibt Antworten aus den Reiseressorts wieder, die sich in der Tendenz mit unseren Erfahrungen bei Tageszeitungen decken. Die zweite Studie präsentiert Antworten von Reiseveranstaltern und Fremdenverkehrsvereinen, wobei es vor allem um Werbung und Werbeträger, Pressearbeit und Direktbetreuung von Journalisten geht. Manche der interessanten Ergebnisse sind für unsere Darstellung weiter hinten im Text (Kap. 8) von Bedeutung.

5.2 Der Markt der Reisemedien

Kathrin Voss

Reisejournalismus - das ist jede Art von Berichterstattung zum Thema Reisen, das ist die große reich bebilderte Reportage genauso wie die kleine Meldung. Reiseberichterstattung findet man heute in einer Vielzahl von Medien. In einer Gesellschaft, in der trotz wirtschaftlicher Krisen immer noch und immer mehr verreist wird und die Reiseziele immer weiter entfernt sind, wird der Bedarf an aktuellen Informationen zum Thema Reisen immer größer. Auch werden Ideen für neue Reiseziele gebraucht.

So **vielfältig** wie die Aufgaben des Reisejournalismus sind, so vielfältig sind auch die Medien, in denen die verschiedenen Formen des Reisejournalismus Einzug gefunden haben. So reicht die Palette heute von der kleinen Lokalzeitung bis hin zum spezialisierten Hochglanzmagazin.

Tageszeitungen bieten ihren Lesern in regelmäßigen oder auch nur in unregelmäßigen Abständen Reiseseiten an, die dann mit den Anzeigen lokaler Reisebüros oder großer Veranstalter gespickt sind. Meist stellen diese Seiten ein Mischung aus Reportagen und praktischen Informationen dar. Auch die obligatorischen Leserreisen, die viele Zeitungen anbieten, werden zu Berichten für die Reiseseite verwertet.

Hauptanbieter von Reiseberichterstattung ist allerdings der **Zeitschriftenmarkt**. Hier reicht das Angebot von reinen Reisezeitschriften, die für ein weitgefächertes Publikum schreiben bis hin zu Special interest-Magazinen, die für ihr Fachpublikum entsprechend zugeschnittene Themen anbieten.

Reine Reisezeitschriften gibt es in zwei sehr verschiedenen Formaten - den monothematischen und den multithematischen Heften. Zu den **monothematische Reisezeitschriften** gehören zum Beispiel *Merian* oder auch *GEO Special*. Sie behandeln ein Reiseziel pro Ausgabe und das in einer sehr ausführlichen Form, die weit über die bloße Beschreibung für den Touristen hinausgeht. Politische und soziale Probleme und Gegebenheiten der Region werden genauso vorgestellt wie die berühmten Sehenswürdigkeiten. Sie erfüllen dadurch eher die Aufgabe eines Reiseführers und sind oft noch Jahre nach dem ersten Erscheinen im Buchhandel erhältlich.

Die **multithematischen Hefte**, dazu gehören zum Beispiel Publikationen wie *GEO SAISON* oder *GLOBO*, bieten hingegen eine Vielfalt an Themen zu unterschiedlichen Reisezielen an. Neben den längeren Reportagen über einzelne Ziele stehen vor allem auch die praktischen Service-Informationen über alles, was mit dem Thema Reisen zu tun hat, im Vordergrund. Neue Flugverbindungen und die aktuellen Trends der Reiseveranstalter werden angekündigt, aber auch Informationen wie Impfschutztabellen und anderes gehören zum Themenspektrum. Reine Reisezeitschriften legen besonderen Wert auf die Optik. Durch brillante Fotos im Hochglanzdruck wollen sie ihren Lesern die Reiseziele näher bringen.

Ein ganz anderer Typ der Reisezeitschriften erfreut sich zunehmender Beliebtheit - die **Servicezeitschrift**, wie zum Beispiel *Fliegen & Sparen* oder *Reise & Preise*. Bei diesem Zeitschriftentyp stehen gut bebilderte Reportagen, die zum Nachreisen anregen sollen, eher im Hintergrund. Wichtiger ist die Vermittlung präziser Informationen. Dem Leser sollen die billigsten Möglichkeiten für den nächsten Urlaub vorgestellt werden. Ein Hauptbestandteil dieser Hefte sind daher auch Listen mit besonders günstigen Angeboten, zum Beispiel von Flugverbindungen in aller Welt oder auch von Pauschalreisen. Damit erfüllen dies Zeitschriften ein Bedürfnis der heutigen Gesellschaft: Es wird zwar immer mehr und auch immer weiter verreist, aber auch der Preis einer Reise erhält in Zeiten der wirtschaftlichen Krise eine immer größere Bedeutung. Die Flut von Reiseveranstaltern, von Fluglinien und ihren Verbindungen und auch von Last-Minute-Angeboten erfordert ein Art der Vorsortierung für den Verbraucher. Diese Marktlücke füllen solche auf Service ausgerichteten Reisezeitschriften.

Ist der Mensch erstmal unterwegs, findet er auf den Flughäfen und in den Flugzeugen eine weitere Art von Reisezeitschriften, denn fast jede Fluggesellschaft bietet ihren Kunden eigene Publikationen an. Für Geschäftsreisende gibt es dann nochmal besondere Publikationen, die sich vor allem durch eine unglaubliches an Service-Informationen auszeichnen. Sie werden zum Beispiel über Hotels verbreitet. Dazu zählt etwa das 'Magazin für internationale Vielflieger' mit dem Titel *Buisiness Traveller*.

Auch im **Special interest-Magazinen** findet man Reiseberichterstattung, die natürlich genau auf das jeweilige Fachpublikum zugeschnitten ist. Hier nur ein kleiner Überblick, wo sich überall Reisejournalismus finden läßt: Dazu zählen Auto-Zeitschriften, wie *ADAC-Motorwelt* oder *auto, motor und sport*, aber auch Zeitschriften, die sich der Gastronomie, dem Essen zugewandt haben. Zu nennen sind hier *Essen & Trinken* oder *Der Feinschmecker*. Es lassen sich auch in Publikationen wie *Ambiente* oder *Schöner Wohnen* Reiseberichte finden. Außerdem bieten natürlich viele **Frauenzeitschriften** wie zum Beispiel die *Brigitte*, ihren Leserinnen Reiseseiten an. Und auch **Lifstyle-Magazine** wie *Max* oder *Fit For Fun* kommen nicht ohne regelmäßige Reisethemen aus. Daneben gibt es dann noch viele richtige Fachzeitschriften, wie zum Beispiel *surfers*, *Yacht*, *Wild und Hund*, *Angler*, die ihrem Publikum speziell auf deren Interessen zugeschnitten Reisearten und Reiseziele vorstellen.

Ein Sonderfall ist die Zeitschrift *GEO*, die sich nicht als Reisemagazin sehen will. Angesichts der vielen wissenschaftlichen Themen, über die regelmäßig berichtet wird, läßt sich *GEO* wohl auch kaum als richtige Reisezeitschrift bezeichnen. Trotzdem erfüllen manche Reportagen über ferne Länder doch einen ähnlichen Zweck, sie entführen den Leser in ein andere Welt, lassen ihn eine Reise in Gedanken machen. Zum Nachreisen eignen sich solche Ziele jedoch eher selten.

Ein weiterer Sonderfall sind die Zeitungen und Zeitschriften, die **Reisen als Wirtschaftsfaktor** behandeln. Sie richten sich an ein Fachpublikum, das vor allem aus Beschäftigten von Reisebüros, Veranstaltern und anderen Unternehmen der Reisebranche besteht. Bunte Reisereportagen findet man darin nur vereinzelt, Wirtschaftsdaten und sachliche Informationen stehen im Vordergrund. Zu diesen Medien zählen zum Beispiel *fvw international*, *Reisebüro Bulletin*, *Touristik Management* oder auch *Touristik Report*.

In den deutschen **Zeitungen** lassen sich höchst unterschiedliche Formen von Reisejournalismus finden, von regelmäßig erscheinenden Beilagen bis hin zu vereinzelten Berichten über Leserreisen reicht das Angebot. Und auch die Ansprüche und Ziele sind sehr verschieden.

Auf der einen Seite steht der service-orientierte Reisejournalismus, der Anregungen und praktische Tips für die nächste Reise vermitteln will. Zu dieser Kategorie lassen sich zum Beispiel *DIE WELT*, *WELT am SONNTAG* und das *Hamburger Abendblatt* zählen, aber auch viele kleinere Tageszeitungen bieten solche Reiseseiten an. Dem gegenüber stehen Zeitungen, die Reisejournalismus eher in Richtung des Feuilletons rücken. Ungewöhnliche Reiseziele und Beschreibungen, gespickt oftmals mit historischen und politischen Hintergrundwissen zeichnen diese Reiseseiten aus. Ein Paradebeispiel für diese Kategorie ist *DIE ZEIT*.

Neben dem Printbereich bieten auch **Hörfunk** und **Fernsehen** Sendungen zum Thema Reisen an, wenn auch längst nicht in dem Umfang wie es die Printmedien tun. So beschränkt sich Reiseberichterstattung im Fernsehen meist auf zwei unterschiedliche Formate, die sich mit den beiden wichtigen Formaten der Reisezeitschriften vergleichen lassen. Das sind zum einen Ratgeber-Sendungen, die eine Mischung aus kürzeren Reportagen und aktuellen Meldungen bieten und im Aufbau und Stil den multithematischen Reiseheften gleichen. Das andere Format entspricht eher den monothematischen Reisezeitschriften. Ein Reiseziel wird durch ein große oder mehrere kleine Reportagen vorgestellt.

Neuestes Medium für Reisejournalismus ist das **Internet**, doch scheint dieses Feld sich noch in der Experimentierphase zu befinden (vgl. Kap. 9.2).

Einige typische Reisemedien - inklusive derer, die hier besprochen werden - mit Auflagenzahlen (IVW bzw. eigene Angaben):

- *abenteuer&reisen* (138.045; IVW 4/96)
- *ADAC reisemagazin* (288.305; IVW 4/96)
- *Brigitte* (1.229.429; IVW 4/96)
- *FAZ* (383.588; IVW 3/96)
- *Fit For Fun* (496.386; IVW 3/96)
- *Fliegen&Sparen* (63.680; IVW 4/96)
- *Frankfurter Rundschau* (185.939; IVW2/96)
- *freizeit&reisen* (10.900; IVW 2/96)
- *fvw international* (33.798; IVW 1/97)
- *GEO* (635.662; IVW 3/96))
- *GEO SAISON* (212.190; IVW 3/96)
- *GLOBO* (145.667; IVW 4/96)
- *Hamburger Abendblatt* (306.564; IVW3/96)
- *Merian* (170.724; IVW 4/96)
- *Reisefieber* (43.000; IVW 3/96)
- *Reise&Preise* (100.000; IVW 4/96)
- *Segeberger Zeitung* (9.805; IVW 4/96)
- *surf* (102.102; IVW 2/96)
- *surfers* (38.000; eigene Angabe)
- *taz - Die Tageszeitung* (61.580; IVW 4/96)
- *Tours* (69.974; IVW 1/96)
- *Outdoor* (71.420; IVW 4/96)
- *DIE ZEIT* (468.774; IVW 3/96)

5.3 *ADAC reisemagazin*

Doris Ehrhardt

Das *ADAC reisemagazin* gehört zu den **monothematischen Reise-Zeitschriften**, das heißt: Jede Ausgabe hat nicht mehrere Zielgebiete zum Thema, sondern nur eines. Obwohl das *ADAC reisemagazin* das letzte einer Reihe von Publikationen war, die um gutverdienende, reisefreudige Leser ins Rennen gingen, ist es heute Marktführer. Das Magazin wird vom *ADAC Verlag* herausgegeben und zusammen mit dem *Axel Springer Verlag* publiziert, wobei Chefredaktion, Vertriebs- und Anzeigenabteilung in München arbeiten, und eine Textredaktion sowie Grafikbüro das Heft in Hamburg erstellen.

Die *ADAC reisemagazin*-Redaktion umfaßt neun Personen: zwei festangestellte und 1997 sieben freie MitarbeiterInnen. Das Magazin erscheint seit 1991 alle zwei Monate und wird bei einem Verkaufspreis von 14,80 Mark zum größten Teil von Abonnenten bezogen, die vor allem aus dem Kreis der *ADAC*-Mitglieder geworben wurden.

Nach **Marktanalysen** wird jede Auflage im Durchschnitt von 2,6 Millionen Deutschen gelesen. Die meisten Leser sind zwischen 30 und 60 Jahre alt, männlich, haben höhere Schulbildung, sind berufstätig und verfügen über ein monatliches Haushaltseinkommen von mindestens 6000 Mark. Im Vergleich zur Gesamtbevölkerung packen die Leser des *ADAC reisemagazins* deutlich häufiger ihre Koffer, mehrmals im Jahr für längere Urlaubsreisen, mindestens neun Mal für Kurz- und Wochenendreisen.

Gemäß der Befragung verstehen sich die Leser als Experten in Sachen Urlaub und Reisen, halten sich für innovativ, sehr aktiv, modern und für Kenner, wenn es um anspruchsvolle Hotels und Restaurants geht. Während ein Teil der Leser das Magazin liest, um abzuschalten und von fremden Regionen zu träumen, nutzt der andere Teil das Heft vorwiegend als Informationsquelle für den nächsten Urlaub.

Entsprechend ist das Heft inhaltlich gestaltet: **reich bebilderte Reportagen zum Träumen und Nachreisen**. Anders als das Logo *ADAC* auf Anhieb vermuten läßt, spielen Reisen mit dem Auto nur ganz selten eine Rolle. Und, abgesehen von einer oder zwei Leserreisen pro Jahr, werden im Heft auch nicht speziell die Reisen promotet, die von der *ADAC Reise GmbH* veranstaltet werden, sondern Reisen für Individualtouristen beschrieben, die unabhängig von den aktuellen Angeboten der Schwesterfirma ausgewählt werden.

Kriterien dieser Auswahl sind „Attraktivität des Zielgebietes, Besucheraufkommen und 'was gibt es unter journalistischen Gesichtspunkten her?'".

Die großen Beiträge im Heft sind hauptsächlich Reportagen und Features sowie jeweils ein Porträt über einen für das Zielgebiet charakteristischen Künstler. Dabei haben Fotos einen großen Stellenwert: „Unsere 'Optik' ist der halbe Erfolg", so der Chefredakteur.

Die Themen variieren von Heft zu Heft, behandeln die Bereiche Kultur und Kunst, Landschaften und Touren, Typen und ethnische Minderheiten, Hotels und Restaurants, Sport und Freizeit. Der Vorlauf eines Heftes bis zur Publikation beträgt 18 Monate.

Da die Recherche-Reisen aus dem redaktionseigenem Etat finanziert werden, kann sich die Zeitschrift eine objektive und kritische Berichterstattung leisten.

Für jede Reportage werden freie Journalisten und Fotografen beauftragt, die, abhängig vom Thema, zwischen sieben Tagen und drei Wochen vor Ort auf Kosten des Verlags recherchieren. Ein Teil der Journalisten und Fotografen stammt aus Deutschland, ein Teil aus dem vorgestellten Zielgebiet.

Im Anschluß an jede der zwölf bis 15 Reportagen pro Heft soll ein **Informationsteil** die praktische Reisegestaltung erleichtern. So enthalten diese Strecken Adressen von Auskunftsbüros, Kurzbeschreibungen von Hotels, Restaurants, Sehenswürdigkeiten und - je nach Ort - auch Bars, Discos und Geschäften.

Eine Übersichtskarte soll dem Leser helfen, die angegebenen Adressen vor Ort leichter zu finden. Zusätzlich gibt es einen ausführlichen **Serviceteil** mit Tips von A bis Z: von Anreise über deutschsprachige Ärzte bis Zollbestimmungen.

Da die Redaktion ihre Leser nicht nur mit interessanten Reportagen und ausgesuchten Bildstrecken gewinnen und halten will, sondern auch mit zuverlässigen Tips für die Reisegestaltung, wird auf die Richtigkeit der Fakten größter Wert gelegt. Deshalb wird pro Heft ein deutschsprachiger Journalist engagiert, der seit vielen Jahren in dem vorgestellten Reiseziel lebt. Er steht der Redaktion für den Verlauf der Produktion des Heftes zur Verfügung, liefert Informationen und kurze Beiträge und überprüft in Zusammenarbeit mit der Redaktion sämtliche Fakten - vom Baujahr einer Kirche bis zu Telefonnummer und Öffnungszeit eine Restaurants.

Werbekunden für das *ADAC reisemagazin* werden von einer Anzeigenabteilung akquiriert, die auch für die *ADAC motorwelt* arbeitet. Die Plazierung der Anzeigen erfolgt in Abstimmung zwischen Redaktion und Anzeigenabteilung.

5.4 *Brigitte*: Ressort *Reise, Umwelt, Freizeit*

Kathrin Voss

Die Zeitschrift *Brigitte* vom Verlag *Gruner + Jahr* gehört zu den klassischen Frauenzeitschriften auf dem deutschen Markt. Dementsprechend richtet sich auch die Reiseberichterstattung an ein ganz bestimmtes Publikum. **Zielgruppe** sind Frauen im Alter zwischen 25 und 50 Jahren (die Hauptgruppe im Alter von 35 bis 40 Jahren), die meist ein eigenes, recht gutes Einkommen haben. Insgesamt wird die Leserschaft auf 3,8 Millionen Leser geschätzt.

Auf das Reiseressort wirkt sich die Zusammensetzung der Leserschaft auch aus. So reisen die meisten *Brigitte*-Leserinnen eher allein und wollen unabhängig sein. Sie interessieren sich für etwas andere Reisen und sind sehr kritisch.

So kann man die Reiseberichte der *Brigitte* in zwei grobe Kategorien unterteilen. Zum einen die Reiseberichte, die direkt zum **Nachreisen** anregen sollen und die Reiseberichte, die für das **Reisen im Kopf** bestimmt sind, die also vor allem fremde Orte und Kulturen vorstellen sollen. Sie können zwar auch Anregung für eigene Vorhaben geben und sind wie alle Reportagen mit einem kleinen Serviceteil ausgestattet. Die Redaktion sieht jedoch auch den anderen, wichtigen Zweck solcher Reportagen - die **Unterhaltung**. So ist die fesselnde Geschichte, die Lust auf die Reise macht, auch das Hauptziel des *Brigitte*-Reiseteils.

Ein **Serviceteil** gehört zu jedem Reisebericht. Er wird meistens von Leuten erstellt, die in den betreffenden Reisegebieten wohnen oder darüber schon Reiseführer geschrieben haben. Größere **Servicehefte** gibt es schon mal für Berichte über beliebte Reiseziele wie Mallorca oder Griechenland. Diese sind dann mit vielen Adressen und praktischen Reiseinformationen gefüllt. Sie werden so konzipiert, daß sie wirklich bei Reisen genutzt werden können, z.B. als herausnehmbares Heft.

Geschrieben wird der größte Teil aller Berichte von **freien Mitarbeitern**, wovon wiederum die meisten sogenannte 'feste Freie' (Pauschalisten) sind. Das sind freie Mitarbeiter, die für ein festes Gehalt für verschiedene Ressorts arbeiten und für gedruckte Berichte nochmals bezahlt werden. Im übrigen arbeiten auch die festen Mitarbeiter des Reiseteils durchaus für die anderen Ressorts der Brigitte. 90 Prozent der Mitarbeiter sind Frauen. Eingesandte Manuskripte werden nur in absoluten Ausnahmefällen gedruckt. Ebenso werden Reaktionsmitglieder oder freie Mitarbeiter nur sehr selten auf Pressereisen geschickt. Berichte entstehen kaum aus diesen Reisen, sie sollen höchstens als Anregung dienen.

So werden die **Reisen alle aus dem eigenen Etat** bezahlt. Die Dauer der Reisen hängt vom Ziel ab, von fünf bis sechs Tagen für ein Städteportrait und bis zu zwei Wochen für entferntere Ziele. Längere Aufenthalte gibt es nur in Ausnahmefällen, zum Beispiel für ein sehr weit entferntes Ziel wie Australien. Daraus entstehen dann meist aber auch noch Berichte und Reportagen für die anderen Ressorts.

Bei der **Auswahl der Themen** werden Reiseziele mit hohem Erlebniswert gesucht. Vor allem 'grüne Ziele', ökologische Reisen, werden in den letzten Jahren bevorzugt ausgewählt. Geschichten über umweltschädliche Reisen oder über Länder, in denen die Menschenrechte verletzt werden, gibt es bei der *Brigitte* nicht. Das ist eine der Grundregeln des Reiseressorts. Trotzdem sollen Schattenseiten und Problematiken nicht ausgespart werden. Ziel ist es jedoch, differenziert darüber zu berichten, das gilt vor allem auch für jede Art von Sexismus. Um Klischees und Stereotypen weitgehend zu vermeiden, werden auch alle Themen und Berichte von mehreren Redakteuren Korrektur gelesen.

Die *Brigitte* bietet pro Ausgabe meist eine längere Reisereportage mit Serviceteil und eigene Meldungen zum Themenbereich Reisen, z.B. über neue Angebote, Änderungen in Visabestimmungen oder ähnliches.

5.5 *Fit for Fun*: Redaktion *Reisen und Abenteuer*

Britta Wormuth

Das Aktiv-Magazin *Fit for Fun* aus dem Haus der *Verlagsgruppe Milchstraße* ist ein innovatives Produkt, das seit der Markteinführung 1994 Jahren Furore auf dem überfluteten Zeitschriftenmarkt macht.

Das Konzept, ein Lifestyle-Magazin mit den Schwerpunkten Sport und Fitneß zu entwickeln und dies expertenmäßig zu hinterlegen, hat den **Zeitgeist** getroffen. **Zielgruppe** sind junge, sportliche Leute im Alter von 18 bis 35 Jahren mit hohem Bildungsstand und einen Nettoeinkommen von ca. DM 5.000,- monatlich.

Fit for Fun greift im Reise- und Abenteuerteil den Spirit des Magazins auf und spezialisiert sich auf eine sportliche Darstellung des Reiselandes. Dieser Teil gliedert sich in die Themenbereiche *Abenteuerbericht*, *Reiseland* und *Reisen-Special*.

Der *Abenteuerbericht* ist in der Regel eine aufregende und einmalige Erlebnisreise, die zum Genießen oder Träumen, weniger jedoch zum Nachmachen einlädt. So zum Beispiel der Bericht über drei Inline-Skater, die mehrere hundert Kilometer entlang der südafrikanischen Küsten rollerbladen und so ein Land auf außergewöhnliche Weise entdecken. Einzigartige Fotos und spannende Erzählungen regen die Phantasie der LeserInnen an und bringen ihnen ein bislang nicht so häufig bereistes Land auf ungewöhnliche Art näher.

Der Bericht über das *Reiseland* zielt hingegen auf die Vorstellung von Reise- und Sportmöglichkeiten in einem Land oder einer Region ab, die anwendbar, buchbar und praktisch sind. Gleichzeitig erhebt das Magazin den Anspruch, eine informative und unterhaltende Geschichte zu erzählen, die einen authentischen Eindruck des bereisten Landes vermittelt. Dazu werden 'echte' Tips präsentiert, die servicemäßig entweder im Artikel aufbereitet oder am Ende der Strecke in einem Adressenteil mit zusätzlichen Preisinformationen zusammengefaßt werden.

Das *Reisen-Special* bietet diverse Service-Elemente wie Travel-Tips und Schnäppchen, besonders ist dabei der Hinweis auf aktuelle Sport-Events und Sport-Reisen zu nennen.

Erstellt wird dieser Reise- und Abenteuerteil von einem Ressortleiter und zwei Redakteurinnen, die die drei Bereiche wechselweise bearbeiten. Bei kleineren Berichten wird zwei bis drei Tage vor Ort recherchiert. Für große Geschichten hingegen ist der jeweilige Mitarbeiter bis zu drei Wochen unterwegs, in der Regel zusammen mit einem Fotographen, die kooperative Zusammenarbeit der beiden vorausgesetzt. Sollte dies nicht der Fall sein, beschafft die Fotoredaktion des Magazins, die aus vier festen MitarbeiterInnen besteht, Fotos über Bildagenturen, die zum Bericht passen und die das *Fit for Fun*- Lebensgefühl vermitteln.

Pro Ausgabe schreiben mehrere **freie Autoren** für *Fit for Fun*, die sich entweder auf ein bestimmtes Thema spezialisiert haben, z.B. 'Skifahren in Italien', oder nach ihrem Schreibstil ausgewählt werden. Sie werden pauschal pro in Auftrag gegebenem Artikel bezahlt.

Die Reisen der Mitarbeiter der *Fit for Fun*-Redaktion sind **Dienstreisen**, die mit begrenztem Etat realisiert und folglich effizient gestaltet werden müssen.

Bei der **Auswahl der Themen** steht die Darstellung von 'noch nicht so breitgetrampelten' Regionen im Vordergrund. Sie sollen sowohl etwas besonderes und aufregendes bieten, als auch für 'jeden' Geldbeutel interessant sein. Weitere Kriterien für die Themenauswahl sind Aktualität, die oftmals auf Insidertips basiert, die Jahreszeit oder auch die Beliebtheit von Reiseregionen. *Fit for Fun* erkennt das steigende Interesse nach Ferne und Fremde sowie den erhöhten Reise-Informationsbedarf der Gesellschaft. Seinen Lesern bietet das Magazin daher einerseits Reiseberichte als Lektüre und andererseits einen **sportlich-informativen Serviceteil** für gezieltes Reisen.

5.6 Das *Reiseblatt* der *FAZ*

Kia Vahland

Wenn ein Reiseziel aufregend, exotisch und schön genannt wird, wird der Ressortleiter des *Reiseblattes* der *Frankfurter Allgemeinen Zeitung* mißtrauisch. Jeder Ort habe „eigene Reize und Erregungen", sagt er dann. Egal, wieviele Kilometer ihn von Frankfurt am Main trennen. Und ‘schön' sei es überall, wo es ‘Möglichkeiten zur Auseinandersetzung' gebe. Ohne Rangordnung: „Die Konfrontation mit dem Leben in Indien steht gleichrangig neben einem Sonnenaufgang in den Bergen."

Weil es überall schön sein kann, ist grundsätzlich auch jede Gegend von Interesse für das *FAZ-Reiseblatt*. Nur **unerforschte Gebiete und Krisenherde bleiben außen vor**, weil das Nachreisen für die Leser zu gefährlich wäre.

Reine Routenbeschreibungen sind bei der *FAZ* nicht gefragt. Eine Reisereportage sei schließlich keine ‘Dia-Schau', heißt es in der Redaktion. Ein Text soll **Hintergründe erklären** anstatt nur den Augenschein zu beschreiben. Er braucht eine Geschichte, die deshalb gut erzählt wird, weil sie **aus dem Leben gegriffen** ist. Dabei richtet sich die Redaktion sowohl an selbstreisende als auch an sesselreisende Leser. **Spezielle Zielgruppen gibt es nicht**. Auch ob ein Land viel oder wenig bereist wird, spielt bei der Themenauswahl keine Rolle.

All die Zielgruppenprofile, Marketingstrategien und Auflagenängste ehrgeiziger Blattmacher scheinen von einer anderen Welt zu sein, wenn der Ressortleiter über die ‘pädagogische Aufgabe' von Reiseberichten sinniert. Er möchte die Leser sensibilisieren und sie zu einem „von Sympathie und Offenheit getragenen Umgang mit Land und Leuten bewegen." Kein Anspruch auf Weltveränderung, aber auf Veränderung von Weltbildern.

Dem Leser etwas auf den Weg mitgeben. Das ist der Wunsch, der immer wieder zu spüren ist bei der Lektüre der Texte. Da titelt ein Kolumnist ‘Essen bildet' und ruft auf zum mutigen Genuß fremder Speisen in fremden Ländern. Essen auf Reisen sei ‘die unmittelbarste aller Erfahrungen' und hinterlasse dauerhaftere kulturelle Eindrücke als jede Sehenswürdigkeit und jeder Sonnenuntergang.

Nicht alle Texte zielen jedoch auf die Reisegewohnheiten der Leser. Auch der **Tourismus als Ganzes** steht auf dem Prüfstein. Die Entwicklungspolitik bestimmter Länder ist genauso Thema wie die Folgen des Flugverkehrs oder

der Bergerschließung. Solche Texte sind Berichte in Essayform oder Kommentare und Glossen. Die Kolumne links oben auf der ersten Seite ist fester Bestandteil des Layouts.

Dieser beobachtende Blick auf touristische Phänomene setzt eine klare Abgrenzung gegenüber den **Werbewünschen der Reisebranche** voraus. Dabei haben es die Reiseredakteure der *FAZ* leichter als ihre Kollegen bei kleineren Blättern. Sie sind nicht auf die Finanzierung von Reisen angewiesen. In der Redaktion entwickelte Themen werden vom Verlag bezahlt. Für Recherchen vor Ort haben die Journalisten zwischen vier und sieben Tage Zeit, bei weiten Reisen auch länger. Einladungen zu **Pressereisen** werden nur akzeptiert, wenn im Gegenzug keine schmeichelnden Texte erwartet werden und wenn auf der Reise Zeit für eigene Recherchen bleibt.

Die *FAZ* beschäftigt in der Reiseredaktion vier Redakteure und 40 regelmäßig schreibende freie Autoren. Hinzu kommen die hauseigenen Fotografen, die die Mehrzahl der Fotos stellen. Seit 30 Jahren hat das *Reiseblatt* den Status eines eigenständigen Ressorts und damit „den gleichen Stellenwert wie jeder andere Teil innerhalb der *Frankfurter Allgemeinen Zeitung*", so der Ressortleiter.

Trotz des über lange Jahre gewachsenen Redaktionsgefüges haben **auch unbekannte Autoren** noch eine Chance, gelesen und gedruckt zu werden. Von Einsteigern erwartet die Redaktion Sprachkenntnisse, politisches und kulturelles Wissen und die Fähigkeit, ihre Reiseerfahrungen vermitteln zu können. Bevor sie ihre Koffer packen, sollten sie genauestens über ihr Gastland informiert sein.

Der Alltag der Festangestellten besteht nur zum kleineren Teil aus Reisen. Themen konzipieren, redigieren, Seiten spiegeln - das sind die tagtäglichen Aufgaben. Besonderes Augenmerk gilt den Bildunterschriften, denen inhaltliche Bedeutung beigemessen wird. Die Fotos selbst sind nicht als schmückendes Beiwerk gedacht, sondern sollen präzise Situationen charakterisieren.

Die Service-Informationen werden in **Infokästen** untergebracht. Sie enthalten in knappen Worten Fakten zur Infrastruktur, zum Klima, Geld und zur Sekundärliteratur. So stören keine nüchternen Zahlen den Erzählfluß der Berichte.

„Reisejournalismus hat eine Zukunft, wenn er vom reinen Abbilden oder vom puren Service abrückt und sich mehr um Hintergrund bemüht", sagt der Ressortleiter. Online-Medien könnten keine Erklärungen bieten, sondern nur reine Reisefakten. Also dürfe der Reisejournalismus in den Zeitungen nicht als leichtes Nebenfeld abgetan werden, sondern müsse die Bedeutung erhalten, die der Tourismus in der Gesellschaft längst habe.

5.7 *fvw international*: Zeitung für die deutsche Tourismusbranche

Kathrin Voss

fvw international - das ist eine 14tägig erscheinende Zeitung, die sich ausschließlich mit dem Thema Reisen beschäftigt. Trotzdem hat *fvw* wenig mit bunt bebilderten Reportagen über die Traumziele dieser Welt zu tun, denn in erster Linie geht es um die **wirtschaftliche Seite des Reisens.** *fvw* steht für Fremdenverkehrswirtschaft und trägt den Untertitel *Zeitung für die deutsche Tourismuswirtschaft.* Es ist ein Wirtschaftsmagazin, das sich an alle Unternehmen der Tourismusbranche wendet. Die Hauptleserschaft besteht daher aus den Beschäftigten von Reisebüros (56%).

Entsprechend diesem Publikum ist auch die Zeitung aufgebaut. Aktuelle Daten aus der Branche, Rechtsfragen, Wirtschaftsdaten über Veranstalter und die neusten Trends auf dem Reisemarkt bestimmen den Inhalt. Daneben werden aber auch gerade erschienende Bücher vorgestellt und Informationen über Reisebürotechnologie und anderes gegeben. Doch auch die große Reisereportage läßt sich in *fvw* finden. Unter der Rubrik *Counter* wird in jeder Ausgabe ein Reiseziel vorgestellt. Diese Berichte werden ausschließlich von freien Mitarbeitern geschrieben, die meist auf Einladung von staatlichen Fremdenverkehrsbüros, Reiseveranstaltern oder Airlines reisen. Oft sind es für Gruppen von Journalisten organisierte Reisen und die freien Mitarbeiter verarbeiten ihre Erlebnissen für verschiedene Printmedien. In den Artikeln selber werden die Geldgeber nicht erwähnt, wohl aber in einem deutlich hervorgehobenen Kasten an der Seite. In dem kleine Serviceteil stehen vor allem allgemeine Informationen über das Reiseziel. Sie sollen genau wie die ganze Reportage, den Mitarbeitern in den Reisebüros helfen, ihre Kunden besser zu beraten.

Trotz der offensichtlichen **Finanzierung der Reisen** durch Veranstalter und Fremdenverkehrsbüros legt *fvw* großen Wert auf objektive Berichterstattung, dazu gehört auch das Offenlegen dieser Geldquellen. Eine weitere Besonderheit ist, daß die Redaktionsmitglieder für ihre Privatreisen keine Ermäßigungen von Veranstaltern annehmen dürfen. Damit will sich *fvw* von der im Reisejournalismus durchaus üblichen Praxis distanzieren.

Neben der Hauptausgabe erstellen die 16 Redakteure und die rund 47 freien Mitarbeiter von *fvw* eine ganze Reihe von Sonderbeilagen. Dazu gehören zum Beispiel die *Counter-Info*-Hefte, die in unregelmäßigen Abständen erscheinen. Sie behandeln jeweils ein bestimmtes Land oder eine Region und bestehen aus Reportagen, Interviews, Meinungen von Veranstaltern und einem größeren Serviceteil. Auch Probleme der Region, die den Reisenden betreffen könnten, werden dargestellt. Alles zusammen soll den Verkäufern in den Reisebüros eine Hilfestellung sein.

Im *Destination-Report* werden je einmal im Jahr verschiedene Großräume (Asien/Pazifik, USA/Kanada, Afrika, Lateinamerika/Karibik, Mittelmeer) unter die Lupe genommen. Dabei geht es mehr um **sachliche Informationen** als um emotionale Reisebeschreibungen. Buchungszahlen, die neuen Angebote der Veranstalter, Trends, Veranstalter-Meinungen und andere Daten und Fakten stehen im Vordergrund.

Auch je einmal im Jahr gibt es die *Fachreports* zu den Themen Bus, Hotel, Informationstechnologie und Schiff. Dabei geht es um die Vermittlung von sachlichen Informationen zu den jeweiligen Thema, wie zum Beispiel neue Angebote, Buchungsmöglichkeiten für die Reisebüros, etc.

Die Wirtschaftsdaten der Tourismusbranche stehen auch bei den jährlich erscheinenden *Dokumentationen* (*Europäische Veranstalter in Zahlen*, *Reisebüroketten/ Kooperationen in Zahlen* und *Der deutsche Veranstaltermarkt in Zahlen*) im Vordergrund. Daneben gibt es Sonderhefte, zum Beispiel zur Internationalen Tourismus-Börse oder zu anderen aktuellen Themen. Reisen als Wirtschaftsfaktor, ohne verträumt-romantische Bilder von Palmenstränden - auch das kann Reisejournalismus sein.

5.8 *GEO SAISON*

Martin Sonnleitner

Vor über 20 Jahren fing alles an. 'Das Auge' Rolf Gillhausen und sein Text-Kollege Rolf Winter erfanden das Magazin *GEO*. Im Laufe der Jahre wurden die drei Ableger des Wissenschaftsjournals geboren: 1981 *GEO Special*, 1987 *GEO Wissen* und *GEO SAISON*. Letzteres arbeitet als Monatsjournal multithematisch ganz auf das Thema Reisen fixiert.

Nach einem einleitenden Vorwort der Chefredakteurin, stößt der Leser zunächst einmal auf Werbung, Tips, Tricks und Trends, bevor die erste Geschichte erscheint. Hier wird schnell deutlich, daß dem Leser **eine imaginäre Welt** suggeriert werden soll. Die Reise möge schon im Sessel oder der U-Bahn beginnen und muß nicht nach London oder Mallorca führen. *GEO SAISON*, das ist das Reisemagazin für den durchschnittlich verdienenden, aufgeklärten Durchschnittsbürger, der sich Reisen leisten kann, aber nicht reisen muß.

Der Redaktion gehören eine Chefredakteurin und ein stellvertretender Chefredakteur an. Weiter besetzen je eine Person die Grafik und das Sekretariat. Den geschriebenen Teil verantworten sechs Textredakteure. Knapp ein Drittel seiner Arbeitszeit verbringt der Redakteur mit dem Schreiben von Beiträgen. Den Rest der Zeit erledigt er sonstige anfallende Schreibtischarbeit: Hierzu gehören konzeptionelle Arbeit, Themen finden und Texte freier Autoren redigieren.

Das Reisen der Redakteure reduziert sich per anno durchschnittlich auf zwei bis drei längere Aufenthalte von ungefähr vierzehn Tagen. Hinzu kommen ein paar Kurztouren. „Es ist für die Recherche hilfreich, macht Spaß und erweitert extrem den Horizont, selber vor Ort zu sein und sich voll ins Geschehen hineinzubegeben", weiß eine Praktikerin zu berichten.

Zum 20. Geburtstag von *GEO* schrieb die *taz*: Oft tolle Fotos, manchmal gute Reportagen und ein Layout wie am ersten Tag.

Noch heute finden sich bei jedem Trödler neben den Kisten mit Büchern und alten Fotoalben stets Kartons voll guterhaltener *GEO*-Ausgaben. Darunter manch legendäres Exemplar - wie die Ausgabe vom August 1981. Damals grinste ein chinesischer Pandabär vom Titel, und im Editorial warb Chefredakteur Rolf Winter für die zugehörige Sensationsstory: „Als erstem westlichem Reporter" sei es einem *GEO*-Fotografen gelungen, Bilder der „legendären, vom Aussterben bedrohten Panda im Naturreservat Wolong" zu schießen. So schwer war das aber gar nicht, denn die abgebildeten Tiere stammten nicht aus der Wildnis, sondern aus einem chinesischen Freigehege, wie der World Wildlife Fund aufdeckte. *GEO's* erster kleiner Skandal...

(Gehrs 1996)

Einmal in der Woche findet auf der Konferenz die Heftbesprechung statt, wobei auf ein ausgewogenes **Verhältnis von langen und kurzen Texten** geachtet wird. Große Themen werden bis zu einem Jahr im voraus geplant. Bei der Text- und Bildauswahl, die gemeinsam und demokratisch (die Chefredakteurin hat ein Veto-Recht) erfolgt, müssen inhaltliche Ausgewogenheit und Balance ebenso berücksichtigt werden, wie die Anforderungen der jeweiligen Saison. Ein Land, über das im Mai berichtet wurde, kann im September nicht schon wieder im Heft erscheinen. Ein klassisches Sommerthema sei Irland, im Winter werden dementsprechend die Skigebiete thematisiert.

Zur Bearbeitung der Themen steht im Hause *Gruner+Jahr* eine Dokumentation zur Verfügung, die sich aus einer Bibliothek und einem Fotoarchiv zusammensetzt. Sie soll jedoch lediglich zur Vorbereitung dienen und den Autoren Vorkenntnisse vermitteln. Man wolle die meisten Geschichten nicht 'kalt', sondern aktuell servieren. Lediglich beim Bildmaterial kommt es vor, daß archivierte Fotos in aktuellen Ausgaben erscheinen.

Bis vor kurzen wurden die **Recherchereisen** bei *GEO SAISON* noch selber bezahlt. Weil die Auflage im Verhältnis zu den Produktionskosten jedoch zu gering war, mußte gespart werden. Also ließ sich die Redaktion auf Sponsorenreisen ein. „Wir schreiben allerdings sowieso nur über Länder, in die gereist werden soll", findet eine klare Abgrenzung zum Politjournalismus statt.

Einige Themen und deren Darstellung würden jedoch heftig diskutiert und sogar gestrichen werden, weil die gegenwärtige Lage des Landes nicht akzeptabel sei. „Wir sind auch kritisch, es geht nicht nur um schöne Seiten," wird von der Redaktion verkündet. „Wir wollen die Leute an den Ort schikken, müssen deshalb die Nachteile erwähnen."

Im Vordergrund jedoch stehen bei *GEO SAISON* die **Reiselust, Erholung und Abenteuer**. Es geht um verrückte, ausgefallene, aber nachvollziehbare Geschichten, die nicht für ein breites Publikum zugänglich sein sollen, wie zum Beispiel eine Höhlentour in Thailand oder Fallschirmspringen in Kalifornien. Man wolle einigermaßen wache Leute ansprechen, die bewußt reisen. Die Zielgruppe sind Leser Anfang 30, aus der Mittelschicht kommend. Mittelmäßig verdienende, die 'ein bißchen intellektuell' sind.

Die **Auseinandersetzung mit dem Fremden** erfordert Zurückhaltung und Offenheit. Eine Redakteurin schildert ihre Herangehensweise, bei der sie Stereotypen vermeiden will, wie folgt: „Ich beobachte sehr viel, versuche die Leute kennenzulernen und spreche sie an, versuche ihnen aber nicht zu nahe zu treten. Vorsicht vor Vorurteilen ist permanent geboten."

Dies wird auch von den freien Autoren und Fotografen erwartet. Ungefähr 50 Mitarbeiter bereichern mit ihren Texten und Bildern die Ausgaben von *GEO SAISON*.

Zieht man ein Fazit, ist bei dem Reisemagazin die Intention erkennbar, Länder dem Leser schmackhaft zu machen.

Im Gegensatz zum grünen *GEO*, das seine Themen von allen Seiten durchleuchtet, soll *GEO SAISON* vordergründig die Sonnenseiten darstellen. Schließlich ist Reisen nach wie vor eines der beliebtesten Hobbies der Deutschen.

5.9 *GLOBO*

Diana Lühmann

GLOBO gehört wie *GEO SAISON* und *abenteuer&reisen* zu den **multithematischen Reisemagazinen** und wurde 1989 von der deutschen Tochter des Schweizer *Ringier-Verlags* und als Partner des amerikanischen *National Geographic Traveler* gegründet. Das Magazin erscheint monatlich, seine Auflage liegt bei 100.000, wobei ein Drittel bis die Hälfte der Hefte von Abonnenten bezogen werden. Außerdem veröffentlicht *GLOBO* jährlich **zwei Sonderhefte**: Die Schwerpunkte lagen 1997 zum einen auf dem Reiseziel Österreich, zum anderen auf dem Urlaubsthema 'Kreuzfahrten'.

Da Service in der *GLOBO*-Redaktion ohnehin großgeschrieben wird, beschäftigt sich eine freie Mitarbeiterin ausschließlich mit dem Beantworten von Leser-Faxen, -Briefen und -Emails. Zusätzlich steht den Lesern in jeder Ausgabe eine Rubrik rund um Fragen zum Thema Reisen zur Verfügung, in der interessante Leserfragen beantwortet und aktuell Wissenswertes für Reisende aufgeführt wird.

Die Leserschaft von *GLOBO* ist der alljährlich durchgeführten Leserbefragung durch das Institut *AWA* zufolge zwischen 30 und 40 Jahren alt, gebildet, anglo-amerikanisch geprägt und verfügt über sehr gute Einkommen. Die Leser reisen viel - und das oft alleine. Sie organisieren ihre Touren und häufigen Kurz- bzw. Wochenendreisen gerne selber und haben Vorlieben für exklusive Gastronomie, Golf und Bergsteigen sowie für Kultur. *GLOBO*-'Stammleser' geben pro Jahr mehr als 14.000 DM fürs Reisen aus und bekleiden drei Mal so häufig die Führungsspitze eines Betriebs als der Durchschnitt der Bundesbürger. *GLOBO* wird von mehr Männern als Frauen gelesen, was sich nach Wunsch des Chefredakteurs jedoch bald wieder ändern soll: Seit dem letzten Jahr wird der für *GLOBO*-Reportagen typische *Guide* um mehr aktuelle Informationen für die Reise ausgebaut. Damit will das Magazin verstärkt die häufig allein reisende und an praktischen Tips interessierte Leserin ansprechen.

Die *GLOBO*-Redaktion mit Sitz in München umfaßt 16 feste Mitarbeiter, wobei das Verhältnis Frauen und Männer ausgeglichen ist. Der Altersdurchschnitt liegt bei durchschnittlich 30 Jahren. Viele der Redaktionsmitglieder haben erhebliche Berufserfahrungen. In einer Ausbildung möglichst im Tages- und Lokaljournalismus sieht der Chefredakteur auch die beste Basis für eine Arbeit im Reisejournalismus, aber auch im Journalismus generell: „Zuerst müssen die journalistischen Grundkenntnisse - etwa die W-Fragen oder 'Wie verfasse ich einen Artikel?' - erlernt werden. Dann kann man sich spezialisieren. Dabei sollte man aber stets offen für neue Arbeitsfelder bleiben und beispielsweise von der Politik noch zur Wirtschaft wechseln können." Für reisejournalistische Reportagen braucht der Journalist jedoch neben handwerklichen Fähigkeiten auch Talent und Sprachgefühl: „Was nützen die interessantesten Informationen, wenn die Dramaturgie einer Zehn-Seiten-Geschichte in sprachlicher Langeweile verödet?"

GLOBO-Redakteure verbringen ihre Arbeit nicht ausschließlich in Routinearbeit am Schreibtisch: „Wichtig ist uns, daß jeder in der Redaktion alle Stufen bis zur Herstellung eines Heftes mitgemacht hat. Und dazu gehört auch die **Recherche vor Ort**." Diese Reisen liegen bei maximal zwei bis drei Wochen und werden aus dem Budget des *Ringier-Verlags* finanziert. „Pressereisen sind die absolute Ausnahme - die anderen Reisen überwiegen mit 99%."

Neben den 16 festen Mitarbeitern greift *GLOBO* auf einen Stamm von 12 bis 20 Autoren sowie sechs bis zehn Fotografen zurück. Bei der Wahl der Fotografen tendiert das Magazin immer mehr zu Fotografen vor Ort. Die freien Autoren sind zwar in der Regel Kenner eines Landes, das aber meist, weil sie in ihrer beruflichen Praxis als Journalist schon viel herumgekommen sind, und nicht, weil sie vor Ort leben.

Ein guter reisejournalistischer Artikel definiert sich in der *GLOBO*-Redaktion über **drei 'Säulen'**:

- Die **Wahl des Themas**: Dabei muß auf die Wünsche der Leser eingegangen und die Aktualität beim Erscheinen des Heftes eingehalten werden. Da *GLOBO*-Leser zum Beispiel oft über ein verlängertes Wochenende verreisen, werden in jedem Heft auf einer Doppelseite 'Fluchtpunkte' für Kurzreisen vorgestellt.
- Die **Recherche**: Vor Ort soll nicht nur anhand von Büchern recherchiert, sondern mit den Menschen gesprochen werden, um ein 'Feeling für die Seele von Land und Leuten' zu bekommen.
- Der **Artikel**: Ein reisejournalistischer Artikel muß spannend geschrieben sein - das Sprachgefühl ist sehr wichtig. Außerdem sind Stereotypen verpönt: Für die Verwendung von 'Paradies' und 'Traum' müßte ein Autor in der Redaktion schon außerordentliche Überzeugungsarbeit leisten. Zudem bemüht sich die Redaktion, Anglizismen zu reduzieren und sie durch deutsche Ausdrücke zu ersetzen.

Die *GLOBO*-Artikel sind im Grunde nicht nur für das 'Reisen im Kopf' angelegt, sondern sollen den Appetit auf das Verreisen anregen und auch bei der Planung der nächsten Reise mit aktuellen Informationen zur Hand gehen. Am Ende jeder Reportage befindet sich deshalb der für *GLOBO* typische *Guide* von ein bis zwei Seiten Länge, so daß im Heft insgesamt um die 12 Seiten konkrete Tips und Ratschläge angeboten werden.

Bei den üblichen sechs langen Reportagen spielen die Bilder ebenfalls eine große Rolle, sind sie doch der Blickfang, der den Leser in die Fremde entführt und zum Reisen anregen soll. Deshalb sind bei *GLOBO* Bildunterschriften genauso wichtig wie die Reportage - und werden mit Sorgfalt formuliert.

Auch für Spaß ist Platz zwischen 'ernsten' Reportagen und Berichten. So ist in *GLOBO* zum Beispiel eine satirische Glosse erschienen, die mit zwinkerndem Auge über die Buchung einer Reise auf den Mond berichtete. Im Gegensatz dazu ist für hämische Verrisse kein Platz: „Dann schreiben wir lieber gar nicht über das Land. Um Land und Leute niederzumachen, sind uns unsere Seiten zu kostbar." Dennoch wird auch in *GLOBO* schon einmal von Reisen in bestimmte Regionen abgeraten, sei es aus medizinischen oder politischen Gründen. Dieses geschieht dann nicht in epischer Breite, sondern in zehn bis 15 Zeilen einer Nachricht an prominenter Stelle im Heft: „Schließlich wissen unsere Leser um die Krisengebiete unserer Erde."

Die **Zukunft des Reisejournalismus** sieht der Chefredakteur von *GLOBO* als Wachstumsfeld, in dem auch multithematische Magazine wie *GLOBO* weiterhin Bestand haben werden: „Reisen wird in unserer Gesellschaft immer alltäglicher. Allerdings hat sich die Faszination am Reisen verändert: Nur, weil man weit weg gewesen ist, erreicht man bei niemandem mehr einen 'Aha-Effekt'. Auf das 'Wie' und 'Was' kommt es an, nicht nur auf das 'Wo' - und so kann das 'Aha-Erlebnis' auch in der Nähe gefunden werden."

Eine Zukunft des Reisejournalismus online kann sich der Chefredakteur durchaus vorstellen, wenn sich dem neuen Medium angepaßte Konzepte durchsetzen und das Angebot im Internet professioneller wird: „Wir alle betrachten das Medium noch viel zu sehr mit den Augen des Printjournalisten. Die neuen Möglichkeiten müssen noch getestet und eigene Formen gefunden werden. Auf jeden Fall wird sich aber der Journalismus durchsetzen und die Amateure werden weitgehend verschwinden - wie sie aus dem Bereich des Privatfernsehens und des Privatradios verschwunden sind."

Noch 1997 wird auch *GLOBO* **online** gehen - wofür ein zusätzlicher Redakteur tätig sein wird. Geplant ist vor allem, den Service rund ums Reisen auszubauen und wie im Heft eine Art *Guide* zu stellen, in dem Termine regelmäßig 'updated' werden und eine Fülle von Daten zur Verfügung stehen.

Auch einen 'chatroom' zu Fragen und Anregungen zum Thema Reisen kann sich die Redaktion vorstellen - Vorbild ist die hauseigene 'Sprechstunde' zu Leserfragen. Nur Reportagen wie im Magazin wird es online nicht geben: „Wer liest sich denn zehn Seiten am Bildschirm durch? Da sind mehr praktische Reise-Informationen gefragt, nach denen man sich vielleicht sogar die Route, die Sehenswürdigkeiten und die Hotels zusammenstellen kann."

5.10 *Hamburger Abendblatt*

Martin Sonnleitner

Hamburg ist Deutschlands Pressemetropole Nummer 1. Hierzu ist sie im Zuge der Nachkriegszeit bis hin zur Gegenwart gewachsen. Die bedeutendste Hamburger Lokalzeitung ist das *Hamburger Abendblatt.*

Seit 1962 arbeitet der Reiseredakteur des *Hamburger Abendblattes* in der Redaktion dieses hanseatischen Renommierblatts. Am längsten im Lokalbereich, dann in der Politik. Es sei die Ausnahme, daß sich ein Journalist vornimmt, Reiseredakteur zu werden, berichtet der Praktiker. „Bei Tageszeitungen wird da sowieso nicht unterschieden. Jemand, der den Job gelernt hat, sollte fast alles können." Nun arbeitet der Routinier seit zehn Jahren im Reiseressort: Eher zufällig sei er dort hingelangt. Weil die Stelle besetzt werden mußte, sei die Wahl auf ihn gefallen. „Der Chefredakteur wird sich schon etwas dabei gedacht haben", kommentiert der Journalist. „Durch eine glückliche Fügung des Schicksals war ich auch privat viel auf Reisen. Seit 1959 jobbte meine Frau bei der *Lufthansa,* was auch den Familienmitgliedern das Reisen vergünstigte." So sei er hineingewachsen in das Geschäft, das sich mit Reisen und Touristik befaßt.

Um möglichst reibungslos arbeiten zu können, müssen eine Menge **Kontakte** geknüpft werden, was man erst nach einer gewissen Zeit als Reiseredakteur geschafft habe. Wozu diese Kontakte vonnöten sind, wird wie folgt beschrieben: „Reisebeschreibungen kommen überwiegend dadurch zustande, daß Einladungen angenommen werden, in der Regel von Fremdenverkehrsämtern oder von Reiseveranstaltern." Am Schreibtisch selektiert der Redakteur dann, welchen Veranstaltungen nachgegangen wird. Das wären jedoch keine Lustveranstaltungen: Sie seien kurz und stressig.

Anschließend entscheidet er, ob das Thema genug Stoff bietet, um darüber schreiben zu können. Es kommt auch vor, daß andere Mitarbeiter des *Hamburger Abendblatts* auf einer ihrer Reisen, sei es privat oder beruflich, auf ein interessantes Thema stoßen und sich an ihren Mitarbeiter aus dem

Reiseressort wenden. Das sei auch eine Frage der redaktionellen Besetzung: „Der Reiseteil des *Hamburger Abendblatt* bin ich. Ich bin ein Einzeltäter."

Die Reiseseiten erscheinen in jeder **Wochenendausgabe**. Für die Realisierung ist der Reiseredakteur alleine verantwortlich. Unter diesen Prämissen gelingt es ihm eher selten, eine Geschichte selber zu recherchieren: „Es bindet einen erheblich an den Schreibtisch, einen hohen Anteil fremder Texte bearbeiten, in Form bringen und Bilder beschaffen zu müssen." Die redaktionsgebundene Arbeit belaufe sich auf ca. 85 Prozent. Einer, der das Blatt mache, könne es nicht nebenbei auch noch vollschreiben.

So bedient sich das Reiseressort im *Hamburger Abendblatt* in einem hohen Maße **freier Mitarbeiter**, und das Angebot an freien Autoren ist groß: Fünf bis zehn Texte werden täglich wieder zurückgeschickt. Meist beauftrage er Mitarbeiter, die er über die Jahre kennengelernt habe, so der Ressortleiter.

Auf dem Schreibtisch häufen sich auch Mitteilungen **kommerzieller Anbieter**: Reise- und PR-Agenturen, Kurdirektoren, Reisefirmen und Veranstalter. Die Redaktion sei nicht verpflichtet, etwas zu nehmen: „Man guckt sich das Angebot an und sucht aus." Die Meldungen werden inhaltlich zusammengefaßt, die Rubriken gekennzeichnet. Es gibt Nachrichten, die rein objektive Tatbestände wiedergeben, und ausgewählte Angebote, in denen der Kommerz zur Sprache kommt. Lobpreisende Adjektive, die sich auf den Mitteilungen der Anbieter wiederfinden, werden jedoch relativiert.

Die **Auswahlprozesse** in der Redaktion richten sich nach dem bekannten Angebot-Nachfrage-Prinzip. Es gibt **Reiseanalysen**, die das Reiseverhalten der deutschen Touristen beschreiben. Fernreisen seien laut jüngster Untersuchungen rückläufig. Von daher wäre es verfehlt, ständig ferne Ziele zu präsentieren. Besonders beliebt sei als Reiseziel immer noch das eigene Land: Deutschland. Man wolle keine speziellen Interessen bedienen, sondern ein **breites Publikum** ansprechen.

Die Reiseseiten erscheinen nur zum Wochenende, also dann, wenn das Abendblatt eine Auflage von über 400.000 Exemplaren hat, ungefähr 100.000 mehr als in der Woche. Der Seitenumfang des Ressorts Reise schwankt: Eher üppig ist er zwischen Mitte Januar und Mitte Mai, wo er bis zu 20 Seiten beträgt. Den Rest des Jahres sind es nur circa sechs Seiten. „Dies hängt vom Anzeigenaufkommen ab, das saisonalen Schwankungen unterliegt", erklärt der Redakteur.

Eine konkrete **Zielgruppe** hat das *Hamburger Abendblatt* nicht. Umfragen haben ergeben, daß die Leser aus allen Alters- und Gesellschaftsschichten kommen. Wichtig sei aber die Abgrenzung zu anderen Ressorts, die aufgrund inhaltlicher Verwandtschaft Dublettengefahr bergen. Die stärkste Affinität weist das Reiseressort zum Wirtschaftsressort auf. Hier müssen eventuelle Berührungspunkte inhaltlich und konzeptionell abgegrenzt werden. Wenn zum Beispiel *TUI* eine Pressekonferenz bezüglich der Geschäftsberichte macht, sei dies 'originär wirtschaftlich'. Touristische Angebote, die auf Konferenzen vorgestellt werden, würden jedoch vom Reiseressorts bearbeitet. Anfang der Woche legt der Reiseredakteur den anderen Ressorts seine Themenplanung für das Wochenende vor. So können tendenzielle Doppelungen vermieden werden.

Es wird deutlich, daß der Reiseredakteur beim *Hamburger Abendblatt*, vielleicht prototypisch für seine Zunft, mehr Fädenzieher im Hintergrund als offensiver Rechercheur ist. Er muß das Gesammelte ordnen, um es in eine angemessene Form zu bringen und ist eher Abenteurer am Schreibtisch als in der Wildnis.

5.11 *Merian*

Achim Griesel

Die Zeitschrift *Merian* des *Jahreszeitenverlags* aus Hamburg ist die älteste Publikation im Bereich Reisejournalismus auf dem deutschen Markt. 1948 gegründet, hat sich die Intention der Zeitschrift nur wenig verändert.

Allerdings widmeten sich die ersten Hefte ausschließlich deutschen Städten, die während des Krieges zerstört wurden. In diesen Heften wurde einerseits das Ausmaß der Zerstörung dokumentiert, andererseits mit Hilfe von Archivbildern und Aussagen Überlebender ein Bild der Städte und ihrer Kultur vor dem Krieg gezeigt, um kulturelle Werte zu bewahren. 1953 wurde mit dem Heft über Paris zum ersten Mal eine Kulturmetropole außerhalb Deutschlands vorgestellt. Auch heute noch gilt das Hauptaugenmerk der Kultur des vorgestellten Reiseziels. Inzwischen liegt die Auflage bei zwölf Ausgaben im Jahr.

„*Merian*, das Monatsheft der Städte und Landschaften" - dieser hauseigene Werbeslogan beschreibt passend die Ziele des Reisemagazins. Monat für Monat soll den Lesern ein anderes Ziel, ob Stadt, Land oder Region, vorgestellt werden, das eine Reise wert ist. Anders als üblich geht die *Merian*-Redaktion dabei den **Weg der Themenhefte**, d.h., daß sich ein Heft auch immer nur mit einem Ziel beschäftigt. Bisher sind knapp 700 Titel erschienen, wobei viele Titel lange auf dem Markt verweilen. Wichtig ist in diesem Zusammenhang, die Philosophie des Verlages zu kennen. *Merian* versteht sich, 'in guter, alter Tradition', als Sammlerobjekt und nicht als reines Kon-

sumprodukt. Die Hefte und ihre Inhalte sind auf Haltbarkeit ausgelegt. Selbst der Serviceteil beinhaltet nur Adressen, bei denen auf Jahre die Authentizität gewährleistet ist. So fließen ebenfalls kaum aktuelle Betrachtungen ein, die ein, zwei Jahre später nicht mehr nachvollziehbar wären. Das *Kulturmagazin für Reisende* will feuilletonartig die schöne, heile Welt, mit dem Ziel beschreiben, vorwiegend kulturelle Hintergründe zu den Reisezielen zu vermitteln, um Verständnis für Land und Leute zu erreichen.
Diese Philosophie spiegelt sich auch in folgenden Punkten wider:

- *Merian*-Hefte sind stets nur in Buchhandlungen oder im Abonnement zu beziehen. So erscheinen sie auch unter dem 'label' des *Hoffmann und Campe Verlags*, Hamburg, der Buchtochter des *Jahreszeiten*-Hauses, heben sich allein dadurch von den 'schnell mal eben am Kiosk gekauften' Zeitschriften ab.

- Die Gestaltung und Verarbeitung - dickes Papier, kartonierter Umschlag mit Schutzrücken - stellt eine optische Aufwertung gegenüber anderen Publikationen dar.

- Mit derzeit 14,80 DM ist *Merian* nicht nur mit die teuerste Reisepublikation, sondern befindet sich preislich auf gleichem Niveau mit Sammlereditionen anderer Printbereiche (z.B. Sammlercomics).

Auch die Auswahl der Themen zeigt, daß es sich bei *Merian* um eine Zeitschrift handelt, die über **Stammleser** verfügt. So kann man es sich erlauben, auch unpopuläre Länder, Städte und Regionen vorzustellen, d.h. Bereiche, in denen weder Tourismus noch Anzeigenkunden reichlich vorhanden sind.

An diesem Umstand orientiert sich die Auswahl und Reihenfolge der zu veröffentlichenden Themen. „Was war noch nicht, was war lange nicht und was hat sich schon wieder verändert?" sind die leitenden Fragen bei der Themenauswahl. Hefte über Städte wie New York werden häufiger neu ausgearbeitet, da sich die Stadt schnell wandelt und die Hefte 'well-seller' sind.

Die Vorlaufzeit für ein Heft beträgt ungefähr ein Jahr. Der Jahresplan wird derart gestaltet, daß populäre Themen in anzeigenschwache Monate und außergewöhnliche Themen in anzeigenstarke Monate gelegt werden, um ein Gleichgewicht bei den Einnahmen aus Anzeigen und Verkauf zu erreichen. Für Planung und Organisation sind die sechs Heftredakteure verantwortlich, wobei jeder Redakteur bis zu zwei Hefte im Jahr eigenverantwortlich betreut.

Die *Merian*-Redaktion umfaßt 25 Mitarbeiter, vom Chefredakteur bis zur Heftassistenz. Der Redakteur konzipiert das Heft, informiert sich über das Ziel durch eine, je nach Ziel, bis zu vierwöchigen Reise und organisiert und instruiert die Autoren. Als Mitarbeiter fungieren stets freie Autoren von hohem Rang oder hoffnungsvolle Nachwuchskräfte, die bereits Veröffentlichungen und Preise vorweisen können. Im Heft *Neuseeland* vom August 1996 schreibt unter anderen der Schriftsteller Sten Nadolny über Europäer, die vom Aussteigen träumten und ein neues Leben in Neuseeland fanden. Der Präsident des nationalen Schriftstellerverbandes Neuseelands, Gordon McLauchlan stellt dar, was seine Landsleute bewegt und worauf sie stolz sind. Auch die international bekannte Autorin Keri Hulme, ihres Zeichens Neuseeländerin, verfaßte exklusiv für *Merian* einen Text über das Leben an der einsamen Westküste ihres Heimatlandes. In keiner anderen Reisepublikation haben so **viele renommierte Schriftsteller** veröffentlicht wie in *Merian*.

Die Reisen der Autoren und Fotografen werden aus Verlagsmitteln bezahlt, die Autoren müssen keinen Bezug zum Zielort haben, kommen aber häufig, speziell bei unpopuläreren Themen, aus dem betreffenden Gebiet. So gelingt eine eindrucksvolle Mischung aus (meist) gefühlvoll vorgetragenem Insiderwissen, (McLauchlan, Hulme) und objektiver Betrachtung (Nadolny). Neben den 'großen Geschichten', die Land, Leute und Leben aufzeigen sollen, gibt es in *Merian* kurze Beiträge über 'In'-Themen und Kultur. Im Heft *Neuseeland* werden sowohl Bungy-Jumping und Rugby als auch Umweltschutzmaßnahmen, Museen, kulturelle Hoffnungsträger und Aushängeschilder vorgestellt. Lady Valerie Solti, Frau des Dirigenten Sir Georg Solti, beschreibt im sogenannten *Corso* ein solches 'Stück' Neuseeland: die Sopranistin Kiri Te Kanawa.

Der **Serviceteil** ist für *Merian* ein „Tribut an den Markt, denn auch ein an Hintergründen interessierter Leser möchte wissen, wo er gut essen und schlafen kann". Allerdings wird bei der Adressenauswahl Wert auf deren Beständigkeit gelegt, weshalb es sich dabei eher um Adressen der gehobeneren Preisklasse handelt. Für die Auswahl sind der Themenautor und der Heftredakteur verantwortlich. Zum Serviceteil gehören aber auch Büchertips zum Thema, Reiseroutenvorschläge am Zielort sowie geschichtliche Fakten und aktuelle Daten.

Eine Besonderheit im Serviceteil sind die Stadtpläne und Karten, die von der Redaktion selbst konzipiert werden. Das Muster dieser Karten ist so detailgenau, daß sie straßenverkehrstauglich sind. Eigens von *Merian* entwickelt und entworfen, stellen diese Karten ein Zugeständnis an den veränderten

Markt dar, wodurch sich *Merian* auch als Reiseführer und nicht nur als heimatliche Vorbereitungs- oder Informationslektüre anbieten möchte.

Das gleiche Ziel wird mit dem Vorhaben verfolgt, *Merian online* über *CompuServe* anzubieten. Dieses Angebot wird in der *Merian*-Redaktion aber schlicht als PR-Maßnahme gesehen, man erwartet dadurch keine neuen Leser. Es soll lediglich auch die junge Generation auf *Merian* aufmerksam machen. Das elektronische Angebot wird durch *Merian*-Städteführer auf CD-ROM ergänzt.

Merian ist die **'große alte Dame' des Reisejournalismus** in Deutschland. Dieser ehrenwerte Ruf ist aber auch ein Manko im Bestreben, junge Leser zu gewinnen. Oft gelten die qualitativ hochstehenden Texte als angestaubt oder zu trocken. *Merian* wird jedoch noch als eines der wenigen verbliebenen, originär gestalteten Produkt angesehen. Es verbindet Kultur- und Reisejournalismus, ohne plakativ schönredend oder überkritisch zu werden.

5.12 *Segeberger Zeitung* und *NordExpress*

Kathrin Voss

Reisejournalismus in kleineren Lokalzeitungen und in örtlichen Anzeigenblättern unterliegt ganz eigenen Gesetzen und Regeln. Die Reiseseiten sind in diesen Publikationen eher zusätzlicher Service für die Leser und nur selten ein wirklich fester Bestandteil des Blattes. Die Berichte über lokale Ereignisse haben im jeden Fall Vorrang, sind sie doch auch der Grund für die Leser, diese Zeitungen in die Hand zu nehmen. Daher **steht der Reisejournalismus weit hinten an**, was sich oft dadurch ausdrückt, daß es kein Reiseressort im eigentlichen Sinne gibt. So ist es auch bei der Lokalzeitung *Segeberger Zeitung* und dem zum selben Verlag gehörenden Anzeigenblatt *NordExpress*, das einmal in der Woche erscheint.

Reisethemen werden von einem Redakteur des Anzeigenblattes *NordExpress* neben der anderen Arbeit erledigt. Er erstellt für das Anzeigenblatt in unregelmäßigen Abständen Reiseseiten, die je nach Platzangebot und Anzeigenaufkommen auch in die Lokalzeitung kommen. Die finanzielle Seite ist dabei ausschlaggebend: Ohne **ausreichendes Anzeigenaufkommen** für diese Reiseseiten, würde es sie nicht geben. Meldungen und kleinere Berichte erscheinen daher fast jede Woche im *NordExpress*, größere Reportagen hingegen nur im Abstand von mehreren Wochen.

Der Alltag des Reiseredakteurs wird somit auch eher von seinen Aufgaben im Lokaljournalismus bestimmt. Nebenbei werden die Pressemeldungen der Touristikunternehmen und der staatlichen Fremdenverkehrsbüros sortiert. Dabei wird darauf geachtet, was den Leser interessieren könnte: Was ist neu? Was ist interessant? Exotische Ziele und **exotische Veranstalter werden aussortiert**. Was nachher, zum Beispiel als Meldung, ins Blatt kommt, wird letztendlich auch durch den Bearbeitungsaufwand entschieden. Pressemitteilungen, die sich leicht in Artikel verwandeln lassen, haben dabei größere Chancen, denn schließlich hat der Lokaljournalismus Priorität, alles andere ist nur zusätzlicher Service.

Die großen Reisereportagen entstehen alle im eigenen Haus und werden von Redakteuren aus allen Ressorts (Lokales, Sport) geschrieben. Zwar kommen auch immer wieder professionelle Reisejournalisten auf die Redaktion zu und wollen ihrer Reportagen verkaufen, aber die geforderten Honorare sind zu hoch. So sind es meist die Privatreisen von Redakteuren und freien Mitarbeitern der Zeitung, die zu Reisereportagen verarbeitet werden. Auch werden ab und zu Einladungen zu Pressereisen angenommen, für die sich die festangestellten Redakteure allerdings Urlaub nehmen müssen. Bei diesen **Reisen** wird darauf geachtet, das sie **für eine Zielgruppe** gedacht sind, die auch in der Leserschaft der Zeitung vertreten ist. So fallen exotische Reiseberichte meist weg, werden aber auch nur sehr selten angeboten. Ziele in der näheren Umgebung, zum Beispiel Skandinavien, werden bevorzugt.

Neben diesen Reisereportagen gibt es von Zeit zu Zeit noch Berichte über Leserreisen, die von der Anzeigenabteilung des Verlages veranstaltet werden. All das geschieht unabhängig von der Redaktion und findet deshalb auch nur selten den Weg in den redaktionellen Teil der Zeitung oder des Anzeigenblattes. Aufgrund des geringen Umfanges solcher Reiseseiten müssen auch die Reisereportagen ganz besonderen Anforderungen entsprechen. In den knapp 120 Zeilen, die hier eine Reportage im Durchschnitt lang ist, ein ganzes Land zu beschreiben ist wohl unmöglich. Deshalb beschränken sich die Berichte meist auf wenige Aspekte des Zieles. Ein besonderer Ort oder ein spezielles Ereignis werden in den Vordergrund gestellt und soll sich wie ein roter Faden durch die ganze Reportage ziehen.

5.13 *surfers*

Astrid Kusser

Die Zeitschrift *surfers* ist ein Special interest-Magazin. Wer nicht selbst surft, hat von den letzten Meldungen über Segel und Boards nicht viel. Dennoch bezeichnet der Chefredakteur und Geschäftsführer des Verlags sein Magazin auch als **Lifestyle**-Produkt. Reportagen über Surf-Reisen und die dazugehörigen Bilder sollen zum Träumen verleiten. Photos sind dabei sehr wichtig und mindestens im A4-Format: muskulöse Männer mit nacktem Oberkörper, im freien Fall an ihr Segel geklammert, während unter ihnen eine Zwölf-Meter-Welle zusammenbricht - und das ganze vor Hawaii. Der Untertitel von *surfers* lautet *the soul magazine*: **Atmosphäre und Gefühl** sind wichtig, das Magazin will nicht nur über die technischen Neuerungen des Sports informieren. Die Texte dazu bedienen sich einiger Wind- und Wellenromantik, wobei auch nicht davor zurückgeschreckt wird, den 'we are family'-Gedanken unter den Surfern zu verkünden.

Mit ihren Reisereportagen wollen die Redakteure ihre Leser gerade nicht mit allen wichtigen Informationen für die nächste Reise versorgen. Vielmehr werden vor Ort Wind und Wellen getestet, gute Spots gesucht und versucht, mit interessanten Leuten ins Gespräch zu kommen. Aus einer Reise entsteht fast immer mehr als eine Geschichte. Als die halbe Redaktion - abgesehen von der Grafikerin allesamt Surfer - einen Monat auf Hawaii verbrachte, wurde das gesamte Heft mit den Erlebnissen und Erfahrungen gefüllt. Im Anhang fanden sich auch mehrere Seiten praktische Informationen für Neuankömmlinge, jedoch überschrieben mit „Keine Angst, wir verraten nicht jede Überraschung, die euch erwartet".

Pro Ausgabe findet sich in *surfers* eine längere Reisereportage, dazu kleinere Berichte über besondere Ereignisse wie Regatten oder Surfertreffen und Meldungen zum Thema Surfspots. Reportagen aus Eigenproduktion werden entweder aus dem Reisebudget der Redaktion bezahlt - oder von **Sponsoren** finanziert. So läßt sich der vor allem für Windsurfen zuständiger Redakteur vom deutschen Fremdenverkehrsverein auf die British Virgin Islands einladen. Problematisch sei das nicht. Zum einen werden nur Einladungen angenommen, die zum Format des Magazins passen. Zum anderen wolle man sowieso die Welt der Windsurfer- und Wellenreiter beschreiben und nicht etwa auf politische oder wirtschaftliche Probleme eines Landes aufmerksam machen.

Für eigene Produktionen bleibt der zuständige Redakteur zwischen einer und mehreren Wochen vor Ort. Selbst zu surfen, ist dabei ein Muß. Die in den Reportagen beschriebene eigene Surfrealität könne nur empfinden, wer selbst unter den Wellen begraben werde und die Wichtigkeit eines perfekten Turns kennt. Reisen ist hier nicht Selbstzweck, sondern dient in erster Linie der Ausübung des Sports.

Die meisten Geschichten kauft die Redaktion bei **freien Mitarbeitern**. Das sind in der Regel Surfer, die nur ausnahmsweise Papier und Schreibmaschine anstelle eines Segels vor Augen haben. Für die Zeitschrift ist das nur von Vorteil, da nicht Reise, Aufenthalt und Spesen finanziert werden müssen, sondern nur Text und Bilder bezahlt werden. Die Autoren leben meist von und vor allem für den Sport und nicht etwa vom Schreiben. Sie haben Verträge mit Firmen, deren Logo sie auf dem Segel tragen oder deren Neopren-Anzüge sie anziehen. Verkaufen sie nun ihre Photos an Zeitschriften, ist das auch gleichzeitig Werbung für ihre Sponsoren. So wie der Sport lebt auch die Zeitschrift von Sponsoren und ihrer Werbung. *Surfers* hat eine Auflage von 38.000 Exemplaren, wovon jeweils ungefähr 24.000 verkauft werden. Für Anzeigenkunden ist die Zeitschrift trotzdem sehr interessant. Ihr Leserprofil ist nahezu perfekt: männlich, zwischen 20 und 30 Jahren, entweder finanziell gut gestellt oder aus Begeisterung dazu bereit, viel in den teuren Sport zu investieren - und im Optimalfall eine Kombination aus beidem.

5.14 *taz- Die Tageszeitung*

Kia Vahland

Taxifahrer haben es schwer mit der Reiseredaktion der *Tageszeitung*. Egal, was für Geschichten sie auf Lager haben - die Chancen, zitiert zu werden, stehen schlecht. Denn einem Autor, der auf einer Reise nur mit Taxifahrern gesprochen hat, mangelt es nach *taz*-Maßstäben an Tuchfühlung mit Land und Leuten. Wer dagegen die Lebensphilosophie einer Bananenverkäuferin oder eines Schuhputzers in Erfahrung bringt, wird schon eher mit Wohlwollen redigiert.

Die Devise der *taz*-Reiseredaktion ist **Lebensnähe**. Das setzt Kennerschaft und eine gute Beobachtungsgabe voraus: „Die Autoren sollen Bescheid wissen über das Reiseland; nicht ahnungslos mit naivem Blick losreisen“, sagt die Reiseredakteurin. Wer diese Erwartung erfüllt, kann sich geradezu literarischer Freiheiten erfreuen. Da darf die Reportage feuilletonistische Töne anschlagen oder politisch brisant sein. Und durch ein gut geschriebenes Stadtporträt kann auch mal eine fiktive Figur führen. Wenn sie nicht gerade Taxifahrer ist.

Eine **gute Story zählt mehr als touristischer Nutzwert**. Es gibt zwar auch die obligatorischen Servicehinweise, aber längst nicht jede Geschichte wird zum Nachreisen gedruckt. Viele Artikel sind eher nüchterne Bestandsaufnahme als Werbemaßnahme: Da ist von Altstadtsanierung die Rede statt vom bunten Orientbazar und von unverträglicher Tourismusindustrie statt von Sonnenuntergangs-Romantik. Das touristische ‘Marketing von Sinnlichkeit’ der ‘Robinsonclubs’ und Erlebnis-Händler wird aufs Korn genommen. Bissig soll es sein; Glossen sind gefragt und Verrisse möglich.

Da *Tageszeitungs*-Leser und -Mitarbeiter sich aber bei allen Übeln dieser Welt ihre Reisefreude bewahrt haben, gibt es **auch lustvoll unpolitische Reiseberichte**. So steht dann ein begeisterter Erlebnisbericht aus der Wüste Tunesiens neben der Warnung vor umweltgefährdendem Oasentourismus.

Im Unterschied zu anderen Tageszeitungen ist der *taz*-Reiseteil in der Regel **monothematisch**. Ein Land steht im Mittelpunkt und wird aus verschiedenen Perspektiven beschrieben. Dazu gehören ausführliche Rezensionen sowohl über Reiseführer als auch über literarische Schilderungen der Gegend. Auch Sachbücher von Freizeittheoretikern werden besprochen, denn eine eigene Freizeitredaktion hat die *taz* nicht. Fotos werden meistens bei externen Fotografen oder Agenturen bestellt. Sie zeigen fast immer Details. Auch bei der Bildauswahl wird also das Allgemeine im Besonderen gesucht.

Die Reiseredaktion der *taz* ist eine **Ein-Frau-Redaktion** mit einem Stamm von 20 festen freien Mitarbeitern. Im Redaktionsalltag nehmen das Organisieren und Redigieren mehr Platz ein als das Reisen und Recherchieren. Geplant wird maximal sechs Wochen im voraus, in der Themenauswahl ist die Redakteurin autark. Die *Tageszeitung* hat erst Ende der 80er Jahre den Reiseteil eingerichtet. „So hat die *taz* damals auf ein **Bedürfnis ihrer Leser** reagiert: Die sind sehr reiselustig, haben einen hohen Bildungsstand und wollen Hintergrundinformationen", so die Reiseredakteurin. Die Zeitung braucht die Reiseseiten noch aus einem anderen Grund: Etliche Groß- und Kleinanzeigen werden hier geschaltet. Und an Inserenten mangelt es dem finanzschwachen Blatt immer.

Auf eins legt die *Tageszeitung* jedoch Wert: Die Nähe von **Anzeigen- und Textteil** ist rein optischer Natur. Inserierende Reiseveranstalter genießen keine größere Aufmerksamkeit als nichtinserierende. Im Grunde müssen sich alle mit kleinen Servicehinweisen begnügen. Weswegen die *taz*-Reiseredaktion auf den Gästelisten der PR-Strategen nicht gerade die Nummer eins ist. „Erstmal sind wir suspekt", sagt die Reiseredakteurin. Das beruht durchaus auf Gegenseitigkeit. An den üblichen 3-Tage-Pressereisen nimmt die *taz* nur selten teil. Die Begründung: In so kurzer Zeit mit dicht gedrängtem Programm seien nur oberflächige Eindrücke von einem Land zu gewinnen.

Ganz ohne externe Partner kommt aber auch die *Tageszeitung* nicht aus. Die *taz* mit ihren chronischen Existenzsorgen kann ihren Autoren keine langen Recherchereisen finanzieren. Also kooperiert die Redaktion mit Fremdenverkehrsämtern und vereinbart maßgeschnittene Pressereisen. So werden die Kosten für Fahrt und Unterkunft gedeckt. Ob die freien Autoren jedoch auch ihre Miete in Deutschland zahlen können, ist bei 1,10 Mark Zeilenhonorar für Auslandsgeschichten eher fraglich.

Nicht alle Artikel sind Auftragsarbeiten. Eine schön formulierte Reportage mit einem klaren Thema hat auch ohne Auftrag eine Chance, in Druck zu gehen. Auch leicht selbstironisch klingende Ich-Reportagen sind möglich. „Allerdings sind die meisten unverlangt eingeschickten Manuskripte nicht verwertbare Tagebucheintragungen", urteilt die Redakteurin. Ein Reisejournalist brauche vor allem eine solide journalistische Vorbildung. Deshalb ihr Tip für Einsteiger: zuerst in anderen Ressorts das journalistische Handwerkszeug lernen und sich erst später an den literarisch anmutenden Reisereportagen versuchen.

Aber Berufserfahrung allein schützt noch nicht vor **Stereotypen** über andere Länder. „Wenn zum Beispiel eine Autorin das alte Macho-Bild von südlichen Ländern ausbreitet, redigiere ich das weg", so die Redakteurin, „die Vermeidung von Stereotypen ist bei der *taz* ungeschriebenes Gesetz." Ihrer Ansicht nach ist der Umgang mit dem Fremden vor allem eine Übungssache: Wer viel reise, könne dabei den Blick für das andere schärfen und eigene Vorurteile ablegen.

Das gilt natürlich auch für die Leser. Eine Beschwerde über den Mangel an Süßstoff in der Karibik ist bestenfalls glossenreif. Die Berichterstattung über schlechten Service im Urlaub überläßt die *taz* ganz der Boulevardpresse. Auch das andere Extrem, nämlich die voyeuristische Abenteuergeschichte über ein unerschlossenes Gebiet, will die Zeitung nicht drucken.

„Ein ziemlich unsauberes Geschäft" ist der Reisejournalismus in Augen der *taz*-Reiseredakteurin. Gerade freie Autoren müßten ständig um ihre journalistische Unabhängigkeit ringen. Das lohne sich aber, denn der Reise- und Freizeitbereich sei ein journalistisches Wachstumsfeld. Auch für Tageszeitungen.

5.15 *DIE ZEIT*

Martin Sonnleitner

„Die Exotik spielt sich hinter dem Schreibtisch ab", entmysthifiziert der Reiseredakteur der *ZEIT* den 'Traumjob Reisejournalist'. Es werden Post und Pressemeldungen bearbeitet und Themen besprochen. Ebenso gehören Kontakte mit den freien Autoren, deren Texte auch noch redigiert werden müssen, sowie Ideenkonferenzen zum redaktionellen Alltag.

Während die Redakteure vor allem organisieren und koordinieren, stammen etwa 80 Prozent der Berichte **aus der Feder freier Mitarbeiter**. Sie selber befinden sich per anno auf fünf bis sechs größeren Reisen von durchschnittlich einer Woche, dazwischen liegen Kurzreisen, wie Programmvorstellungen und auswärtige Pressekonferenzen. „Qua unseres Berufes, müssen wir in die Ferne fahren, freie Autoren reisen mehr, denn sie leben vom Schreiben", stellt der zuständige Redakteur fest.

Pressekonferenzen erfordern im Schnitt einmal pro Woche die Präsenz des Journalisten. Eine ressorteigene Redaktionskonferenz wird zweimal pro Woche vereinbart, einmal in der Woche eine Konferenz der gesamten *ZEIT*-Redaktion. Es arbeiten eine Ressortleiterin, zwei Redakteure und zwei Sekretärinnen im Reiseressort der *ZEIT*.

Die Tourismusbranche sei, ökonomisch betrachtet, eine der wichtigsten Branchen der Welt, weiß der befragte Redakteur, der gelernter Wirtschaftsjournalist ist, zu berichten. Stichworte hierfür wären Fluggesellschaften, Hotelketten, Mietwagen- und Kreditkartenunternehmen. Auch die Tatsache, daß der Tourismus für viele Länder in der Dritten Welt an vorderster Stelle stehe, sei ein Indiz für die global-ökonomische Relevanz der Branche. Obwohl die **Übergänge zum Wirtschaftsressort** fließend seien und sich manchmal überschneiden würden, gelte es, sich thematisch und inhaltlich abzugrenzen.

Um dem Anspruch an den Leser gerecht zu werden, bieten die Reiseseiten der *ZEIT* eine **Mischung aus Aktualität und schönen Lesegeschichten**. Der Leser soll eine Geschichte nicht nur nachreisen, sondern geistig auch nachleben können. Hierzu diene das Reisefeuilleton, welches sich dem Thema Reisen auf kulturellem und unterhaltendem Niveau bediene.

Ebenso will man durch die Darstellung von Trends, Terminen und Themen aktuell sein und sich an der Entwicklung der Branche beteiligen. So schrieb ein Mitarbeiter im letzten Jahr eine längere Geschichte über die Schweiz. Er besuchte vier Wintersportorte. Anhand dieser Orte hat er die Probleme der Schweiz dargestellt, die sie im Moment mit dem Tourismus hat. „Ich wollte erklären, warum die Touristenzahlen ständig zurückgingen und welche Konzepte die Zielgruppen wieder ansprechen könnten."

Das Layout der Reiseseiten in der *ZEIT* ist für den Leser einfach zu durchforsten. Nach den Leitgeschichten stößt der Freund der Ferne auf redaktionell klar getrennte Werbeseiten. Geschickt gelöst ist der Serviceteil. Unter der Seitenüberschrift *Reise-Information-Hintergrund* werden dem Leser notwendige Fakten serviert.

Finanziert werden die Presseeisen aus unterschiedlichen Quellen. „Wir bezahlen die Reisen teilweise selber, der größte Teil kommt jedoch von außen. Es wird eine **Brücke zwischen Werbung und redaktioneller Unabhängigkeit** gebaut. Die Partner werden im Serviceteil erwähnt, haben jedoch keinen Einfluß auf den redaktionellen Inhalt." Freie Autoren seien von Sponsoren abhängiger, die Redaktion verlange jedoch Objektivität.

Beim **Umgang mit dem Fremden** will das Reiseressort der *ZEIT* vermitteln. Wenn ein Land wie Japan der deutschen Mentalität fern liegt, hält es die Redaktion für ihre Aufgabe, andere Kulturkreise dem Leser nahe zu bringen. „Bei einer dreitägigen Inforeise mit 20 Reisejournalisten fällt es schwer, realistische Eindrücke über ein Land zu bekommen.“ Gut sei es, wenn die Gruppe nicht so groß ist. Es wird für sinnvoll gehalten, vorher ein paar Bücher zu lesen. Ebenso sollte man Personen kontakten, „die nicht mit dem Tourismus direkt zu tun haben, sondern sich in der Gesellschaft auskennen", resümiert der befragte Journalist die Prämissen, um einer Toleranz, Verständnis und Neugier verpflichteten Berichterstattung gerecht zu werden. Hierzu sei ein reelles Bild des bereisten Landes von Nöten, man wolle keine Traumwelten suggerieren.

Schließlich ist der potentielle *ZEIT*-Leser geistig anspruchsvoller Natur und wird als ‘Zahnarzt aus Gummersbach’ definiert, und das, obwohl die intellektuelle Wochenzeitung eine Auflage von 465.000 Exemplaren hat.

Die Bedeutung von Reiseteilen nimmt zu. Die Tageszeitung *DIE WELT* wirbt sogar mit der Qualität ihrer Reiseberichterstattung für Abonnenten.[1)]

Einsame Trauminseln, verschwiegene Almenhütten,
elegante Top-Hotels, Tips für Globetrotter
und eine große deutsche Tageszeitung.

Sehr geehrte Leserin,
sehr geehrter Leser,

die Welt hat so viel zu bieten. Wir sorgen dafür, daß Ihnen wirklich nichts entgeht.

DIE WELT - Deutschlands einzige überregionale Tageszeitung aus der Hauptstadt - hat nicht nur ein waches Auge für Politik, Wirtschaft und Kultur, sondern auch für entspanntes Reisen, gepflegtes Speisen und erlebnisreiche Entdeckungstouren. Unsere Korrespondenten berichten aus aller Welt, führen Sie durch quirlige Metropolen, schattige Alleen, zünftige Biergärten, herrschaftliche Hotels und romantische Bistros. Manchmal auch direkt vor Ihrer Haustür.
Ein Service für alle: ob Deutschlandreisender oder Weltenbummler.

In unserem Reise-Teil finden Sie jeden Freitag neue Anregungen für Ihre ganz persönlichen Ausflüge in eine faszinierende Welt. Zweimal im Jahr erscheint zusätzlich unser umfassender Report ‘Reisen’.

(Werbeschreiben an potentielle Abonnenten vom 20. Januar 1997)

1) Wir haben uns um einen Bericht aus der Hamburger Reiseredaktion der *WELT* bemüht. Er kam nicht zustande, vor allem wegen der wenig kooperativen Haltung in der Redaktion.

5.16 Textanhang: Ergebnisse einer repräsentativen Befragung der Reiseressorts deutscher Zeitungen, Tourismusveranstaltern und Fremdenverkehrsvereinen

Der Münchner Reisejournalist Peter Linden hat in Kooperation mit der *Arbeitsgemeinschaft Berufliche Bildung der deutschen Zeitungsverlage* (*ABZV*) eine Befragung der Reiseressorts deutscher Zeitungen durchgeführt, an der sich 71 deutsche Tages-, Sonntags- und Wochenzeitungen beteiligt haben (Studie 1).

Zudem wurden in einem zweiten Lauf 14 Veranstalter und 16 Fremdenverkehrsämter befragt (Studie 2). Die Ergebnisse dieser Erhebung hat uns Peter Linden freundlicherweise zur Verfügung gestellt (Stand 1997):

5.16.1 Studie 1: Reiseressorts deutscher Zeitungen

Ziel und Inhalt der Befragung

Das Anzeigenvolumen aus der Tourismusindustrie hält sich stabil auf hohem Niveau, die Reisteile der Zeitungen sind daher wichtige Werbeträger. In keinem Ressort sind die Umfänge in den vergangenen 30 Jahren so stark gestiegen wie im Reiseressort, wobei Mitte der Sechziger Jahre die Zahl der Werbeseiten die Zahl jener mit redaktionellen Beiträgen überholt hat und die Kluft seither stetig wuchs.

Dennoch scheinen personelle und finanzielle Ausstattung zu stagnieren, dem Reiseressort wird überall ein seiner Bedeutung entsprechender Stellenwert eingeräumt. 71 von 444 deutschen Tages-, Sonntags- und Wochenzeitungen (Stand 1995, zitiert nach: BDZV-Jahrbuch, „Zeitungen 1996“) haben sich an unseren Umfrage zur Gegenwart und Zukunft des Reiseressort beteiligt.

Art der Fragen

Die Fragen an die Leiter der Reiseressorts waren in drei Bereiche eingeteilt. Erstens statische Angaben zur Arbeit im Reiseressort und zu den Honorarsätzen. Zweitens Angaben zur Qualität des Reiseteils und zur Akzeptanz seitens der Leser. Drittens Angaben zur thematischen Aufbereitung nach Darstellungsformen und Zielgebieten.

Ergebnisse der Befragung

1. These: Keine Zeitung kommt heute noch ohne einen Reiseteil aus.

Von 71 befragten Redaktionen gab nur eine (*Frankfurter Allgemeine Sonntagszeitung*) an, „wegen anderer Schwerpunkte“ auf einen Reiseteil zu verzichten. 14 Titel veröffentlichen eine Reisebeilage, 6 haben einen echten Reiseteil und eine Beilage, 62 verfügen über den klassischen Reiseteil.

2. These: Wegen ihrer Leserfreundlichkeit werden Reiseteile bevorzugt an Wochenenden veröffentlicht.

Reisen bedeutet Muße, Muße ist das Gegenteil von Hektik und Streß. Die scheint der Grund zu sein, daß keine einzige Zeitung ihren Reiseteil an einem Montag erscheinen läßt. Zum Wochenende hin wächst die Zahl der Reiseteile: Dienstag (3), Mittwoch (6), Donnerstag (7), Freitag (10). Am Samstag (46) und, falls als Erscheinungsdatum möglich, Sonntag (6) erscheinen insgesamt 52 Reiseteile. *Reutlinger General-Anzeiger* und *Main-Post* veröffentlichen zusätzlich einmal im Jahr eine Sonderbeilage ‘Reise’

3. These: Die Umfänge der Reiseteile schwanken extremer als in anderen Ressorts und sind nicht an journalistische Kriterien gebunden, sondern an das Anzeigenaufkommen.

Die extremsten „zwischen 8 und 32“ sowie „zwischen 3 und 18 Seiten“. Die äußersten Durchschnittswerte lagen bei einer halben Seite und bei 18 Seiten. 42 von 71 Titeln gaben den Durchschnittsumfang mit zwischen einer und drei Seiten an.

4.These: Reiseressorts müssen mit weniger Redakteuren auskommen als andere Ressorts.

Zahlreiche Redaktionen gaben an, das Ressort „Reise“ lediglich nebenbei betreuen zu lassen. Feste Redakteursstellen für die „Reise“ gab es zwischen 0,5 (einmal) und 4,5 (einmal). 27 Reiseredaktionen verfügen über einen Reiseredakteur, 10 über zwei, eine über 2,5 und drei über 3 Redakteursstellen.

5. These: Reiseredakteure kommen kaum zum Reisen. Recherche und Reportage erledigen freie Autoren.

Allein die *Münchner Abendzeitung* gab an, ohne regelmäßige Mitarbeit eines freien Journalisten auszukommen. Ansonsten ergaben sich extrem hohe Zahlen „fester Freier“: 18 Redaktionen beschäftigen bis zu fünf, 12 bis zu zehn, 9 bis zu fünfzehn, 14 Redaktionen sechzehn und mehr. Die übrigen Reiseressorts machten keine exakten Angaben.

6. These: Die freien Autoren werden weniger mit Geld als mit Naturalien entlohnt.

Trotz des hohen Zeitaufwandes und der hohen Spesen bezahlen 57 der 71 Redaktionen Beiträge für das Reiseressorts nicht höher als Beiträge für andere Ressorts, die Entlohnung scheint im Erlebniswert der Arbeit zu liegen.

Bei den übrigen erhalten die Reiseautoren mehr Geld, in zwei Fällen aber nur für Textbeiträge, nicht für Bildmaterial.

7. These: Weil Geld für Autoren fehlt, spielen PR-Texte im Reiseressort eine überdurchschnittliche Rolle.

Nur 7 der an der Umfrage beteiligten Redaktionen kommen ohne PR-Texte aus, 49 verwenden sie „manchmal“, 14 „oft“.

Dies deckt sich mit der Zufriedenheit, die bei der gleichzeitigen Stichproben-Befragung in der Tourismusindustrie gegenüber den Abdruckchancen von Pressediensten geäußert wurde.

8. These: Trotz materieller Probleme fühlen sich Reiseredakteure als kompetente und erfolgreiche Journalisten.

Nur 5mal wurde des Angebot im eigenen Reiseteil als „schlechter als das durchschnittliche redaktionelle Angebot“ bewertet, 53mal „ebenso gut“, 13mal sogar „besser“. Unter diesen 13 befinden sich auffallend viele Wochentitel.

9. These: Innerhalb der Gesamtredaktion sehen sich Reiseredakteure eher negativ bewertet.

Nur 10mal stuften die Reiseredakteure ihr Ressort als „eines der wichtigsten Ressorts“ ein, 45mal „ein Ressort unter vielen“, 16mal gar als „unwesentliches Ressort“.

10.These: Reiseredakteure sehen ihre Arbeit durch die Leser besser bewertet als durch die Kollegen aus anderen Ressorts.

Auf die Frage, welchen Stellenwert die Leser dem Reiseressort zuordneten, antworteten 17 mit „besonders wichtig“, 47 mit „ebenso wichtig wie das übrige redaktionelle Angebot“ und nur 6 mit „eher unwichtig“.

11. These: Reiseredakteure sehen für ihr Ressort überdurchschnittlich gute Entwicklungschancen.

44 sagten in der Umfrage eine „steigende Bedeutung“ des Reiseressorts voraus, 25 sehen die Entwicklung stabil, 1 Redakteur prophezeit „sinkende Bedeutung“. Entsprechend vermuten 15, daß der Umfang des Reiseteils steigen wird, während nur 2 sinkende Seitenzahlen vorhersagen. 51 sehen keine Veränderungen auf sich zukommen. Einmal wurde eine direkte Abhängigkeit vom Anzeigenvolumen angegeben.

12. These: Reiseredakteure arbeiten mehr an konzeptionellen Veränderungen als ihre Kollegen in anderen Ressorts.

Von den 21 Redaktionen, die an einer Umstrukturierung des Reiseteils arbeiten, wurden unter anderem folgende Verbesserungsabsichten genannt: Gezieltere Themenplanung, mehr Reportagen, besseres Layout, mehr Farbbilder, mehr Service, mehr Landkarten, stärkere Orientierung auf regionale Ziele, zusätzliches Freizeitmagazin, Rubrizierung, Produktion eines eigenen Reisemagazins.

13. These: Der Reiseteil ist ein Reportagenteil. Andere Darstellungsformen sind unterrepräsentiert.

Im Durchschnitt bestehen die Reisteile zu etwa 60 Prozent aus Reportagen, wobei 2mal der Spitzenwert von 90 Prozent angegeben wurde und 3mal ein Wert unter 30 Prozent. Es folgen Nachrichten mit 20 und Service mit 18 Prozent sowie 2 Prozent für Glosse und Kommentar. Nur zwei Redaktionen plazierten die Nachricht vor der Reportage, 35 Redaktionen gaben an, ohne Glossen und Kommentar auszukommen.

14. These: Die Wahl des Reiseziele hängt eher von subjektiver Einschätzung als vom Markt ab.

Der grobe Querschnitt ergibt eine Themenverteilung auf die Reiseziele Deutschland:Europa:Übersee von etwa 40:40:20. Individuell traten aber eklatante Unterschiede zutage. Alle drei Zielgebiete erreichten Spitzenwerte von 80 Prozent, die niedrigsten Werte lagen für Deutschland und Übersee bei 10 Prozent, für Europa bei 30 Prozent. Mehrere Redakteure gaben an, die Themenverteilung sei „noch unorganisiert“. Als Schwerpunkte werden besonders häufig die USA, Österreich und die neuen Bundesländer genannt. Es wurden aber auch zahlreiche „exotische“ Schwerpunkte angegeben, die sich weder politisch noch touristisch begründen lassen wie nordamerikanische Kordillieren, Afrika, Asien, Dänemark, Benelux-Länder, Nordrhein-Westfalen.

5.16.2 Studie 2: Reiseveranstalter und Fremdenverkehrsvereine

Ziel und Inhalt der Befragung

Um eine bessere Kooperation zwischen den Reiseressorts der Zeitung und Reiseveranstaltern sowie Fremdenverkehrsämtern zu erzielen, haben wir außer einer repräsentativen Befragung der Zeitungen Deutschlands auch stichprobenartig 14 Veranstalter und 16 Fremdenverkehrsämter befragt. Unter den Veranstaltern sind Hotelketten (6), Airlines (2) sowie Pauschalanbieter (6), die Fremdenverkehrsämter verteilen sich auf Deutschland (2 Bundesländer), Europa (7 Länder) und andere Kontinente (7 Länder).

Art der Fragen

Die Fragen waren in zwei Themenbereiche unterteilt.
Zum ersten ermittelten wir die Art der Zusammenarbeit zwischen Veranstaltern und Medien, die Höhe der Investitionen in klassische Werbung und Direktbetreuung von Journalisten, Trends auf dem Gebiet der Investitionen und Wirkungsgrad eigener Pressedienste.

Zum zweiten erfragten wir die Bewertung einzelner Medien, ein hierarchische Auflistung der fünf besten Reiseteile, eine Beurteilung der inhaltlichen Qualität der Reiseteile sowie positive oder negative Erfahrungen mit unseriösen Journalisten und möglichen Konsequenzen daraus.

Ergebnisse der Befragung

1. These: Die Veranstalter werden in Zukunft mehr Geld in traditionelle Werbung bei Zeitung investieren.

Bei unserer Befragung gab nur ein Fremdenverkehrsamt eines europäischen Landes an, die Aufwendung reduzieren zu wollen. 96,6 Prozent planen für die Zukunft gleiche oder höhere Aufwendungen.

2. These: Die Direktbetreuung von Journalisten wird an Bedeutung gewinnen.

Keiner der 30 Befragten sagt ein Ende der Subventionierung von Pressereisen voraus. 23,3 Prozent wollen die Investition hierfür sogar steigern. Interessanterweise gaben 20 Prozent an, ausschließlich in Direktbetreuung zu investieren, ein Viertel der Befragten verteilt seine Investition zu gleichen Teilen auf klassische Werbung und Direktbetreuung.

3. These: Die Tages- und Wochenzeitung ist wichtigster Werbeträger der Tourismusindustrie.

Über 70 Prozent gaben an, mehr als ein Drittel des Gesamten Werbebudgets für Werbung bei Tages- und Wochenzeitung zu investieren.

4.These: Hauseigene Pressearbeit gilt bei Anbietern als äußerst erfolgreich.

90 Prozent verfügen über eine Presseabteilung mit durchschnittlich zwei Mitarbeitern. 73,3 Prozent der Befragten verfügen über einen regelmäßigen Pressedienst, 46,6 Prozent beurteilen dessen Abdruckchancen als sehr gut.

5. These: Die Tages- und Wochenzeitung gilt der Tourismusindustrie bei weitem als das angesehenste Medium.

63,3 Prozent der Befragen setzten die Zeitung in einer Hierarchie auf Platz eins gegenüber Fernsehen, Hörfunk, Zeitschriften und sogar die eigens aufgeführten Reisezeitschriften. 30 Prozent vergaben Rang zwei hinter Reise- und Fachpublikationen (hiervon zwei Drittel) und TV oder Hörfunk (ein Drittel).

6. These: Überregionale Tageszeitung mit ihren vielfältigen und vorwiegend unabhängig verfaßten Reportagen werden überdurchschnittlich positiv bewertet.

Vier Titel wurden je sechsmal in den Top-Fünf genannt: die *FAZ.*, die *Süddeutsche Zeitung*, die *Frankfurter Rundschau* und die *Westdeutsche Allgemeine.* Unter den wöchentlichen Publikationen erhielten *DIE ZEIT*, die *WELT am SONNTAG* und *Sonntag aktuell* je drei Nennungen. *Sonntag aktuell* gelang dies, obwohl das Blatt allein in Baden-Württemberg erscheint.

Interessant ist, daß Boulevardzeitungen und Regionalzeitungen vor allem von Veranstaltern genannt werden, während die überregionalen Titel sowie die Wochenzeitung die meisten Stimmen von den Fremdenverkehrsämtern erhielten.

7. These: Die Kritik an den Reiseteilen hat zwei Hauptaspekte. Es mangelt an Service und an journalistischer Sorgfalt.

Am häufigsten (9mal) wurden unkomplette oder fehlerhafte Servicekästen moniert, an zweiter Stelle stand seitens der Veranstalter der Kritikpunkt „keine Bereitschaft zur PR“ (4mal). Andererseits wurde von Fremdenverkehrsämtern auch zweimal „zuviel PR“ kritisiert. Die Themenauswahl sei überdies nicht dem Markt angemessen und „unausgewogen“ (5mal), bzw. „zu exotisch“.

Mangel an journalistischer Sorgfalt wurde häufig festgemacht an Klischeehaftigkeit (5mal), Unaktualität (5mal), schlechter Recherche und schlechten Bildern (4mal) sowie „Reiseführerstil“ (3mal).

Da die Kritikpunkte nicht im Multiple-Choice-Verfahren, sondern frei erfragt wurden, kommt diesen Mehrfachnennungen besondere Bedeutung zu.

8. These: Veranstalter und Fremdenverkehrsämter schützen sich gegen unseriöse „Reisejournalisten“. Die Methoden reichen von Gegenrecherche bis zur „Schwarzen Liste“.

Die Stichprobe ergab: 93,3 Prozent waren bereits mit unseriösen Anfragen konfrontiert, 16,6 Prozent nannten als Zusatz, dies sei „häufig" der Fall. Ohne negative Erfahrung blieben ein Fremdenverkehrsamt, das allerdings nach eigenen Angeben kein Budget für Reisejournalisten hat, sowie ein Anbieter von Studienreisen.

Fast alle Befragten reagieren strategisch auf Unseriösität, lediglich ein Fremdenverkehrsamt gab an, im try and error-Verfahren neue Namen zu testen. Die übrigen überprüfen bereits vor Erteilung einer Unterstützung durch Nachfrage bei den Redaktionen (46,6 Prozent), Rückfragen bei Kollegen (20 Prozent), Anforderung von Arbeitsproben (16,6 Prozent). Ein Unternehmen beschäftigt eigens ein Agentur, einmal wurde das Condor-Buch mit den Adressen der Mitglieder des *Vereins deutschen Reisejournalisten* (*VDR*) als Quelle genannt.

Ein kleine Gruppe überprüft lediglich nach der Reise das Resultat (23,3 Prozent), 20 Prozent gaben an, bei Verfehlungen Einträge auf einer „Schwarzen Liste" vorzunehmen und dort vermerkte Personen nicht mehr einzuladen.

6 Aus der Praxis von Reisejournalisten

„Innerhalb der Redaktion unseres Reisemagazins *VOXTOURS* brauchen wir Ihre Unterstützung als TV-Redakteur/in in fester freier Mitarbeit. Sattelfest im redaktionellen Alltag (von der Themenentwicklung bis zur Postproduction), textsicher und abnahmeerfahren sollten Sie für diese vielfältige Aufgabe sein. Weitgereist und welterfahren kennen Sie die Lebensbedingungen im Outback genauso wie die Spielregeln im Tourismus und haben ein Gespür für Geschichten jenseits ausgetretener Pfade. Gute Kontakte im Reisegeschäft, eigene Auslandsdreherfahrungen sowie Kenntnisse der Weltmusiken sind für diese Arbeit von großem Vorteil."

(Stellenanzeige des Fernsehsenders *VOX* in der *ZEIT* v. 6. 9. 1996)

6.1 Einleitung

Hans J. Kleinsteuber

Dieses Kapitel setzt die **subjektive Sichtweise der befragten Reisejournalisten** fort, wie sie schon das vorhergehende Kapitel prägte. Die Art, wie diese Statements von 'Machern' verschiedener Reisemedien gesammelt wurden, stellten wir zu Beginn des Kapitels 5 dar.

Hier werden die Aussagen nach **bestimmten Themen und Schwerpunkten** sozusagen 'querverarbeitet' und präsentiert. Etliche der angeschnittenen Fragen werden in den nachfolgenden Kapiteln wieder aufgegriffen, dann allerdings aus kritischer Distanz.

Am Ende dieses Kapitels findet der Leser zwei Interviews, das erste mit einem Chefredakteur und Herausgeber (Interview mit Peter-Matthias Gaede von *GEO*, Kap. 6.8), das zweite mit einem Autor, der lange als Freier arbeitete und von dem wir auch eine Reportage im Original abdrucken (Interview mit Alexander Smoltczyk, Kap. 6.9).

6.2 Wege zum Reisejournalismus

Britta Wormuth

Die Lebensläufe der von uns befragten Reisejournalisten zeigen, daß es **viele Wege zum Reisejournalismus** gibt - kaum einer hat von Beginn seiner Laufbahn an bzw. durchgängig für dieses Ressort geschrieben. Die Reisejournalisten, mit denen wir gesprochen haben, sind während ihrer Laufbahn in zweifacher Bedeutung 'viel gereist', und selten scheinen sie in ihrer jetzigen Stellung am Ziel zu sein. Stellt sich die Frage, ob man Reisejournalisten vielleicht grundsätzlich als **Wanderer zwischen verschiedenen 'Welten'** begreifen kann? Vielleicht keine Antwort, aber einen Eindruck geben folgende von uns erfaßten beruflichen Lebensläufe.

Ein interviewter Journalist, der jetzt Station in einem renommierten Reisemagazin macht, ist den klassischen Weg über Schülerzeitung, freie Mitarbeit in einer Lokalredaktion und Volontariat bei einer Tageszeitung gegangen. Dann arbeitete er als Korrespondent für eine Nachrichtenagentur und später für eine große Tageszeitung im internationalen Ausland. Ist er als Chefredakteur eines Reisemagazins am Ziel seines Weges?

Nach einem abgeschlossenen Studium der Künste begann eine der befragten Journalistinnen eher zufällig ihre Reise in die mediale Welt, und zwar über ein Volontariat bei einer Tageszeitung. Dann arbeitete sie in Redaktionen thematisch sehr unterschiedlicher Zeitschriften, später als freie Autorin. Nie kreuzte sie dabei ein Reiseressort, und doch hat ihre Reise sie nun zu einem Hochglanzmagazin geführt, das sich ausschließlich mit dem Thema Reisen beschäftigt.

Bei Reisejournalisten, die in relativ jungen Magazinen einen Zwischenstop machen, ist zu beobachten, daß viele eine Journalistenschule besucht, sich dann ihre Wege aber getrennt haben, und sie in Korrespondentenbüros, Nachrichtenagenturen und Redaktionen über die ganze Welt verteilt verschwunden sind. Nun gehen sie - zumindest für eine Weile - wieder einen gemeinsamen Weg und tummeln sich in Reiseressorts von Lifestyle-Magazinen.

Vom Reisen zum Schreiben kam ein junger Surfer, den der Sport um die Welt reisen und darüber schreiben ließ. In einem Volontariat führte er dies fort, eignete sich journalistisches Know-how an und reist fortan als surfender Redakteur von Spot zu Spot, um vom Reisen fürs Reisen zu schreiben.

Ein Wirtschaftswissenschaftler begann seine Reise in die Welt der Medien mit einem Praktikum bei einer Wochenzeitung, daraufhin absolvierte er ein Volontariat, passierte als Wirtschaftsjournalist mehrere Fachzeitschriften und setzte seine Reise fort in das Reiseressort eines klassischen Printmedienvertreters.

Der Chefredakteur eines Hochglanzmagazins begann seine Karriere mit einem Volontariat in der Lokalredaktion einer Boulevardzeitung, schrieb für ein Special interest-Magazin, arbeitete für *stern*, *Spiegel*, *Playboy* und *Bunte*, ist Autor von 12 Büchern und war auch im Fernsehbereich tätig.

Faßt man dies alles zusammen, so gibt es oft **keine gradlinige Karriere in das Reiseressort**. Eher schon sind es Zufälligkeiten, die dorthin führen, und viele sehen darin nicht die Endstation ihres journalistischen Werdegangs. Reisen haben etwas mit Abenteuer und Rastlosigkeit zu tun. Und es scheint, daß auch die Reisejournalisten davon betroffen sind. Mehr als bei vielen ihrer Kollegen erscheint die eigene Karriere als Reise ins Unbekannte. Aber war das nicht zu erwarten?

Einige **Tips für erste Schritte in den Reisejournalismus** können wir aufgrund unserer Gespräche geben:

- In Praktika sollten erste Erfahrungen mit dem Berufsfeld Journalismus gesammelt und die eigenen Fähigkeiten geprüft werden.
- Viele Journalisten empfehlen, bei Tages- und Lokaljournalismus zu beginnen, um sich dort grundlegende Kenntnisse über die Recherche und das Verfassen von Beiträgen zu erwerben.
- Vielseitige freie Mitarbeit bei verschiedenen Medien bringt nicht nur Erfahrungen, sondern schafft auch wichtige Kontakte.
- Reiseredaktionen werden oftmals überflutet mit Reisereportagen von freien Journalisten und Hobby-Schreibern. Deshalb nicht gleich jede Reportage an alle Redaktionen schicken. Vieles landet sofort im Papierkorb. Besondere Reiseziele und ausgefallene Herangehensweise fallen in der Masse eher auf.

6.3 Der Alltag - Abenteuer Schreibtisch?

Astrid Kusser

Die Vorstellung, **daß Reisejournalisten vor allem auf Reisen sind, ist falsch**. Wer fest in einer Redaktion angestellt ist, verbringt die meiste Zeit am Schreibtisch. Ein Redakteur muß den Themenplan der gesamten Ausgabe im Hinterkopf haben und an den Redaktionskonferenzen teilnehmen. Er besucht Pressekonferenzen, sichtet Pressemeldungen, verhandelt mit Sponsoren, hält

Kontakt zu Fotografen und freien Mitarbeitern und redigiert ihre Texte. Auf Reisen ist er lediglich noch sechs bis acht Wochen im Jahr.

Der Großteil der Reisejournalisten steht in einem anderen Arbeitsverhältnis. Sie sind **freie Mitarbeiter** - bisweilen fest bei einer Redaktion - und werden pro Beitrag bezahlt. Sie arbeiten entweder im Auftrag oder reisen auf eigene Faust, und versuchen, die Geschichte im Nachhinein zu verkaufen. Bei letzterem spielen meist Sponsoren eine Rolle, die die Journalisten unter bestimmten Konditionen auf eine Reise einladen. Das teilt der Eingeladene der an einer Reportage interessierten Redaktion oft aber nicht mit - und viele wollen es auch gar nicht wissen, solange der Beitrag erschwinglich ist.

Freie Autoren müssen sich also meist eher selbst um die **Finanzierung ihrer Reise** kümmern. Nicht zuletzt darum ist es für sie auch wichtig, Kontakte zu Leuten vor Ort zu knüpfen und zu pflegen. Sowohl Budget als auch geplante Reisezeit sind eng kalkuliert. Ist man erst einmal vor Ort, muß alles möglichst reibungslos klappen, Verzögerungen kosten Geld. Der berühmte Geheimtip ist da oft auf eigene Faust nur schwer zu beschaffen und Hilfe von Einheimischen willkommen - selbst wenn es manchmal nur der örtliche Fremdenverkehrsverein ist. Auch aktuelle Reiseführer werden zu Rate gezogen.

Im Schnitt wird zwischen drei und sieben Tagen vor Ort recherchiert - **Aufenthalte von mehr als einer Woche sind selten.** Mit Urlaub hat das meist nichts zu tun. Was später dann Anleitung zum Entspannen werden soll, war für den Journalisten selbst ein durchorganisierter Dauerlauf. Ausnahmen von der eben beschriebenen Realität kommen fast ebenso häufig vor. Die traumhaften Seiten über die schönste Zeit des Jahres lassen sich viele Redaktionen eine Menge kosten. Mitarbeiter werden einen Monat nach Hawaii zum Surfen geschickt, um Wind und Wellen zu testen und die Szene kennenzulernen. Andere fliegen gleich die ganze Redaktion nach New York und quartieren sie einige Wochen in einem Loft im Herzen von SoHo ein. Einige große Zeitschriften halten an Grundsätzen fest, z.B. die Reisen nur selbst zu finanzieren und keine Einladungen anzunehmen. Deren Redakteure sind regelmäßig auf Reisen und auf redaktionelles Verständnis von Reisejournalismus verpflichtet. Andere lassen ihre Texte nur von Schriftstellern und Prominenten vor Ort erstellen.

Bis aus einer Idee die fertig gedruckte Geschichte wird, sind viele verschiedene Personen am Werk: Das Konzept entsteht meist in der Redaktion, die dann einen (freien) Mitarbeiter auf die Reise schickt, der wiederum mit Leuten vor Ort und vor allem einem oder mehreren Fotografen zusammenarbeitet. Mit der Erstellung von Serviceteil und Karten beauftragt die Redaktion meist weitere Personen.

Daneben gibt es auch Journalisten, die gelegentlich ihre Urlaubsreise zu einer Geschichte verarbeiten und sie an eine Regionalzeitung verkaufen. Bei den großen Blättern ist das aber die Ausnahme. Die Formate der Publikationen, die das Thema Reise aufnehmen, sind sehr unterschiedlich. Ebenso ist es das jeweilige Verständnis von Reisejournalismus. Vom Alltag 'der' Reisejournalisten zu sprechen, fällt den so Bezeichneten daher selbst schwer: Jede Reise sei anders, jedes Thema speziell und somit ein Monat auch nur schwer mit dem vorhergehenden zu vergleichen.

Abb. nachfolgende Seite: Diese ironische Selbstdarstellung der Arbeit einer Reiseredaktion erschien in der Jubiläumsausgabe der Süddeutschen Zeitung

Drei gegen die Welt – oder: Die Angst vor dem Urlaub

Eingezwängt zwischen technischen Vorgaben, rosaroten Vorurteilen und Erwartungen von Leserschaft, Inserenten, Verlagsleitung und Kollegenschar, gelingt es der Reiseredaktion doch immer wieder, neben Service und Informationen auch Stoff für Träume zu liefern

Von Manfred F. Schröder

Der Reiseredakteur geht für gewöhnlich am Montag (nicht zu früh) ins Büro, sieht nach, über welchen Teil der Welt schon lange nichts mehr berichtet wurde und ob dafür nicht die passende Einladung eines Veranstalters oder einer Fluglinie zu einem Informationsbesuch vorliegt, fährt hin und schreibt – nachdem er einige senkrechte Wände bezwungen hat oder sich einige Wasserfälle hinabtreiben ließ – am Wochenende vom Swimmingpool eines Luxushotels aus: darüber und über die merkwürdigen Völker, geheimnisvollen Wälder und unberührten Traumstrände um ihn herum sowie über diejenigen, die die unberührte Gegend nun zum Touristenmekka machen. Oder – das ist die Alternative – er eilt in genießerischer Vorerwartung ins Büro, um zu sehen, wer ihm wieder einen dieser hinreißenden Artikel über die noch unbekannten Winkel ferner Länder eingesandt hat, die er dem Setzer oder der „Eingeberin" mit der Bemerkung übergeben kann: „Nichts ändern. Das ist reine Literatur." Den Rest überläßt er kundigen Layoutern, die die Reiseseiten ohne Hektik und ohne Zeitdruck so zusammenfügen, daß sie merkwürdigerweise doch immer wieder viereckig werden. Sie tun das oft am Sonntag, wenn andere aus diesen lärmgeplagten Biergärten nicht herauskommen.

Traumlob – Traumjob

Dienstags, wenn der Reiseteil erschienen ist, kommt der Redakteur in die Redaktionskonferenz, wo ihn der Chefredakteur, der ja alles liest, nicht genug loben kann wegen der – erstens – wundervollen Eigenberichte und – zweitens – wegen der intelligenten Auswahl der wundervollen Aufsätze der Mitarbeiter über diese wundervollen Plätze sowie – drittens – wegen der einfallsreichen Anordnung der wundervollen Photos, mit denen die Beiträge verschönt wurden. Der Rest der Woche ist dann den mittags oder abends sich länger hinziehenden Pressekonferenzen mit ausgiebigen Essen in Drei-Sterne-Restaurants gewidmet.

Ohne Übertreibung also ein Traumjob, der sich häufig ins Wochenende hinein fortsetzt: Berichte werden gern inmitten des häuslichen Tumults verfaßt, oder es werden verborgene Bergdörfer erkundet, um der geneigten Leserschaft die beliebten Geheimtips für bisher unentdeckte, preiswerte, idyllische und garantiert regenfreie Wanderziele bieten zu können (die im Winter wiederum total schneesicher sind).

Wo liegt Chuguchak?

Gründe der Arbeitsbeschaffung sind es, daß nicht einem allein soviel Glück gegönnt ist. So sind es eben drei, die sich in diese Vergnügungen teilen – und die gut und gern als jugendlich-dynamisch durchgehen würden, wenn sie nicht aus Bescheidenheit eine solche Charakterisierung zurückweisen würden. Ein weitgehend in Ehren ergrauter Auslandskorrespondent und – der Quote wegen – eine ebenfalls schon einige Zeit dem Volontärsalter entwachsene Expertin für das feine Leben sind es nämlich, die sich mit dem eigentlichen Reiseteil beschäftigen. Eine ebenfalls schon länger in Sand-, Wasser-, Eis- und Steinwüsten erprobte und als unverwüstlich befundene Sportsperson (ebenfalls weiblich) widmet sich der Bergwelt in Sommer und Winter.

Bei ihrer erholsamen, wenn auch gelegentlich mit leichtem sportlichem Einsatz (Kofferschleppen!) verbundenen Tätigkeit werden sie tatkräftig unterstützt von einer erfahrenen Sekretärin, die ihnen mit Frauenpower lästige, die Büroruhe störende Anrufe wie auch sonst alles Unangenehme vom Leib hält und die hartnäkkige Anfragen beantwortet – etwa wenn jemand unbedingt wissen will, wo Chuguchak liegt, nämlich in der Tarbagataj.

Eine hoch befriedigende Tätigkeit also, zumal auch die Verlagsleitung darauf achtet, daß der Reiseteil stets gut placiert und das Verhältnis zwischen redaktionellem Text und Inseraten immer ausgewogen ist, wobei auch die Zahl der bei design-bewußten Lesern wie bei Redakteuren so beliebten Eckfeldanzeigen möglichst hochgehalten wird, um die herum sich Bilder und Text so elegant gruppieren lassen. Zufrieden sind auch die Reiseveranstalter, groß und klein, ebenso wie die Hotels und die Public-Relations-Agenturen, da die Reiseredaktion selbdritt alle ihre Presseverlautbarungen berücksichtigt und auf ihren reichlich bemessenen Seiten leserfreundlich placiert. Zufrieden ist der Verlag, da durch die vorzügliche redaktionelle Arbeit wöchentlich eine Flut von Anzeigen angelockt wird.

Gleichermaßen zufrieden sind die Leser, die über kleinere Fehler (wie sie nun einmal bei der Lässigkeit des Redaktionsbetriebs unterlaufen müssen) großzügig hinwegsehen und die in täglichen körbeweisen Leserbrief-Einsendungen ihrer Begeisterung Luft machen – zumal es der Vierer-Bande trotz all ihrer Bemühungen, den sanften Tourismus zu propagieren, vor Gefahren und Krankheiten im Ausland zu warnen und die Beschwerlichkeiten des Reisens zu schildern, nicht gelungen ist, sie im Lande zu halten. Zufrieden sind auch gelegentlich zum Einsatz gelangende Volontäre und Praktikanten, da es im Büro kaum etwas zu arbeiten, doch immer wieder etwas zu feiern gibt: Von drei Redakteuren hat fast immer einer Geburtstag. Und von der Sekretärin muß beinahe wöchentlich der Abschied in den Urlaub – oder die Wiederkehr – begossen werden. Auch wird die Reiseredaktion von den einschlägigen Büros oder von denen, die ihre Artikel unterbringen durften (und das sind das Jahr über mehr als 200) unablässig mit Champagner bedacht.

Angesichts solcher Umstände fürchtet der Reiseredakteur nichts mehr als den Urlaub: Wo sollte er denn noch hin, wo er noch nicht gewesen wäre – und wo es schöner wäre als dort, wo er sowieso schon ist: bei der Arbeit nämlich.

Vierer-Bande, zum Aufbruch verführt: *Inkognito unterwegs, animiert vom regelmäßigen SZ-Reiseteil mit seinen Darstellungen lohnender Ferienziele und mit der „einfallsreichen Anordnung der wundervollen Photos" . . .*

Photo: Regina Schmeken

(Süddeutsche Zeitung vom 6. Oktober 1995, S. J. 72)

6.4 Auswahlprozesse in den Redaktionen

Kathrin Voss

„Was war noch nicht, was war lange nicht mehr,
und was hat sich schon wieder verändert.“
(Volker Skierka, ehem. Chefredakteur Merian)

Welches Land soll bereist wird? Wer fährt dort hin? Das sind die wichtigen Fragen, die am Anfang jeder Reisereportage stehen. Meistens entscheiden regelmäßige Redaktionskonferenzen über die Reiseziele, über die berichtet werden soll, wobei die Planungen lange im Voraus getätigt werden müssen. **Spontane Reisen und Berichte sind eher die Ausnahme**. Die Ideen für die Themen kommen aus vielen verschiedenen Richtungen. Zum einen werden die Vorschläge der eigenen Redakteure beachtet, ebenso haben freie Autoren und Fotografen, die sich mit ihren Ideen an die Redaktionen wenden, eine Chance. Auch die Reaktionen und Anregungen der **Leser** werden in vielen Zeitungen und Zeitschriften ausgewertet. In manchen Publikationen werden außerdem noch **Statistiken** herangezogen, die Auskunft über die beliebtesten Reiseziele geben.

Ausschlaggebend für ein bestimmtes Ziel können verschiedene Faktoren sein. So werden manche Themen aufgrund ihrer Aktualität ausgewählt, weil dort große Veranstaltungen wie zum Beispiel eine Olympiade geplant sind. Auch Trends werden aufgegriffen, so werden beispielsweise sogenannte ökologische oder ‘grüne’ Reiseziele immer beliebter. Natürlich werden auch die Neuheiten der Touristikbranche beachtet. Zum Teil werden Reiseziele auch nur ausgewählt, weil es für diese Orte Einladungen von Reiseveranstaltern oder Fremdenverkehrsvereinen gibt.

Ist das Ziel erstmal bestimmt, gilt es in vielen Redaktionen, die passenden Autoren und Fotografen zu finden, denn in den wenigsten Fällen schreiben nur die festangestellten Redakteure. Vielmehr werden **freie Autoren und Fotografen** für die Berichte gesucht. Neben den Adressen von Journalisten und Fotografen, mit denen schon zusammengearbeitet wurde, werden deshalb in vielen Redaktionen andere Publikationen gelesen, um auf neue Talente aufmerksam zu werden. So manches Reiseblatt legt dabei Wert auf bekannte Namen und bittet **Schriftsteller und Autoren**, die an dem Zielort leben, für sie zu schreiben. Natürlich gibt es auch Artikel, die von den Redakteuren geschrieben werden. Dabei entscheiden oftmals die persönlichen

Vorlieben und Möglichkeiten (z.B. Sprachkenntnisse) der Mitarbeiter über die Themenvergabe.

Für die Bebilderung der Reportage muß nicht unbedingt extra ein Fotograf engagiert werden, auch wenn das eigentlich der Regelfall ist. Trotzdem werden manchmal Bilder von Bildagenturen oder aus dem eigenen Verlagsarchiv verwendet. Dies ist oftmals aus finanziellen Gründen notwendig.

Bei dem **Serviceteil** verlassen sich die meisten Redaktionen auf fachkundige Autoren, die vor Ort leben und so das Reiseziel besonders gut kennen. Zum Teil sind das auch Autoren, die bereits einen Reiseführer über diese Gegend geschrieben haben. Nur ein geringer Teil der Adressen wird vor Ort vom Redakteur selbst recherchiert.

Wichtigster Faktor für alle Auswahlprozesse ist jedoch die Leserschaft, denn die **Zielgruppe** der jeweiligen Publikation entscheidet darüber, welche Themen machbar sind, welche Autoren passend dafür schreiben und welche Art von Bildern genommen wird kann. Jeder Redakteur, vor allem aber die Chefredakteure haben die Leser, für die sie schreiben, ständig im Hinterkopf, wenn sie die nächste Ausgabe planen.

6.5 Wie sieht die ideale Reisereportage aus?

Martin Sonnleitner

Auf die Frage, was guter Reisejournalismus sei, wird auf Unabhängigkeit und Differenziertheit verwiesen: „Schlechter Reisejournalismus sieht aus, wie die Prospekte von Reiseveranstaltern", schildert eine Redakteurin, wie man es nicht machen sollte. Die Branche erhebt den Anspruch, nichts verschönern zu wollen, Probleme und Schattenseiten einzubeziehen. Ein Kollege verdeutlicht: „Man muß offen sein und darf sich seine Meinung nicht schon vor der Reise bilden." In den Texten soll nach Ansicht der Fachleute ein **Zusammenspiel von Imagination und Realität** vermittelt werden. Eine Geschichte soll gefühlt und eine Stimmung zu einem Land transportiert werden: „Der Text muß anschaulich geschrieben sein, also wie ein Film rüberkommen." Ein anderer Routinier betont: „Guter Reisejournalismus muß fesseln und Lust auf das Reiseziel wecken und sei es nur für das Reisen im Kopf." Man wolle mit Hilfe von Sprache Erlebnisse atmosphärisch und sinnlich wiedergeben und Sympathie für das Fremde schaffen.

Die Distanzierung vom problemorientierten Journalismus wird wie folgt rapportiert: „**Eine Reisereportage sollte immer eine schöne Geschichte sein**. Sie kann zwar Konflikte anklingen lassen, darf jedoch nicht zu problem-orientiert sein. Deswegen lesen Leute keinen Reisejournalismus. Das Lesen sollte ein Genuß sein, Spaß ist vom Urlaub untrennbar. Wir wollen neugierig machen und die Wertung dem Leser überlassen."

Der Redakteur einer Wochenzeitung kommentiert bezüglich der unterschiedlichen Ausrichtungen der Artikel: „Grundsätzlich muß jeder Artikel gut geschrieben sein. Wenn es ein essayistischer Text ist, wird entsprechend mehr Wert auf die Sprache gelegt. Bei einem Text, in dem es um soziale und gesellschaftspolitische Verhältnisse geht, sind fundierte Informationen wichtig."

Anmerkung: Wir haben die befragten Redakteure nach ihren Vorstellungen einer idealen Reportage befragt. Manche nannten uns konkrete Texte. Exemplarisch drucken wir zwei Reportagen ab, die wir für besonders gelungen halten. (siehe Kap. 3)

6.6 Wie steht es mit der Abhängigkeit von der Werbewirtschaft?

Martin Sonnleitner

Diese Frage entpuppt sich als zweischneidiges Schwert. Einerseits ist den Reiseredakteuren klar, daß es ihre journalistische Verpflichtung ist, objektiv zu berichten, andererseits können die Redaktionen nicht auf das Geld der Reiseveranstalter verzichten. Ein Redakteur vertritt die Meinung, würde man dieses hinterfragen, müsse man dasselbe mit dem gesamten Wirtschaftssystem machen.

Die Redakteurin eines Reisemagazins meint, daß monothematische Hefte besonders abhängig seien: „Es ist wie im Modejournalismus. Klamotten von Designern werden vorgestellt, die in der Zeitung inserieren." Sie habe in den letzten Jahren eine eindeutige Gratwanderung der Branche in Richtung Abhängigkeit beobachtet. Printmedien, die mit der Illusion ins konkurrenzstarke Rennen um Leser gegangen sind, ihr Etat selber zu finanzieren, lassen sich ihren Finanzhaushalt längst von Reiseveranstaltern aufbessern.

Redaktionelle Abgrenzungen scheint es in der Branche allerdings doch zu geben. Ein Reisejournalist schildert Fälle, in denen Werbekunden Einfluß auf den textlichen Inhalt nehmen wollten. Die Aufträge wurden abgelehnt. Der Redakteur bemerkt jedoch, daß die festangestellten Redakteure diesbezüglich in einer privilegierten Position seien, **viele Freie hätten diese Freiheit nicht**. Sie würden bei zu großer Kritik aus dem Presseverteiler der Reiseanbieter verschwinden.

Das Ausmaß der Verflechtungen zwischen redaktionellem Teil und der Werbung ist von verschiedenen Faktoren abhängig. Hierbei muß zunächst berücksichtigt werden, um welche Art von Printmedien es sich handelt.

Bei multithematischen Heften sowie bei den sogenannten seriösen Tages- und Wochenzeitungen scheint die inhaltliche Differenz zur Werbung größer zu sein, was bereits am Layout ersichtlich ist.

Monothematische Magazine können leicht durch einen Mangel an optischer Ausdifferenzierung die Sinne des Lesers verwirren.

Noch eindeutiger definiert sich das Special interest-Magazin: „Wir beschreiben sowieso eine heile Welt, wollen Träume beschreiben und nicht auf Probleme aufmerksam machen", umreißt ein Redakteur dieses Genre.

Die Frage, inwieweit subjektive Färbung legitimiert werden kann, ist sicherlich auch vom redaktionellen Anspruch abhängig. Der eine will Spaß vermitteln, bei anderen Reisemedien geht es um eine möglichst genaue Berichterstattung.

Abschließend sollte bei aller Schwierigkeit, redaktionelle Abhängigkeit und Korrumpierbarkeit zu analysieren, festgestellt werden, daß es von jedem einzelnen Journalisten selber abhängt, inwieweit er seiner Pflicht, neutral zu sein, nachkommt oder nicht. (Vgl. hierzu Kap. 8 zu Versuchungen im Reisejournalismus.)

6.7 Wie sieht die Zukunft des Reisejournalismus aus?

Martin Sonnleitner

Die befragten Redakteure sind sich einig, daß Reisejournalismus ein Wachstumsfeld ist.

Hierzu werden folgende Argumente angeführt:

- Der Tourismus wird nicht so schnell stagnieren.
- Die Leute haben viel Freizeit und nutzen diese zum Reisen.
- Mehr Reisen bedeutet einen größeren Bedarf an Informationen.
- Das Bedürfnis nach Ferne und Fremde steigt.
- Reisejournalismus wird wegen der Internationalisierung weiter zunehmen

Die Entwicklungstendenzen werden folgendermaßen beschrieben:

- Es wird aus finanziellen Gründen eine Entwicklung zu Nahzielen geben.
- Es steigt der Bedarf an Vorsortierung dieses riesigen unüberschaubaren Marktes an Klein- und Kleinstanbietern, denn auch die Reisebüros haben kaum noch einen Überblick.
- Der Trend geht zu mehr Service, weniger zu großen Geschichten und Reportagen.
- Die Themen werden immer exklusiver und spezieller. Man sucht die Nische (z.B. Weinführer für Italien).
- Die Abhängigkeit von der Werbung wird größer. Die werbetreibende Wirtschaft fordert Servicegeschichten. Dies führt zu einer Diskrepanz zwischen dem Leser und der Wirtschaft.
- Bilder von hoher Qualität werden immer wichtiger.
- Der Trend geht zu kürzeren Berichten. Die Sprache tritt hinter der Information zurück.

Die Journalisten wurden ebenfalls zu den Entwicklungen und zum gegenwärtigen Stand ihrer Redaktionen, bezüglich Online und Internet, befragt:

Hierbei fiel auf, daß sich drei von zehn befragten Journalisten, beide bei marktführenden Journalen tätig, nicht mit dem Internet auskannten, trotz Online-Aktivitäten ihrer Medien. Bei einem weiteren Magazin beschränken sich die Internet-Aktivitäten auf die Recherche.

Die übrigen Redakteure schildern ihre Eindrücke zum Thema ‘Reise via Datenbahn’ wie folgt:

- Online hat noch keine Zukunftsperspektive, weil die Optik derzeit zu schlecht ist, die in dieser Form von Berichterstattung von äußerster Relevanz ist.
- Reportagen werden online keine Chance haben. Das Internet wird Reisemagazine nicht verdrängen können. Im Sessel wird anders gelesen als vor dem Bildschirm.

Die Kommunikation zwischen Menschen im Internet findet verstärkt statt. Es ermöglicht Reisen, ohne sich vom Ort zu bewegen, durch Kommunikation mit anderen Ländern und anderen Menschen. „Virtuelles Reisen wird jedoch nie das wirkliche Reisen ersetzen können. Man muß die Länder riechen oder schmecken, das geht im Internet nicht.“ (Hierzu vgl. Kap. 9.)

6.8 Interview mit Peter-Matthias Gaede, Chefredakteur von *GEO* und Herausgeber von *GEO SAISON*

- *Wie wurden Sie Reisejournalist?*

Ich bin nicht Reisejournalist geworden, aber ich habe mich unter anderem als Herausgeber von *GEO SAISON* mit Reisejournalismus zu befassen.

Journalist geworden bin ich durch den Vorsatz, es zu werden. Ich habe Sozialwissenschaften in Göttingen studiert; u.a. Kommunikationswissenschaften. Meine ersten Gehversuche im Journalismus habe ich beim Studio des *Hessischen Rundfunks* in Kassel unternommen. Die Journalistenschule *Gruner + Jahr*, damals noch nicht *Henry-Nannen-Schule* heißend, schrieb den ersten Lehrgang aus - ich habe zu den 20 Glücklichen gehört. Danach habe ich drei Jahre bei der *Frankfurter Rundschau* im Lokalen gearbeitet, bin dann zu *GEO* gekommen, und seither ist meine Biographie eher überraschungsfrei, weil ich mich in *GEO* nur intern bewegt habe: vom Reporter zum Chefreporter zum stellvertretenden Chefredakteur zum Chefredakteur, der ich seit 1994 bin.

- *Wo waren Sie als Reporter? Hatten Sie bestimmte regionale Schwerpunkte?*

Ich hatte einen thematischen Schwerpunkt, das waren die politischen Reportagen und die sozialen Reportagen. Ich habe hauptsächlich in Lateinamerika gearbeitet, aber auch in der damaligen Sowjetunion, in Fernost und in den USA. Spezialisierungen geographischer Art, mit denen jemand einen ganzen Erdteil in Geiselhaft nehmen kann, gibt es bei *GEO* nicht. Ich habe mich auf lateinamerikanische Topoi konzentriert: die Militärkaste, den Herbst des Patriarchen, die Kupferarbeiter von Chile, die Campesinos in Kolumbien.

- *War das in Ihrem sozialwissenschaftlichen Studium angelegt, daß Sie sich besonders für politische Themen interessieren?*

Ja; und auch in den 68er-Einflüssen.

- *Meinen Sie, daß Ihr Einstieg optimal für das journalistische Feld war, das Sie jetzt vertreten? Oder würden Sie jungen Leuten eher die Empfehlung geben, es anders zu machen?*

Wenn Sie *GEO* meinen: Das eignet sich nicht als Einstiegsdroge. Sie müssen bei *GEO* die Marathonstrecke von vornherein beherrschen. Sie müssen die spezifische Dramaturgie einer 20-Blatt-Geschichte draufhaben. Als Testfeld für Anfänger im Journalismus ist *GEO* ungeeignet. Es ist gut für Beginner, keinerlei Arroganz gegenüber Tageszeitungen zu entwickeln, denn die sind die Chance, mit den verschiedenen Genres zu spielen.

- *Könnten Sie sich denn vorstellen, daß Sie noch mal in eine ganz andere Art von Printmedium einsteigen, also beispielsweise zu einer Tageszeitung zurückgehen?*

Zur Zeit kann ich mir das nur schwer vorstellen, denn ich habe eine sehr intensive Zweierbeziehung zu den drei Buchstaben GEO.

- *Können Sie etwas zu diesem Gesamtkunstwerk GEO sagen?*

Das ist im Oktober 1996 zwanzig Jahre alt geworden. Es ist ein Magazin, dessen Kraft und Magie, wie wir alle wissen und auch als Autoren akzeptieren müssen, ganz primär aus der Optik kommen. Es ist ein Magazin, das für Menschen gemacht ist, die noch differenzieren können und wollen, die nicht glauben, daß man die Welt in drei Sätzen erzählen, geschweige denn, sie in drei Sätzen verstehen kann. *GEO* ist der Gegenentwurf zu diesem Fast-food-Häppchen-Journalismus, der jetzt spätestens seit Schnippens Essay gegen *Focus* in aller Munde ist. *GEO* ist ein Blatt für Menschen, die mehr als drei Wörter im Wortschatz, mehr als drei Bücher im Buchschrank haben. Die an dem 'Warum' stärker interessiert sind als an dem reinen 'Was', 'Wo', 'Wer', 'Wann'. Ein Magazin, das auch die Einladung zu einer subjektiven Art der Reportage ist, auf der Seite der Bildsprachen, der optischen, visuellen Sprachen. *GEO* hat eine Auflage von gegenwärtig 530.000, eine Reichweite in der Bundesbevölkerung von über drei Millionen Lesern. Das haben wir nur durch eine allmähliche Metamorphose vom Erdkundemagazin, vom Eskapismus für Lehnstuhlreisende, zu einem General interest-Magazin mit hohem Wissenschaftsanteil schaffen können. Geschichten in *GEO* sollen eine überdurchschnittliche Halbwertzeit haben, man soll sie sich eine gewisse Zeit hinter den Spiegel stecken können, man soll mit ihnen Zusammenfassungen latent aktueller Themen haben. Wir sind für Teile unserer Leserschaft, auch eine Art akademischer Austauschdienst, wir sind auch ein Farbklecks in Schulbibliotheken, das wissen wir, wir liegen auf den Vorzimmertischen der Zahnärzte und Ärzte, aber glücklicherweise eben nicht nur dort.

- *Haben Sie eigentlich ein Leitbild, wie Ihr Leser aussieht? Sie sagten 'Lehnstuhlreisender', das impliziert ja, daß man GEO statt der Reise selbst konsumiert. Sehen Sie eher Leute vor sich, denen Sie Informationen zum Nachreisen anbieten? Oder sehen Sie eher Leser, die damit zufrieden sind, mit GEO eine wunderbar durchgestylte Welt virtuell durchreisen zu können?*

Spätestens jetzt muß man zwischen den verschiedenen Mitgliedern der *GEO*-Familie differenzieren. Wir haben uns ja diversifiziert; in einem 'Zellteilungsprozeß' enstanden 1981 die *GEO-Specials* und entstand vor einigen Jahren *GEO SAISON*. Das heißt, das grüne *GEO* entstand ja aus dem *stern* heraus, und als es Henry Nannen damals in einem Brief an die *stern*-Leser vorstellte, sagte er, besser als *GEO* zu lesen, sollte nur sein, selbst in Swaziland oder bei den Korowai oder wo auch immer gewesen zu sein. Mittlerweile ist *GEO* eher ein Magazin für Expeditionen ganz anderer Art. Für Expeditionen in den Blutkreislauf, für Expeditionen in die Mikrokosmen, für die Erhellung gentechnologischer Fragen, Fragen wie Überbevölkerung und natürlich die großen ökologischen Fragen.

Die *Specials* sind, obwohl sie vor *SAISON* gegründet worden sind, das 'missing link' zu dem Nutzwertmagazin *SAISON*. Die *Specials* haben den Anspruch, als Reisemagazine mit einem journalistischen Impetus an ein Land, eine Region, eine Stadt heranzugehen. Auf den vorderen zwei Dritteln Geschichten für Menschen zu präsentieren, die sich gerne einen Reim auf Zusammenhänge machen möchten. Die also nicht einen Swimmingpool buchen, sondern das Land dahinter. Die wissen wollen, wie es am Ende des Strandes weitergeht. Die sich mit einem kosmopolitischen Hirn in eine fremde Kultur begeben und dann dort nicht nur die Sonne auf ihren Bauch scheinen lassen wollen. Das macht sicherlich kein anderes Reisemagazin, in einem *Special* über Rußland eine Reportage über Gulag zu bringen, in einem *Special* über Südafrika eine Reportage aus den Vorort-Zügen von Seweto, in einem New-York-Heft eine Reportage aus einer Crack-Höhle. Das sind dann keine Reisereportagen im klassischen Sinne - zum 'Nachreisen' -, aber Informationen für Menschen, die unter Reisen etwas mehr verstehen als auf dem Schoß des Reiseleiters zu sitzen. Auch bei den *Specials* beginnt der Tag nicht mit einer Schußwunde, aber sie sind schon entschieden mehr der unabhängige, nicht auf dem Ticket von Reiseveranstaltern fahrende Journalismus.

GEO SAISON ist sicherlich das eigentliche Reisemagazin in der *GEO*-Familie. Es ist nach der Devise konzipiert: vorausreisen, vorerleben, vortesten. *GEO SAISON* ist der Pfadfinder in die Restaurants, Hotels, auf die Matratzen und Strände dieser Welt. *GEO SAISON* ist zum Anfassen. Man könnte sagen, die *Specials* sind ein bißchen der Mittelstreckenflug, *SAISON* ist mehr der Inselhopper und der Cityhopper, der Kleinbus, der häufiger anhält, ein Magazin voller Kurzreisen, in dem es wirklich darum geht, Telefonnummern von Hotels zu vermitteln, vorzukosten.

Die grünen Hefte haben sich dagegen noch in einer anderen Richtung Ableger verschafft: die *GEO-Extras*. Die haben keinen seriellen Charakter, sind 'one shots'. Etwa zum Thema Zukunft oder zum Thema Fotografie.

- *Lassen Sie uns zu den Alltagsfragen zurückkehren. Welches sind die Auswahlkriterien in Ihrer Redaktion? Nehmen wir den reisejournalistischen Teil, in dem es um die Darstellung des Fremden geht. Auf was würden Sie besonders achten? Was würden Sie ablehnen? Was würden Sie fördern?*

Ich würde bei jeder Neueinstellung im Textbereich darauf achten, daß die Kollegin oder der Kollege Neugier mitbringt. Daß er am Morgen nicht weiß, wie er am Abend gefunden haben wird. Ich würde darauf achten, daß Dickbrettbohrer eine Chance bekämen. Menschen mit der Fähigkeit zu einer harten Recherche. Es gibt wortgewaltige Menschen zuhauf, es gibt eloquente Menschen zuhauf, es gibt Essayisten und Kommentarschreiber zuhauf. Es gibt aber wenige Journalisten, die sich sozialen Erfahrungen wirklich aussetzen, die Reportagen wirklich als maximale Distanz vom Hotelbar-Journalismus und als maximale Distanz zum Telefon-Journalismus verstehen. Bei *GEO* verlangen wir, daß Leute sich Situationen aussetzen, sie durchleben, sie mitmachen.

- *Wie schützen Sie sich eigentlich gegen Fälschungen, die es auch bei Ihnen ganz vereinzelt gegeben hat?*

Anfang der achtziger Jahre hat ein Fotograf Pandas in einem Reservat fotografiert und behauptet, er habe sie in freier Wildbahn getroffen. Der bis über beide Ohren errötete Chefredakteur entschuldigte sich bei den Lesern, der Fotograf hat seither nicht mehr für uns fotografiert. So etwas ist nicht mehr vorgekommen. Für den Normalfall haben wir eine Dokumentationsabteilung, fünf hochqualifizierte Frauen und Männer stark, die bei uns als unsere 'fact-finding-commission' fingieren. Also jede Geschichte nachrecherchieren.

- *Die gehören zur Redaktion, die sind nicht aus der Dokumentation des Hauses Gruner + Jahr?*

Nein, die gehören zur *GEO*-Redaktion. Diese Kollegen haben den Auftrag, erst einmal gar nichts zu glauben und alles in Frage zu stellen. Der Reporter, der zurückkehrt, muß sich mit seinen Unterlagen, mit Büchern, die er womöglich benutzt hat, mit Zeitschriftenausschnitten, mit seinen Tonbändern oder Notebooks mit dem 'Docker', dem Dokumentationsredakteur, zusammensetzen und alle 'Facts and Figures' überprüfen lassen. Namen, aber auch die Frage, ob der Sonneneinfall auf dem Kontinent XY zu einer bestimmten Jahreszeit um 18 Uhr so gewesen sein kann wie behauptet. Dabei passieren auch uns natürlich ab und zu Fehler. Wir haben es inzwischen mit rund 1800 *GEO*-Geschichten zu tun und an die 70.000 Fotos mit Bildunterschriften gedruckt. Es ist uns einmal der Äquator verrutscht, und unlängst haben wir sogar einen honorigen österreichischen Kirchmann mit einem Geistlichen verwechselt, der besonderer Knabenliebe bezichtigt wurde, weil der Autor zwei Biografien virtuell gemixt hatte und unsere Kontrollinstanzen in der Hetze des Tages leider versagt haben. Solche Sünden sind glücklicherweise die Ausnahme.

- *Mit juristischen Folgen?*

Nein, wir sind auf Knien nach Österreich gekrochen und haben uns tausendmal entschuldigt. Auch vor den Lesern. Glaubwürdigkeit gehört zu dem *GEO*-Konzept. Wir müssen auch streng zu uns selber sein.

- *Gab es Sanktionen gegenüber dem Journalisten? Mußte er das Haus verlassen?*

Es war ein freier Autor, der so schnell seine nächste Geschichte nicht bei uns machen wird. Und dito jene haben es schwer, die, nur weil es besser klingt, aus drei Halbsätzen verschiedener Personen einen machen und ihn einer einzelnen Figur in den Mund legen. Ich gebe zu, daß es nicht immer einfach ist, solche Tricks rechtzeitig zu erkennen.

- *Wo wir im Moment in der ethischen Schublade kramen, zwei Fragen: Wie gehen Sie mit dem Angebot um, als Reisejournalist umsonst befördert zu werden, wenn das mit Gegenerwartungen verbunden ist? Und wie stehen Sie z.B. zu Anzeigen, die sich thematisch an redaktionelle Beiträge anlehnen?*

Reiseredaktionen, speziell jene von Tageszeitungen, sind selten auf Rosen gebettet. Es wird also auf dem Ticket von Veranstaltern tatsächlich gefahren.

Bei seriösen Redaktionen sieht das allerdings so aus, daß sich der Dank in der Nennung der betreffenden Airline im Info-Teil erschöpft. Das ist die ungefährliche Variante. Auch *GEO SAISON* folgt in Einzelfällen Einladungen, allerdings nicht um den Preis eines verordneten Gefälligkeitsjournalismus. Heikel wird's in jenem Graubereich, in dem sich Magazine unter dem winzig klein geschriebenen Wort 'Promotion' tummeln. Und beim 'Product Placement'. Wenn Sie eine Reportage über *Chanel* sehen, und auf jeder Doppelseite ist ein *No. 5*-Flakon abgebildet, dann können Sie da ein paar Nachtigallen trapsen hören. Daß sich die Anzeigenwirtschaft Umfelder sucht und sie auch findet, ist Fakt. Daß sie immer mehr Druck auf Journalisten ausübt, ebenfalls - was Formate und Plazierung ihrer Anzeigen betrifft und bei vielen Magazinen leider auch die Themen.

Bei den *GEO-Specials* hingegen haben wir die Situation, daß wir ein komplettes Schottland-*Special* machen, und wir sind weit und breit die einzigen, die keine doppelseitige Anzeige des schottischen Tourist Boards bekommen. Warum? Weil die Schotten gesagt haben: Dieses Heft ist in toto eine so wunderschöne Werbung für Schottland, da sparen wir uns das Geld für eine Annonce.

- *Sie müßten also Schottland im Vorfeld schlechtmachen, um die Schotten zu Anzeigen zu zwingen, die das Bild geraderücken?*

Ja, aber so ticken wir ja nicht. Bei der Produktion eines Österreich-*Specials*, zum Beispiel, wußten wir um die Not der österreichischen Tourismusindustrie speziell mit den ausbleibenden Deutschen. Wir konnten viele Anzeigen erwarten, mußten den netten Herren der verschiedenen Verkehrsämter aber vorher schon sagen: Erwartet nicht, daß wir die Quotengeschichte aus Vorarlberg, die Quotengeschichte zu Innsbruck, die Quotengeschichte zu Nieder-Österreich bringen, denn so könnten keine journalistischen Produkte entstehen. Wir haben zwar viele Anzeigen bekommen, aber auch beleidigte Reaktionen von jenen, deren Region wir eben nicht vorgestellt haben.

- *Wie wählen Sie überhaupt Ihre Themen aus? Schauen Sie sich da Reisestatistiken an? Suchen Sie eher das Exotische? Ihre Themen müssen Sie ja auf die verschiedenen GEO-Medien verteilen, die da offensichtlich ganz unterschiedlich orientiert sind. Wie gehen Sie da ran?*

Was die *GEO-Specials* betrifft, können wir ohne rot zu werden sagen: Wir gehen nicht danach vor, wo wohl die meisten Anzeigen lauern. Wir hätten sonst kein Special über Amazonien gemacht, keines über das Nordmeer, keines über Argentinien; das sind alles weitgehend anzeigenfreie Hefte geworden. Und daß sie es werden könnten, wußten wir vorher. Die Leser und die Qualität unserer Hefte sind uns wichtiger. Und wichtig ist für uns, uns von *Merian* abzugrenzen, oder von den *ADAC reisemagazinen*. Denen überlassen wir das Kleinteiligere, speziell auch viele Destinationen im europäischen Nahbereich, in denen ein Typus Tourist unterwegs ist, der, sagen wir mal, begrenzt abenteuerlustig ist. Wir gehen mit den *Specials* eher nicht an die Länder und Regionen heran, von denen wir wissen, daß dort vor allem jene hinfahren, die seit dreißig Jahren dasselbe Ferienhaus buchen. Wir versuchen, Ausnahmen bestätigen die Regel, in große offene Räume zu gehen und sind am erfolgreichsten dann, wenn dort Englisch gesprochen wird. Australien, Kanada, die USA und Neuseeland - das sind verläßliche Ziele, nur können wir sie im Interesse unserer Abonnenten auch nicht zu oft wiederholen, ohne Déjà-vu-Erlebnisse zu provozieren. Außerdem: Nicht immer läßt sich aus dem bloßen Handeln nach der Urlauber-Statistik ein erfolgreiches Heft machen. Im Gegenteil. Etwa das Brasilien-*Special* haben sechsmal mehr ‘Lehnstuhlreisende’ als wirklich nach Rio reisende Deutsche gekauft.

- *Haben Sie mal eine Leserumfrage gemacht? So daß Sie da auch erhärtete Zahlen haben?*

Natürlich machen wir Copy-Tests. Aber nur als flankierende Maßnahme, nicht als Guideline für unsere journalistischen Entscheidungen.

- *Die Sie also auch aus dem Bauch heraus treffen?*

Der spielt mit. Und die Entflammbarkeit der beteiligten Redakteure. Wenn jemand auf ein *Special* über das Nordmeer brennt, wird er überzeugende Ideen einbringen. Das ist auf jeden Fall hilfreicher und ertragreicher, als nach Länge mal Breite mal Höhe der Übernachtungsstatistiken vorzugehen.

- *Im Vergleich zu Merian und ADAC sind die Specials wahrscheinlich der Spezialist für das Exotische, für das Weitentfernte und für das, was vielleicht noch ein Kribbeln auslöst. Aber wenn man Amazonien nimmt, oder die Sahara, so sind das ja auch sehr heikle Weltregionen, mit sehr großen Problemen. Dort wünscht man sich unter Umständen keinen einzigen*

Touristen hin. Wie sehen Sie da Ihre Verantwortung gegenüber solchen Regionen?

Wir werden ab und zu mit dem Vorwurf konfrontiert, wir würden, indem wir etwas beschreiben, an dessen Zerstörung mitarbeiten. Und auf den ersten Blick ist da ja auch etwas dran. Andererseits: Journalisten sind in der Regel selten noch die ersten, die einen Raum erobern, sondern wir sind längst schon häufiger auf der Spur von Erdöl-Prospektoren, Holzfällern, Logging-Firmen, auch Ferntouristen. Wir begegnen in Irian Jaya dem Zahnarzt aus Paderborn, dem Extrem-Touristen. Das ist die eine Seite. Dennoch müssen wir uns bewußt sein, daß wir mit dazu beitragen, die letzten weißen Flecken auf der Erde einzufärben. Ich glaube da aber auch an eine gewisse Schutzfunktion, die Journalismus haben kann. Es sind eine Menge Schweinereien in der Welt passiert, gerade deshalb, weil sie keine Öffentlichkeit hatten. Es läßt sich halt besser ein Wald abholzen, ein wertvolles Biotop überschwemmen, wenn es unter Ausschluß der internationalen Öffentlichkeit geschieht. Der Fotograf Nick Nichols zu Beispiel, der fast sein ganzes Leben in den Dienst einer bestimmten Tierfotografie gestellt hat, der davon überzeugt ist, daß er so etwas wie 'die Seele der Tiere' in Bildern einfangen kann, hat einmal gesagt, er versuche, Schutzmauern aus Fotos um sie herum aufzubauen.

Generell sind wir Journalisten mitschuldig am Kleinerwerden der Welt, an den schwindenden Distanzen, an dem Entmystifizieren und halt auch am Entromantisieren der letzten Verborgenheiten dieser Welt. Aber ich halte das nicht nur für schlecht.

- *Sie haben in einem Reportage-Buch von Michael Haller über das Fremde und seine Darstellung im Journalismus geschrieben, über Stereotypen, über vorurteilsbehaftete Darstellung. Sie zeigen Sensibilität gegenüber diesen Problemen. Wie versuchen Sie, damit in der Redaktion umzugehen? Überarbeiten Sie unter Umständen Texte auf 'political correctness' hin?*

Aus tausend anderen Gründen überarbeiten wir fast jeden Text. Ja, wie geht man mit der Darstellung des Fremden um? Das kann wirklich ambivalent sein. Journalistisch attraktiv sind ja, wie wir alle wissen, eher die Exzesse und Extreme als die Normaliät und die Mitte. Jeder Journalist muß schon qua Auftrag das Besondere aus dem Allgemeinen destillieren, muß nach besonderen Exempeln suchen, die für das Ganze stehen. Muß darum bemüht sein, seinem Thema Aufmerksamkeit zu verschaffen. Worauf wir aufpassen müssen, ist, daß er die erstbeste Aufregung nicht für die ganze Wahrheit nimmt. Würde ein Reporter aus Tasmanien ein Deutschland-Porträt anhand des Kölner Karnevals erarbeiten, dürfte er nicht zurückgehen und sagen: Das ist Deutschland. Es besteht die latente Gefahr, daß wir uns umgekehrt genauso verhalten. Wie kann man da gegensteuern? Vor allem, indem man die Sensation der Normalität als solche entdeckt. Wir haben zum Beispiel ein Buch mit dem Titel 'So lebt der Mensch' produziert, das fern alles Sensationellen den Besitz und die Träume von Durchschnittsfamilien in 30 Ländern dieser Erde bilanziert. Ein wunderschönes Buch über die Gemeinsamkeiten und die Antagonismen der 'Weltfamilie', ganz ohne Glamour; und ganz ohne Blut.

Ich glaube, wir können uns vor gewissen Klischees letztlich nur durch gezieltes Überdenken unserer Spontan-Reflexe schützen, und wir werden vorschnellen Urteilen doch nie ganz entkommen. Das liegt im Wesen dreiwöchiger Stippvisiten, die nicht zu verwechseln sind mit dem wirklichen Kennenlernen der Fremde. Mitunter schicken wir Teams mit dem ausdrücklichen Auftrag los, die üblichen Assoziationen, mit denen etwa ein Kontinent wie Afrika in unserem Bewußtsein nistet, zu konterkarieren; Aids, Armut, Bürgerkrieg. Wir sagen dem Team: Konzentriert euch auf die Vitalität, die Überlebenskunst, die Pfiffigkeit, die Cleverness, die Würde von Menschen, die im Elend leben, auf deren Einfallsreichtum. Das ist leichter gesagt als getan, aber notwendig. Es geht darum, diesen 'positiven Kolonialismus' zu verhindern, der für Menschen der sogenannten Dritten Welt nur Mitleid hat, aber kein Gespür für deren Individualität.

- *Ein völlig anderes Thema. Wie gehen Sie bei GEO mit Bildern um? Nach welcher Logik bebildern Sie Ihre Texte? Kann es passieren, daß Sie sagen, wir haben so wunderbare Bilder hier, wir machen eine Reportage danach?*

Ja, das kann passieren. Es kann deshalb passieren, weil Fotografen viel erleben, wenn sie unterwegs sind, und uns entsprechend viele Vorschläge oder komplette Geschichten auftischen. Oder zumindest anfotografierte Stücke. Wir wissen, wie wichtig die Fotografie für *GEO* ist, deswegen suchen wir nach den besten Fotografen der Welt, und das sind längst nicht nur deutsche Fotografen. Wir arbeiten sehr viel mit französischen, mit amerikanischen Fotografen, zum Teil auch mit Fotografen aus Rußland, China, Indien und Lateinamerika. Sie alle haben eine eigene Bildsprache, eine Eigenart, und die lassen wir tunlichst leben. Das heißt, unsere Teams gehen nicht los mit dem Autor als Chef, sondern als zwei gleichberechtigte Journalisten, die dann zum Teil völlig getrennt voneinander arbeiten. Dies ist vielleicht ein Spezifikum von *GEO*, weil wir meist darauf vertrauen können, daß unsere Fotografen schon wissen, wie sie eine Geschichte visuell entwickeln und durcherzählen können. Ein guter Teil der Optik wird aber auch bei *GEO* beschafft, ist also das Ergebnis einer Recherche in der Bildredaktion.

- *Gibt es Geschichten, die vollständig aus der 'Beschaffe' sind? Oder ist das nur eine Ergänzung?*

Die Ergänzung haben wir eher selten, denn wenn wir eine Geschichte bei einem Fotografen in Auftrag geben, dann wollen wir seine Bildsprache nicht verwässern. Aber es gibt natürlich viele Themen, speziell im Wissenschaftsbereich, die von der intelligenten Zusammenstellung von Materialien aus tausenderlei Quellen leben, die ein einzelner so gar nicht fotografieren kann.

6.9 Interview mit dem freien Reporter Alexander Smoltczyk

Um die Reisereportage von der klassischen abzugrenzen und die Unterschiede in den Modalitäten herauszukristalisieren, hat Martin Sonnleitner ein Interview mit Alexander Smoltczyk geführt. Der Kisch-Preisträger arbeitete als Reporter für die *taz*, *Berliner Wochenpost*, war für *GEO* in fernen Regionen und gehört nun einem sechsköpfigen Reporterstamm des *Spiegel* an. Seine erste Reaktion auf unser Anliegen war: "Reisereportagen, das sind doch diese bunten Seiten, da habe ich nichts mit zu tun." Trotzdem wurde er uns vom *GEO*-Chefredakteur empfohlen, als dieser nach beispielhaften Reisereportagen und ihren Autoren gefragt wurde. Wir drucken eine *GEO*-Reportage von Alexander Smoltczyk in Kapitel 3 ab.

- *Werden Reportagen gänzlich von der Redaktion finanziert, unabhängig von der Werbewirtschaft?*

Ich kenne Reisereportagen vom *GEO*, der *Berliner Wochenpost*, *taz* und vom *Spiegel*. Wenn Länder oder Firmen zum Reisen eingeladen haben, wurde dies nicht angenommen. Das Prinzip war: Die Redaktion zahlt die Reise, das Hotel und auch die Essen mit Interviewpartnern. Um die Freiheit zu haben, die Gewissensfreiheit, Sachen so zu schreiben, wie sie empfunden wurden. Es wird schon etwas aufgeschrieben, wie es die Person subjektiv empfunden hat.

- *Ist es wichtig, nicht beeinflußt zu werden?*

Man darf offen für alle möglichen Einflüsse sein - aber nicht gekauft. Es gab ein Beispiel: Nigeria. *Shell* hatte furchtbaren Ärger bekommen wegen der Ermordung von Ken Saro Wiwa und hatte zur Besichtigungstour auf die Ölfelder nach Nigeria eingeladen. Alle sind sie mitgefahren und haben schön berichtet, aber nur ein einziger, der Reporter der *Süddeutschen Zeitung*, hat geschrieben, daß er von *Shell* eingeladen wurde. Das muß man auch machen.

Die anderen seriösen Zeitungen haben es nicht gemacht, haben so getan, als wären sie auf eigene Faust hingefahren. Das ist nicht integer. *GEO* wurde im letzten Jahr von *Shell* angeboten, die ganzen Reisekosten zu übernehmen - und *GEO* hat abgelehnt. Sie haben mich dann auf eigene Kosten hingeschickt.

Man ist dennoch beeinflußt. Ich kam hin, kannte niemanden in der Stadt. Ich hatte zwar alles mögliche gelesen, war aber auf den ersten Kontakt angewiesen. Mir wurde die deutsch-nigerianische Handelskommission empfohlen. Die Frau hat mir sehr geholfen, Gesprächspartner zu finden, die sie aber vorher ausgesucht hatte. Es entstand ein subtiler Druck, den Schrecken in Lagos nicht zu bestätigen. Ich wollte aber andere Leute kennenlernen. Ich habe dann einen Bericht geschrieben, der ziemlich genau das wiedergegeben hat, was ich erfahren hatte. Ich schickte ihr den Bericht, und sie war empört. Sie wollte Hochglanz-Public-Relation haben und nichts über Straßenräuber geschrieben wissen.

Man muß die Gesprächspartner filtern und die Kontakte streuen, um das falsche Bild zu korrigieren. Ich habe, wenn ich eine Geschichte schreibe, trotzdem nie die Garantie, daß ich es richtig wiedergebe.

- *Lauert für einen Reportageschreiber nicht an jeder Ecke die Gefahr, von der Werbewirtschaft bestochen zu werden?*

Jeder, mit dem man spricht, hat die Absicht, den Reporter zu beeinflussen. Durch extreme Höflichkeit, durch Einladungen zu Partys oder in das Gästehaus. So oft kommen Leute ja nicht ins Land. Jeder Bürger eines Landes will ein gutes Bild übermitteln - oder genau das Gegenteil. Die vielen Lobbygruppen machen auch Politik. Von Firmen habe ich dagegen noch nie massive Einflußnahme erlebt, eher Versuche im kleinen Rahmen. Da gibt es schon einen Unterschied zu den reinen Reisemagazinen. Allerdings war ich nie Ressortleiter. Die Firmen melden sich dann beim Chefredakteur.

- *Der Unterschied liegt also im Konzeptionellen. Hefte wie GEO SAISON wollen Reisen schmackhaft machen, GEO will unbeeinflußt Reportagen schreiben?*

Bei *GEO* ist es etwas anderes. Das Prinzip ist, über Reisen zu berichten, die man nicht machen kann. Die weiteste Reise, die ich jemals gemacht habe, war nach Papua-Neuguinea, im Auftrag von *GEO*. Der Auftrag war: „Findet einen unentdeckten Stamm und nehmt mit diesem Kontakt auf." Wir haben vom Flugzeug aus eine Baumhaussiedlung entdeckt. Wir haben mit einem Koordinaten die Längen- und Breitengrade aufgenommen und dann versucht, zu Fuß dort hinzugehen. Die Geschichte war: Wir wollen hingehen und es scheitert. Wir wissen genau, wo die Leute sind, aber die Ureinwohner sind in der Lage, sich gegen Zudringlichkeiten von außen zu verteidigen. Wir bekamen Signale, daß wir nicht weitergehen dürfen, sonst gebe es Ärger. Die Wege waren versperrt. Die Geschichte wurde 700.000 Mal veröffentlicht. Danach tobten die Leute von der Dritten-Welt-Bewegung: „Wie kannst du es wagen, die Koordinaten des unentdeckten Stammes zu verraten?" Dabei war die Geschichte: Auch wenn man weiß, wo sie sind, kommt man nicht hin. Es war eine Ode auf die Selbstverteidigungsfähigkeit dieses Stammes.

Eine andere Geschichte: Es gibt einen Altreporter bei *GEO*, der heißt Uwe George. Der hat in dem Moment aufgehört, Fernreisen zu machen, als er in Südamerika im Amazonasgebiet auf Leute traf, die von einem Reiseveranstalter dorthin geflogen worden sind. Unter dem Thema: „Auf den Spuren von Uwe George." Der Reiseveranstalter hatte dafür gesorgt, daß die Touristen genau die Fotos machen konnten, die von George zehn Jahre vorher im *GEO* erschienen sind. Als George das merkte, sagte er: „Jetzt ist Schluß. Ich bin Schuld daran, daß die Indianer nun auf den Prospekten von Reiseveranstaltern stehen. Hätte ich gewußt, daß ich durch meine Ortsangabe das Leben der Indios gefährde, hätte ich die Geschichte nicht geschrieben."Man muß Spuren verwischen, wo man nur kann, damit sie keiner nachläuft. Teil des 'Systems' ist man sowieso: Man reist mit modernen Mitteln hin und weitet die Grenze noch weiter aus. Wir waren die ersten, die in diesem Gebiet waren. Nach uns werden wahrscheinlich die Missionare kommen. Wir sind Teil einer großen Bewegung, nicht die Pfadfinder.

- *Hat sich bei Ihrer Arbeit, was die redaktionelle Unabhängigkeit angeht, etwas geändert?*

Im Grunde nicht. Die Budgets werden im allgemeinen immer kleiner. Früher konnte man bei *GEO* einen Hubschrauber mieten, aber das ist vorbei. *GEO* war vor 20 Jahren einmalig, jetzt ist die Konkurrenz so groß, daß sie das Geld nicht haben. Es gibt immer weniger Werbeseiten, jetzt muß man sparen. Dadurch ist die Versuchung sicherlich größer, sich Reisen finanzieren zu lassen. Es gab kürzlich einen Artikel in der Zeitschrift der *IG-Medien* über das Aussterben der klassischen Fotoreportage. Sachen werden konserviert. Hefte wie *stern* und *GEO* geben kein Geld mehr aus für Reportagen, die Zeit brauchen und dementsprechend kosten.

- *Ist es beim Geschriebenen ähnlich?*

Ja klar: Die Artikel werden immer kürzer und immer mehr 'durchgebrieft'. Der Idealfall ist, sich gut über ein Land zu informieren und dann alles zu vergessen. Dann einfach drauflosgucken, was riech' ich, was seh' ich, was hör' ich, was erfahr' ich. Das wird immer weniger möglich. Es wird gesagt, man könne fünfzehn Manuskriptblätter schreiben, das ist in der Regel schon sehr viel, und das muß drin sein. Als ich 1989 bei *GEO* angefangen habe, waren drei Wochen das Minimum, heute dauert die Reise 10-14 Tage.

- *Läßt sich hier nicht auch bei den klassische Reportagen eine Tendenz in Richtung Abhängigkeit zur Werbewirtschaft unterstellen?*

Ich habe das noch nicht erlebt, daß Reportagen gekauft werden sollten.

- *Und wenn die Reportagen mit immer weniger Geld zustande kommen müssen?*

Vielleicht ist die Versuchung größer. Die Redaktionen sparen dann einfach. Die Reportage dauert vierzehn Tage, der Fotograf darf nur 80 Bilder belichten statt 120, und während man früher für 500,- Mark Bücher gekauft hat, geht es heute auch mit 100,- Mark. Es gibt kaum festangestellte Reporter, meistens werden freie gebucht.

- *Um noch einmal auf die Reisereportage zu sprechen zu kommen. Kann man bei der Betrachtung des Endproduktes zwingend einen Unterschied zwischen Reportagen aus Reisemagazinen und klassischen Reportagen feststellen?*

Ja, an der Konstruktion des ganzen Textes, der Intensität der Beobachtung. Es gibt in den Reisemagazinen unwahrscheinlich gute Reportagen, der Unterschied ist jedoch die Herangehensweise. Die einen sind Tester, Späher, wollen, daß andere nachreisen. Die anderen reisenden Reporter wollen Abenteuer erleben, eine Geschichte finden, absurde Charakter entdecken. Ich habe die Erfahrung gemacht, je mehr man sich von den großen Touristikhotels in der Dritten Welt fernhält, desto mehr erlebt man auch.

7 Reisejournalismus und die Achtung des Fremden

„'Ein *sutty*, Herr Fogg', erwiederte der Brigadegeneral, 'ist ein Menschenopfer, aber ein freiwilliges. Diese Frau, welche Sie soeben gesehen haben, wird morgen in aller Frühe verbrannt werden.'

'Ei! Die Lumpenkerle!' rief Passepartout, der seine Entrüstung zu äußern sich nicht enthalten konnte. (...)

'Wie', fuhr Phileas Fogg fort, ohne daß seine Stimme die geringste Gemütsbewegung verriet, 'diese barbarischen Gebräuche existieren noch in Indien, und die Engländer haben sie noch nicht abschaffen können?'

'Im größten Teil Indiens', erwiderte Sir Francis Cromarty, 'werden diese Opfer nicht mehr vollzogen, aber wir haben auf diese wilden Gegenden, und besonders das Gebiet des Bundelkund, keinen Einfluß. Der ganze nördliche Abhang des Vindhia ist der Schauplatz unaufhörlichen Mordens und Plünderns.' 'Die Arme!' brummte Passepartout, 'lebendig verbrannt!'

(Quelle: Jules Verne: Reise um die Erde in 80 Tagen, Berlin 1984;
Original: Le tour du monde en 80 jours, 1873)

7.1 Einleitung

Sabine Neumann

Die vorigen Kapitel haben mit ihrer Darstellung der Geschichte, der Darstellungsformen und der Praxis des Reisejournalismus bereits vieles über die Besonderheiten dieses Ressorts erhellt. Besonders die redaktionelle Praxis wurde detailliert dargestellt, Reisejournalisten gaben bereitwillig Auskunft über ihren Beruf, den die meisten von ihnen als Handwerk betrachten. Für eine Theorie, gar eine Philosophie des Reisejournalismus ist in der Praxis meist kein Platz.

Im Rahmen dieses Handbuchs haben wir **einem eher theoretischen Thema** ein Kapitel gewidmet, das sich mit dem Gegenstand des Reisejournalismus beschäftigt - dem Fremden.

Wie sind die Kategorien des Fremden und des Eigenen in unserer Wahrnehmung besetzt? Welche sind die **Wechselwirkungen des Fremden mit dem Eigenen**? Diese Fragestellung, die so xenologietheoretisch klingt, hat doch für die Praxis des Reisejournalismus eine beträchtliche Bedeutung. Denn unser Verhältnis zum Fremden, das als Gegenstand der Berichterstattung im Zentrum der Aufmerksamkeit eines jeden Reisejournalisten stehen muß, ist oft nebelhaft und undifferenziert. Reiseberichterstattung ist von den persönlichen Einstellungen und Stereotypen des Journalisten so sehr geprägt wie kaum ein anderes Ressort. Über eine Landtagswahl, einen Kinofilm oder einen Verkehrsunfall kann man zwar von unterschiedlichen Standpunkten aus berichten, die Kernaussage über die Fakten, die relevant sind, also Nachrichtenwert haben, ist jedoch meist klar, überprüfbar und an den Standards des öffentlichen Interesses orientiert.

Wer dagegen über das Fremde berichtet, muß selbst entscheiden, was relevant bzw. von öffentlichem Interesse ist. Wer beispielsweise über Mauritius schreibt, kann je nach persönlicher Präferenz über eine Badeinsel voller Golfplätze, ein Naturparadies aussterbender Arten, das Opfer einer ökologischen Ausbeutung durch Kolonialismus oder eine wirtschaftlich aufstrebende Inseldemokratie schreiben. Jede dieser Perspektiven ist zwar zutreffend, aber einseitig und für die meisten Leser schon allein der geographischen Entfernung wegen nicht überprüfbar. Aus diesem Grund ist der Reisejournalismus auch am **anfälligsten für die Verbreitung von Stereotypen**. Einen Abriß über Theorie und Praxis des Stereotyps geben zwei Abschnitte dieses Kapitels, das neben entsprechenden Beispielen auch Tips zu deren Vermeidung gibt.

Im Ergebnis sollte klar sein, daß die theoretische Reflexion über das Fremde keineswegs ein reines Gedankenspiel ist, sondern eine praktische Hilfe zu besserem Reisejournalismus, wie es die Intention dieses Handbuchs ist.

7.2 Vom Eigenen und Fremden

Dagmar Rößler

Was unterscheidet das Eigene vom Fremden? Das **Eigene wird im Duden als 'Besitz'** definiert. Seinen Besitz kennt jeder genau und weiß deshalb theoretisch auch, was nicht zum eigenen Besitz gehört. Jenes müßte demnach zum Fremden gehören, wenn das Fremde das Gegenteil zum Eigenen ist. Allerdings kann wohl niemand behaupten, daß alles das ihm fremd ist, was nicht zu seinem Besitz zählt. Sicher ist es kaum möglich, Eigenes und Fremdes trennscharf und eindeutig voneinander abzugrenzen, vielmehr sollte man sich fragen, ob nicht ein beinahe stufenloser Übergang für die Unterscheidung der beiden Begriffe zutreffend ist. Das Gegensatzpaar von Eigenem und Fremdem sei so zu denken, „daß Eigenes und Fremdes sich zwar nicht vermischen, wohl aber ineinandergreifen und aufeinander übergreifen, fern aller Selbstauflösung, fern aber erst recht aller Aneignung des Fremden und aller Assimilation an das Eigene", heißt es bei B.Waldenfels (Waldenfels 1990).

Ein Mensch wird in ein soziales Umfeld hineingeboren und wächst in den meisten Fällen in demselben auf. Er lernt seine Mitmenschen kennen, seine Heimat, seine Sprache. Bevor alle diese Informationen von seinem Gehirn aufgenommen und gespeichert werden, - sozusagen als Erfahrungen - ist der Speicherplatz noch leer und unberührt. Diejenigen Informationen, die als erste vom Gehirn aufgenommen werden, gelten dann als die Normalität, eben als das Eigene. Dieses wiederum setzt sich für jeden Menschen aus anderen Kriterien zusammen, abhängig von der Kultur und dem Lebensraum des Aufwachsens, aber auch von der Art und Weise der Erziehung.

Stellt man sich nun den durchschnittlichen Rezipienten eines Reisejournals vor, setzt sich für ihn das Fremde zusammen aus ungewohnter Kultur, nie gesehener Landschaft, unbekannter Sprache sowie weiteren Details. Zunächst mag es eine Art Furcht vor der Andersartigkeit sein, die das Fremde so befremdlich sein und es als **Bedrohung** erscheinen läßt. Vermutlich ist der Mensch von Natur aus mißtrauisch, und deshalb kommen ihm zunächst bei allem Fremden gewisse Befürchtungen. „Die Angst vor dem Fremden ist 'natürlich'", meint dazu Hark Bohm (Bohm 1990). Gleichzeitig geht von der Fremdartigkeit eine geheimnisvolle Faszination aus, die beim Menschen Neugierde hervorruft, eine Neugierde, die uns zum Fremden hinzieht, uns herausfordert, es zu ergründen und zugänglich zu machen. Denn dann ist das Fremde weniger geheimnisvoll und wirkt auch weniger bedrohlich. Es kann nicht darum gehen, die Furcht vor der Fremdheit zu ignorieren, das käme einem Selbstbetrug gleich. Für Hark Bohm ist klar: „Nur wenn wir die Ängste unserer Mitmenschen akzeptieren, können wir helfen, aus Angst Neugierde, aus Aggression Gastfreundschaft werden zu lassen. Auch eine multikulturelle Gesellschaft, die mit Sicherheit die Zukunft bestimmen wird, muß wie alle Lebensprozesse mit Mühe erarbeitet werden." (Bohm 1990)

Im eigenen Land wird sicher allein die Präsenz einer anderen Kultur bereits als beunruhigend empfunden, da bei vielen das Gefühl entsteht, daß dadurch eigene Traditionen untergraben und verwässert werden. So entstehen Ängste zum Beispiel aus der vermeintlichen Konkurrenz von Deutschen und Ausländern um Arbeitsplätze. Umstritten ist die Frage, inwieweit man sich als Ausländer den Gepflogenheiten eines anderen Landes anpassen sollte, ohne die eigenen Wurzeln völlig aufzugeben. Eventuell wird aber auch einer Kultur durch die Anwesenheit einer anderen eine Art Spiegel vorgehalten, in dem die **eigenen Schwächen und Fehler** zu erkennen sind. Dadurch kann dann ein Gefühl der Abneigung, sogar des Hasses entstehen, so ungerechtfertigt dies auch immer sein mag. Hark Bohm schlägt zur Überwindung der Angst vor dem Fremden folgenden Weg vor: „Bekämpfen müssen wir die Egoisten, die immer wieder bewußt versuchen, aus der Angst vor dem Fremden Aggressionen zu formen. Sie instrumentalisieren damit die verunsicherten Menschen für ihre Machtfantasien. (...) Denn wenn wir genau hinschauen, sind all die Rassistenführer Menschen, die gegenüber ihren eigenen wirklichkeitsfeindlichen Zielen versagt haben.“ (Bohm 1990)

Mit dem 'absoluten Fremden', also fernen Ländern, Kulturen und Lebensbedingungen verhält es sich eher so, daß diese Version der Andersartigkeit Neugierde als Angst erweckt, hin und wieder wird allerdings auch mit Unverständnis reagiert bis hin zu dem Gefühl eines wohligen Grauens. Vielleicht fallen dem einen oder anderen bei solchen Überlegungen Begriffe ein wie **'Zivilisation', 'Wilde' oder 'Rückständigkeit'**. Doch was hat es eigentlich mit der Zivilisation auf sich? Der Duden von 1977 erklärt den Begriff Zivilisation als „Gesittung; Sittenverfeinerung; [äußere] Bildung; die materielle Seite der Kultur [der jeweiligen gesellschaftl. Entwicklungsstufe]“. Von solchen Ansichten muß man sich lösen, will man das Fremde verstehen, denn der Begriff Sitte ist ebenso relativ zu betrachten wie Bildung. Sicher ist für andere Kulturen die unsrige ebenso fremd wie die ihre für uns. Aber das wird meistens außer acht gelassen. Viele betrachten die abendländische Kultur als den Mittelpunkt des irdischen Daseins und alles andere als das Fremde.

Der Philosoph Karl R. Popper schreibt: „Ich glaube, daß unsere abendländische Zivilisation, trotz allem, was man mit vielem Recht an ihr aussetzen kann, die freieste, die gerechteste, die menschlichste, die beste ist, von der wir aus der Geschichte der Menschheit Kenntnis haben. Sie ist die beste - das sollte nicht außer acht bleiben - weil sie die verbesserungsfähigste ist.“ (Popper 1987: 128)

Neben dem Umstand, daß Popper die Bezeichnung 'abendländische Zivilisation' wählt, anstatt des Begriffs Kulturkreis, stört außerdem, daß er einerseits von der Geschichte der Menschheit spricht und andererseits nur das Abendland erwähnt. Als sei es das einzige, in dem die Geschichte der Menschheit stattfand. Dies scheint vor dem Hintergrund, daß das Abendland im Vergleich zu anderen Kulturen erst sehr spät zur Geltung kam, besonders fragwürdig.

Seine Aussage deutet auf eine völlig einseitige Sichtweise hin, nämlich vom Selbst als Subjekt zu dem Anderen als das Objekt. Denker, die sich mit der Wissenschaft vom Eigenen und Fremden, der Xenologie, beschäftigen, bezeichnen diese Sichtweise als unilinear und kritisieren gleichzeitig die traditionellen Ethnowissenschaften: „In der herkömmlichen Anthropologie, bzw. in den Ethnowissenschaften weisen ja die Vektoren, welche die Richtung vom Subjekt zum Objekt festlegen, sozusagen in einem Einbahnsystem aus der europäisch-abendländischen Kultur, die sich zugleich als die 'zivilisierte Welt' schlechthin versteht, stets hin zu den außerhalb des europäischen Kulurkreises angesiedelten Völkern. Von ihnen ist dann die Rede als 'unterentwickelte Völker', 'Primitivkulturen', 'Entwicklungsländer' usw. Hier wird deutlich, daß unsere traditionelle, anthropologische Betrachtungsweise offenbar unter Beibehaltung der Subjekt-Objekt-Spaltung der Erkenntnis nicht nur unilinear ausgerichtet ist, sondern zuzüglich ein hierarchisches Wertungsgefälle aufweist." (Furtwängler 1991)

Hermann Pollig vom Stuttgarter Institut für Auslandsbeziehungen zum Bedürfnis nach Exotik:

„Es muß festgestellt werden, daß nach über hundert Jahren Ethnologie, angesichts weltweiter Informations- und Mediensysteme mit ihrer überreichen Nachrichtenflut das Bild außereuropäischer Kulturen noch immer aus exotischen Stereotypen besteht und das Verständnis wie die Wertung fremder Kulturformen weitgehend nach unangemessenen eurozentrischen Parametern vorgenommen wird. Kuriose Potpourries, zusammengesetzt aus klischeehaften Versatzstücken, wie etwa Palmen, Strand, Meer und Folklore, lassen einer wirklichkeitsnahen Sicht nur wenig Chancen. Exotische Ressourcen sind das Rohmaterial, das zur willkürlichen Disposition steht und als Verbrauchsgut umfassender Vermarktung unterworfen wird. Der Imperativ 'Macht Euch die Erde untertan!' läßt über die Jahrhunderte hinweg keinen Zweifel aufkommen, wie das Verhältnis des christlichen Abendlandes zum Rest der Welt ausgesehen hat. 'Gehet hinaus...!' ist eine weitere Maxime, die klarstellt, wer wem was zu sagen hat. Die christliche, koloniale und poskoloniale Grundeinstellung, daß über die Erde die globale Verfügungsgewalt ausgeübt werden darf, wurde erst im Verlauf dieses Jahrhunderts in Frage gestellt."

(Pollig 1987: 16)

Im Ergebnis dieser Betrachtungen ist es für Reisejournalisten geboten, sich in bezug auf Fremdheit und Andersartigkeit von einer unilinearen Sichtweise zu lösen und sich dem Unbekannten zu nähern, ohne die Lust auf 'Sensationen' und die Suche nach Stereotypen befriedigen zu wollen.

Das Eigene und das Fremde sind **relative Begriffe**, und so muß man mit ihnen auch umgehen.

7.3 Das Problem von Stereotypen und Vorurteilen

Sabine Neumann

Der große Reiz des Reisejournalismus besteht darin, daß er sich mit dem Fremden und Unbekannten beschäftigt und dem Leser oder Zuschauer das Fremde nahe bringt. Kulturelle Kontraste und der Vergleich des Fremden mit dem Eigenen können neue Einsichten in die eigene Kultur und tieferes Verständnis für fremde Kulturen und Menschen schaffen. Unabdingbare Voraussetzung dafür ist vor allem der verantwortliche Umgang des Journalisten mit Sprache und Bildern, die das Fremde zeigen und erklären sollen. Denn gerade im Reiz der Darstellung des Fremden besteht auch die große Gefahr des Reisejournalismus, **statt differenzierter Information lediglich Stereotypen und Vorurteile zu transportieren und zu verbreiten**.

Der Begriff des Stereotyps entstammt der Terminologie der Drucktechnik. Unter Stereotypie versteht man die Abformung der aus beweglichen Lettern gesetzten Originaldruckplatte in eine Pappmatrize, die mit Blei ausgegossen wird. Die beweglichen, frei kombinierbaren Strukturen (der Lettern) werden dabei verfestigt und erstarren unwandelbar.

Der heutige **sozialwissenschaftliche Stereotypenbegriff** wurde erstmals 1922 von dem amerikanischen Journalisten Walter Lippmann definiert. In seinem Standardwerk ‘Public Opinion’ unterscheidet er zwischen der ‘World outside’, der äußeren Welt, und den ‘Pictures in our Heads’, den inneren Vorstellungen der Menschen. Unsere Vorstellungen vom Eigenen und vom Fremden sind festgefügt, wir haben bestimmte, nur schwer wandelbare Bilder in unseren Köpfen. Diese Bilder sind konstruierte Realitäten, die sehr oft nicht mit der objektiven Wirklichkeit übereinstimmen. Ein Beispiel eines solchen Stereotyps: Der typische Ire ist rothaarig. Tatsächlich haben nur 5% (!) der irischen Bevölkerung rote Haare; eine keineswegs repräsentative Anzahl also.

Das Denken in Stereotypen ist für Lippmann eine Form der Weltbewältigung durch das **Reduzieren von Komplexität**. Dies ist zum einen ökonomisch: „Denn der Versuch, alle Dinge frisch und im Detail zu sehen, erschöpft und kommt bei eiligen Angelegenheiten praktisch überhaupt nicht in Frage.“ (Lippmann 1964: 67) Zum anderen wirken Stereotype als Verteidigungsmittel (‘stereotypes as defence’) gegen eine überkomplexe Welt: „Sie bieten vielleicht kein vollständiges Weltbild, aber sie sind das Bild einer möglichen Welt, auf die wir uns eingestellt haben.“ (Lippmann 1964: 71)

Stereotype zeichnen sich im Gegensatz zum kurzlebigeren Image vor allem durch Konstanz und Universalität (Manz 1968) aus, sie durchziehen alle

Themen und Lebensbereiche und sind nur äußerst schwer zu beeinflussen. Sie können wahr (z.B. Deutsche trinken viel Bier) oder falsch (Iren sind rothaarig, s.o.) sein. Stereotype entstehen nicht nur über fremde Länder, Menschen und Kulturen (Hetero-Stereotype), sondern auch über das eigene Land, die eigene Kultur, die eigene Gruppe (Auto-Stereotype).

Woher kommen nun Stereotype, wie entstehen die Bilder in den Köpfen? Die Quellen von Stereotypen liegen vor allem in der persönlichen Sozialisation durch Familie, Schule und Medien. Der Mensch stereotypisiert am wenigsten die eigene Nahwelt, denn er verfügt über deren differenzierte Kenntnis. Die Fernwelt, das Fremde und Unbekannte hingegen, über welches keine differenzierten, sondern bestenfalls ungefähre Kenntnisse vorhanden sind, werden in hohem Maße stereotypisiert. Wir erinnern uns: Stereotype vereinfachen die Komplexität der Welt zu eingängigen Bildern im Kopf.

Der österreichische Kommunikationswissenschaftler Kurt Luger über die Schwierigkeiten bei der Begegnung mit fremden Kulturen:

„Die Medien spielen eine ganz wesentliche Rolle in der Produktion von Erwartungshaltungen, Leitbildern, Stereotypen und Klischees. Wie die österreichischen Heimtfilme der Nachkriegszeit liefern Kataloge, Reiseseiten und Sehnsuchtsliteratur behübschte Realitäten und verlogene Bilder. Würden die Urlaubsziele unter dem Kreuz des Südens oder in den Alpen nicht nur als von Katalog-Indios bzw. von sepplhosentragenden Reservatsösterreichern und Alpenhorn-Schweitzern besiedelte Disneylands angepriesen, entstünden vielleicht nicht jene falschen Erwartungen, bei deren Einlösung sich Touristen wie 'abgekühlte Soldaten' verhalten - so hat Jean Paul Satre diese Invasion genannt.

Insbesondere der Dritte-Welt-Tourismus entpuppt sich daher nicht selten als eine neokolonialistische Veranstaltung ohne Rücksicht auf Menschen, Kulturen und Ökologie in den bereisten Entwicklungsländern. Studien weisen auch nach, daß durch den Ferntourismus, insbesondere bei kürzeren Aufenthalten ohne direkte Begegnung mit den Einheimischen, Vorurteile gegenüber fremden Kulturen eher bestärkt als abgebaut werden. 'Tourismus mit Einsicht' wird aber den Reisewilligen über die Medien kaum nahegebracht; und ethnologische Studien oder sensible Kulturschock-Literatur gelesen zu verschicken ist noch nicht möglich."

(Luger 1994: 11)

Stereotype werden oft mit **Vorurteilen** synonym gesetzt. In der sozialwissenschaftlichen Terminologie ist das allerdings falsch. Beide Phänomene entstehen im Bereich des Vor-Urteils, d.h. vor einer verstandesmäßigen Beschäftigung mit dem Sachverhalt. Doch während Stereotype zumindest einen wahren Kern aufweisen können, insofern also wenigstens zum Teil kognitive Einstellungen reflektieren, sind Vorurteile immer affektiv-emotional gefaßt und von keinerlei Tatsachen getrübt. Deshalb sind Vorurteile immer falsch, während es durchaus zutreffende Stereotype geben kann. Die Vorurteilsforschung stammt aus der Sozialpsychologie und untersucht das Phänomen der Abwertung und Stigmatisierung von Fremdgruppen, die von der eigenen Gruppe streng abgesetzt und ausgegrenzt werden.

Im Reisejournalismus können sowohl Stereotype als auch Vorurteile auftreten bzw. Auswirkungen auf die Berichterstattung haben. Was können Reisejournalisten tun, um faire und differenzierte Berichterstattung zu gewährleisten? Zunächst einmal **sollte der Journalist die eigene Einstellung zu seinem Thema reflektieren**. Nur wer bereit ist, die Bilder im eigenen Kopf bewußt zur Seite zu legen, kann wirklich neue Perspektiven und Eindrücke gewinnen. Vorurteile haben im Reisejournalismus keinen Platz. Guter, lebendiger und interessanter (nicht nur Reise-)Journalismus braucht den unvoreingenommenen Blick, der zumindest als Ideal jedem Journalisten eigen sein sollte. Reisereportagen, die auf dem Boden von Vorurteilen wachsen, verdienen nicht die Bezeichnung Journalismus, sondern sind allenfalls Propaganda.

In der empirischen Analyse von reisejournalistischen Produkten findet man echte Vorurteile (glücklicherweise) relativ selten. Vorurteile sind immer falsch, deshalb fallen sie unter Umständen leichter als solche auf. Relativ oft trifft man in der Reiseberichterstattung allerdings auf Stereotype. Einige von ihnen sind bereits so stark verfestigt, daß kaum jemand sie mehr als Stereotype zu erkennen vermag. Die 'grüne Insel', das ist natürlich Irland. Und der 'schwarze Kontinent' ist ein immer wieder gern verwendetes Synonym für Afrika, auch wenn das Bild aus rassistischem Blickwinkel stammt. Wer einen herkömmlichen Reiseartikel über Mauritius liest, erfährt im Sinne des Exotismus von Korallenriffen, Segelmöglichkeiten und paradiesischen Badebuchten, aber nicht von einer funktionierenden Demokratie und einer florierenden Textilindustrie. Hierin liegt das Kernproblem des Umgangs mit Stereotypen, nämlich dem Eingehen des Journalisten auf die **Erwartungen seiner Zielgruppe**. Ganz ohne Stereotype auszukommen, heißt die Erwartungen der Leser oder Zuschauer oftmals zu enttäuschen. Die Rezipienten, von denen jeder seinen eigenen Vorrat an Stereotypen mit sich herumträgt, brauchen eine Art Wiedererkennungsfaktor. Eine Reportage über Schottland, in der kein einziger Kiltträger, keine Dudelsackmusik und kein Hochlandrind auftaucht, wirkt auf den durchschnittlichen Rezipienten nicht vollständig oder auch langweilig, weil nichts Bekanntes darin vorkommt und die Erwartung des Rezipienten enttäuscht wird.

Was also soll der Reisejournalist tun, wenn er in der journalistischen Realität ganz ohne Stereotypen offenbar nicht auskommen kann? Am wichtigsten erscheint mir der verantwortliche, kritische Umgang mit dem Stereotyp. Wo es vermieden werden kann, sollte es zugunsten von differenzierter, informativer Berichterstattung verschwinden. Platte, trivial-exotistische und rassistische Stereotype (‘schwarzer Kontinent’) gehören nicht in einen guten Reisejournalismus.

Statt dessen kann man **mit dem Stereotyp auch überlegt umgehen**, man kann es als solches kenntlich machen und gegebenenfalls verifizieren oder falsifizieren. Für den Leser oder Zuschauer ergibt dieses unter Umständen eine neue Perspektive, eigene Stereotype werden als solche erkannt, das Bild im Kopf wird differenzierter, die Informationsteilchen werden neu kombiniert - und das Stereotyp wird im besten Fall durch ein Bild ersetzt, das näher an der objektiven Wirklichkeit liegt. Und damit wird der eigentliche Zweck des Reisejournalismus, das Fremde nahe zu bringen, erfüllt.

7.4 Stereotypen in reisejournalistischen Artikeln

Undine Kayser

7.4.1 Kommunikationsmechanismen begünstigen Stereotypen

Im Kommunikationsprozeß zwischen Mensch und Umwelt wird zunächst Information aus einem Überfluß an Wahrnehmungen selektiert, dann abstrahiert, interpretiert und ins eigene Denk- und Werteschema eingeordnet. Dieser automatische **Prozeß der ‘selektiven Wahrnehmung’** läuft ununterbrochen ab, wenn wir unsere Umwelt ‘sinnlich’ betrachten, also hören, sehen, riechen, fühlen und schmecken. Sie schützt das Gehirn vor Überanstrengung durch zuviel Information. Selektion und Abstraktion von Information helfen, komplexe Zusammenhänge zu vereinfachen. Sie bedeuten aber auch immer eine Verallgemeinerung der speziellen Information und können so Grundlage von Stereotypen sein. Dazu wird die vereinfachte Information, wenn sie vom Gehirn interpretiert wird, bewertet.

Selbst in einer bekannten Umgebung ergeben sich aus diesem Prozeß Schwierigkeiten und Mißverständnisse. Der amerikanische Kommunikations-Psychologe Paul Watzlawick gibt ein überspitztes Beispiel eines solchen Mißverständnisses:

7.4.2 Die Geschichte mit dem Hammer

Ein Mann will ein Bild aufhängen. Den Nagel hat er, nicht aber den Hammer. Also beschließt unser Mann, hinüberzugehen und ihn auszuborgen. Doch da kommt ihm ein Zweifel: Was, wenn der Nachbar mir den Hammer nicht leihen will? Gestern schon grüßte er mich nur so flüchtig. Aber vielleicht war die Eile nur vorgeschützt, und er hat etwas gegen mich. Und was? Ich habe ihm nichts angetan; der bildet sich da etwas ein. Wenn jemand von mir ein Werkzeug borgen wollte, ich gäbe es ihm sofort. Und warum er nicht? Wie kann man einem Mitmenschen einen so einfachen Gefallen abschlagen? Leute wie dieser Kerl vergiften einem das Leben.

Und dann bildet er sich noch ein, ich sei auf ihn angewiesen. Nur weil er einen Hammer hat. Jetzt reichts mir wirklich. Und so stürmt er hinüber, läutet, der Nachbar öffnet, doch bevor er „Guten Tag“ sagen kann, schreit ihn unser Mann an: „Behalten sie ihren Hammer, sie Rüpel!“ (Watzlawick 1983: 37) Der Mann hatte nur eine Information, die Eile seines Nachbarn. Diese kurze Information hat er aus der Begegnung mit dem Nachbarn ausgewählt. Vielleicht hat der Nachbar auch beim Gruß gelächelt oder sah besonders gestreßt aus, aber das erinnert der Mann nicht mehr. Er mißt dieser Eile eine Bedeutung zu: Sie war nur vorgeschützt. Und er interpretiert die Eile: Der Nachbar hat etwas gegen mich. Entsprechend der Ursache-Folge-Beziehung, die er aufgestellt hat: „Eile - vorgeschützt - Nachbar mag mich nicht“, handelt der Mann. Doch seine Handlungsweise ist völlig unpassend für die gegebene Situation. Inwiefern begünstigt dieser Kommunikationsprozeß die Entstehung von Stereotypen im Reisejournalismus?

7.4.3 Selektive Wahrnehmung

In einer unbekannten Umgebung ist es noch leichter, Eindrücke (die durch die selektive Wahrnehmung schon verfälscht sein können) inadequat zu interpretieren. In einem fremden Land ergeben sich umso leichter Mißverständnisse, zumal **unterschiedliche Wertvorstellungen in bezug auf Moral, Ethik, Religion**, etc. bestehen. Dazu ein weiteres Beispiel der selektiven Wahrnehmung: Drei Männer in einem Land XY sehen das gleiche Mädchen, A ein Iraner, B ein Deutscher, C ein Amerikaner. Dem Iraner geht als erstes durch den Kopf: „Sie trägt keinen Schleier, sie ist eine Ungläubige“. Der Deutsche denkt: „Holla, die sieht aber gut aus!“ während der Amerikaner sich ekelt: „Ieh, die hat ja unrasierte Beine wie ein Tier.“ Alle drei haben ihrem kulturellen Denk- und Werteschema entsprechend Information über das Mädchen ausgewählt. Stereotypen (und zwar drei ganz unterschiedliche) würden die drei dann prägen, wenn sie nach diesem Eindruck in ihrem Heimatland erzählen würden: A: „Die Mädchen in XY sind ungläubig.“, B: „Die Mädchen in XY sind echt heiß.“, C: „Die Mädchen in XY sind abstoßend.“ Nach der selektiven Wahrnehmung des Mädchens haben die Männer ihre Information, den Werten ihrer Kultur entsprechend beurteilt und als allgemeingültig weitergegeben. Ähnliches kann dem Journalisten passieren, der in ein fremdes Land reist und später darüber berichtet.

7.4.4 Befremdende Eindrücke

In einer anderen Kultur fällt uns zunächst alles auf, was unser Gehirn als fremd und unbekannt registriert. Unter dem **Begriff ‘Kultur’** sollen in diesem Kontext alle Elemente verstanden werden, die das Zusammenleben von Menschen in einer Gruppe ausmachen (anthropologischer Kulturbegriff). Alle neuen Eindrücke der Kultur werden sofort in unser bestehendes Denk- und Werteschema eingeordnet, befremdende Wahrnehmungen dabei besonders genau analysiert. Um etwas gänzlich Fremdes später wiederzugeben, zu erzählen oder zu beschreiben, brauchen wir viele Worte, suchen nach Vergleichen und abstrahieren, um anderen Angehörigen unserer Kultur unsere Erlebnisse zu veranschaulichen. Innerhalb dieses Prozesses kann es zur **Prägung von Stereotypen** kommen, wenn die Informationen, die im Gedächtnis haften bleiben, (meistens, weil sie vereinfacht und deshalb eingänglich sind), als allgemeingültig angesehen und weitergegeben werden. Stereotypen entstehen erst, wenn das völlig Fremde vertrauter wird, also im Laufe von wiederholten Erzählungen bzw. Beschreibungen, denn Stereotypen über ein Land entstehen immer erst durch das gemeinsame Wissen einer Gruppe um bestimmte stereotype Information darüber. Achim Schmitz-Forte hat 470 Reisebeschreibungen aus 35 Jahren untersucht und kommt zu folgendem Ergebnis: „Je fremder der Gegenstand des Berichtens, desto schwieriger ist es, ihn einfach durch ein Etikett zu *repräsentieren.* Der Autor muß wenigstens oberflächlich zu beschreiben versuchen, was im Kopf des Lesers einfach noch nicht präsent ist.“ (Schmitz-Forte 1992: 21)

Das heißt konkret für den Reisejournalisten: Wäre es nicht besser, **unvoreingenommen und völlig unvorbereitet einer fremden Kultur zu begegnen**, um Stereotypen zu vermeiden? Sind somit in einem Bericht über ein exotisches, unbekanntes Land wie Papua Neuguinea weniger Stereotypen zu finden als in einem Artikel über Frankreich? Schmitz-Forte schreibt dazu: „Je fremder die Umgebung, in die ein Reisender (oder Reisejournalist) gerät, desto gröber sind die Erwartungshaltungen strukturiert. Je gröber die Erwartungshaltung, desto größer ist potentiell die Diskrepanz zwischen der erlebten Realität und dem Vorurteil." (Schmitz-Forte 1992: 21) Schmitz-Forte findet in seiner Untersuchung zwei Reaktionsmuster: „Zum einen: Stereotypen werden aufgebrochen, es entsteht Raum für ein vergleichsweise wenig vorselektiertes Erleben, für neue Eindrücke, neue Information, neue Bewertungen und ein (zumindest modifiziertes) Urteil nach der Erfahrung. Zum anderen: das Gegenteil. Die Wahrnehmung wird radikal selektiert, bis soviel von den unbekannten, bedrohlichen Eindrücken ausgeblendet ist, daß sich eine gewisse Vertrauheit einstellt." (Schmitz-Forte 1992: 22) Hier wird die Chance, aber auch die Gefahr des unvoreingenommenen Erlebens deutlich.

Dazu kommt, daß **wir von den meisten Kulturen der Welt bereits eine Vorstellung haben**, die sich aus Medieneindrücken und persönlichen Erzählungen zusammensetzt. Der Reisejournalist wird sich in der Regel auf seine Recherche in der fremden Kultur vorbereiten. Er wird Reiseführer lesen und andere Reportagen über das Land, in jedem Fall aber wird er eine Erwartungshaltung haben, ein Bild des Landes, über das er schreibt. Dazu kommen äußere Zwänge: Vielleicht hat der Chefredakteur bereits deutlich gemacht, wie er sich den Bericht über das Land vorstellt, welche Aspekte beschrieben werden und welche unter den Tisch fallen sollen? All diese Faktoren tragen zur Prägung von Stereotypen bei, wenn es darum geht, dem potentiellen Reisenden ein neues Land, dem Leser zu Hause eine fremde Kultur vorzustellen.

7.4.5 Vertraute Eindrücke

Wie steht es dagegen mit Berichten über eine mehr oder minder 'bekannte fremde' Kultur? Im Ausland wirkt scheinbar Bekanntes auf den ersten Blick wohltuend vertraut, jedoch nur, weil wir es innerhalb unseres eigenen kulturellen Bezugssystemes verstehen. Das bedeutet noch nicht, daß es im richtigen Kontext der anderen Kultur verstanden worden ist, deren Bezugssystem wir nicht kennen. Dieser Aspekt des Wahrnehmungsprozesses ist besonders problematisch, denn gerade **das Vertraute** würde sich vielleicht bei näherem Hinsehen als **fremd und erforschenwert**, herausstellen. Das Gehirn signalisiert jedoch: „Das kennst Du, da brauchst Du nicht genauer hinsehen." In vielen Fällen stecken hinter gleichen oder ähnlichen Verhaltensweisen unterschiedliche Bedeutungen. Ein einfaches Beispiel: In Rumänien bedeutet Kopfnicken ein 'nein' und Kopfschütteln ein 'ja'.

Als bekannt läßt das Gehirn all das gelten, was wir bereits von der anderen Kultur wußten und deshalb erwartet haben. Dabei kommt ein psychologischer Aspekt ins Spiel: „Ich habe es gewußt und nun ist es wirklich so." Wir fühlen uns bestätigt. Habe ich erwartet, daß es in Irland besonders grün ist, so wird mir die grüne hügelige Landschaft im Süden der Insel vertraut vorkommen. Im Gegensatz zum karg-felsigen Connemara im Westen, das dieser Erwartung nicht entspricht und mir fremd und un-irisch erscheint. Meine Erfahrung, die ich später weitergebe, wird durch meine vorherige Erwartungshaltung geprägt sein. Das Berichten über eine „fremde Kultur", von der ich schon viel weiß, lädt also förmlich dazu ein, bestehende Stereotypen weiter zu verwenden.

Eine junge Amerikanerin aus Ohio verbrachte vor einigen Jahren ein Austauschjahr auf der Insel Sylt. Nach einigen Wochen hatte sie einen Artikel für ihre Schülerzeitung daheim in den USA geschrieben. Sie erzählte darin von ihrem Leben in Deutschland und berichtete unter anderem: „Übrigens stimmt es tatsächlich: die Deutschen fahren entweder *Mercedes*, *Porsche* oder *BMW*." Alles, was die Schülerin von Deutschland kennengelernt hatte, war der Sommer auf der Insel Sylt. Sie sah die Touristen mit ihren teuren Autos. Das überzeugende 'die Deutschen' hat sie aber deshalb eingefügt, weil sie diesen Stereotyp aus Amerika kannte, ihn auf Sylt bestätigt fand und verallgemeinerte. Sie hatte **bereits ein fertiges Bild im Kopf**, was für Autos die meisten Deutschen fahren würden, und hat den Stereotyp, als sie ihn bestätigt fand, bedenkenlos weitergegeben, ohne ihn zu hinterfragen. Walter Lippmann formulierte bereits in den 20er Jahren: „We do not first see and then define, we define first and then see." (Lippmann 1922: 81) Damit meint er, daß wir genau nach dem Bild suchen, das wir schon im Kopf hatten, bevor wir einer Situation begegnet sind. Man interpretiert also nicht das Gesehene neu, sondern sucht darin das, was der eigenen Vorstellung davon entspricht.

In Reiseberichten werden sowohl im Umgang mit fremden als auch mit vertrauten Eindrücken Stereotypen verwendet. Dahinter steckt oft keine Absicht, denn um kritisch mit der eigenen Wahrnehmung umgehen zu können, muß man sich immer wieder bewußt machen, wie die beschriebenen Wahrnehmungsprozesse funktionieren.

Dabei spielt auch der Zeitmangel der Journalisten eine Rolle. Die Recherche in einem fremden Land ist in der Regel zu kurz, um sich eingehend mit einem Land und seinen Menschen zu befassen. Ein vollständiges, differenziertes Verständnis der Kultur ist auch nicht das Ziel eines Reisejournalisten, vielmehr präsentiert er nur einen kleinen Teil davon und diesen unter touristischen Gesichtspunkten. Aber selbst in kurzer Zeit kann man sich mehr oder weniger **auf Land und Leute einlassen**, kann versuchen, **Fremdes zu begreifen**, ohne es grundsätzlich abzulehnen, kann sich darin üben, scheinbar Bekanntes zu hinterfragen und neue Wertvorstellungen kennenlernen, ohne sie zu bewerten.

Die Darstellung Asiens als Projektionsfläche europäisch-exotischer Träume:

„Natürlich: Thailand ist ein einziger Puff. Und ‘Prostitution’, das ist so ein unpassendes Europäer-Wort dafür und in Asien vollkommen fehl am Platz: Männern Liebe geben, das sind die Thailänderinnen schon aus Tradition gewohnt, für sie ist es die natürlichste Sache der Welt.

Stammtisch-Parolen, die man immer wieder hört. Der Barbesitzer auf der Reeperbahn weiß es (besser?), flotte Schreiber verbreiten sie immer wieder, dem Pauschaltouristen verschaffen sie in Asien ein anregendes Prickeln in der Magengegend, und auch die als seriös geltende FAZ preßt es in die klugen Köpfe: „Die meisten Mädchen finden nichts dabei.“

Europäer haben hinter der Höflichkeit Asiens, dem unergründlichen Lächeln und der Anmut der Asiatinnen seit jeher besondere Verlockungen verspürt. Heuter werden die Sehnsüchte perfekt kommerziell ausgebeutet - ob fernöstliche Fluglinien mit dem Gesicht einer Stewardess werben, BILD in Serien wie „Heiße Fracht aus Bangkok“ Käuferwünsche regelmäßig in den nächsten Auflagenzuwachs ummünzt oder Reisende zu den ‘letzten Paradiesen’ in der Südsee verschifft werden und dort traditionellen Tänzen im Baströckchen zusehen und mit Steingeld bezahlen (um später festzustellen, daß ein Bier umgerechnet acht Mark gekostet hat).

Renommierte Reiseführer, die den Urlaub erst so recht zu einem Genuß werden lassen sollen, gewinnen dem Mythos der Asiatin nicht nur immer wieder neue alte Seiten ab, sie geben stets auch Hinweise auf den praktischen Gebrauchswert von Frauen. „Die Fremden-Prostitution hat ein interessantes Phänomen hervorgebracht: taubstumme junge Mädchen sind äußerst beliebt und können Rekordzahlen an Kunden aufweisen, da zum einen das Problem der sprachlichen Verständigung entfällt und sie zum anderen im ‘Wunschlesen’ konkurrenzlos sind.“ Erst als diese Passage in der Neuauflage des Bangkok-Baedekers 1986 einigen Lerser(inne)n auffiel und Baedeker in die Schlagzeilen kam, bemerkte der Verlag seine Schamlosigkeit und zog den Band zurück.“

(Wilke-Lammer / Lammer 1987: 106)

7.4.6 Stereotypen und ihre Verbreitung

Reisejournalisten spielen eine nicht unwesentliche Rolle bei der Prägung und Weiterverbreitung von Stereotypen. Sie nehmen eine Vermittlerposition ein in einer Branche, die wesentlich prägt, wie Kulturen einander hautnah begegnen, dem Tourismus. **Reisejournalisten** sind häufig ein Bindeglied zwischen den Rucksackreisenden, die dem Tourismus immer einen Schritt voraus sind, wenn es um die Entdeckung noch wenig erschlossener Regionen geht, und den späteren Pauschaltouristen. Sie prägen das Bild einer andereren Kultur in ihrem Heimatland, indem sie beschreiben, was ihrer Ansicht nach sehenwert ist, was abstoßend-fremd und was faszinierend-anziehend ist. Sie sind sozusagen **'Katalysatoren der Kultur'**, die aus einer Vielzahl von positiven und negativen Erlebnismöglichkeiten das herauskristallisieren, was einen Besuch wert macht. Den Lesern ist oft nicht bewußt, daß es sich bei einer Reisereportage um einen subjektiven, beschränkten Blick handelt. Der Wirklichkeitsausschnitt, den der Journalist präsentiert, wird für sie zum ersten 'persönlichen' Eindruck von der fremden Kultur. Das macht den Leser anfällig für Stereotypen, denn sie schaffen ein schnelles, leicht vorstellbares Bild. Auf diese Weise prägen Reisejournalisten entscheidend, mit welcher Einstellung sich reisende Leser einer Kultur nähern, ob mit Respekt oder Respektlosigkeit. Und sie schaffen eine Erwartungshaltung bei den Reisenden, die sich nicht selten in ein hartnäckiges PR-Image verwandelt, wie z.B. in den Ländern der Südsee, in denen blütenbekränzte Tänzer den Touristen am Flughafen erwarten.

7.4.7 Stereotypen - eine Frage von Nähe und Distanz des Reisejournalisten zur fremden Kultur?

Zur besonderen Verantwortung der Reisejournalisten gehört es, bewußt mit Stereotypen umzugehen, immer wieder kritisch die eigene Wahrnehmung zu überprüfen. Verwendet der Reisejournalist, der ein Land gut kennt, weniger Stereotypen? **Vertrautheit mit einer anderen Kultur schützt gerade nicht vor der Verwendung von Stereotypen**. Auch in den beliebten 'Kenner-Berichten' finden sich zahlreiche. Man könnte die Reisejournalisten in 'Insider' und 'Outsider' einteilen, die - je nach Wissensstand - aus verschiedenem Blickwinkel über eine fremde Kultur berichten. Der Versuch soll hier gewagt werden, auch auf die Gefahr hin, mit dieser Kategorisierung neue Stereotypen zu schaffen.

Der **Insider** kennt das zu beschreibende Land wie seine Westentasche. Er ist entweder langjähriger Besucher des Landes oder hat sogar dort gelebt. Sein Tonfall ist der des **gelassen-erfahrenen Kenners**, der zu jeder Sehenswürdigkeit die Geschichte, zu jeder kulturellen Eigenheit eine Anekdote zu erzählen weiß. All das **feit ihn aber keineswegs gegen den Gebrauch von Stereotypen**. Lippmann spricht von der 'mirror-image-attitude' (Lippmann 1922), wenn die 'Opfer' eines Stereotypen diesen akzeptieren und sogar selber weiter gebrauchen. Das Stereotyp der Insel Sylt etwa als die 'Insel der Schönen und Reichen' wird gleichermaßen von PR und von Journalisten genutzt, obwohl ein Tag vor Ort reichen würde, um festzustellen, daß das 'Körnchen Wahrheit', das der Stereotyp besessen haben mag, längst bis zur Unkenntlichkeit geschrumpft ist. Gerade der Insider sollte in der Lage sein, einseitige Stereotypen (Iren sind rothaarige Guinnesstrinker, die singend in der Kneipe anzutreffen sind...) zu identifizieren, und zu differenzieren, d.h. sowohl den Wahrheitsgehalt zu erkennen, den sie enthalten mögen, ohne ihn in der Beschreibung zu übertreiben, als auch kulturelle Phänomene in den historischen und gesellschaftlichen Kontext der jeweiligen Kultur zu stellen.

Der **Outsider** dagegen kennt das besuchte Land gar nicht oder nur wenig. Er hat einen **'jungfräulichen' Blick** zum Geschehen und wird hauptsächlich seine Beobachtungen beschreiben. Er wird die Dinge ähnlich erleben wie der Leser, der das Land dann zum ersten Mal besucht. Dadurch wird die Perspektive des Outsiders reizvoll, denn nur er weiß um die Schwierigkeiten, die den Neuling erwarten, um Dinge, die der Insider schon längst als selbstverständliches Wissen voraussetzt. So sieht eine amerikanische Journalistin auf Sylt nichts von den 'Schönen und Reichen', sie bemerkt vielmehr „einen Strand voller Leute in Körben, dicke Nackte, alte Nackte, Hardcore-Nudisten" (Jessel 1994: 81).

Wenn der Outsider aber Phänomenen, die er nicht versteht, mit Unverständnis begegnet, läuft er Gefahr, Stereotypen zu prägen, indem er Dinge aus seiner eigenen Sichtweise interpretiert und beurteilt. Das können sowohl positive als auch negative Stereotypen sein. Derjenige, der positiv und mit großer Begeisterung die spirituelle 'Unschuld und Unverdorbenheit' eines tibetischen Bergvolkes anpreist, entwirft ebenso einen Stereotyp wie derjenige, der angewidert von den blutigen Ritualen afrikanischer Buschvölker berichtet.

Diese Typisierung zeigt, daß die Entstehung von Stereotypen und ihre Verbreitung nicht nur von der Nähe bzw. Distanz des Journalisten zur jeweiligen Kultur abhängig ist. Im heutigen Reisejournalismus sind Stereotypen bei 'Insidern' und 'Outsidern' gleichermaßen zu finden.

7.4.8 Stereotypen - wo und wie sind sie in Reiseberichten zu finden?

Stereotypen können auf verschiedenen Ebenen eines Reiseberichtes auftauchen, beginnend bei der **Themenauswahl**. Schreibe ich den zwanzigsten Artikel über eine Pub-Tour in Irland oder hat das Land noch andere interessante Aspekte zu bieten? Wenn New York, dann muß es Harlem sein, oder die Bronx oder war da noch was?

Die **Recherche** bzw. später **die Auswahl aus dem recherchierten Material** sind ebenfalls besonders anfällig für Stereotypen. Was wählt der Journalist aus der Fülle von Informationsmaterial, das er gesammelt hat? Nach welchen Kriterien selektiert er? Beschreibt er Alltägliches oder Außergewöhnliches? Wählt er eher Erlebnisse, die ihm vertraut waren, die vielleicht leichter zu beschreiben sind und bei denen er davon ausgehen kann, daß der Leser Vorwissen besitzt oder nimmt er die exotische, sensationelle Story? Und wenn er eine Geschichte auswählt, wie geht er mit bekannten Stereotypen um?

Im Falle einer Sensationsstory wäre die Frage, ob der Journalist sie als solche kennzeichnet oder ob er einen außergewöhnlichen Vorfall als alltäglich porträtiert und so eine völlig falsche Erwartungshaltung beim Leser schafft. Oft ist schon die äußerliche Beschreibung der Menschen eines Landes stereotyp: der Chinese trägt natürlich maoblau, der skandinavische Hüne dagegen ist hellblond und der Amerikaner entweder fett oder ein Cowboy. Mit diesem Bild im Kopf fahren viele Reisejournalisten los, suchen und finden es im fremden Land und konzentrieren ihre Beschreibung darauf.

Auch die **Sprache und der Sprachstil**, tragen entscheidend dazu bei, ob ein Reisebericht stereotyp ist oder nicht. Adjektive können einem Text wertenden Charakter geben. Achim Schmitz-Forte gibt in seiner Untersuchung eine unsystematische Auswahl: „berühmt, unvergeßlich, herrlich, sehenswert, edel, meisterlich, großartig, romantisch usw." (Schmitz-Forte 1992: 17). Negativbeispiele wären „unheimlich, schauerlich, ekelhaft, unakzeptabel, unmöglich, grauenhaft, abstoßend", usw.

Diese **Platzhalter-Adjektive** beschreiben eine emotionale Wertung, sie spielen mit Gefühlen, die jeder von uns kennt, aber nicht unbedingt gleich empfindet. So ermöglichen sie dem Leser, seine eigene Interpretation von 'herrlich' oder 'unmöglich' in den Text einzusetzen. Die 'herrliche' Bergwelt oder der 'herrliche' Strand vermitteln keine Vorstellung darüber, wie sie wirklich aussehen. Der Strand könnte mit oder ohne Palmen sein, er könnte aus Lavasteinen bestehen oder auch voller gutaussehender Menschen sein. Was nützt dem Leser der Begriff 'herrlich'?

Die Wahl des bestimmten oder **unbestimmten Artikels** trägt ebenfalls zur Stereotypenbildung bei. Ist es 'der' Amerikaner (generell) und 'die' Irin (schlechthin), die ich beschreibe oder handelt es sich um eine bestimmte Person? Spreche ich von 'den' Franzosen, beschreibe ich 'die' Schweden oder die Menschen, denen ich wirklich begnet bin?

Mit dem Begriff 'Sprachstil' ist in diesem Fall der **Tonfall** eines Berichts gemeint, der plaudernd, ironisch, schwärmerisch, abwertend usw. sein kann. Ich kann einen Stereotypen ironisch präsentieren und dadurch entlarven: „Mein Freund Paddy, der natürlich rote Haare hat und literweise Guinness in seinem Bauch verschwinden lassen kann, ist ein Bilderbuch-Ire."

Aber nicht nur Sprache, auch **Bilder und Layout** können Träger von Stereotypen sein. Bilder von Deutschland in ausländischen Reisemagazinen zeigen meistens Burgen am Rhein, Schloß Neuschwanstein, Menschen in Lederhosen und das Münchner Oktoberfest. In einer Irland-Reportage ist das Foto eines rothaariges, sommersprossigen Jungen abgebildet. Darunter steht kurioserweise: „Minderheit: Nur wenige Iren sind rothaarig." Dies wird im Text nicht weiter erläutert. Das Foto zeigt den Stereotypen, während die Bildunterschrift ihn entlarvt und widerlegt (Schwer 1996: 34). Zudem haben die Ganzseitenfotos dieses Artikels über die „grüne Insel" alle einen grünen Rahmen, wie überhaupt die Farbe grün im Layout vieler Irland-Berichte dominiert.

Es scheint, als ob mit Bildern und im Layout hemmungsloser mit Stereotypen gearbeitet wird als im Text. Vielleicht weil an den gleichen Orten immer wieder dieselben Bilder problemlos zu kriegen sind? Oder einfach die Bilder vom Fremdenverkehrsamt benutzt werden, das sein Image pflegen möchte? Wie beim Text ist ein Bild nicht von Anfang an stereotyp, sondern nur durch fortwährende Wiederholung im Zusammenhang mit dem Text. Der Text hat in der Regel die Vorreiterrolle bei der Prägung von Stereotypen.

Eine bewußte und kritische Überprüfung von Themenwahl, Informationsauswahl, des Sprachgebrauchs und der Auswahl von Fotos und Layout in Bezug auf Stereotypen zu gewährleisten, liegt jedoch nicht allein in der Verantwortung des schreibenden Journalisten. Hier müssen alle Beteiligten zusammenarbeiten, Auftraggeber, Journalist, Fotograf und Layouter.

8 Licht und Schatten im Reisejournalismus: Korrumpierbarkeit und ethische Aspekte

„Die Tourismusindustrie ist der größte Wirtschaftszweig der Welt. (...) In der Reiseindustruie werden im Jahr weltweit 3,5 Billionen DM umgesetzt. (...) Tourismusunternehmen sind mit über 200 Millionen Beschäftigten weltweit der größte Arbeitgeber.“ (Scherer 1995: 21f)

8.1 Einleitung

Hans J. Kleinsteuber

Reisejournalisten haben **keinen guten Ruf** - und dafür gibt es einige Gründe. Oft gelten sie - gemeinsam mit den Autojournalisten - als diejenigen, die besonders beeinflußbar sind durch Sponsoren und PR-Abteilungen. Andere sagen es präziser: Manche unter ihnen sind korrumpierbar. Machen wir eine einfache Rechnung auf: Die Reise zu einem attraktiven Reiseziel in Lateinamerika kostet, sagen wir DM 5.000. Der Reiseschreiber erhält von einer gutzahlenden Zeitung ein Honorar für die Reportage von vielleicht DM 1.000; dazu kommen Einnahmen für einige Fotos und Zweitverwertungen. Vergleicht man das mit der Berichterstattung über den örtlichen Kaninchenzüchterverein, so kommt unvermeidlich ein Zuschußgeschäft heraus. Nun gut, das Reiseziel ist sicherlich interessanter als der Verein in der Vorstadt. Und wenn ein sowieso schon geplanter Urlaub über eine Reportage mitfinanziert wird - umso besser.Dennoch gilt für den professionellen Reisejournalisten - besonders wenn er nicht fest angestellt ist -, daß Einsatz und Erfolg in einem schlechten Verhältnis zueinander stehen. Da bieten wiederum **Touristikveranstalter und Fremdenverkehrspromotoren** ihre Dienste an. Journalisten werden oft auf eine Gratis-Reise eingeladen, mit Hintergedanken freilich, denn es wird ein Jubelartikel als Gegenleistung erwartet. Dazu steht zu befürchten, daß der Chefredakteur das auch noch gut findet, weil sein Reisekostenetat viel zu klein ist, um all die Reisen bezahlen zu können. Außerdem sitzt ihm die Anzeigenabteilung im Nacken, die wiederum freundliche Reportagen benötigt, um begleitende Werbung akquirieren zu können. Auf den Journalisten wirken folglich viele Versuchungen ein, die ihn in immer neue Entscheidungsnöte zwischen Moral und Business zwingen.

Im ersten Teil dieses Kapitels geht es um die Verquickung zwischen redaktioneller Arbeit und der Tourismusindustrie. Da zeigen sich beide Seiten allzuoft im selben Boot sitzend und heraus kommt ein Art **'Amigo-Journalismus'**. Für den sind nicht nur die Verlockungen der PR-Abteilungen schuld, es sind die Journalisten selbst, die sich auf zweifelhafte Tauschgeschäfte einlassen. Aus der Sicht der PR-Leute erschienen sie oft als leicht 'kaufbar', die schlimmsten unter ihnen werden als **'Schnorrergilde'** empfunden. (Ortlepp 1995: 10) Die lassen sich ihre Reisebedürfnisse elegant von der Industrie finanzieren. Dann - aber leider erst dann - wird es den Öffentlichkeitsarbeitern zu viel, die sich gegenseitig vor diesen Klinkenputzern warnen. Für einen hoffnungsfrohen Reisejournalisten ist es dann möglicherweise zu spät, wenn sein Ruf dauerhaft geschädigt ist.

Die Befunde, was die Rahmenbedingungen der Reiseberichterstattung anbetrifft, stimmen überwiegend betrüblich. Aber ein Handbuch sollte mehr bieten als ein Lamento darüber, daß die Schreiber über die 'Paradiese' dieser Welt mitunter auf den Strich gehen. Für eine kritische Bewertung steht die noch recht junge Herangehensweise via Medienethik zur Verfügung. In Medienpraxis und Kommunikationswissenschaft reflektiert sie über die Normen und Maßstäbe im Dschungel des real praktizierten Journalismus. Hier werden Vorstellungen darüber entwickelt, was geht und was nicht mehr tolerabel ist, über das was sich gehört und worauf man empört mit dem Finger zeigen muß. Der medienethische Diskurs geht meist vom konkreten Beispiel aus, um dann grundsätzliche Regeln aufzustellen. In den entsprechenden Büchern kommt Reisejournalismus freilich so gut wie nicht vor, meist geht es um zentrale Ressorts. Ist er zu unwichtig oder wird er gleich als ethisch hoffnungslos aufgegeben?

Wir vermitteln hier einige Grundzüge der Ethikdebatte. Auch wenn deren Begriffe aus der Wissenschaft kommen, wird sie vor allem unter Journalisten geführt. In Deutschland vor allem innerhalb der *Vereinigung Deutscher Reisejournalisten* (*VDRJ*). Die ethische Debatte hat in den USA eine sehr viel längere Tradition und wird weitaus intensiver betreiben. Ein wichtiges Resultat sind Ethik-Codes, die von den professionellen Organisationen erstellt werden und ihre Mitglieder in Form **freiwilliger Selbstverpflichtungen** binden. Die Codes bestimmen die Kommunikation mit den Auftraggebern der Journalisten, definieren wie weit beide Seiten gehen dürfen und welche Grenzen einzuhalten sind. Wir dokumentieren den *Code of Ethics* der bedeutendsten Fachvereinigung *Society of American Travel Writers* (*SATW*).

Die Mitglieder haben sich an diese Regeln zu halten, Verstöße werden von einem eigens dafür etablierten *Ethics's Committee* geahndet, im Extremfall mit Ausschluß aus der Organisation. Der schädigt nachhaltig, weil die Redaktionen die Zusammenarbeit mit 'sauberen' Journalisten vorziehen. Hier sind Wegweisungen in einen besseren Journalismus angelegt.

8.2 Versuchungen im Reisejournalismus

Hans J. Kleinsteuber

Dieser Abschnitt widmet sich den vielfältigen Versuchungen, denen jeder Reisejournalist ausgesetzt ist. Eigentlich ist alles ganz einfach. Der Pressekodex des Deutschen Presserats stellt in seiner Ziffer 15 klar, wie sich Journalisten verhalten sollen, wenn es um Korrumpierungsversuche von außen geht. **Wer sich bestechen läßt, handelt unehrenhaft und berufswidrig.**

Ziffer 15 Pressekodex

Die Annahme und Gewährung von Vorteilen jeder Art, die geeignet sein könnten, die Entscheidungsfreiheit von Verlag und Redaktion zu beeinträchtigen, sind mit dem Ansehen, der Unabhängigkeit und der Aufgabe der Presse unvereinbar. Wer sich für die Verbreitung oder Unterdrückung von Nachrichten bestechen läßt, handelt unehrenhaft und berufswidrig.

Richtlinie 15.1 - Einladungen und Geschenke

Die Gefahr einer Beeinträchtigung der Entscheidungsfreiheit von Verlagen und Redaktionen sowie der unabhängigen Urteilsbildung der Journalisten besteht, wenn Redakteure und redaktionelle Mitarbeiter Einladungen oder Geschenke annehmen, deren Wert das im gesellschaftlichen Verkehr übliche und im Rahmen der beruflichen Tätigkeit notwendige Maß übersteigt. Schon der Anschein, die Entscheidungsfreiheit von Verlag und Redaktion könne durch Gewährung von Einladungen oder Geschenken beeinträchtigt werden, ist zu vermeiden.

Geschenke sind wirtschaftliche und ideelle Vergünstigungen jeder Art. Die Annahme von Werbeartikeln zum täglichen Gebrauch oder sonstiger geringwertiger Gegenstände zu traditionellen Gelegenheiten ist unbedenklich.

Recherche und Berichterstattung dürfen durch die Vergabe oder Annahme von Geschenken, Rabatten oder Einladungen nicht beeinflußt, behindert oder gar verhindert werden. Verlage und Journalisten sollten darauf bestehen, daß Informationen unabhängig von der Annahme eines Geschenks oder einer Einladung gegeben werden.

(Deutscher Presserat: Publizistische Grundsätze (Pressekodex), Bonn, Stand 1996)

Gibt es Grund für derartige Festlegungen? Ganz sicherlich. Unter Journalisten wird seit Jahren das **'Amigo-Syndrom'** diskutiert. Amigos waren einst die politischen Kumpel süddeutscher Spitzenpolitiker, die auf der Grundlage enger Kontakte Vorteile für beide Seiten einheimsten. Was die Journalisten seinerzeit im politischen Sumpf ausgruben, gilt häufig genug auch für sie selbst. Warum sollten sie auch bessere Menschen sein? Wenn sich Politiker Brasilien-Reisen bezahlen lassen, wie damals bekannt wurde, warum sollten Journalisten dies nicht tun? (Tillmanns 1995)

8.2.1 Die Reise-Amigos

In der Branche ist bekannt, daß es für viele Weltregionen, für Reiseveranstalter und Transportunternehmen PR-Agenturen gibt, die Journalisten auf eine nette Reise einladen, wenn dabei ein freundlicher Artikel über den Sponsor herauskommt. „Reisejournalisten und Reiseveranstalter leben in enger Symbiose" und was dabei herauskommt ist **„Urlaub auf lau"** (so im *Spiegel special* zu Journalisten 1995). Im Ergebnis werden gerade die Reisejournalisten von den PR-Agenturen als besonders 'bestechlich' einge-schätzt, ein Schicksal, das sie mit den Motor-Kollegen teilen. Zumindest sind hier die Übergänge zwischen akzeptabler Zusammenarbeit und schlichtem 'Einkaufen' fließend, wobei aus Perspektive der **PR-Agenturen** alles recht normal erscheint. Ein konkretes Beispiel ist hier eine Kreuzfahrt: „Die müssen schließlich einen Journalisten an Bord haben, wenn er Schiffe und Routen 'testen' soll. Bilanz: Pressekonferenzen könne man nun nicht mehr im kalten Hamburg organisieren, dann komme doch keiner. Nein, es müsse schon Tokio sein, dann sei die Maschine auch voll." (Flöper 1995)

Tatsächlich reicht der Anruf bei entsprechenden Agenturen aus und eine Einladung incl. Flug in der Business Class und Spitzenbewirtung vor Ort kann durchaus das Resultat sein. Zumindest, wenn der Journalist glaubwürdig ein bekanntes Medium vertritt oder für seine industriefreundliche Berichterstattung bereits bekannt ist. Weil das so ist, sparen wiederum viele Redaktionen beim Reise-Ressort und erwarten von ihren Autoren, daß sie sich die Reise für ihre Reportage selbst besorgen. Entsprechend kollidiert die Praxis auf ganzer Linie mit oben zitierten publizistischen Grundsätzen.

Die Ausgangslage zeigt die zynischen Seiten des real praktizierten Journalismus, und jeder Beteiligte wird für sich entscheiden müssen, wie weit er dabei gehen will. Das *MediumMagazin* gibt die folgenden Ratschläge (Spaeth 1996). Dort wird im Detail über das Gratis-Geschäft mit den Reisen berichtet und es wird sogar eine Liste der PR-Agenturen für Pressekontakte in Sachen Reisestories abgedruckt. Der Tip des Praktikers ist, sich bei den Agenturen zu melden, die den noch unbekannten Journalisten bitten werden, als Beleg bereits geschriebene Artikel einzusenden. Sind die vorhanden und fällt die Prüfung zufriedenstellend aus, so erscheint eine Einladung durchaus möglich. Der Autor warnt freilich vor der Illusion, daß dabei ein erholsamer Strandurlaub herauskommt. Diese **Informationsreisen** dienen der Öffentlichkeitsarbeit und sind entsprechend kurz und kompakt angelegt. Nach Abschluß der Reise wird die PR-Agentur Druck machen und will alsbald Ergebnisse sehen. Denn auch die Agenturleute müssen gegenüber ihren Auftraggebern Erfolge vorweisen. Diese Agenturen stehen wieder in heftiger Konkurrenz gegeneinander und müssen sich oft jährlich um die PR-Etats bedeutender Reiseziele bewerben.

Sicherlich bieten sich diese Möglichkeiten für den Einstieg in die Branche an, als Dauertätigkeit eines Journalisten, der davon leben will, ist das allerdings ein höchst unberechenbares Geschäft, zudem wenig befriedigend. Das dabei seriöser Reisejournalismus herauskommt, ist kaum wahrscheinlich und auf Dauer wird der Autor damit seine Reputation ruinieren.

Letztlich müssen immer beide Seiten gesehen werden. Die **Vermarkter von Reisezielen** gehen davon aus, daß sich ein redaktioneller Bericht mit freundlicher Tendenz über ihre Region besser rechnet, als eine Anzeige in demselben Medium. Darum sind sie bereit, in einen korrumpierbaren Journalisten zu 'investieren'. Ob diese Rechnung tatsächlich aufgeht, sei dahingestellt. Weiterhin gehen sie davon aus, daß sie das Meinungsklima bezüglich ihrer Region ständig pflegen müssen, denn das Reisegeschäft ist enorm von öffentlichen Meinungskonjunkturen abhängig. Dabei geht es einerseits um Moden, bestimmte Urlaubsorte gelten als 'in', andere als 'out'. Das hat mit den realen Qualitäten der Reiseziele oft wenig zu tun. Dazu kommen bestimmte Katastrophenmeldungen aus den Urlaubsgebieten - Touristenmorde in Florida, Bombenanschläge in der Türkei -, die sich in enormen Einbußen an Buchungen und Einnahmen niederschlagen. Auch dabei geht es nicht um reale Bedrohungen - die gibt es immer und auch bei 'sicheren' Reisezielen -, sondern um die sehr subjektiven Einschätzungen der potentiellen Reisekunden. So meint die Reiseindustrie, diesen unwägbaren Folgen des 'Sensationsjournalismus' mit intensiver eigener Pflege der öffentlichen Meinung entgegenwirken zu müssen. Spricht man mit beiden Seiten, so wird gern die Verrohung der Sitten bei der jeweils anderen beklagt. Man wird offen darüber sprechen müssen, bevor es hier zu einer Wende kommt.

8.2.2 Zur Bedeutung von Reisewerbung

Während die Versuchungen von PR und Reise-Amigos vor allem im individuellen Bereich der Beziehung einzelner Medienakteure untereinander angesiedelt sind, gibt es auch strukturelle, den Verlag als ganzes betreffende Querverbindungen, die qualitätsvollen Reisejournalismus bedrohen: Die Werbung rund um den Reiseteil.

Zuerst einmal einige Fakten: Die Reise-Gesellschaften stehen auf der Skala der besonders werbeintensiven Branchen in Deutschland auf Platz 25. Das waren 1994 in Deutschland 224 Mio DM an **Brutto-Werbe-Investitionen**, die 1995 auf beachtliche 271 Mio anwuchsen. Das entspricht einem Wachstum von stolzen 20,8 Prozent. (*ZAW* 1996: 12) Im Gesamtvolumen der Werbung macht das allerdings nicht mehr als etwa ein Neuntel dessen aus, was die Auto-Branche ausgibt (1995: 2.418 Mio), die auf Platz Eins rangiert. Doch sind die Wachstumraten der Reisebranche in letzten Jahre exzeptionell hoch gewesen und steigen weiter überdurchschnittlich an (Gesamtanstieg der Werbung 1995 nur 5,5 Prozent). Dazu kommt, daß die Zahlen nur die halbe Wahrheit wiedergeben. **Die Statistik nimmt die Besonderheiten der Reisebranche nur unzureichend zur Kenntnis**. Die hier interessierenden Werbetreibenden umfaßt deutlich mehr Unternehmen als nur Reisegesellschaften (wie es etwas mißverständlich heißt), also etwa *TUI* und *Neckermann*. Hierzu gehören sicherlich auch Fluggesellschaften, Hotelketten und manche mehr, die auch - aber nicht nur - für Reisen werben.

> Tourismus gilt inzwischen als beachtliche Wirtschaftsbranche. Fast 70 Mrd DM gaben die Deutschen 1995 für ihr liebstes Hobby aus. Dieses Geld landet in den Kassen einer weit gefächerten und international tätigen Tourismusindustrie. Nehmen wir als Beispiel den Touristikkonzern *TUI*, der sich aus einem ehemals mittellständischen Unternehmen in den letzten 30 Jahren zu einem Dienstleistungskonzern entwickelt hat und heute zu den 300 größten Unternehmen des Landes zählt. Er transportiert ca. 5 Mio Gäste im Jahr an ihre 'Traumziele'. Die *TUI*-Unternemensgruppe setzt sich aus weltweit ca. 100 Unternehmen zusammen. Dazu zählen neben den konventionellen Veranstaltern auch Hotelgesellschaften, Clubanlagen, Reiseagenturen, Beteiligungen an Reisebüroketten und Anteile am Reservierungssystem *START*.

Letztlich wird man das Gesamtvolumen der Reisewerbung nicht präzise angeben können. Im folgenden werden einige Zahlen aus der Nielsen-Forschung präsentiert, welche Größenordnungen wiedergeben und nach

Werbemedien aufschlüsseln. Ganz sicherlich stimmt aber: Die Reisebranche boomt trotz der allgemeinen wirtschaftlichen Stagnation und die Werbung ist gleichermaßen Voraussetzung wie Konsequenz dieser Hochkonjunktur.

Werbeausgaben von Reise-Gesellschaften und verwandten Branchen im Jahr 1995:

Branche	total in 1.000 DM	TZ	PZ	FZ	TV	HF	PL
Reise-Gesell-schaften	26.004	39 %	25 %	4 %	25 %	6 %	
Hotels/ Hotel-Ketten	2.139	55 %	27 %	6 %	8 %	4 %	1 %
Luftfahrt	10.728	32 %	50 %	5 %	2 %	11 %	
Schif-fahrt	1.571	48 %	35 %	16 %	1 %		
Straßen- u. Schie-nenver-kehr	7.439	65 %	16 %	3 %	1 %	7 %	8 %

TZ=Tageszeitungen
PZ=Publikumszeitschriften
FZ=Fachzeitschriften
TV=Fernsehen
HF=Hörfunk
PL=Plakat

Daten der *Nielsen Werbeforschung S+P*

8.2.3 Redaktioneller Teil und Anzeigen

Wer sich den Reiseteil einer Zeitung oder die Reportage in einer einschlägigen Zeitschrift vornimmt, dem fällt sofort auf: Es gibt eine unverkennbare **Nähe der redaktionellen Teile zu reisebezogener Werbung**. Eine typische Wochenendbeilage, übertitelt Reisen, steigt mit einigen längeren und bunt bebilderten Reportagen ein, doch je weiter man nach hinten blättert, umso umfangreicher werden werbende Teile, und die kommen fast ausnahmslos von Reiseveranstaltern Transporteuren, Reisezielen und Übernachtungsbetrieben. Während die Reportagen eher von großflächiger Werbung größerer Anbieter begleitet werden, finden wir auf den hinteren Seiten oft eine Unzahl kleiner Anzeigen, bis hin zu zweizeiligen Angeboten für ein Ferienheim oder einen Spezialveranstalter. Etwas anders sieht es bei den einschlägigen Zeitschriften aus. Hier fehlen die ganz kleinen Anzeigen oft, stattdessen finden wir die Reportagen mit Werbung zu eben den Zielen garniert, die auch im Beitrag beschrieben werden.

Aus dem *Reise-Journal* der Zeitungsgruppe *WAZ*:

Im redaktionellen Teil zum Thema 'Kreuzfahrten'):
„Die 'Calypso' schreibt auf einer 17-tägigen Tour von Bremerhaven nach Nizza 'Hobby aktiv' auf ihre Fahnen. Unterwegs können die Freizeitkapitäne allerlei lernen. Vom Filmen bis zum Steptanz. (Transocean Tours)"

In einer Anzeige:
„Calypso - die heitere Urlaubsinsel. Traumhafte Ostsee. 7.6.-18.6.1997: Hamburg-Gotland... Transocean Tours. Der Seereisen-Spezialist."

Leserreisen-Service-Center der Zeitungsgruppe *WAZ*:
„Ostern in Fernost erleben. Kreuzfahrt mit der MS Calypso..."

(*Reisejournal* vom 1. März 1997)

Letzteres setzt eine differenzierte Kooperation zwischen Redaktion und Anzeigenabteilung voraus, die so eigentlich nicht vorkommen sollte. Solche Koppelgeschäfte gelten als nicht zulässig; das Gesetz gegen Wettbewerbsbeschränkungen sieht darin eine Erschleichung von Wettbewerbsvorteilen und auf einen solchen **'Vorteil auf Gegenleistung'** stehen erhebliche Strafen. (Holm 1995) Auf der anderen Seite kommt Werbung mitten im Reiseteil natürlich besonders nahe an den Leser heran, kann doch vermutet werden, daß der Interessierte auch mehr oder minder konkrete Absichten hegt, eine Reise zu buchen. Aber genau hier liegt das Problem: Der Werbeeffekt würde sich ins Gegenteil verkehren, wenn Kritik geübt wird. Der Anzeigenkunde fühlte sich düpiert und wäre wohl erst einmal verloren. Vielleicht kann man es aber auch anders sehen: Indem jemand wirbt, darf er damit rechnen, nicht im Text angeschwärzt zu werden. Auf jeden Fall bewegen wir uns hier auf sehr heiklem Terrain.

Einen ähnlich dichten Zusammenhang zwischen Text und Reklame, bei dem manche Beiträge wie eine Art Umfeld oder schmückendes Beiwerk für Werbung wirken, finden wir eigentlich nur noch bei den Auto-Beilagen. Nun sind es gerade die Motor-Redakteure, die aus eben diesem Grund einen eher schlechten Leumund in der Redaktion genießen. Manchmal kommt auch ein wenig Neid dazu, wenn sie wieder einmal von der Industrie mit großzügigen Leistungen verwöhnt werden - neue Modelle werden gern in Monte Carlo oder Las Vegas vorgestellt. Eine derartige Hofierung der Redakteure erfolgt natürlich immer mit Hintergedanken: Die Berichterstattung soll entsprechend freundlich sein; ist sie es einmal nicht, kann der Betreffende von der Einladungsliste gestrichen werden. Ganz so schlimm ist es sicherlich beim Reisejournalismus nicht, wobei dahingestellt sein mag, ob dies wegen der Unbestechlichkeit der Schreibenden der Fall ist, oder weil die Reiseindustrie dann doch nicht die Größe und Werbeintensität der Automobilbranche erreicht.

Der Direktor Presse und PR der *TUI*, Rainer Ortlepp, über die Vermarktung von Reisen und die Zusammenarbeit mit Journalisten:

„Was macht nun ein Reiseveranstalter wie die *TUI*, der z.B. ein neues Zielgebiet in seinen Katalog aufnimmt, wie in diesem Jahr verstärkt die USA?

Wir basteln uns einen Kommunikationsplan und setzen alle Instrumente der Presse- und PR-Arbeit ein, um z.B. eben USA-Themen für die Medien aufzubereiten und interessant zu machen. Pressemitteilungen zu speziellen USA-Highlights, PR-Aktionen, Gewinnspiele usw.

Was wir nicht machen, ... ist über die Anzeigenabteilung Druck auf die Redaktionen auszuüben oder gar redaktionellen Raum zu kaufen. Dies wird allerdings leider in letzter Zeit immer mehr ein Thema.

Aber zurück zu meinem Kommunikationsplan. Bestandteil sind natürlich auch Pressereisen. Ob nun als einzelreisender Journalist, ob als Fernsehteam oder aber als Journalisten-Gruppenreisen. Wir laden also - professionell nach Zielgruppeninteressen ausgewählt - je nach Anlaß acht bis zwölf Reisejournalisten zu einer mehrtägigen Informationstour in das Zielgebiet ein. Wir stellen Hotels und Ausflüge vor, vermittel Interviews mit den *TUI*-Partnern vor Ort, halten ein kleines Pressegespräch ab, um über Hintergründe, Wachstumschancen und Infrastruktur des Landes oder der Stadt zu informieren, und stellen letztlich das Unternehmen als das vor, was es ist: ein touristischer Dienstleistungskonzern."

(Ortlepp 1995: 5)

Nach den gesetzlichen Vorgaben und dem Selbstverständnis des professionellen Journalisten gilt es, eine **strikte Trennung von redaktionellem Teil und Werbung** zu beachten. Der Alltag sieht anders aus. Beiträge und Reklame ergänzen sich und mitunter ist man unsicher, was eigentlich im Mittelpunkt steht. Es gibt sicherlich verschiedene Gründe, warum ein Leser die Reiseseiten aufblättert. Er mag darin ganz allgemein Anregungen und Informationen suchen, vielleicht um den nächsten Urlaub zu planen oder er sucht nach spezifischen Reisezielen und aktuellen Informationen. Vielleicht will er auch nur Reisegefühle entwickeln, im Traum von fremden Ländern schwelgen. Ganz sicher sucht er höchst selten nach der Werbung, welche die Beiträge einrahmt. Andererseits wird er für gutgemachte Reiseanzeigen hier offener sein, als wenn sie sich irgendwo sonst im Blatt verstecken.

Wie lange wird aber die Reisewirtschaft noch inserieren, wenn in den Artikeln kritische Sichtweisen von schlechter Organisation, Schmutz in Hotelbädern oder verdreckten Stränden vorherrschen? Andererseits: Wird in den Reiseberichten nur gejubelt, wird der Leser schnell müde werden und die Schreibe nicht ernst nehmen. Oft weiß er es auch besser: Rio de Janeiros Copacabana ist ebenso reizvoll wie unsicher und Irland leuchtet sattgrün, weil es besonders viel regnet. Mit anderen Worten: Redaktion und Werbung stehen in einem ständigen Dreieck von Spannungen: Zwischen den Belangen der Schreiber, der möglichst wahrhaftig und lebendig schreiben möchte, dem Leser, der konkrete und ehrliche Informationen erwartet und der Industrie, die ihr Produkt im besten Licht dargestellt sehen möchte. Das Ergebnis des daraus resultierenden mehrfachen Spagats wird immer aus einem Kompromiß bestehen.

8.2.4 Medien werden zu Reiseveranstaltern

Es gibt noch weitere Interessenkollisionen. Nehmen wir nur den Fall der beliebten **'Leserreisen'**. Aus welchen Gründen auch immer, es gibt eine lange Tradition, daß Verlagshäuser im Verbund mit Veranstaltern Ausflüge für ihre Leser organisieren.

Geworben wird dafür an hervorgehobener Stelle in den Zeitungen, ohne daß es sich um Anzeigen im eigentlichen Sinne handelt. Vielmehr wird dabei an das 'Wir-Gefühl' der Leser-'Gemeinde' appelliert, die eben mehr Gemeinsamkeiten habe, als das Lesen desselben Blattes. Auch hier ist kaum vorstellbar, daß das im Blatt angepriesene Ziel von einem Redakteur gleichzeitig in düsteren Farben geschildert wird.

Ganz finster sieht es im Bereich der 'Regenbogenpresse' aus, also bei den Zeitschriften mit einem eher schlichten journalistischen Konzept. In der Frauenzeitschrift *bella* werden z.B. Reiseziele in Form einer Reisereportage präsentiert („Mit dem Traumschiff vom Bosporus in die Adria"). Gleichwohl handelt es sich um eine *bella*-Leserreise. In einem Pseudo-Serviceteil (*Tips und Preise*) wird besagte Reise mit Preisen und Konditionen inklusive Adresse und Telefonnummer dargestellt. Die ganze Aufmachung könnte auch als Katalogseite eines Reiseveranstalters durchgehen - und erfüllt anscheinend auch dieselbe Aufgabe...

Inzwischen steigen auch Radio- und Fernsehanbieter in diese **seltsamen Koppelgeschäfte** ein. Ein Fachorgan der Reisebranche berichtet über die Aktivitäten eines Senders: „'Wir führen derzeit die vierte Zuschauerreise durch', sagt Isabelle Hen-Wollmaker, beim Hamburger Pay-TV-Sender *Premiere* zuständig für Kundenbindung. Es handelt sich um drei Einzelreisen zur Fußball-Europameisterschaft 1996 in England, exklusiv für die 1,2 Mill. Abonnenten aufgelegt vom Sportreisen-Spezialist *Vieten Tours* in Meerbusch." (Peymani 1996: 16) Der Edelsender *Premiere* bezuschußt diese Reisen sogar und läßt sie jeweils von einem bekannten Sportreporter oder einem Sportler begleiten.

Eine andere problematische Vermischung von Programm und Werbung findet sich, wenn in die Reiseberichterstattung Gewinnspiele einbezogen werden. Oder wenn Medien und Reiseveranstalter gemeinsam für sich und ihre Leistungen werben.

Nehmen wir die *Nix wie weg*-Kampagne von *Sat1*. Dazu heißt es wörtlich in einer Anzeige: „Festhalten Freunde, das gab's noch nie: *SAT1* und *L'TUR*, Europas Nr. 1 für günstige Last-Minute-Reisen, starten eines der größten Gewinnspiele aller Zeiten. Wir verschenken 1.111 Reisegutscheine im Gesamtwert von 1,2 Mio. DM und einen Porsche 911 Cabrio." (Anzeige *Der Spiegel*, Nr. 16, 1996, S. 51).

Sat1 verbindet z.B. auch in seiner 'Reisezeit' (regelmäßiger Beitrag im *Morgenmagazin*) freundliche PR-Berichte mit Hinweisen auf Reisebüros und -veranstalter. Dabei wird etwa ein einwöchiger Urlaub auf Teneriffa ausgelost: für denjenigen, der die Hauptstadt der Insel anzugeben weiß, die gerade vorher in leuchtenden Farben geschildert wurde. Das alles hat mit Promotion viel, aber mit Journalismus nichts mehr zu tun.

8.2.5 Der Reisejournalist als Gratwanderer

Versuchungen für die Beteiligten gibt es also genug. Mitunter werden dabei nicht nur die Grenzen des guten Geschmacks strapaziert, sondern auch die **Grenzen des Presserechts**. Public Relations für Reiseveranstalter im laufenden Programm verhöhnt den Zuschauer und untergräbt ganz sicherlich die Glaubwürdigkeit des Artikels. Keinesfalls sollte sich der Reiseredakteur zum Schönschreiber der Reisebranche degradieren lassen.

Ein Beitrag ist viel glaubwürdiger, wenn er nicht nur die Schönheiten des Reiseziels schildert (dazu ist der Reiseprospekt da), sondern auch auf Schwächen und Probleme hinweist. Das dient nicht zuletzt auch der **Glaubwürdigkeit** in den Augen der Leser, die genau wissen, daß wahrhaftige Traumziele immer nur aus Träumen gesponnen sind. Jedes Paradies hat auch seine Kehrseite. Es dient letztlich auch der Reiseindustrie, die kein Interesse daran haben kann, daß ihre Kunden mit **medienerzeugten Illusionen** ein Ziel anreisen, das für sie nicht geeignet ist. Das Ergebnis sind Frustationen oder - schlimmer noch - nachfolgende Rückforderungen und Rechtsstreitigkeiten, die niemandem (außer den beteiligten Anwaltskanzleien) etwas nützen.

Darauf sollte ein Autor hinweisen, wenn er aufgefordert wird, einen potenten Annoncen-Geber per Reportage zu umjubeln. Schließlich muß auch der Redakteur auf notwendige Distanz achten, wenn er seinen Ruf wahren will. Das notorisch schlechte Image der Motorredakteure ist nicht zufällig entstanden und der Reiseredakteur steht ständig vor ähnlichen Verlockungen.

Interessenkollisionen sind im Alltag ständig gegeben und dürfen nicht unter den Teppich gekehrt werden. Verleger müssen darauf achten, daß sich ihre Redakteure fair und korrekt verhalten. Umgekehrt müssen sie die Rahmenbedingungen in der Redaktion so schaffen, daß ein Journalist nicht auf das Schönschreiben für Veranstalter angewiesen ist.

Wer als Chef eine Reisereportage in Auftrag gibt und deren Finanzierung nicht klärt, verhält sich verlogen und zwingt den Untergebenen auf die Amigo-Tour. Die zweifelhafte Qualität des Reisejournalismus in unserem Lande ist ganz sicher nicht nur ein Problem der Journalisten sondern auch ihrer Brötchengeber.

Ein besonders schäbiges Beispiel für mangelnden Instinkt bei den immer neu entstehenden Konflikten gab der Kölner Verleger Neven *DuMont*. Ein Redakteur seines *Kölner Stadt-Anzeigers* beschrieb alltägliche Praktiken im Reisegewerbe: *DuMont* kontrolliert auch den gleichnamigen Reisebuchverlag, der wiederum am Reiseveranstalter *Klingenberg* beteiligt ist. Geschildert wird ein völlig normaler Vorgang, daß nämlich von den Veranstaltern oft

Reiseführer als Service am Kunden mitgeliefert werden. Aus welchem Verlag diese kommen und welchen Veranstalter sie vielleicht empfehlen, kann sich jeder ausrechnen.

Der Reiseredakteur thematisierte diese Zusammenhänge und wurde nach 25 Jahren Beschäftigung im Hause fristlos gekündigt. (Röper 1996). Und die Zeitungen des Verlegers berichteten nicht darüber, das taten umso mehr die anderen Blätter. Erst massive Proteste weit über Köln hinaus brachten die Wiedereinstellung.

Der Vorgang war auch Thema einer Dokumentation bei *Kanal 4*, einem Anbieter, der ein Fensterprogrmm bei *RTL* gestaltet. Nun weigerte sich *RTL*, dieses zu senden. Erst eine einstweilige Verfügung beim Landesgericht bahnte den Weg zur Ausstrahlung. In dem Beitrag war der Verleger DuMont, in Köln eine einflußreiche Figur, in seiner Funktion als ehemaliger Karnevalsprinz (nicht eben günstig) dargestellt worden.

Unsere Verleger müssen wohl noch lernen, daß die wirtschaftlichen Vorgänge rund um ihre Zeitungen auch für die Leser interessant sind. Die eigenen wirtschaftlichen Verflechtungen dürfen kein Tabu der deutschen Presse sein; der Leser dar Offenheit erwarten.

Nicht nur dieses Beispiel unterstreicht, daß **mehr Transparenz** viel mit **publizistischer Qualität** zu tun hat. Warum sollte es nicht zur Regel werden, daß in einer Reisereportage vermerkt ist, wie sie finanziert wurde? Umsonst - so lautet eine alte Volks-weisheit - ist schließlich nichts zu haben, schon gar nicht eine Reise in ferne Gefilde.

Vorbilder für einen verantwortlichen Umgang mit den ständigen Versuchungen der Reisebranche bieten sicherlich die seriösen Zeitungen oder öffentlich-rechtliche TV-Magazine wie *Unterwegs* vom *SWF*. Sie setzen sich differenziert und ohne Schönmalerei mit ihren Reisezielen auseinander.

Ein Blick in den Reiseteil der *ZEIT* oder der *FAZ* unterstreicht, daß es nicht die Werbung an sich ist, die korrumpiert. Es geht auch ohne Koppelgeschäfte und der Leser schätzt, daß dies der Unabhängigkeit und Seriosität zugute kommt.

Die Probleme entstehen erst, wenn Grundprinzipien journalistischer Professionalität nicht mehr eingehalten werden können: Sei es, weil Werbende unanständige Forderungen stellen, sei es, weil der Verlag auch schmutziges Geld annimmt oder auch, weil Redakteure allzu willfährig auf Geldgeber reagieren.

8.3 Grundfragen journalistischer Ethik

Katharina Griese und Hans J. Kleinsteuber

Ethik beschäftigt sich mit dem **Wesen des Guten, der Tugend, der Gerechtigkeit, mit den Regeln von moralischer und sittlicher Richtigkeit**. Der Begriff der Ethik stammt aus der Philosophie und meint den Bereich, in dem Moral, also Anweisungen zum richtigen Handeln, erörtert wird. Journalistische Ethik ist eigentlich der falsche Begriff, geht es doch eher um Moral im reisejournalistischen Alltag. Aber Moral klingt allzusehr nach erhobenem Zeigefinger.

Aus der jahrtausendalten Diskussion um ethische Grundwerte - wie die Sicherung einer sittlichen Gesinnung oder die Wahrung der Menschenwürde - sind im Bereich der Medienethik ganz konkrete Handreichungen übriggeblieben. In die Debatte ging vor allem die Unterscheidung in **Gesinnungs- und Verantwortungsethik** durch den Soziologen Max Weber ein. Gesinnungsethik beurteilt die Richtigkeit des Handelns auf der Grundlage von Überzeugung (z.B.: religiösen Geboten), Verantwortungsethik betont dagegen, daß jeder selbst für die vorhersehbaren Folgen seines Handelns aufzukommen hat. (Weber 1964: 58)

Für den journalistischen Alltag ist vor allem der zweite Ansatz von Bedeutung: Der Journalist muß immer einstehen können für das, was er produziert. Der weltliche Richter sorgt dafür, daß gesetzliche Regeln eingehalten werden, daß er nicht verleumdet oder Plagiat begeht. Den Rest muß er mit seinem Gewissen ausmachen. Und nicht nur mit dem, dazu kommen der eigene Kollegenkreis, die Profession als Ganzes, die Fachverbände, die Kritiker seiner Arbeit, die Leser, die Betroffenen seiner Beiträge draußen in den bereisten Ländern. Wenn er ihnen allen mit gutem Gewissen in die Augen schauen kann, dann sollte auch der Reisebeitrag ethisch in Ordnung sein.

8.3.1 Recherche auf eigene Rechnung

Moral und Ethik versus leere Kassen - ein Problem, mit dem sich wohl jede Redaktion auseinandersetzen muß. Damit stehen und fallen die **Qualität der Recherche, die Objektivität und Relevanz sowie der Wahrheitsgehalt der vermittelten Informationen.** Nicht nur der wankelmütige Journalist ist da bereits manchen Versuchungen im Reisejournalismus unterlegen. Die Frage ist, wer kann es sich leisten, 'nein' zu sagen - leider oft nur die Großen der Branche.

Der Verlag *Gruner+Jahr* aus Hamburg gehört mit seinen Publikationen zweifelsohne zu diesem elitären Kreis. In der Redaktion der *GEO*-Magazine orientiert sich die Art der Recherche an dem Ziel, das der entsprechende Beitrag verfolgt. Die Reportagen in der 'grünen' *GEO* beispielsweise sollen dem Leser einen Eindruck des Fremden und Einzigartigen vermitteln sowie sein Interesse für andere Kulturen und Lebensweisen wecken. Solche Darstellungen basieren oft auf Erlebnissen von Forschungsreisenden. Der Beitrag „Die Furcht des Donnergottes“ (de Vallombreuse 1994), ein Bericht über das Leben von Höhlenmenschen auf den Philippinen, entstand aus der Zusammenarbeit von *GEO*-Redakteuren und Ethnologen.

Solche 'Reise-Reportagen' sind wohl die ehrlichsten, da sie dem Leser mehr als pure Unterhaltung bieten, aber in den seltensten Fällen zum Kofferpacken auffordern sollen. Ethik besteht hier gerade darin, nicht zum Reisen anzuregen.

Anders ist es bei der Reiseberichterstattung über touristisch bereits erschlossene Gebiete. Wer nicht nur den Swimmingpool bucht, sondern auch das Land dahinter, möchte eine realistische Darstellung über Land und Leute. Hier liegt eine hohe Eigenverantwortung in der Arbeit des Journalisten, aber gleichzeitig auch ein großes Problem.

Das Budget für Reisekosten in den Redaktionen ist knapp bemessen und auch die 'freien' Mitarbeiter müssen wirtschaftlich denken. Zusätzlich wird der Markt von Reiseberichterstattungen aller Art überschwemmt, was den Preis der Produkte deutlich drückt. Somit ist die 'Recherche auf eigene Rechnung' für die meisten Redaktionen und 'freien' Journalisten finanziell nicht mehr möglich. Ohne Sponsoring von Reiseveranstaltern, z.B. in Form von vergünstigten Flügen oder Übernachtungsrabatten, läuft selten etwas in der Branche.

Es stellt sich die **Frage nach der moralisch vertretbaren Grenze** und ob unter diesen Voraussetzungen eine realistische Reiseberichterstattung überhaupt noch möglich ist.

Eins erscheint klar zu sein, den persönlichen Überzeugungen des einzelnen Journalisten wird hier ein Spiegel vorgehalten. Wer mit Reisejournalismus seine Brötchen verdient, behauptet vielleicht, er könne es sich nicht leisten, von miserablen Zuständen eines Reiselandes zu berichten, die den Leser eher abschrecken denn zur Urlaubsbuchung einladen. Doch Reisejournalismus wird für den Leser gemacht und in diesem Sinne sollte die journalistische Entscheidungsfreiheit gewahrt werden.

8.3.2 Reisejournalismus und der Schutz des Menschen und seiner Umwelt

Es gibt nur noch wenige Plätze auf der Welt, die nicht touristisch erschlossen sind. In sehr vielen Ländern der Erde sind die Menschen durch den Tourismus dem Wohlstand und den Problemen der Industrieländer nähergekommen. Doch der Preis den sie zahlen ist oft sehr hoch, denn es gilt, sich den Wünschen der Pauschaltouristen anzupassen.

Das Geschäft mit der Reise boomt, den Reiselustigen verlangt es nach immer mehr Exotik und Abenteuer. Hier **setzen Reisejournalisten Trends**, in der Vergangenheit oft ohne Rücksicht auf Verluste. Stimmen von Natur- und Umweltschützern wurden immer lauter, denn wo einst die Plätze an der Sonne gerühmt wurden, machen sich längst schon die Schatten breit. Die Redakteure der Zeitschrift *Kosmos* verstehen sich zwar nicht als Reisejournalisten, setzen jedoch um so mehr Akzente für umweltbewußtes Reisen und den 'sanften Tourismus'. Sie informieren in ihren Beiträgen über Umweltschäden als Folge des Massentourismus. So wird in dem Beitrag „Alptraum - Alpenraum" (von Stamm 1995: 33) verdeutlicht, wie durch den ständig expandierenden Skitourismus Bergwälder sterben und das Ökosystem Alpen aus den Fugen gerät. Der Tourismus ist eine Industrie wie andere Industrien auch. Er handelt mit Rohstoffen, allerdings mit dem Unterschied, daß der Mensch zum Rohstoff gebracht wird und nicht der Rohstoff zum Menschen. Der Effekt ist derselbe: Den bereisten Rohstofflieferanten bringt er in einem bestimmten Zyklus Geld, ohne jedoch tragfähige, eigenständige Infrastrukturen aufzubauen. Tourismus verbraucht Land, Leute und Ressourcen (Burghoff/Kresta 1995: 7).

Ein Reisejournalist, der über die faszinierendsten Plätze unserer Erde schreibt, sollte **sich über die Folgen seine Reportage bewußt sein**. Es gilt nicht, das letzte Stückchen unberührte Natur mit Hotels und Mietwagenfirmen zu verbauen, im Gegenteil. Es liegt in der Verantwortung des Reisejournalisten, die Flora und Fauna der Reiseziele nicht rücksichtslos preiszugeben, sondern den Lesern Zusammenhänge zu verdeutlichen, zu informieren und auch aufzuklären. Wer von fremden Ländern berichtet, kann Brücken des Verständnisses für andere Kulturen und Lebensarten bauen. Reisejournalismus erfordert einen behutsamen Umgang mit der Darstellung fremder Lebensweisen. „Das Verstehen der Kultur eines Volkes führt dazu, seine Normalität zu enthüllen, ohne daß seine Besonderheit dabei zu kurz käme. Es macht sie erreichbar: in den Kontext ihrer eigenen Alltäglichkeiten gestellt, schwindet ihre Unverständlichkeit." (Luger 1994: 12). Jeder weiß, daß Glück nicht mit Geld zu erkaufen ist und Tourismus ist nicht das Heilmittel des armen Mannes, auch wenn es leider oft behauptet wird.

Die Journalistinnen Christel Burghoff und Edith Kresta über Chancen und Grenzen eines ‘besseren Tourismus’:

„Sozial- und umweltverträglicher Tourismus ist eine Spielart des modernen Tourismus. Sie ist ressourcenschonender und mittelstandsorientierter in das natürliche und soziale Gefüge einer Region eingepaßt. So wird die Landschaft nicht mehr um jeden Preis mit einer großindustriellen Infrastruktur überzogen. Das Begriffspaar sozial- und umweltverträglich suggeriert eine Wende zum Positiven: zum sozialpolitisch Wünschenswerten und zum umwelpolitisch Gebotenen. Diese Wende ist Programm: zur Sanierung der Umwelt zwar, aber in erster Linie als spezifisches Produkt. Auch sozial- und umweltverträglicher Tourismus wird von wirtschaftlichen Interessen diktiert. Der schonende Umgang mit Mensch und Natur in der Oase verhindert nicht, daß auch mit ‘sanften’ Urlaubspaketen neue Umweltschäden entstehen...

Er ist eine halbherzige Kompromißformel zwischen dem Konsumprodukt Urlaub und der Einsicht in seine zerstörerischen Auswirkungen. Ein Besänftigungsprogramm für die weiterhin ungebrochene Expansion des Urlaubsgeschäfts.“

(Bergoff/Kresta 1995: 99ff)

Viele Defizite sind im Bereich des vernünftigen Reisens entstanden, Schuld ist nicht zuletzt auch die Reiseberichterstattung. Ein treffendes Beispiel ist hier sicherlich Ägypten. Wer kennt sie nicht, die faszinierenden Bilder atemberaubender Tempel, verschleierter Menschen und die Schilderungen der weiten Klänge der Gebetsgesänge. Reisejournalisten brachten sie zu Papier, die ‘Märchen aus 1000 und einer Nacht’. Gekoppelt mit günstigen Angeboten verschiedener Reiseveranstalter hatten sie eine Flut von Touristen zur Folge. Zahlreiche Kreuzfahrtschiffe befördern täglich Hunderte Touristen auf dem Nil von Tempel zu Tempel. Das Land ist dem Ansturm oft nicht gewachsen, so versinkt der Fluß im Müll, Flora und Fauna des ‘Märchenlandes’ sind ernstlich bedroht. Wo einerseits die Menschen vom blühenden Handel mit den Touristen profitieren, macht sich andererseits der Haß breit, auf die, die ‘halbnackt’ und respektlos durch die heiligen Stätten der Götter schlendern und achtlos ihre Cola-Dosen überall hinwerfen. Hier wird Tourismus zur Quelle (und zum Angriffsziel) von Fundamentalisten, geschürt durch unser mangelndes Verständnis für diese fremde Kultur und unzureichende Information, besonders von Seiten der Medien. Dies ist nur ein Beispiel, es gibt viele andere. Hier ist professioneller Reisejournalismus gefragt, damit es gar nicht erst soweit kommt. **Die Welt vor unserer Haustür ist kein Zoo und auch keine Müllhalde**, das sollte den Lesern verdeutlicht werden. Reisejournalismus sollte der 'Nach mir die Sintflut'- Mentalität entgegenwirken.

Peter-Matthias Gaede, Chefredakteur des *GEO*-Magazins, sagte in einem Interview: „Um einen seltenen Vogel zu schützen, muß man den Wald schützen, und um den Wald zu schützen, muß man den Menschen etwas zu essen geben.“ Massentourismus ist alles andere als Entwicklungshilfe. Der Weg zur ethischen Selbstkontrolle ist steinig und unbequem, doch einige Journalisten gehen ihn bereits.

8.3.3 Vereinigung deutscher Reisejournalisten (VDRJ)

Seit fast vierzig Jahren gibt es die ***Vereinigung Deutscher Reisejournalisten (VDRJ)***. Sie ist mit der publizistischen und wirtschaftliche Bedeutung von Reise und Tourismus gewachsen und zählt heute weit über hundert Mitglieder, zu denen Redakteure und selbständige Journalisten zählen.

Die *VDRJ* ist eine Arbeitsgemeinschaft von Gleichgesinnten im Bereich des Reisejournalismus, welchen die Mitglieder als Information, Service und Unterhaltung für den Verbraucher betrachten. Die Mitglieder der *VDRJ* lehnen 'Schönfärberei' und 'Hofberichterstattung' sowie die Koppelung von Reisebericht und Werbeanzeigen der Reiseindustrie strikt ab.

Wer Mitglied werden möchte, muß nicht nur über jahrelange Erfahrungen als Reisejournalist verfügen, sondern er muß vor allem 'sauber' sein, d.h. er darf die Ethik nicht Geschenken opfern. Die *VDRJ* fordert angemessene Honorare, um Recherchen wieder bezahlbar zu machen (*VDRJ 1989*).

„Ein **verantwortungsvoller Reisejournalist** fühlt sich nicht nur seinen Lesern gegenüber verantwortlich, denen er kein geschöntes, sondern ein möglichst realistisches Bild der betreffenden Region schildern möchte“, so *VDRJ*-Ge-schäftsführerin Liselotte Nückel. „Er wird versuchen, den Leser zum 'richti-gen' Reisen zu führen. Selbstverständlich fühlt er sich auch den Folgen des Tourismus (den er ja mit angeregt hat) gegenüber verantwortlich, weist auf diese hin und warnt vor Schäden an den Ressourcen, der Landschaft, den gewachsenen Kulturen und den Menschen. Wir gelten den Naturschützern als Multiplikatoren, sie zeigen uns überall gern ihre Projekte, und wir greifen gern ihre Themen auf.“ (Nückel 1996)

Die *VDRJ* macht auf Menschen und Institutionen aufmerksam, die sich für verantwortliches Reisen einsetzen. In diesem Sinne vergibt die *VDRJ* alljährlich einen **Preis für besondere Verdienste** um den Tourismus auf der *Internationalen Tourismusbörse* (*ITB*) in Berlin. Im Jahr 1995 ging dieser an Horst Xylander für seine Pionierleistungen auf dem Gebiet der Studienreisen per Fahrrad. Als Gründer und Unternehmer der *ROTALIS Sport- und Kulturreisen* in Baldham veranstaltet er seit 1973 Radwanderreisen durch Europa. Die Gruppen bestehen trotz gestiegener Nachfrage aus maximal zwanzig Personen und zwei Reisebegleitern. Sie radeln abseits der großen Straßen durch verschiedene Länder.

Die Aktivitäten des *VDRJ* beziehen sich nicht nur auf das Bundesgebiet, so zeichnete der Verein vor einigen Jahren Celik Gülersoy, den Präsidenten des *Türkischen Touring- und Automobilclubs*, für seinen Einsatz zur Erhaltung kulturhistorischer Denkmäler in der Türkei aus.

In 1996 wurde der *VDRJ*-Preis an den Umweltbeauftragten der *Touristik Union International GmbH & Co. KG* (*TUI*), Hannover, Dr. Wolf Michael Iwand verliehen. Er hat es sich zum Ziel gemacht, durch langfristig angelegte, systematische Problemlösungen, die Belastungen der Umwelt durch den Tourismus zu reduzieren. So sind mit seiner Hilfe Müllkippen auf den Balearen verschwunden, wurden Kläranlagen optimiert und lokale Lösungen zur Nutzung alternativer Energien gefunden. Sicher ist der Selbstzweck unbestritten, dennoch, würden alle Reiseveranstalter sich offen mit den Umweltschäden durch Tourismus auseinandersetzen, wären wir beim Thema Ethik schon einen großen Schritt weiter.

8.3.4 Reiseethik in den USA - Amerika als Vorreiter

Ob Musik, Film oder Freizeitsport, die Trends der USA setzen sich oft mit Zeitverzögerung in Europa fort. Auch bezüglich der Ethik im Reisejournalismus sind die Amerikaner schon einen großen Schritt weiter. Wo in deutschen Redaktionen noch mit den Schultern gezuckt wird, wenn man nach ethischen Richtlinien fragt, gibt es **in den USA bei allen Journalistn-Organisationen Satzungen, die das Thema Ethik ausführlich behandeln** und zu deren Einhaltung sich jedes Mitglied schriftlich verpflichten muß.

Was in Deutschland die kleine *VDRJ* verkörpert, nämlich ein Element journalistischer Selbstkontrolle auf freiwilliger Basis, das leistet in den USA die sehr viel größere ***Society of American Travel Writers*** (***SATW***). In ihrem ***Code of Ethics*** wird zusammengetragen, was sich an ethischen Regeln über die Jahre herausgeschält hat. (Wir dokumentieren ihn unter Kap. 8.4.) Der Selbstdarstellung von *SATW* folgend, sind die Mitglieder 'professionelle

Reise-Kommunikatoren', für die strenge Maßstäbe anzusetzen sind. Wenn es auf Presse-Reisen geht, die auch in den USA üblich sind, so gilt es viele Regeln zu beachten. So darf kein *SATW*-Mitglied Zahlungen akzeptieren im Zusammenhang mit einer Übereinkunft, freundliches Material über ein Reiseziel zu produzieren.

Die *SATW* hat auch andere Wege entwickelt, die Qualität der Reiseberichterstattung zu erhöhen. Dazu zählen eine eigene Publication *The Travel Writer*, in der gemeinsame Probleme erörtert werden, ein jährlich erscheinendes Register der Mitglieder mit Angabe der Fachgebiete und die Zusammenarbeit mit universiären Journalistenschulen. In einem jährlich ausgeschriebenen Wettbewerb (*Lowell Thomas Travel Journalism Award*) werden Preise in Gold, Silber und Bronze vergeben. 1995 lagen der Jury über 1.000 Produkte zur Beurteilung vor, entschieden wurde nach 21 Kategorien. Dazu zählen z.B die besten Reiseteile in Tageszeitungen, die besten Reisemagazine, prämiert werden aber auch recht spezielle Beiträge wie der beste selbstbebilderte Artikel, die beste Seereisen-Reportage, der beste Service-orientierte Artikel für Konsumenten, der beste Umwelt-Bericht für Touristen (The Travel Writer, May 1996).

Weitere Fachorganisationen, die reisende Journalisten in den USA erfassen, sind die *Outdoor Writers Association of America*, die *Travel Journalists Guild* und die *International Food, Wine & Travel Writers Association.* Sie haben ähnliche **Bestimmungen zur Selbstkontrolle** formuliert und binden ihre Mitglieder entsprechend. Auf der Gegenseite der Verlage finden sich - auch dies eine amerikanische Eigenheit - vergleichbare Codizes mit entsprechenden Selbstbindungen. So zählt zur Hausphilosophie der *New York Times* und ihrer berühmten *Travel Section*, daß ein Autor niemals mehr als einem Herren dienen kann. Daher werden keine Artikel publiziert, die aus einer Reise hervorgehen, die von einer Fluggesellschaft, einem Hotel oder einer vergleichbaren Organisation bezahlt wurde. So wird es auch den Lesern garantiert, entsprechend hoch ist die **Glaubwürdigkeit der Berichte**. Andere Publikationen sind nicht so streng, doch lassen sie sich vorher den Grad der Unterstützung erklären und durchforsten die Artikel nach verborgener Werbung (Zobel 1992: 292ff). Wie man sieht, wird der Grad, bis zu dem Reisejournalisten verführbar sind, wesentlich von der Haltung der Verlegerseite mitgestaltet. Einseitige Schuldzuweisungen auf Kosten der Autoren sind deshalb nicht zulässig.

Was amerikanische Quellen zu ethischen Fragen so erfrischend macht, ist ihre Nähe zur Praxis. Es geht nicht um akademische Dispute, sondern um praktische Probleme. Diejenigen, die sich auf Kosten Dritter durchmogeln und kostenlose Leistungen 'abstauben', werden gern 'Freebies' genannt. Während deren Strategie aus ethischen Gründen abzulehnen ist, bestimmt sie faktisch das Verhalten vieler Journalisten mit. Umso kurioser ist diese kleine Geschichte: Ein Autor von City-Führern erklärt ganz offen, daß er sich seit Jahren in den später von ihm besprochenen Restaurants zu erkennen gebe und darauf kostenlos schmause. Das gehe immer gut, nur einmal habe ihm der Manager die Speise verweigert - weil der selbst ein Jahr als falscher Journalist und Kritiker aufgetreten sei, um sich durchzuschlagen (Zobel 1992: 294). 'Freebie Ethics', das ist die Frage nach den immer neuen Gratwanderungen zwischen Überlebensbedürfnis und gutem Gewissen. Freilich sind sich alle Beteiligten wieder an einem Punkt einig, nämlich, daß die Reisen der Journalisten großzügig mit der Steuererklärung verrechnet werden können. Dafür zu sorgen, zählt zu den Aufgaben der Berufsverbände.

Eine **ethische Grundhaltung hat viel mit Professionalisierung zu tun**. Der Reisejournalist muß in den Stand kommen, bestimmte Zumutungen, die an ihn herangetragen werden, ablehnen zu können. Die professionelle Vereinigung muß ihn darin unterstützen, indem sie 'unkeusche' Angebote öffentlich macht und anprangert. Das wird nur dann glaubwürdig praktiziert, wenn auch die 'schwarzen Schafe' unter den Journalisten öffentlich kritisiert werden können. Selbst wenn die Realitäten heute ganz anders aussehen, müssen die Visionen eines besseren Reisejournalismus immer wieder beschworen werden. Vorbilder dafür gibt es genug. Ihre Umsetzung steht im ureigensten Interesse der Reisejournalisten, deren Renommee dadurch nachhaltig gehoben wird, aber auch ihrer Arbeitgeber, die an der Verbreitung von Plattheiten und Vorurteilen in ihren Blättern kein Interesse haben können.

8.4 Textanhang: *Society of American Travel Writers (SATW): Code of Ethics*

All members of the *Society of American Travel Writers* - Actives and Associates - subscribe to the highest standards of professionalism and, by accepting membership, agree to abide by the *Code of Ethics* of the Society.

The Code is comprised of Principles and Rules, and Procedures for enforcement.

The Principles represent the highest standards of conduct toward which all members should strive, and represent the overriding concepts from which the specific rules are derived.

The Rules are mandatory. They state the minimum level of conduct below which no member of *SATW* can fall without being subject to disciplinary action. The rules are uniform applied to all members.
The Procedures set forth the process by which violators of the rules will be investigated and disciplined. Disciplinary action, which may be imposed by the *Ethics Committee* of *SATW*, may range from a reprimand to suspension or expulsion from membership in the Society.

Principle I

***SATW* members are professional travel communicators and should always strive to maintain the highest professional standards.**

Rules

1. Members shall not engage in plagiarism or infringement of the rights, including copyright, of others.
2. No member shall publish information about a destination about which he or she has no first-hand knowledge unless the member uses reliable sources of information.
3. No member shall misrepresent his or her *SATW* membership category or status.
4. No member shall falsely represent his or her credentials or word output as part of any *SATW* membership review or listing.
5. No member shall use the *SATW* name or insignia except to designate his or her membership, and no member may use official *SATW* stationary except for the conduct of official business of the Society.
6. Members shall not engage in conduct that embarrasses the Society or that will otherwise harm its reputation or professionalism.

Principle II

***SATW* members should conduct business in a professional manner.**

1. No member shall knowingly sell that rights that he or she does not own.
2. No member shall permit his or her byline to appear as sole author on word not produced by him of her, nor shall a member be listed as co-author of a work to which he or she has not contributed.

3. When photographs or editorial have been furnished by others, a member shall so advise the publisher.
4. No member shall deliberately misrepresent his or her participation in a press trip in order to secure an editorial assignment.
5. Associate members shall not accept nor pay money for acquiring new accounts, except for proposal fees, and shall not offer cash or any others form of payment to editors or writers in exchange for editorial coverage purporting to be objective unbiased reporting of information.

Principle III

***SATW* members should maintain the highest standards of professionalism on press trips.**

Rules

1. No member shall deliberately misrepresent the status of an assignment in order to secure participation in a press trip.
2. All assistants accompanying a member on a press trip shall be fully qualified assistants; all others accompanying a member must be identified a guest. The participation of guest on press trips is subject to the restrictions of the host and at no time shall a guest attend in place of a member.
3. A member shall personally pay for all services required by that member that are personal, or over and above the services voluntarily provided by the host.

Principle IV

***SATW* Members Shoul Avoid Conflicts of Interest.**

Rules

1. No member shall accept payment or courtesies in exchange for an agreement to produce material about a travel destination, service or supplier that is contrary to his or her own professional appraisal.
2. Members who are or have been employed by or associated with a travel destination, service firm or supplier shall disclose that fact to all potential editors and/or publishers prior to accepting an assignment relating to that destination or involving that service firm or supplier.

Procedures

As provided in the Procedures section below, The Society shall discipline members found guilty of violations of the *SATW* Ethics Code, as well as for conduct detrimental to the best interests of the Society.

1. Complaints of suspected violations of any rule of the *SATW Code of Ethics* must be made in writing, signed by the complainant(s), and sent to the Society's Ethics Director at the Society's headquarters office.
2. The Executive Director will immediately forward copies of the complainant to the members of the Society's *Ethics Committee* and the President.
3. The *Ethics Committee* will promptly investigate all complaints forwarded to it and, within 60 days, shall determine if the complaint shall be dismissed, investigated further, or set for a hearing.
4. If the complaint is dismissed, the *Ethics Committee* will notify the complainant(s) and the President of the committee's decision, which shall be final.
5. If the *Ethics Committee* determines that the complaint should be investigated further, the committee shall notify the member of the complaint and by whom it was made, and advise him or her of the right to present evidence relating to the complaint. The *Ethics Committee* may interview by telephone, by mail, or in person, either members or others who have information relevant to the complaint.
6. If the *Ethics Committee* determines after further investigation that a violation has occurred for which is appropriate, the committee shall prepare a written report detailing its finding of the facts, the nature of the misconduct so established, and the form of the reprimand imposed; a copy of the report will be sent to the charged party, the complainant(s), and the President. The decision of the *Ethics Committee* shall be final unless appealed by the charged party to the Executive Committee within 60 days of the decision; the request for an appeal must be made within that time frame by certified mail to the President at the Society's headquarters office.
7. If the *Ethics Committee* determines after further investigation that a violation has occurred for which suspension or expulsion from membership may be appropriate, the *Ethics Committee* shall hold a hearing by telephone conference call or at a location mutually convenient for all parties. Notice shall be given to the charged party, the Complainant(s), and the President at least 60 days prior to the date set hearing. The charged party may appear with counsel at his or her own expense. The Chairman of the

Ethics Committee shall preside over the hearing, which shall be conducted in an informal manner, with or without the presence of *SATW*'s legal counsel. At the option of the charged party, a hearing may be waived and the complaint resolved by documents submitted in response by both the charged party and the complainant(s). After the conclusion of the hearing, the full committee shall decide by four-fifth vote to suspend or expel the charged member. The decision of the *Ethics Committee* shall be final unless appealed by the charged party to the Executive Committee within 60 days of notice of the decision; the request for an appeal must be made within that time frame by certified mail to the President at the Society's headquarters office.

8. Upon any appeal filed by a charged party subject to reprimand, suspension or expulsion, the Executive committee shall hold a hearing by telephone conference call or at the next regularly scheduled meeting of the Board of Directors. The charged party may appear at the appeal hearing with counsel at his or her own expense, The President shall preside over the appeal hearing, which shall be conducted in an informal manner, with or without the presence of *SATW's* legal counsel. At the option of the charged party, an appeal hearing may be waived and the appeal resolved by documents submitted in response by both the charged party and the complainant. After the conclusion of the hearing, the full committee shall decide by four-fifth vote (with the President not voting) to uphold or reverse the decision of the *Ethics Committee.*
9. All proceedings of the *Ethics Committee* and all appeal proceedings of the Executive Committee shall be held in closed sessions, unless open sessions are requested by the charged party. All evidence submitted to either committee shall be maintained in the strictest of confidence.
10. A suspension may be imposed for any definite period of time. At the conclusion of the suspension period, no formal action is required for reinstatement of membership. A member who is expelled cannot be reinstated or reapply for membership.

9 Die Zukunft des Reisejournalismus

„Bei der Reiseplanung gehen wir neue, multimediale Wege. Gemeinsam mit *BOSCH* haben wir *MERIAN scout*, den ersten elektronischen Reiseführer für Autonavigationssysteme, realisiert. *MERIAN* online ist der heißeste Surf-Tip im *CompuServe*-Netz. Und die intelligente Verbindung von Stadtführer und Reiseführer auf CD ROM heißt *MERIAN screen*. Ob im Auto oder im PC, unsere elektronischen Wegweiser begleiten Sie mit den besten Empfehlungen aus der *MERIAN*-Datenbank."

(Aus der *MERIAN*-Eigenwerbung)

9.1 Einleitung

Hans J. Kleinsteuber

In diesem Kapitel werden Perspektiven des Reisejournalismus erarbeitet. In den letzten Jahrzehnten hatte diese Richtung journalistischer Arbeit bereits einen stürmischen Aufschwung durchgemacht. Er hat sich differenziert und diversifiziert, er hat viele Erscheinungsformen angenommen. Derzeit gibt es kaum noch ein Printmedium, das nicht zumindest zwischendurch Reisen thematisiert, etwa die Autozeitschrift mit dem Motorwandern oder das Sportorgan mit Schilderung der nächsten Weltmeister-Stadt. Dazu ist die Reiseberichterstattung in Radio und Fernsehen hineingekrochen, auch wenn sich der Umfang in Grenzen hält. Hier wollen wir versuchen zu analysieren, wie es weitergeht. Dabei sei auf den Abschnitt verwiesen, in dem die Reisejournalisten selbst die Zukunft entwerfen (Kap. 6.7).

Die **Trends der Zukunft** sollen vorab unter einigen Stichworten zusammengefasst werden:

Globalisierung: Noch nie in der Geschichte der technischen Kommunikation war es so einfach und kostengünstig, Informationen an fremden Punkten aufzuspüren und abzufragen. Speziell das 'distanzvernichtende' Internet bietet Zugang zu den entferntesten Informationen, so als seien sie an der nächsten Ecke zu bekommen. Diese Möglichkeit wird ergänzt um die

Tatsache, daß immer mehr Menschen immer weiter reisen, die virtuelle Distanzüberwindung also von der realen Möglichkeit begleitet wird, Entfernungen schneller, einfacher und kostengünstiger als jemals zuvor zu überwinden. Diese Chancen haben schon in der Vergangenheit für immer mehr Nachfrage nach Reiseinformationen gesorgt und es gibt keinen Grund, diese Tendenz nicht in die Zukunft zu extrapolieren. Globalisierung findet so gleichermaßen real und virtuell statt.

Für den Journalisten wird es damit höchst einfach, sich auf der Homepage der Stadt Montreal 'einzuloggen' und sich über das nächste Musikfestival mitsamt Übernachtungsmöglichkeiten zu informieren. Dazu kann er noch das aktuelle Wetter abrufen und Fragen in der Touristikzentrale hinterlassen, wie es zur Zeit des Festivals erwartet wird. Der Journalist wird sich mit diesen - heute in vielen Industriestaaten schon verfügbaren - neuen Formen der Netz-Recherche vertraut machen müssen. Das Problem freilich ist, daß sich auch jeder andere Netznutzer dieser Möglichkeiten bedienen, die traditionelle Schleusenfunktion des Journalisten unterlaufen werden kann. Was dem Journalisten nutzt, macht ihn tendenziell auch überflüssig.

Interaktivierung und Individualisierung: Die Möglichkeiten der neuen Netze schaffen bei erster Annäherung neue Übertragungsmöglichkeiten, die Zeitung wird elektronisch übermittelt, die Fernsehsendung um ihre Webpage ergänzt. Aber das ist nur der Einstieg, denn tendenziell werden alle vertrauten Formen der Masseninformierung durch Massenmedien überflüssig, Jeder kann sich zukünftig selbst und individuell bedienen. Wo früher der Journalist Pakete der Informierung schnürte - in Form von Zeitungen oder Fernsehmagazinen - kann sich jeder Interessent nun seine maßgeschneiderten Informationen ins Haus holen: die individuell zusammengestellte elektronische Zeitung oder auch nur Berichte, die sich mit dem nächsten geplanten Reiseziel beschäftigen. Wo früher aus wenigen Zentren Medieninhalte gestaltet wurden, werden jetzt immer mehr individuell abrufbare Informationen zur Verfügung gestellt. Im daraus resultierenden Ozean von Daten wird die Orientierung zur zentralen Aufgabe. Und die bietet sich als Chance für den Journalisten, der nun seinen 'Rezipienten' sicher durch die Informationsmeere navigiert. So besehen wird der Journalist, wenn auch unter veränderten Vorzeichen, wichtiger als jemals zuvor.

Zwei-Klassen-Informationsgesellschaft: Die Beobachtung, daß Reisen und die darauf bezogenen Medien auch in Zukunft noch an Bedeutung zunehmen, darf nicht zu schlichten Extrapolationen verleiten. Etwa dem Prinzip folgend, daß dann mehr von den jetzt vertrauten Reisemedien nachgefragt würden. In der Gesellschaft beobachten wir vielfältige Prozesse der Polarisierung, eine wachsende Wissenskluft etwa zwischen den 'Information Poor' und den 'Information Rich'. Sie wird begleitet von einem gleichzeitigen Wachsen des Massentourismus in riesige, nahezu industriell betriebene Gettos für Niedrigverdiener á la Mallorca und dem individuellen und edlen Unterwegssein der Connoisseure in Luxus-Lodges. Entsprechend werden sich die Medien entwickeln, hier die schlichten, stereotypisierten Berichte, dort die aufwendig produzierten Hochglanzmagazine für die feine Klientel. In beide wird sich die Touristikindustrie mit ihren Interessen hineindrängeln wollen, freilich mit sehr unterschiedlichen Strategien. Wird sich der Massentourismus auch weiterhin an die Massenmedien hängen, so werden sie sich gegenseitig stabilisieren. Für die feine Art, individuell zu reisen wird sich das Angebot der Netze als immer attraktiver erweisen. Letztere zu bedienen, erfordert zudem erhebliche Vorinvestitionen und Kenntnisse im Umgang mit vernetzten Computern, was wiederum die 'Information Rich' auszeichnet.

Konvergenz: Eine besondere Qualität der digitalen Technik liegt darin, daß sie bisher getrennte Medien und Vorgänge miteinander zu verknüpfen und sie ineinander zu verweben vermag. Die Tätigkeiten der Veranstalter und der Reiseinteressenten, der Reisejournalisten und die der Reisebüros werden nun über dasselbe Netz abgewickelt. Was bedeutet es für eine Reisereportage, wenn der Text an vielen Schlüsselbegriffen mit 'Links' versehen ist, also mit Verknüpfungen zu den jeweiligen Organisationen und Anbietern? Bei der Erwähnung eines Landes wird zu den Grenzbehörden durchgestellt, die Visa- und Zollbestimmungen mitteilen, bei Nennung einer Stadt wird mit einem Click die Touristikzentrale angesteuert, bei Hotelvorschlägen direkt mit der Buchungszentrale verbunden, bei Restaurants mit Speisekarte und Tischreservierung. So besehen, bekommt der Serviceteil, bisher eher stiefmütterlich von den schreibenden Kollegen behandelt, eine völlig neue Bedeutung, ermöglicht er doch ganz konkrete Reisevorbereitungen im Internet. Im nun enorm aufgewerteten Service-Teil wird der Journalist quasi zum Lotsen im Cyberspace, bietet Leistungsmerkmale an, die bisher Reisebüros vorbehalten blieben. Es gibt viele Prognosen, daß aus genau diesen Gründen die Arbeitsplätze typischer 'Mittelsleute' - wie der Mitarbeiter von Reisebüros - von den neuen Netzen bedroht werden.

Da sind Potentiale, aber auch offensichtliche Grenzen. Nach einer Untersuchung der *Handelsblatt*-Gruppe zählen Reiseleistungen mit einem Anteil von 26,5 Prozent zu den beliebsten Angeboten im Internet. Nach einer anderen Analyse des *stern* können sich 40 Prozent der Netznutzer vorstellen, Reisen via Datenhighway zu buchen. (*Wirtschaftswoche* v. 6. Febr. 1997)

Inzwischen bieten die großen Hotelketten ihre Zimmer im Hypertext an, mitunter inklusive Bildern vom Quartier und Tabellen mit den Preisen. Freilich, die Realitäten sehen viel nüchterner aus. Genutzt werden die Möglichkeiten bisher, zumindest von Privatleuten, kaum. Dafür gibt es gute Gründe. Derzeit erweist sich der Datenaustausch auf beiden Seiten als nicht sicher, weder kann der Buchende sicher sein, daß sein Begehr ankommt, noch vermag sich das Hotel auf seine Bestellung verlassen. 'Witzbolde' sollen schon ganze Hotels mit ihren Vorausbuchungen belegt haben, erschienen ist dann niemand.

Was hier präsentiert wurde, sind **Ideen und erste Ansätze, keine verläßlichen Prognosen**. Dazu sind die Zukunftsperspektiven viel zu unsicher, haben sich frühere Voraussagen nicht bewahrheitet. Die neuen Techniken werden auf jeden Fall die Karten neu verteilen. Vielleicht versuchen nun die Reisebüros selbst in den Journalismus einzusteigen, wenn es stimmt, daß zukünftig Reportagen und Serviceteile unmittelbar die Plattformen für den Start in eine Reise abgeben. Wie verhalten sich die PR-Leute, denen es das Netz einfacher als heute machen wird, sich verborgen zu halten? Wird, wer harmlos ein Reiseziel in die Suchmaschine eingibt, direkt auf die Web-Seiten der Veranstaltern geleitet? Das Interesse der Tourismusindustrie, ihre Ware in geschönten Reiseberichten zu vermarkten, könnte sich weiter erhöhen und als schmerzlicher Druck für die Journalisten spürbar werden. Wird sie Druck machen, daß sich in Zukunft die Reportagen kaum mehr von ihren Katalogseiten unterscheiden? Vielleicht gelingt es ihr, die notwendigerweise begrenzte Zahl der Links in ihrem Sinne zu kontrollieren, also die per Reportage stimulierte Nachfrage gerade auf ihre Adressen zu lenken. Wie immer sich das Szenario entwickelt, der Reisejournalismus im Cyberspace wird ein ganz anderer sein, als der im uns so vertrauten Gutenberg-Zeitalter.

9.2 Neue Präsentationsformen: Reisejournalismus online

Johannes Broermann

Cyberspace, Internet, World Wide Web, Online-Dienste - ein neues Medium ist entdeckt und wächst. Wer in dieser virtuellen Welt nach Reisenden sucht, der erhält eine ganze Menge Verweise (sogenannte Links) zu 'Surf'-Reisen - **den Reisen durchs Netz**. Es scheint, als wolle jeder Surfer von seinen längsten Wartezeiten, schönsten Fotos und den seiner Meinung nach am besten gestalteten Netzseiten berichten. Doch wie steht's mit dem Reisejournalismus von der Erde - kommt er vor in der Welt der Netze?

Und wie! In den verschiedensten Formen: ob als reines online-Magazin, als bloße Wiedergabe der im Handel erhältlichen Druckversion oder als Werbung für das Hochglanzmagazin am Kiosk. Mischformen bleiben natürlich nicht aus. Nur von den Rundfunkveranstaltern konnte Anfang 1997 noch keine Reiseredaktion im Netz entdeckt werden. Allerdings mußte sich die Recherche auf den deutschsprachigen Raum und im wesentlichen auf das World Wide Web (WWW) beschränken. Ausgewertet wurde zusätzlich das Angebot von CompuServe. Exemplarisch werden die Ergebnisse an einzelnen Beispielen deutlich gemacht. Die **Schnellebigkeit des Internets** läßt keine andere Darstellung zu.

9.2.1 Reise-Online-Magazine

Sie wurden erst durch Online-Publishing möglich: die **Internet-Magazine**. Ausschließlich online zu erhalten, scheuen sie sich am wenigsten, die neuen Möglichkeiten auszureizen.

travelbook

Erst seit dem Frühjahr 1996 ist *travelbook* im Internet. Das „Reisemagazin im Internet", wie es sich im Untertitel nennt, bietet in seinem Magazin-Teil Reportagen, die auch in gedruckten Magazinen stehen könnten. Doch anders aufbereitet: Der Text und die dazugehörigen Bilder sind voneinander getrennt. Der Leser kann wählen, ob er den Bericht vor dem Lesen 'downloaded', also herunterläd, oder online liest. Die Fotos präsentiert *travelbook* in Form einer 'Diashow'. Alle paar Sekunden wird auf dem Bildschirm ein neues Foto aufgebaut. Leider sind die Zeiten so kurz, daß viele Bildunterschriften einfach nur vor den eigenen Augen hinweghuschen - vorausgesetzt der permanente Stau auf der Datenautobahn hält sich in Grenzen.

Travelbook wäre natürlich kein Internet-Magazin, wenn es sich nicht der Technik der Links bedienen würde, mit denen Verknüpfungen zu anderen Angeboten im Internet hergestellt werden. Dabei reicht das Anklicken besonders gekennzeichneter Worte per Maustaste und die angekündigte nächste Seite erscheint.

Bei *travelbook* finden sich Links zu Reisetips sowie Buchhinweisen mit weiterem Link auf das Gesamtverzeichnis des entsprechenden Verlags. Bisher kann online nur weiteres Informationsmaterial angefordert werden, aber warum sollte es nicht schon bald die Online-Bestellung geben? Wie sehr es sich bei den Buchtips um Werbung handelt, wird daran deutlich, daß Reiseführer nur aus einem Verlag angepriesen werden. Damit ist der Netz-Surfer auch schon mitten im Service-Teil von *travelbook* angelangt. Nicht nur Verlage, auch Hotelketten, Reiseveranstalter und Fluglinien können offensichtlich unter *Service* direkt werben. Ähnlich sieht es hinter den Rubriken *News*, *Trends* und *Tips* aus. Viele Texte scheinen unbearbeitete PR-Mitteilungen zu sein.

Neben dem *Magazin* ist daher vor allem noch die Rubrik *Links* zu gebrauchen, die mittlerweile schon selbst wieder unterteilt ist in *Land&Leute*, *Hin&Weg* sowie *Freunde&Finden*. Dort finden sich nicht nur Verweise auf die Werbepartner, sondern eben auch auf Informationsquellen anderer Anbieter - sozusagen der eigentliche Serviceteil.

Beispielsweise kann das *CIA Factbook* angeklickt werden, in dem Daten zu allen Ländern der Erde abrufbar sind. Zeitweilig gab es auch einen Link zur *NBC Wetterkarte*. Vermutlich hat die Redaktion gemerkt, daß das Angebot für eine Reisewettervorhersage eigentlich ziemlich dürftig war: Bei *NBC* gibt es nur das Wetter der USA sowie das Weltwetter. Wetter-Links bot *travelbook* Anfang 1997 nicht mehr an.

TraXXX

„Willkommen bei *TraXXX*, der *Travel & Traffic-Line* aus dem Hause *Burda*." Willkommen bei einem noch stärkern Gemisch aus Information und Werbung. Dennoch versprechen die Macher, alles zu bieten, „was Reisen schöner macht." Dazu gehören u.a. Devisenkurse, ein Wetterbericht von *meteo consult*, Staumeldungen, ein Kleinanzeigenmarkt des *ADAC*, ein Reisebüro, ein Veranstaltungskalender und der Hinweis auf *Burda*-Magazine. Die Internet-Ausgabe von *Holiday* (s.u.) ist ebenso einsehbar wie die von *Tour*.

9.2.2 Reise-Printmagazine online

Mit Vorliebe nutzen auch Printmedien das Netz weitgehend zu Werbezwekken. Da baut sich dann in mühevoller Rechenarbeit mit hohem Zeitverlust die bunte Titelseite auf dem Bildschirm auf. Doch außer einer kurzen Inhaltsangabe des zuletzt erschienen Heftes und dem Link auf die Seite mit dem (Probeabo-) Bestellformular ist nichts zu erfahren.

GEO SAISON

In dieser Art präsentiert sich beispielsweise *GEO SAISON*. Hinter den Links zu den einzelnen Themen im Heft finden sich nur ein, zwei Anreißersätze und der Hinweis auf welcher Seitenzahl im Printheft weitergelesen werden kann.

So heißt es zum *GEO SAISON*-Heft New York unter dem Link „Fränkische Schweiz" lediglich „Wo die Hexen tanzen. Seite 84" (*http:// www.geo.de /hefte/saison/96/07/f_schweiz.html*). Hier wird also überhaupt kein redaktioneller Inhalt geboten, keine einzige Kostprobe, das Heft ist gefälligst zu kaufen: reine Werbung im Netz.

Wie sieht die Reisereportage der Zukunft aus? Die Zeitschrift *Das Internet Programm* gibt die Antwort. Unter nicht gerade origineller Betitelung 'Oh la la, la France' findet sich neben den üblichen Belanglosigkeiten („In Frankreich wird geflirtet...") eine Auflistung interessanter Web-Seiten zum Thema. Einige Beispiele:

http://www.lonelyplanet.com
→ „Infos übers Land und Bilder von dort hat die Online-Version von Lonely Planet - nicht schlecht, um sich auf den Urlaub einzustimmen. Einige lohnende Reiseziele werden vorgestellt, aber leider nur sehr wenige - auch wenn die Auswahl nicht schlecht ist."

http://www.mmania.com/cur/home
→ „The virtual Baguette - eine nicht immer ganz ernst gemeinte Fundgrube für Frankreich-Freaks."

http://www.pariscope.fr
→ „P@riscope ist randvoll mit Infos über die Hauptstadt: Shopping, Nightlife, Restaurants und was man sonst noch braucht."

http://www.city.net
→ „Exite's Städtenetz bietet Informationen im Überfluß. Aktuelle Wetterdaten, Verkehr, Persönlichkeiten, virtuelle Stadtrundgänge und Karten - es gibt nichts, was es nicht gibt."

(*Das Internet Programm*, Juni 1997: 86-89)

Holiday

Eine Abstufung bietet *Holiday* an. Der Vergleich zwischen dem Original und seinem virtuellen Pendant fällt für das Heft Juli/August 1996 so aus: Von den sechs Reportagen im Heft können drei im Volltext online abgerufen werden. Ansonsten ist von den 152 Heftseiten nur das Inhaltsverzeichnis einzusehen.

Sofern in den Reportagen Zusatzinformationen (*Service*) in eigenen Kästen angeboten wurden, kommen diese online nicht mehr vor. Die Texte werden vermutlich wörtlich übernommen, vereinzelt sind noch Trennstriche aus dem Satz für das Papier erhalten geblieben und tauchen mitten im Schriftbild auf. Die Bebilderung wurde stark zurückgefahren. Während im Original in der Regel mehr Fotoseiten als Textseiten vorhanden sind, ist das Verhältnis online umgekehrt.

Und noch ein umgekehrtes Verhältnis: Die Reportage „Stille Straßen“ (im Heft S. 100ff) hat zu einzelnen Stichworten Anmerkungen direkt am Rand, so als wenn es jetzt Links auch gedruckt geben würde. Online fehlen diese Hinweise. Überhaupt scheint das Online-Layout erheblich leseunfreundlicher zu sein: Es gibt nur eine Spalte. Ausgehend von Standard-Einstellungen eines Netbrowsers geht sie zwar nicht über die gesamte Bildschirmbreite, ist aber breiter als im Heft. Dort druckt *Holiday* bis zu fünf Spalten.

9.2.3 Reiseredaktionen online

Nicht nur ausgesprochene Reisemagazine drängen in den Cyberspace, allgemeiner ausgerichtete Blätter sind genauso vertreten. Das heißt aber noch lange nicht, daß auch die dazugehörigen Reiseredaktionen ein neues Mitteilungsmedium gefunden haben. Obwohl Tageszeitungen zumeist einmal in der Woche einen Reiseteil mitliefern, ist er im Netz nicht immer erhältlich.

Reise und Erholung der *Süddeutschen Zeitung*

Die Internetausgabe der *Süddeutschen Zeitung* erscheint mit Reiseteil. Entsprechend den anderen Ressorts sind die Beiträge nicht weiter für das Internet aufbereitet. Der Abruf ist nur am Erscheinungstag problemlos möglich. Wer im Archiv suchen will muß auf Volltext-Recherche verzichten. Ohne genaue Eingabe des Erscheinungsdatums ist ein Text unauffindbar. Links zu anderen Internet-Angeboten fehlen, ebenso Fotos, obwohl beim Anblick der Printausgabe der Eindruck entstehen kann, gerade auf die werde viel Wert gelegt. Fazit: Das vorhandene Material wird lediglich in geringerem Umfang auf einem anderem Vertriebsweg angeboten.

Schweriner Volkszeitung

Ganz anders sieht es bei der *Schweriner Volkszeitung* aus. Bei ihr kann zwar niemand einen Reiseteil im herkömmlichen Sinne finden, dafür gibt es aber einen virtuellen Spaziergang durch Mecklenburg-Vorpommern (*http://hamburg.bda.de:800/bda/nat/hn/SVZ/inhalt/vtour/index.html*). Bis Juli 1996 existierten darin erst einige Orte im westlichen Landesteil, aber das angestrebte Ziel läßt sich schon erahnen. Einzelne Orte werden mit ihrer Geschichte und ihren Sehenswürdigkeiten aufbereitet. Tips für die Anreise, für Unternehmungen in der Umgebung und Links auf Nachbarstädte runden das Angebot ab.

CompuServe Reisen

CompuServe enthält einen eigenen Menüpunkt zum Reisen. Neben Reise-Diskussionsforen bietet das Menü die Angebote kommerzieller Touristikanbieter. Beispielsweise präsentiert die *Deutsche Bahn AG* ihre Fahrplandatenbank. Im Vergleich mit der im Handel erhältlichen Fahrplan-CD-ROM ist der Bedienungskomfort leider schlechter. Sobald allgemeine Informationen zur Bahn angeklickt werden, lädt sich automatisch per Web-Browser das Angebot im WWW. Allerdings ist unter *CompuServe* die Fahrkartenbestellung online möglich - ein Vorteil, den das Internet noch nicht so sicher bietet.

Wenn überhaupt von journalistischen Inhalten gesprochen werden kann, dann beim Angebot von *Merian*. In dessen Online-Datenbanken finden sich Informationen zu Restaurants, Hotels und Veranstaltungsorten mit kurzen Bewertungen. Doch wer auf einzelne *Merian*-Ausgaben gehofft hat, wird enttäuscht. Noch nicht mal eine Übersicht der lieferbaren Hefte wird angeboten - das Probeabo-Bestellformular ist allerdings vorhanden.

9.2.4 Ausblick

Die Möglichkeiten der **Darstellung journalistischer Inhalte scheinen unbegrenzt im elektronischen Datenverbund**. Für den potentiellen Reisenden ist es natürlich sehr praktisch, wenn Reisereportagen mit tagesaktuellen Informationen (Wetter, politische Lage) verknüpt sind und die online-Buchung des gleichen Trips spielend leicht ist. Vorsicht ist allerdings angebracht, sobald die journalistische Darstellung nicht mehr unabhängig von den Werbepartnern auftritt. Die indirekte Lenkung des Verbrauchers ist, verglichen mit bisherigen Medien, viel einfacher geworden - die Links machen es möglich. Gerade hier könnte eine **neue Herausforderung des Reisejournalisten** liegen, seinen Lesern **qualitativ hochwertige Links im Zusammenhang mit seinen Texten anzubieten**. Darüber hinaus wird die Darstellungsform seiner Arbeit immer wichtiger. Nicht zuletzt soll sie ja im Datendschungel auffallen, möglichst viele Netzsurfer sollen sich auf der Seite einklicken. Dabei sind Dinge zu beachten, die auch für andere Netzangebote zutreffen. So gilt es, ein anspruchsvolles Layout zu realisieren und trotzdem kurze Ladezeiten auf den Computer des Lesers zu ermöglichen. Dank der realen Erde haben Reisejournalisten in der virtuellen Welt etwas zu bieten.

Online-Adressen zum Thema Reisen

travelbook	*http://www.travelbook.de*
CIA Factbook	*http://www.odci.gov/sia/publications/95fact*
ABC Wetterkarte	*http://www.intellicast.com*
TraXXX	*http://www.traxxx.de*
GEO SAISON	*http://www.geo.de/hefte/saison/index.html*
Holiday	*http://www.traxxx.de/holiday*
Süddeutsche Zeitung	*http://www.dw.gmd.de/sz*
Schweriner Volkszeitung	*http://hamburg.bda.de:800/bda/nat/hn/SVZ/inhalt/vtour/index.html*
Mecklenburg Vorpommern	*http://hamburg.bda.de:800/bda/nat/hn/SVZ/inhalz/vtour/index.html*

9.3 Zukunft der Reisemedien: CD ROM

Verena Wolff

Die ausführlichsten und ansehnlichsten Darstellungen eines Reiseziels sind auf **CD ROM** möglich. Per Mausklick kann man sich z.B. zu einen imaginären Spaziergang durch den New Yorker Central Park aufmachen. Dabei erfährt man gleich, welche Sport- und Freizeitmöglichkeiten der Central Park zu bieten hat, wie hoch die Leihgebühr für ein Fahrrad oder Roller Skates sind oder wo man weitere elf Leute für ein Volleyballmatch finden kann.

> Knut Föckler, Deutschland-Manager von *Microsoft Network* (und ehemaliger Unterhaltungschef von *SAT1*) zur Zukunft der Kommunikation:
>
> **Herr Professor Föckler, sind Sie als ehemaliger Fernsehmann nicht gelangweilt, wenn Sie im Web surfen?**
>
> **Föckler:** Nein, im Gegenteil. Ich kann jederzeit die Unterhaltung abrufen, die ich möchte. Und zwar mit der gewaltigen Flexibilität dieses Mediums.
>
> **Aber welche TV-Konsument, der sich abends aufs Sofa lümmelt und berieseln läßt, will schon so viel Aktivität?**
>
> **Föckler:** Ich glaube, eine ganze Menge. Ich selbst beispielsweise bin noch nie auf die Idee gekommen, mit einem TV-Gerät zu verreisen. Dagegen macht es ungeheuren Spaß, mit einem Laptop unterwegs zu sein und weltweit Unterhaltung, Informationen et cetera abzurufen.
>
> **Dennoch kann ein aktives Medium dem passiven Fernsehen keine echte Konkurrenz machen, behaupten Kritiker.**
>
> **Föckler.** Das sehe ich anders. Sie und ich unterhalten uns ja jetzt auch aktiv, und ich habe nicht das Gefühl, daß einer von uns in Passivität verfällt. Das heißt: Unterhaltung kann durchaus ein aktiver Prozeß sein. Sie ist nur deshalb passiv geworden, weil das Fernsehen ausschließlich Eigenware anbieten kann ...
>
> (Föckler 1997: 81)

Wem nicht nach Sport in New York zumute ist, informiert sich über die Vereinsgeschichte der New Yorker Baseball-Mannschaften. Oder legt sich zum Beispiel einen City-Guide London in den PC und läßt sich das Interieur der exklusivsten Hotels Londons vorführen, um schon mal zu überlegen, wo er beim nächsten Städtetrip sein müdes Haupt zur Ruhe bettet!

Da die CD ROM eine **viel größere Speicherkapazität** hat als ein gemeines Buch, hat man natürlich auch viel mehr Möglichkeiten, eine Stadt oder ein Land zu präsentieren. Eine CD ROM ist eine Art **Zwischending zu Reisevideo, Diashow und Bildband** mit der Möglichkeit, unzählige Informationen bereit zu halten und räumliche Eindrücke vermitteln zu können. Es gibt sogenannte 'slide shows', kommentierte Diashows, die bestimmte sehenswerte Viertel einer Stadt vorführen oder Festlichkeiten zu verschiedenen Ereignissen beschreiben.

Die CD ROM bietet eine interessante Möglichkeit, eine Stadt vorzustellen und dabei viele Informationen zu vermitteln. Damit es beim 'Spaziergänger' nicht zu einem 'information overload' kommt, können die Infos auch separat und in aller Ruhe jederzeit wieder abgerufen werden. In einem Städteführer (z.B. London oder New York) werden ca. 300 Hotels und ebenso viele Restaurants vorgestellt, die später kategorisiert abgerufen werden können (Lage, Kategorie und Preise). Die Restaurants sind z. B. nach Lage, Nationalität und Preisklasse kategorisiert. Will man also im Londoner West End ein Hotel finden, das drei Sterne hat und pro Nacht zwischen 50 und 100 Pfund Sterling kostet, klickt man auf die jeweiligen Kategorieren und bekommt die entsprechenden Angebote mitsamt Beschreibung und Photos auf den Bildschirm, hin und wieder versehen mit einer Anekdote. Bei den Restaurants bekommt man häufig noch das ideale Menü 'serviert'. Unzählige Möglichkeiten also, die in einem Reiseführer gar nicht realisierbar wären. Sie würden viel zu viele Seiten füllen und die Informationen können nicht so übersichtlich kategorisiert und präsentiert werden, wie das bei einer CD ROM der Fall ist. Allerdings ist eine CD ROM als Reisebegleiter etwas unpraktisch, denn wer trägt auf seinem Stadtrundgang schon gerne seinen Labtop unter dem Arm? Außerdem sind die Produktionskosten für einen solchen 'Silberling' natürlich sehr viel höher als für eine Zeitschrift, so wird der Reisende sich eher überlegen, ob er zehn Mark für eine Zeitschrift ausgibt oder hundert Mark für eine CD ROM.

Trotzdem bietet die CD ROM eine gute und allumfassende Vorbereitungsmöglichkeit, vor allem bei Städtereisen. Sie bietet die Möglichkeit, **schnell und gezielt bestimmte Informationen** abrufen zu können. Als Zwischenstufe zwischen Buch und Internet ist sie ferner einer größeren Zahl an Nutzern zugänglich, denn mehr Kunden haben ein CD ROM-Laufwerk zu Hause als einen Zugang zum Internet.

Literaturverzeichnis

Adam, H. C./ Fabian, R. (1981): Frühe Reisen mit der Kamera, Hamburg.

Aigner, Gottfried (1992): Ressort Reise. Neue Verantwortung im Reisejournalismus, München.

Albertson, Lesley A. (1977): Telecommunication as a Travel Substitute: Some Psychlogical, Organizational, and Social Aspects, in: Journal of Communication, Nr. 2, S. 32-43.

Appelbaum, Judith (1992): Traveling the Rocky Road to Readers, in: Media Studies Journal, Nr. 3, S. 73-80.

Appeldorn, Werner van (1970): Der dokumentarische Film, Bonn.

Arbeit im Paradies (1996): Interview mit Gerd Ludwig und Tom Kennedy im National Geographic, in: MediumMagazin, Nr. 2, S. 64f.

Autorenkollektiv der Sektion Journalistik der Karl-Marx-Universität Leipzig (Hg.) (1988): Einführung in die journalistische Methodik, 2. durchgesehene Auflage, Leipzig.

Baden in klaren Gewässern (1996): Funk Uhr v. 20.-26.07., S. 74.

Bausinger, Hermann/Breyer, Klaus/Korff, Gottfried (Hg.) (1991): Reisekultur. Von der Pilgerfahrt zum modernen Tourismus, München.

Bausinger, Hermann (1996): Wie die Deutschen zu Reiseweltmeistern werden, in: Aus der Geschichte der Bundesrepublik Deutschland (Hg.): Endlich Urlaub! Die Deutschen reisen, Bonn, S. 25-32.

Becker, Christoph/Job, Hubert/ Witzel, Anke (1996): Tourismus und nachhaltige Entwicklung. Grundlagen und praktische Ansätze für den mitteleuropäischen Raum.

Becker, Hans (1938): Das Feuilleton der Berliner Tagespresse von 1848-1852. Ein Beitrag zur Geschichte des deutschen Feuilletons, Würzburg.

Benedikt, Bene (1995): Wie Reiseträume ins Blatt kommen, in: Guilino, Heidie (Hg.): Reisejournalismus als Berufsfeld. Kulturvermittlung, Service, Tourismuskritik, Eichstätt, S. 15-21.

Berquist, Goodwin (1990): The Retorical Travels of Robert T. Oliver, in: Rhetoric Review, Nr. 1, S. 173-183.

Beyrer, Klaus (1991): Im Coupé - Vom Zeitvertreib der Kutschfahrten, in: Bausinger u. a.: Reisekultur. Von der Pilgerfahrt zum modernen Tourismus, München, S. 137-146.

Bird, S. Elizabeth (1992): Travels in Nowhere Land: Ethnography and the „Impossible" Audience, in: Critical Studies in Mass Communication, Nr. 9, S. 250-260.

Blum, Joachim (1995): Auch Fotos müssen redigiert werden, in: Sage & Schreibe Nr. 7.

Bohm, Hark (1990): Fremde machen Angst, in: Klöckner, M./Twornschka, U. (Hg.): Miteinander - was sonst?, Köln/Wien, S. 22f.

Brendel, Detlef/Grobe, Bernd E. (1976): Journalistisches Grundwissen, München.

Brenner, Peter J. (Hg.) (1989): Der Reisebericht. Die Entwicklung einer Gattung in der deutschen Literatur, Frankfurt a. M..

Bryant, Jennings (1986): The Road Most Traveled: Yet Another Cultivation Critique, in: Journal of Broadcasting and Electronic Media, Nr. 2, S. 50-69.

Buchholz, A, Schult G., (Hg.) (1990): Fernseh-Journalismus, München.

Burgett, Gordon (1991): The Travel Writer`s Guide, Rocklin CA.

Burghoff, Christel/ Kresta, Edith (1995): Schöne Ferien. Tourismus zwischen Biotop und künstlichen Paradiesen, München.

Cudden, J. A. (1992): The Penguin Dictionary of Literary Terms and Literary Theory, London.

Crichton, Michael (1989): Travels, London.

Deutscher Presserat (1996): Publizistische Grundsätze (Pressekodex), Bonn.

Enos, Richard Leo (1992): Why Georgias of Leontini Traveled to Athen: A Study of Recent Epigraphical Evidence, in: Rhetoric Review Nr. 1, S. 1-15.

Enzensberger, Hans Magnus (1962): Eine Theorie des Tourismus.

Erskine, John, u. a. (1917): The Cambridge History of American Literature, Cambridge.

Fasel, Christoph/ Schneider, Wolf (1995): Schöne neue Kunstwelt, in: Spiegel special, Nr. 8, S. 31-33.

Faul, Stephanie (1997): Die Amerikaner pauschal, Frankfurt a. M. (Original: The Xenophobe´s Guide to The Americans, London 1994).

Fiedler, Tanja (1997): Amerika - O´zapft is in Tschortscha, in: stern. Nr. 8, S. 112f.

Fischer, Volkhard (1992): Ausländerstereotype und Gedächtnis, Hamburg.

Flöper, Berthold L. (Hg.) (1992): Ratgeber Freie Journalisten, 2. Auflage, Berlin.

Flöper, Berthold L. (1995): Umworben und bedrängt. Wann wird der Journalist zum 'Amigo'?, in: Die Zeitung, Nr. 1, S. 20.

Föckler, Knut (1997): Sexapeal gewinnen! (Interview), in: Wirtschaftswoche vom 27. 02., S. 81ff.

Florida ganz privat (1996): GEO SAISON Nr. 3, S. 12.

Frei, Bruno (1934): Von Reportagen und Reportern. Einige Bemerkungen zu Egon Erwin Kisch´s neuem Buch „Eintritt verboten“, in: Der Gegenangriff, 2. Jahrgang, Nr. 42, S. 4.

Frey, Barbara (1945): Der Reisebericht in der deutschen Tageszeitung. Untersuchungen über Funktion und journalistische Umformung eines zeitungsfremden Stoffes von den Anfängen bis zum Beginn des 20. Jahrhunderts, Heidelberg (Diss. Phil.).

Friedrich, M. u. a. (1984): Die Fremden sehen, München.

Furtwängler, Jürgen P.(1992): Das Selbst und das Fremde - Versuch zur Eröffnung einer psychoxenologischen Perspektive, in: Duala-M'bedy, L. J. Bonny (Hg.): Das Begehren des Fremden. Tagungsbericht 1991 des Kaiserwerthers Instituts für Xenologie, Essen.

Ganser, Armin (1995): Reisejournalismus - für die Leser oder die Reiseindustrie, in: Guilino, Heidie (Hg.): Reisejournalismus als Berufsfeld, Eichstätt, S. 32-42.

Gerhardt, Rudolf (1996): Lesebuch für Schreiber. Vom journalistischen Umgang mit der Sprache. Ein Ratgeber in Beispielen, 4. Auflage, Frankfurt a. M.

Gehrs, Oliver (1996): Reisen im Kopf, in: taz vom 31. 08.

Glaser, Horst Albert (Hg.) (1983): Deutsche Reiseliteratur. Eine Sozialgeschichte, Reinbek.

Griep, Wolfgang (1980): Reiseliteratur im späten 18. Jahrhundert, in: Rolf Grimminger (Hg.): Hansers Sozialgeschichte der deutschen Literatur vom 16. Jahrhundert bis zur Gegenwart, München.

Groth, Ernst (1941): Die Zeitung im Dienste des Fremdenverkehrs. Die Reisebeilage der Tageszeitung und ihre politische Aufgabe, Leipzig (Diss. Phil.).

Günther, Carmen (1996): Im Land der großen Mutter, in: GLOBO Sonderheft Kanada, S. 103.

Guilino, Heidie (Hg.) (1995): Reisejournalismus als Berufsfeld. Kulturvermittlung, Service, Tourismuskritik, Eichstätt, S. 5-8.

Guilino, Heidie (1995): Von der Schwierigkeit, übers Reisen zu schreiben, in: Guilino, Heidie (Hg.): Reisejournalismus als Berufsfeld. Kulturvermittlung, Service, Tourismuskritik, Eichstätt, S. 5-8.

Guilino, Heidi (1996): Reisejournalismus: Träume im Test, in: journalist, Nr. 6, S. 10-18.

Haake, Wilmont (1967): Reisebericht, Reisefeuilleton und Reisewerbung, in: Jahrbuch der Absatz- und Verbrauchsforschung, Nr. 3, S. 306-326.

Hager, Martin (1997): Ein wahres Schottendasein, in: taz vom 18. 01. 1997.

Haller, Michael (1991): Recherchieren. Ein Handbuch für Journalisten, 4. überarb. Auflage, München.

Haller, Michael (1995): Die Reportage. Ein Handbuch für Journalisten, 3., überarb. Auflage München.

Hamburger Journalistenschule (1996): Der Bildtext. Materialsammlung zum Unterricht, Hamburg.

Heinrichs, Hans-Jürgen (1993): Die geheimen Wunder des Reisens, Graz.

Hennig, Christoph (1977): Reiselust - Touristen, Tourismus und Urlaubskultur, Frankfurt.

Hennig, Christoph (1995): Die Lust der Lemminge. In: DIE ZEIT, Nr. 26. S. 51f.

Herbers, Klaus (1986): Der Jakobsweg. Mit einem mittelalterlichen Pilgerführer unterwegs nach Santiago de Compostela, Tübingen.

Herman, Helmut (1990): Das Reise Foto-Buch, Reinbek.

Hofstätter, Peter R. (1949): Die Psychologie der öffentlichen Meinung, Wien.

Holm, Carsten (1995): Urlaub auf Lau, in: Die Journalisten, Spiegel special, Nr. 1, S. 112.

Jessel, Hans (Hg.) (1994): Das große Sylt Buch, Hamburg.

Junge, Gabriele (1982): Die Presse und ihre Bedeutung für den Fremdenverkehr. Gezielter Einsatz der Presse in der Praxis, München.

Kalb, Gertrud (1981): Bildungsreise und literarischer Reisebericht - Studien zur englischen Reiseliteratur (1700-1850), Nürnberg.

Kieffer, Rob (1997): Die mörderische Eiffel, in: DIE ZEIT, Nr. 5, S. 57.

King, Elisabeth (1996): All the World Loves Paris, in: The Age v. 24.08., Brisbane, Travel Sec. S. 1.

Kleinsteuber, Hans J. (1992): Stereotype, Images und Vorurteile - Die Bilder in den Köpfen der Menschen, in: Wissenschaft und Fortschritt, Nr. 42, S. 50-53.

Koch, Walter A. (1990): Natürlichkeit der Sprache und Kultur, Bochum.

Kreuzfahrt für Behinderte (1996): Süddeutsche Zeitung v. 09. 07., S. 34.

Kreuzer, Helmut/ Rümm, Karl (1979): Fernsehsendungen und ihre Formen, Stuttgart.

Krohn, Heinrich (1987): Welche Lust gewährt das Reisen! Mit Kutsche, Schiff und Eisenbahn, München.

LaRoche, Walter von (1992): Einführung in den praktischen Journalismus. Mit genauer Beschreibung aller Ausbildungswege, 12., neu überarbeitete Auflage, München/Leipzig.

Lippmann, Walter (1922): Public Opinion, New York (deutsch: Die öffentliche Meinung, München 1964.)

Loppow, Bernd/Krohn, Olaf (1995): Überall ist Paradise Island. Ein Silvester-Cocktail aus Reiseberichten des vergangenen Jahres - oder was die klischeefeste Sonne-, Strand- und Säuselprosa enthüllt, in: DIE ZEIT, Nr. 1, S. 43.

Luger, Kurt (1994): Fluchthelfer in die Paradiese, in: aviso, Nr. 12, S. 9-12.

Märtin, Ralf-Peter (1987): Lust am Reisen. Ein Lesebuch, München.

Manz, Wolfgang (1968): Das Stereotyp. Zur Operationalisierung eines sozialwissenschaftlichen Begriffs, Meisenheim.

Martels, Zweder van (Hg.) (1994): Travel Fact and Fiction. Studies on Fiction, Literary Tradition, Scholary Discovery and Observations in Travel Writing, Leiden/New York.

Marquart, Alfred (1982): Bericht, in: Roloff, Eckart Klaus (Hg.): Journalistische Textgattungen, Oldenburg und München, S. 15.

Mast, Claudia (Hg.) (1996): ABC des Journalismus. Projektteam Lokaljournalisten, München.

Maugham, Sommerset (1951): Betörende Südsee, Zürich 1951.

Meyer, Werner (1995): Der Bildtext, in: MediumMagazin, Nr. 12, S. 54-57.

Mit Indianern Iglus bauen (1996): Süddeutsche Zeitung v. 09. 07., S. 38.

Newby, Eric (1985): A Book of Travellers` Talk, London.

Nobel, Rolf (1997): Der Fotoreporter ist tot, es lebe der Fotoreporter, in: 'M', Nr. 3, S. 6f.

Nückel, Liselotte (1996): Brief vom VDRJ Ettlingen (03.10.), Ettlingen.

O `Gara, Elaine (1989): Travel Writer`s Markets. Where to Set Your Travel Articles and Place Your Press Releases, Harvard MA.

O´Neil, L. Peat (1996): Travel Writing: A Guide to Research, Writing, and Selling, Cincinnati, Ohio.

Opaschowski, Horst W. (1989): Tourismusforschung, Opladen.

Ortlepp, Rainer (1995): Reise-PR zwischen Recherche und Bestechung, Hannover (vervielfältigtes Manuskript eines Vortrags).

Osmasreiter, Pia (1982): Travels Through the British Isles - Die Funktion des Reiseberichts im 18. Jahrhundert, Heidelberg.

Paulot, Bruno (Hg.) (1982): Ein Bild und mehr als tausend Worte, Düsseldorf.

Peymani, Bijan (1996): Lukratives Geschäft vor allem für Spezialisten, in: fvw international - Die Zeitung für die deutsche Tourismuswirtschaft, Nr. 14, S.16-18.

Pilgern zu Luther (1996): Süddeutsche Zeitung v. 09. 07., S. 34.

Pohl, Klaus (Hg.) (1983): Ansichten der Ferne. Reisephotographie von 1815 bis heute, Gießen.

Pollig, Hermann (1987): Exotische Wetten - Europäische Phantasien, in: Institut für Auslandsbeziehungen (Hg.): Exotische Wetten - Europäische Phantasien, Stuttgart, S. 16-25.

Popper, Karl R. (1987): Auf der Suche nach einer besseren Welt. Vorträge und Aufsätze aus dreißig Jahren, München/Zürich.

Possin, Hans-Joachim (1972): Das Thema des Reisens in der englischen Literatur des 18. Jahrhunderts, Tübingen.

Prahl, Hans-Werner und Steinecke, A. (Hg.) (1981): Tourismus. Arbeitstexte für den Unterricht, Stuttgart.

Pürer, Heinz (1991): Praktischer Journalismus in Zeitung, Radio und Fernsehen, München.

Pursche, Peter (1996): Schmeißen Sie den Gecko raus!, in: GEO SAISON Nr. 5, S. 86/87.

Reiners, Ludwig (1976): Stilkunst. Ein Lehrbuch deutscher Prosa, München.

Ribeiro, Joao Ubaldo (1991): Wo der Blick ins Leere geht. Betrachtungen eines Brasilianers über die Deutschen, in: DIE ZEIT, Nr. 41, S. 89f.

Richter, Dieter (1991): Die Angst des Reisenden, die Gefahren der Reise, in: Bausinger u. a.: Reisekultur. Von der Pilgerfahrt zum modernen Tourismus, München, S. 100-108.

Röper, Horst (1983): Elektronische Berichterstattung. Formen und Folgen der neuen Fernsehproduktion, Hamburg.

Röper, Horst (1996): Redakteure unter Druck, in: DIE ZEIT v. 23. 08., S. 49.

Rogers, Raymond S.(1982): Movement on the Periphery: Foreign Travel as a First Amendment Right, in: Free Speech Yearbook, Nr. 21, S. 50-69.

Rogers Brown, Sharon (1993): American Travel Narratives as a Literary Genre from 1542 to 1832 - The Act of a Perpetual Journey, New York.

Roloff, Eckart Klaus (1982): Journalistische Textgattungen, Oldenburg/München.

Ruhe bitte! (1996): Hamburger Abendblatt v. 3./4. 8., S. 105.

Schaefer, Thomas (1996): Mord in der Idylle, in: DIE ZEIT, Nr. 29, S. 47.

Scharnberg, Manfred (1996): Glaubwürdiger als der Papst, in: MediumMagazin, Nr. 2, S. 62f.

Scheer, Brigitte (1995): Special: Tourismus, Reinbek (rororo special).

Schilb, John (1992): „Traveling Theory“ and Defining of New Rhetorics, in: Rhetoric Review, Nr. 1, S. 34-48.

Schmitz-Forte, Achim (1992): Reisejournalismus. Eine Analyse unter publizistischen, ökonomischen und ethischen Aspekten, Hamburg.

Schmitz-Forte, Achim (1995): Die journalistische Reisebeschreibung nach 1945 am Beispiel des Kölner Stadt-Anzeigers und der Süddeutschen Zeitung, Frankfurt.

Schneider, Wolf/Raue, Paul-Josef (1996): Handbuch des Journalismus, Reinbek.

Schönbach, Klaus (1977): Die Norm der Trennung von Nachricht und Meldung, Freiburg.

Schult, G./ Buchholz, A. (Hg.) (1990): Fernseh-Journalismus. Ein Handbuch für Ausbildung und Praxis, München.

Schulz, Winfried (1990): Die Konstruktion von Realität in den Nachrichtenmedien, 2. Auflage, Freiburg (Breisgau).

Schwartz, David A. (1973): How Fast Does News Travel? in: Public Opinion Quarterly, Nr. 4, S. 625-627.

Schwer, Bernd (1996): Links ab in Richtung Küste, in: GEO SAISON, Nr. 5, S. 22-35.

Shnayerson, Robert (1996): Die Suche nach dem Paradies, in: GEO SAISON, Nr. 12, S. 62-74 (Fotos: Dennis Marisco).

Sichtermann, Barbara (1995): Wir bleiben Schnüffeltiere, in: Spiegel special, Nr. 8, S. 28-30.

Simon, Dennis M/Ostrom, Charles W. Jr. (1989): The impact of televised speeches and foreign travel on presidential approval, in: Public Opinion Quarterly, Nr. 1, S. 58-82.

Spaeth, Andreas (1996): Bei Anruf Flug, in: MediumMagazin, Nr. 2, S. 70-73.

Spode, Hasso (1996): „Zu den Eigentümlichkeiten unserer Zeit gehört das Massenreisen" - Die Entstehung des modernen Tourismus, in: Haus der Geschichte der Bundesrepublik Deutschlang (Hg.): Endlich Urlaub - Die Deutschen reisen, Köln, S. 13-19.

Stamm, Peter von (1995): Alptraum - Alpentraum, in: Kosmos, Nr. 2, S. 27-33.

Stein, Conrad (1996): Auf du und du mit der Natur, in: GLOBO Sonderheft Kanada, S. 118-120.

Stewart William E. (1978): Die Reisebeschreibung und ihre Theorie im Deutschland des 18. Jahrhunderts, Bonn.

Stout, Janis P. (1983): The Journey Narrative in American Literature, Patterns and Departures, Westport/Conneticut.

Tillmanns, Lutz (1995): Auf Capri den Dosenöffner testen. Korrumpiertheit im Journalismus, in: Sage & Schreibe, Nr. 8, S. 12f.

Traub, Hans (1982): Bericht, in: Roloff, Eckart Klaus (Hg.): Journalistische Textgattungen, Oldenburg und München.

Underwood, Bruce/Rodrigues, Blanca/Uresti, Sandra Leal (1979): Travel News and Ads in Mexican Newspapers, in: Journalism Quartelerly, Nr. 4, S. 868-870.

Unterwegs sein (1995): Themenheft von ZEIT-Magazin, Nr. 40.

Vallombreuse, Pierren de/ Vallombreuse Doujy de (1994): In der Furcht des Donnergottes, in: GEO, Nr. 12, S. 37-54.

Vorlaufer, Karl (1996): Tourismus in Entwicklungsländern. Möglichkeiten und Grenzen einer nachhaltigen Entwicklung durch Fremdenverkehr, Darmstadt.

Wadenfels, B. (1990): Der Stachel des Fremden, Frankfurt a. M..

Wagner, Friedrich A. (1962): Sinn und Unsinn der Reisebeilage, in: Die Anzeige, 1. Märzheft, S. 30.

Waller, Klaus (1982): Fotografie und Zeitung. Die alltägliche Manipulation, Düsseldorf.

Waller, Klaus (1984): Bildunterschrift, in: Beifuß, Blume, Rauch: Bildjournalismus, München, S. 193-200.

Watzlawick, Paul (1983): Anleitung zum Unglücklichsein, München.

Weber, Max (1964): Politik als Beruf, München.

Weischenberg, Siegfried (1988): Nachrichtenschreiben, Opladen.

Weissbusch, Siegfried (1996): Langsamer in die Zukunft, in: GLOBO Sonderheft Südsee und Hawaii, S. 67.

Wember, Bernhard (1983): Wie informiert das Fernsehen?, München.

Wie der Luxus in die Wälder kam (1996): GLOBO Sonderheft Kanada, S. 103.

Wilke-Lammer, Renate/Lammer, Eckehard (1987): Sexotik - Biedermann im Paradies, in: Institut für Auslandsbeziehungen (Hg.): Exotische Wetten - Europäische Phantasien, Stuttgart, S. 106-113.

Wilpert, Gero von (1964): Sachwörterbuch der Literatur, 4., verbesserte und erweiterte Auflage, Stuttgart.

Wood, Larry (1977): Is Travel Writing a Growing Profession? in: Journalism Quarterly, Nr. 4, S. 761-764.

Wuthenow, Ralph-Rainer (1980): Erfahrene Welt. Europäische Reiseliteratur im Zeitalter der Aufklärung, Frankfurt a. M..

ZAW (Zentralverband der deutschen Werbewirtschaft) (1996): Werbung in Deutschland, Bonn.

Zimmer, Dieter E. (1991): Der Garten Eden, in: ZEIT-Magazin, Nr. 46, S. 56-64.

Zinsser, William (Hg.) (1991): They Went: The Art and Craft of Travel Writing, Boston.

Zobel, Louise Purwin (1992): The Travel Writer`s Handbook. How to Write and Set For Own Travel Experience, Chicago (Ill.).

Autorenverzeichnis

Johannes Broermann
Jahrgang 1974, Studium der Geographie, Soziologie und Journalistik in Hamburg und Genf, Stipendiat des *Instituts für publizistische Nachwuchsförderung* (München), journalistische Tätigkeit als freier Mitarbeiter diverser Zeitungen.

Doris Ehrhardt
Geboren 1965 in München, Zeitschriftenvolontariat, Arbeit als Film-, dann als Reiseredakteurin (für das Reisemagazin *GLOBO*), Studium der Politischen Wissenschaft und Journalistik in München und Hamburg, seit 1992 freie Journalistin mit dem Schwerpunktthema Reise.

Nikolas Fentrop
Geboren 1958, Studium der Biologie in Hamburg und Australien, freie Unternehmertätigkeit mit dem Schwerpunkt Marketing, Ergänzungsstudium am *Institut für Journalistik* in Hamburg und besonders viel und gern gereist.

Katharina Griese (geb. Richter)
Geboren 1970 in Hagenow (Mecklenburg), arbeitete 1989/90 in verschiedenen Ressorts der *Schweriner Volkszeitung*, seit 1995 Studium der Psychologie und Journalistik an der *Universität Hamburg*.

Achim Griesel
Jahrgang 1968, Bankkaufmann, Student der Politischen Wissenschaft und Journalistik an der *Universität Hamburg*, freier Mitarbeiter des *Pinneberger Tageblatts* und der *Tagesschau*-Redaktion des *NDR Fernsehen Hamburg*.

Frank Höfer
Jahrgang 1969, Tageszeitungsvolontariat, Arbeit für Zeitungen und Zeitschriften, Studium der Geographie und Ethnologie.

Undine Kayser
Jahrgang 1973, Studium der Germanistik, Amerikanistik und Journalistik an der *Universität Hamburg*, freie Mitarbeit: *sh:z-Verlag*, *Syltmagazin*, Erfahrungen in Print, Radio und PR, Schwerpunkte der Tätigkeiten: interkulturelle Begegnungen und internationale Zusammenarbeit.

Hans J. Kleinsteuber
Geboren 1943, Professor für Politische Wissenschaft und Journalistik an der *Universität Hamburg*.

Astrid Kusser
Geboren 1974 in Passau, studiert Geschichte, Journalistik und Politische Wissenschaft an der *Universität Hamburg*, Praktika bei der *Passauer Neuen Presse* und bei *Spiegel TV*.

Peter Linden
Jahrgang 1959, Studium der Germanistik und Romanistik an der *Ludwig-Maximilians-Universität* in München, 1985-1993 Redakteur der *Süddeutschen Zeitung*, seitdem freie Tätigkeit für u.a. *Süddeutsche Zeitung*, *DIE ZEIT* und *Merian*, Lehraufträge über Reisejournalismus u.a. an der *Deutschen Journalistenschule* in München.

Diana Lühmann
Geboren 1975, Studium der Sozial- und Wirtschaftsgeschichte, Politischen Wissenschaft und Journalistik in Hamburg, diverse Praktika in den Bereichen Zeitung, Zeitschrift, Neue Medien und PR, freie Mitarbeit bei *WELT am SONNTAG*.

Sabine Neumann
Jahrgang 1972, Studium der Ostslavistik, Journalistik und Politischen Wissenschaft in Hamburg, Praktika u.a. bei *Rundblick*, *Focus* und *WELT am SONNTAG*, tätig als freie Journalistin.

Michael Pahl
Geboren 1973 in Husum, seit 1994 Studium der Geschichte, Journalistik und Romanistik (Spanisch) an der *Universität Hamburg*, Praktika u.a. bei *Husumer Nachrichten* und *Kieler Nachrichten*, *Evangelischer Rundfunkdienst Nord*, *KSDT Radio San Diego*, *Deutsches Schauspielhaus* (Öffentlichkeitsarbeit).

Dagmar Rößler
Jahrgang 1976, mehrere Praktika im lokalen Bereich einer Tageszeitung, Studium der Romanistik in Hamburg, Studienaufenthalt in Coimbra, freie Mitarbeit für eine Tageszeitung.

Martin Sonnleitner
Jahrgang 1967, freier Sportreporter (*taz-Die Tageszeitung*, *Hamburg Regionalsport*) und Fernsehjournalist (*RTL*), Studium der Soziologie und Journalistik.

Marina Tischer
Jahrgang 1968, Ausbildung zur Verlagskauffrau, Diplom-Studiengang Sportwissenschaft und Journalistik, Nebentätigkeit als Researcherin in einer Personalberatung.

Kia Vahland
Jahrgang 1970, Tageszeitungsvolontariat, Arbeit als Lokal- und Fernsehredakteurin, Studium der Kunstgeschichte und Politischen Wissenschaft in Rom, Hamburg und Dijon, freie Reisejournalistin.

Sonja Valentin
Jahrgang 1971, Studium der Germanistik, Anglistik und Journalistik in Hamburg und London, hat zwei Jahre in England gelebt und war eins davon als assistant teacher tätig, Arbeit als Übersetzerin, Mitarbeit bei einer Film-Co-Produktion *BBC/Goethe Institut*, Tätigkeiten im Bereich Kultur und Theater (Theaterpädagogik, Regiehospitanzen, Dramaturgie, Öffentlichkeitsarbeit).

Kathrin Voss
Jahrgang 1974, Studium der Politischen Wissenschaft und Journalistik in Hamburg, Praktika bei diversen Medien, freie Mitarbeiterin der *Segeberger Zeitung* und freie Autorin.

Alex Weck
Seit 1986 Journalist, Internationaler Print-/Bildreporter, Hörfunkkorrespondent, TV-Volontariat, TV-Redakteur, Autor/Regie (u.a. für Reiseformate auf *VOX*, *SAT1*), Studium der Politischen Wissenschaft, Ethnologie und Journalistik in München und Hamburg sowie Fortbildungslehrgang zum Kommunikationswirt A/V Medien an der *Hanseatischen Akademie.*

Sonja Wielow
Jahrgang 1972, Studium der Anglistik, Neueren Literatur und Journalistik in Hamburg, Praktika u.a. an der *Kunsthalle Hamburg* und bei *Das Sonntagsblatt*, Magisterarbeit zum Thema 'Indien in der britischen Literatur'.

Verena Wolff
Geboren 1976, freie Mitarbeiterin der *Westdeutschen Allgemeinen Zeitung* und bei *Bertelsmann T1 New Media*, Praktika beim Radio und in der Öffentlichkeitsarbeit, Studium der Amerikanistik, Journalistik und Internationalen Politik in Hamburg.

Britta Wormuth
Geboren 1971, Studium der Betriebswirtschaftslehre und Journalistik an der *Universität Hamburg*, Aufenthalt an der *Perdue University* in Indiana, freie Journalistin und Grafikerin.